CATHERINE COOKSON

CATHERINE COOKSON

TILLY TROTTER

TILLY TROTTER WED

TILLY TROTTER WIDOWED

CHANCELLOR
PRESS

Tilly Trotter first published in Great Britain in 1977
by William Heinemann Ltd
Tilly Trotter Wed first published in Great Britain in 1981
by William Heinemann Ltd
Tilly Trotter Widowed first published in Great Britain in 1982
by William Heinemann Ltd

This collected edition first published in Great Britain in 1993
by Chancellor Press
an imprint of Reed International Books Ltd
Michelin House, 81 Fulham Road, London SW3 6RB
and Auckland, Melbourne, Singapore and Toronto

Reprinted 1994

A CIP catalogue record for this book is available from
the British Library

ISBN 1 85152 466 5

Printed and bound in Great Britain by The Bath Press

CONTENTS

CONTENTS

TILLY TROTTER

PART ONE

❧ The Old Life ❧

∽ 1 ᧡

He urged his horse up the rise, then stopped at the summit as he always did and sat gazing about him. The sky was high today, clear and blue, not resting as it usually did on the far low hills away to his left, or on the masts of the ships not so far away that lined the river. From this point he could see the town of South Shields lying in a bustling huddle along the banks of the river right to where it made its way into the North Sea.

From Tyne Dock to where the village of Jarrow began the land was bare of all but a cottage and a farmstead here and there, but once his eyes lit on Jarrow itself he had the feeling of bustle again, even if it were in a lesser way: the little shipyard he knew would be busy, and at the salt pans along the river where the work would be ceaseless.

Then came Hebburn. He knew it to be there, but it was obscured from his view by a series of hillocks. Always a shadow of pity rose in him when he looked upon any town, even the great Newcastle, for he could never understand how men, given the choice, would want to live among the bustle and hustle and, for the majority of them, stink and muck. But then again the majority of them had little choice. Yet if the chance were given them would they want to live out here in the open country? . . .

Open country! The words were now scornful in his mind. He looked down towards the earth. There was a mine underneath his horse's feet. How often did the miners enjoy the open country? Once a week? Some of them were so worn out that all the Sunday privilege meant to them was bed.

He urged on his horse again, impatience in his 'Get up there!' Now why was it that on this monthly visit to William Trotter he should, winter or summer, pause on that knoll and ask himself questions that had nothing whatsoever to do with him or his life? Here he was a prosperous farmer, well set-up; oh yes, he knew his own value. He would have liked another inch or two to his stature but five foot ten and a half wasn't bad, not when you had breadth to go with it; and the hair on his head was as thick as a horse's mane, and the colour of chestnut into the bargain. As for his face, well, the looking-glass had told him there were handsomer men but they were only to be found among the fops. His was a strong manly face; all strong faces had big noses. His mouth in proportion was large, and that was as it should be. And he had all his teeth; the bottom set as wide as they were high and as white as salt would make them. It wasn't everybody who could reach twenty-four and brag that he hadn't as yet had one tooth broken or pulled. Jeff Barnes had three missing in the front and him not twenty yet, all because he couldn't stand a bit of faceache, and him the size of a house end! No, his face, as his mother used to say, would get him past in a crowd . . . but only just. He used to laugh at his mother: she had been a joker.

At the bottom of the knoll he was still on a rise and as he turned the horse on to a narrow bridle path he was now looking over a mass of woody land where in the far distance a row of ornamental chimneys pierced the sky, and on the sight of them he again pulled his horse to a stop; and as he did so he now asked himself: Could the rumour be true? Was the Sopwith mine finished, or running out? Because if it was that would be the finish of the family and the Manor. But in a way it could be the making of himself, it could bring about the realisation of a dream. Yet if the place and the land and farm went under the hammer could he go to Mr Mark and say, 'I have money to buy me farm'? He couldn't for there was very little left of the big lot and the first thing Mr Mark would likely say would be, 'Where did you get such money from?' And what would he say to that? 'An uncle died in Australia'? People did say things like that. He hadn't an uncle in Australia and Mark Sopwith would know that. There had been Sopwiths in the Manor for the last three hundred years and there had been Bentwoods on Brook Farm for as long, and each knew the history of the other.

He urged his horse on again and the thought in his mind now was, I hope to God it is just a rumour. Aye, I do, for all their sakes.

He entered a narrow belt of wood and when he emerged a few minutes later it was as if he had come into a new country, so changed was the scene. Beyond the stretch of moorland lay a huddle of houses known as Rosier's Village. They were mean two-roomed, mud-floored, miners' cottages housing the workers in the mine that lay half a mile beyond, and the land between the houses and the mine seemed to be dotted with black coal mounds. Although there were only three of them, they nevertheless dominated the landscape.

As his eyes dwelt on the panorama of industry he wondered how it was that one mine owner, such as Rosier, could flourish when a man of more ability and stature such as Sopwith could go to the wall. He supposed the answer could be given in two parts: first, although, so he understood, Rosier had his troubles with water and explosions and the like, as every mine owner had, his was a shaft mine whereas Sopwith's was a drift mine; and the second part of the answer lay in luck, which, in the coal industry, meant good seams and bad seams, although it was said that luck, bad luck, was just an excuse for poor prospecting.

Even when he was well past the village the stench of it still clung to his nostrils. He had ridden a further two miles or more before he came in sight of his destination. It was a thatched cottage, and it lay just off the bridle-path sheltered in a flat-bottomed hollow, and within the boundary of the Sopwith estate. It had a large square of cultivated garden in front and a paddock behind, all neatly railed in. Away to the left of him the land dropped slightly before rising to a grass-covered hill which halfway up levelled itself into a narrow plateau, then rose upwards again and on to an apparently flat head.

He rode down to the cottage, dismounted and tied his horse to the gatepost. When he unlatched the gate and went up the path the geese in the paddock set up a chattering and screeching, and this seemed to be the signal for a door to open. When he reached it he spoke to the old woman standing there, saying, 'They're as good as watch-dogs those two.'

'Oh, hello, Simon. 'Tis good to see you. Come away in. Come away in. Isn't it a beautiful day?'

'It is, Annie. It is,' he said, following her inside.

'I was just saying to William there' – she thrust her hand out towards the bed that was inset in the wall at the far end of the room – 'give us one or two more days like this an' we'll have him outside.'

'Why not. Why not indeed. . . . How are you, William?'

The man in the bed pulled himself up out of the feather tick and leant forward, holding out his hand. 'As you see me, as you see me, Simon; no better, no worse.'

'Well, that's something.'

As Simon Bentwood spoke he opened the buttons of his double-breasted coat and inserted his finger in his high neckerchief as he exclaimed, 'It's been a hot ride.'

'I've got something for that. And take your coat off. Ginger or herb?'

Simon was on the point of saying, 'Ginger,' when he remembered that the last pint of ginger beer he'd drunk here had filled him with wind and he'd been up half the night. She had put so much root ginger into it it had burnt his innards. 'Herb,' he said. 'Thanks, Annie.'

'Herb,' she repeated; 'I thought you liked ginger.'

'I like them both, but I can have a change, can't I?' He flapped his hand towards her, and, laughing, she turned from him and hurried across the long stone-floored room, her humped hips swinging her faded serge skirt.

When she disappeared through a door at the far end of the room Simon took a seat by the bed and, looking at the old man, he asked quietly, 'And how goes it?'

'Aw.' William Trotter now lay back into the denseness of the feather-filled pillows and muttered slowly, 'Not so good at times, Simon.'

'Pain worse?'

'I can't say it is, it's always been worse.' He gave a wry smile now through his bewhiskered face.

'I might be able to come by a bottle of the real stuff shortly; I understand the lads are going out again.'

'That would be good, Simon. Aw, that would be good. There's nothing like a drop of the real stuff. But it's funny that the real stuff has to come from foreign parts, now isn't it?'

'Aye, it is when you come to think of it, William; yes, it is. But then of course brandy has to come from foreign parts.'

'Aye, aye; yes, I remember the last lot, I slept like a baby for nights.' The old man now turned and looked towards Simon and, his words slow and meaningful, he said, 'Sleep's a wonderful thing you know, Simon, it's the best thing that God has given us, sleep. I think He bestowed it on us as an apprenticeship to death, 'cos that's what it will be, death, just a long sleep.'

'Yes, William, yes, I . . . I agree with you there, just a long sleep. Ah . . . !' He turned, on a forced laugh, and greeted Annie Trotter as she came back into the room carrying a grey hen by the handle: 'There you are then. Mind, you've taken your time.'

'Away with you. Taken me time! I'm not as young as I used to be; it's difficult to get under the house, Tilly usually does the crawling.'

'Where is she, by the way?'

'Oh, out gathering wood as usual. She's for ever sawing branches off and sawing them up. I'd like to bet there's not a cleaner line of trees in the county than those in Sop's Wood. It's a good job Mr Mark doesn't mind her stripping the trees head high, but I must say this for her she does it properly, as good as any man, for there's no sap runs after she's finished; she tars every spot.'

'I'm worried.'

Simon now looked at William again and he asked, 'Worried? What about?'

'Her . . . Tilly. Fifteen gone, coming up sixteen, she should be in place, in good service learnin' to be a woman 'stead of rangin' around like a half-scalded young colt; it wouldn't surprise me if one day she decided to wear trousers.'

'Ho! I don't think you need worry about that; she'll never do anything silly, not Tilly, she's got a head on her shoulders.'

'Oh, I know that, I know that, Simon. The trouble is she's got too much head on her shoulders. Do you know, she can read and write as good as the parson hissel.'

'And dance.'

Simon turned quickly to Annie who was in the act of handing him a mug of herb beer and he said, 'Dance?'

'Aye. You don't know the latest. It's the parson's wife, Mrs Ross.'

'The parson's wife?' Simon screwed up his face.

'Aye, aren't I tellin' you? She must have thought that Tilly needed some gentlewomanly accomplishments or some such, and so what does she do? She shows her how to dance. Takes her into the vicarage indeed! Plays a tune on the spinet, then down into the cellar they go and there she takes her through a minet . . . no, minuet. That's it.'

'*Mrs Ross, the parsons' wife!*' Simon's face was stretched now in one wide grin.

'Aye. But oh, Simon, don't let on. Now don't say a word 'cos once that got about, God help her. Well, I mean if it was anybody else they could dance until their toes wore down to their knees, but she's the parson's wife and as ignorant, so I hear, poor dear, of how to be a parson's wife as I am to be the lady of the manor.' Now she was laughing. Her two forearms underneath her flagging breasts, she rocked backwards and forwards for a moment, and the tears were spurting from her eyes as she asked, 'Have you seen her?'

'Yes, oh yes; she's there sitting in the front pew every Sunday and that front pew hasn't seen anything so pretty for many a year, I can tell you.'

'Is she bonny then?'

He put his head on one side, then thought for a moment before answering. 'Aye,' he said, 'she's more than bonny. But she's not beautiful. What she's got is an air about her, she's alive . . . Aye, that's the word. Now that's funny' – he wagged his finger now at Annie – 'she's got the same quality about her as Tilly has.'

'Like our Tilly? And her a parson's wife! Aw no!'

This had come from the bed, and Simon turned to the old man and said, 'Aye, William, it's a kind of glowing quality, spritey. Aw, I'm not the one for words, I can only say she looks alive.'

'Well' – William nodded his head slowly – 'all I can say is, if she looks and acts like Tilly she shouldn't have married a parson.'

'Oh, I don't know, William, Parson Ross had a pretty thin time with the other one. She'd have frightened the devil in hell, she would, and did sometimes I think. But I must confess I meself have wondered if he's been wise with his second choice. She comes from quite a family I hear. Oh yes, quite a family. Got a cousin or some such in the new young queen's household, high up at that, so they say. I'm also told that both families were neighbours years ago, away in Dorset. He was the youngest of seven boys, and thereby thrown into the church. Anyway, I can tell you this, she's made a different fellow out of him. He's not so much blood and thunder these days, more love thy neighbour. You know what I mean? An' you know something more? She never takes her eyes off him all the time he's preaching. I've watched her. But on the other hand he never looks at her. He daren' t. . . . I think the fellow's in love.' He threw his head back and laughed, but it was a self-conscious laugh.

Annie stood looking at him, her face straight; then she said, 'But about this dancing. It's the last thing on God's earth I would have thought our Tilly would have wanted to do, 'cos as you know she's only happy when she's got a saw in her hand or an axe. She can get through a log better than I ever could, an' she's dug every inch of that ground out there as well as William ever did. She's always wanted to do the things that a lad would want to do, an' it's worried me. But I think it's gona worry me more now that she wants to dance.'

'She's a girl, Annie.' Simon's face, too, was straight now. 'And she might grow into a bonny one I've been thinking.'

'Aw, I doubt it; she hasn't a bit of figure to her frame. Comin' up sixteen, she should be developin', but look at her! Like a yard of pump water, as straight as a die.'

'There's plenty of time . . . and some fellows like them thin.' He was smiling now, but Annie shook her head at him as she said, 'I've yet to meet one. Nobody buys a cow with its ribs sticking through if there's a fat one aside it.'

'She's no cow and don't you refer to her as such, Annie Trotter!'

Annie turned her face sharply towards the bed and cried, 'An' don't you bark at me, William Trotter, else I'll give you what for! I've got you where I want you. You'll keep a civil tongue in your head.' She now bounced her head at him before turning and winking at Simon; then glancing towards the window, she said, 'There she comes over the top.'

Simon now bent his back and looked out of the small window away towards the mound and to where a young girl was leaping down the hill as a wild goat might. Of a sudden she came to a stop, and the reason was evident for there emerged from behind a clump of gorse the figure of a young man.

'Who's that with her? Can you see, Simon?'

Simon made no reply but he narrowed his eyes, and it wasn't until the two figures were halfway down the lower part of the hill that he said, 'McGrath. Hal McGrath.'

'Oh no! Him again?' Annie straightened her back, and as she did so Simon turned from the window and put his hand into his pocket; he drew out a sovereign and, handing it to her, said, 'Better take it afore she comes.'

'Oh thanks, Simon. Thanks.' She nodded up at him.

He stared at her for a moment, bit on his lip, then said, 'What do you think he's after? Do you think he's got his eye on her, or is it the other thing?'

'Hopes to kill two birds with one stone I should say.' They both looked towards the bed. 'He's been round here every Sunday for months past.'

Simon looked at Annie again and his voice came from deep in his throat as he muttered, 'He won't give up, will he?'

'Not while there's a breath in him, if I know anything about Hal McGrath. He's his father over again, an' his father afore him.'

'Does she ask any questions, I mean about . . . ?' He pointed towards her hand that was now clutching the sovereign against her breast, and she blinked her eyes and looked away for a moment before she said, 'A year or so ago she asked where we got the money from to buy the flour, meat and such. She provides our other needs from the garden and, as you know, she has done since William took to his bed, so I . . . I had to give her some sort of an answer. I said it was money you borrowed from us some years ago. Well, not you, your father.'

'That was as good as anything. Did she believe you?'

'It seemed to satisfy her. I remember she said, "I like people who pay their debts."'

'Huh! debts.' He turned again towards the window and, once more bending his back, he said, 'She's left him; she's running like a hare and he's standing like a stook.'

When a few minutes later the cottage door burst open it was as if a fresh wind had suddenly blown into the room. Tilly Trotter was tall for her age, being now five foot five and a half inches. She was wearing a faded cotton dress and it hung straight from her shoulders to the uppers of her thick boots, and nowhere was there an undulation. Her neck was long and tinted brown with wind and weather, as was her face; yet here there was a flush of pink to the tint on her high cheekbones. Her eyes, now bright and laughing, looked as if they had taken up the colour of her skin, the only difference being that the brown of her skin was matt while the brown of her eyes was clear and deep. Her hair was dark, darker than brown and thick, and it should at her age have been either piled high on the top of her head or in a decorous knot at the back, but it was hanging in two long plaits tied at the back of her neck with what at one time had been a piece of blue ribbon and joined at the ends with a similar piece. Her mouth, full-lipped, was now wide with welcome as she gabbled breathlessly, 'Hello, Simon.' Then without pause she said, 'Why didn't you come and rescue me? Do you know who I've just been accosted by, an' that's the word, accosted, which means waylaid?' She now nodded towards the bed. 'That Hal McGrath's been at me again. You'd never guess, not in a month of Sundays, what he's just asked.' She now dropped with a flop on to a wooden chair by the side of the long bare wooden table that was placed in the middle of the room; then leaning her head back on her shoulders, she looked up towards the low ceiling and pulled her nose down as if in an effort to meet her chin before she brought out, 'He wants to court me. Him, Hal McGrath! And you know what I told him?' She rolled her eyes from one to the other. 'I told him I'd sooner walk out with one of Tillson's pigs. I did! I did!' She was now laughing loudly.

'Court you!' Sitting straight up in the bed and his voice a loud growl now, William repeated, 'Court you!'

'Yes, Granda, that's what he said. He wanted to court me cause he thought – ' The laughter slid from her face, her voice dropped as she lowered her chin on to her chest, and she ended shyly, 'He said I . . . I was ready for it . . . courtin'.'

'That bloody gormless clot!'

Annie was now bending over the bed pressing her husband down into the pillows, saying soothingly, 'There now! There now! Don't frash yourself. Didn't you hear what she said? She'd sooner walk out with one of Tillson's pigs. There now. There now. Settle down, settle down.'

Simon now stood pulling on his coat; his face was set and stiff, and when he fastened the last button he looked down on Tilly where she was still sitting at the table, her hands clasped on it in front of her now, and he said, 'keep clear of him, Tilly.'

She looked back at him and, her voice as sober as his, she said, 'Oh, I keep clear of him, Simon, I dodge him whenever I can, but he's been round here a lot lately – "

Annie's voice cut in on her now, saying, 'Go and get me some water, we're nearly run dry.'

Tilly got up immediately from the table but stopped in front of Simon and said, 'Ta-rah, Simon,' and he answered, 'Ta-rah, Tilly'; then moving his head to take in both the old man and woman he brought out on an embarrassed laugh, 'I came over with me news today but here I am on the point of going and never spilled it . . . I'm going to be married.'

'*Married? No!*' Annie moved two steps towards him, then stopped; William sat up in the bed again but said nothing; and Tilly looked up into his face and after a moment asked quietly, 'Who you marryin', Simon?'

'Mary . . . Mary Forster. You wouldn't know her, she's not from this part, she's from over beyond Felling way.'

'So far away from your farm!' It was Annie speaking again, and he turned his head to her and said, 'Oh, it's only five miles or so and you know what they say, a warm heart and a galloping horse can jump that.'

'When is it gona be, Simon?'

He was again looking at Tilly. 'We're calling the banns next Sunday,' he said.

'Oh!' She nodded her head and smiled faintly, and there was silence in the room until he broke it with a laugh, and his voice was loud now as he bent towards her, saying, 'And you can come and dance at me wedding.'

'Yes.' She nodded at him now, answering his smile. 'I'll come and dance at your wedding, Simon.'

'But don't bring the parson's wife with you.' He had spoken in a mock whisper and he shot his glance towards the two old people before letting his eyes rest on her again; and she too glanced sharply towards her grandparents before she said soberly, 'Don't say nothing about that, will you, Simon, because the Reverend doesn't like her to dance, I mean Mrs Ross.'

'Oh, your secret's safe with me.' He had bent forward until his laughing face was on a level with hers, but as he looked into her eyes the smile slid from it, and when he straightened up his voice was hearty and loud once more as he cried, 'Well now! I must be off, cows can tell the time better than me.'

'Have you still got Randy?'

He turned to Annie, saying as he made for the door, 'Oh yes, yes; but he's so damned lazy, he falls asleep with his head in their ribs and his slobbers almost dripping into the milk. But young Bill and Ally are good lads, they'll come on with the years. Oh, by the way.' He turned and directed his gaze now towards William, saying, 'I forgot to tell you, you'll never guess who applied to me for a job. He did it on the quiet like, on the side – he'd have to of course – Big McGrath's youngest, Steve, the fourteen-year-old you know. He waylaid me one night last week and asked if there would be any chance. I had to laugh at him. I said, "Does your da know you're asking to be set on?" but he only shook his head. And then I said to him soberly like, "It's no use, lad. I'd set you on the morrow because you look strong and fit, but you know what would happen; your da would come after you and haul you out. You are all in the pit, and for good."

'And you know what he answered to that?' He looked from one to the other now. 'He just said, "Not me, not me for good, I'm getting out," and turned on his heels. It's funny, that young 'un isn't like any of the others, he's not like a McGrath at all; not as we know McGraths, eh, William?'

'All McGraths are the same beneath the skin, Simon. Never trust a McGrath.'

'Perhaps you're right. Keep rested now.' He nodded towards the old man, and William said, 'Aye. Aye.'

'Ta-rah for now,' he said, his glance taking them all in, then went out, closing the door behind him.

Annie was the first to move. She went towards the open fireplace where the kale pot was hanging from a spit and, reaching up to the mantelpiece above it, she took down a wooden tea caddy and placed the sovereign gently in the bottom of it; then replacing the caddy, she turned and, looking at Tilly, said, 'I thought I told you to go for water.'

'You only said that to get me out of the room, Gran; the butt's half full outside, you know it is. What's it you don't want me to hear?'

'Now don't you be perky, miss.'

'I'm not being perky, Gran.' Tilly walked towards the table, then round it to the side that faced the fire and her grandmother who was now opposite to her, and her grandfather who lay in the bed to the left of her, and, looking from one to the other, she said, 'You're always tellin' me I'm comin' up sixteen and that I should act like a young woman, yet there's things you keep from me, an' always have done. Like the sovereign up there that Simon brings every month. And did you know he was gona be married? Did it come as big a surprise to you as you let on it was?'

'Of course it was a surprise to me, an' to your granda there.' Annie's voice was harsh now. 'It's the first breath of it we've heard. We never knew he was even courtin', did we, William?' She turned and looked towards the bed, and William shook his head slowly and looked at Tilly as he said, 'No, girl, it was news to us. Now if it had been Rose Benton, or that Fanny Hutchinson, yes, her who's been after him for years, I could have understood it, but I've never heard of this one. What did he say her name was?'

'Mary Forster.'

They both looked from under their lids at Tilly, and after a moment Annie, too, said, 'Mary Forster.' Then shaking her head, she added, 'Never heard one of any such name.'

'Well, that's explained that!' The tone of Tilly's voice was such that her grandparents gaped at her in surprise as she went on, 'But about the other thing.' She nodded her head towards the tea caddy. 'And don't tell me again that Simon's paying back some money he's owin' you. I could never imagine you havin' that much to lend him that it would take all those years for him to clear his debt, so what's it all about? I'm entitled to know. . . .'

William now began to cough, a racking tormented cough, and Annie, going to him quickly, brought him up on the pillows and thumped his back and as she was doing it she turned her head towards Tilly and cried, 'See what your niggling pestering's done! It's days since he had a turn. Scald some honey and bring it here, sharp. . . . You an' your entitled to know. Huh!'

Tilly, her whole attitude changed now, ran towards an oak dresser at the far end of the room and, taking a jar from it, she quickly returned to the table and scooped out two spoonfuls of honey into a mug; she then went to the fire and after dipping the mug quickly into the kale pot of simmering water she stirred the contents with a small wooden spoon, before going to the bed and handing the mug to her grandmother.

Between gasps the old man sipped at the hot honeyed water; then lay back on his pillows, his chest heaving like bellows all the while.

Tilly stood by the bed, her expression contrite and her voice equally so as she said, 'I'm sorry, Granda. I'm sorry if I've upset you.'

'No, no' – he took hold of her hand – 'you'd never upset me, me dear. You're a good girl; you always have been, and I'll tell you something else . . . when I can get me breath.' He pulled at the air for some seconds; then smiling at her, he said, 'You've been the joy of me life since you came into it.'

'Oh, Granda!' She bent now and laid her face against his hairy cheek and there was a break in her voice as she again said, 'Oh, Granda!'

Then the emotion and sentiment was shattered by her grandmother's level tone, saying now, 'I didn't want water but I did want wood an' I'll have to have it, that's if you two want a meal the night.'

Tilly moved from the bed and as she passed her grandmother the old woman turned towards her and they exchanged glances that held no resentment on either side.

At the back of the cottage, a roughly paved open yard was bordered on one side by two outhouses: one had been a stable and the other a harness-room. The harness-room was now used for storing vegetables and the stable for the storage of wood. Outside the stable there was a sawing cradle and on it lay a thick branch of a tree that she had brought down from the wood only that morning. She put her hand on it and, turning her body half round, leaned against the cradle and looked across the paddock and beyond to where the land dropped far away before rising again to the woods that edged the Sopwith estate; and for once, looking over the landscape, she didn't think consciously, by! it's bonny, because she was feeling slightly sick inside.

Simon was going to be married. She was still under the shock of the announcement; she had never imagined Simon getting married. But why hadn't she imagined it? A good-looking strapping farmer like him with his kindness and sense of fun. She had loved him for so many things, but mostly for his kindness and sense of fun.

She could remember the very first day she had seen him, it was the day her mother had brought her to this cottage. She was five years old. She could remember what she was dressed in, a black serge dress and a short black coat and bonnet; she was wearing black because her father had fallen over a steep cliff in Shields and was drowned. Her granda took off her coat and sat her on a chair; then together with her grandmother, he helped to get her mother up the steep stairs and to the bedroom because her mother was sick.

She was sitting by the fire when the door opened and a man and boy entered, and the boy came over to her and said, 'And who are you when you're out?' And he laughed down on her; but she didn't laugh back, she began to cry and he said, 'There now. There now,' and brought a barley sugar from his pocket and gave it to her.

And when her granda came down the stairs he and the man talked. It was on that day too that she first heard the name McGrath spoken, and also a swear word, for the man said, 'Bugger me eyes that for a tale, your Fred to fall over a cliff!'

The boy then asked her name, and when she told him 'Tilly', he said 'Tilly Trotter! Now that's a daft name, Tilly Trotter.' And she remembered her grandfather shouting at the boy, saying, 'Don't you call the child daft, Simon! Her name's Matilda,' and the man said to the boy, 'Get outside! I'll deal with you later. It's you that's daft.'

But the boy didn't go outside. She could see him now standing straight and looking at her grandfather and his father and saying, 'I heard tell Mr McGrath was there waiting for the boat an' all, he wasn't on his shift, he had slipped it. Bill Nelson heard his father talking.' And at that the two men came up to the boy, and somehow the boy no longer seemed a boy but a man.

From that time she had always looked upon Simon as a man and someone who belonged to her. But he was no longer hers. She felt a desire to cry, and the desire was strange for she rarely cried. She'd had nothing in her life to make her cry, her days had been free, happy, and filled with love; moreover she hadn't been sent into service, or into the fields – or yet down the mine.

She was seven when her mother died, and she had scarcely missed her for the two people back in that room had wrapped her round with loving care from that day until this moment, and she had tried to repay them not only with love but with work. Even so, she knew that they could not have survived these past few years since her grandfather had taken to his bed had it not been for that monthly sovereign.

But why? Why did Simon feel bound to bring that money? He must do, for to her knowledge he had never missed a month during the last six years. And before that he had accompanied his father on similar missions. There was something here she couldn't understand. And look what happened when she probed, it forced her grandfather to have a turn.

Would Simon's wife probe? She could give herself no answer.

She turned quickly about and went into the stable and, picking up a straw skip, she flung in small logs; then, scooping up handfuls of chips from a wooden bin, she threw these with equal force on top of the logs. With a heave she lifted up the weighty skip and with her arms stretched wide gripping it she went towards the back door. Here, she pressed the basket against the stanchion and, her head turned over her shoulder, she once again looked at the wide landscape, but now as if saying good-bye to it, for there had come over her a foreboding feeling as if she had suddenly stepped out of one life into another, and she felt that never again would she know the lightness of spirit that had caused her to run down the hills, or skip the burns like a deer; nor yet sit in the moonlight on the knoll and let the day seep from her and the night enter into a silent patch that lay deep within her and from which there oozed understanding – understanding which in turn she could not understand, for she had not as yet served her time in tribulations. But in this moment she sensed that that time was not far ahead.

As she pushed open the door and went through the scullery her mind skipped back a step into the long childhood she had just left and she said to herself, 'Perhaps if my breasts had developed more he would have noticed me.'

2

Simon stood with his back against the farm gate and looked up at his landlord, Mr Mark Sopwith, and he returned the smile of the older man, nodding as he said, "Tis true, 'tis true; tomorrow as ever was I let the halter be put about me neck.' He turned now and nodded towards the head of the horse, and Mark Sopwith, laughing too, said, 'There's many a worse situation; it all depends on the temper of the rider.'

'Oh, I know the temper of the rider; I can manage the rider.'

'Oh well!' Mark Sopwith now pursed his lips and made a slow movement with his head from shoulder to shoulder. 'You can't wear the halter and be the rider, that's an utter impossibility.'

'You're right there. You're right there.' Simon jerked his chin upwards now, and the action spoke against himself and he said, 'I've always been one to have me cake and eat it. By the way, sir, may I ask, is it true what I'm hearin'?'

'It all depends, rumours always have a spice of truth in them.' Mark Sopwith's face was straight now. 'What have you been hearing?'

'Well – ' Simon now kicked at a pebble in the road so raising a cloud of dust, and he watched the pebble skitting away over the surface before looking straight up into Mark Sopwith's face and adding, 'They're saying the mine's all but finished since the water's come in.'

Mark Sopwith did not answer but he stared down at Simon, then presently said, 'There's such things as pumps. The water did come in, but it's gone. And you can set another rumour around; my mine isn't finished, nor likely to be.'

'I'm glad of that, sir, I really am.'

'Thank you. Ah well!' The stiffness went out of his face and tone again as he said, 'I must be off now, but you have my best wishes for a happy life after tomorrow.

'Thank you, sir.'

Mark Sopwith was just about to press his knees into the horse's flanks when his action was checked by the sight of a rider coming round the bend in the road a few yards ahead. The rider was a girl – no a woman, and she sat her mount as if moulded to it. A few trotting steps of the horse and she was abreast of them, and she drew the beast to a stop and looked at them, and both men returned her look, their eyes wide with interest.

'Good-morning.'

'Good-morning, ma'am.' They both answered her almost simultaneously. Mark Sopwith raised his hat but Simon, hatless, didn't put his fingers to his forehead.

'I'm speaking to Mr Sopwith?' She was looking directly at Mark now and he inclined his head and said, 'That's so, ma'am.'

'I'm Lady Myton.'

'Oh, how do you do? I'm . . . I'm sorry I haven't been able to call on you yet, I . . .'

The lady now smiled, then gave a chuckling laugh as she said, 'I've called on you just this very morning but I was told that you were out and that your wife was indisposed.'

Simon, standing straight, stared from one to the other of the riders. He noted that Mr Sopwith's face had lost its sallowness and was now a warm pink; he also noted that the lady was amused. He had heard that a lordship had taken over Dean House and that he was an oldish fellow with a young wife. Well, from what he could see she wasn't all that young, nearing thirty he would say, but by! she had a figure on her; and the boldness in those eyes was what one would expect to see in the face of some wench sloshing out the beer in an inn.

With almost a start he realised her eyes were being levelled on him and the head was being held enquiringly to one side, and he also knew that his landlord was being put to a little disadvantage wondering whether or not he should introduce him. He felt his spine stiffening a little, and the action became registered in his expression as he looked up at his landlord.

'This is Farmer Bentwood, a tenant of mine.'

She was again looking at Mark Sopwith, and it was a number of seconds before she inclined her head towards Simon, but he still didn't, as he should have done, raise his hand to his forehead and say, 'Good-day, me lady,' but returned her the same salute, inclining his head just the slightest, which action seemed to annoy Mr Sopwith for, backing his horse, a manoeuvre which caused Simon to skip to one side, he brought its head round in the same direction as that of Lady Myton's mount and now level with her and, his knee almost touching her skirt, he said, 'Have you any destination in view or are you just out for a canter?'

'I'm just out for a canter.' She accompanied her words with a deep obeisance of her head.

'Then perhaps you'll do me the honour of riding with me back to the house and there make the acquaintance of my wife?'

'Surely.'

As they both started their horses Mark Sopwith turned and looked down on Simon, saying, 'Good-bye, Bentwood, and a merry wedding tomorrow.'

At this Lady Myton pulled up her horse and twisted round in the saddle. 'You're going to be married tomorrow?'

He paused before he said quietly, 'Yes, me lady.'

'Well, may I too wish you a merry wedding, Mr ... Farmer ... what did you say your name was?'

'Bentwood, Simon Bentwood.' He stressed his name. His face was straight, but hers was wide and laughing as she repeated, 'Simon Bentwood. Well, again I say a merry wedding, Farmer Simon Bentwood,' and on this she spurred the horse sharply forward, leaving Mark Sopwith to follow behind her; that was until they reached the end of the winding road, for there he shouted, 'Turn right here on to the bridle path.' He himself now took the lead, putting his horse into a gallop and then knowing a feeling of satisfaction and of not a little amusement that though she was close on his tail she would, he guessed, even from this short acquaintance, be annoyed that she couldn't pass him and show off her horsemanship because he had recognised at once she was one of those women who once seated on a horse would go hell for leather over walls, ditches, fences ... and over farmlands. Yes, they were no respecters of farmlands. Likely, that was what Bentwood had recognised in her that had made him act out of place, because his manner had not been respectful.

When the path eventually widened out he drew his horse to a walk and as she came abreast of him he looked at her, but she gave him no indication of annoyance. She was looking away to the right, down towards a cottage, and she remarked, 'That's a pretty cottage and a well-tended garden. That's something I've noticed in the short time I've been here' – she glanced at him now – 'the cottages have very untidy gardens; some with a few vegetables, nothing pretty.'

'That's the Trotters' place. It's within the boundary of my land. Old man and woman Trotter live there. It's their young granddaughter who keeps the place tidy. There she is now coming up from the burn. She does the work of a man. She can fell a tree as good as the next; she's got one of my copses as clean as a whistle.'

'You allow her to saw your trees down?'

'No, only limb so far up; it's good for them.'

As they drew nearer the cottage the girl came closer into view, and Lady Myton said, 'She looks very young, rather fragile.'

'Oh, I shouldn't judge her on her thinness, she's as strong as a young colt.'

When the girl saw them she didn't stop but went on towards the back of the cottage, carrying the two wooden buckets full of water, and as they passed the paddock Lady Myton said, 'So this is all part of your estate?'

'Yes, what's left of it.' There was a wry smile on his face as he said, 'Half our land was sold to enhance your property about fifty years ago.'

'You must have been very short of money.'

'We were.'

'And now?'

'Things haven't altered very much.'

'But you have a mine?'

'Yes.'

'Doesn't that make money?'

He sighed. 'The only way mines seem to make money is if you go abroad or live in London and leave them to managers. If you stay at home and look after the people's interests you lose all along the line.'

'The Rosiers, I understand, do very well.'

His face became straight. He levelled his glance now towards his hand that was gripping the reins as he muttered, 'Ruthless people generally do . . . do very well.'

There was silence between them for a moment. They reined the horses away from each other to avoid a deep pothole in the road and when they came together again she said, 'You sound as if you don't care for the Rosiers, why?'

It was on the point of his tongue to say, 'Whether I care for them or not, madam, is no business of yours,' for of a sudden he was realising that he hadn't been in the company of this woman for half an hour and she was questioning him as any close friend might. But when he turned and looked at the expression in those large deep blue eyes it wiped away any sting with which he might have threaded his next words. 'You're a most inquisitive lady,' he said.

Her answer was to put her head back and let out what he considered a most unladylike laugh, and, her eyes twinkling now, she looked at him and said, 'You know some people are with me a full day before they realise what a very nosey person I am.'

He was now laughing with her, but his was a gentle chuckle, and as he kept his eyes on her he felt a stirring in his blood that he had never imagined he would experience again, for here he was, forty-two years old, with a son of twenty by his first wife, three sons and a daughter by his second, and she in decline, a mortgage on his estate that was choking him, a mine that was barely meeting his men's wages, and a household that was in chaos because it had no controlling hand. He had imagined there was no space left in him wherein was harboured a remnant of the emotions of youth; desire of the body yes, but not the excitement with which it had first made itself known. It was in this moment as if the spring of his manhood had just burst through the earth.

When she now suddenly put her horse into a gallop and they entered another bridle path that led towards the back drive, which in its turn led towards his house, he allowed her to take the lead.

At the beginning of the nineteenth century the account books showed Highfield Manor's staff amounted to thirty-two people in all; this included six gardeners and four in the stable yard. Today the account books named only thirteen on the staff, which numbered a coachman and three gardeners but did not take into account Mr Burgess, the tutor, and Miss Mabel Venner Price, who was Mrs Sopwith's companion-maid.

The depletion of the staff showed itself not only in the ornamental gardens that surrounded the house but in the house itself. Mr Pike, the butler, who had been with the family for sixty years no longer appeared in the hall whenever Robert Simes, the footman, answered the doorbell, for he was mostly otherwise engaged doing, as he mournfully stated, the work of lesser men; nor did Mrs Lucas, the housekeeper, make her appearance from nowhere, as her predecessor would have done, to greet her master. When Mrs Lucas appeared it was usually to say in her own stiff, polite, guarded way that she could get no help from the mistress or that she herself couldn't be expected to run an establishment like this on such a depleted staff; or, would he order Mr Burgess, the tutor, to come down to the staff room for his meals? It would be one less to take up to the nursery floor. But generally when she waylaid him it was to complain about the children: they were entirely out of hand; the nursemaid had no control over them, nor for that matter had the tutor. Would he speak to Master Matthew because where Matthew went the others followed?

Of late, Mark had dreaded entering the house because from the ground floor to the top he was met with complaints. He looked back with deep nostalgia to the time when in London, or abroad, or even at the mine, all he longed for was to get back to his home. Now at the mine, all he wanted was to get away from it; and the same feeling was in him with regard to his home.

He stood aside and opened the door to allow his elegant visitor to enter the hall, and as he did so he looked about him. Then calling across to where the footman was disappearing into the dining-room, he shouted, 'Simes!' and when the man turned and walked towards them across the marble-tiled floor he pointed to Lady Myton who was holding out her riding crop and gloves, then asked, 'Your mistress, is she still in her room?'

The man blinked once before he answered, 'Yes, master,' and Mark knew he could have added, 'Does she ever leave it?'

'Will you come this way?' He now led the visitor across the wide hall and up the broad faded red-carpeted staircase and on to a wide gallery, also carpeted in the same fading red, and of which the walls were almost obliterated by ornately framed paintings, mostly portraits. He glanced at her as they crossed the gallery and there was a twinkle in his eye as he noted the fact that she wasn't, as was usual, carrying the train of her riding habit over her arm, but was allowing it to trail the floor. She was determined to be different, this lady.

He was about to lead the way down a long corridor when a succession of high squeals caused them both to look towards the far end from where a staircase led upwards; and now scampering down it and into their sight came three children. Two were boys, the third, a smaller girl. It was she who was screaming the loudest, and apparently she had cause to, for from the top of her head streaming down her face and on to her frilled pinafore was a thick blue substance.

'Matthew! Luke! Jessie Ann!'

For a moment he appeared to forget about his companion and, striding to the children who seemed oblivious of them and who were now making for the main staircase, he brought them to a halt with another loud bellow: 'Stop! Stop this minute!'

As if governed by one mind, they skidded to a stop that brought them into a huddle, and the younger of the two boys, Luke, a dark-haired, dark-eyed, mischievous-faced seven-year-old, now flapped his hand wildly in the air to get rid of the blue substance that he had picked up from being in contact with his sister's pinafore.

'What is this? What is the meaning of this? Jessie Ann, what have you done?'

'Oh, Papa. Papa.' She came towards him now, but, backing slightly from her, he cried, 'Get yourself away! Where is Dewhurst?' He was now speaking to his elder son Matthew and he, endeavouring to keep a straight face, muttered, 'In the nursery, Papa, crying.'

Mark closed his eyes, then was about to issue another order when Lady Myton's voice, threaded with laughter, broke in. 'Somebody's been having a game,' she said. She was standing by Mark's side now, bending slightly forward, looking into the three upturned faces, and Jessie Ann stopped her snivelling for a moment when the lady said, 'Was it from the top of the door?'

As Jessie Ann nodded slowly the boys shrieked in chorus, 'Yes, yes, ma'am! It was for Dewhurst, but she had Jessie Ann alongside her.' They remained now staring their admiration at the lady who had been clever enough to guess how Jessie Ann had become covered with the paste.

'I never thought of using paste, I never got beyond water.'

The boys now giggled and the small girl sniffed, then screwed up her face and sneezed violently in an effort to rid her nostrils of the paste.

'Get upstairs, all of you! And don't dare leave the floor again until I see you. Understand?'

'Yes, Papa.'

'Yes, Papa.'

Jessie Ann couldn't make any retort, she was still sneezing, but her brothers, each grabbing an arm, pulled her towards the nursery stairs again and as they did so Mrs Lucas appeared at the end of the corridor.

Going quickly towards her and his voice seeming to be strained through his narrowed lips, he said, 'Mrs Lucas, will you kindly attend to your duty and contain that commotion upstairs' – he pointed towards the disappearing figures – 'and also see that they don't come down on to this floor unless they are escorted. You may remember that we have been over this particular matter before.'

Mrs Lucas, her hands joined at her waist, pressed them into it so causing her already full breasts to push out her black alpaca bodice and puff out a small white apron that appeared like a patch on the front of her wide skirt, and looking straight at her master and ignoring the visitor as if she weren't there, she said, 'My various duties take me from one end of the establishment to the other, sir; I cannot spend my time in the nursery. Moreover, there is a nursemaid, and a tutor there.'

'I'm well aware of that, Mrs Lucas' – he endeavoured to control the tremble of anger in his voice – 'and I was under the impression that the nursemaid at least came into your province. But no more! No more!' He wagged his hand almost in front of her face. 'Go up there this moment and restore order!'

The housekeeper stretched her neck out of the narrow white-starched collar that bordered her dress; she inclined her head just the slightest; then with a step that expressed her ruffled indignation, she passed between her master and his guest and went towards the staircase.

Now Mark, turning and walking slowly towards a deep-bayed window in the corridor, stood for a moment with his hand across his eyes; then turning again and looking towards where Lady Myton still stood, he made a helpless gesture with his shoulders and outstretched hands as he said, 'What can I say? I'm . . . I'm very sorry you have had to be subjected to this scene.'

'Don't be silly!' She moved towards him and when she stood opposite him she smiled openly into his face as she said, 'I've enjoyed every minute of it. It took me back; I used to do the same. I loathe nursemaids, governesses and all their kin. They were always changing my nursemaids. I led them a hell of a life.'

He was looking into her eyes and seconds passed before his chest jerked and there came from the back of his throat a low rumbling, and now he was laughing with her. But it was a smothered laughter, and after a moment, still looking at her, he said softly, 'You're a very refreshing person. But I suppose you know that?'

'No, no . . . well, I've never been called refreshing before; it sounds like one of those fizzy drinks. And that takes me back to the nursery too because when I used to belch, and I did often and on purpose' – she nodded her head now – 'I had a nurse who used to squeeze a lemon into a glass of water, then put a great dollop of bicarb in, and when it fizzed, which it did straightaway, she used to make me drink it, almost pouring it down my throat. But no, I haven't been referred to as refreshing; exciting yes, enticing yes, amusing yes, and – ' she paused, and pursing her lips ended, 'and one great lump of a bitch. The last, I may say, is a purely female comment.'

He said nothing but continued to gaze at her, with open admiration in his look now, then giving a little huh! of a laugh he took her arm and turned her about and led her further along the corridor, and when he drew her to a stop opposite a grey-painted door he glanced at her for a moment before tapping twice on it with his knuckles.

Having entered the room, he immediately stood aside to allow her to pass him, and he closed the door deliberately before leading her across the room towards the window where, on a chaise-longue, lay his wife.

Eileen Sopwith was thirty-seven years old. She had a fair complexion, grey eyes, a delicate tint of skin, and hair that had once been a very fair blonde but which was now of a mousy hue. She had taken to this couch four years ago, and had not put her foot outside her apartments since. She only moved from the couch to be helped to the water closet and to bed in the adjoining room at night. She passed most of her time reading or doing embroidery – she took great pains in embroidering pinafores and dresses for her daughter – and the most trying moments of her day were when her four children were filed decorously in to greet her. It took only five minutes for them to say their 'Good-morning, Mama. How are you, Mama?' and for her to answer them and to add, 'Be good children,' but even this exhausted her.

The expression on her face rarely altered, mostly showing a patient resignation, as did also her voice. Her visitors were few and far between, and then they were nearly always members of her own family.

So when her husband now ushered into her room the startling looking stranger in a riding habit, her mouth was brought slightly agape and her head up from the satin pillow. For a moment she was on the point of calling, 'Mabel! Mabel!' because very few people got past Mabel, but here was her husband leading a woman, a healthy, vigorous striding person, towards her.

She wasn't called upon to speak because Mark was saying, 'This is Lady Myton, Eileen. She had called earlier but you weren't quite ready for visitors, so when I came across her on my way home I assured her you would be pleased to see her. They have taken Dean House you know.'

As Eileen Sopwith took her eyes from her husband and lowered her head in a slight acknowledgement of the visitor, Agnes Myton held out her hand, saying, 'I'm delighted to meet you. I had called to bring you an invitation to a little dinner we are putting on next week but perhaps it would be too much for you.'

'Yes, yes, I'm afraid it would.'

'That's such a pity. You being our nearest neighbours, I had hoped – ' she shrugged her shoulders. 'Well, what's a dinner party, I can always call.'

'Please be seated.'

She turned and smiled her thanks at Mark as he pressed a chair under her thick riding skirt and after she was seated there was a moment's silence before, laughing now, she said, 'I've made the acquaintance of your charming family.'

Eileen Sopwith now turned a quick enquiring glance on her husband and he, smiling down at her, said, 'Yes. Yes, they made their presence felt, up to some prank.' His head bobbed.

'Have . . . have you any children?'

'No, I'm afraid not. But there's plenty of time, I've only been married just over a year.' She ended on a laugh as if she had expressed something amusing.

Eileen Sopwith stared at her visitor but said nothing, while Mark put in quickly, 'I suppose you find this part of the country very stale after London. I am, of course, taking it for granted you did live in London?'

'Yes, yes, we had a house there, and another in Warwickshire, but he sold them both up, Billy, you know. His people originally came from this part, so I understand, a hundred years or so ago. He's always wanted to live up here, he says he finds more to do here than in London. He came up at the back end of last year in all that terrible weather just to be here for the Mansion House sale in Newcastle; there were some pieces he wanted for our place you know. Moreover, he's very interested in engineering; and there were some bridges going up at the time. I've forgotten the name of them.' She shrugged her shoulders and glanced up at Mark, and he said, 'Oh yes, the railway viaducts over the Ouseburn and Willington Dean.'

She nodded at him and said, 'Yes, those are the places; I can never remember names. . . . The first place he took me to when I came up here was the New Theatre at Newcastle, rather splendid, and it was a great evening. I've never laughed so much for a long time, not only at the play but at the people. Really' – she glanced back up at him – 'you'll likely get on your provincial high horse when I say this, but I could hardly understand a word any of them said.'

When Mark made no immediate reply to this because the word provincial had annoyed him somewhat she cried loudly, 'There! there! I told you.'

'Are . . . are you returning to London soon or are you making this your permanent home?'

The quiet question from the chaise-longue cut in on her laughter and she answered, 'Oh no, no, we've just come from there, well, only a fortnight ago. We were to come up much earlier but then the King died and the Queen was proclaimed and Billy had to be there. I think Billy is going to love it here, in fact I'm sure of it, but as yet I cannot speak for myself, except I know I am going to enjoy the riding, the land is so open and wild . . . like the people.' She turned her head again and glanced up at Mark and her expression invited contradiction.

It was at this point that the door opened and the companion entered, and her hesitation and the look on her face as she stood with her hand still on the door handle showed her surprise, and also her displeasure.

The latter was immediately evident to Mark, who, bent on mollifying her, put out his hand towards her while looking at Lady Myton, and saying, 'This is Miss Mabel Venner Price, my wife's companion, Lady Myton.'

The title, lady, seemed to have little effect for Miss Price's countenance didn't change; her mouth opened, the square chin dropped and she dipped the smallest of curtsies as she said, 'Your Ladyship.'

Lady Agnes acknowledged the salute by a mere inclining of her head, which gesture reminded Mark of the look she had bestowed on young Bentwood. Apparently she had a manner she kept precisely for menials, and the condescension was, to his mind, overdone.

She was a madam all right, but a very likeable madam, oh yes, a very likeable madam.

He watched her now making her farewells to Eileen and it was apparent that Eileen had been stirred slightly out of herself by her visitor. Well, that was a good thing an' all. There were times when he had his doubts about his wife's malaise, yet both Doctor Kemp and Doctor Fellows had said she must have no more children, something to do with her womb; and the man he had brought down from Edinburgh had gone further, stating that the pain she had in the sides of her stomach were from her ovaries and that there was really no cure unless nature took a hand and settled things internally, which it often did. Well, nature was a long time in taking a hand and he had asked himself often of late, would he know when it had? He missed the warmth of her body – she no longer allowed him to lie beside her at night. When he explained he could love her without taking her she had been shocked.

How was it, he wondered, that the common woman managed to carry on. There were women in his mine crawling on their hands and knees, pulling and shoving bogies full of coal less than a week after giving birth. Often when he had gone down the mine with the manager they had come across couples sporting and more in a side roadway on the bare rock earth, and while Yarrow scattered them, crying, 'I'll cuddle you! Begod, I'll cuddle you!' he himself had been filled with envy. He often thought about the word cuddle. It was a beautiful word, warm in itself.

'Shall we be going then?'

'Oh yes, yes.'

He hadn't been conscious of staring at her all the while he had been thinking, but he was now conscious of his wife's eyes being tight on him as he turned to her and said, 'I'll be up shortly.'

When Mabel Price opened the door for them he smiled at her but her cheeks made no answering movement.

They had reached the main hall before they spoke again. Looking at her, he said, 'I feel very embarrassed, you have been offered no refreshment whatever,' and she put out her hand and gently tapped his sleeve with two fingers as she said, 'Please don't apologise, there is nothing to apologise for. The visit itself has been refreshment enough.' Then her head on one side, she asked, 'Can I depend upon you coming to dinner a fortnight tonight?'

There was the slightest pause before he answered, 'Most certainly. I shall be pleased to.'

Their eyes held for a moment longer, then she turned about, walked towards the door where the footman was now standing with her crop and gloves, and taking them from him as if she had picked them up from a hallstand she went out and on to the broad terrace, then walked down the three shallow steps on to the grass-spattered gravel and to where Fred Leyburn, the coachman-cum-groom-cum-handyman was holding her horse.

Mark himself helped her up into the saddle; then taking the reins from the coachman, he dismissed him with a lift of his head, and handing the reins up to her, he said, 'Until today fortnight then,' and she, looking down at him, her face unsmiling now but her gaze steady, replied, 'Until today fortnight . . . if not before.' With that, she spurred her horse and was gone galloping along the drive, and he stood and watched her until she disappeared from his sight before turning and running up the steps and into the house again.

At the bottom of the main staircase he paused a moment, his fingers pressed on his lower lip. He knew he should go straight to the nursery, take Matthew's breeches down and thrash him – he had promised him that the very next time he played a dirty prank on Dewhurst he would lather him – but were he to do so there would likely be screaming, and when the sound reached Eileen, as it surely would because Matthew had a great pair of lungs on him, she would either have one of her real bad turns or punish him with her weapon of hurt silence for the next few days.

Running once more, he took the stairs two at a time. He was panting when he reached the gallery and as he drew himself to a walk he asked himself why the hurry.

When he entered his wife's bedroom again, Mabel Price was adjusting a light silk cover over her mistress's knees and she turned an unsmiling face towards her master before walking past him and leaving the room.

'What's the matter with her?' Mark looked towards the closed door.

'She didn't like your visitor.'

'My visitor! She came to see you.'

Eileen Sopwith ignored this remark and went on, 'She has heard rumours.'

'Yes, yes, I bet she has. If there's any rumours to be sifted out our dear Miss Price will be the first down the hole.'

'You mustn't talk like that about her, Mark, she's a very good friend to me, quite indispensable.'

'And does that allow her to be rude to guests?'

'Lady Myton wasn't a guest, Mark, she came here uninvited.'

'She came here as a neighbour, hoping, I think, for a neighbourly response. She likely wants to make friends.'

'By what I hear she's quite adept at making friends.'

He stood looking down at his wife while she smoothed out a fine lawn handkerchief with her forefinger and thumb. 'Did you know she'd been married before?'

'No, I didn't. . . . But you knew I'd been married before' – he now leant towards her – 'didn't you, Eileen, and that didn't stamp me as a villain.'

'It is different with a woman, and I'm not blaming her for being married before, but I do now understand the reason why they came here in rather a hurry. Her name was coupled with that of a certain gentleman in London, and her husband was for thrashing him.'

He screwed up his face now as he said, 'You've learned all this in the last few minutes, and may I ask where Price got her information?'

'Yes, you may ask, Mark, that is if you don't shout.' There was a pause now while she stared at him before continuing, 'It should happen that their coachman is a distant relation to Simes, second cousin or some such.'

'Really!'

'Yes, really.'

His head took on its bobbing motion as it was apt to do when he was angry or annoyed, and he said, 'I suppose Lord Myton challenged some young fellow to a duel because he admired his wife? . . . Oh!' – he flung one arm wide – 'why do you listen to such clap-trap, Eileen? Myton, I understand, is well into his sixties and past thrashing anyone or anything, even his dogs.' He sighed, then said quietly, 'Why do you listen to Price?'

He watched her lips quiver and when she brought out in a thin piping voice, 'I have no one else to listen to, you spare me very little of your time these days,' he dropped down on to the edge of the couch and, taking her hands in his, he said patiently, 'I've told you, Eileen, I can't be in two or three places at once, I'm up to my neck at the mine. There was a time when I could leave everything to Yarrow but not any more, things are critical. Come on, smile.' He cupped her chin in his hand, then said brightly, 'You'll never guess who is being married tomorrow. . . . Young Bentwood, the farmer, you know.'

'Really!' She smiled faintly at him and nodded her head as she repeated, 'Young Bentwood. Dear! Dear! I haven't seen him for years. He . . . he was quite a presentable young man.'

'Oh, he's that all right. A bit cocky, knows his own value, but he's a good farmer. He's made a better job of that place than his father did.'

'Do you know whom he's marrying?'

'A girl, I think.' He laughed and wagged her hand now, and she turned her face from him, saying, 'Oh, Mark!'

'No, I don't really know anything about her.'

'Do you think we should make them a present?'

'A present? Yes, I suppose so. But what?'

'Yes, what?' She put her head back on the pillow and thought for a moment, then said, 'A little silver, a little silver milk jug or sugar basin. There's a lot in the cabinets downstairs, one piece would never be missed.'

'No, you're right, and it's a nice gesture.' He moved his head down towards her and kissed her lightly on the cheek, then repeated, 'A nice gesture, very thoughtful. When I come back later I'll bring some pieces up and you can choose.'

'Yes, do that. Oh, by the way, Mark' – she put out her hand to him now in a gentle pleading gesture as he moved from the bed – 'Go up to the nursery and speak to Matthew but please, please, be gentle. I know he's been naughty. Mabel tells me she went up and remonstrated with him. He's upset Dewhurst again. But the girl is weak, she has no control over the children. I . . . I don't know what's going to be done.'

He turned fully about now and in a manner that swept away his easy-going kindliness of the moment before, he said, 'I know what should be done, I've known what should be done for some time and we'll have to talk about this, Eileen. That boy should be sent away to school.'

'No, no, I won't have it, I've told you. I won't even discuss it. And . . . and anyway, boarding schools cost money and you're continually telling me that the household expenses must be cut down. No, no, I won't have it. Leave me. Please leave me.'

He left her with her hands thrashing the top of the silk coverlet, but he did not go up to the nursery. Running down the stairs once more, but his haste now conditioned by acute irritation, he burst out of the house, hurried across the courtyard and to the stables, and within minutes he was mounted and riding now towards the mine.

He couldn't understand the woman, he couldn't. She could only bear to see the children for a few minutes each day, yet the very mention of sending them away to school upset her. . . . No, no; he just couldn't understand the woman. Or any woman for that matter. Lady Myton who seemed to see life as a joke, or perhaps more accurately as a stage on which to play out her affairs and the cuckolding of her husband. Women were enigmas, and botheration, the lot of them.

🙠 3 · 🙢

'Aye, you do look bonny. Doesn't she, William?'

'Aye. Aye, she'll pass.'

They both looked smilingly at Tilly standing straight but with head slightly bowed.

'You should have gone to the church. Shouldn't she, William?'

'Yes, I should have thought you would have liked to see Simon wed because there's no one been kinder to you since you first set foot in this house.'

'No, you're right there, William,' Annie put in, nodding her head. 'An' you would have got a ride in one of the brakes, both there and back. An' that treat doesn't come upon you every day, now does it? And I'm sure Simon would be puzzled and a bit hurt likely. I wish I'd had the chance, I do, I do.'

Tilly's chin drooped a little further towards her chest. She knew that they were both staring at her waiting for an explanation which she had refused to voice over the past days because she could not say to them, 'I couldn't bear to see him married' but she knew she had to say something, so what she said, and in a mumble, was, 'It's me frock.'

'Your frock!' They voiced the words, one after the other. 'What's wrong with your frock? You look as fresh as a sprig in it.'

'Aw, Gran!' She had lifted her head now and also had caught hold of the skirt of the dress at each side pulling it to its full width as she exclaimed somewhat reproachfully, 'It's washed out! It's been turned up and turned down so many times it's got dizzy an' doesn't know if it's comin' or goin'.'

At this there was silence for a moment. Then as William eased himself from his elbow and lay back on his pillows and let out a deep grunt of a chuckle, Annie put her fingers across her mouth while Tilly, her head once again drooping, joined her smothered laughter to theirs.

As she had said, her dress was washed out. Its original colour of deep pink was only to be seen now under the ten rows of pintucks that ran shoulder to shoulder across her flat breast. When it was bought five years ago in the rag market in Newcastle for ninepence, the sleeves had been much too long; even after the cuffs had been turned up twice they still reached her knuckles; as for the gored bell-shaped skirt, its six-inch hem had been turned up another nine inches. There had been no thought at that time of cutting off either the bottom of the dress or the ends of the sleeves because Tilly was sprouting 'Like a corn stalk gone mad,' as Annie was apt to exclaim almost daily. And so as Tilly grew the dress was lengthened, until the day came when the six-inch hem was reduced to three inches and the dress was now of an embarrassing length reaching only to the top of her boots; in fact she knew she would be indecent if she had been wearing shoes, for her ankles would have been entirely exposed.

'Go on, get yourself off, lass, else you'll be late. The jollification will be over afore you get there. And look – " Annie reached up towards Tilly's bonnet, saying, 'Loosen some of your hair, a strand or two to bring over your ears.'

'Oh, Gran! I don't like it fluffed around me face.'

'I'm not fluffin' it around your face. There' – she patted the two dark brown curls of hair lying now in front of Tilly's ears – 'they show up your skin, set it off like.'

'Aw, Gran!'

'And stop saying, Aw, Gran! There you are.' She turned her about and pushed her towards the door. 'Enjoy yourself. Take everything in because we want to hear all about it the morrow. And tell Simon again that we wish him happiness. Tell him we wish him everything that he wishes for himself, and more 'cos he deserves it! Away with you.'

Tilly turned in the open doorway and, looking towards the bed, said softly, 'Bye-bye, Granda.'

'Bye-bye, lass. keep your back straight, your head up, an' remember you're bonny.'

'Now, now, now, don't say, Aw Gran or Granda again, else I'll slap your cheek for you.'

One final push from Annie sent Tilly towards the gate, and there she turned and waved her hand before hurrying along the bridle path.

She hurried until she knew she was out of sight of the cottage, and then her step slowed. It would be all over now; he'd be firmly wed, and to that girl! Woman. Twenty-four, he said she was, but she looked older. Her round blue eyes and fair fluffy hair didn't make her appear like a young woman. Not that her face looked old, it was just something in her manner. She had only met her the once when coming out of church and she knew she hadn't liked her. And it wasn't only because she was marrying Simon, she was the kind of woman she would never have liked. She had hinted as much to Mrs Ross.

Wasn't that funny! She was always telling herself it was funny, how she could talk to the parson's wife openly, even more so than she could to her granny. Sometimes she thought that the parson's wife and herself were about the same age, but Mrs Ross was all of twenty-six, she admitted so herself. She had never known anyone quite like her, life would be very dull without her, without their reading lessons and their talks. She wondered if she would dance the day. Perhaps not, not in the open. And anyway she mightn't be there for the wedding had taken place in Pelaw. Still, if the parson should happen to be there and Mrs Ross joined in the dancing, wouldn't that cause a stir?

For a moment she forgot the sickness in her heart as she imagined the straight faces and nodding heads of some of the villagers should the parson's wife forget herself so far as to allow her feet to hop.

She was glad she didn't live in the village, there was always bickering among one or other of them, mostly the churchgoers. She knew that Simon had come in for quite a bit of gossip because he had chosen a girl from so far away when all around him were, as her granda had said, lasses like ripe plums waiting for him to catch them falling.

She came to the burn. It was running gaily today, the water gurgling and struggling to make its way in between the rocks. She crossed it carefully because the water had risen slightly during the last few days owing to recent rainfalls, and was lapping over some of the stepping stones.

As she reached the further bank and bent forward to pull herself up on to the path she espied the head and shoulders of a boy half hidden by the bushes that bordered a small pool to the side of the burn. As she straightened up the boy rose from the bank but didn't come towards her, and she looked at him over the top of the bushes, saying, 'Hello, Steve.'

'Hi there, Tilly!'

'You fishin'?'

'No, no, just sitting watchin'. There's a salmon here. I don't know how he got up this far.'

'Oh!' She went round the bushes, her face eager. 'Are you going to catch him?'

'No.' He shook his head.

'No?' She was looking at him in surprise now, and again he said, 'No; I just like watchin' him. I don't think anybody knows he's here.'

'I'm sure they don't else he wouldn't be here long.'

'You're right.'

She stared at him. His face was solemn, unsmiling. He didn't look like any one of the McGraths, he didn't talk like any one of the McGraths, he didn't act like any one of the McGraths. She had at one time wondered if he had been stolen as a baby, but her granda had disabused her of that idea for he remembered the day Steve was born because he had helped to carry his father home drunk from the hills. There had been a still going and the hard stuff was running freely.

'You goin' to the weddin'?' he asked.

'Yes.' She moved her head once and while he stood looking at her she looked at him. He wasn't very tall for his age. He had a long face and sandy-coloured hair that looked strong, even wiry in parts for strands of it stood up straight from the crown of his head. His shoulders were thick but his legs looked thin, even skinny, below his moleskin knee pants. His movements were quick, jerky; yet when he spoke his words always came slowly, as if he had to think up each one before uttering it.

He didn't speak further, and so she said, 'Well, I'll have to be goin', else it'll be over.'

'You look different the day.'

'Do I?'

'Aye, bonny.'

She half turned away, then faced him again, and she smiled rather sadly at him as she said, 'Ta, thanks, Steve, but I don't believe you. I'll never look bonny 'cos I've got no flesh on me.'

'That's daft.' His words came surprisingly quickly now, and he added to them, 'You haven't to have loads of fat stickin' out of you like a cow's udders to be bonny.'

For a moment her face remained straight, and then her mouth sprang wide and her head went back before drooping forward, and as she laughed his chuckle slowly joined hers.

'You are funny, Steve,' she said, taking out a handkerchief and drying her eyes. 'I didn't feel like laughin' the day, but it was the way you said it.'

'Aye' – he jerked his head to the side – 'I can be funny at times, that's what they say, but mostly I keep me mouth shut, I find it pays.' His face was straight again, as was hers now, and she folded her handkerchief carefully and tucked it in the cuff of her dress before saying, 'Well now, I must be off this time. Ta-rah, Steve.'

'Ta-rah, Tilly.'

She had gone beyond the bushes when his voice came at her in a hissing whisper, calling, 'Don't let on about this fish,' and she called back, 'Why, no! I won't say a word.'

But as she went on she wondered why he should be sitting watching a fish, especially a salmon. He was a funny lad, was Steve, but nice. She had always liked him. She wished that the rest of his family took after him.

She had just reached the coach road when a brake full of people passed her, and they waved their hands and shouted unintelligible greetings to her. But the driver didn't pull the horses to a stop to give her a lift, and she stood where she was well back on the verge of the road until the vehicle disappeared into the distance because she didn't want to walk in the dust that the horses and the wheels had thrown up.

The sounds of jollification came to her while she was still quite some distance from the farm, and she slowed her step. She wished she needn't go, she didn't want to see Simon, or his new wife. She had been thinking over the past week that it would be better if she never clapped eyes on Simon Bentwood again, but she knew this would be difficult because they never knew which day he would pop in with the monthly sovereign. That business was still troubling her; she even lay awake at nights now wondering about it.

As she went through a gateless gap in the stone walls and crossed the farmyard towards the front of the house she saw that the whole place seemed transformed. It wasn't only that there were a lot of people milling about, but on the lawn there were two long tables set in the form of a T, both weighed down with food; and there was a tent at the far end of the lawn and the open flaps showed the big head of a beer barrel and a laughing man busily filling tankards.

She stood shyly by one of the long windows that were on each side of the front door. Simon's father had had these put in some years ago at his own expense and had had to pay tax for doing it, so she had been told. As she stood looking on the gay milling scene she chided herself for wondering at this particular moment if the money for the windows had come out of the same coffer as the monthly sovereign, and she was telling herself to stop it, because the matter seemed to be getting between her and her wits, when she heard her name being called loudly, and she turned to see Simon coming down the two steps that led from the front door. The next minute he was holding her hand and she was looking into his face. His eyes were bright, his mouth was wide. 'Where've you been?' he cried at her. 'I thought you weren't coming. And why didn't you come to the church, eh?' He was bending towards her, his face level with hers. 'Come' – he was pulling her now – 'come and see Mary.'

He tugged her up the steps and into the farm sitting-room to where his bride was standing in her white dress.

Tilly mouthed her good wishes as her granny had told her to. 'I hope you have a very happy life,' she said, 'and never want for nothing; an' that's from me granny and granda an' all.'

'Oh thank you. Thank you.' The words were polite, stilted. The lids blinked rapidly over the blue eyes and as the bow-shaped mouth moved into a wider smile Tilly thought grudgingly, She's bonny, I suppose, and I can see what got Simon. Oh aye. Her look went to where the white lace dipped deeply between the full breasts, then swept downwards to the tight-laced waist, and as her eyes lowered towards the floor her practical mind told her that there was all of ten yards of satin or more in the skirt of the dress.

'Oh, how kind of you.'

She found herself nudged aside by the churchwarden and his wife, Mr and Mrs Fossett. Mrs Fossett was being gushing, as usual. 'Oh, you do look beautiful, Mrs Bentwood. And what a wedding! what a spread! The village has seen nothin' like it for years.' Then came the sting as it always did from Mrs Fossett's barbed tongue. ''Twas ... 'twas a pity though you couldn't have been married in our church. Oh, that would have given the stamp to the day. But there, there. . . . I would like you to accept this little gift. It's really nothing, although it's very old, it belonged to my great-grandmother.'

As she spoke she was unwrapping a small parcel, and when the paper fell away it showed a flower vase of no apparent attraction.

'Oh, thank you. Thank you.'

As Tilly looked at the bride she was asking herself if that was all she was ever going to say; but she was wrong, for now the new Mrs Bentwood led the way to a table at the end of the room and there, from amid a number of presents she picked up a fluted sugar basin and, holding it up for all to see, she said, 'Mr Sopwith himself called in earlier on and brought us this. It's a present from his wife.' There was a pause before she ended, 'It's solid silver; it's from their collection.'

'Oh! Oh!' Mrs Fossett's voice was cool. She nodded her head, then said, 'Very nice. Very nice.'

'Enough. Enough of presents for the time being. Come on, it's time we had something to eat. . . . Mrs Bentwood – " Simon now playfully caught hold of his bride's arm and in a masterful voice demanded, 'Aren't you going to see to my victuals, woman?'

There was general laughter and the company in the room followed the bride and bridegroom outside on to the lawn. All except Tilly. She remained behind for a moment and looked round the room. She had often been in this room. She'd had her dreams about this room. It was a bonny room; it wasn't like other rooms in the house, dim because of the small windows. Old Mr Bentwood had known what he was doing when he'd had these windows put in.

She turned and made for the door and as she did so she saw Mrs Ross, the parson's wife, passing, and Mrs Ross saw her and, coming quickly up the steps, she said, 'Hello, Tilly,' and not waiting for Tilly's greeting, she added in a voice that was low and rapid and was backed by a mischievous gurgle, 'Have you seen the vicar? I should have been here an hour ago but I got caught up with a class.' Her voice sank even lower now and her eyes seemed to sparkle more as she brought her face close to Tilly's and whispered, 'I've got three pitmen. Aha! Aha!' Her head moved in little jerks now. 'What do you think of that? Three pitmen!'

Tilly's voice was as conspiratorial as hers and her eyes shone as she repeated, 'Three . . . for learnin'?'

'Ssh!' The parson's wife now looked from side to side. 'Not a word. They came of their own accord, said they wanted to learn their letters. Of course it's dangerous' – she straightened her back – 'I mean for them. Should Mr Rosier get to know they'll be dismissed their work. Dreadful. Dreadful, when you come to think of it.'

''Tis, 'tis awful.' Tilly nodded vigorously. 'Just because they want to learn their letters!'

'They were as black as the devil himself.' The parson's wife was gurgling again. 'They hadn't washed, you see. Well, if they had got tidied up to come to the vicarage someone would have noticed. But they were supposedly on their way home from their shift, as they said.'

'But where did you learn them? I mean, where did you take them?'

'In the summer-house at the bottom of the garden.'

'Oh, Mrs Ross!' Tilly had her hand over her mouth now. Then her face straight, she said, 'What about the parson?'

At this Mrs Ross cast her eyes towards the ceiling and said, 'Heigh-ho! nonny-no! skull, hair and feathers flying.'

'He'll be very vexed?'

Mrs Ross now turned her head to the side as if considering, then said, 'I really don't know, Tilly. I've thought about it and somehow I think he might even turn a blind eye... seeing they are men. Oh, it's different for men. As you know he doesn't hold with women learning. I can't understand that about Geor... Mr Ross, because he is wide you know, Tilly, very wide in his views.'

'Yes, yes, I know, Mrs Ross. Yes, I know. Oh my!' She looked past the parson's wife out on to the lawn as she whispered now, 'They are sitting down at the tables. Should we be going?'

'Dear! dear! yes.' Mrs Ross swung round so quickly that the skirt of her grey alpaca dress formed itself for a moment into a bell and it looked to Tilly as if she were about to run down the steps and across the lawn. This thought made her want to laugh; just think of the faces if the parson's wife was seen running across the lawn! She loved Mrs Ross. She did, she did.... Could you love a woman? Yes, she supposed you could, like you loved God. And she was the nearest thing she knew to God. Eeh! that somehow sounded like blasphemy. Yet she was. Yes, she was; she was better and kinder than anybody she knew. What's more, she was of *the class*, and you didn't get much kindness from *the class*, did you? Not really. You usually had to work for the kindness you got from *the class*. And yet *the class*, in the form of Mr Sopwith, had been kind to her granda and her great-granda by letting them have the cottage. But then her great-granda had worked for the Sopwiths from he was six years old, and her granda had worked in the Sopwith mine since he was eight. Still, he hadn't got the cottage because he had worked in the mine, because so many men worked in the mine and they didn't get cottages, he had got the cottage because he had dived into the lake in the bitter cold weather and saved Mr Mark Sopwith, as he was now, from drowning. The lad had gone out in a boat when he shouldn't and it had capsized and he couldn't swim, and his father had been on the shore and stood there helpless, and her granda had dived in and brought him out almost dead. The young lad had survived without hurt, but her granda had always had his chest after that. Her granda shouldn't have been in the Sopwith grounds that day, he was after a rabbit and could have been had up for poaching, but old Mr Sopwith, who was religious, said that God had sent him, and for saving his son's life he had let him have the cottage free for as long as he should live.

Her mind was wandering. Everybody was laughing and shouting all up and down the tables and all towards the bride and bridegroom. Someone pushed a great chunk of hare pie in front of her. She didn't like hare, it was too strong, but she nibbled at it out of politeness.

She lost count of the time she sat at the table. Everybody was talking, but she hadn't much to say. Mrs Ross was now at the top table seated next to the parson, and she herself was stuck between Mr Fairweather and Bessie Bradshaw, the wife of the innkeeper. She didn't know Mrs Bradshaw very well, only that no one ever called her Mrs Bradshaw, it was always Bessie. She knew Mr Fairweather because he was one of the sidesmen at the church, but she had never liked him, he always sang the hymns louder and longer than anybody else, and his amens were like an echo, they came so long after the prayer was finished. But now he was laughing a lot; he'd had his tankard filled four times to her knowledge. There was a tankard of home-brewed beer in front of her, too, but she had only sipped at it because it was bitter; it had a different bitterness to the herb beer her granny made, she liked that.

The whole table now seemed to rock to its feet as somebody cried, 'The fiddlers! The fiddlers!' and there at the other side of the lawn two fiddlers were dragging their bows across the strings while the man with a melodeon began to pull it in and out.

She was glad to get to her feet, but as she was lifting one booted foot decorously over the form she squealed and almost jumped in the air; then turning angrily about, her face flushed, she stared at Mr Fairweather and in no small voice she cried, 'Don't you dare do that to me, Mr Fairweather!' whereupon Andy Fairweather, the usually staid church sidesman, put his head back and laughed, saying, ''Tis a weddin', girl. 'Tis a weddin'.'

'Wedding or no' – she backed from him, her hand to her bottom – 'you keep your hands to yourself.'

There was much laughter from the bottom of the table and as the company made towards the far end of the lawn somebody chokingly spluttered, 'Andy Fairweather put his finger in her backside.'

'Never! Andy Fairweather? Ho! Ho!'

''Tis the wedding. 'Tis the wedding. There'll be more than backsides probed the night.'

She wanted to go home, she wasn't enjoying this wedding, not a bit. But she had known she wouldn't before she came.

'Here, Tilly! what you looking so solemn about?' It was Simon, and once again he had hold of her hand. 'Not a smile on your face. I saw you at the bottom of the table. And what was that business with Andy Fairweather?'

She turned her head to the side, then looked down as she simplified things by muttering, 'He nipped me . . . my . . .'

'Oh! Oh! . . . Andy Fairweather nipped your . . . ? Well! Well?'

As she looked into his face she saw that he was straining not to laugh; then his mouth springing wide, he said, 'See the funny side of it, Tilly: Andy Fairweather nipping anybody. My! the ale must have spread right down to his innards for him to do that. Next time you see him in church claiming kinship with the Almighty, just think of him the day, eh?' He jerked her hand in his and she bit on her lip and began to laugh. 'Come on, there's a nice lad over here, his people are neighbours of Mary's. Come on, give him a dance.'

'No! no!' She pulled back from his hand, but he held on to her tightly, saying, 'Look, I won't enjoy me wedding if I see you sitting with a face like a wet week-end. Come on.' But as he tugged her across the lawn, weaving in and out of the company, his wife's voice suddenly arrested him, saying, 'Simon! Simon! Come here a minute.'

He stopped and looked over the heads of the group surrounding her and, his chin up, he called to her, 'In two ticks, Mary. Be with you in two ticks.' The next minute he had pulled Tilly to a stop opposite a young boy of seventeen. 'Bobby, this is Tilly, a great friend of mine. Now I want you to look after her, give her a dance. What about it?'

'Aye, yes, yes, Simon.'

Simon was now peering down into Tilly's face. His own mock stern, his voice imitating a growl, he ordered her, 'Enjoy yourself, Miss Tilly Trotter. Do you hear? Enjoy yourself.' Then on a laugh he patted her cheek and turning from her hurried to his bride.

Tilly looked at the boy and the boy looked at Tilly, and neither of them found a word to say to each other.

When in embarrassment she turned from him and went and sat on a weather-worn oak bench that was set against a low hedge bordering the lawn, he paused for a full minute before following her and taking his place by her side.

Then together they sat in silence and watched women clearing the tables and carrying the remnants of the food around the side of the house and into the barn where later in the evening the jollification would continue.

The lawn finally cleared, the fiddlers and the melodeon player struck up a lively tune, and almost immediately Simon, leading his bride into the middle of the lawn, cried, 'Come on, let's go!' And this was the signal for the men to grab their partners and start the dance.

The musicians played polkas and jigs, and the dancers danced, some in step and some out of it, stopping between times to refresh themselves from the barrel. Once Simon waved to Tilly telling her to get to her feet, but she shook her head.

She was on the point of getting up and walking away from her tongue-tied companion when she saw Simon weaving his way towards her. Then he was standing over them, looking from one to the other and demanding, 'What's the matter with you two? This is a wedding not a funeral! Come on.' He pulled her up, and the next minute he was whirling her over the grass. One, two, three, hop! One, two, three, hop! They went into the polka and, laughing, he cried to her, 'By! you're as light as a feather.' Then bending his mouth down to her ear, he said, 'She taught you well.'

She had no breath for speaking and so she just shook her head at him and went on lifting her feet: One, two, three, hop! One, two, three, hop! When he almost swung her into the air, so light did she feel she could imagine she hadn't any boots on.

At last the music stopped; he held her tightly against him for a moment; then looking down into her face, he said, 'What about that, eh?'

"Twas wonderful, Simon. Wonderful.'

'Well, you go on now and take Bobby.'

'No! No! I'm not going back to him, he's never opened his mouth.'

'Well, did you open yours?'

'No.'

'Well then. . . . I've got to go, but enjoy yourself.' His face became straight for a moment as he ended, 'I want you to enjoy yourself, Tilly, and be happy with me the day.'

She could find no answer to give him, not even to say politely, 'I will, I will. Don't worry, I'll enjoy meself.'

'Simon!' A man was pulling at his sleeve. 'Your missus is calling you. By! you're going to get it.'

'Oh aye. Oh aye. Comin' George. I'm comin'.' Without further words he turned from her.

She watched him but he did not make directly towards where his wife was sitting below the house steps; instead he went towards the beer tent, and when he was handed a tankard of beer she saw him put it to his mouth and almost drain it at one go.

He would be drunk before the night was over. Men usually got drunk on their wedding night, at least those who drank did. Would she like the man she married to get drunk on her wedding night? A stupid question to ask herself 'cos she would never marry. With or without the chance she would never marry.

She looked about her. What could she do? Who could she talk to? There were three old village women sitting alongside the wall at the far end of the house; she'd go and talk to them, she was used to talking to old people. She got on well with old people; likely it was having lived with her granda and grandma all these years.

Two hours later, when the light was beginning to go, she knew she could now make her excuses and go home. She had talked to the old women, she had been in the kitchen and helped to wash up, she had been in the barn and filled plates with odds and ends and carried empty ones back into the house. The guests had now sorted themselves out, those who were going home had already left such as the parson and Mrs Ross and the old people who were tired. One brake-load had set off an hour ago back to Felling. She went up the steps into the house to say good-bye to Simon and his wife. There was nobody in the front room. She went out into the passage, then into the hall; and there they were, he had his arms around her and was kissing her.

Her muttering, 'Oh, I'm sorry!' brought them apart, yet still holding.

''Tis all right, Tilly, 'tis all right.' His voice was slurred and he held out one hand towards her, but she remained standing, saying, 'I'm off now; I just wanted to say thank you.' She didn't look at Simon but at his wife. 'It . . . it was a lovely wedding. Good-night.' She was about to add, 'I wish you happiness,' when Simon made to come towards her but was stopped by his wife, her hand on his arm. He remained still, asking now, 'You'll be all right?'

'Yes, yes. Aye, of course, thank you. Thank you.' She nodded to both of them, then backed into the doorway before turning and going hastily out.

She had begun to make her way towards the farmyard when she saw Mr Fairweather and Mr Laudimer, another sidesman at the church, standing together. They were laughing and had their hands on each other's shoulders. She didn't want to pass them. She looked towards the far end of the lawn. There was a gate that led into a meadow, and further on there was a bridle path that would bring her out near the toll bridge and the coach road, and from there she could pick up her usual route home.

A few minutes later she had let herself through the gate and had walked across the meadow and swung herself over a low stone wall and so on to the bridle path that ran alongside it.

She must have gone about a mile along the path when she saw galloping towards her a horse and rider. Jumping to the side she pressed tight against the hedge to allow them to pass, but the man drew the horse up almost opposite her. She recognised him as Mr Sopwith, and he, recognising her, said, 'Hello there.'

'Hel . . . Good-evenin', sir.'

'You're some way from home, aren't you?'

'Yes. Yes, sir; I've been to Mr Bentwood's weddin'.'

'Oh, the wedding. Oh yes, yes.' He nodded down at her smiling. Then casting his eyes about him, he asked, 'Did you happen to see a lady on a horse further along this road?'

'No, sir, no; I haven't met anyone but yourself.'

'Oh. Well, thank you. Good-night.'

'Good . . . good-night, sir.'

He rode on again, putting the horse into a gallop, and she watched him for a moment before going on her way. . . .

As Mark came to the meadow he took the horse over the stone wall, then again drew it to a stop, and once more he looked about him; then settling himself in the seat, he brought his teeth tightly together for a moment before muttering aloud, 'Damn!' She was playing cat and mouse with him: she was very much the cat and he didn't like being put in the position of the mouse. 'All prizes must be won,' she had said, doubtless considering herself as being a very big prize. Well, he'd had enough; he would return home. He had ridden like an escaping hare hither and thither for the past hour, and likely she was back in her house laughing up her sleeve.

What was the matter with him anyway? Why had he allowed himself to get in this state? She was coming between him and his sleep. He felt he would know no peace until he'd had her. But then what? Would the taste of her consume him or would he be brought to his senses and the fire in him quenched? It had happened before. Many years ago, he had become enamoured of a woman, so much so that he had thought life would be worthless without her. Janet, his first wife, had known. He had hurt her terribly but he hadn't been able to help himself. Once he had conquered, however, the woman had gone sour on him and he had sworn never again, never, never again. Yet here he was galloping the countryside after a will-o'-the-wisp. Except that Lady Agnes Myton was no will-o'-the-wisp, she was a full-blooded, alluring, maddening woman.

He rode along by the wall, jumped a hedge, and came on to the coach road, and in the distance he could hear the faint sound of a fiddle being played. . . . Farmer Bentwood's wedding was still in full swing.

As he put his horse into a gallop he damned and blasted Lady Agnes Myton. He was tired, as he also knew was his mount, and he doubted if he would make home before dark. Again he damned her.

Then at a turning in the road his horse shied from one side to the other as the figure of a boy came bursting through the hedge.

'What the hell!' Mark Sopwith pulled himself straight in the saddle and, glaring, bent towards the boy who had paused in his run and was gasping as he spluttered, 'Sorry, mister. Sorry,' and quickly drawing in one long breath, he raced off down the road, leaving Mark still glaring after him.

Now what had he been up to? Poaching? But if someone was after him he wouldn't have stopped to say he was sorry. He turned the horse around, allowing it to move at a walking pace now. . . .

Steve McGrath was a good runner. He had won a race at the hill fair last year, beating lads three and four years older than himself, but that race hadn't taken it out of him like this one was doing. The sweat was running down his groin and his short moleskin breeks were sticking to his buttocks.

He didn't seem to hear the music until he stopped to hug the end of the brick wall that bordered the farmyard and the gateless drive-in. There was a pain in his chest, his feet were sore and his legs at this moment were like jelly and threatening to give way beneath him. He tried to call out to someone crossing the yard, but his voice came out as a croak.

A minute later he stumbled into the yard and, catching hold of a man's arm, said, 'Mister! Mister! Where will I find Mr Bentwood?'

The man turned a laughing face down on him.

'With his bride, lad, with his bride, where else? Tripping the light fantastic.' He pointed towards the barn from where was coming the loud noise of the fiddles and the whining of the melodeon.

'Will you get him, mister, will you get him for me?'

'Get him for you?' The man peered down at him. 'You're young McGrath, aren't you? Aye yes, young McGrath. What do you want with him?'

'I must get him, talk to him, I've got somethin' to tell him.'

'You can tell him nowt this night, lad; I should say he's past listenin'.'

'Mister! Mister!' He was clutching at the man now. 'Tell him, will you? Tell him somebody is going to get hurt, somebody he knows. Ask him if I can see him a minute. Go on, will you, will you? Please! Please!'

'Who's gona get hurt?'

'Just . . . just somebody, somebody he knows.'

'Oh! Oh, well, well, if that's it.' The man turned about and with a gait that spoke of his having imbibed not a little from the barrel, he made his way into the barn.

Steve moved to the side to get out of the way of people who were coming and going, all laughing and joking. He stood with his back pressed against the stone wall of the cow byre but keeping his eyes on the great open doors of the barn and, fascinated, he watched the scene within.

The whole place was lit with lanterns. Some people were dancing, and some people were standing drinking, and some were sitting round the walls eating, but all had their mouths open and were laughing.

So immersed had he become for the moment in the scene that he didn't realise Simon was coming towards him, nor that the bride was standing just within the barn and that she alone wasn't smiling.

'What is it boy? What do you want?'

'Oh. Oh, Mr Bentwood, it's . . . it's Tilly. She needs somebody to see to her. I . . . I couldn't, I mean on her way home, because there's three of them.'

'What on earth are you talkin' about, boy?' Simon's brain was not very clear, it was fogged with ale and not a little with happiness and expectation of his wedding night, and his voice now was full of impatience as he demanded, 'Speak clearly, boy! what you gettin' at?'

Steve swallowed a mouthful of spittle before he said slowly, 'She'll . . . she'll have to have somebody to guide her home, perhaps more than one, 'cos they're gona net her.'

'Net her?' Simon was now bending over him and he repeated, 'Net her? What you on about, lad?'

'It's . . . it's our Hal and Mick and Ned Wheeler. Our Hal said, well, she wouldn't have him the clean way so she's gona have him t'other way.' He bit his lip and his head drooped.

Simon straightened his back and looked around him. In his glance he saw his wife staring enquiringly towards him, and he raised his hand as if to say, 'I'll be there in a minute,' then taking the boy by the shoulder, he pushed him into the cowshed and seeming now to sober up, he said, 'Make it quick, boy, explain yourself!'

'They're waitin' for her. They've a net rigged up in a tree. She's strong, Tilly, wiry, an' our Hal knew she'd fight like a chained bitch, an' so they're gona net her an' . . . an' – ' He turned his head to the side, bit hard on his lip again, then muttered, 'He's gona take her down, then she'll have to have him.'

'What!'

The boy looked up into Simon's face which was now twisted in disbelief and he said, 'He'd murder me if he knew I'd split. But it was our George, I heard him tellin' me dad and me dad was for it. George wouldn't go along with them and me dad went for him and said he was soft. And then he said – ' He stopped and shook his head, and Simon cried impatiently, 'Yes! yes! what did he say?'

'I don't know what it meant, it . . . it was about somethin' they wanted to find out, it seemed to be mixed up with money, and if he got Tilly he'd find out. It was double Dutch. . . .'

'My God!' Simon now pushed his hand up through his hair.

'You'll take her home?'

'She's gone, boy, this fifteen or twenty minutes or more. . . . Come on. . . . No, wait. Where are they going to do this?'

'Billings Flat near the wood. Eeh! God, they could have her by now.' He put his hand to his mouth, then muttered, 'But I . . . I can't come along of you 'cos he'd . . . he'd brain me.'

Simon didn't hear the boy's protest, he was already running towards the barn where his bride was still standing. When he reached her he took her by the hands and pulled her aside, out into the yard, across it and into the dairy, and there, holding her hands against his chest, he said, 'Listen, me dear, there's something come up, I've . . . I've got to leave you, but I won't be a half-hour or more.'

'Where . . . where are you going?'

'It's' – he closed his eyes and shook his head – 'it's nothing, just a little bit of business.'

'Business? Business that can't wait on this special night! What did that boy want?'

'He had come to tell me something. I'll . . . I'll explain it all when I come back.

I tell you I won't be more than half an hour. keep things going. Anyway I won't be missed, only by you I hope.' He jerked her hard against him and kissed her upon the lips. Then looking at her again, he said, 'It's been a grand day, and it's not over yet, is it?'

'I hope not.' She was smiling at him now. 'Don't be long.'

'I won't, I won't, I promise.' He kissed her again quickly; then pulling her out through the door, he pushed her gently towards the barn before he himself turned and ran into the stable.

Simon was quite used to riding bare-back though not in tight breeches; but there was no time to stop and saddle the mare, and within minutes he was out of the yard, causing some of the guests to stand and gape as if they couldn't believe their eyes, for wasn't that the bridegroom riding out on his own!

Billings Flat was all of two miles from the farm and about half a mile from the cottage. To anyone for whom the name conjured up an open area, this particular piece of land was misnamed, for the path ran at the bottom of a shallow stretch of land bordered on each side by trees which were intertwined here and there with great shrouds of ivy, the Flat itself being more than twenty yards in length and only in winter when the trees were bare did full light penetrate it.

Simon knew that he could cut off a further mile by taking his horse straight across his fields. This would be against his principles for he hated even the hunt to cross his fields either on horse or on foot; but this was a case of needs must when the devil drove, and the devil was driving him now because he swore inside himself that if Hal McGrath had taken Tilly down then he wouldn't live long to enjoy his victory.

Tilly hadn't hurried on her way home. Again as of late, she'd had the desire to cry, and that was something she mustn't do, not until she got into bed because else how would she explain her red eyes to her granny and granda: she was returning from a wedding and they were sitting up waiting to hear all the news. And she knew that she'd have to make things up, at least about herself, how she had eaten a grand tea and drunk Simon's home-brewed ale, and danced. And then she would have to tell them what the bride looked like and how Simon, too, had appeared. Well, she could be truthful about Simon for she would say to them he looked happy.

She stepped out of the twilight into Billings Flat. She blinked her eyes and turned her gaze towards the ground, being careful where she placed her feet for the roots of the trees spread across the path in places and had tripped her up many a time before today. She had never been afraid passing through Billings Flat. Many people were; the village women in particular would never come this way after dark, for it was said that the long hollow had once been a burial ground, and that at one time it had been dug over and the bodies carted away. But her granda said that this was all nonsense because it would take a few hundred bodies lying side by side to fill the Flat.

She was halfway along it and could see through the dim funnel where the trees ended and the twilight in comparison showed almost bright, when something came flying out of the heavens at her like a bird with extended wings and brought a high piercing scream from her. The thing now had her on the ground trapping her arms and legs and she continued to thrash and scream until the wind was knocked completely out of her as a body, a human body, pressed down on her and fingers digging into her cheeks clamped her mouth shut.

Her eyes, wide in a petrified gaze, were now peering through the mesh of a net and into a face, and she knew the face. There were other figures at each side of her holding her arms tight to the ground. She wanted to yell out in agony because one forearm was being bent over a rut in the path.

She couldn't believe this was happening to her until Hal McGrath, his breath fanning her face now, said between gasps, 'You've got some fight in you, skinny as you are, that's your choppin' 'n sawin', I'll . . . I'll put that to use an' all. Now listen . . . listen, Tilly Trotter. I asked you squarely, I wanted to court you proper, I gave you a chance but you'd have none of it. Well now, you wouldn't take it the decent way, you'll take it t'other an' when your belly's full I'll come an' claim me own. Your two old 'uns won't last much longer, then what'll you do? You know what happens to lasses who get taken down, it's the house or the whore shop. . . . Go . . . God Almighty!'

This exclamation was wrenched from him as Tilly, gathering every fraction of strength she had left in her body, surprised them all by getting one leg free from under the side of McGrath's body and, twisting herself, brought her knee up with all the force she could muster into McGrath's groin, so causing him for a moment to release the pressure on her mouth; and now, her strong teeth going through the net dug into the side of his hand.

'You bloody vixen you! God!' He thrust his doubled fist between his legs. Then as the men on each side of him scrambled to hold her thrashing limbs she let out another blood-curdling scream. But this was throttled at its height by a hand again clapping itself over her mouth. And now McGrath was growling, 'Get the net off her; it'll be here and now. By God! it will. It will.'

When her skirt was flung over her head the hand left her mouth and again she screamed, but once more the wind was knocked out of her body.

It was as somebody laughed that she cried from the essence of her soul 'Oh God! No! No! No! Please. No! No! No!' and it was as if instantly He had heard her prayer, for her hands were released and she heard a voice that hadn't spoken before gabbling, 'Somebody comin'. Hal! Hal man! stop. Stop! somebody comin'. A horseman an' more than one about somewhere, I know, I know, I can hear 'em. Let's be gone! Let's be gone!' Then another voice, full of panic now said, 'Give over, Hal man. Listen, they're comin'. I'm off. I'm off.'

The next minute the weight was wrenched from her. She lay inert, the skirt and petticoats still over her head, her body trembling from head to foot, aware of her indecent appearance yet not able to exert the strength needed to pull her clothes down and see what was happening about her.

She had a strange feeling on her and felt that she must be going to faint. But she had never fainted before, only ladies fainted, and then only when in church. Dimly she was aware of the sound of thuds and groans and curses and of horses' hooves trampling quite near her. She heard a woman's voice and a man's voice, both strange, then her skirt and petticoats were pulled down from her face and her shoulders were brought upwards, and the woman was saying, 'Really! Really!

They're savages! Hadn't I just said they were savages.' Then turning to the man, she said, 'Stop him before he kills him, whoever he is.'

Mark Sopwith now ran towards where Simon had Hal McGrath pressed against a tree, his fingers around his throat, while McGrath's hands were gripping the wrists in an endeavour to free himself.

'Leave go! Leave go, man! you'll choke him to death. Leave go, I tell you!' Mark Sopwith brought the side of his hand sharply down across Simon's forearm, and as if a spring had released his hands Simon dropped them away from McGrath's throat and stumbled backwards.

His face was bleeding from a cut above his eye; the sleeve of his wedding coat was wrenched partly from the shoulder. His head thrust forward, his hands hanging limply by his side now, he stood gasping, his eyes tight on McGrath who, with hands clutching his own throat, sidled drunkenly from the tree.

It was Mark Sopwith who spoke now. Peering through the dusk he said in some surprise, 'You're McGrath, aren't you, the blacksmith at the mine? Yes. Yes. Well! I'll deal with you later. Now get! Clear out. Go on!'

Hal McGrath didn't immediately obey the order but, looking from one to the other of the men, he said, "'Twas nought to do with either of you, nowt! I was courtin' her. 'Twas family business, courtin'.'

'And her screaming her head off? Go on, on your way before I myself decide to have a go at you. And by the way' – he held up his hand – 'show yourself at the office on Monday; my manager will have something to say to you.'

McGrath's face twisted as he stared at the mine owner; then muttering curses, he turned from them.

Both men now went to where Tilly was still sitting on the ground, but Lady Myton was no longer bending over her, she was standing dusting her gloved hands together. Looking towards them, she said, 'She's got the shakes, she's been badly frightened.'

Simon passed her without a word and, dropping on to his hunkers at Tilly's side, he put his arm around her shoulders, saying hesitantly, 'Are . . . are you all right?'

The words 'all right' had a twofold meaning, and after a moment, as if she were considering, she moved her head slowly downwards.

'Come on, I'll get you home.'

When he lifted her gently to her feet her legs threatened to give way beneath her and she leant against him, her head pillowed on his breast.

'The farmer, isn't it?'

Simon turned and peered at Lady Myton, but he gave her no answer, just stared at her as she continued, a chuckle in her voice now, 'It's your wedding day, I understand. What brought you here, you couldn't have heard her screaming from your farm?'

'No, me lady, I didn't hear her screaming from my farm' – his words were slow and heavy – 'I was warned of what was going to happen to her.'

'Oh, and you got here just in time . . . I think so anyway.'

'Come.' He now turned from them and led Tilly towards where his horse was standing calmly munching at the grass on the side of the bank, and after he had lifted her on to its bare back he turned his head and looked towards Mark Sopwith, saying, 'Thanks. Thanks for your help, sir.'

'I was no help, except to stop you killing him. You just could have you know.'

'Pity I didn't.' He now bent his knees, then with a heave of his body he, too, was sitting astride the horse, his arms around Tilly gripping the reins. Slowly he urged the animal forward and when it passed Lady Myton he did not look towards her or give her any word of farewell, although she was standing looking up at him. . . .

Mark Sopwith went back along the road and, gathering up the reins of the two horses which had also been contentedly munching at the grass on the bank, he brought them forward, and when he reached Lady Myton she lifted her gaze from the departing figures and, looking at him, she said, 'Well! Well! an interesting interlude.' Then after a moment's pause she added, 'The interruption came at a most crucial part of our conversation. If I remember rightly' – her head drooped to one side now – 'you were about to extract your winnings, Mr Sopwith.'

As he handed her the reins of her horse he could scarcely make out the outline of her face but he knew that she was laughing at him, and he also knew that she didn't think he would be ungentlemanly enough at this stage to, as she said, extract his winnings from her.

Well, she was mistaken for there would be no better time than the present, nor place for that matter, to prove her wrong, and if it lay with him he would extract his winnings to the full before the night was out because she had led him a dance. It was as if she had been in a position all evening to watch his every move for when, disgruntled, he had been making his way home she had stepped out on him, elegantly straight in the saddle, some little distance from the Flat, and what she had said was, 'Good-evening, Mr Sopwith. Were you looking for me?'

When, having dismounted, he had gone to her she had extended her arms towards him and he had helped her down from the saddle. Having lifted her to the ground, he had kept his hold on her as he answered her, saying, 'No, Lady Myton, you weren't even in my thoughts.'

He had still been holding her, their faces close together, their eyes telling each other that a certain kind of relationship was about to begin, when a girl's scream brought them apart.

It could have been a girlish scream of delight, but neither of them was sure, and they waited for it to be repeated, then were about to resume their own affairs when it came again.

When he moved from her and held his ear cocked, she had enquired coolly, 'What do you think it might be, some yokel causing his lady love to squeal with delight?'

'That was no squeal of delight.'

A few minutes later another scream was abruptly cut off and so he quickly helped her to mount, then turning in the direction of Billings Flat, he said, 'Follow me.'

'What? What did you say?'

He had turned towards her and said slowly, 'I said follow me.'

'Oh, I thought that was what you said.'

He knew that she was annoyed, yet once they reached the scene in which the

Trotter girl was involved her attitude changed, and he had the idea she had really been amused by it all.

And now she was awaiting developments. Well, he wouldn't keep her waiting any longer.

At the end of the Flat he took the reins from her and now quickly urged the horses towards a low bank. Once up it, he doubled them back and now led them along the higher ground beyond the belt of trees that bordered the Flat.

Here the belt thinned out into saplings and scrub land, and after not more than a minute's walk he tied the horses to a tree, then turned and waited until she came stumbling towards him. He could see her face now. Her eyes were wide and filled with amusement, her mouth was laughing. She didn't speak, but he did and what he said was, 'I'm ready for the prize-giving.'

He knew that she was about to laugh and loud, but just as Tilly's scream had been smothered, so was her laughter now as he, putting his arms about her, swung her from her feet. The next minute they had both tumbled on to the ground, and there they lay staring at each other for a moment, but only for a moment.

As often happened in his life, the prize turned out in the end to be somewhat of a surprise holding a negative quality, because, whereas he knew who was master in the beginning, at the end he was not at all sure, and he was made to wonder how an elderly man like her husband coped with such passion, that was if he attempted to cope at all. Perhaps it was lack of his coping that made her so ravenous.

It had been a very unusual night, but strangely he wasn't feeling elated, not even temporarily happy.

As Simon helped Tilly into the cottage Annie, turning in her chair before the fire where she had been dozing, put her hands to her lips and muttered, 'God in heaven! what's happened?'

In a matter of seconds she was pulling herself from the chair and glancing towards the bed where William was now easing himself on to his side, his face showing the same amazement as hers, and turning, she said again, 'What is it. What is it? What's happened?' She was now standing in front of Tilly, and Tilly, throwing herself into the old woman's arms, began to sob, spluttering as she did so, 'Oh Gran! Gran!'

Holding her tightly, Annie looked up at Simon, at his blood-smeared face and at his rent coat, and in a voice that was a mere whisper she asked him again, 'What's happened, lad? What's happened to you? And why are you here this night of all nights?'

Simon, dropping into a chair at the side of the table, didn't answer her directly, but looking towards William, he said, 'Doesn't take long in the telling. McGrath tried to take her down, the dirty bugger! But besides that, he netted her in order to do it.'

'Netted her?' William's face was screwed up.

'Aye, you know the old game, the net slung up atween a couple of accommodatin' trees, with a slip knot and a pole. The last time I heard of it being used was years ago when they wanted to trap a good pony. Safer way than chasing your guts out across the moor.'

'Netted her?' William looked towards where his beloved child, as he thought of her, was now sitting crouched low on a cracket before the fire, and Annie, standing by her side, stroking her hair. 'God above! if I only had the use of me legs.'

He turned his head now and looked at Simon and ended, 'They'll stop at nothin', they're so sure it's here.'

'Yes, William, yes, they're sure it's here.'

They both started somewhat and Annie actually stumbled backwards as Tilly, swinging her body round from the stool, cried now, 'What's here? He isn't only after me, it's somethin' else and . . . and I've got a right to know; after tonight I've got a right to know. Granda!' – she appealed to him, her head thrust out and falling to the side and the tears raining down her face – 'this business of the money, I've a right to know.'

There was silence in the room for a moment, except for the wind blowing down the chimney, and when the fire hissed and the log of wood parted in the middle and dropped gently away to each side of the hearth, William, lying back on his pillow, drew in a short painful breath before he said, 'Aye, aye, lass, you've got a right to know. But I think you've had enough for one night, we'll talk about it the morrow.'

'No, no, you're always sayin' never put off till the morrow what can be done the day, or the morrow never comes, or some such. The morrow, you'll have another excuse. And you an' all, Gran,' she said, her voice breaking as she now turned and looked at her grandmother.

Annie bowed her head as if against a piercing truth.

'Come; sit down.' Simon had risen from the chair and now, his arm about her shoulders, he brought her to the end of the table and pressed her down into a chair that was facing the bed, and he said, 'Go ahead, William; or . . . or shall I tell her as I know it?'

William's eyes were closed, his head was turned slightly away as he muttered, 'Aye, Simon; aye, 'tis best.'

Simon now pulled his chair towards the end of the table and, sitting down, he leant his forearm on it and looking at her, where she had turned her face half towards him, he said, 'It's some thirty years this August. That correct, William?'

William made no verbal reply; he merely acknowledged with a small movement of his hand, and Simon went on, 'Well, it was on this summer's day, a Sunday it was, your granda there was taking the air because that was the only day in the week the pitman had to himself. He had walked a good way and was hot and tired and he lay down amidst some gorse and dosed off. Now, as your granda said, when he heard the commotion beyond the gorse he lay still thinking it was a courting couple having a tussle. But then he realised he wasn't listening to a tussle but to a man gasping as if he were struggling with something heavy. Your granda then turned on his side and carefully edged himself along by the scrub until he could see just beyond it. Well, he found himself looking on to part of the fell that was covered with boulders; he had just earlier on become acquainted with these boulders when he had walked in between them before coming to the grassy patch where he had lain down, and what he saw then stretched his eyes, so he's told me many times, and I can believe him, for there was McGrath, Hal McGrath's father you know, who was blacksmith in the village then as he still is today, struggling with one of the outcrops of rock. Eventually he moved it; but he moved it in the direction in which your granda was looking, so he couldn't see what was going on beyond. But after a time, Big McGrath struggled with the rock again and placed it where it was before, then straightened up, dusted his hands, and walked calmly away into the fading light.

'Your granda there' – Simon now nodded towards the bed – 'was naturally set to wondering. He stayed where he was for some time to let McGrath get well away, then he went round and examined this great lump of rock. And he marvelled that any one man could move it. He himself tried but he couldn't even rock it. Then your granda got to thinking.

'Well, things were very bad in the country about this time; jobs were scarce; farmers, such as my father, had had to dismiss some of their hands because of taxation and the like; the whole country was in a state of unrest. We think it's bad enough now but around that time two men not a mile from this spot were sent to Botany Bay for stealing a sheep. One of them had lost two children in three months through starvation; but that was no excuse, he was lucky to get off with his life. The village, our village, was one of the hardest hit around these parts because half of the workers were on the land and four farmers went broke within one year. There were near riots. You know the big houses that still lie between here and Harton village, well, they used to put guards round them at nights with dogs to stop the peasantry, as they called them, raiding the vegetable gardens or the chicken runs. It had been said there wasn't a rabbit to be seen between Westoe village and Gateshead not for many a year. . . . So how, your granda asked himself, did the McGraths always appear to manage, always appear to be well fed and well shod, because fewer farms meant not only fewer farm workers but also fewer horses to be shod and Big McGrath worked the forge himself. The Rosier mine and Sopwith's had their own blacksmiths, so how did it come about that the McGraths were not only surviving but surviving well? The answer, your granda considered, lay under this stone. But how to move it?

'Now you knew, didn't you, William?' – he inclined his head towards the bed – 'that should you go into the village and ask one of your neighbours to come and help you find out what McGrath had hidden under that stone, and should the findings show money, because money was the only thing that bought food in those days, for people had nothing left to exchange; well, you knew that should they help themselves the change in their fortunes would soon be noticed.'

Simon looked at Tilly again. Her face white, her eyes wide and unblinking, held his for some seconds, until he wetted his lips and went on, 'You see, men like the miners were working for starvation wages. Often a husband and wife had to go down below just keep themselves alive. Aye, and take their young 'uns with them, five or six years old. There were about three dozen Sopwith's men in the village at that time living in hovels; and as you know some of them are still there; and your granda was one of them.

'Anyway' – he inclined his head again towards the bed – 'your granda was determined to see what Big McGrath had got buried, but he was at a loss to know where to go for help. Well, he began to walk home. Now on his road he had to pass our farm; and it didn't look as it does today. My father, so I understand, was at the end of his tether both financially and domestically. You see my mother had had five miscarriages before she had her sixth child, and that had lived only a month. Moreover, it was only five months to Christmas and the rent to the owner, Mr Sopwith, was then due. Now old Sopwith was going through hard times too, at least so he gave out; he wasn't as lenient as the present one, with him it was no rent, no farm; and what was more he was badly liked because he had enclosed some free pasture on the north side of his land. People said it was because his own father had had to sell half the estate in order to keep going. But hard times with the gentry and hard times with the people were horses of a different colour. The gentry could still have their servants by the dozen, go up to London Town, lavish presents on their wives and children; but what was more important in the eyes of the ordinary man, they could still eat.

'Anyway, I'm going off the subject, which your mind is apt to do because these issues are still with us the day. Now who should your granda see when passing the farmyard but my own father. Now it says in the Bible, cast thy bread upon the waters and it shall be returned to you a thousandfold; well, I translate that, Tilly, in this way, do a good turn for anybody and if they're decent folk they'll repay you in some way. So it should happen that a few years afore this when there was a strike at the mine my father had given your granda there free milk, mostly skimmed of course, nevertheless free milk every day during the time they were off; he had also thrown in a stone of taties every week. Your granda there never forgot this, so when he saw my father coming towards him across the yard, to use his own words, he thought, here's a man who is as much in need of an extra shilling or two as anybody in these parts, and so what did he do, he told him what he had seen. And my father, after listening to him in silence, simply said, "Come on, show me."

'It was a good mile back to the spot and it was getting dark, and when there it took them both every ounce of their strength to budge the stone an inch. But gradually, gradually, they moved it to the side, and there in the dim light below them was a hole, and in it was a tin box. Not an ordinary tin box you know, but one of those that travel on coaches, steel bound and locked; the gentry sometimes use them for carrying jewellery or money in when travelling from one estate to another, or in a mail coach when hundreds of pounds had to be taken to where they were building the railroads. Anyway' – Simon's voice dropped now – 'that box wasn't only full of golden guineas but round it there were a number of leather bags also full. But these ones were mixed with silver.

'Well, your granda there and my father peered at each other, and it was my father who said, "What about it, Trotter?" and your granda answered, "We'll take it. But. where will we put it?"

'My father thought a minute and then said, "I've got the very place, the dry well." It's a well that drained out in my father's time after he had made an extension to the seed room and had roughly slabbed over it. It is three or four years ago since I looked down it. It was still dry then, a bit soggy at the bottom but that's all. Anyway, water or not, guineas don't melt.

'So they cleared the hole of its secret and they replaced the stone and in the now dark night they skitted along that road, keeping to the hedgerow like two highwaymen with their loot.' For the first time Simon's face went into a smile as he added, 'There's little more to tell. They counted the money. There was close on a thousand pounds. They were both amazed and slightly drunk with the happening, but when they sat down and thought things out they faced a snag, and that was, they wouldn't be able to use the money, not openly, not in any way that would show a difference in their style of living. It was easier for my father because any extra money he had a mind to spend he could put out as profit from the farm, but not so William there. William was getting twelve shillings a week; even a shilling spent extra could bring suspicion on him because they knew that McGrath, once he had made the discovery, would have his sons taping everybody in the village and beyond. And so your granda decided to have five shillings a week for as long as it would last, but he would spend it far afield, like in Shields.... So there you are, now you know why I bring the sovereign every month.' Simon let out a long, slow breath and leaned back in the chair and ended, 'And what McGrath's after an' all.'

Tilly's eyes were wide, her mouth was slightly agape. She stared at Simon for some time before she turned her head slowly and looked towards her grand-father, then towards her grandmother who was seated at the top of the table. But now it was Annie who spoke. Sadly, she said, 'The times, hinny, I've been tempted to ask for more in order to buy you some decent clothes. An' I might have chanced it except that I made a mistake one day. 'Twas some weeks after they had brought William back from the pit. They thought he would die an' I couldn't leave him and we were in need of meat, candles, and flour an' such, an' you being on ten years old and a sensible child into the bargain, I told you what was needed. And so I wrapped the sovereign in a rag and pinned it in the pocket of your petticoat an' gave you a penny for the carrier cart into Shields. Well, you came back as proud as punch with all the messages an' the change intact, an' when I asked you how you got on you told me that one woman at the bacon stall wanted to know how a little thing like you had come by a sovereign, an' you said your granny had given it to you to do the messages with. And then you caught sight of Bella McGrath at another stall an' simply to point out to the woman your honesty you said, "That's Mrs McGrath from the village, she knows me an' me granny." An' you went to her and brought her to the bacon stall an' said to her, "You do know me an' me granny, Mrs McGrath, don't you?" An' Bella McGrath said, "I do, I do indeed. But what for are you askin'?" An' you explained to her about the sovereign.' Annie now sighed and shook her head as she ended, 'It was from then, hinny, that this business all started. The McGraths knew, like everybody else did, that William being bad, there'd be no money coming in, so from that day to this they've never let up. You see, they think we've got it hidden here. They've worked it out that there must still be a good deal left. That's why Hal McGrath's bent on having you; it's one way of getting his hands on the remainder of it.'

Tilly could find no words to express what she was feeling. The whole business sounded too fantastic to be believed, yet she knew it was true, too true. They had been living on stolen money for years. They had stolen it from McGrath, but whom had McGrath stolen it from? All that money, all those sovereigns, and she had been the means, the innocent means of giving her grandfather away and of bringing on herself the raping attack tonight. She shuddered visibly and bent her head. She would feel his body on top of her for the rest of her days, and his hands clawing at her bare flesh. Instinctively, she brought her legs tight together under the table.

'Don't worry, he won't come near you again.' Simon's hand came across the table and covered her joined ones.

As she looked back into his face she thought, I've spoilt his wedding. And yet the question she asked him now had nothing whatever to do with his wedding: 'Where did Mr McGrath get the money from? Was he a highwayman?'

'No, not him' – Simon shook his head – 'he would never have the guts. But his cousin was transported three or four years previous. He was one of three men who held up a coach on its way to Scotland, it was on the road between Gosforth and Morpeth, a lonely stretch. One of the men was shot by the guard, the other two escaped. McGrath's cousin was picked up from a description some weeks later when he was at the hoppings in Newcastle; one of the gentry who had been in the coach spotted him and informed the constables. It couldn't really be proved against him, it was only hearsay, but still it was enough to send him to Botany Bay; otherwise it would have been his neck. William' – he looked towards the bed again – 'you remember him, don't you, McGrath's cousin?'

'Aye, aye, I do indeed. He was a small fellow, quiet, dark, quick on his feet. Around that time there were two or three big hold-ups. They never found who did them, but the money in that box told the tale all right. The only thing I can't understand, and never have been able to, is why he let Big McGrath have the keeping of it 'cos he himself lived in Glasgow in one of those tenements they said that you wouldn't house a rat in.'

'Here' – Annie was now standing by Simon's side, she had placed a dish of water on the table – 'let me clean up that cut. You are in a mess. My goodness!' She dabbed at his face with a wet cloth. 'This needs a needle and thread else you're going to have a scar there. Here, dry your face.' She handed him a rough towel, then added, 'I'm sorry I can't do anything with your coat, that's a tailor's job. By! your wife will go mad when she sees you. And this to happen on your wedding night. 'Tis sorry I am to the heart, Simon.'

He stood up and, handing her the towel back, he smiled and only just in time stopped himself from saying, 'It isn't every man who saves another woman from being raped on his wedding night and gets his face bashed into the bargain' because Tilly wasn't a woman, she was a girl, still a girl, a sweet girl, a lovable girl. He looked at her and as he met her wide, warm, troubled gaze, he turned on himself: Aw, to hell! Let him get out of here and back to Mary. Aye, back to Mary. And what would she say to him? Aye, what would she say? Would she overlook his running off like that and greet him with open arms when he turned up like this? Huh! he doubted it. Well anyway, the quicker he got back and tested her temper the better.

'Good-night, William. Good-night, Tilly. Good-night, Annie.'

William muttered 'Good-night, lad, and thanks, thanks for what you've done the night.'

Tilly gave him no farewell. She just stood and watched him as her grandmother handed him a lantern, saying, 'You'll need this now.'

'Aye, yes I'll need it now.'

She opened the door for him and as he stepped out into the dark, she said, 'Tell your wife I'm sorry you were fetched away and are going back to her like this. I . . . I hope she understands.'

He made no answer, but as he went swiftly down the path towards the gate and his horse he thought, I hope she does an' all.

But Mary Bentwood was never to understand this night, nor to forgive him until the day she died.

✍ 4 ✍

The light of the candle lantern set in the middle of the vestry table illuminated the six faces gathered around it, those of the churchwarden Mr Septimus Fossett and the five sidesmen: Burk Laudimer the wheelwright, Andy Fairweather the carpenter, George Knight the cooper and gravedigger, Tom Pearson the painter and odd-job man, and Randy Simmons, Simon Bentwood's cowman.

Mr Fossett had just finished speaking, and it was Andy Fairweather who answered him, saying, 'Aye, 'tis as you said a serious business. And that's why we're here, we're responsible men, responsible for the conduct of the church. Well, what I mean is to see that those who run it act decent like.'

'But she doesn't run it' – Tom Pearson's voice held a note of protest – 'be parson that is responsible.'

'Aye, but he's responsible for his wife.' Two voices came at him now, Andy Fairweather's and George Knight's.

'Aye, well, yes, you're right there.' Burk Laudimer was nodding his head now. 'But she be different class. We knew that from the start. She comes from the gentry, an' we all know what they're like. Like bitches in season they skitter about.'

'Aw, shut tha mouth!' Tom Pearson not only nodded angrily towards Burk Laudimer, but he thrust his pointing finger across the table at him, crying, 'We're not talkin' of bitches but of the parson's wife.'

' . . . One and the same thing p'raps.'

'Now, now, Burk' – Septimus Fossett nodded his head disapprovingly down the table – 'this is no time to be funny, 'tis no light subject we're dealing with. Now tell us, you're sure what you saw?'

'As true as God's me judge. An' as I said, you haven't only got to take me word for it, there was Andy. You saw them with your own eyes, didn't you, Andy?'

'Aye, aye, I did, Burk. You're right, I did. There they were in this very room, this table pushed back to the wall there, an' dancin' they were.' The carpenter's voice now dropping to a low mutter, he went on, 'Astonishin' it was to see in a place of worship an' all, their arms about each other. And her singin'! An' no hymn. Oh no! no! No hymn. A lilt she was singin', a dancin' lilt, and as Burk here has told you – I saw it as well as him – when they parted they up with their skirts like a pair of whores on the waterfront at Shields. Halfway up their calves they pulled them, and started prancin' about. Now 'twould have been bad enough if it had been in a barn or in the room across yonder' – he thumbed over his shoulder – 'where she holds what she calls her Sunday School, but I suppose that was too small a place for them to have their fling. . . . But now listen.' He rolled his eyes from one staring member to the other. 'I'll tell you somethin', I don't blame the parson's wife altogether. No, no, I don't, 'cos I think she's been led astray, aye she has, and by that young Tilly Trotter.'

'Ah, don't be daft man.'

'Now, Tom Pearson, don't you tell me I'm daft, I know what I'm talkin' about.'

'Well, you're the only one.' Tom Pearson turned his head away from the table and looked into the deep shadows as he said, 'Led away by Tilly Trotter! She's only a bit of a lass, not yet on sixteen.'

'She's no bit of a lass, not in the ordinary way I'd say. An' what's more, she's above herself, has been for years. There's always been something fishy about her; an' about her old grandparents an' all. Old Trotter's never done a hand's turn for years, but they never seem to want. Have you ever thought of that? An' can you tell me another thing' – he now cast his glance again around the table – 'why should Simon Bentwood ride off on his weddin' night to see that she was all right just 'cos he heard that Hal McGrath was for takin' her? Leaves his bride he does an' all the bridal party; in the midst of the jollifications he rides off and comes back hours later, a slit brow, a black eye, an' his clothes torn off his back through fightin' Hal McGrath for her. Now I ask you, is that usual goin' on for a groom on his weddin' day? An' look at the rumpus that came after. Randy there' – he pointed down the table – 'said there was hell to pay. An' the lads didn't see them up to bed that night. An' moreover there was high jinks in the house the next day. That girl, I'm tellin' you, is a creator of trouble, in fact she's witch-like in some ways. Have you ever seen the way she looks at . . . ?'

'Oh, for goodness sake!' Tom Pearson got to his feet. 'I've never heard such bloody rubbish in me life.'

'No language in here, Tom. Remember where you are.' The churchwarden's voice was stern.

'Not so much rubbish, Tom.' It was George Knight, the gravedigger now.

His thin piping voice seemed to check the anger of the two men and they both looked at him, and he, nodding from one to the other, said, 'That was a strange business about Pete Gladwish's dog, now you must admit that. It was strange that was. It was.'

'Aye, it might have been' – Tom Pearson's voice was also quiet now – 'but what has that to do with young Tilly Trotter?'

'More than something, Tom, more than something, so some folks say. Pete's dog was a ratter, you know that yourself, an' one of the best terriers for miles. An' the old fellow lived on his winnings, didn't he? Saturda' night in the pit I've seen that dog kill fifty rats in as many minutes, or less. Aye, or less. Then comes the night that he's takin' him over Boldon way, and they meet up – with young Tilly on the road, an' you know what happened? She stroked the dog. Talked to it, Pete said, and the bloomin' beast then didn't want to come along of him, tugged to follow her. An' that night he didn't even want to go in the pit. Can you imagine a terrier seeing a rat an' not wanting to go after it? Why, when they see them swarming down in the pit they nearly go mad to get at 'em. But, Pete said, that dog just stood there, dazed like. Well, he knocked the daylights out of it and took it home and chained it up, and what happened? Well, you live in this village as well as I do an' you know what happened, the dog was gone the next mornin', wasn't it, and it's never been seen hilt nor hair of since. It wasn't until this business of the weddin' an' the sort of enticing away of Farmer Bentwood on the most special night of his life that old Pete got thinkin' about the night Tilly Trotter stroked his dog; he hadn't linked it up afore. And to my mind there's something in it. . . .'

'To your mind, George, there's always something in it, even in an empty pea-pod.'

'Pity the stocks are no longer in the square.'

'Why, are you thinkin' of sitting in them?'

Burk Laudimer now turned on Tom Pearson, crying, 'I don't know why you were asked in on this meetin', you're for her, aren't you, for the pair of 'em? When they're dancing on the altar next and drinkin' out of the font you'll say that ain't witchery. Just high spirits, you'll say.'

'Aye, I might an' all.' Tom Pearson nodded at them; then looking up the table to where the churchwarden sat, his face grim, he said, 'Well, I've got a job to finish, I'm off, but have you made up your mind what you're gona do?'

Mr Fossett put the palms of his hands flat on the table before him and surveyed the five of them for a moment before he said, 'Yes, I've made up me mind, an' being churchwarden 'tis me duty as I see it to carry it out.'

'And what are you gona carry out?' Tom Pearson asked.

The churchwarden's head swung from side to side before he answered, 'Just the fact that the parson will have to put a stop to her gallop, he'll tell her she must behave or else.'

'Or else what?'

'Well' – again Mr Fossett's head was wagging – 'we can't have disgrace brought on the church, an' his wife acting like a light woman can bring nothin' but disgrace on the church.'

'You're right. You're right.' His supporters nodded confirmation of this; then simultaneously they rose and the meeting was at an end. . . .

Outside in the churchyard they dispersed to go their separate ways, with the exception of Burk Laudimer and Andy Fairweather. As if of one mind they both stood looking up into the darkening sky, then they turned together and walked down by the side of the church and, cutting across between the gravestones, made for a small gate in the low stone wall that surrounded the cemetery. But before going through it, Burk Laudimer came to a stop and, looking at his companion, said under his breath, 'Do you remember the tale of old Cissy Clackett?'

'Cissy Clackett? . . . You mean Cissy Clackett over there?' He pointed to the right of him where the tall grass was almost obliterating the small headstones.

'Aye, that Cissy Clackett.' Burk Laudimer now turned from the gate and made his way into the long grass until he came to a side wall close to which was a headstone so green with moss that the inscription on it was almost obliterated, and he turned to Andy Fairweather and, his words slow and low, he said, 'She was buried seventeen twenty-four and as the story goes she just escaped being burnt, they had stopped doing them then. But now, listen here' – he now bent his head close to that of Andy Fairweather – 'Old Annie Trotter was a Page before she married, wasn't she?'

'I don't know.'

'Well, she was; and you should know 'cos you've lived in the village as long as me, and your people afore you. Anyway, the Pages took their names from the male side, didn't they, but on the female side they were the Clacketts and they went back right to old Cissy here.' He now went to clap his hand on top of the headstone but stopped suddenly as if in fear, and he rubbed his palm up and down his thigh again before he went on, 'This thing runs right through families, the female side – always the female side – and from all the evidence we've heard the night, an' what I've suspected for a long time, young Tilly Trotter's picked up the thread.'

'Eeh! Well, 'tis a funny thing to say, Burk.'

''Tis true, these things run in families, like boss eyes and harelips.'

'Aye, I've got to agree with you there; aye, you're right there.'

They both turned now and made their way back to the gate, through it and into a sunken road that led down into the village.

Presently Burk Laudimer said, 'Gona call in?'

Andy Fairweather hesitated, saying now, 'Oh, I don't know the night; I'm not feelin' too clever, heavy tea I think.'

'Aw, come on, a mug of Bessie's brew will cure that.'

'I don't think we should, Burk. If Fossett gets to hear about it he won't like it.'

'Damn Fossett I say! I do what I like in me own time. I pay me respects on Sunday, I do me duty, but there's nobody goin' to stop me wettin' me whistle when I want to.'

Andy Fairweather lowered his head for a moment, then gave a shaky laugh and turned with Burk Laudimer round the curve of the narrow street where the houses seemed to bow to each other from each side of the road and into an open square in the middle of which was a round of rough grass, and at the centre of this a flat stone measuring about six foot square.

On the far side of the green was a row of cottages sitting well back and fronted by small gardens, and on the near side, that to which the two men were now making their way, was a crescent of what appeared to be workshops. The end one gave evidence of being the blacksmith's shop by the faint glow coming through the open doorway. The wheelwright's next door was distinguished by its swinging board with its trade-mark painted on it. A space divided it from the baker's shop, and another opening beyond the baker's provided space for the vehicles belonging to the patrons of the inn. Beyond the inn were two cottages, stone-faced and sturdy looking, one occupied by the cobbler, the other by a breeches maker who was also a hosier, for he could knit stockings as well as any woman, better in fact some said. But then of course he wasn't really a man, having been stunted in his youth and only four foot in height. The grocer's shop took up the space of two cottages, and it needed every inch because with the exception of meat, it sold most things necessary to the village life.

The crescent now straggled away in an untidy end covered by a row of small cottages which housed the drover, who was also the mole catcher, the thatcher whose wife was the district midwife, and also the families of Andy Fairweather, George Knight, Tom Pearson, Burk Laudimer and lastly the McGraths.

Mr Septimus Fossett, as behoved his standing in the church and the fact that he owned the draper's shop on the outskirts of Harton village, had a house fifty yards away. It possessed all of five rooms and had wooden floors, even in the kitchen. Moreover, the railings on the south side of his back garden touched on the grounds of the first of the gentlemen's residences which led towards Harton village, then on to Westoe village. But unfortunately and irritatingly so, its back windows looked on to the row of cottages lying down in the valley below. These were the habitations of Rosier's mine-workers.

As Burk Laudimer and Andy Fairweather entered the inn it was the adult section of the McGrath family that their eyes encountered, for Big Bill the father, Hal, and Mick were seated side by side on an oak settle that ran at right angles to one side of the deep-based open fire, and opposite them on a similar settle sat four men, two being middle-aged and two decidedly old-aged. It was the elder of the latter, Charlie Stevenson, now turned eighty, who, wiping his ale dripping unkempt moustache with the back of his hand looked towards the newcomers and croaked, 'Hie! there, Burk.'

'Hello, Charlie.' Burk Laudimer nodded at the old man, then at his companion, saying, 'Evenin', Peg-Leg,' and the man with the rough crutch by his side grinned at him toothlessly and bounced his head two or three times but made no reply.

It was towards the younger of the other two men that Andy Fairweather spoke, saying, 'Why, Billy, don't often see you round here,' and Billy Fogget, the carrier, replied, 'Visitin' me sister, Andy, visitin' me sister.'

'Who's lookin' after your cart?'

'Oh, me lad is for the next few days, he's got to learn.'

When Bessie Bradshaw now called from behind the rough counter 'What's it to be?' Laudimer and Fairweather looked at each other; then it was Andy Fairweather who said, 'Mild.'

Having pulled two stools from under a rough table, they brought them to the front of the fire, placing them between the settles, and the conversation became general, in the course of which most of the attention was given to the carrier for he travelled places and knew about goings on. He told them about taking cart-loads of folk up to the New Theatre in Newcastle that had just been opened; that he only charged half as much as they would have paid by coach, but that they paid extra when it was raining for then he supplied covers for them, penny for sacks, tuppence for oilcloth. He told them he had spoken to people who had been to London and had glimpsed royalty; and when he told them he was in Newcastle on June 21st when news had come in that the King was dead and that the young Princess Victoria was now Queen, the four men on the settle sat open-mouthed.

The three McGrath men, too, seemed interested, because Fogget, being a natural story-teller, had the art of holding his audience; that was until Peg-Leg Dickens, speaking for the first time, said, 'Wonderful thing 'tis to travel. Me, I travelled world till I got this.' He patted the stump of his leg. 'But now times are different, nowt happens here, one day like t'other, nowt happens here.'

He was shaking his head as Billy Fogget's companion Joe Rowlands, who was the hedger and ditcher, put in on a grunt of a laugh, 'Aa wouldn't say that. It all depends what you're after for amusement; aye, it does. I get mine. Things I see nobody'd believe' – he nodded now towards Burk Laudimer – 'but Dick and Bessie there.' He turned his head to include the host and hostess now. 'They know 'tis right, don't you, Bessie? Don't you, Dick?'

'About Sopwith?' Bessie Bradshaw heaved up her flagging breasts with her forearms, then laughed and said, 'Put nowt past the gentry. Never put nowt past the gentry. As for the new 'un, she's a flyer if I ever saw one. Went past here like the divil in a gale of wind yesterday. Thinks she owns the county that one, an' not in it five minutes.'

'What's this all about?' Andy Fairweather now looked at Joe Rowlands who, sensing he had the attention of the company, appeared in no hurry to explain further. Taking a long drink from his mug, he then wiped each side of his mouth with his knuckles before directing his gaze down to the floor. And there he let it remain for some seconds; then slowly raising his head he looked around the company from under his brows before saying, 'I see things on me travels, I see things you'd never believe. First time you see 'em you think you're mistaken, but not second time. No, not second time.'

'Well, go on, go on, you're lettin' it drip like treacle in the workhouse.'

There was a guffawing now at Burk Laudimer's remark and old Charlie Stevenson spluttered, 'Aye, go on, go on, Joe, it's spice you've got in your gob I can tell, I can tell, so spit it out, man, spit it out.'

Joe Rowlands was laughing now at the old man. Nodding his head towards him, he said, 'Aye, spice. Aye, spice, Charlie, 'twas spice all right. Well – ' his eyes again travelled round the company and, his voice dropping now, he brought them into the circle of expectation by beginning, 'It was on this night, the night that this village won't forget, Farmer Bentwood's wedding, you mind . . . what's been said about it, an' the divil's fagarties that took place. Well, I see some of what happens but only at the end of it. I heard the shoutin' an' the bashin' from a distance. I was takin' a short cut over from Lord Redhead's place, you know where our Fanny's man works on the estate, an' he had a bit of something for me' – he nodded and winked knowingly – ' "twas in the shape of a bird, you understand.' He pressed his lips together for a moment. 'So there I was comin' back pathways, never expecting to meet anybody 'cos I was goin' to drop down into Billings Flat. Anyway, there was this hullabaloo, an' me with what I had with me, well, I didn't want to show me face. I stayed up top of bank. There's rough ground there, you know round top of Billings Flat.' He was nodding to each one in turn now. 'I couldn't hear exactly what was going on but it was a rumpus right enough an' voices shouting and horses gallopin'. Then things went quiet and I was just about to get up and continue on me way when I hear the sound of horses coming towards me, and so I lay doggo and there who did I see, eh? Who did I see?' He paused, but no one broke the silence. 'Mr Sopwith himsel'. An' who was with him? The new lady from Dean House, Lady Myton.' He paused again. 'Now there they were right in front of me, an' I could see them plain from where I was lying atween two boulders. He said something to her which I couldn't catch; then as if he were picking up a sack of corn he had her off her feet and on her back. But it was no rapin' 'cos God she was willin'. Aye, God! I'll say that for him, she was willin'.'

There was silence in the room now; then for the first time one of the McGrath men spoke. It was Hal. His voice quiet, soft and flat, he said, 'You sure of this?'

The insult to his integrity brought Joe Rowlands to his feet and he barked at Hal McGrath, crying, 'I'm not a bloody liar! What do you think I've been tellin' you, you think I made it up?'

'No, no –' Hal McGrath's voice was quiet, even pacifying – 'only it's a night of tales goin' round.' He cast his glance towards the carrier.

''Tis no tale,' Joe Rowlands interrupted him. ''Twas as I said, I could hardly believe me eyes the first time but when I came across it again then there was no mistakin'. No, it was no mistakin'. They passed me on the road they did with never a glance in my direction. I touched me cap but neither of them seemed to see me. I was in the ditch when they passed, but happenin' to go up the bank a few minutes later I saw them cutting up on to the fells an' it struck me where they were makin' for, the same place again. Well, I couldn't beat them to it an' get there afore they did 'cos it was a good half mile away an' there were three stone walls to jump, an' me jumping days are over. But what I did do was to skitter up through Fletcher's Copse and up to the mound near Trotter's cottage, and from there if I couldn't see exactly what they were up to I could tell the time of their goin' in and their comin' out. Well, from the time they reached the outcrop to the time they came out of it was a full half-hour, and as I guessed they didn't go out the way they came in, but they came out t'other end. They were a good way off from the mound but I could see them clearly although they were protected on each side by trees, and their parting was not "Good-bye, Mr Sopwith." "Good-bye, Lady Myton," for she was hanging on to him like a bitch in heat and he was over her likewise. So there it is, the truth.'

He looked full at Hal McGrath, who said, 'Well! well! Aye, as you said, Joe, the things what happen round here, it isn't as quiet as you think.'

'No, you're right there.' Burk Laudimer was nodding in his direction now, and not to be outdone in the tale-telling he said solemnly, 'Things happen in the open and beyond closed doors, which is the worse I wouldn't know. Andy and I here have just come from a meetin' in the vestry, an important meetin', and the result could have percussions on this village. Aye yes; yes, indeed.'

'What kind of percussions?' Dick Bradshaw's voice came from behind the bar and his mind they all knew was linking the percussions with business, and Burk Laudimer, looking towards him, said smarmily, 'Oh, it wouldn't affect you, Dick, it wouldn't affect you. But the vicarage it would. Aye, yes, it would that, the vicarage.'

'The vicarage?'

'Aye, the vicarage.'

'The vicarage?'

The question came from different throats now, then Peg-Leg Dickens said, 'What's wrong with parson then?'

''Tisn't parson, Peg-Leg, 'tisn't parson, 'tis his wife.'

'His wife?'

'Aye.' He nodded at him; then bending forward and his voice dropping a number of tones, he murmured, 'She and that young Tilly Trotter up to larks in the vestry.'

'Up to larks?' The carrier's round eyes were bright, his face was poked forward. He looked from one to the other; then his gaze resting on the three McGrath men sitting straight and silent, he laughed as he repeated, 'Up to larks?' expecting them to join in his amusement. However, they neither smiled nor moved but waited for Burk Laudimer to continue, and he did.

'Dancin' they've been, dancin' together, their skirts almost up to their thighs, kickin' their legs up.'

There was a murmur of 'Never! never! not parson's wife.'

'Aye, parson's wife.' His voice was louder now. 'But I don't blame parson's wife, no, no, 'tis young Trotter that I blame, as has been mentioned by Joe there. There was divil's fagarties to play on Farmer Bentwood's weddin' night, weren't there, but who started it?' He now turned his head and looked at Hal McGrath and said, 'No blame attached to you, Hal; no, no, courtin's courtin' all the world over, an' as you said you tried to do it honest with her 'cos she had led you on; if she hadn't asked for it you wouldn't have attempted to give her it, would you now? No, no; so no blame's attached to you. And for Sopwith to sack you, 'twas a bloody shame, 'twas. She's trouble that girl, she's trouble. You're best off without her. Aye, I'd say, 'cos I was just pointin' out to Andy here back in the cemetery that old tombstone of Cissy Clackett, you know. Remember Cissy Clackett?' His head was again bobbing from one to the other; and the bobs were being returned, particularly from the two old men. 'Well, she comes from that stock, young Trotter does. An' the thread runs strong in the female. As I said an' all back there in the vestry, it's a pity the stocks are not in use no more. Aye, it is that, for I'd put her in meself, I would that. An' as I was sayin' to Andy here an' all, there was Pete Gladwish's dog. That was a funny business now, wasn't it? Eh, wasn't it?'

When a silence fell on the room again, Big Bill McGrath turned his head slowly towards the counter and said quietly, 'Fill 'em up all round, Bessie, small 'uns.'

'Good, good. Oh, that's kind of you, Bill.' They all stirred on their seats.

'Aye, aye, 'tis.'

After half pints of ale were distributed among the men the conversation flagged somewhat, but when Burk Laudimer and Andy Fairweather rose to take their leave, the three McGrath men rose too, saying it was time for them to hit the road, and they all went out into the dark night together. They did not, however, immediately make their ways to their respective homes, but stood outside the inn talking for quite some time.

⁌ 5 ⁊

Parson Ross was only thirty-five years old but his slightly stooped shoulders, long face, and thinning hair made him appear a man in his middle forties. He was tall and thin, and usually had a sallow complexion, but at this moment his skin was suffused to a dull red, and his wide straight lips trembled slightly as he pressed them together, at the same time shaking his head as he looked at his wife.

Ellen Ross at twenty-six was what could be called petite. She hardly reached her husband's shoulder. Her hair was light brown, her eyes a startling clear blue; her manner and speech were quick and when she talked she had the habit of moving her hands, each gesture seeming to add emphasis to her words, as they did now. 'They are spiteful, those men are spiteful. I've never liked them from the first. And churchwarden or no churchwarden, Mr Fossett's an old granny. As for the wheelwright, well!' She grimaced and threw her arms wide as if pressing something away to each side of her.

George Ross now closed his eyes for a moment as he said with strained patience, 'You are getting away from the point, Ellen. Were you or were you not dancing with Tilly Trotter in the vestry?'

'*Yes! Yes! Yes!* All right if you say we were dancing we were dancing, but as I've already told you, it was the first time it had happened there, and . . . and it was all over in a matter of seconds. And we didn't move the benches back; we went round the table once.'

Ellen looked at her husband as he closed his eyes again while his head slowly drooped towards his chest and, her voice pleading now, she whispered, 'Oh! George, George, I'm so sorry if this has distressed you, but it all started so innocently. One day in the summer-house after I had taken Tilly for her letters I remarked that there was a barn dance being held outside of Westoe village and I asked her if she was going, and sadly, that was it . . . that was it, George. There was so much sadness in her voice when she replied she never went to barn dances, that in fact she couldn't dance at all, she had never danced. Well, George, you know yourself what used to happen on birthdays and anniversaries at home when Mother played the spinet and Robert the violin, you were there, and you enjoyed it you did. Our drawing-room was gayer than any court ball; you said so yourself.'

The vicar slowly raised his head now and looked with infinite sadness at his wife as he said softly, 'That was before we were married, Ellen. When you agreed to become my wife you knew there would be responsibilities, and these responsibilities would be heavily laden with decorum. We talked about this, didn't we?'

'Yes, George.' Her voice was flat, her hands remained still, joined tightly together at her waist now.

'The first Mrs Ross was. . . .'

'Oh! Oh no! George.' Her hands had sprung apart and her head was shaking widely. 'Please, don't tell me again of the first Mrs Ross's qualities. If you do I shall scream.'

'Ellen! Ellen! Ellen! Calm yourself. Dear! Dear!' He stared sadly at her. 'I wasn't going to do any such thing except to admit that an excess of decorum can have its drawbacks when it impinges on happiness.'

'Oh, I'm sorry. I'm sorry, George.' She moved a step nearer to him and, putting out her hands, she gripped his and, looking up into his face, she said softly, 'I will try, George. Honestly and faithfully, I give you my promise that from today I will try to be different.'

The parson stared down into the face he so dearly loved. Then his nose twitched, his eyelids blinked, he wetted his lips and, his voice now soft and unlike its previous tone, he said, 'Oh, Ellen, Ellen, I do so want you to be happy, and . . . and, I would like to add, I want you to be free to take the line your active mind directs, but . . . but I am hampered, my very position hampers us both.'

'I know, I know, my dear.'

'Well now, Ellen, I'm sorry to have to say this, but you must stop seeing Tilly.'

Now it was her eyes that blinked and her whole face twitched and she glanced to the side before she said, 'Not even teach her her letters?'

'Not even that, my dear. They . . . the villagers, they have strange ideas about Tilly, weird, stupid ideas, but these ideas could make them dangerous.'

'What . . . what kind of ideas?' Her head had swung quickly round towards him again.

'Well ' he became embarrassed for a moment and his lips worked in and out before he answered, 'She is apparently a descendant of an old lady who . . . who is buried in the churchyard. Her name was Cissy Clackett and she was . . . well, they seem to think she had supernatural powers.'

'A witch?'

'Yes, yes, I suppose she would in those days have been called a witch.'

Ellen's hands jerked quickly away from her husband's and her body bristled with indignation as she cried, 'And they're saying that Tilly is a witch! Tilly Trotter a witch!'

'My dear, you must have realised yourself that most of the villagers are ignorant people and ignorant people thrive on superstition. . . .'

'But Tilly a witch, huh!' She gave a mirthless laugh. 'I have never heard anything so stupid in my life. She's a sweet, kind, quite innocent girl, and I've never heard her say a wrong word about anyone, not even about that horrible McGrath man.' She paused for a moment while they stared at each other; then in a high, clear voice, like someone asking a question of the platform, she said, 'Are they intending to burn Tilly Trotter, sir?'

'Don't be silly, Ellen.'

'I am not being silly, at least not any more silly than the villagers or anyone else who takes notice of them.'

'Ellen!'

Although his voice held a stern reprimand it seemingly had no effect on her now for, swinging round from him and walking to the far end of the drawing-room, she looked out of the window for a moment before turning again with the same swinging movement and facing him across the room as she cried, 'And what sentence are they likely to put on me should they discover that I sit alone for an hour at a time in the summer-house with three coal-begrimed pitmen?'

'What! What did you say?'

'I think you heard, George, what I said. I sit alone at least one hour a week, sometimes two hours a week, with three very dirty, ignorant miners from Mr Rosier's pit.'

The vicar's long face seemed to take on inches. His mouth dropped into a gape, his eyebrows moved up towards his receding hair, and as he walked towards her his gait could have suggested that he had been indulging early in the day. An arm's length from her he stopped and his head moved with a small unbelieving motion as he said, 'No! no! Ellen, you couldn't, not Mr Rosier's men. Do you know what you're doing?'

'Yes, yes, I do. I am helping them to express themselves; I am pushing them through the thick barrier of ignorance, the ignorance that you yourself say is prevalent in this village. But these men are different, they've had enough of ignorance, they have at last realised the power that lies in the pen, and in being able to read the written word.'

The parson now drew in a long breath and let it out slowly before he said in a flat unemotional tone, 'And of what help, may I ask, will this knowledge be to them when they are dismissed from their work, and not only dismissed but more probably they and their families turned out of their cottages?'

Her lids were blinking again and it was some seconds before she said, 'They . . . they know the risk they are taking and, as one of them has already said, except for the cold they'd have to endure during the winter he'd rather sleep on the hillside, in fact bring his family up there, than in the hovels that Mr Rosier provides for the men who work for him.'

The parson's face was a deep red now, there were beads of sweat on his brow, and he seemed to find difficulty in speaking. 'This must stop and at once. You have gone too far, Ellen. You are young, you know nothing about the privations of these men, what can happen to them when they are without work. Outside this very parish last year a man died on the road through starvation. He was found stiff in a ditch. He was one of Rosier's men. You haven't as yet seen people standing for hours waiting for a bowl of weak soup; you haven't as yet seen a child tugging at the breast that held no milk. You have a lot to learn, Ellen. Now tell me, when are you seeing these men again?'

It was some time before she answered him. Her hands hanging slack by her sides, her head bent, she seemed for the moment defeated as she whispered, 'They're . . . they're waiting for me now in . . . in the summer-house.'

'Dear God! Dear God!'

Ellen's head came up slowly. The fact that her husband had used God's name outside of prayer or when in the pulpit showed how deeply troubled he was, and so she was torn inside between the hope of bringing the glory of reading and writing to the poor and the love, the deep passionate love, she had for this man.

Sensing some of her feelings, his manner softened. He put his hand out and gently took her arm, saying, 'Come, we will settle the matter now at once. They will understand. Put on your cloak and bonnet.'

His last command brought a slight stiffening to her body. Put on her cloak and bonnet to go down to the summer-house! But it melted away on the thought that, as he said, she was the parson's wife, she was going out in the open and her head must be covered, as must her dress.

A few minutes later they were walking side by side over the stone flags of the large hall, through the heavy oak door, across the narrow terrace and down the six broad stone steps that led on to the gravel drive.

The drive curved away to the iron gates that gave on to the road, but since they were going to the bottom of the garden they took the path along past the three mullioned windows and were about to go under the topiary archway leading into the flower garden when the sound of running steps and a voice calling 'Parson! Parson!' brought them to a stop, and they both looked to where Tom Pearson hurried panting up the drive towards them.

When the painter came to a stop in front of them he was unable to speak, and the parson said with some concern, 'What is it, Tom? Something wrong?'

'Don't know, parson, don't know for sure yet, but I fear something could go wrong, and badly so.'

'Your family?'

'Oh no! No! No, not me family.' Tom Pearson now glanced towards Ellen and muttered in a gasping shy manner, ''Tis young Tilly Trotter I fear, ma'am.'

'Tilly! What's happened to her?'

'Don't know, ma'am, not yet, but things could.'

'Speak up, Tom.' The parson's voice was brisk now. 'What can happen to Tilly?'

'Well – ' Tom swallowed deeply, drew some spittle into his mouth, made as if to get rid of it, changed his mind, swallowed again, then blurted out, ''Tis the stocks, the old stocks that used to be on the slab in the centre of the village years gone by; been lying in Tillson's barn this age. I wouldn't have believed it, wouldn't have known nowt about it but for young Steve McGrath. I found him crying, poor little devil, in the wood, Hal had thrashed the daylights out of him, I think he's broken the boy's arm. I told him to go to Sep Logan, he knows more about bones than most, but the lad had been and Sep, like everybody else seemingly, was away to the fair, except the three concerned, Burk Laudimer, Andy Fairweather, and Hal McGrath himself.'

'But . . . but what about Tilly? What about her?'

'I'm comin' to that, ma'am. They set up the stocks again in the old barn and Laudimer sent his young Frank with some sort of a message; apparently young Steve was on his way to tip Tilly the wink but Hal McGrath sensed what he was up to and by! he has lathered that lad, there won't be a place on him that's not black and blue the morrer. But . . . I knew it was no good me goin' on me own, I couldn't tackle the three of 'em and . . . and it's authority they want' – he was looking at the vicar – 'brawn alone won't stop 'em, Parson.'

Again Ellen heard her husband murmur 'Dear God! Dear God!' Then without further words the three of them were going through the garden at a pace between a trot and a run.

It was when they came to the side path which would lead them into the vegetable garden and so into the meadow beyond that Ellen, glancing over the long lawn which ran right up to the very steps of the summer-house, stopped and cried, 'The miners! George. I'll bring the miners.'

'No! No!' He paused in his walk and again said, 'No, no.' Yet there was a doubt now in the words and she, sensing it, ran from him lifting her skirts above her shoes as she did so, and when she burst into the summer-house the three grimed men rose slowly from the slatted wooden bench while their caps remained on their heads and were nodding towards her when she startled them by crying, 'Come! Come quickly. You can help us. My ... my friend, I mean a young girl, she's in trouble with some men. The vicar and I would ... would be obliged if you would come and ... and help us.'

'Is it a fight, ma'am?'

They were out of the door now, following her running steps towards the parson and Tom Pearson, and she had almost reached her husband before she answered them, saying, 'It well might be. It well might be.'

The parson gave no explanation to the miners; instead, after glancing at them with a look of dismay, all he said was, 'We'd better hurry.'

A wall separated the boundary of the vicarage from the meadow. It was a low wall and the men were over it in a moment and the parson, about to follow them, turned and looked at his wife and said, 'Run to the gate, my dear.' He pointed to the far end of the meadow, but for answer Ellen caused a shiver of shock to run through him while at the same time evoking a thrill of admiration from the men as she sat on top of the wall, pausing a moment as if in deference to her husband's feelings to spread her skirts over her ankles before swinging them to the other side.

They were all running again now. 'Where we making for, sir?' One of the pitmen turned his head and shouted towards the minister, and George Ross called back, 'The barn. Tillson's barn. It's in the far end of the other field. We ... we must cross the road.'

Having crossed the meadow, this time they went through a gate, over the road, jumped a narrow ditch, climbed a bank, they were now in a large field. It was rutted here and there with outcrops of rock which made it unsuitable for farming and the sparse grass in between the outcrops hardly afforded enough grass even for a few sheep, yet at the far side of this field there had at one time been a farmhouse. But all that remained of the house now were the foundations buried among long tangled grass. Many years previous a fire had destroyed the house and most of the outbuildings, leaving only the barn whose timbers had stood the outrage of time for two hundred years and were still persevering; only time it seemed was now winning the battle, for the roof had fallen in a number of places, and the owner of the barn, Mr Tillson, who now farmed about half a mile away, did not consider the place even worth attention. If it was used at all it was as a questionable shelter for those travelling the road or at some season in the year when the village children would decide to scramble over it.

That a commotion was going on inside the barn became evident to them all as they neared it, and when the parson, with the help of the miners, dragged open the half-door they were all brought into a moment's amazed silence at the scene before them.

Their entry also brought to a frozen halt the three men who were in the act of aiming something they had cupped in their hands at the bedraggled and gagged figure pinioned by arms, legs and head in the stocks.

Again the parson said, 'Oh my God!' but now it was merely a whisper on a long soft outgoing breath, but the exclamations from the three pitmen were anything but soft. Their curses rang round the barn as they cried, first one, 'Why you bugger in hell!' Then 'You bloody maniacs!' And lastly as they seemed to leap forward of one accord the smallest and broadest of the three men yelled, 'Stocks! Bloody stocks!'

What followed was a mêlée of blows and curses and figures slipping on the overturned box of rotten apples.

The parson was yelling now, his voice higher than ever he had allowed it to go in his life before; he was screaming at the combating men, 'Give over! Cease I say! Stop it this moment all of you, stop it!' But when no one paid any heed to him he edged himself along by the barn wall, closely followed by Tom Pearson. They were making their way towards the top end and the stocks but before they reached them they were both thrown together by the combined force of the joined bodies of Andy Fairweather and one of the pitmen.

Ellen Ross had remained standing in the open doorway, her hands clapped tightly over her mouth, and moving from one foot to the other as if she was doing a standing march, but now seeing that her husband was being impeded in his efforts to reach Tilly, she ran blindly from the doorway and, weaving her way between the battling men, reached the end of the stocks, and as she moaned 'Oh Tilly! Tilly!' she reached out and touched the bent shoulders pressed against the wood.

As her eyes darted over the back of the stocks she saw that the top section, which clamped Tilly's head down, was held in place by long wooden spikes set in sockets at each side. Gripping one of them she wrenched it back and forward and when she managed to ease it upwards it came away so quickly that she stumbled backwards. It was at this moment she saw, within an arm's length of her, that her brightest pupil was about to be given a final blow by Burk Laudimer. Laudimer had his fist upraised and her instinct told her that if it reached its aim Sam Drew would fall to the floor because his body was only being kept upright by the fact that Laudimer had him held by the front of his jacket.

Ellen never remembered turning the long peg in her hand, nor could she ever believe that even in her anger she had enough strength to fell a man, but when her swinging arm, her hand now gripping the narrow end of the peg, came in contact with Laudimer's neck, he became quite still for what appeared a long second. His left hand was still holding Sam Drew by the coat while his right arm, fist doubled, was raised in the air. So many things happened in that second, blood spurted from a hole in his neck, he screamed a high wild scream, at the same time loosening his hold on Sam Drew and swinging round to confront the parson's wife.

Ellen was still standing, her arm half extended; her hand was open now and the peg was lying across it but there was no blood on it, not what you could see.

Following the scream there fell on the barn a silence; then the parson and Tom Pearson came rushing towards the stocks, not to release Tilly, but for both to stand stock-still. Their eyes darted between the huddled prostrate figure on the barn floor and Ellen looking like a piece of sculpture carved in stone presenting an offering of a stock peg.

'What . . . what have you done?' The parson was now kneeling by the side of Burk Laudimer and, tearing a handkerchief from his pocket, he thrust it around the man's neck, then cried, 'Give me something quick! A scarf, anything to bind him.'

Tom Pearson wasn't even wearing a scarf or a neckerchief, he had on a high-breasted coat buttoned up to under his chin. Andy Fairweather was in no position to offer any assistance for he was lying slumped against the far wall. It was Hal McGrath who stumbled forward tearing at his white knotted neckerchief, and as he handed it down to the parson, the parson let his eyes rest on him for a moment and in a voice that no one in that place had ever heard him use before he said, 'You've got a lot to answer for this day, Hal McGrath.'

McGrath looked down on him where he was now tying the neckerchief around Burk Laudimer's neck in an effort to hold the pad of the handkerchief in place, and he said, 'I ain't the only one likely who'll have a lot to answer for, ours was only a bit fun.'

'Do you call this a bit fun?' It was Tom Pearson speaking now as he wrenched the pegs from out of their newly made sockets.

'Enough to turn anybody's reason. Fun you call it? You should be strung up, the lot of you.'

When at last Tom Pearson, with the help of one of the miners, had Tilly free, they laid her down on the rough floor. Her eyes were closed, her face looked ashen, she could have been dead. Tom Pearson clasped her hands, then tapped each cheek, saying, 'Come on. Come on, Tilly. Wake up. Wake up.'

'Is . . . is she all right?' It was a small voice above them and both Tom and the pitmen looked up at the parson's wife. Her face, too, was white and all her perkiness, as Tom Pearson called her vivacity, seemed to have left her.

'Tom.' It was the parson calling now, and when Tom Pearson rose from his knees and went and stood by his side he noted that the parson too, in some subtle way, seemed strange. He would even have put the word frightened to the look in his eyes, and there was no command now in his voice as he said, 'I . . . I can't stop the bleeding and . . . and I don't think it would be safe to move him at this stage. Will . . . will you go and get the doctor?'

'But it will take me all of an hour, parson, to get to Harton and back.'

'Run to the vicarage. Get Jimmy to harness the trap.' His voice was still quiet, flat, it was as if he were saying 'Hurry' but at the same time implying that his errand would be fruitless.

As Tom Pearson now turned to run out of the barn he glanced towards the pitmen still kneeling by Tilly's side and called, 'Will you see to her, see her home?' and one man answered, 'Don't worry; we'll see her all right.'

It was as the pitman spoke that Tilly opened her eyes, and she stared into the man's face for a full minute before, her lips trembling and her memory returning, the tears sprang from her eyes and rained down her brown mushed-apple-smeared face.

'There, there! It's all right. Can you stand, hinny?'

She made no answer, and the man helped her to her feet and as she stood wavering on her shaking legs Sam Drew said, 'Come on, let's get out of here' and to this his companions said, 'Quicker the better.'

As they went to turn away, Sam Drew paused and, looking at Ellen, who was standing silently gazing towards her husband who was still on his knees, said, 'Thanks, missis, you saved me bacon; he could have done for me. An' he would have an' all if he had got the chance, I could see it in his eyes.' Then looking towards where his late opponent lay by the side of the parson's kneeling figure, he added, 'Don't worry, missis, he'll be all right, 'tis only the good die young,' and on this the three men turned away, two of them supporting Tilly, and went out of the barn.

Ellen stood and watched them. There was a non-reality about herself and the whole proceedings. She had never spoken to Tilly, never commiserated with her. It was strange but she had the feeling she was saying good-bye to her for ever.

'Oh God above! what's happening to us? 'Tis the money. It all started with the money. Money's a curse. I've always said it, money's a curse. But lass! lass! to do that to you, to put you in the stocks. Why God above! there's been no stocks used for many and many a long year. Then to even make a place for your head. Oh dear God! Oh me bairn! Me bairn!'

They were sitting on a box in the woodshed and Annie had her arms around Tilly, cradling her head and rocking her as if she was indeed a bairn again. Presently she released her and, passing her fingers gently around Tilly's smeared face, she said, 'Wash yourself. Go down to the stream and wash yourself and tidy yourself up. But for God's sake don't let an inkling of this get to your granda 'cos it would finish him off. He's bad, you know he's bad, if he has another turn like yesterday it'll be the end of him. I'll . . . I'll tell him that the message that came from the parson's wife' – she now gritted her teeth together as she repeated – 'supposedly from the parson's wife,' and it was a second or two before she went on, 'I'll tell him she wanted a hand with her scholars like, eh?'

Tilly made no response, she just rose to her feet and walked to the door of the woodshed where she leant against the stanchion and looked up into the clear high sky. And her thoughts sprang upwards too. She asked God why, why was He allowing all these things to happen to her? She had done no harm to anyone, she wished no harm on anyone – except to Hal McGrath, for added to the other business she would always remember the feeling of his hands again on her body after he had thrust her legs through the holes of the stocks.

It came to her now as she stared upwards that she would never know happiness until she could leave this place. . . . Yet she could never leave it as long as it held the two people she loved and who needed her. She was like the linnet in the cage hanging outside the grocer's shop in the village which sang all day to the world it couldn't see: they had poked its eyes out because they said blind linnets sang better.

She walked down through the back garden, crossed the field and when she reached the burn she lay down on the grass and, bending over the water, she sluiced handfuls of it over her face and head. That done, she took a rag from her pocket and after wetting it in the burn she went into a thicket and there, lifting her skirt, she washed her thighs in an endeavour to erase the feeling of Hal McGrath's hands at least from her skin if not from her mind. . . .

When she returned to the house she endeavoured to go about her duties as usual, but William noticed the change in her and he remarked, 'You look peaky, lass, bloodless somehow. You're not eating enough, is that it?'

'I . . . I suppose so, Granda.'

'It's a pity you don't like cabbage, and you grow them fine, there's a lot of goodness in cabbage.'

'Yes, Granda.'

'Are you feelin' bad, lass?'

'No, Granda.'

'Are you tired then?'

'Yes; yes, I'm feelin' a bit tired.'

'She's growin'.' This was Annie's voice from where she was placing some griddle cakes on the hanging black griddle pan.

'Aye, yes; yes, she's growin', and into a bonny lass, a bonny, bonny lass.' His voice faded away and his head sank into the pillow, and Tilly and her granny exchanged glances. . . .

It was almost dark when there came a knock on the door and it was opened before either Tilly or her granny could get to answer it. To their surprise they saw Simon standing there.

Annie's first words to him were, 'Anything wrong, Simon?'

He made no reply for a moment but looked through the lamplight from one to the other, then turned his gaze towards the bed and William, and Annie, sensing trouble, said quickly 'William's not too clever, he . . . he had a turn yesterday.'

'Oh. Oh.'

'Anything . . . anything wrong, Simon?' William's words were slow and halting, and Simon called to him, 'No, no; just on me way back from the fair, I thought I'd look in, see . . . see how you were doing.'

'Aha.' This was all the comment William made before closing his eyes again.

'You all right?' Simon now asked softly looking full at Tilly, and after a moment she answered, 'Yes, yes, I'm all right, Simon.'

'Well, that's fine, that's fine. I . . . I just thought I'd look in.' He glanced again towards the bed and making sure now that William's eyes were closed he made a quick motion with his hand towards both Annie and Tilly, and they understanding the motion followed him to the door, which he opened quietly and went outside.

In the deep gloom they stood peering at him, and it was Tilly he looked at as he said, 'You had a bad day then?'

'Yes; yes, Simon.' She turned her head away.

'They're devils. I'll do for that McGrath yet.'

'No, no, Simon' – Annie put her hand on his arm – 'no violence like that. No, no.'

'No violence, Annie?' His voice had a strange note to it now. 'No violence you say! Well, I haven't only come to see if Tilly was all right, I've come with some news, violent news, bad news.' He was again looking at Tilly. 'Tom Pearson said you were dazed and you mightn't have taken in what happened. Do . . . do you remember the fight that took place?'

'Just . . . just dimly, Simon. I think I fainted like. I must have 'cos everything went black.'

'Well, I must tell you because you'll know soon enough, they'll . . . they'll be coming to question you.'

'They? Who's they?' Annie's voice was sharp.

'The police, Annie. The police.'

'What!' They both said the word, Annie sharply and Tilly in a whisper.

'Apparently three pitmen that the parson's wife was teaching their letters to, went with them, I mean the parson and missis, when Tom Pearson told them that Hal McGrath, Burk Laudimer and Andy Fairweather had Tilly in the old barn in the stocks, and apparently from what I can gather there was a fight, and Laudimer was knocking daylights out of one of the pitmen, who was almost at his end, when Mrs Ross who had taken a peg out of the stocks to release you Tilly, saw this little fellow being knocked silly by Laudimer and God knows why, because she's a refined lady, but she hits him on the neck with the peg. But of course she didn't know that there was a nail in the top end, it was placed there I suppose to stop the peg slipping further into the socket. Well, it went into Laudimer's neck.' He stopped, swallowed, looked from one side to the other, and now in a mumble he finished, 'He . . . he bled to death.'

'No! No!' Tilly backed from him, her head shaking. 'No! Mrs Ross could never have done that. No! no! She's small, not strong.'

'It's all right, Tilly, it's all right. Now, now stop trembling.'

Both Simon and Annie had hold of her now, but so violently was her body shaking that they shook with her.

'Get her round to the back, Simon, William, . . . William mustn't be disturbed . . .'

Once more they were in the woodshed, and Tilly was crying loudly now, 'Oh no! no! they'll hurt her, they'll do something to her. She's lovely, lovely, a lovely woman. An' all through me, all through me.'

'Hold her fast, Simon. I'll go an' get a drop of William's laudanum, she'll go off her head else.'

In the dark he held her while, with her arms about him, she clung to him, crying all the while, 'Because of me, because of me. There's a curse on me. There must be, there must be, Simon, there must be a curse on me.'

'Ssh! Ssh!'

And with one arm tightly around her waist and the other cupping her shoulders he thought, And there's a curse on me, a blind curse. Why in the name of God couldn't I see where me heart lay. Oh Tilly! Tilly! There, there, there my love, my love.

಄ 6 ಄

'Why don't you go and live across there?'

'Look, Mary. . . .'

'Don't look Mary me. Yesterday you went to the old fellow's funeral. He was buried at ten o'clock in the morning but you never landed back here until almost dark. Do you think the farm can run itself?'

'No, I don't think the farm can run itself.' Simon's tone now had changed from one pleading for understanding to an angry yell. 'I was born and brought up on it and for the last ten years have worked from dawn till dusk, and far into the night. I've made it what it is, so don't you say to me do I think the farm can run itself. And what's more, let's get this out into the open once and for all, the Trotters are my friends, our families have been close for years. . . .'

'Huh! a miner and a farmer friends?' Her words were a mutter but he picked them up and cried at her, 'Yes, a miner and a farmer; but not an ignorant miner, William Trotter was one of the wisest men I've ever known. Well, now he's gone and his wife, an ailing old woman, and Tilly, but a lass, are alone . . .'

'But a lass!' Mary Bentwood flounced round so quickly that her heavy wool skirt billowed; then as quickly again she turned towards him, her voice as loud as his now as she cried, 'That girl's a menace! From the day I wed she has got into my hair. I've got her to thank for my wedding night and the week that followed and this thing that's been between us ever since. They're saying roundabout that she's a witch and not a good one, a bad one, one that creates trouble. A man is dead, and it wasn't really the parson's wife who brought him low, that poor woman would have had no need to go to the barn that day if it hadn't been for that . . . that creature.'

'Don't' – Simon's voice was low now, his words thick – 'don't speak of her like that. She's naught but the victim of circumstances. She's too attractive for her own good, and women, aye women like you Mary, sense this. Yes, yes' – he nodded at her, his head bouncing on his shoulders now – 'I'm telling you the truth, and men, aye, men, although they mightn't know it, want her. She's got something about her that they want and because she won't give it their feelings turn to hate.'

'Aw! Oh!' Mary Bentwood's face was now wearing an unpleasant smile that slowly mounted into a broad sneer, and after staring at her husband for a moment she asked, 'Are you speaking of your own feelings, Simon?'

'Oh my God! woman' – again his head was shaking, but slowly now – 'you'll drive me mad afore you're finished.'

'Huh! Huh! Five months we've been married and now I'm driving you mad.

All right, I'm driving you mad. Well, what I'm going to tell you now might add to it, and it's just this, Simon Bentwood, when you're away from the farm I don't work, the milk can go sour, the churns green, but I don't do a hand's turn when you're gone from this house other than the days you're at market. Now there you have it. And I'll add to that, I didn't promise to be your wife in order to be a slavey.'

He stared at her for a full minute before he inclined his head towards her once, saying now, 'Very well, have it your way. You don't work, then I get someone in who will, and I'll hand the housekeeping over to her every week. You can sit on your backside and pick your nails, or sew fine seams for your frocks, as you seem to have done all your life. Anyway, now we know where we stand. I'm away to give me men their orders and they'll see that the farm, at least outside, doesn't drop to pieces until I return from Newcastle.'

Simon now turned from his wife and went across the room and as he opened the door into the hall her screaming voice seemed to thrust him forward as she cried, 'I hate you! Simon Bentwood. I hate you, your old farm and everything about you and it.'

He closed the sitting-room door quietly, then standing still, his shoulders hunched, he screwed up his eyes tightly and bit on his lip before straightening up again and, this time thrusting back his shoulders, he crossed the hall, went through the kitchen and out into the yard to where his trap was waiting for him.

Simon loved Newcastle. The first time he had visited it he had gone on foot. As a lad of thirteen he had walked the ten miles to watch the hoppings on the town moor; but even on that day his interest had been caught by the sight of the amazingly beautiful buildings. He remembered he had left the town moor in the early afternoon and wandered through streets and crescents and terraces, imagining that they couldn't be real because no man could build so high and so decoratively with great lumps of stone. In the village it took the masons and the carpenters all their time to erect a double-storied house. Of course round about the village were the big houses of the gentry, but at that early age, he didn't imagine these had been built by the hand of man either.

Since those days he had not once visited the city without leaving himself time, if only half an hour, to wander about; and now in the twelve years that had passed the changes that had come about were amazing. The bridges he found fascinating, but the streets even more so because these were where people actually lived.

There was the new Jesmond Road and the Leazes Crescent with its rounded gable ends, and the beautiful Leazes Terrace, four great windows high; as for Eldon Square, he always imagined that Mr Dobson, the designer, must have thought it up during the period of his life when he was happiest. And Mr Grainger, who built the Square, well, what had *he* thought when he put the last touches to the long handsome wrought-iron balconies?

Strangely, after each visit to the city he would experience a day or two of unrest. Although within himself he was aware that he had been born to farm the land, he realised there were other avenues in life that could give a man intense satisfaction, for once a street, a terrace, a church was built it was there.

You could move on to other things, greater things, express greater dreams, but on the land life covered but one year at a time, your long efforts were whipped up with the scythe or ended when you struck the fatal blow at an animal you had come in a way to like – he wouldn't go as far as to say love. . . .

But here he was in Newcastle today and it would be the one time he wouldn't walk its elegant streets that spoke of wealth and comfort, but which he recognised in his heart housed only a small portion of the population, for at the other end of the city there were rows of hovels that he wouldn't put his pigs into.

As he drove the trap towards the courthouse his mind was a turmoil of emotions, private emotions. His marriage had gone sour on him right from that first night. He knew he had made a mistake in picking Mary for a mate, but he also knew he'd have to live with his mistake.

His horse was brought to a standstill in the midst of a mêlée of traffic. There were gentlemen's coaches, beer drays, ragmen's flat carts laden with stinking rags and their horses with heads bent as if in sorrow at their plight. There were meat carts and vegetable barrows; there were fish carts and knackers' vans, the latter displaying their trade by the legs of the dead animals sticking out from the back, one animal piled on top of the other as if they had been instantly massacred, which he hoped was the way they had died, for some men made killing a slow business.

The din was indescribable; Simon's call to his horse to be steady was lost to his own ears. The pavements along each side of the road were full of people. These in a way were fortunate because they were walking on flagstones, a new acquisition to the streets, but the road where the traffic was jammed was still made up of mud and broken stones.

When at last there was a movement and Simon turned his horse's head towards a lane that led off at the top of the street he found his passage again blocked. Standing up in the trap he could see that the hostelry ahead where he usually left his horse was jammed full. He looked to the side of him where a man in a similar trap to his own shouted, 'The town's out, it must be the case at the courthouse, the parson's wife,' and he nodded; but Simon didn't return the nod. He glanced behind him. No one had turned in from the main road to block his return passage and so, jumping down from the trap, he took the horse's head and eased her backwards, to the main road where he mounted the trap and rode onwards.

Agitated inside, he pulled out a lever watch from his waistcoat pocket. It said quarter past eleven. The case would have already begun and Tilly, looking round for just one friend, would encounter nothing but the hostile gaze of the villagers. And these would undoubtedly be making a day of it. Oh yes, they'd be making a day of it all right.

He did not at this moment think of what might happen to the parson's wife; she had lawyers and big men on her side, her family were important. Anyway, she was only being charged with manslaughter, not murder, and whatever her sentence, one way or another, she'd be gone from the village after today. But not so Tilly, Tilly had to live there, as long as her granny was alive Tilly would stay there. But what would happen to her? Apart from Tom Pearson and himself, aye, and young Steve, there wasn't one soul in that whole place that had a good word for her. After Laudimer died they would have killed her. Now that was strange for it wasn't she who had struck the blow; but they'd worked it all back to the beginning: the parson's wife was in the pickle she was because of Tilly Trotter.

My God! if only he could get out of this jam.

It was a full half-hour later when he found a stable where he could leave the horse and trap, and from there it was all of a ten-minute run back to the court house. And run he did; but when he tried to enter the building his way was blocked by the spectators. The outer hall was a mass of people, yet all strangely quiet, until he began to thrust himself between them, when there were angry murmurs. But he took no notice. Some made way for him, thinking he was some kind of an official, that was until he came to the main doors leading into the courtroom itself, and there he was confronted by an officer of the law.

'How . . . how far is it on?'

'Over halfway I should say, sir.'

'The main witnesses, have they . . . ?'

'Yes, I think so. The young lass is on the stand now.'

'Please let me in.' Simon brought his face close to that of the officer, saying again, 'Please, let me in. You . . . you see I' – he gulped in his throat – 'I'm about the only friend she has.'

They stared into each other's eyes for a moment; then the officer said, 'Well, even if I could, sir, I doubt if you'd make it, it's as bad in there as it is out here, it's crammed.'

'Let me try, please.' His hand came out of his pocket and slid unobtrusively in front of him and pressed something into the officer's hand and the officer not taking his eyes from Simon's now, said, 'Well, you can have a try, sir,' and on this he turned the big handle of one of the double doors, and as he opened it a number of people almost fell backwards. Simon, pressing himself forward with the aid of the policeman, forced himself into the throng, and the door was pushed slowly behind him; and there he was looking to where Tilly stood on a railed dais gazing towards the bench and the man who was speaking to her. . . .

'You have heard what the other witnesses in this case have said. To their mind you are the cause of Mrs Ellen Ross being present here today and being charged with manslaughter. One of them has definitely stated that you have some . . . well' – the judge now looked down at the bench, then over it and on to the head of the clerk standing below before he raised his eyes to the witness box again – 'occult power. You understand what I mean by that?'

'No . . . o, no . . . o, sir.'

'Well, in ordinary terms it means that you dabble in witchcraft.'

Everyone in the courtroom had their gaze fixed on Tilly waiting for her answer, but she didn't reply, not even to make a motion of her head, and Simon gazing at her cried voicelessly, 'She knows as much about witchcraft as an unborn child. Oh, Tilly! Tilly!'

'Well, do you dabble in witchcraft?'

'No, sir. No! No!' Her words were slow but emphatic now. 'I . . . I never . . . never have, never. I . . . I don't know nothing about witchcraft.'

'It has been stated that you enticed the parson's wife to dance in a place that is usually considered part of holy ground, namely the vestry. Did you do this?'

For the first time Tilly took her eyes from the judge and looked towards Ellen Ross and when Ellen shook her head at her she looked at the judge again, then mumbled, 'We did a step or two, sir.'

'She didn't! I taught her to dance.' Ellen Ross's voice ringing through the courtroom caused the whole place to buzz; and now there were two men standing in front of her and talking to her.

The judge struck the bench with a mallet and after the hubbub had slowly died away he, looking at Tilly again, said, 'You danced in the vestry?' and after a moment Tilly said, 'Yes, sir.'

'What else did you do in the vestry?'

'Nothing, sir, only a few steps up and down.'

Looking at the bench once again, the judge was heard to mutter to himself, 'Only a few steps up and down'; then raising his head his next question was, 'Do you hold yourself accountable for being here today? Do you in any way think that you are responsible for the death of Burk Laudimer?'

'No, sir. No, sir.'

'But you have heard the prosecuting counsel say that you are responsible inasmuch as the accused, Mrs Ellen Ross, would never have gone to your assistance had you not been put in the stocks, and you would not have been put in the stocks had you not been seen to be dancing on holy ground. So can you still say that you don't feel at least partly responsible for what is happening in this court today?'

As Tilly drooped her head Simon groaned inwardly. These men with their words and their cleverness, they could make out black was white. He allowed his own head to hang for a moment, or was it two or three, but he brought it up sharply as the judge said, 'Mark my words well, young woman. Now you may stand down.'

He watched her stumbling down the two steps, then being led to the end seat of the front row, and when she sat down he could no longer see anything of her. But the courtroom became astir again. 'Call Hal McGrath . . . Hal McGrath.'

McGrath dressed in his Sunday best, his hair brushed back from his low forehead, a clean white neckerchief knotted below his Adam's apple, his grey worsted coat tightly buttoned across his chest, stood with his cap in both hands, his mien that of a quiet country man.

'You are Hal McGrath? You are said to be the man responsible for putting the girl, Tilly Trotter, into the stocks?'

There was a pause before McGrath spoke, and then he said, 'Yes, sir, 'twas me.'

'Why did you do this?'

'Just . . . just for a joke, sir.'

'Nothing more?'

'Well' – McGrath's head swung from side to side – 'I'd been a-courtin' her and she'd egged me on like; then she threw me off so I suppose, sir, 'twas, 'twas a bit spite in it.'

'You're honest, I'll say that for you.'

Again Simon hung his head and missed something that was being said by the judge, but McGrath's answer to it was, 'Yes, sir, I'd heard tell of things she'd done like an' 'twas a bit odd, but I thought, well, when we were wed I'd knock that all out of her.'

This answer evoked loud guffaws and brought the eyes of the judge on all those present.

'Do you in any way hold yourself responsible for the death of Burk Laudimer?'

'Well' – McGrath looked from one side then the other – 'no, sir. No, sir, t'ain't me what hit him.'

'No, it wasn't you that hit him' – the judge's voice was stern now – 'but had you not put that girl in the stocks then Mrs Ross would have had no need to go to her rescue, nor to call in the aid of three miners, nor in defence of one of them to strike a blow that inadvertently brought about the death of a man.' There was a pause now before the judge asked, 'Do you still want to marry this girl?'

There was another pause before Hall McGrath muttered, 'Aye, sir.'

'Then I hope it may come about, and it could be the making of her. Stand down.'

Simon leant against the door and closed his eyes. He was raging inside. Marry Hal McGrath and be the makings of her. He would do for him first before he saw that happen to her.

'Call Mrs Ellen Ross.'

The parson's wife was on the stand. After the preliminary questioning by the counsel the judge addressed her and it was evident to everyone in court that he was speaking to her in a manner that he hadn't used to any previous witness that day.

'You are very interested in education, is that not so, Mrs Ross?'

'Yes, my lord.' Ellen's voice came as a thin whisper.

'It is your desire to educate the labouring classes?'

There was a pause, and again she said, 'Yes, my lord.'

'Have you now come to the conclusion that your decision to do so was ill-advised?'

'No, my lord.' Her voice was stronger, her manner slightly more alert, and undoubtedly she had nonplussed the judge for again he looked down at the bench, then on to the head of the clerk before continuing, 'You don't think it ill-advised that because you desired to teach three pitmen their letters they are now out of employment?'

When she made no reply to this the judge waited a few minutes before going on, 'Well now, tell me, do you not think it would have been wiser if you had refrained from teaching the girl, Tilly Trotter, her letters and attempting to coach her into refinements that are far above her station, such as dancing gavottes and such like?'

The whole court stared at Ellen as, her chin coming up now, she said, 'Country people dance, your honour, farm labourers and such, as do the people in the lower end of this city.'

It was evident now by the judge's tone that his sympathy for the parson's wife was waning a little, for his voice was crisp as he said briefly, 'There's dancing and dancing as you well know; as the classes differ so do their types of recreation, and this, I think, has been proved by the very fact that this case is being tried in this court today.'

The assembled people watched the judge purse his lips, then look towards an object lying on the bench; and, pointing to it, he seemed to address it as he said, 'This is the implement that caused the death of a man. Had you any idea that it had a nail in its end when you picked it up?'

He was now looking at her, and her voice trembled a little as she answered, 'No, my lord, of course not, no.'

'Why did you aim the blow at the deceased man? Was it because he was one of the men that put the girl in the stocks or was it because he was attacking one of the workmen you had come to look upon as a sort of protégé?'

Some seconds passed before Ellen gave her answer, and then she said, 'I don't know, my lord. My intention was to thrust the man aside because I could see that Mr Drew was in a bad way and . . . and the further blow would have felled him to the ground.'

'Yes, yes.' The judge was now looking down at the bench again. The court waited; then lifting his head he said abruptly, 'You may stand down.'

As the defence counsel stepped forward to present his side of the case there was a stir in the middle of the court as a woman fainted, and when they brought her limp body towards the doors Simon was pressed outside into the hall once again, and when he attempted to return into the courtroom it was only to find that the door was closed with someone else having obviously taken his place and pressed against the door. The policeman, remembering the tip, spoke apologetically, saying, 'Sorry, sir, that's how things go. You couldn't get another pin in there.'

Seeing it was no use trying any further persuasion, Simon turned about and pushed through the throng and out into the open air. All he could do now was wait until the case was over. . . .

It was almost an hour later when the courtroom doors opened and the people surged through the hall and into the street. It was now that Simon forced his way back through them and into the courtroom. The bench was empty, but before it he saw the parson standing, his wife enfolded in his arms, and about them a number of men. But standing alone at the far end of the long front seat was Tilly, and he made his way straight towards her and without preamble took her hand and said, 'I was outside, I didn't hear how it went.'

Tilly looked up into his face and muttered slowly, as if coming out of a dream, 'She's free. Thank God!'

'Come.' As he turned her about and went to walk up the aisle, he glimpsed from the side of his eye the parson's wife turning from her husband's arms and looking towards them.

But Tilly didn't notice for her head was down, and she kept it down until they were well away from the court walking up a comparatively quiet street and then she stopped and, looking up at Simon, she said, ''Twas awful, Simon, awful, to say I was a witch. Simon, what has come upon me?'

'Nothing, nothing, me dear. Don't let it trouble you.'

She shook her head hard now as if throwing off his soft words as she said bitterly, 'But it does trouble me, Simon, it does. I've . . . I've never done any harm to anyone, not even to wish them harm, that is not until the last business, then I wished, I even prayed, that God would strike Hal McGrath, I did. But that is the one and only time I've ever wished bad on anybody. They're even saying I spirited Pete Gladwish's dog away. Can you understand it, Simon?' Her voice had risen. 'What'll they say I've done next? I'm afeared, Simon.'

'Now! now!' He gripped her hands tightly. 'No one's going to do anything more to you; I'll keep a look out.'

'No, no, don't.' She now pulled her hands away from his and began walking up the street again, and she had her head turned from him as she went on, '"Tis best if you keep away from me, they're sayin' things.'

'Who's sayin' things?' His voice was grim.

'Oh, all of them.' She moved her head wearily now.

'Well, what are they saying?'

Her voice harsh again, she cried, 'They're sayin' I'm the cause of your marriage going wrong.'

He pulled her to a sharp stop, demanding now, 'Who said my marriage is going wrong?'

'Oh, it's no matter, I just heard.'

'You must have heard it from somebody. Who said it?'

She lifted her head and looked him in the eyes now as she replied, 'Randy Simmons has put it about that you're always fightin' and it's 'cos of what happened on your marriage night. Oh, Simon, Simon, I'm sorry.'

'Damned lot of rot! Never heard such idiot talk in me life. Don't you believe a word of it.' He bent towards her now. 'Do you hear! don't you believe a word of it. You know, it's funny' – he straightened up – 'I've read things like this, about every now and again a village going mad. They've nothing to do except their grind, nothing to interest them after, so they hatch up something like a – ' he had almost brought out 'a witch hunt' but substituted quickly, 'a scandal and run a gossip shop.'

Slowly she turned from him and began to walk again, and presently she said quietly, 'If it wasn't for me granny I would leave the place an' go miles away. I could get work, perhaps in a big house, somewhere where I wasn't known.'

'Well, you can't leave, you know you can't, you've got your granny, and she needs you, more so now than ever before 'cos she's lost William.'

They walked on in silence until she broke it by saying, 'I miss me granda, Simon. He was always kind to me. He never gave me a harsh word in his life. I . . . I suppose' – she dropped her head slightly to the side as if thinking back – 'between them they spoilt me. I was lucky to have been brought up by them. Aye, I was.'

He cast his glance towards her. Lucky, she said, and here she was walking through the streets of Newcastle dressed as the poorest of the poor would be in this city. Her short blue coat was green in parts; her serge skirt had been darned in various places near the hem; her hat was a flat straw one and unadorned; her boots had seen better days, one toe showing it had recently been very roughly cobbled. He would like to take her into a restaurant and give her a meal but her appearance might suggest he had picked her up from the street. He wished also he were able to take her into one of the fashionable new dress shops with their huge glass windows and say, 'Rig her out'; but were he to do so he wouldn't now be able to pay out of his own pocket. What the old couple didn't know was that the money had run out some time back, for his father had not only spent his own share, he had dipped into William's side too; and so he himself had sworn that as long as they needed it the sovereign a month would be forthcoming. Up to the time of his marriage the carrying out of this resolution had been easy, but since, what he had discovered, among other things, was that his wife had a nose for keeping accounts, and he knew that in the future he was going to be hard pushed to explain where the regular payment went.

And so he said, 'There's a shop not far from here, would you like some pies and peas? They're good; I generally have a plate when I come into the city.'

She hesitated, then said, 'I'm not hungry, Simon.'

'Aw, come on; you'll be hungry when you smell these.' He took her arm and hurried her forward now and within a few minutes they were standing among others scooping up the hot pies and peas, and he smiled at her, saying, 'Good?' and she answered, but without a smile, 'Yes, very tasty, Simon, very tasty.'

As he was finishing the last mouthful of pie, Simon, glancing over the mingled customers towards the open door, saw white flakes falling and exclaimed on a mutter, 'Oh, not snow!' then looking at Tilly who had only half finished her food, he said, 'We'll have to be moving, Tilly; look, it's starting to snow.'

'Aye; I don't really want any more, Simon.' She put the plate down.

'Are you sure?'

'Yes; 'twas nice but I'm not hungry.'

'Come on then.'

Fifteen minutes later they were crossing the bridge into Gateshead amidst heavy falling snow and it was almost an hour later before they came to the outskirts of the village. It was still snowing but not so heavily here, although the ground showed a good spread of it. It was at the point where the roads branched that Tilly said, 'Stop here, Simon; I'll make me way over the fields.'

'You'll do no such thing.'

'Simon – ' she leant forward and gripped the hand that held the reins and her voice no longer sounded like that of a young girl but of a knowing woman as she said, 'You know what will happen if you're seen drivin' with me through the village. They'll say . . .'

'What'll they say?' He jerked his finger towards her. 'Well, let them say, but you're not going to end up stiff in the fields because of their dirty tongues, so sit tight.'

She sat tight with her head bowed, in fact she crouched down on the seat hoping that she'd pass unrecognised. Because of the state of the weather there was no one in the village street, but that wasn't to say that the sound of a neighing horse or the muffled tramp of its feet didn't bring at least some of them to their windows.

When they eventually reached the cottage gate it was to see Annie with her face to the window, and as Tilly got down from the trap she said, 'Are you comin' in, Simon?' and he answered, 'No, I'd better be getting back while the going's good. But listen.' He bent towards her where she was standing in the road now, her hand extended on the back rails, and he leant sideways and covered it

with his own as he said, 'At the slightest sign of trouble, make for the farm . . .
I'm going to have a word with young Steve on the quiet; he'll keep me in touch.'

'No, no!' She shook her head. 'Don't ask Steve to do anything more, Simon.
The poor lad, look at the state he was in; and his arm will never be the same
again.'

'Well, in spite of that he's still for you, very much for you. He's a good lad, is
Steve. How he came to be bred of that crew, God alone knows. Now look, get
yourself in, there's your granny at the door, you'll catch your death in this.'

She stared up at him for a moment longer; then in pulling her hand from
underneath his she let her fingers rest against his for a moment as she said, 'I
don't know what I'd . . . we'd do without you, Simon; but please, for your own
sake an' . . . an' your wife's, keep your distance.'

He blinked some snowflakes from his eyes before he answered, 'That'll be up
to me. Go on; good-night to you.'

'Good-night, Simon.'

Annie had the door open and her first words were 'Oh, lass, I thought you
were never comin'.' Then she added, 'That was Simon; why didn't he come in?'

'He's got to get back, the roads are gettin' thick.'

'Here, give me that coat off you, you look frozen. Come to the fire.'

Tilly had only one sleeve out of her coat before Annie was tugging at her arm
and pulling her forward towards the fireplace where she pushed her down into
a chair, saying, 'I've got some broth boiling.' She inclined her head towards the
spit. 'It's been on the bubble these past two hours. Ah, lass!' Her voice suddenly
sank deep into her chest and, the tears springing from her eyes, she said, 'I . . . I
thought they had done somethin' to you, kept you or somethin'. I thought you
were never coming. I . . . I didn't know how I was goin' to go on without
you. Aw! me bairn.'

'Aw, Granny.' It was too much on top of all that had happened, and Tilly leant
forward and laid her head against Annie's breast, and the old woman held her
tightly while they both cried. Then Annie, recovering first, muttered, 'This won't
get any broth down you an' you're as cold as clay.' This latter remark seemed
to remind her of William for she now added, 'Me poor lad. Me dear lad.'

It wasn't until after she had served up the plate of broth and Tilly had forced
herself to eat it that Annie now asked, 'How did it go?'

'She got off.'

'Thanks be to God!'

'What did they ask you?'

'Aw, Granny.' Tilly now put the bowl on to her knees and she bent her head
over it as she murmured, 'It was awful, awful. All of it was awful, but . . . but
when the judge asked me had . . . had I practised witchcraft. . . .'

'What!'

'Aye, Granny. They're makin' out in the' village that I'm a witch. It isn't just
the McGraths now, 'tis everybody, and they're blamin' me for the lot.'

'They're mad, stark starin' mad.'

'And you know what, Granny' – Tilly's voice rose now – 'the judge asked
McGrath did he want to marry me and he said aye, and he would knock the
witchcraft out of me. And the judge said it was a good thing. Aw, Granny, I
thought I would die.'

Annie looked at the face before her, the beloved face, and all she saw in it was purity. Her bairn was bonny, lovely; aye, too much so really, and in spite of having no figure to speak of, she had something, an air about her, a quality, something she couldn't give a name to. But . . . witchcraft! What would they say next? But this was serious, very serious, much more so than McGrath's thinking they had money hidden here. Oh aye, more so. Feeling suddenly weak she sat down on the settle by the side of Tilly, and after a moment she said, 'Thank God we've got Simon. As long as he lives he'll let nothing bad happen to you.' And to herself she added, 'Married or no.'

The fire had been banked down. Tilly was lying by the side of her grandmother in the walled bed. She had lain there each night since they had boxed William and set him out on the table in the middle of the room until it was time to take him to his last resting place.

Her granny was quiet; she didn't know whether she was asleep or not but for herself sleep was far away, her mind was going over the details of the day from the moment she had got off the back of the carrier cart and Mr Fogget, the carter, had pointed out the way to the courthouse. But he had done so without looking at her, and the other passengers from the village had remained seated in the cart and let her go on ahead. No one had spoken to her on the journey, in fact Mrs Summers, whose husband worked in the Sopwiths' gardens, had pulled her skirt aside when she sat down beside her.

The thought of wanting to die had been in her mind a lot of late but never more so than at the moment when she entered that courthouse. It was as if she was the person about to be judged, and she knew that in a great many minds this was so.

She lay wide-eyed in the stillness. There were no night sounds tonight, the snow had muffled them. The fire wasn't crackling. The only sounds were the short soft gasping breaths of her granny.

Then she was sitting bolt upright in the bed, her hand pressed tight against the stone wall to her side. Someone was coming up the path. She wasn't dreaming. No, she wasn't dreaming. They had stopped outside the door, and now her heart seemed to leap in her breast when there came two short raps on the door.

She was immediately aware that her granny had not been asleep because now she was resting on her elbow and whispering, 'Who in the name of God can this be at this time?'

As Tilly went to crawl over her to reach the edge of the bed, Annie's hand stayed her, saying, 'No, no; stay were you are.'

When the raps came again and a soft murmur came to them, saying, 'Tilly! Tilly!' Tilly turned her head to stare down at her grandmother, and although she couldn't see her face she knew that her granny was staring at her, and she whispered, 'I think 'tis Mrs Ross.'

'Mrs Ross at this time of the night! Dear God! Dear God! what now?' Annie was muttering as she painfully swung her legs out of the bed. By this time Tilly was at the door and, pulling her coat over her nightgown, she paused before calling, 'Who's there?'

'Me, Tilly, Ellen Ross.'

Tilly turned the key in the lock, withdrew the top and bottom bolts and pulled the door ajar.

The world outside looked white and against the whiteness stood the small dark form of the parson's wife. 'Come in. Come in.'

When the door was closed and they were standing in the dark room, Tilly said quickly, 'Stay where you are, ma'am, stay where you are till I light the lamp.'

When the lamp was alight it showed Ellen Ross leaning against the door and Annie standing supporting herself against the edge of the table.

It was as if the heightening of the flame drew Ellen Ross towards the table too and as she came within the halo of the light Tilly glanced at her for a moment; then turning quickly, she grabbed the bellows and blew on the dying embers of the fire. Immediately these flared she turned towards the table again, saying, 'Come and sit down, ma'am, you look froze. Take your cape off a minute;' and she put her hands out to take the hip-length fur cape partly covering the long grey melton cloth coat. But Ellen Ross shook her head and, putting her gloved hands to the collar, gripped it as she said, 'I ... I can't stay, but I had to come and see you to ... to say good-bye.'

It was Annie who now spoke, saying, 'Well, sit down a moment, ma'am.'

Ellen nodded at the old woman, then took a seat by the side of the reviving fire and as she looked at it her head drooped on to her chest and the voice in which she now spoke was tear-filled. 'I ... I had to come and say how sorry I was, I am ... I am for all the trouble I have brought on you.'

Tilly walked slowly towards her now and, standing before her, looked down on the bent head as she said, 'There's no blame attached to you, ma'am; there's only one person who bears the guilt for this and that's McGrath.'

'Yes, yes, I think that's right, but ... but my interference hasn't helped; oh no, no, it hasn't helped.' She now looked up at Tilly. Her face was wet as she said, 'I have ruined George ... my husband's life; he can no longer follow his vocation, at least not in this country. He has already arranged that we should go abroad; he is to be a missionary.'

'Oh, ma'am!' There was a break in Tilly's voice, and again she muttered, 'Oh, ma'am!'

Ellen now looked towards Annie, who was on the settle opposite to her, and she addressed her as if she would understand what she was now about to say. 'My ... my people want me to return home but ... but that would mean separating from my husband. As much as I would love to, because my family are very understanding people, I feel I must abide with my husband, for that is as little as I can do for all the trouble I have caused him. Where he goes I go, I must go.'

'And you're right, ma'am, you're right.'

'Yes, yes, I think I am. But ... but life will never be the same again. I shall carry the burden of that man's death with me to my grave.'

'You weren't to blame for that, ma'am. That part of the business links straight up with Hal McGrath.'

'Yes, I suppose you're right, Tilly. But ... but tell me, he won't get his own way? I mean you will never marry him, will you Tilly? No matter what happens you couldn't ...'

'Oh no! No!' Tilly was shaking her head in wide sweeps. 'Never! Never! I'd sooner die first.'

'And I'd sooner see her dead first.' Annie was nodding her head violently now. 'I'd kill him afore he'd lay a hand on her.'

The fire suddenly blazed upwards, the lamp flickered, there was a whining of wind round the chimney. Ellen Ross shivered; then getting to her feet, she said, 'I . . . I have to return.'

'It must have been dangerous for you coming, ma'am; the roads are bad, an' you didn't carry a light.' Although Annie had referred to the roads her words also implied there was danger from another quarter, and to this Ellen answered, 'I'm safe in the fact that not many people will venture out tonight, and the snow has made it quite light.'

'I'll put my things on me and go back with you to the crossroads.'

As Tilly spoke the protests came from both Annie and Ellen Ross saying, 'No! No!' and Ellen now added, 'I'm warmly wrapped and I'm not afraid. Believe me, I'm not afraid. I don't think there's anything could happen to me in life now that could make me really afraid. The last few weeks I have lived with fear and I have faced it, and conquered it.'

'Well, it's good-bye, Mrs Trotter.' Ellen walked towards the old woman and took her outstretched hand. 'I used to think it would be nice to grow old hereabouts, but it wasn't to be.'

'Good-bye, me dear, and God go with you.'

Tilly had walked towards the door, and when Ellen came up to her she suddenly put out her arms and drew Tilly tightly into her embrace, and after a moment's hesitation, Tilly returned the embrace with equal intensity. Then Ellen kissed her on each cheek and, her face again flowing with tears and her voice breaking, she said, 'Promise me one thing, promise me you'll keep up your reading and your writing; no matter what happens you'll do a little each day. Promise me, Tilly.'

Tilly had no voice with which to answer that promise but gulping in her throat and screwing up her eyes tight, she made a deep obeisance with her head.

'Good-bye, my dear, I'll never forget you. I . . . I would like to say I will write, but I . . . I may not be able to because I . . . I prom. . . .' Her voice ended abruptly and she turned blindly to the door and, slowly opening it, went out into the night and she didn't look back.

Tilly watched the dark figure seeming to glide over the snow; she watched her go through the gate; she watched her until she became lost in the night; then she closed the door, locked it, bolted it top and bottom, and, leaning her head against it in the crook of her elbow, she sobbed aloud.

cᴏ 7 ᴏ

A week went by; then a month; then two months, and nothing happened. Tilly
never went into the village, and only from a distance did she see any of the
villagers, except Tom Pearson and young Steve. On the day she found a couple
of dead rabbits in the woodshed she thanked Steve on the Sunday afternoon
when she went down to the burn and saw him sitting on the bank. Sunday being
his only free day from the pit he had made it a rule, she knew, to be at the burn
in the afternoon; and she was glad of this because it was someone to pass a
word with, someone young. But on that particular Sunday afternoon after she
had thanked him for the rabbits he had said that it wasn't he who had put them
in the woodshed but he had a good idea who had; it would be Tom Pearson
because he was known to be a dab hand at poaching. She had felt slightly
warmed inside that day knowing that besides Simon and Steve she had another
friend, one who apparently wasn't afraid of the villagers.

One person she hadn't seen even a glimpse of over the past weeks was Hal
McGrath, and she wondered if Simon had gone for him. However, she had not
asked him because the subject she felt was best buried; and deep in her mind
she wished that McGrath could be buried with it.

Yesterday Simon had brought the sovereign. His face had looked frozen and
pinched, and there was a kind of sadness about him. But perhaps it was due to
the weather. For the past fortnight it had hardly stopped raining, and even under
better weather conditions farmers always found this a heavy time. He'd had
little to say, just asked them if they were all right and if they had been troubled
by anyone. When she had said 'No', his answer had been, 'Well, that's as it
should be.'

When he left without even having a drink of hot ginger beer her granny had
said, 'He's more troubled than we are, he's not happy, you can see it in his face.'

This morning the rain had stopped but the wind was high and the air biting,
and when she was pulling her coat on Annie said, 'Don't put your hat on, it'll
be blown away afore you get out of the gate. Look, take my shawl' – she pulled
the shawl from her shoulders – 'put it round your head and cross it over and
I'll tie it behind your waist.'

'No, no, Granny' – she put out a protesting hand – 'I'll be all right. I've got
me scarf, I'll put that round me head.'

'Don't be silly, girl, that piece of wool wouldn't keep the wind out of a flute.
Here' – she was already putting the shawl over Tilly's head; then crossing it
over, she turned her around and knotted it under her shoulder blades – 'There,
at least you'll be warm.'

'What about you?'

'I'm in the house, aren't I, an' there's a roarin' fire there and enough wood in to keep me going for a week; you've got a four-mile walk afore you each way.'

'I don't mind the walk, Granny.'

And she didn't mind the walk. She no longer took the carrier cart into Shields for the necessities because it would already be laden with villagers. Instead she now went into Jarrow for her shopping.

The shops in Jarrow were of poor quality compared with those in Shields because Jarrow was little more than an enlarged village, nor was the quality of the food as good as that which could be purchased in the market place in Shields. Still, they could live without bread, substituting potato cake in place of it rather than sit that ride out among the villagers, or even walk along the road into Harton village just to get flour; for that way she was sure to bump into one or the other she knew, and someone who didn't want to know her.

Ready now for the road, she stood waiting while her granny went to the tea caddy on the mantelpiece and took out the sovereign, and as she handed it to her she said, 'What would we do without Simon? Although I've cursed that money many a time of late, it helped to put my William decently away.' Then her chin jerking, she said, 'That'll be another thing to puzzle them, where we got the money for an oak coffin. Well, let it puzzle 'em; he wasn't going to his last bed in any deal box. Now away with you, and get back well afore dark, won't you?'

'Yes, Granny. An' mind you don't go outside, or it'll be you who'll catch your death, not me. Sit warm aside the fire. I won't be all that long.' She leant slightly forward and touched her grandmother's cheek, letting her fingers linger on it for a moment; and Annie put up her hand and gripped it tight, and, her lips trembling slightly, she muttered, as she was wont to do when her feelings were troubled, 'Aw! lass. Aw! lass.'

Turning quickly away, Tilly went out, but she was no sooner on the path than the wind caught her skirt and swirled it up to the bottom of her coat and when she reached the gate she turned, laughing, and waved her hand to Annie who was at the window and indicated what the wind had done to her skirt. And Annie waved back.

The shortest cut to Jarrow led through Rosier's village but she always skirted that; news spread, at least bad news and who knew but the Rosier villagers would hold her responsible for the three pitmen losing their jobs, and their cottages. The Rosier pit lay about a mile from the village, and she skirted that too. Once or twice when she had seen the men coming out of the gates following their shift, to avoid running into them she had swung herself over a wall or hidden in a thicket, until they were past.

But this morning, on a narrow path, her head down against the wind, she glanced upwards to see a solitary pitman coming towards her. He wasn't a man but a young boy, and when he came nearer she stopped, as he stopped, and as she exclaimed brightly, 'Why! hello, Steve,' he said, 'Hello, Tilly.'

'Just finished a shift?'

'Aye, but it's been over half an hour or so. I . . . I had something to see to, that's why I'm late gettin' home. . . . Where you goin'?'

'Into Jarrow for some groceries.'

'Oh, aye. Aye.' He nodded his head in understanding; then looking about him, he said, 'How long will it take you?'

'Oh, I should be there in another twenty minutes or so and I spend about half an hour in the shops. It takes me about three hours altogether.'

He shook his head as if that wasn't what he was meaning, then said, 'Would you like me to come along of you?'

'Oh no, no.' She gave a small laugh. 'An' look at you, you're dead on your feet. Have . . . have you been on a double shift?'

'No, no; just the twelve hours.'

Some part of her mind repeated, Just twelve hours. Twelve hours down there! She said, ''Tis a long time to be down below, an' you must be hungry an' want a wash.'

'Aye, both.' He laughed now; then his face becoming suddenly serious, he stepped close up to her and, half turning his back against the wind, he asked, 'Has anybody been about your place lately, Tilly?'

Her face and voice were serious as she answered, 'No, nobody.'

'You haven't seen our Hal or Mick, nor our George?'

'No, no, none of them. Why?' She swallowed deeply now before she could ask the question, 'Are they up to something again?' She watched him droop his head; and now she was looking down on to his greasy black cap as she again said, with a tremble in her voice now, 'Are they?'

The wind carried his answer away and she bent down and said, 'What did you say?'

He lifted his head to the side and the whites of his eyes seemed to grow larger in his black face and she watched his mouth open and shut twice before he said, 'I think they're hatching something, Tilly. What, I don't know. They're wary of me, never say nowt in front of me. An' since our Hal gave me this' – he lifted his arm upwards – 'he hasn't touched me again because me ma threatened him. But . . . but I think you'd better be on your guard, Tilly. I . . . I think you should get in touch with Farmer Bentwood and tell him what I've just said.'

Her stomach seemed to be loose within its cage, her whole body was trembling, she had the desire to be sick.

'Try not to worry. I . . . I might just be imaginin' things but I thought it best to put you on your guard. Anyway, I'd hurry up now and get back afore dark.'

'Aye, aye, Steve. And . . . and thanks.'

'You're welcome, Tilly. I wish I could do more, I wish – ' he put his dirty hand out towards her, then withdrew it sharply and saying, 'Take care. Go on now, an' take care,' he turned from her and hurried away.

She, too, turned and walked along the road, but she didn't hurry because of a sudden her legs seemed to have lost their power. Like a child who didn't know which way to turn, she wanted to sit down on the side of the road and cry until someone should come to her aid. Well, there was only one person who could come to her aid and as soon as she got back she would go to him. She'd risk annoying his wife, but she'd go to him.

Her arms were breaking. Although she had only bought a half stone of flour, a pound of bacon ends, a pound of hough meat, a marrow bone and a few dry goods, each mile she walked seemed to add to the weight, and she had just passed the Rosier village and was within the last mile home when she smelt the smoke. At first she thought it was Mr Sopwith's woodman burning the scrub; he liked his places kept clear did Mr Sopwith. Of course he hadn't the men now to do all he would like on the estate and some of it was like a jungle, so he seemed pleased that she kept the little wood clear of brambles and undergrowth. She stopped for a moment and changed the half stone of flour over into the crook of her left arm and picked the bass bag up with her right hand. But as she went to walk on again she put her head back and sniffed. The smell of burning was heavy, not like brushwood or leaves burning.

She had gone another hundred yards or so when she paused for a moment; then some instinct rising in her, she actually leapt forward and ran. Leaping and stumbling, she came to the beginning of the bridle path that led to the cottage, and there, her head back and her mouth open, she cried aloud, 'Oh Lord! Lord!' for a great pall of smoke was blotting out the road and the surrounding sky.

When she came in sight of the cottage she let out a high cry, dropped her packages, oblivious at the moment that the flour bag had split, and raced towards the blazing building. There were a number of people standing on the pathway and one of them caught her arm and said, 'It's no use. Everything possible's been done, but it's no use.'

Her wild agonised glance looked up into the face of Mark Sopwith, then at the other three men standing near. One she vaguely recognised as the pitman Mrs Ross had defended and the other two looked like Mr Sopwith's men. She actually grabbed at Mark Sopwith's coat as she cried, 'Me granny! Me granny!'

'It's all right, she's safe. It's all right. Come' – he took her arm – 'she's round the back with the farmer.'

When he went to draw her over the vegetable patch giving the blazing cottage a wide berth, she pulled herself to a halt for a moment and, looking at the flames leaping heavenwards through the aperture that had once been the roof, she moaned aloud, and Mark Sopwith said, 'Come. Come.'

At the back of the house she looked towards the woodshed. All the wood had been dragged outside, but she recognised that only half of it was lying about. The byre door was open but there was no one in there. She glanced at Mark Sopwith again and he motioned his head down towards the bottom of the garden where stood a rickety outdoor closet and next to it an equally rickety shed in which, over the years, unused or worn out household objects had been thrown. She now pulled herself away from Mark Sopwith's grasp and raced towards it.

Gasping, she stood gripping each side of the doorway. Lying on some sacks was her granny, and kneeling by her side and almost taking up all the remaining space were two people: one was Simon and the other was a young girl she hadn't seen before.

Simon immediately got to his feet and, holding her arms, said, 'It's all right. It's all right.'

'What . . . what have they done to her?' Her voice was high, almost on the point of a scream, and now he gripped her shoulders as he shouted at her, 'It's all right! It's all right! I'm telling you.'

'They . . . they burnt her?'

'No, no' – he shook her again – 'we found her down here. She's . . . she's had a bit of a seizure.'

'Oh God! Oh God!' She thrust past him and dropped on to her knees beside the inert figure and tenderly now she cupped the wrinkled face between her palms and whimpered, 'Oh, Granny! Granny!'

The girl kneeling opposite her said in thick rough tones, 'Don't frash yourself, lass; you can't do nowt by frashing yourself. She's alive. It's just likely a stroke she's had. Me Aunt Hunisett, she got a shock when they told her her man was drowned, she went just like this, but she's alive the day and well, as well as can be expected. There now. There now.' The girl put out her hand and patted Tilly's shoulder and Tilly, looking through her streaming eyes at her, whimpered now, 'They're cruel. They're cruel.'

'Aye, those are the very words our Sam said; cruel buggers, the lot of 'em. 'Twas him an' me saw the fire first an' the poor old girl going mad outside. We tried all we could with buckets from the rain barrel but it was like spittin' against the wind. Then the old lady here up and had a seizure, fell at our feet she did. 'Twas no use puttin' her into one of your outhouses, they were too near the house, this was the only safe place, and I stayed alongside of her while our Sam ran back to the big house. An' it was fortunate Mr Sopwith was just mountin' to go to the mine, an' he galloped along here. But what could he do? Nowt, because the whole place looked like hell let loose. But he was in a state 'cos he thought you were inside, miss, an' he gallops off again to the farmer, so our Sam said, an' he comes tearing up with his men, an' that's the whole of it. Except the farmer there.' She nodded her head towards the opening of the hut. 'They had to stop him going in. And I think he would have gone, only a lad from the village said you had gone shoppin', and at the news he went down like a pricked balloon. There now. There now, I talk too much. But I always do in cases like this, accidents like. When me dad was killed in the pit two years gone I never stopped talkin' for a week.'

Tilly looked at the girl. She didn't look much older than herself but she sounded like a woman. She said to her now as if she could give her the answer, 'Where am I going to put her? She can't stay here, she'll die of cold.'

The girl considered for a moment, her head on one side, then said, 'Well, we're packed like sardines since we got the push from Rosier's an' the cottage; but we were lucky to get into Mr Sopwith's row. They're a bit cleaner his cottages, but no bigger. One room's got a stone floor and that's something. But there's nine of us there still.' She smiled. 'As me ma says, if you can't lie down to sleep tack yoursel' to the wall. We'd find a corner for you; as you say, the old girl can't stay out in this.'

'You mean . . . you mean your mother wouldn't mind?'

'No, me ma won't mind; she takes life as it comes. As she says, she had to take us an' we've been far from God's blessin'.' Her smile had turned into a wide grin and for the moment Tilly almost forgot she was in the midst of tragedy. Here was someone kind, a stranger, an utter stranger offering to take them in, and making light of it.

Her attention was brought from the girl as Annie stirred and slowly opened her eyes. Her hand came up and grabbed at Tilly's arm, and her mouth opened and shut but no sound came from it.

'It's all right, Gran, it's all right. It's going to be all right. I'm here, I'm here.'

Again Annie's mouth opened and shut but still no sound came from it, and the girl at the other side from her remarked, 'Aye, she's had a stroke an' I bet it's down the left side.' She now lifted Annie's left arm and when it dropped lifelessly back on to her skirt she nodded at Tilly and said, 'Aye, I thought so; it's usually on the left side.'

At this point Simon's voice came to her, saying, 'They're not going into the house, neither of them, I'll take them back home with me.' And Mark Sopwith's reply was, 'That's good of you, I'm glad of that. They were a decent couple and they brought the girl up well.'

When Simon entered the hut again Tilly looked at him with the feelings of her heart shining through her wet eyes, and he said to her, 'Move out of the way a minute.' Then nodding at the girl at the other side of Annie, he added, 'You'll both have to get outside because I've got to lift her up.'

'But you can't carry her all the way.'

'I'm not aiming to.' He glanced at Tilly as she made for the door. 'I've got the farm cart outside. I was on the road to the miller's when I met Mr Sopwith. The cart's at the end of the bridle path.' He stooped down and gently gathered Annie up into his arms and, his body bent, he eased himself out of the hut doorway; then hitching his burden close up against his breast, he cut across the vegetable patch, round the side of the blazing cottage and through the gate into the road where there were now a number of villagers standing, and when, passing through them, he heard the remark, ''Tis a blaze, isn't it?' he paused and cried at the man, 'Yes, 'tis a blaze, and somebody's responsible for the blaze, and by God! he or they'll suffer for it.'

Their faces shamefaced, some of them looked away, while others continued to stare at him; but no one gave him any answer. And when Mark Sopwith led Tilly through the gate they had the grace to turn their heads away; that was until, as if digging her feet into the ground, she pulled herself to a halt and, looking around them, she cried, 'You've given me a name, you say I've the power to curse, well, if me granny dies, I'll curse each and every one of you. Remember that. You'll do no more to me or mine without paying for it! No, by God! you won't.'

The eyes blinked, here and there a head bowed as if in fear, one or two turned away; then, her glance full of scorn sweeping over them, she hurried on, without the aid of Mark Sopwith now, and he, turning and looking at the villagers, said sternly, 'She's right. Someone will pay for this.'

When one man dared to voice his opinion and say, 'Fires are apt to start in thatched cottages, sir,' he turned on him, saying, 'This fire was deliberately set. There was almost a bonfire blazing in the centre of that room when I first saw it. It was a prepared fire, and the scattered wood from the shed adds proof to this. Now you can go back to the village and tell them what I said, someone will pay for this, not only because it is my property but because of the damage that has been done to two people, whose only crime was to keep themselves to themselves. Now get away with you, all of you, you've seen enough . . . I hope.'

Without further words they obeyed him, some hurrying along the bridle path; but when these came in sight of the cart with the inert figure lying along it and the girl kneeling beside it, they stayed their step. Mr Sopwith was one thing but Simon Bentwood was another, for hadn't he put it around that should anyone lay a finger on the pair up at the cottage they'd have to answer to him; and they guessed what the result of his answer would be, it would be the horsewhip, and he had a thick, strong arm. So they climbed the banks and made their several ways back to the village by varying routes.

But Simon drove straight through the village, straight through the main street that had as many people in it as was to be seen on a fair day, but no one called to him; no one passed any remark, but all their eyes noted the girl in the back supporting the head of the old woman who looked dead. . . .

'What in the name of . . . !'

Mary Bentwood's voice was cut off by Simon saying, 'Get out of that! Out of the way!'

'What did you say?'

Walking sideways through the kitchen door with Annie in his arms, he almost yelled now, 'You heard. I said get out of the way.'

'What do you think you're doing?' Her voice was a hoarse whisper now as she followed him up the long, stone-flagged kitchen to the door at the far end. But he didn't answer her, he simply turned his back to the door, thrust it open with his buttocks, stumbled across the hall and into the sitting-room, and there he laid Annie on the couch. Then straightening his back, he turned to his enraged wife, saying a little more calmly now, 'They've burnt them out.'

'Burnt them out?'

'Yes, that's what I said, right down to the ground. It's a wonder they spared her.' He looked down at the inert form of Annie.

'And the other one?' Mary Bentwood now jerked her head backwards towards the door, and Simon, putting stress on the name, said, 'Tilly? Tilly was in Jarrow shopping, and she came back to find a blazing house.'

'I hope her conscience is pricking her then.'

'Oh, woman!' he glared at her now; then walking sharply across the room he said, 'She's got to have a doctor.'

'Here' – she reached the door before him and she stood with her back to it facing him – 'let's get this straight, Simon Bentwood. What do you intend to do with these two?'

'What do you think? They're staying here for the time being.'

'Oh no! no! they're not. A sick woman like that and her, that girl!'

'Mary' – he leant towards her, his voice deceptively soft now – 'I've told you before, they're my lifelong friends. Until I can get them fixed up some place they're staying here.'

Mary Bentwood pressed her flat hands to each side of her against the door now and, her broad chest heaving, she said, 'I'll not have that girl in my house.'

'Well, that's where we differ. I'm going to have her in *mine*, Mary. And if I'm not mistaken, you've been grumbling for weeks that you haven't enough help in the house so she can come to your assistance in that way.'

'I'll . . . I'll walk out, I'll go home.'

'Oh well, that's up to you. Now get out of me way!' He took her by the shoulder and thrust her aside almost overbalancing her, leaving her standing in the doorway glaring after him as he hurried across the hall; her face was red, her eyes wild with temper that touched on fury.

In the kitchen Tilly was standing near the dresser. Her face was devoid of all colour, her eyes looking like saucers in her head, and when she said, 'Can I go to her?' he said, 'In a minute, Tilly. I'm going to send Randy for the doctor. Just take your coat off and sit down by the fire. Make a cup of something, Peggy.'

The woman standing at the far end of the kitchen peeling potatoes turned her head in a nonchalant way and said, 'Aye, master, aye.'

When Tilly hesitated to walk towards the fire he took her arm and, his voice a whisper now, he said, 'It'll be all right, it'll be all right. I'll . . . I'll explain things to you in a minute.' And then he left her.

She was standing by the fire looking down on the big black pan simmering on the hob when the far door opened and Mary Bentwood came slowly into the room, and walking past Tilly as if she weren't there, she spoke to her woman, saying, 'Leave that and see to the churn in the dairy.'

'But I've just come from there, ma'am,' Peggy Fullbright said.

'Then go back again.'

'Aye, ma'am.'

As soon as the woman left the kitchen, Mary Bentwood walked towards the fireplace and, standing in front of Tilly who had been awaiting her coming, she ground out between strong white clenched teeth, 'You're not staying in my house, girl! You understand? Your granny can stay until she's fit to be moved but you'll find some place else to sleep.'

'Aye, she will, and it'll be upstairs for the present.'

They both swung round towards the door where Simon was standing. He moved to the table and, looking at his wife, his voice harsh and deep, he said, 'Let's hear no more of it. She's staying; they're both staying until I can get them fixed up in a place of their own. This much I'll grant you, I'll see to the business right away.'

He hadn't looked at Tilly, but now he said, 'Go in to your granny, she's in the front room.'

Tilly looked from one to the other before, her head bowed, she turned and went hastily from the kitchen. But no sooner was the door closed on her than Mary Bentwood cried, 'By God! I'll make you pay for this day. You see if I don't. Oh! you see if I don't.' Her last words were slow and ominous and to them he replied on a long sigh, 'Everything in life has to be paid for and I've never been in debt yet, so there's no doubt, my dear, that you will, and with interest.' He turned and he, too, went out of the kitchen and towards the sitting-room.

PART TWO

ৡ The New Life ৡ

∽ 1 ∾

Four days later Annie died. She died without speaking except through the pain and love she expressed with her eyes whenever she looked at Tilly; and she was buried three days afterwards. A very short laying-out, as the men said in the yard, but the quicker the old 'un went the quicker the young one would leave and things would get back to normal.

Besides the new parson the Reverend Portman, George Knight the gravedigger, the master, and that Tilly Trotter, there was one other person whose presence surprised them as much as did the presence of Tilly, the latter only because everyone knew it wasn't right for a female to attend a funeral, especially that of a relative. But Mark Sopwith's appearance in the cemetery just as, with the help of Tom Pearson and the hedger, they were carrying the coffin from the cart, caused eyebrows to be raised. He had ridden up to the gate, left his horse there, then joined the small cortège to the graveside.

When the first clod fell on the coffin Tilly closed her eyes tightly and her mind gabbled, Oh, Granny! Granny! What am I gona do without you? Oh, Granny! Granny!

She wasn't really aware of someone turning her from the graveside until she was once again standing by the farm cart, then through her blurred tear-streaming eyes she jaw Simon and Mr Sopwith standing apart talking.

Presently, Mr Sopwith went to his horse and Simon came back to her. It was when he said, 'Come on, get up,' that her tears stopped flowing. She took out her handkerchief and slowly wiped her face; then looking at him, she spoke as someone would who had suddenly put on years and jumped into adulthood. 'I'll . . . I'll never be able to thank you, Simon, for all you've done for me granny and me. And also me granda. But it's finished now. From now on I'll have to stand on me own two feet.'

'What you talking about? Come along! it's cold standing here. Get up.'

'No, Simon, no.' She pulled her arm from his grip. 'I'm not going back to your house.'

'What! . . . Now don't be silly; where do you think you'll go?'

'I'm . . . I'm goin' to the cottage. I was there yesterday. The woodshed and the byre are all right, they're dry.'

'Don't be a fool! You can't live there.'

'I can for a little while anyway; and then . . . then I'll go into service or some such.'

'Well, until you go into service you're coming back. . . .'

'No! Simon.'

He stared at her, amazed at the authority in her voice. She neither looked nor sounded like young Tilly. He knew that not one word, not one deprecating look, not one insinuating nod had missed her during the past few days. She had been aware of Mary's feelings towards her from the first, and they must have pierced deep for her now to be refusing the shelter of his home; and in weather like this too, for the spring had seemingly forgotten to materialise. Instinctively he pulled the collar of his coat high around his neck; and then said weakly, 'But where will you sleep?'

'There's plenty of dry straw and they left enough wood for me to make another fire.' Although her voice was now low, her words implied deep hard bitterness. 'The woodshed has a boiler in the corner; it used to be the pot house. I'll get by, never fear. And anyway, it'll only be for a short time.'

Simon hung his head, every decent instinct telling him to thrust her into the cart and take her back to his home; yet he knew that if she returned there there would be hell to pay. Mary had a deep ingrained hate of her; she had the power of looking beyond the eyes had Mary, she could sense hidden feelings, like a terrier smelling a rat. . . . But for this girl to go back there among the burnt-out ruins of that cottage and to live in the woodshed. . . . Well perhaps, when he came to think of it, she'd be happier there. Aye, and perhaps she'd be safer there an' all, at least for a time, for if some of those maniacs in the village got going again God knows what would happen to her. There was one thing he would like to find out, that was who started the fire . . . deliberately started the fire. Apparently it wasn't Hal McGrath for he had proved he was nowhere near the village on that day. He had cleaned up immediately after his shift, so he had said, and gone to Cooksons' foundry in Shields to pick up some pieces of iron for his father, and Billy Fogget had sworn that he was on his cart early that morning. That he had also visited Cooksons' was verified by the gaffer who had served him.

Well, whoever had perpetrated the deed that had brought on Annie's end would let it slip out one day, he had no doubt, and until then he could wait. In a way he was glad it wasn't McGrath because that fact had prevented bloodshed.

'Ta-rah! Simon. Don't worry about me, I'll be all right.'

'Wait!' He pulled at her coat with one hand while thrusting his other into the back pocket of his breeches; then pressing something into her hand, he said, 'That'll tide you over.'

She looked at the two sovereigns and was about to refuse them when she thought, Well, it's me granda's money. But even as she thought this she asked, 'How much money is there left . . . of me granda's, I mean?'

When she saw his face redden and his tongue come over his lips before he said, 'Oh, a bit,' she stared at him then said softly, 'There isn't any left, is there?' And now he sighed and said, 'No.' But he didn't add, 'There should be.'

'How long has it been finished?'

'Oh. Oh, I can't remember. Not long.' He shook his head, and for a moment she looked perplexed.

Twice she opened her mouth to speak before she said, 'Well, I thank you for them, both of them; and for me an' all. But now I can't take this.' She held out the two sovereigns to him. But he thrust her hand away, saying, 'Don't be a fool, Tilly. How are you going to live?'

She looked downwards to where her boots were showing below her old skirt; then, her fingers closing over the coins, she said, 'Thanks, Simon.' And with one last look at him she slowly turned away.

But she hadn't taken two steps before his voice halted her, saying, 'I'll drop in and see how you are. I'll bring you a blanket or two.'

'No, Simon.' She was facing him again, and as she stared at him over the distance she shook her head, saying now, 'Please, please, don't come near me.'

'Don't be daft, girl!'

'I'm not bein' daft. They'll be watchin', talkin', waitin'.'

'Who will?' It was a silly question to ask, and he knew that she thought so too when all the answer she gave him was one slow movement of her head before turning from him and walking away.

∽ 2 ∾

She had been living in the woodshed two days. The first day she cleared it out, swept the narrow pot chimney and got the fire to burn, brought in some dry sacks and clean straw from the byre, raked among the burnt embers of the cottage until she found the frying pan, the kale pot and a few other cooking utensils. In one place her foot had slipped through some mushed wood and disclosed red embers still burning. As she worked the slightest unusual sound had brought her head up. There was fear in her still, but a fear threaded now with anger.

The first night lying on the straw on the stone floor she had lain awake and seen herself standing in the middle of the village yelling at each house in turn and the occupants cowering behind their curtains. Later, her dreams picked up her retaliation and there she was again in the village, but behind the main street now and facing the McGrath house, and she was screaming, 'You murdered me granny, and in a way you've killed the parson an' Mrs Ross for they'll never know real happiness again. An' you've tried to befoul me. But you won't! You won't! Hal McGrath, nor no one else. Let anybody venture near me again an' they'll take what they get.'

The remnants of the dream had helped to stiffen her back when early this morning she had taken the long walk into Jarrow, but on this particular return journey her arms weren't aching for her purchases had been meagre. She had planned that if she could last out till the fair she would go to the hirings in Newcastle and get a position in some house, no matter how lowly, any place that would take her miles away from this area.

Arriving at the ruins of the cottage, she stopped within the broken gate sensing that she wasn't alone. The outer wall, still standing, blocked her view of the yard but she knew there was someone there, and she was backing towards the road again when round by the smoke-begrimed wall she saw young Steve McGrath and she drew in a long breath before moving towards him.

'Hello, Tilly,' he said. 'I've fetched you a couple of blankets, and there's some bacon and odds wrapped inside.'

'Oh' – she moved her head slowly – 'that's kind of you, Steve. But . . . but where did you get the blankets and the rest?'

'They're not from me; Farmer Bentwood asked me to pick them up on the quiet like an' last night he slipped them out on to the road, an' I hid them in the thicket down by the burn 'cos I didn't want to come up here in the dark an' frighten you. They're a bit damp, the blankets. 'Cos they would be, lying in the thicket, wouldn't they?' He sounded apologetic.

'Ta. Thank you, Steve.'

'How you farin'?'

'Oh, all right, Steve.'

'I put them in the byre, I couldn't get into the woodshed.'

'No, I locked it up.'

'You're right, you're right an' all to do that.'

He now turned from her and looked through the gaping hole that had been the scullery window and what he said was, 'Wicked . . . wicked,' then looking at her again he added, 'He's bad, rotten. He was born rotten; he'll die rotten, putrid. Aye, putrid.'

'Who?' Although she knew to whom he was referring, she still didn't know why he was connecting his brother with the fire, but when he said, 'Our Hal,' she moved a step nearer to him and said, 'But . . . but he was gone, he was in Shields when it happened.'

'Aye' – his chin moved upwards, stretching his thin neck out of his coat collar – 'but he had it planned, he had it all set up.'

'Aw no! No!'

'Aye. Aye, Tilly. An' I think you should know just to be on the safe side, but keep it to yoursel'. I'm tellin' you in case you let your guard down against him 'cos he can be smoothed-tongued when he likes; aye, like the devil. An' like the devil he coached the other two well, our Mick and George. They watched you leave the house that mornin', then they went in and brought your granny out. And then they tore the place apart lookin' for the money, they even chopped at the beams. He had worked it all out for them. They even dug the bricks out of the side of the fireplace thinking there might be a loose one there, but they found nowt.' His head drooped to the side now. 'But they made sure not to leave empty-handed, they took the odds and ends, like your granny's bits of pewter an' the tea caddy, an' the big brass tongs and other bits and pieces.'

She was leaning against the wall now, the bass bag at her feet, one hand held tightly across her mouth, and when he said, 'He means to have you, Tilly. That's . . . that's why I'm tellin' you, just . . . just to put you on your guard. I think' – he bit on his lip and his eyelids blinked – 'your best plan would be to do a bunk, clear out somewhere 'cos . . . 'cos if he made you marry him your life would be. . . .'

'Marry him!' She was standing away from the wall now actually glaring down at him as she cried, 'Marry your Hal! Oh! Steve. You know what I'd do first? I'd cut me throat. Aye, I would, I swear on it, I'd cut me throat afore your Hal puts another finger on me. An' . . . an' should he come near me an' me hands are free, an' by God! I'll see they're free this time, I'll leave me mark on him. I will! Steve, I will! I've stood enough. He's . . . he's a murderer. He killed me granny and it was him that was the means of Burk Laudimer dying. As you say, he's a devil.'

She stood gasping now and when he said, 'I only told you to put you on your guard. You won't tell Farmer Bentwood? 'Cos . . . 'cos I feel there'd be trouble, big trouble if he knew.'

She turned from him without answering and went behind the wall and, taking a large key from the pocket of her skirt, she opened the woodshed door, and when she went inside he followed her and, looking around the small warm space, he said, with not a little admiration in his voice, 'Eeh! by! you've got it cosy, Tilly. I wouldn't mind livin' here meself.'

When she looked at him the half-smile slipped in embarrassment from his face and he stammered, 'I . . . I was only meaning'. . . .'

'Yes, yes, I know.' She put her hand on his shoulder. 'You're a good friend, Steve. I haven't many of them an' I appreciate all you've done, and all you would do for me, but . . . but I'm not gona live in this little hole all me life. As you said, I'd best go away, I'd already made up me mind to do just that. It's gettin' a place. You see I'm well past sixteen and I'm not trained, not for anything. I realise I've had it too easy.'

'Not you, not you, Tilly. You've done a man's work around here, and you looked after the old couple for years.'

'That was happy work.' Her fingers began picking at the front of her coat as if trying to unloosen the threads, and she repeated, 'Aye, happy work. It'll never come again.'

'I wish I was older.'

'What?'

He looked towards the boiler in the corner of the shed. The fire below it was giving off a good heat and he bent down on his hunkers and held his hands towards the iron door enclosing the fire and he repeated, 'I wish I was older.'

'You'll soon be old.'

'It's now I want age. If . . . if I was older I would take care of you.'

'Oh! Steve.' Her hand was out towards him again about to drop on to his cap when she hesitated and withdrew it. She knew, without being told, what he meant by taking care of her, and at this moment she wished he was older, as old as his brother Hal, as big as his brother Hal, as strong as him, stronger, able to stand up to him, to frighten him. But there was nothing or no one on God's earth, she imagined, able to frighten Hal McGrath, only distance from him would give her any safety and rid her of the complications that life was heaping upon her, that involved Simon and his wife, and Steve here. Yes, Steve, because she realised that his feelings for her could bring him into danger; it had already, in a way, crippled his arm for he would never be able to straighten it again. And so her voice held a sharp note as she said, 'If you see Farmer Bentwood thank him for the blankets and . . . and the food.'

He rose to his feet and, his face now as straight as hers, he said, 'Aye. Aye, I will.'

He had left the hut and taken some steps along by the wall when he turned and, looking over his shoulder, he warned, 'Keep your eyes open and your door locked.'

She didn't answer, she just stood and watched him go.

And now the twilight had set in and with it another long night before her. There was enough chopped small wood to keep her going. She had forced herself to eat some belly pork which she had toasted at the fire opening, and a couple of potatoes cooked in the boiler; but it had been no effort to drink two mugs of black tea – she wanted to keep on drinking.

It was as she decided the time had come to bolt the door that she heard the muted sound of a horse's hooves coming along the bridle path. Quickly she moved outside to where the back door of the cottage had been. This gave her a clear view through the living-room and out through the gap that had been the front door, and through narrowed gaze she recognised the rider as Mr Sopwith.

While he was dismounting she moved slowly until she reached the end of the wall, but she did not go further to meet him.

For a moment he stayed his approach and looked at her kindly before saying, 'How are you, Tilly?'

'All right, sir.'

'I understand you are living here?'

'Yes, if you don't mind, sir, just for the time being.'

'But I do mind.' He passed her now and walked towards the open door of the woodshed and, glancing inside, he was surprised to note that it was both warm and tidy, and, he surmised, far cleaner than some of his cottages, though it was many years since he had been inside one. He turned to her now and said, 'You can't stay here . . . I mean for your own good. How would you like to go into service?'

'Service, sir? I . . . I would like that very much, sir.'

'Ah yes, well, that's the first step, you're willing. But having been brought up solitary, you don't know much about children, do you?'

'No, sir.'

'Are you willing to learn?'

'Yes, sir. Oh yes, sir.'

'Well, I understand the nursemaid that looks after my children has left suddenly, in tears I understand.' He smiled now. 'You see, my four are a little wild. I'm packing two off to school shortly, but in the meantime they all need some attention. Are you willing to take them on?' Again he smiled at her.

Four children! As he said, and rightly, she knew nothing about children. She couldn't remember playing with children because the village children rarely got out this far; sometimes on a holiday she would see them playing down by the burn, but she had always been too shy to join them. More than once she had lain hidden and watched them at play, especially the miners' children because they, too, worked down the pit, and so they usually came in a group by themselves on a Sunday in the summer and would swim like fish in the water and yell and shout and struggle with each other. They always enjoyed the water, the miners' children.

'Are you deterred?'

'Pardon, sir?'

'Have I put you off accepting the position?'

'Oh no, sir. No, sir. I'll take it and gladly, an' . . . an' do me best.'

'Well, you can do no more. But I must warn you, you may have a rough time of it.'

'I'm used to rough times, sir.'

Her face had been straight, her voice low, and he stared at her for a moment as he thought, Yes, yes, indeed, you're used to hard times; and likely, looking as she did, there were many more ahead of her. There was something about her. It was in the eyes perhaps, they seemed to draw you. This had likely frightened the villagers and yet at the same time had the power to attract the men, like that McGrath individual in particular.

There had been McGraths in the village as long as there had been Sopwiths in the Manor, and strangely history noted that every generation of McGraths brought its own particular kind of trouble; highway robbers, sheep stealers, wife abductors.

Wife abductors. The word brought his chain of thinking to a halt for it had reminded him, that's if he needed reminding, there was that dinner tonight with the Mytons. Agnes delighted in making a cuckold of the old man, and he had the idea that Lord Billy wasn't unaware of it, which made him think that maybe he wasn't unaware of his own part in her latest escapade. That he was merely one in a long string of offside suitors he recognised, and he was sorry that he had ever started the affair, but Agnes had a quality about her. Like this girl here, only of a different appeal. Yet perhaps not all that different, for this slim girl, who still had a childish look about her, had certainly aroused the fires in the man McGrath.

'Can you come along to the house tonight, you don't want to sleep here any longer than is necessary . . . do you?'

'No, sir. I mean yes, yes, I could come tonight.'

'Have you any belongings?'

'Only what I stand up in, sir, and a few pots back there.' She inclined her head towards the woodshed.

'Well, you won't have need of . . . the pots.' He laughed gently. 'Be there within the hour. Ask for Mrs Lucas, she is the housekeeper, I shall tell her to expect you. . . . All right?'

'All right, sir. And thank you.'

He had half turned from her when, looking at her again, he smiled broadly and said, 'I would reserve your thanks, my crew are little demons, they'll likely put you through it. But I give you leave to take a firm hand with them. Do whatever you think is necessary to curb their high spirits.'

'Yes, sir. Yes, sir.' As she watched him go, her mind was in a turmoil, one part of it thanking God she had a post, the other frightening her in a number of different ways: She was going into a big house where there were lots of servants. Would they be like the villagers? And then there were the children. Terrors he had called them. How would she manage them? Suddenly she smiled to herself, a small tentative smile, as she thought, Well, I can only follow me granny's pattern with meself: smacked me backside when I was bad, an' a bit of taffy when I was good.

*

The night was already settled in firmly before she reached the Manor gates. Timorously she went through them, passed the lodge from where no one called out to ask her business, then almost groped her way for half a mile up the drive until it opened out to show, standing beyond a large lawn, a big house, some windows illuminated, others like great black eyes.

She skirted the lawn, went round the side of the house and came upon a courtyard lit by a lantern swinging from a bracket. She now made her way to the far end from where the sound of muffled voices was coming. There were four doors in this wall, but she didn't stop until she was opposite the end one. This one was partly open and the voices were clearer now, and mixed with laughter. She leant forward and knocked on the door and waited a full minute before knocking again, louder this time. The chatter ceased abruptly and presently the door was pulled open to reveal a girl of about her own age who peered at her, then said, 'Oh, 'tis you from the cottage, is it?'

'Aye, yes.'

'Oh well then, you'd better come in.'

The girl's face was straight and she stood aside to let Tilly pass her before closing the door. They were now in a small room which she could see was used as a cloakroom of sorts for, hanging from the pegs, were rough coats and shawls, and along one wall a number of pairs of boots ranging from heavy hob-nailed ones down to slippers. The room was also lit by a lantern hanging from a bracket and Tilly almost hit her head against it as she followed the girl into the kitchen.

Just within the doorway of the long stone-flagged room she stopped and gazed at the scene before her. Sitting around a table opposite a great open fireplace were a number of people, three men and four women, and all their heads were turned towards her. No one spoke until the girl who had shown her in said, 'She's here.'

'I've got eyes in me head, haven't I?' This came from a short and enormously fat woman who was sitting at the head of the table and who turned now and looked at the man who was sitting at the foot of the table, saying under her breath, 'You better go and tell Mrs Lucas, hadn't you?'

'It can wait. Anyway, she won't thank me if I break into their meal.'

'Sit down, lass.' It was one of the two men from the bottom end of the table speaking to her now, and this remark brought a dark look on him from the cook and the footman, and as if they had spoken their displeasure aloud he leaned forward and looked along the table towards the top end, saying, 'Well, she's the master's choice, whatever she be, and it would pay some of us not to forget that.'

This remark seemed to affect the whole table for those sitting round it moved uneasily on the forms; and now Jane Brackett, the cook, taking control of the situation before Robert Simes could challenge her position as head of the table, lifted her small, thick arm and, pointing to a cracket near the fire, said, 'Sit yourself down; you'll be seen to in a minute.'

Tilly sat down. Her heart was thumping against her ribs, her mouth was dry, she knew her eyes were stretched wide as they were apt to do when she was nervous or upset. For a moment she imagined she was back in the courtroom, so thick was the hostility in the air about her. But then there appeared a ray of warm light as a young woman, rising from the table and going to a delf rack, quickly took down a mug and returned to the table and poured out a cup of tea from the huge teapot that was resting on a stand between the cook and the footman.

So taken aback by this forward action, the cook was lost for words for some moments; then she demanded, 'And what do you think you're doin', Phyllis Coates?'

'Well, you can see what I'm doin', can't you, Mrs Brackett?' The answer sounded perky and was given with a grin. 'I'm pourin' out a cup of tea.' She nudged the cook now with her elbow. 'Live and let live. We'll wait and see how things turn out. Anyway – ' she bent close to the cook's ear now and whispered something which brought from Jane Brackett the retort, 'I'm not afeared of charms or any such damn nonsense.' Yet there was no conviction in the words and her voice was muted.

Phyllis Coates was first housemaid at the Manor. She was thirty years old and had started in the kitchen twenty years ago as scullery maid. She was of medium height, and thin, with a pleasant face and happy disposition. She considered herself fortunate to hold the position that she did, and much more so because in a year or two's time she was to marry Fred Leyburn the coachman. She had taken her cue from Fred. He had been kind to the lass, telling her to take a seat, so she would be an' all, she would lose nothing by it.

Bending down to Tilly now, she said, 'Would you like a shive?'

'No; no, thank you.'

'Go on, you must be hungry.'

She went to the table again and amid silence took from her own plate a large crust of new bread and having put on it half the ham that was still on her plate she brought it to Tilly, saying, 'There. There, get it down you,' and bending further until their faces were on a level, she grinned at her and said, 'People never look so bad when you've got a full belly.'

If Tilly could have smiled she would have at that moment, but a softness came into her eyes and she had the desire to cry; and she almost did when the girl's hand lightly touched her shoulder and patted it twice.

There was silence until Phyllis returned to the table; then it seemed as if everybody was bent on speaking at once. And this went on for some time until the cook, her voice high and strident now, said, 'Sup up your last, Ada Tennant, else your backside will get glued to that form.'

Tilly saw the girl who had let her in gulp at her mug, then quickly rise from the form and go to the sink at the far end of the kitchen where the dishes were piled high on each side of it.

'And you, Maggie Short, get along and see if Mrs Lucas an' that lot's finished.'

'Yes; yes, Cook.' The girl rose hastily from the table and, wiping her mouth with the back of her hand, went up the kitchen towards the far door with the cook's voice following her: 'Straighten your cap and pull your apron down else you'll hear about it if she sees you like that. And . . . and tell her that – ' She now paused and, looking towards Tilly, said, 'What's your name again?'

'Tilly, Tilly Trotter.'

There was an audible giggle from the table, but the cook did nothing to stop it; instead, looking at the kitchen-maid, she said, 'Tell her that she's come, the Trotter girl.'

'No need to do any such thing.' Robert Simes the footman had risen to his feet now. 'I'll see to this matter. Come along you.' He jerked his head. It was a gesture one might have used to raise a dog from the hearth, and Tilly rose from the cracket and followed him.

He didn't wait for her as he passed through the green-baized door at the end of the kitchen and it swung noiselessly into her face. She paused a moment before pressing it open again and when she found herself in a broad corridor with doors going off at each side, she again paused, only to be jolted forward by Simes's voice, calling, 'Come on! Look slippy.' He hadn't turned his head while speaking to her.

He was standing now outside a door, the last but one in the corridor. She saw him knock on it, and she was standing to the side of him when a voice from inside said, 'Come.'

He opened the door but did not go over the threshold, and his tone now dropping to one of polite subservience, he said, 'It's the girl, Mrs Lucas, she's come.'

'Oh.' There was a murmur from inside the room, and presently a woman of medium height wearing a grey alpaca dress, the bodice of which seemed moulded to her thin body, stood confronting the footman, who had now taken a step back into the corridor.

Staring unblinking at the thin-lipped, sharp-nosed face of the housekeeper, Tilly experienced another tremor of apprehension as the round dark eyes swept over her. She knew, even if the atmosphere hadn't warned her, that her history had preceded her; she was already feeling that she had been thrust back into the middle of the village.

The housekeeper was now joined by the butler. Mr Pike was a man nearing seventy. He had a long, tired face, his shoulders were slightly stooped, and when he looked at her his eyes gave nothing away – his gaze was neutral.

'Well, let's get it over. Come, girl,' said the housekeeper.

'Does she want to see her tonight?'

The housekeeper turned her head to look at the butler. 'My order from Her Ladyship Price was to take her up as soon as she arrived.'

'I don't think the mistress will thank you for taking her up at this time of night.'

'What has the mistress got to do with it when that one's about? Come on, you.'

Again it was as if the command were being given to a dog.

Tilly followed the housekeeper and that part of her not filled with fear and apprehension noted that the woman didn't seem to take steps as she walked, her head didn't bob or her arms swing, it was as if her feet were attached to wheels beneath the hem of the full alpaca skirt. She was reminded of a toy she once had called Bad Weather Jack and Fine Weather Jane: according to the atmosphere they glided in and out of miniature doors set in a box painted to represent a house.

She followed her up a narrow staircase on to a small landing, then up a short flight of four stairs and through yet another green-baized door; and now she was walking across what was to her the biggest room she had ever seen. She only vaguely took in that it was partly railed in and that a broad stairway led from the centre down to the ground floor because the housekeeper had now turned and was gliding quickly up an even broader and longer corridor than the one below. The length of it was indicated by the three coloured lamps set at intervals on tables along its walls. Everything about her seemed to be wrapped in a soft red glow: the carpet was red, the wallpaper was red; there were deep red colours reflecting from some of the pictures hanging between the doors. She was dazed by the wonder of it, even transported out of herself for a moment; that was until the housekeeper came to a stop and, her voice a muted hiss, she said, 'Only speak when you're spoken to. And keep your head down until you're told to lift it. You heard what I said?' The last words were delivered in an almost inaudible whisper, and for answer Tilly nodded once. 'Then when I speak to you answer "Yes, Mrs Lucas".'

Her head already bent forward, Tilly looked up under her eyelids at the housekeeper and obediently said, 'Yes, Mrs Lucas.'

The housekeeper glared at her. Why did the mistress want to see this girl? It wasn't her place to engage staff. She was acting like an ordinary small-house mistress, the engaging of staff was the duty of the housekeeper. There was something fishy here. Another of Madam Price's tactics, she'd be bound.

In answer to the housekeeper's knock on the door, Mabel Price opened it and, after looking from one to the other, she turned her head and said quietly, 'It's the girl, madam.'

'Oh, I'll see her now.'

As the housekeeper went to draw Tilly forward Miss Price said, 'It's quite all right, Mrs Lucas, you won't be needed.'

The women exchanged looks that only they could have translated; then Miss Price, touching Tilly's shoulder with the tip of her finger, indicated that she enter the room, almost at the same time closing the door on the housekeeper; then her fingers still on Tilly's shoulder, she pressed her forward until she was standing about a yard from the couch on which a lady was lying. She could only see the shape of her lower body underneath what looked like a silk rug because, obeying orders, she had her head down and her eyes directed towards the floor.

'Look at me, girl.'

Slowly Tilly raised her head and looked at the lady; and she thought she was beautiful, sickly looking, but beautiful.

'My husband has recommended you as nursemaid for our children, but he tells me you have no previous experience. Is that so?'

'Yes, ma'am.'

'Do you like children?'

There was a pause, 'Yes, ma'am.'

'How old are you?'

'Gone sixteen, ma'am.'

'You have lived on the estate since you were very young, I understand?'

'Yes, ma'am.'

'Your grandmother and grandfather died, did they not?'

'Yes, ma'am.'

'And there was the unfortunate business of your cottage being burned down, at least my husband's cottage being burned down.'

Another pause. 'Yes, ma'am.'

'Well, Trotter, I hope you realise that you are very fortunate to be given this position, having had no previous experience.'

'Yes, ma'am.'

'You will find that my children are very high-spirited. I . . . I expect you to control them, to a certain extent.'

'Yes, ma'am.'

'How long you remain in my service depends on their reaction to you, you understand?'

'Yes, ma'am.'

'You may go now, and Miss Price will instruct you as to your duties.'

'Yes, ma'am.'

She was about to turn away when she was hissed at again. It was a different hiss from the housekeeper's, it was a high, thin, refined hiss. 'Thank the mistress,' it said.

She gulped; then with head down and eyes cast towards the thick grey carpet, she said, 'Thank you, ma'am,'

A few minutes later, after having led her not into the corridor but through a dressing-room and into what Tilly took to be a closet, for it held two hand basins on stands with big copper watering cans to the side, while in the corner was a wooden seat with a hole in it and on the top a decorated porcelain lid, and underneath a porcelain pail with beautiful paintings on it and a square straw-bound handle dangling down the side of it, Mabel Price looked at the new nursery maid with deep interest. She knew all about her, her business with the parson's wife, the murder of that man, the case in Newcastle, the cottage being burned down because she was a witch, and as she stared at her she wondered why it was that the master had insisted on taking her into his employ. One thing was certain, if the mistress had got wind of the witch business Miss Tilly Trotter wouldn't have got through the back door of this house. That's why he had warned her. And how he had warned her! Almost threatened her. 'You say one word about this girl to the mistress, Price,' he had said, 'and you'll be outside those gates quicker than you've ever passed through them before. And no pleading from the mistress will make me change my mind. You understand me?'

Oh, she understood him all right. She understood that at times he was no gentleman and if it hadn't been that he was deep in the clutches of the Myton piece she might have put two and two together. But this girl before her was just that, a girl; she was sixteen but she didn't look it, she didn't act it. He had been wild about the cottage being burned down, furious in fact, and if he had found who had done it they would certainly have gone along the line. Likely he was just sorry for this individual. As for her being a witch, she looked as much like a witch as the Virgin Mary did. Funny that, her mind linking her up with the Virgin Mary. She supposed it was because she had already been linked up with the church through the parson's wife. Well, anyway, by the look of her she wouldn't reign long upstairs because that bunch would eat her alive. Time would tell, and in her estimation it would take very little time before Tilly Trotter was trotting down the drive again Tilly Trotter, what a name!

But why had the mistress insisted on seeing her herself? Did she think that he was up to something with her? Well, if she did, it was one thing she wouldn't confide in her. She knew that.

'Before we go upstairs you had better know where you stand' – it was strange to Tilly to realise that although this woman looked refined and appeared so when talking to her mistress, the words she used were ordinary – 'the ins and outs of your position. Your wages will be five pounds a year. Should you get yourself up to anything, misbehave in any way, you can be dismissed without notice. Should you take it in your mind to leave without giving a full month's notice you'll have to refund so much for each day, threepence or threepence farthing.' She shook her head at the difference. 'You'll be supplied with uniform which'll only be yours as long as you're in service here. You'll be allowed time to go to church on a Sunday morning and one full day off a month. If you break anything through carelessness it'll be charged against you. You understand?'

'Yes; yes, m. . . .'

'You call me miss.'

'Yes, miss.'

'Come on then.'

She was again in the broad corridor. They now turned into a narrower one at the end of which was a steep flight of stairs. The stairs were dark and the only guidance she had was from a narrow handrail and the sound of Mabel Price's steps on the bare boards, but when she emerged at the top she found herself on a square landing lit by two lamps. There were a number of doors going off this landing and Mabel Price, lifting up a lamp, went to the first door and, thrusting it open and holding the lamp high above her head, said, 'This is the children's school and day-room.'

In the moment of time she had for looking round the room Tilly saw a large rocking horse, a doll's house, and various other toys scattered about the room. She noticed that a fire had burned low in the grate which was now covered by a large black-mesh screen.

The next room she was shown was a small bedroom, the main furniture being two single iron beds. In one lay a small child curled up fast asleep. 'That's John,' Mabel Price said; 'he's the baby.' In the other bed a little girl was sitting up, her arms hugging her knees, and when Mabel Price ordered, 'Lie down, Jessie Ann, and go to sleep,' the girl made no movement whatever but stared at Tilly, and it was to her she spoke, saying in a voice that held laughter, 'You're the new one then?'

Tilly said nothing to this, but Mabel Price, going to the child, pushed her roughly backwards and pulled the covers up almost smothering her face as she said, 'Get yourself to sleep. If you're not gone in five minutes I'll inform your mama.'

For answer the child simply said, 'Huh!'

As if she had been exposed to defeat, Mabel Price marched out of the room with no order for Tilly to follow her; but Tilly did and closed the door gently behind her.

They were in the next room now. This room was a little larger, but also sparsely furnished. The eldest boy was sitting at the foot of his bed, his long blue-striped nightshirt and his fair curly hair framing his round face giving him an angelic look. His brother was tucked well down under the bedclothes, but both boys' eyes were bright with expectancy.

Mabel Price began without any introduction. 'That's Matthew there' – she pointed to the cherub 'he's ten. And this is Luke, he's eight.'

She was standing by the bedside, the lamp, held over the boy, showing only his dark hair and bright eyes. Then throwing her glance from one to the other, she added without indicating Tilly in any way, 'This is the new maid. Any of your carry-on and I'm to inform your father. Those are his words, and remember them! Now you get into bed.' She pointed to Matthew, but the boy, instead of obeying her, simply returned her stare and she went out as if once again she were suffering defeat.

On the landing she opened another door but did not enter. Simply pointing into it, she said, 'That's the closet. You will see that they wash themselves well every morning. You'll have to stand over them, it'll be no use trusting them to do it themselves. They are called at half past seven. You start at six prompt. You clean out the schoolroom, the closet, and your own room.' She now pushed open another door and, marching inside, pointed to a battered chest of drawers on which was a half burnt candle in a candlestick. 'Light the candle from the lamp,' she said.

Quickly Tilly brought the candle forward and, holding it over the long glass funnel of the lamp, she waited until it was alight, feeling all the while that this woman would go for her because of the grease spluttering on to the burning wick below. But Mabel Price seemed to ignore this and said, 'This is your room, not that you'll be in it much. But to get on with your morning's work. You light the fire in the schoolroom; then after you've cleaned and tidied it up, you set the children's breakfast out. You'll find the crockery in the cupboard there. At half past seven you awake them and see that they're washed, as I told you. Their breakfast is brought up at eight. Having seen to them starting the meal you then go down to the kitchen for your own breakfast. You have from eight till half past for your meal. Ada Tennant, the scullery maid, takes your place up here while you're downstairs. At nine o'clock Mrs Lucas, the housekeeper, does her inspection. At quarter past nine if the weather is fine you take the children for a brisk walk round the garden. They begin their lessons with Mr Burgess, their tutor, at ten o'clock. In the meantime you empty all the slops, and see that you wash out the buckets well. Then you see to their clothes and necessary mending. That's as far as I'll go now. Have you taken that in?'

Tilly stared at the woman for almost ten seconds before she could make herself say, 'Yes, miss.'

'Well, I'll know tomorrow whether you have or not. Anyway, should you want to know anything, you come to me. My room is the fourth one along the corridor from the mistress's, it's the end door. I'm in charge up here, not Mrs Lucas, understand that?'

'Yes, miss.'

'Well, you'd better get to bed, not that you'll be allowed to go to bed at this hour every night, but you've got a lot to get into that head of yours, so you'll have time to think over my instructions.'

Alone now, Tilly looked round the room. Even the soft glow from the candle didn't lend any warmth to it and the patchwork quilt on the bed did nothing to brighten it. All the furniture it possessed was the bed, the chest of drawers, a stool, and a rickety table with a chipped jug and basin on it. Two hooks on the back of the door was all the wardrobe the room afforded.

Up under the roof in the cottage she'd had clippy rugs on the floor but these boards were bare, with not a thread of covering to them. The knobs on her brass bed had been polished bright, the curtains on her window, although faded, had been crisp and clean, but the window in this room didn't require curtains because it was let partly into the roof.

She dropped down on to the edge of the bed. Her mind was in a turmoil; she had met so many people during the last hour and apart from two of them they had all been alien to her. Yet not only to her, for there was alienation among themselves. She had sensed it from the moment she entered the house; each was trying to get the better of the others in some way. And those children, what was she to make of them? Well, she would soon find out in that quarter, she was sure of that. But the staff, they were another kettle of fish altogether. She'd have to go careful; if she pleased one, she'd offend the other, and she'd have to find who she wanted to please and who she didn't mind offending. Her granny used to say speak the truth and shame the devil, but she already knew that this wasn't the kind of house where it would be wise to speak the truth. . . . And the mistress of it? She didn't know what to make of her. A grand lady doubtless, but cold; somehow not alive. No, no; that wasn't what she meant. Oh, what did it matter, she had tomorrow to face. Six o'clock in the morning . . . prompt, which meant rising before that. But how would she know when it was time to get up? She should have asked her, that woman, Miss Price. Likely there would be a knocker-up. Well, she could think no more, she was tired and weary in both mind and body. . . . It must be nice to be dead, just to lie there still and have no worries.

She shook her head at herself, she mustn't start to think like that again. She'd got a job, wasn't that what she wanted? A job, and she must learn how to do it, and learn quickly or else. . . . Aye, or else.

3

She started the following day by learning how one knew when it was time to get up when her shoulder was roughly shaken and a voice said briefly, 'Up!'

She came quickly out of sleep to peer at Ada Tennant and when the girl again cried, 'Up!' she surprised her by answering as abruptly, 'All right! All right!' and when the scullery maid backed three steps away from her and the grease of her candle spilt over before she turned towards the door, she knew a moment of victory, and again one of her granny's sayings came to her: 'Give what you get. I never believed in a soft word turning away wrath.'

Her mind was clear. Strangely, she remembered nearly all the instructions that Miss Price had given her last night and she went about them with agility; until she attempted to wake the children. When gently she shook Matthew's shoulder the boy's fist came out and struck her a blow on the arm. It was as if he had been waiting for her coming. She stood for a moment, her body half bent over the bed gripping the place where the boy's fist had hit her, her arm was paining because it had been no light blow; then as if she had stepped out of her timid body she was amazed at her next reaction for, her hands on the boy's shoulders, she was pinning him to the bed. Bringing her face down to his, she whispered, 'Don't you ever do that again because whatever you do to me I'll give you twice as much back.' She paused while their eyes bored into each other in the lamplight and for a moment she imagined she was holding down Hal McGrath, and then she asked him, 'Do you understand me?'

It was evident to her that he was so taken aback by her reaction that for a moment she seemed to have stunned him, and not him alone for Luke, sitting up in bed, stopped rubbing his eyes and gaped at her, his mouth partly open. Then she turned to him and said, 'It's time to get up.'

After a moment's hesitation he pulled the bedclothes back, but when he went to put his feet on the floor his brother cried at him, 'Stay where you are! There's plenty of time.'

Tilly looked hard at the boy for a moment before going to the other bed. Here she finished what Luke had begun: pulling the bedclothes right to the bottom of the bed, she put her hand gently on the boy's elbow and eased him to his feet; then looking from one to the other, she said, 'You'll be in the closet in five minutes.'

It wasn't until she stood on the landing that she realised her legs were trembling, and she asked herself, 'What made me go on like that? Well, start the way you mean to go on.' It was as if her granny were at her side, directing her.

In the next room she had no trouble with Jessie Ann, but the four-year-old John seemed a chip off his ten-year-old brother and when she tried to lift him from the bed he kicked and kept saying, 'Don't wanna!' and as he kept repeating this she thought, He speaks no better than a village child.

The first incident in the nursery war took place in the closet when Matthew purposely kicked over a bucket of slops. As the water spread across the floor the others screeched with glee and jumped out of the way, but Tilly stood in the midst of it, and as she looked at the excrement floating around her feet she could at that moment have been sick. But there was her grandmother again seeming to shout at her now. ''Tis no time for a weak stomach, go for him or else you'll not last long here.' And so, instinctively, she reached out and gripped the boy's arm and pulled him in his slippered feet towards her. For a moment he was again too taken aback to fight; even when he attempted to she held his arms against his sides, and her grip was surprisingly strong. She had not wielded an axe or used a saw to no avail during all her young days and the strength of her hands must have got through to him for, like the little bully he was, he whined and said, 'It was an accident. I tripped, I did. Didn't I, Luke, I tripped?'

Staring into his face again, Tilly said, 'You didn't trip, you did it on purpose' – her voice was quiet now – 'but I'm tellin' you this, you do this again an' I'll make you clean it up, every last drop.' And she added, 'Your father has given me the position to look after you, an' I'll do it gladly, but any more of such pranks and I'll go right to him an' let him deal with you.'

The boy was truly astounded: maids didn't react like this, they cried, they whined, they pleaded, they brought extras and titbits from the kitchen to placate him.

But the boy's surprise was nothing to the surprise Tilly herself was feeling. It was as if on this day she were being reborn. Like the little lizards who shed their skins, the fearful, frightened Tilly Trotter was sliding away from her. If she could get the better of this fellow she felt she would lose her fear of people, all people. . . . No, not all people; there was one man she would always fear. But he was miles away beyond the walls of this house, wherein was encased another world. He had no hope of getting at her here, and she would see that she didn't meet up with him on her day off a month. Oh aye; aye, she would see to that.

'Go now, get your clothes on.' She addressed the two older boys and, looking at Jessie Ann, she said, 'Take John' – she wasn't even sure of their names – 'and I'll be along to dress you in a few minutes. Away now. But before you go out there, wipe your slippers on the mat.'

They wiped their slippers and they went away, all of them, without a word but with backward glances. They couldn't make this one out; she had got the better of Matthew, and they had never known anyone get the better of Matthew.

When the door closed on them she looked at the filth around her feet and again her stomach heaved. But heave or not, it had to be cleared up and so, grimly, she set about the task.

She didn't realise that this particular nursery breakfast was an unusually quiet affair. There were no spoonfuls of porridge splashed over the table; the bread and butter was not stuck downwards on to its surface; and so when Ada Tennant came into the room she stood for a moment gazing at the four children all quietly eating their meal. Then turning to Tilly, she was about to make some remark when she changed her mind. Her eyes widened just the slightest and what she said now and in a civil manner was, 'Your breakfast's waitin'.'

'Thank you.'

Ada Tennant's eyes widened still further. It was likely true the rumour about her, must be. An' the way she spoke! She hadn't said 'Ta' but 'Thank you', just as if she was educated. And look at this lot sittin' here like lambs. But how long would it last? Then the rumour was utterly confirmed when Tilly turned in the open doorway and, looking towards the children, said, 'Behave yourselves mind.'

When the door closed on Tilly, Ada Tennant gazed at it. It was as if she knew the minute her back was turned they would start, and she had given them a warning.

She herself had started to work here when she was eight years old, now she was fourteen. She had seen this lot grow up, and for the past three years it had been her morning chore to attend them at breakfast, and she had dreaded it. She still did. She turned and looked at the children and, taking advantage of the new lass's authority, she said, 'You heard what she said, so get on with it.'

And they got on with it.

Breakfast was almost finished when Tilly entered the kitchen, and it seemed to her now that when she left the top floor she had also left her new-found courage behind. Two men were leaving by the far door; and the only ones seated at the table now were the cook and Phyllis Coates, the first housemaid. Amy Stiles, the second housemaid, was filling copper cans of hot water from a boiler attached to a second fireplace in the kitchen. Tilly hadn't noticed this last night. It was an enclosed fire with a boiler on one side and a round oven on the other, and as she turned and looked towards it the cook spoke. What she said was, 'Are you tea or beer?'

'Pardon. What?'

'I said are you tea or beer?'

'I . . . I would like tea please.'

'Well, get it.' Cook jerked her head towards the stove.

After a moment's hesitation Tilly made her way towards the stove. At the same time Phyllis Coates rose from the table, smiled at Tilly, pointed to the dresser and said, 'Bring a mug an' a plate' and when Tilly did this, she muttered under her breath, 'You help yourself from the pot.' She pointed to a huge brown teapot standing on the hearth near a heap of hot ashes. 'But first come and fill your plate, the porridge is finished.' And on this she walked along the room to the round oven. Tilly followed her and watched her pull open the iron door to disclose a large dripping tin in which there were a few strips of sizzling bacon.

'Mostly fat left,' Phyllis said, 'but help yourself if you want any.'

Tilly helped herself to one narrow slice of the bacon; then after placing her plate on the table she filled her mug with the black tea from the pot, and when she sat down at the table Phyllis Coates pushed towards her the end of a crusty loaf.

As Tilly ate the bread and bacon and drank the bitter tea she noted that there was a basin full of sugar opposite the cook; also a platter with a large lump of butter on it and a brown stone jar that evidently held some breakfast preserve. But she was grateful for the bacon and bread and the tea, and when she had finished Cook was still sitting at the table but had as yet exchanged no word with her, in fact she had hardly looked in her direction.

It hadn't taken her ten minutes to eat her meal and when she rose from the table Phyllis Coates rose with her, and when Cook spoke to Phyllis, saying, 'You're goin' about your business early this mornin' then?' the first housemaid answered, 'It'll take me, with the old dragon due in a fortnight's time. She'll have her eyes in every corner.'

'Well, she won't find any mucky corners in my kitchen.'

'She'll find mucky corners in heaven, that one.'

This last retort was made as Phyllis Coates followed Tilly through the door and into the broad passage. She walked by Tilly's side to the end of it where it turned towards the back stairs, but once round the corner she pulled her to a stop and, her voice rapid and her tone low, she said, 'Don't let Ma Brackett frighten you. She's only over the kitchen, she's got no other say in the house. The one you've got to look out for is Miss Price.' She raised her eyebrows upwards. 'She's the one who rules the roost here. Not the housekeeper, Mrs Lucas; she thinks she does but it's only in name, it's Miss Price who has the say. An' watch out for Simes. That's the footman, you know. He's a crawler, he'd give his mother away for a shillin' that one. Mr Pike, the butler, the old fella, he's all right. Amy Stiles, she's my second, she's all right an' all. Not much up top but she's all right. An' take no notice of Maggie Short. She's as ignorant as a pig that one. An' Ada Tennant, you know the scullery maid, the one who's up in the nursery now, she's got a slate loose.' She tapped her head. 'Outside there's three gardeners an' my Fred. That's Fred Leyburn. He's the coachman.' She smiled now. 'We're walkin' out. Should get married shortly.'

For the first time in weeks Tilly smiled widely, and she said, 'I hope you'll be happy.'

'Ta, thanks. He's a good man. He's been married afore, his wife died, but he's a good man. It was him who said last night when we had a minute, "Put her wise" – that was you – "to the set-up inside, you know, who's what an' everything." She drew her head back into her shoulders and surveyed Tilly for a moment. Then shaking her head, she said, 'I must admit you're a different kettle of fish from Nancy . . . Nancy Dewhurst, that's the one whose place you've taken. She was older than you by years, eighteen she was, but didn't look half as sensible; cried her eyes out every day. Of course mind, they'll likely bring you to tears an' all afore you're much older, I mean that lot in the nursery. Real hell-bent little devils they are, especially Master Matthew. Oh! that one, he's got somethin' missing an' that's his horns. Well there, I must get on. You see, the mistress's mother is comin' in a fortnight's time, comes twice a year when the roads are passable. She lives near Scarborough. Oh and don't you know she's here! Everybody runs around like scalded cats for a month. An' you know we're very understaffed. There used to be twice as many in the house at one time, when the wings were open. Well, when I first come years ago there were over thirty servants inside and out, now there's about half that many. But they expect the same out of us. Oh aye; yes they expect the same out of us. Anyway' – she smiled again – 'if you want to know anything, I'll be around the first floor till twelve.'

'Thank you. Thank you very much.'

'You're welcome.'

As Tilly turned away she called softly to her, 'Keep your full breakfast half-hour, you'll need it afore the day's out,' and for answer Tilly nodded at her, then went towards the stairs.

Again she was feeling confident, and again a strange feeling of courage was rising in her. She had a friend, in fact she had two friends, the housemaid and the coachman. Well, that wasn't bad for a start, now was it? No; no, it wasn't. She ran up the whole flight of stairs to the nursery floor.

At twenty past nine she was standing in the schoolroom and protests were coming at her from all sides. They didn't want to go out for a walk, it was cold, they wanted to stay in and play. Matthew had some beetles in a box and they were going to race them.

She let them go on with their protests for some minutes; then, holding up her hand, she said, 'Very well. I shall go downstairs and tell your mother you don't want to go out. I would go to your father but I saw him leavin' for the mine some time ago.'

Go and tell their mother! They looked at this new creature, and they really could see her doing just that, especially Matthew. If they upset their mother their father would be told and that would bring up the question again of being sent to boarding school. He didn't want to go away to school, he liked his life here. He was wise enough to know that he would have no dominion over anyone at boarding school; in fact, he was aware that the tables would be turned and he would have to obey. He didn't like obeying. But for some strange reason he knew that he had better obey this thin, weak-looking girl who had a grip like iron and who had the habit of staring you out. He turned to his brother and said, 'Aw, come on,' and immediately Luke and Jessie Ann repeated, 'Yes, come on.' But John just stood, and when she held out her hand and said to him, 'Come along,' he looked up at her and said, 'I've w . . . wet myself.'

At this the others doubled up with laughter and, as if their young brother had scored off her for them, they cried almost in one voice, 'He always wets himself.'

She looked down on the boy and, her voice and face stiff, she said, 'You're too big to wet yourself; you should go to the closet.'

Jessie Ann, her wide grey eyes full of mischief, tossed her long ringlets first from one shoulder then to the other and cried, 'He'll go on wetting himself until he's put into trousers, and he won't have them until he's five. Luke wetted himself until he was five, didn't you, Luke?'

Tilly gazed at the little boy, who had every appearance of a girl, dressed in a blue cordroy velvet dress with a white frill at the neck, his thick straight brown hair hanging on to his shoulders. He looked more of a girl than did Jessie Ann. She felt like taking him up in her arms and hugging him, wet as he was underneath; but these were children who, she surmised, at the slightest show of softness in her would make her life unbearable so that she, too, would be crying every day. Well, she wasn't going to cry every day, she had finished with crying, she was going to get on with this job. So, bending down to the small boy and watched by the other three, she said, 'Well, I'll change you this time, John, but if you wet yourself again you'll keep your wet pants on till they dry on you. An' you won't like that, will you now?'

'N-no.'

'Well then. An' should you wet yourself just afore we are goin' out into the garden then we'll leave you behind 'cos I won't be able to waste time changin' you.'

Where was she getting the words from to talk to children like this? She who had had little to say except to her grandma and granda and, of course, Mrs Ross, dear, dear Mrs Ross. Funny – she straightened up and stood looking over the children's heads for a moment – wasn't it strange, but she felt she was acting in much the same way as Mrs Ross would do when dealing with children; in fact she was speaking to them as Mrs Ross had spoken to her Sunday School. She smiled to herself, and when she again looked at the children her voice was brisk and had a happy sound, and, looking at Jessie Ann, she said, 'Bring me a pair of clean pantaloons from the cupboard.'

'What!' Jessie Ann looked as surprised as if she had been told to jump out of the window, and so Tilly leant towards the round fair face and in words slow and clear she said, 'You heard what I said, Jessie Ann. Bring me a pair of John's pantaloons from the cupboard.'

After a moment's pause Jessie Ann did just that, she brought a pair of small pantaloons and handed them to Tilly. . . .

The play area in the garden was a stretch of lawn which was bordered by the vegetable garden on one side and a stretch of woodland on the other, and when the children began to play desultorily with a ball she stood watching; until Matthew aimed it directly at her, not for her to catch she understood but with the intention of hitting her, and when she caught it she kept it in her hand for a moment, then threw it to Luke; and Luke threw it to Jessie; and Jessie, after a pause, threw it back again to Tilly; and now Tilly threw it to John, and he ran away with it and they all chased him, and she among them; and when the little boy fell and the other children tumbled on top of him and he began to cry, it was then she picked him up and held him in her arms and her hand cupping the back of his head pressed it into her shoulder as she said, 'There now. There now. 'Tis all right, you're not dead,' while the others stood looking at her in amazement. After a while the play went on.

When they returned to the nursery it was to find an old man sitting there. He rose from a chair before the fire and as she went to take her coat off she looked at him and said, 'Good-morning, sir,' and he answered, 'Good-morning.' Then poking his head forward, he added, 'Your name is?'

'Trotter. Tilly Trotter, sir.'

'Tilly Trotter. Trotter Tilly. Tilly Trotter.' Matthew had his head back now chanting her name, and Mr Burgess, looking at the boy, said, 'Don't be silly, Matthew. It's a nice name, it's a singing name; a name you can associate with alliteration. . . . Ah, now that's a word we can use this morning, Matthew. You will find out what alliteration means and give me some examples, eh, like, Miss Tilly Trotter?' He smiled at Tilly and Tilly smiled back at him. Then she stood looking at him as he marshalled the children towards the table. Here could be a third friend. He spoke kindly, he looked kindly. Again she was reminded of Mrs Ross. This man knew words like Mrs Ross did. And then she started visibly as he said, 'You . . . you were acquainted with Mrs Ross?'

It was a long moment before she answered, 'Yes, sir.'

'They . . . they were friends of mine.' As he inclined his head towards her she wanted to say, 'I'm sorry, sir.' And she was sorry that he had lost his friends, sorry as she was that she had lost Mrs Ross.

'She taught you to read and write, did she not . . . Mrs Ross?'

'Yes, sir.'

As they looked at each other she knew that he knew all about her. Yet he was being civil to her, nice to her; he didn't blame her for what had happened to his friends.

'The world is yours if you can read and write.'

Again she answered, 'Yes, sir.'

Now he turned from her, saying to the children, 'Well, what are we waiting for? Let's begin! for there's no time to waste, life is short; at the longest it's short.'

She noticed, with not a little surprise, that the children obeyed him, even Matthew did. They fetched their slates and pencils from a cupboard and took their places around the bare wooden table.

Unobtrusively now, she made her way out of the room and crossed the landing to her own room. Here she hung up her coat and hat and, slumping down on to the side of her bed for a moment, she thought, That's that! The worst is over, I'm set.

It was fortunate in this moment she didn't realise that her battle, the real battle of her life, had not yet even begun.

At eleven o'clock she took a tray of hot milk and biscuits to the schoolroom. But just within the doorway she stopped. The tutor was speaking and he was making the words sound like a lilt, like music. He was saying, 'The boy saw that the land was green, as in the beginning, and water swept, as in the beginning, and as beautiful and mysterious, as in the beginning; and he knew that it was the seasons that made it so for without the seasons what would there be. . . . Devastation! And he asked from where do the seasons get their orders? And the answer came, from the sun. . . . Ah, now we'll talk about the sun, shall we?'

He stopped and looked towards Tilly still standing with the tray of steaming mugs in her hand, and he said, 'Well now, the sun can wait; here is Miss Trotter with refreshment.'

He had called her Miss Trotter. It was the first time in her life she had been called Miss Trotter. It sounded nice somehow.

She handed the children the mugs, and a large one of tea with milk and sugar in it she placed before him; then having set the plate of biscuits in the middle of the table, she withdrew.

The children hadn't spoken. Mr Burgess, she thought, was a wonderful man, so . . . so like Mrs Ross. The Sunday School children hadn't talked either when Mrs Ross was speaking.

At dinnertime the meal was good, and she noted that she was given a fair share like everyone else; but no one spoke to her, except Phyllis Coates and the coachman. Somehow, it didn't seem to matter. When Mrs Lucas had inspected the nursery floor she had hardly said two words to her, although all during her inspection she had kept muttering, 'Hm! Hm!' However, in the afternoon Miss Price had been more verbal, much more verbal.

'You are not to say "you" to the children,' she said; 'you'll address them in the following manner: Master Matthew, Master Luke, Master John, and Miss Jessie Ann. You understand?'

She had said she understood.

'And go down at once and tell Mrs Lucas to fit you up with suitable uniform.'

When she had carried out this order, Mrs Lucas had not been at all pleased; she had muttered something under her breath that sounded like bitch. But then it couldn't possibly have been – a woman in Mrs Lucas's position wouldn't call anyone in Miss Price's position a bitch.

Towards the end of the day she had one pleasant surprise. The master came up to the nursery and, after talking to the children, he called her out on to the landing, and there he said, 'Well, how's it gone?'

'Very well, sir,' she had answered.

'Do you think you can manage them?'

'I'm having a good try, sir.'

'They haven't played any of their tricks on you yet?'

'Not as yet, sir.'

'There's plenty of time.' He had smiled at her. 'Look out for Matthew; he's a rip, as I've already indicated.'

'I'll look out for him, sir.'

'That's right. Good-night, Trotter.'

As he turned from her she said, 'Sir,' and he looked towards her again. 'Yes?'

'I would just like to say thank you for . . . for givin' me the post, sir.'

''Tis nothing. 'Tis nothing.' He shook his head, smiled once more at her, then went quickly from the landing; and she stood until the sound of his feet running down the stairs was smothered in the carpet of the lower floor. . . .

She had seen them to bed, she had tidied up the schoolroom, carried down the last slops from the closet, washed out the pails, then by the light of the candle she had taken in the waist of the print dress she was to wear tomorrow and moved the buttons on the bodice and on the cuffs. It was ten o'clock now and she was dying with sleep. Getting out of her dress, stockings and shoes, she left on her bodice and petticoat to sleep in and, pulling the cover back, she got into bed, thrust her feet down, then only just in time smothered a high scream as the thing jumped around her legs.

Within a split second she was standing on the floor again. Gulping in her throat, she groped around for the candle, then made her way out on to the lighted landing and lit her candle from the lamp. Back in the room she held it in her shaking hand over the bed; and there, as startled as she was, sat a large frog.

A gurgle came into her throat and steadied the trembling of her hand. The little devil! And he was a devil. He wasn't just an imp like some young lads, he was a devil. It was in his eyes, and she was going to have trouble with him if she didn't do something about it. These were the kind of tricks which could scare the daylights out of you, and once he got away with it they would get worse. What should she do? She leant forward and picked up the frog just as he was about to make another leap. She had handled numerous frogs, having had to save many of them from losing legs when they took refuge under pieces of wood she had been about to chop.

She turned and looked towards the door. They were both likely out there, the two older ones anyway, waiting to hear her scream.

. . . Do unto others as you'd have them do to you. Her granny was again in her head, but her saying was a little confused now with her grandfather's laughing remark to his wife's parable: Do for others before they do for you. Anyway, she would give Master Matthew tit for tat, and see how that worked.

Silently she crept out of the room and into the boys' room. They were now both tucked well down in bed, but instinctively she knew that Matthew was very much awake and had only just scrambled into his bed. Placing the candlestick on the box table to the side of the bed, she gently pulled down the bedclothes that half covered the boy's face, and as gently she lifted up the neck of his nightshirt, then with a quick movement she thrust the frog down on to his chest.

The result of her action frightened her more than when the frog had jumped up her bare legs, for when the animal's clammy body flopped against the boy's bare flesh he let out an ear-splitting scream, and then another, before jumping out of bed and shaking madly at his nightshirt.

When the frog leapt on to her bare feet before making its escape under the bed, she took no heed but, gripping the boy's shoulders and shaking him, she cried, 'Whist! whist!' and when he became quiet she bent down to his gasping mouth and said, 'Tit for tat. I told you, didn't I?'

She turned her head now quickly towards the door when she heard running steps on the stairs, and she had only just pushed him back into bed when the door was burst open and Mark Sopwith appeared.

'What is it? What's wrong?'

The boy was sitting up in bed and he stammered, 'Fa . . . Father, Fa . . . Father.'

Mark took hold of him, then said, 'What's the matter? Did you have a dream?'

The boy now glanced from his father towards Tilly and it was she who stammered now, 'Ye . . . ye . . . yes. Yes, he had a dream, a night . . . nightmare.'

'What is it? What's wrong? The mistress is upset.'

They all looked towards Mabel Price who had burst in and was standing at the foot of the bed dressed in a blue dressing-gown with her hair hanging down her back in two plaits, and Mark said, 'He's had a nightmare. Too much supper likely. It's all right. . . . Tell your mistress he's all right. I'll be down presently.' His tone was curt and held a dismissal, and after looking from one to the other she left the room.

'Settle down now, you're all right.' He pressed his son back into the pillows, and when the boy said again, 'Father,' he asked, 'What is it?'

There was a long pause before Matthew muttered, 'Nothing, nothing.'

'There now, go to sleep.' He tucked the clothes around the boy's shoulders; then nodding to Tilly, he beckoned her out of the room.

On the landing he looked at her standing in her petticoat and bodice. He hadn't realised before that she was only partly undressed. She must, he imagined, have been getting ready for bed. Although she was tall, almost as tall as himself, she looked like a very young girl, for her face had a childlike quality. He said, 'Did he have a lot to eat tonight?'

'No, sir . . . and' – her head drooped – 'and it wasn't a nightmare.'

'No?' It was a question.

'Well, you see, sir, when I got into bed I was startled like 'cos I found . . . well, he'd put a frog in me bed, and . . . and I thought the only way to get the better of him was tit for tat. He . . . he must have been waitin' for me screamin' and . . . and I just stopped meself, but . . . but I didn't think he'd be frightened like that when I put it down his shirt.'

'You put the frog down his shirt?'

'Yes, sir.' Her head drooped still further. She didn't know why she was telling this man the truth, she felt that she must be mad, he could put her out of the door this minute for treating his children so, gentry's children were allowed to do things that others weren't, especially to servants. She should never have thought tit for tat, not in this household.

Mark looked at her lowered head. Her face certainly portrayed her character for she was still a child. There had been no adult vindictiveness behind her action, and perhaps it would teach Master Matthew a lesson. He needed teaching a lesson, and likely he had taken it in for he hadn't given her away. Yet he knew that his son's reticence in this matter hadn't been to save the nursemaid but to avert his own displeasure and so bring nearer the threat of boarding school. Well, little did he know it but the threat was upon him. He said now, 'I can understand your motive but ... but you must have scared him badly.'

'I'm feared I did, sir, and ... and I'm very sorry.'

'Well' – he smiled a wry smile – 'don't be too sorry. Though I wouldn't take such drastic measures again. Still, for the short time he'll have with you I think you'll manage him.'

Her eyes widened and she whispered now, 'You're ... you're not dismissing me, sir?'

'No, no.' He shook his head. 'I'm sending him and his brother to boarding school. They don't know it yet' – and now he poked his head close to hers as he ended, 'In fact their mother doesn't know it yet, so – " He tapped his lips with his forefinger, and she smiled back at him and answered, 'Aye, sir, not a word.'

'Well now, get away to bed and I'll go down and tell the mistress that you haven't tried to bewitch him.'

It was the wrong thing to have said and they both knew it.

'Good-night, Trotter.'

'Good-night, sir.'

Strange girl, strange girl. The thought ran through his mind as, slowly this time, he went down the bare stairs, while Tilly, getting into bed once more, thought, He didn't mean nothing; he's a nice man, a very nice man. He put her in mind of her granda, though he wasn't so old.

❧ 4 ❧

The day the boys went to boarding school was a day of tears, lamentations, recrimination, and the revelation to Tilly of how a house is run below stairs.

At ten o'clock in the morning she had taken all the children to their mother's room. They were all crying, Jessie Ann most of all, and when their mother joined in Tilly could hardly stop her own tears from flowing. What had touched her more than anything was the young bully's attitude towards herself not an hour ago; while she was helping him into his new clothes he had drooped his head and pressed it against her waist as he muttered, 'I don't want to go, Trotter; I'd ... I'd behave if I could stay.'

For the first time in their acquaintance she put her arms about him and said, 'It won't be for ever, Master Matthew. There's the holidays and they're long. You'll be home for Christmas an' just think of the parties you'll have.'

He had raised his head and, looking up into her face, she had seen the frightened boy behind the bully as he said, 'It . . . it will all be so different, I won't know what to do; and they'll be big boys.'

'You'll hold your own, Master Matthew. Never fear, you'll hold your own. And you're not going to the end of the world, just outside Newcastle. And when you come back at Christmas we'll have some carry-on, like we did last week. You said you didn't enjoy it but I know you did when we played "Pat-a-cake, Pat-a-cake" and "Here we go round the mulberry bush", and' – she had bent her knees until her face was level with his – 'I'll let you put another frog in me bed, and I promise you I won't stick it down your nightshirt.' But his answer to this had been like one from an adult, for all he had said was, 'Oh! Trotter.'

Now she was marshalling them out of the room and Mabel Price was saying, 'There now. There now. No more tears, not from big boys, no more tears.' And the master was bending over the mistress soothing her. But that she wasn't soothed was evident when her voice, raised unusually high, reached the landing, saying, 'I shall never forgive you, Mark, never!'

Then she was standing with most of the staff on the steps watching Fred Leyburn driving the master and the boys away.

It was an event, and for many of the staff a happy event, that that little rip was leaving them, at least for a time; and Tilly should have been the happiest among them, but strangely she wasn't. In a way, in a very odd way, she would miss him, much more than she would Luke.

'Come along about your business, all of you!' Mrs Lucas was floating up the steps now and her voice scattered the rest.

On her way upstairs Tilly was joined by Mr Burgess who had just arrived. 'Well,' he said, 'I've missed the departure, I saw the coach going out of the gate. Best thing that could happen to those two, by far the best thing.'

'But you taught them well, Mr Burgess.'

'Learning isn't enough, Trotter, if it isn't associated with your fellow men and women.' He inclined his head towards her and smiled. 'Learning is only of any use when it helps people to live with one another, put up with one another, and in this narrow establishment what I could have taught that boy would have helped him not at all.'

She was amazed to think that he thought this house a narrow establishment and yet in a faint way she knew what he meant.

He said now in an undertone, 'Have you read the book that I gave you?'

'Yes. But . . . but I don't understand it.'

'You will as you read it again and again.'

'One thing seems to turn against the other and it hasn't a story.'

'Well, I wouldn't say that now; Voltaire is telling you of life. When I gave you the book I thought perhaps I was starting you at the top of literature instead of at the bottom, but from now on when you read lower down in the scale you will understand more for having read the top bars first, if you follow me.'

No, she didn't. Anyway, not quite. But she liked listening to him and she had learned a lot from him. He had given her two books, not just loaned them to her, given them to her, but the only time she had a chance to read was by the candle at night, and then she soon ran out of light because she was allowed only two candles a week. But lately she had conceived the idea of saving the droppings and moulding them and putting a string through them. She daren't look at her books during the day in case Miss Price came on them, but what she did do, and what she could do without being questioned, was look at the children's work and now and again listen to Mr Burgess teaching them. . . .

The mistress was in great distress all day, she knew this by the activity below. She had left her day couch and returned to bed, and by eight o'clock that night the master hadn't come home. Then at supper there was revealed to her another side of the master's character, which startled and depressed her. It was when Amy Stiles said, 'Doesn't take you all day to go to Newcastle and back; you'd have thought he'd have come right home knowin' the state the mistress was in.'

'Which mistress?' There had been a snigger at this and Frank Summers, the head gardener, repeated, 'Aye, you've said it, which mistress. She's a whore that one; her rightful place is on the Shields waterfront.'

'An' she's all airs and graces.' Again Amy Stiles was talking. 'How she dare come in this house and visit the mistress God above knows. She's brass-faced, that's what she is, brass-faced. They say she treats them all up at Dean House like dirt 'neath her feet. And another thing they say' – she looked round the table now – 'the old fellow knows what's going on.'

'How do you know that?' Phyllis Coates looked at Amy for a second.

'How do I know that? Well, because our Willy knows the still-room maid, Peggy Frost. She thinks the old boy's dotty, but wily dotty, you know. At the table he calls her, me darling, me dearest, and she's always kissing him on the head, and she's always saying funny things to make him laugh. And he laughs, a great belly laugh.'

'By! By! you are well informed.' Phyllis Coates was nodding her head.

'Don't be funny, but I know this. 'Tis said she's got more than one on the string an' the master might be playing second fiddle.'

''Tis said! 'Tis said!' Phyllis Coates tossed her head. 'The things you hear, Amy. You know' – she now looked round the table, thumbing towards her companion – 'she should be writing a book, she's got the 'magination.'

There was laughter at this, but it died away when the cook said, 'Well! enough. Let them up there attend to their business and we down here'll attend to ours. 'Tis Saturday and the end of the month, let's get down to it.' Then as if she had said something she regretted she glanced sharply at Tilly and now added, 'You finished?'

'Yes, Mrs Brackett.'

'Well, you can go.'

'Why should she?'

They all looked at Phyllis Coates. 'She's been here on two months, she's one of us, she should have her share accordin' to her place.'

There was a long silence following this remark, then the cook muttered, 'It'll be coppers only then.'

'Well, coppers are not to be sneezed at.' Now Phyllis Coates turned and smiled at Tilly, and as Tilly rose to leave the table she said, 'Sit down.'

What followed next didn't seem real to Tilly. The cook brought to the table a box holding silver and copper and, tipping it on to the board, she spread it out with her hands; then taking from the ample pocket of her white apron a notebook, she wet her finger on her tongue and licked over its pages before she began to read: 'Grocer an' meat exchange brought total twenty-five shillings; fishmonger and poultry exchange, eighteen shillings and ninepence; miller, two pounds seven and fourpence.' She lifted her head and looked about her. 'That was with putting a penny on the stone, an' things, instead of three farthings like last month; I don't see why Mrs Lucas should have the plums.'

'I'm with you.' Robert Simes nodded towards her. 'Her and Mr Pike come off very nicely at their own end, thank you very much. Oh, I know what I know. Only nine bottles to the dozen!' He tapped the side of his nose with his finger, and to this the cook said, 'You needn't tell me, I'm not blind or daft, I wasn't born yesterday;' then went on: 'Now the eggs an' vegetables an' fruit that went to the market, that was good this month with the currants an' things, eight pounds two and sixpence.' There were nods of approval all round the table. Wetting her pencil between her lips, the cook began to add up the sum and after a long pause she said, 'Twelve pounds, thirteen and sevenpence I make it.'

'Is that all?'

The cook looked at Robert Simes and she nodded, saying emphatically, 'That's all!'

'Lord! old Pike used to make nearly as much as that on the wine bill at one time.'

'Aye, at one time we all did well, but this house is not as it was at one time, and we all know that an' all, don't we?' The cook's double chins were flapping against the starched collar of her print dress and there were murmurs of, 'Aye. Aye.'

'Well now, to share it out.' The cook now put her hand among the silver and coppers and, separating the coins, she said again, 'Well now, three five to you, Robert.' She pushed three pounds five towards the footman. 'The same for meself.' She extracted another three pounds five. 'Two pounds for you, Phyllis, and two pounds for Fred. You can take his.' She pushed four sovereigns down the table. 'One for you, Amy.' She handed a sovereign to the second housemaid. 'Fourteen shillings for you, Maggie, although you haven't deserved it, you haven't worked for it.' The girl giggled as she picked up the four half-crowns and four single shillings from the table. 'Now that leaves. . . . What does it leave?'

Everybody at the table knew that the cook was aware of what it left, she had had it all worked out before she had tipped up the box, and now she said, 'Nine and sevenpence, so what are we going to do with that?'

'Well, 'tis mine.' Ada Tennant was bobbing her head.

'We said Trotter was in on this, didn't we?' Phyllis Coates was staring across the table at the cook now and the cook muttered, 'Well it better be halved then.'

''Tisn't fair and you know it, Cook. By rights Trotter's above me and Amy here.'

'That'll be the day.' The cook now cast an almost vehement glance at Tilly, and as Tilly was about to say, 'I don't want anything,' the cook said, 'Half or nothing.'

When the four and ninepence ha'penny was pushed down the table towards her, Tilly hesitated in picking it up, until she glanced at Phyllis Coates and Phyllis's eyebrows sent out a message by moving rapidly up and down.

When Tilly lifted up the coins she felt for a moment that they were burning her fingers, it was like stolen money. And in a way it was stolen because they were doing the master and thinking nothing of it; even Phyllis seemed to accept it as her right.

A few minutes later, after she had left the table, Phyllis caught up with her at the bottom of the attic stairs and, her voice a husky whisper, she said, 'Don't you worry, you'll have your full share next month. Fred'll see to it.'

'I don't want it. I mean . . . well – ' She looked down on Phyllis from the first step of the stairs and although she knew it might turn her friend against her she couldn't resist saying, 'It somehow feels like stealin'.'

Phyllis was in no way insulted by this remark, it only proved to her how naive this lass was in the ways of a household such as this, and so she punched Tilly gently in the arm as she said, 'Don't be daft. How do you think we get things together who are soon to be married? or them who've got their old age to face? 'cos take it from me, the gentry do nowt for you. Twelve pounds a year I get and they think they're giving me gold dust. And Fred gets twenty-five and his uniform. We wont' be able to set up a very big establishment on that. No' – she now patted Tilly's arm – 'take all you can get, lass, and ask for more. It's the only way to survive in this life. And don't let it worry you, the thought of stealin'. My God! no, 'cos they'd have the last drop of blood out of you, the gentry. An' the master's no better than the rest, although he does a good turn here and there when it pleases him; like letting people stay in a cottage. But if he's put out, you're out. As for the mistress, well she got rid of the whole laundry staff, four of them, 'cos her lawn petticoats got put in with the coloureds. That's why we only have two dailies. You mark my words, girl. Now go on and don't look so depressed. Why, it should be the happiest night of your life; you've got rid of that little bugger, haven't you? an' that's all he was, a little bugger.'

Tilly lowered her head, biting on her lip to stop herself from laughing. Yes, she supposed that all Phyllis had said was true, especially about the little bugger. It sounded so funny though, coming from her, for she had never heard her swear before. She leant towards her and said softly, 'I'm glad you're my friend, Phyllis,' and Phyllis, pleased and embarrassed, gave her such a push that she almost fell on to the stairs as she said, 'Get away with you! Go on an' get to bed.' And on this she turned and ran down the passage back to the kitchen, and Tilly went upstairs four and ninepence ha'penny richer.

It was her third Sunday off. The summer was at its height, the sky was high, and the sun was hot, so hot that it penetrated the crown of her straw hat and lay warm on her head. She was glad of the thin dress she was wearing; it was a cotton one that Phyllis had given her. She'd had to let the hem down and again take in the waist. Her waist and hips were so narrow that she had to put tucks in everything she wore.

She was making her way, as usual, towards the cottage, for the simple reason she had nowhere else to go. If she'd had even a half-day on a Saturday she could have gone into Shields and seen the market, but she couldn't gather up the courage to ask either Mrs Lucas or Miss Price to change her day. But she was content. Life was running smoothly, she had been in service for three months, and the two remaining children she was finding were manageable; she was learning things from Mr Burgess; she had Phyllis and Fred for friends and also Katie Drew. Yes, she could class Katie Drew as a friend for on the two previous Sundays she had visited the ruined cottage she had met Katie and her brother, Sam, somewhere along the road. In fact, she now looked forward to meeting them, she expected to meet them.

On her first Sunday off she had almost shunned going to the cottage in case she should run into Hal McGrath, but when she had met up with Sam and Katie Drew she felt safe; and on her following Sunday off they had been there again, and here they were now coming towards her. She had the desire to run and meet them, and when Katie left her brother and ran, she, too, ran, then they both stopped simultaneously and said, 'Hello.'

'How you getting on, Tilly?'

'Fine, Katie. Are you all right?'

'Aye. . . . Isn't it a lovely day?'

'Yes, beautiful. I'm sweatin'.'

'You're not the only one. Sam here' – she nodded to Sam who had now joined them – 'he's just said he'll need a scraper to get his trousers off.'

Tilly looked at Sam and Sam looked at her. He had on his Sunday suit and a clean neckerchief. His face, she knew, had been scrubbed yet there remained on it the marks of the pit, especially around his eyes. His lashes seemed to be stained with coal dust and there were blue indentations on his brow, the insignia of a pitman.

'Hello there,' he said.

'Hello, Sam . . . Isn't it hot?'

'Can't be hot enough for me.'

'You said your clothes were stickin' to you.' His sister pushed him and he pretended to fall over, and when he straightened up, he said, 'Aye, they are, but I like them that way. I'll think about this all day the morrow.'

'Me an' all,' Katie said, nodding her head, and Tilly was amazed when she thought of the morrow and the depth of the pit that this fifteen-year-old girl, who looked twenty if a day, could still smile. Yet because both of them spent most of their lives in the bowels of the earth they seemed to savour the daylight more than she did. Their enjoyment of the sun oozed from them. They walked with their faces held up towards the sky. Funny that, she thought, for she was in the habit of walking with her head down looking towards the earth.

'We've been round the cottage; someone's been sleeping in the byre.'

'Well, they would find good shelter.'

'Aye, there's that in it.' Sam was nodding at her. 'It must be hellish being on the road, not having a roof over your head. An' there's many like that the day, God help them. But it won't go on, not for ever.' He looked at Tilly and, nodding slowly, he repeated, 'No, it won't go on for ever. We're comin' alive to the fact that we're human beings, not animals, an' we've got the rights of human beings. Things are movin'. The masters will have to look out for themselves afore long, you'll see. They won't always have the upper hand, it'll be wor turn some day. I mightn't live to see it, but wor turn'll come, an' then God help 'em.'

'They're not all alike, Sopwith's not bad.'

'There isn't a pin to choose atween them.' He leant in front of Tilly and glared at his sister. But she laughed at him, saying, 'Aw, don't get on your high horse, man, it's Sunda'. And anyway, just think where would we be the day if Sopwith hadn't taken you on and given us the cottage.'

'He wouldn't have taken us on if he didn't need men, he didn't do it out of any charity. None of his kind do owt for charity; they make you pay interest in sweat, all of 'em. An' the cottage, what is it after all, two rooms.'

'Aw now, our Sam' – Katie stepped in front of him now – 'fair's fair. What did we have in the other place? Mud floors. There's a solid stone one in this. And the pittle isn't oozing up a through it from the middens. Now be fair.'

'Listen to her!' He was laughing now as he looked at Tilly. 'You haven't got to ask whose side she's on. She does as much work for him as a man, an' he pays her half as much, an' she still stands up for him. Aw . . . women!'

'Aye, women!' Katie was nodding at him, laughing with him now. 'Where would you be without us? I know where you'd be, you'd still be an urge in me dad's belly.'

'Well, here we are back again.' They looked at Tilly and she stepped over the broken gate and led the way up the path, and as always she wanted to turn her eyes away from the burnt out shell of her home. The saddening effect it had on her didn't seem to lessen, and when she rounded the side wall and came into the yard she stood still, looking towards the byre; then shaking her head, she turned abruptly about and walked back to the gate.

The brother and sister looked at each other, then followed her in silence.

On the bridle path Katie said, 'What time have you got to be in the day?' and Tilly answered, 'I've got another half-hour 'cos it's still light, half past six the day.'

'Well, 'tis only on three. I tell you what. Would you like to come back to our house an' have a sup tea?'

Tilly smiled down on Katie into the round homely face that would never know prettiness but which had such a quality of kindness in the eyes that to her in this moment it almost appeared beautiful, and she said, 'Oh yes, thank you very much, I'd like that. Aye, yes, I would.'

'Well, what we waitin' for?' It was Sam who now turned from them and strode ahead; and as they followed him they both began to laugh, not knowing why, except perhaps they realised that for a few hours they were free; perhaps because it was a beautiful, warm sunny day; but most of all perhaps they realised they were young and that for a fleeting moment they were experiencing a spurt of joy, which is the natural gift of youth.

It was a two-mile walk to the Drews' cottage. It lay to the north of the estate, and was reached by an angled bend that led off the coach road. The cottages were situated on the very boundary of the Sopwith estate and within half a mile of the pit. There were sixteen cottages in the two rows. The Drews' home was in the end cottage of the second row and when Tilly entered it on this hot steamy Sunday afternoon, it appeared to her like a small cramped box after the spaciousness of the Manor. Not only was it small and cramped, but it had a mixed odour which she likened to the smell that emanated from soot and soap-suds, the last soap-suds in the poss tub at the end of the day's wash, an arid, body sweating odour. The small room seemed crammed with people and she stood just within the open door as Katie introduced her, speaking first to a big woman whose bony frame seemed devoid of flesh. 'Ma, this is Tilly, the lass I told you about.'

The woman stopped cutting slices of bread from a big loaf on the end of a table which was surprisingly covered with a white tablecloth, and she paused for a moment and smiled at Tilly as she said, 'Well, come in, lass, come in. That's if you can get in. But, as they say, never grumble about being crowded until you can't shut your door. You're welcome. Sit down. Get your backside off that cracket, our Arthur, and let the lass take the weight off her legs.'

When Arthur, a grinning boy of twelve, sidled off the low stool, then stood with his back against the whitewashed wall near the small open fireplace, Tilly wanted to protest that she didn't mind standing, but feeling very awkward all of a sudden she sat down on the low cracket and looked shyly around the sea of eyes surveying her. Some were looking at her from under their brows, others straight at her. She was wondering why they were all crammed into this room on this rare and lovely day when she was given the answer; it was as if she had asked for it.

Continuing cutting the bread, Mrs Drew said, 'Sunday, we're all together for Sunday tea. Rain, hail, sun or snow, 'tis one time in the week I have me troubles all around me at one go.'

'Aw, Ma. Ma!' The same protest came from different quarters of the room.

'Do you like workin' up at the big house?'

'Yes; yes, thank you.' Tilly nodded to Mrs Drew, and the big woman, scooping up the slices of bread in handfuls on to a large coloured flat dish, said, 'Well, it's one thing, you get trained to be quick in big houses, not like this lot here.' She pointed to a tall young woman and a smaller one who were taking down crockery from the hooks on an old black-wood Welsh dresser, the back of which Tilly noticed in some surprise was forming a kind of high headboard to a double iron bed along the edge of which were sitting two young boys and a youth.

'Oh, Ma. Ma!' It was the same laughing protest.

'Are those griddle cakes finished?' Mrs Drew now looked towards a plump child who was kneeling before the fire turning pats of round pastry which were resting on an iron shelf, which in turn was resting on top of a flattened mound of hot ash.

Before the child could answer, Sam Drew, bending over his sister, said, 'She's been scoffin' 'em, Ma.'

The small girl, her face red from the heat of the fire, sat back on her hunkers, crying, 'Oh, our Sam! our Sam! I've never touched one,' slapping out at her brother as she said so. And he slapped playfully back at her; then looking at Tilly, he said, 'This lot must look like a menagerie to you.'

She smiled but could find no reply to this. He was right, they did look like a menagerie.

'Well, if you've got a good memory I'll start at the top and work downwards.

That one over there' – Sam pointed to a short, thick man sitting at the edge of the table – 'that's me big brother, our Henry, twenty-four he is, an' married, lock an' chain you know.'

Ignoring his brother's clenched fist, he went on, 'Then there's me next.' He thumbed his chest. 'Then comes our Peg, that one who's slow with the crockery.' He pointed to the taller of the two girls moving between the table and the delf rack. 'And then Bill. He's seventeen, him sittin' on the bed, the daft-looking one.'

'I'll daft you, our Sam, if you don't look out.'

'I'm lookin' out, so get on with it.' Sam grinned at his younger brother, then said, 'And his two daft companions, there's Arthur there on the left, he's twelve, and Georgie, he's the one that looks like a donkey about to bray, he's ten.'

'Oh, our Sam!' This came from different parts of the room now.

'Then there's our Katie, who's not right in the top storey. . . .'

'Oh, you wait, our Sam!'

'And the best of the bunch is Jimmy there. He's a natural scarecrow, aren't you, Jimmy? A penny a day he can earn standin' in the fields.'

'Oh, our Sam! Our Sam!'

'And then there's my Fanny.' He bent and rubbed his fingers in the thick brown hair of the kneeling child, saying, 'She's seven, aren't you, Fanny? An' she's goin' down the pit next year, aren't you, Fanny?'

'Now you shut your mouth, our Sam!' It was his mother turning on him now, no laughter in her face. 'Don't joke about her goin' down the pit. She's not seein' top nor bottom of the pit except over my dead body.'

'I was only funnin', Ma.'

'Well, don't fun about that; the pit's got the rest of yous, but they're not gettin' her. Nor Jimmy there. There's two of you I aim to give daylight to.'

'Aye, Ma; aye, you're right' – Sam's voice was very subdued now – ''tis nowt to joke about.'

Mrs Drew had stopped pouring out mugs of tea and she now looked at Tilly; but for some seconds she did not speak. When she did her voice, although low, held a deep note of bitterness as she said, 'The pit took four of mine in seven years, me man included, so you can see me reason for stickin' out for two of them, can't you?'

'Yes; yes, Mrs Drew.'

'Well now, that said, let's eat.'

It was, Tilly imagined, as if the tall gaunt woman had suddenly turned a knob somewhere inside her being and switched off the bitter memories, for now her voice was jovial again as she cried at her daughter, 'Peg, bring the china cup, we've got company.'

When Peg brought the fragile china cup and saucer to the table and handed it to her mother, Mrs Drew took the saucer between her finger and thumb and gently placed it on the table; then looking at Tilly, she asked, 'You like your tea with milk, lass?'

'Oh yes, please.'

'An' you can have sugar an' all if you like.' This was from the upturned face of Fanny. They all laughed and there was a chorus: 'And you can have sugar if you like' in imitation of the small girl, and she, swinging her head from side to side, exclaimed, 'Aw yous! you're always scoffin', yous!'

'And now we're all here we'll start. I said, we're all here' – Mrs Drew now looked again at Tilly as she placed the china cup and saucer before her – 'except there's my Alec. He's on a double shift – it's the water down there – he'll be dead beat when he does come up. Shouldn't be allowed, twenty-four hours under at one time! and he only a bit of a lad.'

'He's eighteen, he's older than me an' I've done a double shift.'

'Oh listen!' Sam held up his hand. 'Hero Bill's done a double shift.' He leant towards his younger brother now, saying, 'Aye, but it wasn't in water standin' up to your neck.' Then, his tone altering, he said, 'Somethin's got to be done. By God! somethin's got to be done.'

'Now! now!' It was his mother's voice again. ''Tis Sunday, we've got company, no more pit talk.'

Since only nine could be seated at the table, two of the younger boys, Arthur and Georgie, remained seated on the bed, and when their mother ordered them to come to the table to get their shives, thick slices of bread with a piece of cheese in the middle, she looked from one to the other as they approached and said, 'You don't deserve nowt either of you; 'tis a wonder you're not in jail.'

'Why, what have they been up to?' Henry, the married son, said, turning his head towards them. 'What's this? What you been up to, you two now?'

When they didn't answer he looked at his mother and she, evidently trying to suppress a smile, made her voice sound harsher than ever as she said, 'What have they been up to? Just tried to burn the Mytons' place down, that's all.'

'What!'

There were splutters from different members at the table. Some of them choked, so much so that Katie had to be thumped on the back before their mother went on, 'They were scrumpin' apples an' one of the gardeners caught them, an' being kind to them instead of taking them up to the house an' then callin' the polis, he thumped them well and roundly, bumped their heads together, kicked their backsides and set them flyin'. And what do you think they did last night as ever was?'

'Well, what did they do, I'm waitin'?' Henry asked.

Again the table was convulsed with laughter, and it was Sam who now said, 'They stuffed straw up half a dozen drainpipes, you know the old trick, an' set fire to them.'

'No!'

'Aye.'

'At the Myton place? Oh my God! I wish I'd been there. Eeh! you young buggers!' He turned and looked towards the bed where the two boys were sitting with their heads hanging but with their shoulders shaking with laughter.

'And not content with that' – the mother nodded at her eldest son – 'they went back into the orchard and helped themselves to apples, not windfalls this time but from the trees. My God! when they told me that I was sick. To try a second time! God! they're lucky they weren't caught. Anyway' – she grinned now – 'three good stones of them they brought in. As they said, they could have brought a cartload 'cos everybody was too busy pullin' the burning straw out of the drainpipes.'

'They'll end up in Australia those two.' It was Sam now nodding towards them.

'They'll never live to reach Australia.'

As Tilly watched Mrs Drew's head move slowly back and forward there was rising in her a swirl of merriment such as she had never felt in her life before, and when Mrs Drew ended, 'Swing they will, the both of them, from the cross-roads an' we'll all have a field day,' the laughter burst from her throat. It surprised not only herself but all those at the table, because they had never heard anyone laugh like it. It was a high wavering sound that swelled and swelled until, holding her waist, she turned from the table and rocked herself. She laughed until she cried; she couldn't stop laughing, not even when Katie, herself doubled up with laughter, put her arm about her and begged, 'Give over. Give over.' Nor when Sam lifted her chin and, his own mouth wide, cried, 'That's good. That's good.' And he kept repeating this until he realised her face was crumpling and that the water running down it was no longer caused by merriment; and so, straightening up, he looked round the table and raised his hand, saying, 'Enough is enough.'

The noise in the room gradually subsided, and Tilly turned to the table again and, her head bowed, murmured, 'I'm sorry.'

'Sorry, lass? You've got nowt to be sorry for. We've never had such release in this room for many a long day. It's good to laugh, it's the salve for sores. Aye, it's the salve for sores. Drink your tea, lass.'

Gratefully now Tilly drank her tea. Then she looked at the sea of faces about her, warm, caring faces, and she thought she had never felt such closeness as there was in this family. Most of them spent their lives underground, even the girls; but there was a happiness here that she envied, a happiness here that she longed to share. She looked across the now silent table at Mrs Drew as she said, 'It's lovely tea, lovely.'

⤷ 5 ↶

It was Guy Fawkes Day, and afterwards Mark Sopwith always looked back on this particular day as the time when the catastrophe began.

It started badly. Eileen Sopwith was still weepy over a letter she'd had from Matthew saying he hated the school and wanted to come home; added to this, she was irritated by the fact that her husband's son, Harry, the only issue of his first marriage and now in his second year at Cambridge studying law, had decided – without asking her permission – to join them for the long Christmas vacation. She had never liked Harry, although since her marriage to his father she had seen him only during the school holidays. But even as a boy his manner had annoyed her. He had an air of aloofness that was disconcerting and when she looked at him she saw his mother in him and so was reminded that she wasn't the first woman in her husband's life.

That she was of an intensely jealous disposition Mark had found out after Matthew was born, for she begrudged his affection for the child feeling that it detracted from his love for her. Even after John was born and she had decided to become an invalid, her jealousy hadn't lessened. Her possessiveness for the children, he understood well enough, was designed to alienate their affection away from himself so that he would be more likely to turn to her, not to receive love but to give it in the form of petting and fussing.

She liked to feel his fingers going through her hair, she liked to feel him fondling her hands, even stroking the pale skin of her arms inside the elbows; but never did she allow his hands near her breasts, she was an invalid now and mustn't be distressed in that way. Had she not borne him four children? Was he not satisfied? He was forty-three years old and she thirty-eight. Good moral people should be past that kind of thing. It went with the begetting of children and Mark knew only too well she had begot all she intended to beget.

But as yet on this day it wasn't she who was the main issue.

He always breakfasted alone. The breakfast-room he considered the cosiest room in the house. It was in this room he had tasted his first meal downstairs, but that hadn't been until he was twelve years old and had been attending boarding school for four years.

He breakfasted light, never more than one egg, one slice of bacon, and a kidney. He had never been able to stand fish for breakfast. He was sitting back in his chair wiping his mouth on a napkin but his mind was three miles away . . . no five, away in the mine where the weak spot was. He must get Rice along there this morning and look at that stretch himself. The pump was having a job to clear it of water. One of the women had nearly drowned there last week; and he didn't want that again, it gave the pit a bad name. They hadn't had an accident now for three years, and even then it had really been nothing, only two dead; not like the Jarrow lot, a hundred odd at one go. Twenty-two colliers had died at Rosier's pit last year. He wished to God he didn't need the mine, the worry of it was beginning to tell on him; his grey hairs were thickening at the temples and his face was becoming lined. Agnes had tactlessly pointed this out to him the other day.

Agnes. There was another worry; he hadn't seen her now for three weeks. They had parted with hot words. He really didn't care if he never saw her for another three weeks, or three months, or ever, but he doubted if she'd let him go that easy. She was like a leech, that girl . . . that woman, for she was no girl, she was a hungry, devouring, body-consuming woman. He had met a few women in his time, intimately so, but never one like her. The saying that you could have too much of a good thing applied to everything. There might have been a time when he would have doubted this, but not any more.

He rumpled his table napkin, threw it on the table, and as he rose to his feet the door opened and Simes said, 'There's a gentleman to see you, sir.'

'A gentleman! at this hour. Who is it?'

'Mr Rosier, sir.'

Mark did not repeat the name Rosier, but his brows drew darkly together and he paused for a long moment before he said, 'Where've you put him?'

'In the library, sir.'

'I'll be there in a minute.'

'Very good, sir.'

When the man had closed the door, Mark stood rubbing the cleft below his lower lip with his first two fingers. Rosier at this time in the morning! now what would he be after? Well, there were only two things that interested Rosier, his mine and his money. Which could have brought him here? He had understood he was still abroad taking his tall, stately, socially ambitious wife on a tour of America. He moved his head slightly back and forwards before straightening his cravat and smoothing down the pockets of his long jacket; then he left the room, crossed the hall and entered the library.

George Daniel Rosier had been gazing at the portrait hanging over the empty fireplace and he turned abruptly when the door opened. He was a small man, his complexion was swarthy, his hair was thin with just a touch of grey here and there. His nose was long and protruding, it was the largest feature of his face. He looked a common man; three generations gone, his people had been mill workers. The stigma was still on him, and he fought it by bluster. How he had come to be chosen by a daughter of the landed gentry was a puzzle to everyone. Well, perhaps not everyone, certainly not to Agnes Rosier for she was already past the choosing age when he married her, and she was tired of refined poverty. Within a year of the marriage she had borne him a son who was now four years old. She had also almost trebled the servants in his household and nearly driven him mad, not with the fact that she wanted to entertain those in high places, but with the cost to his pocket for such entertainments.

His mine was a good one as mines went, but being the taskmaster that he was, he drove his overseers and they in turn drove the men and women under them, with the result that his mine became noted for unrest among the workers. Time and again he had threatened to bring the Irish in but had been sensible enough, as yet, to withhold his hand in that direction. But with this latest business of education rampant among the scum, he could see himself bringing a shipload over. Yet he wanted to avoid the trouble and expense this would cost him, and that was why he was here this morning.

'Good-morning.' It was Mark speaking, and to this Rosier replied briefly, 'Morning.'

'What is the trouble, something happened at your place?'

'No, there's nothing happened at my place, not as yet; and there's nothing happened at your place as yet; but you go on enticing my colliers away and something will happen.'

'What are you talking about?' Mark's voice was stiff.

'Now! now!' Rosier turned his head to the side and looked towards the window; then jerking his chin back he glared at Mark as he said, 'The three fellows you took on recently, the three my overseer dismissed.'

'What about it? I took them on because I needed men. Your overseer broke their bond, not them. Apparently he didn't want them on the job.'

'You know as well as I do why they were dismissed. Look, Sopwith, as man to man –' Rosier's nose twitched, his lips pursed and he brought his shoulders almost up to his chin as he said, 'You let these fellows get reading and writing and you know as well as I do that'll be the beginning of the end.'

'I don't agree with you.'

'Aw, don't be so damned naive, man.'

'I'm not damned naive, and I'll thank you not to infer that I am. You've got a rule that your men don't learn to read or write, well, I have no such rule in my pit and if I need men I'll take them if they come asking for work whether they can read or write or not.'

'You will, will you?'

'Yes, I will!'

'Well' – Rosier gave a broken laugh now – 'by what I hear, things are not going too brightly for you. You had water below before I went away but now I understand they are up to their necks in it. You had to close one road, how many have you left open?'

'As many as you have.'

'Never! never!' Now the laugh was derisive. 'You only need your pump to stop and you'll have your men and horses floating out through the drift.'

Mark stared at the small man. He was raging inside but endeavoured not to show it; and so, keeping his voice as level as possible, he said, 'Why precisely did you come here this morning?'

'I told you, just to warn you that you're a bloody fool if you let them get away with this reading and writing business. But there is one thing more. . . . Well, seeing that you're up against it and are hard pressed for money. . . . Oh! Oh! Oh!' He jerked his head with each word. 'Rumours travel even as far as America. Anyway, I came with a friendly gesture and I give it to you now, if you need money I'll be willing to advance it.'

'You will?'

'Yes; I said I will and I will.'

'May I ask what guarantee you'd like?'

'Oh well, that could be gone into.'

'No, no, no; let's get down to business straightaway. I presume you would like a share in the mine. Is that not so, say a half share?'

Rosier's eyebrows moved up, his nose stretched downwards, his lips pursed again, his shoulders once more tried to cover his jawbone and with a nonchalant air he muttered, 'Why yes, something along those lines.'

Mark stared at the man for a moment; then turning slowly about, he went to the door and, opening it, said, 'Good-morning, Rosier. When I need your help I'll call upon you, and at a respectable hour.'

'Huh! Huh! Well, take it like that if you will but I'll tell you something.' He was now facing Mark in the doorway. 'I bet you a shilling it won't be very long before you're swallowing your words. You'll see.' He bounced his head towards Mark and again he said, 'You'll see.'

As Rosier stamped across the hall, Robert Simes was standing waiting at the door.

Mark stood where he was until the door had closed on his visitor, and he remained there until he heard the sound of the carriage going down the gravel drive; then he turned and went back into the room and over towards the fireplace where he took his fist and beat it hard against the edge of the marble mantelpiece, saying as he did so, 'Damn and blast him to hell!'

He had never liked Rosier; his father had never liked the elder Rosier, in fact his father had never recognised the man, looking upon him as an upstart. But everything George Rosier had said was right. He was up against it, he needed money badly, and if his pumps went his mine would go too.

The thought spun him round and seemingly as if his mere presence at the mine would be enough to hold back the water and so avert final disaster, he hurried out of the room, calling to Simes to tell Leyburn to bring round his horse immediately, and without paying his usual morning visit to his wife, he went to a cupboard at the end of the hall, donned his cloak and hat and hurried out.

Jane Forefoot-Meadows was a lady in her own right when she married John Forefoot-Meadows. He, too, had been born and bred in the upper class, so when their only daughter Eileen said she wished to marry Mr Mark Sopwith, if they didn't actually scowl on the affair, their frowns were evident. True, he came of an old well-known family, but he was a widower with a young son; that he was a mine owner didn't carry much weight with them, for from what they gathered it was a drift mine employing not more than fifty men and thirty women and children at the most. There were mine owners and mine owners. Moreover, Mr Mark Sopwith lived north of Durham and that was such a long, long way off, it would mean that they would hardly ever see their dear daughter during the winter, the roads being what they were and themselves no longer young.

Jane Forefoot-Meadows was a possessive mother; it was doubtful if she would have welcomed any man for her daughter's husband, but from the beginning she had disliked Mark Sopwith and never bothered to hide her feelings for him. Whenever they met she managed to convey to him how she pitied her daughter's existence in Highfield Manor, in a house that wasn't properly staffed, and the children being brought up without capable nursemaids or tutors. But unlike her daughter, she hadn't been aghast at Mark sending his sons to boarding school; at least, so she surmised, there they would have proper grounding. Truthfully she knew she wasn't fond of any of her grandchildren, she only suffered them because her daughter had given them birth.

After John was born and her daughter took to the sofa, she'd had a talk with Doctor Fellows, in fact it had been at her instigation that Doctor Kemp had called in Doctor Fellows. It was from Doctor Fellows's guarded replies to her questions that she guessed there was nothing seriously wrong with her daughter, that she was merely using the weapon of many such women in her position. Her decline was a fence against her husband's sensual appetite, and she was with her in the erecting of such a barrier. She'd never had to erect such a barrier herself for her husband wasn't an emotional man, and she thanked God for it. In fact she often wondered how she had conceived a child at all. She would not put the term impotent to her husband, she just imagined him to be not inclined that way, and that suited her.

But her son-in-law was very much inclined that way if all rumours were true, and the rumour that had brought her flying to the Manor this particular day was no rumour. Oh no, it was no rumour. She had been so incensed by what she had heard that she had wanted to start out on the journey last night; only the fact that she was afraid of the dark had stopped her, but the coach had been ordered at first light this morning, and here she was now springing a surprise on the whole household, not least of all on her daughter, for when she marched into the room Eileen almost jumped from the sofa, crying, 'Mama! Mama! what has brought you?'

'You may well ask. But don't excite yourself.' She held up a hand. 'Here Price, take my bonnet and cloak,' she called, then turned her back towards the maid, and Mabel Price, as much astonished as was her mistress, sprang forward, relieved the tall, dominant figure of her cloak and bonnet, then with a free hand pulled a chair to the side of the sofa. Without even a word of thanks or a glance towards her, Mrs Meadows took the seat; then stretching out her arms, she held her daughter, making a sort of soft moaning sound as she did so.

'Is there anything wrong with Papa?'

'No! no!' Jane Forefoot-Meadows straightened herself. 'Not more than usual. His gout is worse of course, and he coughs louder each day, but he still goes on. No, no; nothing wrong with him.'

'Then . . . then what has brought you? Are you ill?'

'Now do I look ill, my dear?' Jane Forefoot-Meadows raised her plucked eyebrows high and touched lightly each rouged cheek with her fingers.

'No, no, Mama, you look extremely well, and I am so glad to note this.'

'Well, I wish I could say that you look extremely well too, my dear, for I'm afraid that the news I have to bring you' – she now turned her head and for the first time looked at Mabel Price and, her voice seeming to come out of the top of her nose, she said briefly, 'Leave us.'

Mabel Price hesitated only a moment before turning sulkily away and going out of the room.

'Now, my dear – ' Jane Forefoot-Meadows tapped her daughter's hand which she was still holding between her own and asked softly, 'How are you?'

'As usual, Mama. The slightest exertion tires me and I do miss the boys. Not that I saw much of them admittedly, but I knew they were there above me.' She raised her eyes to the ceiling. 'And at times I heard their laughter; it was so refreshing. Now very little sound comes from above, and Matthew hates the school. But Mark is obdurate.' Her face tightened. 'This is a point he will not budge on. I've begged him. Mama, I've begged him. . . .'

'Mark! Mark!' Jane Forefoot-Meadows tossed her head to the side now; then bending forward, she looked straight into her daughter's eyes as she asked, 'Do you know a person by the name of Lady Agnes Myton?'

'Oh yes, Mama, she's a neighbour, she visits at times.'

'She what?' Mrs Forefoot-Meadows drew herself away from the sofa as if she were stung by this latest news, and she repeated on an even higher tone, 'She what?'

'As I said, Mama, she's a neighbour, she visits. . . . Lord Myton took Dean House. You know Dean House, well he took it last year.'

'Yes, I know Dean House and I have heard a little of Lord Myton. I've also heard a lot of his wife, and that she should dare to visit you . . . well! my dear.'

Eileen Sopwith now pressed herself back into the satin pillows of the chaise-longue and, her face straight and her words coming from her almost closed lips, said, 'What are you meaning to infer, Mama?'

'Well – ' Mrs Forefoot-Meadows now rose to her feet and, throwing one arm wide in a dramatic gesture, she said, 'Do I have to explain further?'

'Yes, I'm afraid you do, Mama.'

'Tut! Tut! The very fact that I'm here should be explanatory enough. You can't be aware, I presume, that she and Mark are having an affair. And this is no new thing; apparently it started when she was hardly settled in the house. She is his mistress and she makes no secret of it.'

Eileen Sopwith was now holding her throat with her hands, and her face had gone a shade paler than its usual tint. She tried to speak but words wouldn't come, and so, looking at her mother who had again sat down, she listened to her saying in a low excited whisper, 'You remember Betty Carville, Nancy Stillwell's daughter who married Sir James? Well, apparently she and Agnes Myton were at the same Ladies' Seminary and Agnes Myton was over there visiting last week and, being the trollop that she is, she regaled Betty Carville with the story of her amours. And not satisfied with your husband, apparently she has her eyes set on someone else too, a workman of some sort. Can you believe it? a farm worker. I couldn't get the gist of all Nancy Stillwell had to tell me because I was so shocked at hearing about Mark. Nancy said that Betty said that Agnes Myton said she was having the time of her life; it was much more fun than London . . . and you know what happened in London.' Mrs Forefoot-Meadows again rose from her chair, adding as if in answer to a question, 'Well . . . no, no; it is better that you don't know. Disgrace that was, utter disgrace. Myton's an imbecile else he wouldn't stand for it. Yet I understand, but I don't know how far it is true, that he went for one of her swains. Was going to run him through with a sword or shoot him or something. So when he finds out about this, if he doesn't already know – ' She turned again and looked at her daughter; then, her voice dropping to a warm sympathetic tone, she rushed to the sofa and enfolding Eileen's stiff body in her arms, cried, 'Oh my dear! my dear! Don't . . . don't upset yourself. . . . Now I've got it all worked out. You're coming back with me, you can't possibly stay here, and you're bringing the children. No! no! don't argue.' She shook her head even though Eileen had neither moved nor spoken. 'I know I'm not very fond of gambolling youngsters, but your happiness comes first. Oh my dear! my dear! that this should have come upon you. Didn't you know this was going on?' Releasing her hold, she stared at her daughter; but she, to her mother's surprise, pushed her firmly aside as she slowly swung her legs from the couch and sat on the edge of it. She then stood up and walked somewhat unsteadily towards the window and looked out.

Had she known this was going on? Hadn't she suspected something from the first? Perhaps; but her suspicions had been allayed because she had seen no change in him, no elation . . . no despondency. His manner had continued to be the same towards her, except when they quarrelled over the children being sent away to school, then he had yelled at her. But to think that he and that woman . . . all these months! How long had she been resident in Dean House? Over a year. The whole countryside must be aware of it.

It was as if her mother had picked up her thought for her voice came stridently across the room, saying now, 'It's the talk of the county, it has even closed doors to her. Haven't you had the slightest suspicion?'

It was now she turned on her mother and, speaking for the first time, she said, 'No, Mama, I've had no suspicion. What do I know of what's going on in the world, tied to this room as I am? In fact I don't know what's going on in my own household.'

'Well, that's your own fault, my dear.'

They stared at each other now in silence until Eileen said with deep indignation, 'Mama!'

'Oh my dear, don't look like that. And don't take on that haughty air; you and I know why you took to the couch. There are other ways you could have gained your liberty from his bed: gone visiting, or gone abroad for a time, or come to me. Yes' – her voice sank now – 'yes, you could have come to me. How often have I asked you to? But no, you choose to be incarcerated, and that is the word, my dear, incarcerated in this padded tomb, and you have refused to be disturbed. You know you have. Yes, you know you have.' She nodded her head vigorously. 'But, my dear,' she went on whilst walking towards her daughter with outstretched arms, 'all I ever wanted in life, all I want now, is your happiness, your welfare. Come home with me. Gradually you will regain the strength you have lost while lying on that thing' – she thrust her hand disdainfully back towards the chaise-longue – 'because, you know, a few more years and you wouldn't be able to use your legs at all. It happened to Sylvia Harrington. Oh yes, it did.' Her head made a deep obeisance at this. 'And Sarah de Court became unbalanced.'

'Oh! Mama, Mama, be quiet!' Eileen stumbled past her mother and, grabbing at the side of the chaise-longue, she sat down on it with a slight plop, and when her mother, standing in front of her, demanded, 'Well, what are you going to do?' she looked up at her and said pleadingly, 'Oh, Mama, don't you realise this has come as a shock to me? Just . . . just give me a little time.'

'All the time in the world, my dear.' Mrs Meadows bent over her, her voice and manner expressing her deep solicitude. 'All the time in the world. All the time in the world.' Then she added, 'What time do you expect him back?'

'It . . . it could be this evening.'

'I wouldn't wait till then.'

Again they were staring at each other. 'Is he at the mine?'

'Yes, I think so.'

'Then I would send for him, my dear.'

'Oh! Mama.'

'Well, just ask yourself the question: Do you want to go on living in this house knowing that he is having his daily satisfaction with another woman, and also knowing, my dear, and this is what you've got to face, that you are tied here for the rest of your life, tied to this chaise-longue, which you will be as I warned you if you stay on it much longer? Now do you want that? Or do you want to come home, have your health restored, and live again? Scarborough is a wonderful place in the winter season. You know that, you used to enjoy it.'

'I never did, Mama.'

'Yes, you did in your early days. You only stopped enjoying it when you thought that you'd never be married; then you jumped at the first man that asked you.'

'That isn't fair, Mama.' Eileen's head was up. 'He wasn't the first man who asked me, there were others but you didn't approve.'

'And rightly so; they weren't fit to be your husband.'

'But you thought Mark was.'

'No, we didn't, we had our misgivings, but you were so bent on it. Anyway, my dear, I must go now and refresh myself in the closet. Then I will have something to eat and we'll talk again. But if you take my advice you will send for him, and now.'

Eileen watched her mother leave the room; then once again she was on her feet and walking towards the window. Here she stood gripping the curtains and looking down on to the gardens.

There was a deep bitterness inside her, but it was a bitterness born of hurt vanity rather than of lost love. She knew that she had never really loved Mark Sopwith. In the first place she had wanted him, or rather she had wanted to be a wife. But being a wife had turned out a disappointment to her. Marriage had been full of perplexities, painful perplexities that seemed to be of no concern to her husband. Never having been married before, nor been intimate with any other man, she had no one with whom to compare him, and so she couldn't say if he was a better or worse husband than the usual run of such. She only knew that, like her mother, she was possessive of what she owned, love didn't come into it. You didn't love a house or a horse, they were merely possessions, accessories to living. She reached out her hand and, lifting a silver bell from a table, she rang it, and within seconds Price had entered the room.

'Yes, madam?' Her manner was subservient but her eyes and her whole expression were eager; she had heard bits and pieces of what had been said and she knew what was afoot, although as yet she didn't know what the outcome was going to be. The only thing she hoped was that her mistress wouldn't take any notice of her mother and go off. Although she would likely take her along with her, life in the Forefoot-Meadows' household wouldn't be like it was here. She had been there only once before and the hierarchy in the servants' hall was stiffer than what it had been above stairs. In this household she could throw her weight about, she had power, but what would her standing be in Waterford Place? Something between the upper housemaid and the footman. Oh Lord! she hoped it wouldn't come to that.

'Tell Mr Pike to get a message to the master at the mine and ask him to return, he is needed here.'

'Yes, yes, madam.'

A few minutes later, having passed on the message to him, Pike looked at her and said, 'What's afoot? What brought the old girl?' and her answer was, 'You'll know soon enough.'

It was a full two hours later when Mark entered the house. The message had been delivered to him when he was well below ground and examining a road that was almost three foot under water, and the conditions underground were such that he couldn't leave without trying to find a way out of a desperate situation, for if the pumps couldn't keep the water below this level then it would rise, and if it should branch into the main roadway, well, that would be that.

The first intimation he had that his mother-in-law was in the house was when he said to the butler, who was at the door awaiting him, 'What is it? What's wrong?'

'Nothing that I know, sir, except that Mrs Forefoot-Meadows has arrived.'

Mark screwed up his face as he peered at the old man. They sent for him because his mother-in-law had arrived? Had his father-in-law died? Was that what had brought her? Of course not, she wouldn't be here if that were the case. She had only been gone a short while from the house, and her departure had filled him with pleasure. And so what had brought her today? Something of import surely.

He ran up the stairs, across the gallery, along the corridor, and as he tapped on his wife's door so he thrust it open and was surprised to see her sitting in a chair by the window. It must be two years or more since she had sat up like that; at least, since he had seen her in such a position.

The only other person in the room was Price and he turned his head and looked at her. Following his wordless command she left the room. He walked towards Eileen and stood looking down at her. Her face looked tight, her eyes hard. She had never had a nice-shaped mouth and now it looked a mere slit. He was the first to speak. 'I understand your mama has arrived, is something wrong?'

He saw her swallow deeply before saying, 'Well, it all depends on how one views the word wrong. She came to bring me some news, but some people wouldn't consider her news bad, they would likely look upon it with some amusement, whereas others would be shocked by it. Myself, I'm not only shocked and astounded, I am hurt and humiliated.'

Before she could say another word he realised what was coming, and his own features fell into a stiff mould and, unblinking, he looked at her and waited.

When she spoke, her words were precise and to the point, and her voice was not that of the invalid he had come to know holding a thread of soft whining, but was hard and brittle. 'I understand that I am the last person in the county to know that you have a mistress,' she said. 'I'm not unaware that a number of men take mistresses but generally they do it discreetly, at least the gentlemen among them do. But not only is your affair with that Myton woman the talk of the county, *your slut'* – she almost spat the words out – 'has made it a cause for amusement in Scarborough. What is more, she has even coupled you with workmen who also supply her needs.'

His head was buzzing. He tried to speak but found he couldn't put into words the fact that he had been trying hard for months now to break the association, and that in any case it had been a hole in a corner affair at best. The description was accurate, too, because their love-making had mostly taken place in a hollow in a corner of the wood above Billings Flat. And so how could news of it have got around other than through that ravenous bitch spouting it out to her friends.

The words he now used surprised even himself as in a quiet, weary tone he said, 'I'm not of such importance that Scarborough would bother to find much entertainment in my doings, be they right or wrong, and I'm assuming that my fame has reached Scarborough.'

'You admit it then?' She had pulled herself to her feet and was holding on to the back of a chair now, and he turned to her, saying, 'What do you expect me to do? Your mother has given you her version, and you haven't asked me for any explanation.'

' . . . As if there could be one.'

'Oh yes. Oh yes, Eileen, there could be one.' His voice had risen suddenly and there was an angry light in his eye as he poked his head towards her now and said, 'How long is it since I've lain with you? How long is it since you've even let me touch you? Years. I am a man, I have bodily needs, it's got nothing to do with affection or love or care of family, they are just needs, like the need to eat or drink. If you don't eat you starve, if you don't drink you die of thirst. If a man doesn't have a woman then he also dies in his mind; one can go crazy with such a need. If I had taken one of the sluts from the kitchen would you have felt any better about it, because that is the usual pattern? I could have taken Price, your dear, dear Price. Oh yes, yes' – he tossed his head from shoulder to shoulder now – 'her invitation has been in her eyes since you took to that couch. What would you have thought of that, eh?'

'How dare you say such a thing! *Price!*'

'Oh! Eileen, for God's sake don't be so naive! But you're not naive; no, not really, you are blind, you have made yourself blind like you made yourself an invalid. Oh you haven't hoodwinked me all the way, that couch has been an escape. I knew it, your mother knew it, so don't blame me entirely for what I did and for what – ' He only just stopped himself from adding, 'I intend to go on doing.' And he would go on doing so, but not with Agnes Myton.

He turned abruptly from her now and walked the length of the room and back. She was still standing staring at him when he asked, 'Well, what do you intend to do?'

It was a full minute before she answered him. 'I'm going home with my mother,' she said.

Well, he hadn't been surprised at that either. He knew that that was what the old girl would have advised her daughter to do. However, after a month or so at Waterford Place, she would, if he knew anything about her, be glad to come back, no matter what the conditions. But then she surprised him, in fact shocked him, by saying, 'And I have no intention of returning here, ever. I shall take the children with me of course.'

'*You'll what!*'

'You heard what I said, Mark. I shall take the children with me.'

'*You, will not.*'

'Oh yes, I shall. Mark. If you don't let me have them without fuss then I shall take them legally. I shall take the matter to court.'

He screwed up his eyes into narrow slits. He didn't know this woman. He stared at her, the while she returned his look with her grey eyes that had taken on a slaty deepness, and as he stared the probing of his mind revealed to him, like a door being thrust open, that she was using his indiscretion as a form of escape and that once away from this house and him she would no longer remain an invalid. He saw that the determination that had kept her riveted to her couch would now be turned into energy to bring her back to an ordinary way of living. For a moment he saw himself through her eyes like some primitive jailer, guarding a captive chained to a wall yet ignorant of why he was holding a prisoner at all. He also knew in this moment that he could let her go without the slightest compunction; but it was a different kettle of fish altogether as regards the children. Yet what could he do if the children were here alone. Of course they wouldn't be alone, there was Trotter upstairs. But there would be no mistress to guide Trotter, or any of the others.

She astounded him still further with her coolness when, her voice breaking into his thoughts, she said, 'If you don't put any obstacle in my way I shall make it possible for the children to visit you at times. Should you cause an obstruction now, then my papa will place the matter in the hands of our family solicitor, Mr Weldon, and it will have to be settled legally.'

My God! He put his hand to his head and turned from her, and again he walked the length of the room. He couldn't believe it. This was his delicate sickly wife talking. What a pity, he thought now with a wry humour, that he hadn't openly shown his infidelity immediately after she had refused him her bed. Oh, he gibed at himself, let him be fair, she herself had never refused him her bed, she had got dear old Doctor Kemp to pave that part for her. Still, if she had known from the beginning she'd a rival it might, who knew, have assisted in a cure.

But what did it matter, he was tired. He was tired of so many things, the mine, his home that was only half run, his stables that were now almost empty of thoroughbreds, of Lady Agnes, oh yes, of Lady Agnes, and of Eileen. Yes, he turned and looked at her, he had been tired of Eileen for a long time. Let her go. But the children. . . . Well – he bowed his head now – what could he do? Life was a burden, you either shouldered it or you threw off your pack, took up your gun, went into the woods and, placing the muzzle against the throb in your temple, you just moved your first finger, then peace; nothing, nothing, just peace. He turned slowly and walked out of the room.

ൟ 6 ൹

Tilly wanted to cry, not only because of the uncertainty of the future but because she was going to lose Jessie Ann and John, for since Matthew and Luke had been at school life in the nursery had become a kind of holiday. And then there was Mr Burgess. What was to become of him? He had assured her not to worry, there were always children who needed coaching and he had an abode. His three-roomed, long attic cottage was a palace, he had told her.

She had seen his palace, and she didn't think much of it, at least the contents. There was hardly any furniture in it, a chair, a small table, a dresser, and in the bedroom a single rough bed, but what it lacked in furniture it made up with books, for there were books of all kinds, shapes, and sizes on rough home-made shelves around the walls. The only comfort she could see in the place was the open fireplace; there wasn't an ornament or a picture in the cottage, nor yet a bit of decent china. Yes, he had his abode, but he couldn't have saved any money because after he was paid once a month he always trudged into Newcastle and bought more books. She considered him worse off in a way than any of the staff, or even the miners. Oh, much worse off.

The whole house was in an upheaval. She had been packing the children's clothes all day. All the servants were in a state, not knowing what was going to happen. The only good thing, from their point of view, about this whole situation was that they were getting rid of Price, because she was going with the mistress.

Tilly hadn't really had time to consider her own fate, she only knew that once the children had left the house she wouldn't be needed and that Mrs Lucas would then make short work of her. Mrs Lucas didn't like her no more than did the cook. In a way, they were like the villagers; every time they looked at her there was suspicion in their eyes.

Jessie Ann, who was standing by her side, now said, 'Don't put my fuzzy-wuzzy in the trunk, Trotter, I like my fuzzy-wuzzy.' She lifted out the negro doll with the corkscrew hair and held it tightly in her arms; then looking up at Tilly, she said, 'Why won't you come with me, Trotter?'

'Well, Miss Jessie Ann, because . . . because it's a long way and . . . and anyway, you'll have another nursemaid waiting at that end.'

'Don't wan' n'other.' It was John speaking, and Tilly looked tenderly down on him. In spite of Mr Burgess's efforts he still spoke, she thought, like a village child. Mr Burgess said it was an impediment which time would erase.

As she bent down to pick him up, she straightened his dress, saying almost tearfully, 'You'll go into knickerbockers now.'

'Don' w-wan bockers.'

Jessie Ann laughed and Tilly smiled and she held the boy pressed close to her for a moment, and as she did so Phyllis Coates slid quietly round the nursery door, hissing, 'Tilly!'

'Aye, what is it?'

'There's . . . there's a lad at the back door, he says he wants to see you. He's a pit lad by the look of him. Cook sent him packing, or she tried to, but he stood his ground and said he wanted to see you private for a minute. It might have got round about the business, you know' – she jerked her chin – 'he might think you're goin' away with the bairns.'

'What's his name? What's he look like? Is . . . is he a man? You said a lad, but did you mean a man?'

'No, no, he's not a man, a lad about fifteen or so.'

Tilly let out a long drawn breath. For a moment she had thought that Hal McGrath had dared to come to the house. She wouldn't put anything past him. Last night she had lain in bed wondering where she would go from here. In any case it would be in a direction away from the village, for once he got wind that she was no longer protected by the house she hadn't a doubt but that he would come after her again. But from the description that Phyllis was giving her the visitor could be no other than Steve. Why should he come here though?

'Tell him . . . tell him I'm not free, not till after the morrow when they go,' she said.

'Look' – Phyllis took the child from her arms – 'go on, slip down the back way, you needn't go through the kitchen. Go through the still-room and out that door; you can whistle him down the yard.'

When she hesitated, Phyllis pushed her, saying, 'Go on, they can't do much more to you, you'll be out on your heels the morrow, anyway.'

Yes, Phyllis was right, an escapade like this could at any other time have brought on the sack, but she was already for the sack, so what matter.

When she reached a corner of the yard she saw Steve standing looking over the half-door of a horse box, and she did whistle him. He turned sharply, then came towards her at a run. His face was bright, his eyes laughing. He began straightaway, saying, 'I had to see you, I've some good news. Our Hal's gone for a sailor.'

Her eyes widened and her mouth opened into a gape before she repeated, 'Gone for a sailor?'

'Aye; him and wor Mick an' all. George was with them. They were on the quay in Newcastle. They got into a fight, George said, with three other fellows, proper sailors, 'cos they were scoffing them. Our Hal and Mick said they couldn't paddle canoes and the sailors jumped them. Our George run for it an' hid behind a warehouse an' he saw two fellows come off a big ship an' talk to the sailors; then together they hoisted our Hal and Mick up the gangway, an' the last our George saw of them was when these fellows seemed to be dropping them down a hatchway.'

Steve now bowed his head and, putting his hand round his waist, he began to laugh; then looking up at Tilly, he said, 'I've laughed more since yesterday than I've done in me life, I think, 'cos our George was afraid to come in and tell me ma and da what had happened to their shining pair. You see an hour or so after they were took on board the ship up anchor an' went off, and when George asked some fella on the quay where it was bound for he said some place like the Indies.... Aw! Tilly' – he caught hold of her arm – 'can you imagine what they'll be like when they wake up? Our Hal's always hated the water, he wouldn't go swimmin' in the burn with the other lads. The great big "I am" hated the water.' He now threw his head back and when his laugh rang out, Tilly, her own face creased with smiles, cried at him, 'Ssh! Ssh! you'll have the kitchen lot out on us.' Then pulling him round the corner and through an archway from where a narrow path led to the middens, she looked at him and whispered, 'Oh, Steve, 'tis the best news I've heard in me life I think. I was worried sick. You see, I'll likely be out of a job the morrow.'

'Why?' His voice was sharp. 'They sackin' you?'

'No, no. Well, not sackin' me, but the mistress is leavin' to go to her mother's house. There's been trouble atween her and the master and she's taking the children with her.'

'Aw' – he shook his head – 'nobody's allowed to have good news, are they, not without bad followin'?'

'Oh, I don't mind now, well, not so much. But I liked it back there' – she jerked her head towards the high wall – 'yet the thought of meeting up with your Hal again was terrifyin' me.'

'Well, you're safe now for a year, perhaps two or three. Me da said if the ship was bound for the Indies it could be for trading an' they mightn't see these shores again for years. Eeh! he did go on, nearly went mad. Me ma didn't, she just said, "Bloody fools." And you know, Tilly, from the stories I've heard 'bout ships an' sailors he'll get his deserts all right.' Without pausing a moment, he looked up at her and, the smile sliding from his face, he said, "Twas my birthday yesterday, I was sixteen, Tilly.'

'Oh you were, Steve? Oh I'm so glad. May it return again and again.'

'Thank you, Tilly. I wish I'd been eighteen.'

'You will be soon enough.'

'Do you like me, Tilly?'

'Like you? Of course I do, Steve. You know I do, you're my friend.' She stressed the word, then said quicKly, 'I'll . . . I'll have to be goin', one of the maids is standin' in for me, there'll be trouble if she's caught.'

'Oh aye, aye. But wait a minute.'

As she moved away he put his arm out to her and checked her, saying, 'Where will you go? I want to know.'

'I haven't really thought. I could go back to the woodshed at the cottage, but I think I might go and see Mrs Drew. She's a nice woman. You know, you saw Katie that day an' her brother Sam. Mrs Drew will tell me what to do, and they'll take me in for a night, I'm sure, until I find me feet.'

'Can I come and see you there?'

There was a pause before she said, 'Why yes, Steve, of course. Now I really must be goin'. Thank you. Thank you for your news, Steve. Oh aye, aye, thank you.'

'It's all right, Tilly. I . . . I don't mind what I do, for you.' His voice trailed away.

She walked backwards from him for a number of steps before, smiling and nodding at him, she said, 'Will you be able to find your way out?'

'Aye, I found it in, I'll find it out.'

On this she turned and ran back through the archway and into the yard; but once having passed into the still-room she paused for a moment and closed her eyes. It was a good job, she thought, Steve was only sixteen, else she'd be having trouble with him. No, no; that was the wrong word to use about Steve, she owed Steve a lot, not trouble. Well, she said to herself, you know what I mean. Then as quietly as possible she scurried out of the room, along the passage and then came to a dead stop for there, with their backs to her, were the housekeeper and the butler, and the housekeeper's voice not unduly low was saying, 'Tomorrow I'll come into me own, then I'll sort them out, all of them. There'll be changes here, and I'm starting with Cook. I'm going to put a stop to her fiddling on the side right away. In future I'll be in that kitchen to meet the tradesmen from the top to the bottom of them. In any case there won't be so many pickings after this with six less.'

'Six less?' It was a quiet enquiry from the butler, and she said 'Yes, six. The mistress and the children and Madam Price; then there's the old man, Burgess, and that weird witch of a girl who gets on me nerves every time I look at her. That's one I'll be glad to see the back of, and once the mistress is out of this house she'll be the first to take her bundle, you'll see.'

And Tilly saw. At twelve o'clock the next day only half an hour after the coach had left taking the mistress, her mother, and the children away, she was walking down the back drive with her bundle.

Only Phyllis had wished her good-bye and God-speed; the rest of the staff paid no attention to her, they were too taken up with the war that was going on between the housekeeper and the cook. They all really knew that because of Mrs Lucas's seniority she would win, nevertheless they were interested in the battle even though they all stood to lose by the inevitable outcome.

Tilly had not heard one of them say, not even Phyllis, that they were sorry the mistress was going, nor to ask what the master was going to do now he would be left on his own. Strangely, she hadn't seen the master since this business had flared up three days ago, and to her knowledge he hadn't seen the children. He certainly hadn't come up to the nursery, unless he had done so while she was dead asleep. She was sorry for him. Of course, he hadn't acted right by his wife, but then, as they had said around the table time and time again, the mistress was no use to him in the way a wife should be, so perhaps he wasn't entirely to blame. She still liked him, she still thought he was a kind man. Anyway, he'd been kind to her.

When she reached the lower gates she stood outside the disused lodge and looked at the gaping windows. Nobody had lived in there for years they said. It was almost overgrown with grass, as were the gates that were never closed now. This part of the estate had been sadly neglected. She wished she could have a little house like that. It would be lovely, like living in the cottage again.

She stood looking at it for a moment while she thought, If Mrs Drew can't take me in I'll come back and sleep there the night. The master wouldn't mind I'm sure. And the thought directed her steps through the tall grass and weeds to the window. Through it, the room appeared dark and she couldn't see anything. She pushed her way now along the wall and round to the back of the lodge, and there to her surprise she found a pathway had been made leading from the back door away into the long grass and the thicket of the wood beyond. So somebody came here.

She was passing the narrow scullery window next to the back door when she heard the rustle of footsteps coming through the dried grass, and she turned and almost dived into a thicket behind her.

The footsteps seemed to come to a stop just near her head. Then her mouth slowly opened and she stifled an exclamation as she saw a hand come down through the grass, turn over a small stone and take something from under it. She next heard a key grating in the lock of the back door and before she had time hardly to close her mouth the key grated again; then the hand came through the grass and placed it under the stone once more.

When the footsteps died away she laid her face down among the stems and let out one long-drawn breath after another. Then she asked herself why she was afraid of anyone seeing her round by the lodge. Well, she told herself, they would put two and two together and think she was going to stay there and the next thing that would happen would be Mrs Lucas bearing down upon her.

She now put out her hand and unearthed the key and, looking at it, she asked herself who it was had gone in and out of there so quickly, and why? Getting up, she turned and looked in the direction of the wood. Whoever it was had come from the house, and this wasn't their first trip not by a long chalk. She nodded to herself.

She went quickly to the door and inserted the key; then she was standing in what had been the scullery and the reason for the secret visit was immediately apparent. On a bench within an arm's length of her stood a skip holding at least three dozen eggs, and next to it lay a whole sucking pig that must have been recently slaughtered; on the floor below the bench were two other skips, one full of plums and the other holding large luscious bunches of grapes.

Eeh! the things that went on. All this pinched from the small stock. She shook her head. The Manor didn't have a home farm, but there were a hundred or so hens in the lower meadows and three sties full of pigs. Mr Pilby, besides helping in the garden, looked after the livestock, but Mr Summers was the chief one outside and he looked after the greenhouses. Her head was still shaking as she thought, They're all at it inside and out. Yet both Mr Summers and Mr Pilby were as mean as muck; she'd had personal experience of this. One day when she was out with the children and she'd pulled an apple off a tree, Mr Summers had gone for her. And to think they were doing this all the time. They were robbing the master. Did they think of it that way?

She could have understood it if they were slipping something to somebody outside who was out of work or who never saw a grape or an apple for that matter, but to sell it in piles like this. A feeling of anger rising in her, she turned abruptly away and, after locking the door, she replaced the key and went round the lodge and into the road.

One thing was clear. If Mrs Drew couldn't take her in she couldn't go back to that place and sleep, she'd have to make her way to the shed behind the cottage. . . . But what if there was a tramp in it?

Now not only did her head shake but her whole body gave an impatient jerk; she'd have to meet that trouble when she came to it. Let her get to Mrs Drew's first. . . .

Biddy Drew hailed her with warmth but with some surprise, saying, 'What brings you at this time of the day, lass?'

'I've . . . I've lost me job, Mrs Drew.'

'They sacked you?'

'Wasn't like that, no. The mistress . . . well, there's been trouble and she's gone back to her mother an' taken the bairns with her and so I'm not needed any more.'

'Huh! I said it all along, 'tisn't only the poor that have their troubles. Well, come along in, lass, that's if you can get in. As you see I'm up to me eyes in soap-suds; twice a week I have to be at it. I pick me day 'cos I like to get them dried outside; if not, you have them hangin' round the room for evermore. Look, push that lot off there' – she pointed to a large mound of pit clothes lying on the form – 'and sit yourself down. I'll put the kettle on; I'm in need of a drink meself, me tongue's hangin' out.'

Tilly didn't sit down but she placed her bundle on the form and said, 'Can I help you?'

'Help me?' Biddy turned and looked at her; then smiling widely, she said, 'Aye, well, you might. But you'll have to take your hat and coat off first, wouldn't you, lass? Then we'll have that sup tea an' a bit crack, an' then we'll get goin'.'

Tilly took off her hat and coat and hung them on the nail on the back of the door leading into the other room and as she did so, she said, 'Where's everybody the day?'

'Oh, Peg, Katie and Sam are down below' – Biddy nodded her head towards the floor – 'Bill and Arthur were on back shift, they're asleep in there.' She nodded now towards the other room and when Tilly drew her lips together and said quietly, 'Oh,' Biddy said, 'You needn't whisper, lass, the militia could go marching through here an' it wouldn't disturb either of them once they got their heads down. Fanny and Jimmy are in the fields at Richardson's farm, cleanin' up.' The smile sliding from her face, she said, 'It's hard work for a bairn of seven, but she's in the air and light and that's something.'

As they sat down on the bench, mugs of steaming weak tea in their hands, there came a high cry from behind the fireplace wall, and when Tilly turned sharply and looked behind her, Biddy laughed and said, 'Oh that's Annie Waters. She's as deaf as a stone; some of them must have got into bed without washin' and she's hauling them out. Seven she's got an' all men. They're all down below an' they're a mucky lot. Pit dust or not, they're still mucky.' She smiled tolerantly, then said, 'Well, lass, come on, let us have your news.'

Tilly gave her the news, and when she had finished, Biddy, inclining her head towards her, said quietly, 'Well, he's no better or no worse than any of the rest of them. The gentry were ever like that. As me mother used to say, if one doesn't satisfy a man, ten won't. But on the other hand there's some women, lass, worse than men, and when you get a woman inclined that way, well, nothin'll stop her except that she should be taken to bed every year with a bairn. But about your Lady Myton, well, that lady is makin' a name for hersel', I can tell you that. It isn't the first time I've heard about her. And she's a right madam, but in the high and mighty way you know, servants are scum 'neath her feet. There's gentry and gentry, lass, and some of them would use you like cattle. The McCanns at the far end of the row' – she jerked her head towards the door – 'their Peggy was sent home from her place outside Newcastle. The lasses in that house used to be sent from the kitchen upstairs to a special room and there the dirty old bugger had his way with them. And one of the stable lads was always blamed for it. By the way' – she leant forward and asked Tilly a personal question now and Tilly, the colour flooding to her face, lowered her eyes as she said, 'Yes, me granny told me, Mrs Drew, after I started when I was thirteen.'

'Aw well, you know all about it then. But nevertheless, lass, take care, keep your eyes open and your skirt down an' you'll be all right.'

'Yes, Mrs Drew.'

Biddy finished the last of her tea; then getting to her feet, she said, 'Of course there's black and white in all classes, lass; 'tisn't only the gentry for there's the keeker up at the pit, Dave Rice, he'd have you on your back afore you could say give over if he had his way. I meself have had to fight him off afore this. Dirty old bugger! The last time he had a go at me I threatened to put me pick shaft where it had never been afore if he didn't leave over.'

'You were down the mine, Mrs Drew?' Tilly's eyes widened.

'Fifteen years, lass, fifteen years.' She turned her head away now and looked towards the open doorway leading into the mud road and, her voice dropping, she said, "Twasn't bad as I got older, but I was but a bit of a bairn when I first went down. God! I was scared to death, crawling, crawling, crawling, day after day, me knees and me hands bleedin'. I didn't know what it was all about.' She turned and looked at Tilly. 'A child can't take it in, you know; that's why I'm not for lettin' my Fanny or Jimmy go down. The others have had to in order that we should eat, but we're not doin' so bad now an' they're all with me in this to keep the last two clear of that bloody black hole.' Her voice ended on a bitter note; then her tone changing quickly again, she said, 'Well, let's for the wash-tub, lass. If you're goin' to help, take this lot there and put them through the mangle. It's out in the back under the lean-to, you know where. Then hang them on the line.'

'Yes, Mrs Drew.' As Tilly went to pick up the tin bath of wet clothes she paused for a moment and said, 'About tonight, Mrs brew, do you think . . . do you think I could stay here until I get fixed up the morrow some place?'

'Where else, lass? Where else? It might be on the mat in front of the fire, or you might have to stand up against the wall.' She laughed, then said, 'Go on, go on, you'll always have a place to rest your head here.'

Warmed, and almost on the point of tears, which kindness always evoked in her, she went out through the back door to the lean-to where an iron mangle stood, its wooden rollers worn thin in the middle. It was of a type similar to the one that she had used in the cottage and so it was no hardship to wring out the clothes; but when it came to pegging them out, which meant her going into the lane which was bordered by the middens, her stomach almost heaved with the smell. But then she chided herself, for what did the smell matter when she had been received with such kindness.

As she went between the mangle and the clothes line it came to her that instead of going into Shields the morrow to look for a place she could perhaps get a job in the mine beside Katie and stay in this family, this family that seemed bound together with love and warmth. Oh, she would like that. Oh, she would. She'd do anything if she could only stay with this family.

༺ **7** ༻

It was Katie who said, 'You go down the pit? Don't be daft! you'd never last five minutes down there, not you.'

That was three days ago; since then she had tramped daily around Shields only to find that all respectable posts required a reference, and sometimes not only one but three. She had thought of going back and asking the master for one, but then that would mean facing the staff in the house again. She had thought, too, of Simon; he would have spoken up highly for her, she was sure, but she couldn't bring herself to go to the farm because likely or not she'd meet his wife.

Days could pass now when she never thought of Simon, but the moment his name came into her mind the pain came into her heart. Still, she was able to tell herself now that time would erase this feeling. It would have to, because she didn't see herself as going on alone all her days, she needed someone, someone to love and to love her. Yet the real need in her was not so much for someone to love her but to be kind to her; she treasured kindness.

So it was as she lay in bed facing Katie who had young Fanny curled into her back, that she again put her suggestion to her. This time, her voice a whispered hiss, Katie said, 'You haven't any idea, lass, what it's like down there. I'm used to it but I'd give my eye teeth if I could get a job up top. And yet at the same time I tell meself I should thank God I've got work, that we've all got work, 'cos what else is there for us around here? But you down there? No, Tilly; I can't see you down there, ever. An' our Sam won't hear of it either. . . . You'll get work, work that'll suit you like what you've been doin'.'

'I won't, Katie; as I've told you, I've got no references, an' all I was offered today was a job in a pub on the waterfront. I was told about this place from the woman who gets people jobs. You have to pay sixpence and after I gave it to her she gave me two addresses, and as I said, one was the pub. It was awful. There were women in there, Katie . . . oh, you wouldn't believe it!'

'Oh, I believe it all right' – Katie's voice sounded practical – 'I believe it 'cos I've seen it. You haven't to go any further than the Cock and Bull on the coach road. Stand out there on a Saturday night in the summer and you'll see some things that you've never seen afore, especially when they start throwing them out. What was the other job?'

'It . . . it was a kind of boarding-house, and she said I'd . . . I'd have to live in. I nearly thought about taking it until she said she didn't mind me not havin' references – it was something about the place. I got out as quickly as I could, an' she came after me to the door.'

'You were lucky' – Katie started to shake with laughter – 'you might have landed up in bed with a Swede.'

'Oh, Katie!'

They pushed at each other, and Fanny cried, 'Stop kickin', our Katie,' and a male voice from the other end of the room said, 'Shut up yous over there, I want to get to sleep.'

'Shut up yoursel'!' hissed Katie. 'You shouldn't be listenin'.'

'I wasn't an' I want none of your old lip, else I'll come an' pull you out of bed.'

'We wouldn't have far to fall, would we?' Katie was laughing again, and Tilly chuckled with her because their bed was merely a straw-filled mattress on the floor, and this made out of hessian bags. But still it was warm, and when half an hour ago she had dropped into it, it had seemed as soft as a down couch to her for her legs were aching and her feet were blistered with walking.

When Katie put her arms around her she shyly did the same, and soon, their heads together, they went to sleep.

At four o'clock in the morning Biddy gently shook Katie. She was lying on her back and she muttered a protest, but then, blinking the dead sleep from her eyes she quietly stepped over Tilly and, pulling on her over clothes that were lying on the floor by the side of the shaky-down, she stumbled into the kitchen and blinked in the lamplight.

Peg, who slept with her mother in the kitchen, was already dressed and gulping at some hot porridge, as was Sam. No one spoke; not even when the three of them went out of the door and Biddy closed it behind them: sleep was still on them, the morning was bitter, there was a day's grind ahead, what was there to say?

Three mornings later there was an addition to their number. Tilly was with them and, breaking the rule, Biddy patted her on the shoulder and said, 'God be with you, lass'; then added to herself as she closed the door on the blackness and the bitter frost, 'You'll need Him.'

Tilly's heart was thumping against her ribs as she followed Katie round the end of a row of bogies, then almost brushed against the flank of a horse that was being led towards a huddle of buildings set at the side of a wide slope which disappeared into the ground.

The scene was lit by swaying candle lamps, the candles held in place inside rude tin boxes.

'Keep close if you don't want to be trampled by the cuddies,' Katie said, pulling Tilly towards her as they went between a group of horses hardly discernible as they stood in deep shadow.

'Come on, this way, and mind what I told you, don't be afraid to answer him back, and if he asks if you're willin' to be bonded say, Why aye ... what else?'

Tilly made no answer, but, as Katie had bidden her she kept close to her side. And then they were standing at the window of a wooden hut and a man was peering at them. Tilly couldn't distinguish his face because he was standing against the light, she only saw that he was short and thin. But that didn't make him uncommon, all the men who went down mines seemed to be short and thin. It was his voice that made him different, it was deep and rollicking and he seemed to sing his words. 'Aye, well, here you are, Katie Drew, and half a day gone!'

'Stop your carry on, Mr Rice, it's too early in the mornin'. I've brought her.' She nodded towards Tilly.

'Aye, I'm not blind, I didn't think she was your shadda. Well now, lass, I suppose she's told you all there is to know. You know somethin'?' He leaned towards her from the window. 'She thinks she knows more about this bloody hole in the ground than I do. You willin' to be bonded, lass?'

'Yes ... aye.'

'Well, if that's the case you know what you're in for, and I'm tellin' you something, you're lucky. If Katie here hadn't spoke for you you'd never have been set on; there's a queue from here to Jarrow for a job like this.'

'Stop your kiddin', Mr Rice; you know damn fine anybody's got to be on their last legs afore they go down that bloody hole.' She jerked her head to the side. 'Anyway, I'll take her in.'

'Aye, you will after she signs. Come in here a minute.'

Katie pushed Tilly before her and into the hut and to the front of a high desk on which there were two ledgers. Dave Rice, opening one of them, said, 'Give us your full name, then you can write your cross.'

Tilly slanted her eyes towards Katie and a small tremor of Katie's head sent a warning to her, so what she said was, 'Tilly Trotter.'

'Married?' There was a grin on his face now as he poked it towards her.

'No,' she said.

'Then it's Tilly Trotter, spinster.' After writing her name in the ledger he put the date to the side of it; then stabbing the pen on to the paper, he said, 'Put it there'; and she put her cross by the side of her name.

His face straight now, he said, 'You know the rates, twelve shillings a fortnight. But that depends, of course, on how much they bring out. You'll be workin' marrer with Katie and Florrie Connor, isn't it?' He turned and glanced at Katie and she said, 'You know as well as I do.'

'Cheeky monkey you!' He grinned at Katie now. 'It's about time you had your arse smacked. I'll have to see about it.'

'That'll be the day. Come on.' She tugged at Tilly's arm, and they were hardly out of earshot of the hut when she said, 'Mean bugger that. You watch out for 'im, if you're not along of me. Now hold your hand a minute.' She pulled Tilly to a stop and, lifting her lantern, she peered at her through its flickering light, saying, 'Now I've warned you, you're gona get a gliff when you get along inbye, 'cos I'm gona tell you something here and now, Miss Nursery Maid from the big house' – she punched her gently in the shoulder – 'in a couple of days' time you'll realise that the cleanest things, in all ways, down here are the horses. An' at bait time keep your eyes straight ahead an' don't take no notice of what you see on the thill.'

'The what?'

'The thill, the floor, you know at the coal seam, it's called that, the thill. As I said, keep your eyes straight ahead 'cos things go on round corners that'll likely make your hair rise on your scalp. I suppose it's true what our Sam said last night, you should have kept on lookin' for a decent position. Still here you are, you've signed up an' you can't get out of it unless you go and die like Florrie Thompson, whose job you've got. But it wasn't the coal that killed her, it was the consumption. . . . Aw! come on, here's the squad.' She half turned to where the group of men, women, and children were making their way towards the incline and she added, 'I thought we'd get to the face afore they came, I wanted to show you things quiet like. Not that it's ever quiet down here, but with the crew around us . . . aw, come on, come on, put a move on.'

Bewildered, her innards seeming to have broken loose in the casing of her stomach, she scurried now to keep up with Katie's trotting steps. She was afraid as she'd never been afraid before. This was a different kind of fear. The fear associated with Hal McGrath had come and gone from time to time but this particular fear she felt was going to be permanent. She was walking into a world that didn't belong to any kind of life she had yet imagined. She was going along what appeared to be a tunnel with iron rails down the middle, and she went to step in between them for easier walking when Katie with a bawl that nearly took her head off cried, 'Do you want to be run over afore you start? Don't be so bloody gormless, lass, that's the rolley way. Look.' She pointed ahead to where a young lad was coming towards them leading a horse, and as they came nearer, Tilly could see the three bogies full of coal rattling behind the horse.

It seemed that she had been walking and stumbling for an interminable time when the tunnel widened out into a bay, which in comparison to the tunnel was well lit by the lanterns hanging on nails stuck into two square supporting pillars which were holding up the roof. The rolley line now met up with others coming out of different roads, and on these there were more horses dragging more tubs.

For a moment she stood transfixed at the sight of a man squatting in the corner doing his business. His moleskin trousers were dangling over his knees and the rest of his body was bare.

'What cheer, Katie!'

'What cheer, Danny!'

Katie didn't look towards the squatting man as she answered him but she nevertheless appeared unaffected by his pose.

'This way.' Katie was tugging again at Tilly's arm, and now they were going down one of the side roads. It was impossible to imagine they were going any deeper into the mine, but this was made more evident to her when the road on which they were now stumbling along began to go steeply downward. Moreover, it was much narrower than the main one and the roof seemed much lower, for after bumping her head against a spar of wood that was being held in place by two pit props all the sympathy she got from Katie in answer to her exclamation of pain was, 'You'll larn.'

That she was learning was evident when on the sound of a horse's hooves and the rattle of the wagons she pressed herself into an aperture seemingly scraped out of the wall between the pit props until the horse and bogies had passed.

She noticed that the leader of the horse was but a small boy, and that the horse was not a horse like those in the first part of the mine, this was a small Galloway pony. She had often wondered why when these ponies were let out in the fields they kicked their heels and seemed to go mad for a while, but now she could tell why. Oh yes, she could tell why.

When a few minutes later she let out a stifled scream as a rat the size of a small cat ran almost over her feet Katie stopped for a moment and after laughing said quietly, 'Don't be feared of them 'cos you'll have to get used to them. In fact there's one along here we call Charlie, an' he's a cheeky little bugger is Charlie.'

Tilly gulped in her throat but said nothing, although she thought it was strange how Katie kept swearing down here, yet she hadn't heard her swear at home. . . . Would she become like Katie?

'We're nearly there. . . . Look! watch out for that sump.' She pulled Tilly to the side of the roadway. 'It looks just a little puddle but it'll take you past your knees if you go in. They'll be filling it in shortly. Never walk on smooth coal dust, take my tip, or you'll find yourself swimmin'. An' you just might one of these days, if that doesn't hold – ' She jerked her thumb towards the low roof. 'Seam up there's flooded out and it drips through.' She raised her lantern and pointed to where water was oozing through a fissure in the roof, then added reassuringly, 'Don't worry, it'll hold the day. And for a good few more I hope.'

Once again the road opened out and immediately they stepped into a hive of activity. If Tilly hadn't known different she would have imagined that the small figures darting here and there were a number of children playing, except that their voices were raucous and that most of their words were profane. They looked like imps for only the whites of their eyes and the grey of their open mouths and tongues showed any colour.

As she stood, her eyes staring, there arose in her a feeling which mounted; amazement mingled with compassion and expressed itself in horror. Then her mouth widened and her chin drooped as she saw come crawling from a side road a small creature. She couldn't at first make out whether it was a girl or a boy, but it looked no bigger than Master John. It was a boy and he was in harness, but the harness was strapped round his waist and extended between his legs and it wasn't made of leather but of chain, and the chain was attached to a shallow skip loaded to a point with coal.

She watched as a man unbuckled the harness and slowly the child rose from his hands and knees and stood swaying for a moment, then rubbed his black knuckle into his eyes as if he were arising from sleep.

She was unaware that she had been gripping Katie's arm, and Katie, recognising her feelings, shouted above the hubbub, 'Oh, he's older than he looks; that's Billy Snaith, he's ten. Hello there, Billy.'

There was a pause of seconds before the child answered wearily, 'Hello, Katie.'

'Tired?'

'Aye, I'm jiggered. What's it like up top?'

'Cold but dry.'

His reply, if he made any, was lost when a raucous voice shouted above the mêlée, 'Come on the lot of yous if you want to go! Well, alreet, if you want to stay I don't mind puttin' you on another shift.'

The answer to this was murmurs and growls from the incoming shift. But what was amazing Tilly more than anything was the apparent acceptance of this way of life, and also the humour threading it. Yet there was no sign of humour in the line of straggling children making their way to the outside world.

'That's the low drift lot.' Katie nodded towards the departing children. 'The road in there's too low for a Galloway to get in.'

'Why don't they make it bigger?'

In the enquiry there was a note in Tilly's voice that could have touched on anger, and Katie laughed as she said, 'Don't ask me. I suppose they would if they could; it's got something to do with the seams.' She nodded up towards the uneven stone roof. 'It means cutting through that an' some of it won't be cut through, an' there are places where it would be dangerous to try 'cos there's the water to contend with. Look at that pump there.' She pointed across the space. 'Goin' hell for leather all the time twenty-four hours a day. It's like tryin' to drain the Tyne. Anyway, we're lucky we can walk in to our place, an' believe me I do think meself lucky' – she was nodding at Tilly now – 'cos I was three years on that shift where Billy is, and by! it was a long 'un. The day I was moved to the fourth road' – she pointed ahead of her – 'I wouldn't have called the Queen me aunt. Yet I cried all that first night – relief I think it was.'

Tilly made no response to this; her mind was in a whirl with the overlying pattern of horror.

They were in a small group now, people in front and people behind, but there was no talking until they came on a single bogey, one boy pulling in front, a second almost horizontal adding his puny efforts as he pushed at the iron contraption laden with coal. And then someone shouted, 'Better get a move on, Robbie, else you'll catch it.'

The boy in front paused, turned his head slowly and looked at the man; then seeming to draw his shoulders up over his head he moved on again.

'Don't linger.' Katie was pulling at Tilly's arm, impatience in her voice now; then she whispered, 'If you stopped every time you saw that you wouldn't last long down here, now I'm tellin' you so if you mean to work, an' you'll have to 'cos you've bonded yourself, you'll have to buck up.' It was as if her warning was final.

They now arrived at what Tilly took to be a dead end, for it looked like a long blank wall except that there were men hacking at it. They had hardly reached them when one of the men turned and shouted, 'You've taken your time; we'll be up to our bloody necks in it if you don't get crackin'!'

This was answered by a mouthful of cursing from a woman among the group and there was a ripple of laughter accompanied by bustle, and Katie whispered, 'That's big Meggie. She keeps them in their place, caution she is in more ways than one. Keep on the right side of her.' The last was a whisper almost in Tilly's ear. 'Now here's what you do. Your bait? Where's your bait? . . . . Oh my God!' She reached out and snatched Tilly's bait from a shelf of rock and on a laugh she said, 'You're green all right, that wouldn't last two minutes there. That's what I'd give it, two minutes afore Charlie'd be at it. Look, you see the knot in the string, you hang it up here, like this.' She demonstrated by hanging the small parcel of food from a nail in a beam and allowing it to dangle downwards. 'There! He hasn't learned to walk the tight-rope yet but some day I bet he does; he's a clever 'un is Charlie.'

'Why . . . why don't you kill them, I mean him, the rat?'

'Oh, we kill 'em, but not Charlie. The blokes are superstitious about Charlie. As long as Charlie shows his face they guess they're all right. They say he can smell fire damp better than any of their new-fangled ideas, an' I believe that's true, like I believe safety lamps is dangerous. Our lads won't use them, they stuck out against them. There was war on at first but they stuck out an' we've hardly lost any men in the last twenty years, well, not to speak of, not compared with others. There's been hundreds killed in mines along here. Me ma remembers Heaton Colliery. Seventy-five killed in a flood there. . . . Look' – she broke off – 'don't stand there like a stook, do what I'm at, take that shovel an' fill that skip, like this.' She thrust her shovel into a heap of coal and she had filled the skip within a few minutes.

Tilly took the shovel and began to fill a skip. Shovelling was no hardship, her muscles were attuned to the saw; what was troubling her was the coal dust in her throat that seemed to be choking her, the coal dust in her eyes that was blurring her limited vision in the dim light, and the noise, the bustle; and then . . . the lifting up of the skip on to the shoulders of the children. Some fell to their knees with the weight of them before they got adjusted, and the children didn't go down the road she and the others had come up because this had the rolley lines laid on it; they went by a narrow by-pass disappearing into blackness as if walking into the mouth of hell. Before she had been at the work an hour she was associating the whole place with hell and its horrors.

When time had passed to which she couldn't put a name, a halt was called and, dropping her shovel, she went and leant against the wall and slowly slid down to the floor; and there Katie joined her. She had brought a can with her and, taking the lid off it, she handed it to Tilly, saying, 'Here, wash your throat, an' spit the first mouthful out.'

Tilly gulped at the tepid water and it tasted like wine, and had swallowed half of it before she aimed to spit it out.

'You've done well for a starter.'

Tilly made no answer.

'You'll get used to it after a bit. You're achin' now I know, but in a day or so you won't know that you've got any arms or legs, or back, 'cos they'll all work together; it's only your throat that'll trouble you.'

A man came and sat down at the other side of Tilly. He was naked except for a pair of ragged drawers. 'How's it goin', lass?' he asked.

Tilly did not know how to answer him; the answer she couldn't give him was 'All right'; it was Katie who replied for her, saying, 'She's a bit winded, Micky; but as I was tellin' her, in a week or so's time it'll only be the dust that'll worry her. I'm right, aren't I, Micky?'

'Aye, lass, aye, you're right. 'Tis the dust that's the trouble. Gets you, the dust.' He took a swill from his can; then wiping his cleaned washed lips with the back of his black hand, he added, 'And finally in the end. Aye, 'tis as you say, Katie, the dust. Anyway, it mightn't trouble you for very much longer. Do you know what I was hearin' when I was in Shields t'other Sunday? A fellow was spoutin' and he was sayin' that there's one or two blokes up in London Town trying to get a bill out to stop bairns and lasses being down here, an' in factories an' all, that is until a certain age. But he's tryin' to potch women and children in mines altogether.'

'Is that true, Micky?'

'Aye, I heard it from this fellow's own lips, lass. And what's more, I saw him gettin' run in. He had a big crowd round him, Sunday strollers you know, and the polis took him for breakin' the peace.'

Katie was silent for a moment before she said, 'I was gona say bloody lot of silly Holy Joes up there tryin' to take the bread out of wor mouths, but I don't know, it could be the best thing that could happen, that's if they give us other jobs.'

'Aye, that's it, lass, if they give you other jobs, but where are the jobs for lasses and women, only service, or the fields. You've got your pick, but whichever you choose you're under a bloody master, aren't you? Well, there's one thing, lass' – he now gripped Tilly's knee tightly – 'you haven't got to get dressed up for this lark, have you? Wear nowt if you like. Aye, wear nowt. What about it, eh, Katie?' He leaned over Tilly and peered at Katie and she pushed at him, saying with a laugh, 'Go on you! you're a Micky drippin'.'

'Well, here we go!' He pulled himself to his feet; then looking round at the squatting figures, he said, 'Where's big Meggie . . . as if I didn't know? That lass should be in a bull pen.'

A voice from the other side of the roadway shouted, 'What d'ya think her secret is, Micky? Twenty-two years old an' never been dropped yet; she should have had 'em by the litter with her carry-on.'

There was muffled laughter as the various figures rose from the ground and the process of shovelling started all over again. Push in the shovel, lift, throw. Push in the shovel, lift, throw. When the rhythm stopped a small back was waiting to be laden with your efforts.

Push in the shovel, lift, throw. Push in the shovel, lift, throw. Dear God in Heaven! she could never stand this. That place in Shields serving in the bar appeared like paradise to her now; even the boarding-house job seemed attractive. She'd have to tell Katie when they got out of here . . . when they got out of here. Would this work ever stop?

Some time during the day it stopped for half an hour, then again for a break to sit down by the wall and drink from the can.

Three o'clock in the afternoon and a final halt was called. She had lost count of time. She couldn't hear what Katie was saying. Later, she couldn't recall the walk from the face to outbye. She only knew she was aware that some of the children didn't accompany them. It was later Katie told her that a few of them were on twelve hour shifts; two hours overtime she said, whether they liked it or not; they had to clear the face for the next shift.

At one part of the road when coming out she had been aware of walking through water and of some of the men stopping and discussing it saying that the landing box must be overflowing.

And she recalled standing at the mouth of the mine amid the sweating horses and blackened men and looking upwards towards the bright sky. The sun was shining, two larks were competing with each other in a chorus of sound, and as she gazed upwards the wind lifted her hair from her brow. And she could have stood like this, she felt, for ever but Katie, practical to the last, said, 'You can sniff it all the way home. Come on, lass.'

And when she arrived home Biddy did for her what she had never done for her own children. In the narrow confines of the scullery she eased her into the tin bath and gently she washed the grime from her, hair and all. Then after helping her to dry herself she slipped over her head a stiff calico nightdress and led her to the shaky-down, and there she let her sleep for four hours before awakening her and giving her a meal. It was a bowl of mutton broth and dumplings and she brought it to the bed in a basin placed on a tin tray, and while Tilly sat up and then sleepily ate it, Katie lay snoring solidly by her side. And when she had finished the meal Biddy took the bowl from her, saying quietly, 'Away you go, put your head down, lass; your first day's over. It'll never seem so bad again.'

8

The days turned into weeks and the weeks into months, and Tilly learned what it was to work in water up to her knees. She learned not to pass out when she saw a man injured by a fall of stone or coal, or saw one trapped in the brokens where he had been pulling the pillars in order to drop a roof. She learned how to make her own candles with cotton wicks and ox tallow because this worked out cheaper than paying the viewer to supply you with them. And she learned to trust Charlie. This happened on the day one of the men, seeing the rat standing on his hind legs sniffing before scurrying away up the road, cried to them, 'Run for it!'

The brattice, a wooden partition which aided the currents of air to flow, had in some way blocked the flow and a small child detailed to watch at the air door had fallen asleep. This time the build-up of gas was slight, but nevertheless it could have caused an explosion if touched off by a candle lamp. There was jollification the following day when Charlie returned, and pieces of bait were put on the shelf for him. Charlie, the men swore, was a better gas detector than any canary.

Tilly also learned that most people look alike when covered in coal dust, for twice in as many months she had passed close to the master and he hadn't even given her a second glance. She had wondered that if he noticed her name on the books whether he might seek her out and speak to her. But then, she supposed, he never saw the names of his workers; this was left to the viewer.

One thing she knew for certain and that was she hated every day she went down into the depths of the earth, and that if there were the slightest chance of other work she would jump at it, even working in the fields. But there were queues for those jobs and the field managers picked their own gangs. Anyway, during the winter there was no work for them.

Another thing worrying her was Sam. She could read the signs all too clearly. He had laughed at Steve's first visit to the house to ask how she was, but when the lad put in an appearance on both the following two Sundays he hadn't laughed or chipped her as the others had done. She had wanted to say, 'Steve is like a brother to me, no more, no less,' but that would have left the road open for him, so she said nothing and let them assume what they liked about her and Steve.

Then something happened that made Sam show his hand. It was on a Sunday at the end of her fourth week down the mine. The family had gathered as usual, the children had been out playing in the road, and it was young Jimmy who rushed in gabbling, 'Tilly! Tilly! there's a gent on a horse askin' for you.'

Tilly had risen to her feet. There were two people she knew who rode horses, one was the master, the other was Simon, and she knew it wouldn't be the master who'd come looking for her. She felt her face turn scarlet and, looking round the now silent company, she sidled from the form as she said, 'I'll ... I'll be back in a minute.'

'Do you know who it is?' It was Biddy asking the question, and she looked at her and said, 'Yes, I think so, Mrs Drew. It'll likely be Si ... Farmer Bentwood. He's ... he's the friend I told you about who looked after me granny and granda.'

'Oh, aye, lass, aye. Well, ask him in. He'll have to squeeze, but ask him in.'

She did not say 'Yes' or 'No' to this but simply thanked Mrs Drew. She didn't want Simon to see this over-crowded room, he wouldn't understand her living in such conditions; nor would he understand the warmth and happiness they engendered.

He was standing by his horse's head in the muddy road. Several doors were open along the row and heads were peering out. She was embarrassed by the situation, she knew what they would be thinking: why was a lass like her being visited by a man on a horse and dressed as he was? for he could be taken for a gentleman.

'Hello, Tilly.'

'Hello, Simon.'

'I ... I didn't know where you had gone until ... until the other day.'

'Oh, I've been here some weeks now.'

'My God!' The words came from under his breath as he looked up and down the row; then he said, 'Look, we can't stand here, come for a walk.'

She looked behind her towards the half open door before muttering, 'I'll get me hat and coat.'

Back in the room she passed through them and addressed herself to Biddy as she said, 'I'm ... I'm just going for a short walk, I ... I won't be long, I'm gettin' me hat and coat.'

There was silence again as she returned pulling on her coat and it was Sam who spoke now, saying, 'Why can't you ask your visitor in?'

She glanced at him as she said, 'He ... he hasn't got much time.'

Out in the road again, walking by Simon's side, her eyes cast downwards, she realised that she hadn't walked like this for some time now, it was as if she were ashamed. For the last few weeks she had held her head high; perhaps it was because she wanted to look at the sky and drink in the air.

'Why didn't you come to me after you left the Manor?' He was muttering his words for they were still in the row.

And she answered low, 'You should know the answer to that.'

They had passed the end of the row and were in the open country before he spoke again. 'I could have at least seen that you were decently housed.'

She turned on him now, her voice high. 'I am decently housed. I'm happier with them' – she jerked her head backwards – 'than ever I've been in me life with anybody ... well, except me granda and grandma. But they were old; back there, the Drews, well, they're all youngish, and the place might look awful but they're clean, an' they're good, an' it might surprise you, Simon, but they're happy.'

He pulled the horse to a standstill and looked at her. 'And you, you're happy, working down the pit, because that's what they tell me you're doing?'

She swallowed and looked to the side now as she said, 'No, I can't say I'm happy workin' down the pit, but . . . but I have them to come back to.'

'Look' – he bent towards her – 'I'll give you the money; you can get a decent room in Shields until you find a place to go into service or some such, but . . . but I can't bear the thought of you down there' – he now thumbed angrily towards the ground – 'and the things that I hear go on. They act like beasts.'

'No, they don't. Well, perhaps a few of them do' – her voice was raised again – 'but you can't judge them all alike. As for acting like beasts, there's plenty of them up top, and you should know that. I've just escaped one because he's gone to sea.'

'I know, I know.' His tone was quiet now. 'Yet Tilly' – he shook his head slowly – 'I somehow feel responsible for you. . . .'

'Well, you needn't, I'm responsible for meself and workin' for me livin'; I'm on me own feet, and what's more I'm not hounded any longer. Even over there' – she pointed in the direction of the Manor – 'they would have burnt me alive, aye, and I'm not kiddin'. Take us back a few years and they would have had me burnt alive. They were as bad as the villagers, except for a couple of them, and the tutor.'

He stared at her in silence for a moment, then said, 'Does he know that you are working in his mine . . . Sopwith?'

'I don't know, and it wouldn't matter if he did. But I do know this: if he had offered to keep me on in a job below stairs I would have refused it, an' I was badly in need of a roof over me head at the time. Such was the feeling against me that I'm tellin' you I would have refused it because they, all of them' – again she thumbed in the direction of the Manor – 'they're a lot of thieves an' scroungers an' not fit to wipe any one of the Drews' boots. Diddling him, the master, at all turns. You've never seen anything like it.'

'Diddling?' He raised his eyebrows and smiled weakly at her. 'Well, everybody knows that goes on.'

'Aye, it might, a bit here and there, but not to the extent that lot takes it to. You know nothing, Simon. If your men were robbing you like the staff rob Mr Sopwith you'd go broke within weeks, I'm tellin' you.'

'Well, that's his look out. He's got a housekeeper, hasn't he?'

'Huh! housekeeper. Anyway, that's over and done with, I'm here and I'm gona remain here till something better turns up. But whatever it is I'm stayin' along with the Drews as long as they'll have me.'

'So I needn't have worried?'

She looked him full in the face now, saying quietly, 'No, you needn't have worried, Simon.'

Again there was a long pause; and when he eventually spoke his voice was soft and full of meaning as he said, 'I'll always worry over you, Tilly. No matter what comes my way in life, nor no matter how I change, my feelings for you will remain the same as they've always been.'

She stared into his face for some seconds before saying quietly, 'Good, like they were when I was a little girl.'

Her eyes were unblinking and he closed his own for a moment and bit on his lip before looking at her again and murmuring, 'Just as you say, Tilly, like they were when you were a little girl.'

His gaze was hot on her belying his words and she turned her head to the side, saying slowly now, 'I may be starting courtin' soon.'

When he made no answer she looked at him again. 'Sam, he's the eldest, he wants me; he's a good fellow.'

'And you? You want him?'

She forced herself to look straight into his eyes as she answered, 'Yes, because I can't see I'll do any better and I'll have a house of me own and . . .'

'Huh! a house of your own,' he broke in, his voice almost a shout now as he cried, 'Don't be silly, a house of your own! I wouldn't use any one of those along that row for sties.'

'No, perhaps you wouldn't.' Her voice was almost as loud as his; but then, taking a deep breath and her tone changing, she said, 'But then you're very fortunate, Simon. You've always been very fortunate ; in fact, you don't know you're born. Now I've got to go back, Mrs Drew likes us all there at teatime on a Sunday . . . in the sty.'

'I'm . . . I'm sorry.' His head was turned to the side now and she answered, 'Yes, so am I. . . . Good-bye, Simon.' Her voice was soft, but he didn't answer and she turned away. Pulling her coat closer around her neck, she bent her head and ran back to the row.

Simon stood and watched her until the door closed on her, and then, turning towards the horse, he put his two hands on the saddle and bent his head towards them as he muttered to himself, 'Well, I tried, so what has to be will be. Let things take their course.'

༒ **9** ༒

Mark Sopwith was experiencing a deep loneliness which was making him feel as if he were hollow right through. The house appeared empty, and even when there was a movement in it it seemed to be at a slower pace. Mrs Lucas had assured him that he had no need to worry about the household, she would see that it ran as smoothly as before.

It was Pike who presented him with the monthly accounts. These, he noticed, were reduced hardly at all, yet there were six people less to feed. But he let it pass, at least for the present; there were more serious problems on his mind. This morning he was to make a thorough inspection of the mine with his agent. The day before yesterday they had repaired the clack-valve in the pump on the fourth level and the water there was now much lower. They had also had a new bucket attached, a heavier type which helped with the downstroke in the cylinder. Yet things were still not right; there was more seepage coming in from the upper level, and this was likely being fed by a spring near the burn having diverted itself. Springs were hell to locate; they caused more trouble than the river because you knew where the river was.

Then his private affairs: he'd had one polite note from Eileen saying that the children were well and happy and that when they broke up for the Christmas holidays, weather permitting, she'd allow them to come and stay overnight.

His teeth had clenched hard on that line – she would allow them to come and stay overnight. Was this to be the pattern of the future, his children for one night? No, he wasn't going to stand for that. All right, let her have a legal separation, then he'd put in a legal claim, and in that way he'd have his children for so many months, well, at least weeks in the year.

He had breakfasted at the same time as usual but this morning he did not rise from the table immediately he had finished, but remained seated staring towards the bright glowing fire to the right of him; and as he did so he asked himself again if this was to be the pattern of his life. He couldn't marry again unless she divorced him. And if he took a mistress it would mean seeing her only at intervals, whereas what he needed at this moment was a companion more than a mistress, a loving companion, someone to sit opposite him, smile at him, listen to him, touch his hand – he didn't want to roll with her. . . . All right, if that too should happen to be in the picture it would be a bonus, but he just wanted a woman near him, close, warm. He had friends, or rather he'd had friends before this affair had flared into the open. Since Eileen left he had seen Albert Cragg just once, and then Bernice hadn't shown her face. Only Albert had called, and he had the nerve to convey diplomatically to him that Bernice, having been a friend of Eileen's . . . well, he understood, didn't he?. . . . Yes, yes, he understood.

John Tolman had called too, but also unaccompanied by Joan. Only Olive and Stanley Fieldman had visited together, when Stan in his hearty way had thumped him on the back as he said, 'You'll ride the waves, laddie. Never fear, you'll ride the waves.' That was the only reference he had made to the scandal of which he had become the chief figure. But what about Agnes? Olive Fieldman hadn't been as reticent as her husband and he gathered from what she said that Agnes's escapades had become so notorious that every decent door was now closed to her. But as Olive had pointed out, it didn't seem to worry her in the least; she was a most remarkable person.

Yes, Agnes was indeed a most remarkable person. She wasn't really a woman at all, merely a ravenous collection of primeval instincts, with a ruthless disregard for everything and everyone who didn't suit her purpose. It didn't seem to trouble her in the least that she was blatantly violating the standards of the society in which she moved.

He rose and went to the fire and, holding his hands out to the flame, he asked of it, 'What am I going to do?' and the answer came tersely, 'Get down to business. Robinson will be waiting for you.'

It could have been about eleven o'clock. Tilly had just loaded a full skip on to Betty Pringle's back. Betty was eleven years old, her body was thin and her shoulders permanently stooped, and her face, when it was washed, gave one the impression of age, even when she laughed, for her eyes never smiled.

Betty never complained, even when the skip was piled so high that the coal stuck in her neck she said nothing. Her father had been killed in this mine three years ago and she and her twelve-year-old brother were the only means of support for her mother, who was ailing with 'the sickness'.

At first Tilly had barely filled the child's skip, but this had brought the barrow man storming up the roadway saying he would report them both to the keeker and they would have their money docked if the skips weren't filled properly, for it was taking him twice as long to get his corves filled and therefore he was behind in taking his loads outbye. And so from then Tilly filled the skips to the required measure, and spat out the coal dust not only to clear her throat but as a significant reply to what she thought of the barrow man.

Indeed Tilly was learning, and fast.

Today the work was excruciating. Straightening her back, she went hurriedly towards the shelf where Katie kept the tin box holding the candles. To get to the shelf she had to splash through water that came up to her calves. She didn't mind; it was warm and for a moment it washed the grit from out of her clogs.

Tempers were on edge along the whole face; the hewers were swearing at the putters, the putters were swearing at the women and children because they couldn't keep pace with transporting the coal from the face to the middle landing; everything about them was sodden wet; everybody was working in water. It was into this atmosphere that one of the putters came running back from the middle road with the news that Alf, the horseman, had just told him that the boss, the master, the check weighman, and the agent were all on their way up to number four face.

'Well, let the buggers come,' was the general comment. 'Oh aye, especially him. Let him see the real conditions in his bloody mine. Another foot and we can't go on. Aye, let him come. Let them all come.'

Half an hour later they came, in single file: the check weighman first, then Mark, followed by the agent; and they were all wearing high knee-boots.

They stopped almost opposite to where Tilly and Katie were working. No one had stopped work and no one spoke. The voiceless silence was eerie, there was only the tapping of the picks and the grating of the shovels. Then the check weighman said, 'It's risen in the last hour.' He stuck a rod in the ground, then added, 'Four inches.'

'Well, it can't be all coming from number three drift; you've seen to that, haven't you? the pump's working?' Mark had turned to the check weighman and he answered, 'Aye, sir, we've seen to that. But it's up above I fear the trouble is.' He pointed towards the roof. ''Tis as if there were a leak in the river and it was finding its outlet here 'cos we're touching on river level at this point.'

It was as the agent spoke for the first time, saying, 'And that's quite possible. Yet we checked the fissures just a short while ago,' that a strange noise alerted everybody. The men at the face stayed their picks in mid-air, and when a big rat that was perched on a shelf suddenly leapt forward and scampered down the road away into the dimness, a weird cry rang round the enclosed space. It galvanised everybody. Men, women, and children, tumbling and yelling, made for the road, and the check weighman's voice above everyone else's now seemed to verge on a scream as he cried, 'Run! Run, sir!' But even as the man thrust out his arm to grab Mark, a wave of water swept them all forward like matchwood.

Tilly heard herself yell as she lost her footing and sprawled into the water. She could swim a little, having taught herself in the burn, but now the motions of her flaying arms were impeded by bodies and clutching hands, and faces with wide open mouths confronting her one minute then spun away from her the next. The whole terrifying nightmare scene was lit by a lantern here and there on shelves where the water had not yet reached.

She was swallowing the filthy water in great gulps, she knew she was dying and it was no use struggling, but she struggled. Her hand went out sideways and found a rung of a ladder and she clung on to it realising it was the ladder leading up to some old workings where they had been dropping the roof only last week, and that if she could get in there she'd be safe.

As she attempted to pull herself upwards a hand came out and grabbed her shoulder, the nails digging into her flesh, and as she was dragged upwards the water, having billowed her skirt, left her knees bare and they scraped against the rough stone, but her agonised crying out was mixed with relief when she felt her feet touch solid ground although still under the water.

There was no light now and in the pitch blackness she kept tight hold of the hand. As she gasped for breath a whimper came from the side of her, and she put out her other hand and touched a small head that was just above the water and, gasping, she said, 'Who is it?'

'Betty. Me, Betty Pringle.'

'Oh, Betty; thank God you're safe, at least for the present. And ... and who are you?' She brought her hand now from Betty to touch her rescuer, and when she felt the sodden cloth of a coat she realised that he must be one of the three men, the weighman, the agent ... or the master. She wouldn't know until he spoke, but he didn't speak. And now she stammered, 'This ... this is the old workin'. They ... they were dropping the roof, but it'll likely be dry further in.'

The hand was still holding hers but the man said nothing, and she thought, He's stunned; whichever one of them it is he's stunned.

'Hang on to me.' Her words were meant for both the man and Betty. The man still held her hand and after feeling the child grab at her skirt she moved forward, and the man came behind her.

The lay of the ground told her they were moving upwards, but they hadn't gone more than a dozen steps when the earth below them shook, and the roof above them shook. It seemed to Tilly in this moment that the whole world was rocking; and then she was screaming again, as was Betty.

She didn't know whether it was the man who threw her forward or whether it was the upheaving of the earth, but she seemed to fly through space before her head hit something and a blankness descended on her.

When she came round the earth was steady again but her mouth was filled with dust. There was no water here. Slowly she raised herself upwards, but when she tried to stand she was impeded by something across her legs. Her groping fingers told her that these were two pit props, and when she felt the rocks on top of them she realised that they might have saved her from broken shins.

She tried to call out but the words stuck in her throat. She listened. There was no sound, only the sound within her, the terror that was rushing up to her throat to find release.

When at last she found her voice it was small, she could hardly hear it herself, and she said, 'Is anybody there?'

There was no answer. She pulled herself clear of the props and began to crawl round on her hands and knees. She was muttering to herself now: 'There's been a fall, it's a fall, the mouth of the old workings must have caved in. 'Twas the water; it couldn't stand up against the water. . . . Is anybody there? Betty! Betty!' Her voice was getting stronger, and now she was yelling. 'Mister! Mister!' She had been climbing over mangled stones and props but now suddenly she could move no further forward because the stones and the props had become a steep wall.

'Oh my God! Oh my God! they must be under there, the man and Betty.' She started calling again, 'Mister! Mister!' Betty!' She stood up now, groping at the stones, and like someone demented she started to pull at them and throw them behind her.

When her foot touched something soft she dropped on to her knees and, groping blindly, she moved her hands over it, then almost shouted in her relief. It was the man. Like her, he too had been knocked out. But then her fingers tracing his body, her relief sank into dismay; he was lying on his back with his legs above him, and these had been caught. Her fingers moved down over one trouser to where his knee should be, but all she could feel here was a great block of stone. His other leg was hanging downwards and only the foot was caught above the ankle, fastened tight by a pit prop which in turn was weighed down by the wall of stone.

Now her hands were running over his face, then she was undoing his jacket, then his waistcoat. When her fingers touched his shirt her hands became still for her touch told her what the material was made of, fine flannel, a material so thin it was almost like silk. The children had had shirts like this. Oh my God! the master. When her fingers went through his vest and on to his flesh her head turned to the side as if listening, and when the beat of his heart came to her hand it seemed to pass up her arm and shock her into vitalised life, for now, lifting Mark's head she cried, 'Sir! Sir! wake up.' When she got no response she edged herself forward so that she was half sitting, half leaning among the debris, and in this position and supporting his head against her thigh, she now started patting his face, like a mother trying to restore a child to life and gabbling all the while, 'Come on. Come on. Please, please, wake up. Oh! sir, do wake up, please.'

For the moment she had forgotten about Betty; then her head turning from one side to the other in the darkness she called, 'Betty! Are you there, Betty? Can you hear me, Betty?' And as she called once again the head resting against her moved and Mark let out a long agonised groan.

'That's it, sir, wake up. Wake up.'

'What! What!'

She kept patting his face. 'Come on, wake up. Wake up properly. Oh! please wake up.'

'What is it? What happened?'

'There was a fall, sir. You . . . you pulled me out of the water and . . . and we came into the drift and there was a fall.'

'A fall?'

'Yes, sir.'

'I can't move.'

'No, sir, your feet are caught, but . . . but it'll be all right, they'll come, they always come and get people out, they won't be long.'

'Who . . . who are you? I . . . I know you, don't I?'

'I'm Trotter, sir. I . . . I used to be the children's nurse.'

'Ah, Trotter. Trotter.' His voice faded away and once again she was patting his face, saying, 'Come on. Oh! come on, sir, wake up properly. Please wake up. Look, they'll get us out, they have special men for gettin' people out. Sam is one of them, Katie's brother. Aw come on, come on, sir. Can you hear me, sir?'

When he groaned she said, 'That's it, that's it, keep awake. That's what they say you've got to do, keep awake. You haven't got to move about, just keep awake.'

'I can't move.'

'No, but you soon will. Are you hurtin', sir?'

'Hurting? No, I'm not hurting, Trotter. I . . . I just don't feel anything. Yes, yes, I do, my neck is stiff, I'm lying . . . rather twisted.'

When she shifted amid the tumbled stones, jagged edges here and there pierced her flesh; then she eased his head up between her small breasts and asked softly, 'Is that better?'

'Yes; yes, thank you.' Again his voice from a whisper faded away; and there was silence about her once more, and it was as terrifying as the blackness. This was like no blackness she had ever experienced before. No matter how long a road in the mine there had always been a glimmer of light somewhere; but this blackness was encasing her like a shroud. She could be in her grave, buried alive. . . .

Her body trembled violently and she coughed, jerking his head on her breast, and he moaned and said, 'Oo . . . h! Oo . . . h! How long ago did it happen? I . . . I seem to have been asleep.'

'Not long, sir; about half an hour I should say.'

'Is that all?'

There was a surprised note in his voice. Then his words spaced, he said, 'I . . . wish . . . I . . . could . . . move.'

She made no answer, and again slowly he asked, 'Do you think you might be able to move the stones from my feet, Trotter?'

Some seconds passed before she muttered, 'I . . . I'd better not, sir; the . . . the way you're lying I could bring the rest down on top of you.'

'Yes, yes, of course.'

'They won't be long, sir, they won't be long.'

'The . . . the little girl?'

She didn't answer, and he muttered, 'Oh! dear, dear. Oh! dear.'

She sat now quite still saying no word. She didn't know whether he had fallen asleep again but it didn't seem to matter, her body was cramped, she felt weary, sort of bad, ill. Her mind was now picturing light. She saw herself walking over the open land back from Jarrow to the cottage, and she realised that time passed differently when it was spent in light. You didn't really think of time in the daylight not unless you had to get somewhere in a hurry. There were so many things that showed up in the light and took up time, like the sky and the grass and cows in a field, and the burn. She liked the burn. Some days when it was running low and the water just dribbled over the stones it appeared to be talking, chatting. And then there were the larks. They made you forget time. You put your head back and tried to follow their flight, but even when you couldn't see them any more you could hear them. . . .

The scream that ran through her head seemed to be mixed up with the lark song and she pulled herself upwards crying loudly, 'What is it? What is it?' She felt his arms flaying and realised that she must have slipped while she dozed, for her groping hands now found his head resting against a stone. Now she was to the side of him, her arms about his shoulders pushing him upwards, and when his scream turned to a shuddering moan she felt his face pressed tight into her shoulder and she stammered, 'Are . . . are . . . are you in pain?'

His mouth was moving against her neck; she felt his tongue come out and he gulped several times before he said, 'Yes.'

''Tis bad?'

'Yes.' The word seemed to have required effort and she could feel the air leaving his chest and his shoulders hunching.

She said in an apology now, 'I . . . I must have dozed an' you slipped. Look.' She put out one hand now and felt the twisted surface of the stones to the side of them, and coming to a crevice she put her hand in and pulled gently, then a little harder, and when she felt the stone was tightly fixed she said again, 'Look, if you could put your hand in here and hang on for a few minutes, I . . . I could rake some stones and props from along there and build up under you so as you could rest. It's . . . it's the way you are lying that's hurtin' you. Can you do it?'

He twisted his body round and her hand guided his into the small cleft, and now he muttered, 'Yes, yes; go ahead.'

Like a mole now she scrambled here and there and pulled the loose debris towards him. Once she lost her direction and when, feeling the wall again, her hands didn't find him she yelled, 'Where are you?'

'I'm . . . I'm here.' His voice came from just to the side of her, not an arm's length away, and she gasped as if in relief and stumbled towards him, dragging two broken props.

As she gradually built up the mound she kept easing him upwards, saying, 'Is that better?' and when he didn't give her any answer she knew that the angle of the stones was still not right.

Not until she had built up the support until it had almost reached her waist did he say, 'Yes, that's better, thank you, thank you.'

'Is . . . is the pain any easier?'

'Yes, yes, it's bearable now. It's . . . it's mostly down my right side; I don't feel much at all in the left leg.'

'Well, your right is just caught a little bit just round the ankle.'

'It's . . . it's likely cramp.'

'Yes, yes, it could be cramp, sir.'

She slumped down exhausted by the side of the pile, and presently he said, 'Where are you, Trotter?'

'I'm here, sir.'

'Would . . . would you give me your hand, Trotter?'

'Yes, sir.' She put her hand out gropingly towards him, but when she felt his fingers entwine with hers she could feel her change of colour even in the darkness. Just a short while ago she had been holding him, his face had been pressed into her neck, and his head had lain between her breasts, but that contact was different from this. He had asked to hold her hand.

'Hands are comforting things, don't you think, Trotter?'

'We'd ... we'd come badly off without them, sir.' She felt she had said something funny and she smiled in the darkness, and as if he had seen her smile he answered, 'Indeed we would, Trotter. Indeed we would. How old are you, Trotter?'

'Coming up eighteen, sir.'

'I never knew you were in the mine. In fact if I had known this was your intention I would have endeavoured to put you off.'

'I ... I needed work, sir.'

'Yes, I can understand that, but this is the lowest type of work for a woman, and I shouldn't think you're suited to it.'

'They tell me I'm quite good at it, sir.'

'How long have you been here?'

'Since three days after I left the Manor, sir.'

He didn't speak for some minutes and then he said, 'I should have seen to you but ... but as you know the house was in an upheaval.'

'Yes, sir. Oh, I understand, sir.'

'Why didn't you go to the farm to your friend Bentwood? He was a friend, wasn't he?'

'Yes, sir.'

'You stayed there after the fire, didn't you?'

'Only for a short time, sir. I ... I left the day me grandma was buried. I went back to the cottage. That's ... that's when you found me there and kindly offered me the post.'

'But ... but why couldn't you stay on the farm? I am sure he could have found you something to do. I thought about that at the time. Why didn't you?'

When she didn't answer he said, 'I'm ... I'm sorry, I appear to be probing into something.'

Her fingers were now gripped so tightly that she wanted to cry out, and when the darkness was filled with a long shuddering groan she got to her knees; then putting out her other arm, she placed it around his shoulders and held him to her, saying, 'There, there. There, there.'

'Oh-my-God!' He released the grip on her hand and she put it up to his face. It was running with sweat. Tears in her eyes now and in her voice, she said, 'If only I could do something for you.'

It was a long moment before he answered, 'You are doing something for me, Trotter, you're here. There ... there, it's gone, I don't feel anything at all now. It just comes in spasms. I ... I suppose I'm not used to pain. When I come to think of it, I've never been ill in my life. Toothache yes. I ... I once had two teeth pulled and I remember I raised Cain. ... What is it? What is it? Oh, please, don't cry. Now, now, don't cry like that. Look –' his hand was on her cheek now and his voice was soft as he said, 'What am I going to do if you fail me? I shouldn't have thought you were the kind to have vapours, Trotter?'

'N ... no, sir; I'll never have the vapours.'

'Good; I really didn't think you would. Sit by me and rest. You know I ... I don't think we should be talking, they say it uses up the oxygen. But ... but the air seems quite clear. What do you think?'

She sniffed and said, 'Yes. Yes, sir, it does since the dust's settled. Would there be any way fresh air could get in, sir?'

He thought a moment before he answered, 'No, I don't think so, Trotter, not from inside anyway. If this fall is not too thick and it hasn't affected the main roadway there's a chance there might be a crevice among the stones. Yet – ' his voice sank almost to a whisper as he ended, 'I think that's too long a shot to hope for.'

The grip of his fingers slackened once more and she realised he had fallen asleep again, but now she made no effort to rouse him because she, too, was feeling tired and she told herself she'd have a doze for a little while, it would do her good, and also pass the time until she heard them knocking, because that's what they did, the rescuers, they knocked on the stones and you answered.

How many times had he said he was dry during these last hours, or was it days? It must be days. Her head was muzzy, she wanted to sleep. It was some time ago that he had said, 'The air's going, Trotter, start knocking again.'

She had knocked for a short time, but she had no strength in her arms now, they didn't seem to belong to her, she just wanted to sleep. But when she fell asleep she was always awakened by his groaning. He didn't cry out loudly any more, he just groaned, and when it went on too long she forced herself to kneel and hold him.

She was holding him now and he was gasping for breath. She no longer said, 'Does it hurt?' or 'They'll come soon, sir', and when his words came slow and soft, as if pressed down by the atmosphere, saying, 'I ... I think the end is almost near, Trotter,' she did not contradict him, for she knew within herself the end was almost near. But somehow she wasn't afraid, she would be warm if she was dead. She felt sure of that, warm all the time. Not like now, burning one minute and cold the next, but just warm and comfortable.

'It's all right. Sit down, you're tired. Just give me your hand.'

She slumped down again while keeping hold of his hand.

'Do you believe in God, Trotter?'

'I don't know, sir. Sometimes yes and sometimes not. My ... my granny did, and granda too.'

'They were a nice couple.'

'Yes, yes, they were.'

'Trotter.'

'Yes?' She was aware that she wasn't adding 'sir' so much now when she answered him, but what did it matter?

'I'm going to tell you something. I ... I was lonely this morning. Or was it yesterday, or some other time? But I remember I was lonely, and now I don't feel lonely any more. Strange, but I don't.'

'That's good,' she said wearily. She wished he would stop talking so she wouldn't have to answer. She felt a bit sick, more than a bit sick, she was feeling bad, real bad.

As if he had heard her wish he said no more, and after a time she forced herself to kneel up and to put her ear towards his mouth to see if he were still breathing. And when she slumped down again it was to ponder on the thought that the reverence she seemed to have had for him while in the Manor was gone. He could have been the check weighman or the agent or Sam. . . . Sam had wanted to marry her, he had told her so, and contrary to what she had said to Simon her reply had been no, and a definite no, even though she had said it in a nice way telling him that she didn't want to marry anybody yet, but that she liked him. And in answer to a further question he had put to her, she had said, no, she hadn't anybody in her eye. Sam would be very sorry about her going. Would Simon? Yes, oh yes, Simon would be sorry. And he'd blame himself. Anyway, why bother to think. Her teeth were chattering again. Why was she cold? It wasn't cold in here, anything but. She moved slightly to make her position easier on the stones because the way he was holding her hand her arm was being pressed against the jagged end of a prop. Then a most strange thing happened: the wall of rock just below where the master's feet must be pinned opened and out stepped her granny and granda, and they came and sat one each side of her and she felt a happiness that she hadn't experienced before. And it didn't matter that they didn't speak or answer her questions, they were there.

It was three and a half days before the rescuers got through to them, and the way hadn't been made through the fall of stone. This would have been impossible because the fall had blocked the main road too. They came through the side of the drift, just a foot to the side of where the last prop had been pulled from the roof.

When they found them they knew it was impossible to remove Mark Sopwith without amputating both feet, in fact one leg below the knee. As for the girl, she was still breathing when they brought her out but they thought there was little chance that she would live. They carried her through the crowd lining the bank; sightseers had come from as far away as Newcastle and Gateshead because it wasn't every day that the owner of a mine got a taste of what his men often got. Such was the feeling.

It was as they placed Tilly in a covered cart that Biddy pushed her way forward and demanded, 'Where are you takin' her?'

'The hospital, the workhouse hospital in Shields.'

She turned and looked at Sam; then they both stood and watched the tail board being put into place.

'Has she got a chance?' It was Katie now speaking to one of the men, and his answer was, 'Hard to say, lass, but I doubt it. The only good thing that can be said for her is she's whole, unlike the boss who's lost his feet.'

'My God!' The murmur carried the news round the crowd.

When half an hour later they moved the closely wrapped form of Mark into the daylight an open landau was waiting with planks laid from door to door, and a mattress on top of these; and so with one man at each horse's head and another two supporting the temporary platform on which Mark now lay, they slowly drove him home.

PART THREE

The Workings
of the Witch

ᥫᩚ 1 ᥫᩚ

For one full week he existed in a nightmare in which he imagined that he had no feet. As a child he had been subject to bad dreams; an unknown fear would overtake him and when he went to scream no sound came and he would wake up sweating, the bed clothes in a heap about him.

As he grew older the intervals between the nightmares lengthened but the intensity remained, and in some way his mind had taught him to recognise the experience of the nightmare when in the midst of it and he would wake himself up, saying, 'It's only a dream. It's only a dream.'

But now the nightmare had been with him solidly for seven days and when he was in the midst of it he would yell at himself, 'It's only a dream. It's only a dream,' but unlike his awakening in years past he now recognised the nightmare as real, and not being able to bear the thought he forced himself to descend into the phantasy of the dream again. When on the seventh day he could no longer dream he made himself look down the bed towards the hump of the wire cage that covered the place where his feet should be and, even now clinging to his dream, he told himself they must be there because they were paining.

As he gazed down the coverlet a strange face intruded itself in front of the cage and a strange voice said, 'Ah! we're awake. There now, you feel better this morning?'

He looked up at the bulbous bosom covered in a white starched apron and at the round face above it topped by the frilled white cap, but he made no reply, and the voice went on, 'Now we'll have some soup, won't we?'

A minute later he almost screamed aloud as the nurse, her arms underneath his oxters, attempted to prop him up against his pillows. What he did was to take his hands and with all the strength he could gather push violently at her; and as she reeled away the set smile slipped from her face and, indignantly, she said, 'Now! now! I was only trying to make you comfortable.'

'Well, don't do it like a dray horse.' His voice sounded strange to his ears – it was hoarse, cracked.

'Doctor Kemp is on his way up,' she said stiffly.

His answer was to turn an almost ferocious glance on her. There was a wild anger inside of him, he wanted to claw, smash, rend. He looked down at his hands where his fingers like talons were grabbing up fistsful of the silk counterpane.

The door opened and Simes stood aside and ushered Doctor Kemp into the room.

The doctor was a small man. He looked robust, jolly and well fed, and his voice matched his appearance in heartiness. 'Well! well! now this is better, we are really awake at last. Well done! nurse. You've got him looking bright and. . . .'

'Shut up!'

Both the doctor and the nurse stared at him in amazement and when he added, 'Get out!' while flicking a finger in the direction of the nurse, Doctor Kemp put in, 'Now! now! what's all this about?'

'Oh my God!' Mark now lay back on the pillow, grabbed the front of his head with outstretched hand and cried, 'Don't ask such bloody silly questions.' And glaring again at the nurse, he said, 'Did you hear me? Get out.' And on a wave of indignation the nurse went out.

'That isn't very kind.' Doctor Kemp's face was straight. 'Nurse Bailey has looked after you very well this last week.'

Had he been conforming to pattern Mark should have said, 'I'm sorry,' but what he did say was, 'Tell me about this?' stabbing his finger towards the bottom of the bed.

'Ah well, it had to be done.'

'Why? In the name of God, why? Couldn't they have removed the stones?'

'Yes, they could' – Doctor Kemp's voice was as loud as Mark's now – 'but you would have been dead by the time they got you out, along with those attempting to move the fall from the inside. I did what I had to do.'

'You did it then?'

'Yes, yes, I amputated, and only just in time. They were going rotten on you, man. You'll be lucky even now, let me tell you, if you get off without gangrene setting in.'

'Thank you, thank you, that's good to know.'

'Well, you're alive, you should be grateful.'

'What! you've taken off my feet and you tell me I should be grateful!' The spittle ran down his chin as he finished, and he wiped it roughly off with the side of his hand.

'Life is life after all. It could have been worse.'

'Could it? Really! tell me how.'

'Yes, I'll tell you how.' The doctor was standing close to him now, his plump body pressed against the side of the high bed. 'You could have been blinded, as one of your men was three years ago; you could have been caught up to the hips with no hope of ever getting out of that bed again; but as it is you'll be able to get about on a wooden leg and with the help of crutches.'

Mark closed his eyes, then sank deeper into the pillows. Of a sudden his anger seemed to be seeping away with his strength, he felt tired. It seemed a long moment before he spoke again, and then he said, 'Eileen, I suppose she was told?'

'Yes.'

'But she hasn't been?'

'No. But your mother-in-law came. She stayed two days, but you didn't recognise her or anyone else at that time. I told her I would keep her informed, which I have done.'

'And Eileen didn't come?' The words were soft, almost as if spoken to himself, but the doctor answered, 'She's a sick woman, you must take that into account.'

Mark turned his head slowly and looked at Doctor Kemp, and he said, with almost a sneer on his face, 'I wish I were as well as she is at this moment. As for being sick, you know how sick she is, don't you, Doctor?'

'She has the usual woman's complaints.' The doctor had turned from the bed now and was going through his bag which he had placed on a table, and he said, 'I must have the nurse in, and if I may offer you advice I would say be civil to her because you're likely to be together for some weeks yet.'

Mark said nothing to this; instead, he asked, 'Were many killed?'

'No, no; only a girl.'

'A girl?' The word brought him up in the bed supporting himself on his stiffened arms and he turned towards the doctor and said, 'She died then, Trotter? Aw no! No!'

'No, it wasn't the girl Trotter, it was a small child, Pringle. Her father died almost in the same area three years ago, you remember?'

Yes, yes, he remembered. And so it was the small girl who had died, a child he had pulled out of the water. It was all coming back now like pictures shown by a magic lantern. Trotter, she had held him and comforted him. During all that time he had not seen her face but he could see her plainly in his mind's eye.

'The girl, Trotter, what happened to her? Was she all right?'

'No, she wasn't all right, and she still isn't. She got pneumonia.'

'Where is she now?'

'The hospital, the House hospital in Shields.'

He lay back on his pillows again. The workhouse hospital. He knew what that was like. And she had pneumonia. Pneumonia needed care. She had come through that dreadful ordeal in the black hole only to die under the rough care that one would receive in the workhouse hospital.

'Nurse.' Doctor Kemp was calling, and when the nurse entered the room the atmosphere became chilly indeed.

It was when the examination was over, the bandages changed, and Nurse Bailey was handing the dish of blood-stained wrappings through the half opened doorway to Amy Stiles that Mark said in an undertone, 'I would prefer a man to look after me.'

'You have a man at nights, Simes is with you then, but you require a nurse. And I have great faith in Nurse Bailey, so be a good fellow and be civil to her.'

Just before the doctor left, Mark said, 'The mine, how is it?' and Doctor Kemp busied himself with his bag for some seconds before he answered. 'There's plenty of time to go into that,' he said; 'you get your strength back and then you can deal with those matters. Now be a good fellow.' He nodded towards him as if to a small boy, then went out, followed by the nurse, and Mark, lying back exhausted, said half aloud, 'Well, that's the end of that then. The end of so many things.?' Then presently he added, 'Pity I didn't let Rosier carry half the weight after all.'

╭∾ 2 ∾╮

When Tilly saw the tall figure of Biddy Drew marching up the narrow ward she half rose from the stool by the side of her bed before sinking back on to it again, but when Biddy stood over her her hands were extended out to greet her.

'Aw, Mrs Drew, it's good to see you.'

'An' you, lass, an' you.'

Their joined hands wagged up and down for a moment. Then straightening herself, Biddy looked about the ward, sniffed hard, and shook her head before she exclaimed, 'My God! lass, Katie said it was bad, the smell's worse than our middens.'

'You get used to it.'

When Biddy went to sit down on the side of the bed Tilly hissed quietly, 'You're not allowed to sit on the bed, Mrs Drew, they . . . they don't like it.'

'Well, like it or not, lass, I'm gettin' off me legs for a minute,' and so saying, she sat down.

Tilly, smiling weakly at her, moved her head as she said, 'Oh, 'tis good to see you.'

'I would have come afore this but I've been hard pushed. Still, Katie an' Sam have kept me posted as to how you're going on. By! you were thin afore, lass, but you'd make a good clothes' prop now.

'Yes, I would, wouldn't I. . . . How are things?'

'Not much better, lass, I'm sorry to say, except that Sam's been set on· in a candle factory. But what he's gettin' there won't keep him in shoe leather. 'Tis a bad time of the year for work for anybody, the winter.' She now leant forward and gripped Tilly's wrist as she said, 'I want to thank you, lass, for lettin' us have what was in your bundle. It saw us through a couple of weeks, it was a godsend. And I'll repay you sometime, I will, I promise you I will.'

'You've repaid me already, Mrs Drew; you gave me a home when I needed one badly.'

'Aye, well, that's what I've come about the day. When are you coming back to it?'

'Well, they told me I can only stay in the ward another two or three days and then I've got to go into the House.'

'You're goin' into no house, except me own. The House indeed!' She tossed her head. 'I've heard about the House, an' my God! this is bad enough.'

'Most of them are old people.'

'I can see that, lass.'

'Anyway, I suppose I should be grateful they pulled me round. By the way, how did you get here? Did you walk all that way?'

'Well, I set out to walk, lass, but I was lucky, there was a cart passin' takin' stuff into the market. It was from the Manor. One of the gardeners was driving it and he gave me a lift. All talk he was about the goin's on there.'

'Did . . . did he say how the master was?'

'Oh aye, he talked about little else. Turned out a real tartar, he was saying, going a bit off his head he thinks.'

'The master going off his head? No!'

'Well, that's what he said. Anyway, he's making himself felt, feet or no.'

At this Tilly bowed her head and bit on her lip, she couldn't bear to think of him without feet. She had lain at nights thinking about what he must have gone through when they cut them off and her thoughts had made her vomit.

'Sacked the nurse he did last week.' Biddy was laughing now. 'Threw something at her, the gardener said. There's war on in the house because everything's upside down. He has the footman looking after him and by all accounts he's not having a pleasant time of it either. Swears like a trooper, he says, and was never known to swear afore. Well, it seems that he's rousing them, and by what you told me afore, lass, it'll do some of them good. . . . Have you had anybody else to see you?'

'Yes; Steve came. You know the boy, Steve McGrath. And . . . and Simon, Mr Bentwood you know, the farmer, he's been every week.' She turned her head away and after a moment Biddy said quietly, 'And what does he propose to do for you, lass?'

She looked quickly up at the older woman and she saw that there was nothing that Biddy didn't guess at; then lowering her eyes again, she said, 'He . . . he wants to get me a room, or . . . or some place in Shields.'

'And what then?'

'What do you mean, Mrs Drew, what then?'

'You know what I mean, lass. Some farmers are still rich enough to afford a kept woman on the side, is that what you intend to be?'

'Oh no! No!' Tilly shook her head. 'I wouldn't, Mrs Drew.'

'I know you wouldn't, lass. Well, what you've got to do is, as soon as the doctor passes you clear of this ward, an' you say that's in a day or so, well then you've got to make your way back home. You can get the carrier cart from the market, that's if you can't get word to any of us to come an' fetch you. It'll take you beyond the village, not a mile from our door. Do you think you'll be able to manage that?'

'Oh yes, Mrs Drew, yes. And thank you. The journey can't come soon enough for me.'

They looked hard at each other, then gripped hands.

Three days later Tilly made the journey from the workhouse back to the pit row. She caught the carrier cart from the market place, but when she alighted at the turnpike road she felt that her legs wouldn't carry her as far as the house.

It was three o'clock in the afternoon and there was a slight flurry of snow falling. Before she was halfway there she'd had to stop several times and rest with her back against a tree or a stone wall or a gate leading into a field; and when eventually she arrived frozen and looking on the point of collapse, Biddy dragged off her outer clothes and her boots and chafed her frozen limbs all the while ordering those about her to put a hot brick in the bed, to put on the bone soup that was to be their evening meal to heat, and Tilly took all the ministrations' without uttering a word.

Within half an hour she was tucked up warmly on the shaky-down. And there she lay for the next few days. The day following her getting up, she was sitting before the fire when a knock came on the door, and when Biddy opened it there stood a young woman warmly dressed who said, 'I'm from the Manor, I'm Phyllis Coates, the master sent me an' . . . and Mr Leyburn.' She jerked her head to the side, indicating a man standing by the side of a coach. 'Could I have a word please with Tilly, Tilly Trotter?'

'Come in.' Biddy's voice was quiet. She was asking herself why she hadn't heard the coach coming up to the door. But then there was a thin hard-caked layer of snow on the ground. She looked towards the coachman before shutting the door; then she walked slowly towards the fire where the visitor was bending over Tilly.

'Hello, Tilly. How are you?'

'Oh, fine, fine, Phyllis. 'Tis nice to see you. It was good of you to call.'

'Well, I haven't come on me own.' She turned to where Biddy was pushing a wooden chair towards her and said, 'Ta . . . thanks'; then sitting down, she began rapidly, ''Tisn't me at all that should be here, 'tis Mrs Lucas, but . . . but she couldn't come. She made an excuse, the snow, but the master had given orders that she was to come and ask you to go and visit him.'

'Visit him?' The repeated words were a mere whisper.

'Yes' – Phyllis nodded – 'that was the order that came down from upstairs. It wasn't given to Simes, it was given to Pike and he told Mrs Lucas. But you don't look up to goin' for a drive, I'll say that straightaway.'

'I'm . . . I'm all right, Phyllis, just a bit wobbly on me legs.'

Tilly now watched Phyllis glance round the room, and her glance which took in Fanny, Jimmy, and Arthur, who were sitting close to one side of the dull fire, showed that she found the stark poverty distasteful.

'The master's kept in touch about your condition through Doctor Kemp, and . . . and he ordered Mrs Lucas to send you stuff from the kitchen. Of course you know I'm upstairs most of the time, and she said she did, but I've got me doubts . . . did she?'

'No, Phyllis, no, I've received nothing from the Manor.'

'Eeh! the old bitch.' Phyllis now turned and glanced at Biddy, saying, 'It's the housekeeper, she always had it in for Tilly here. But now she won't be able to do much 'cos the master wants to see her. Do you think she's fit to travel?'

Biddy seemed to consider for a moment. She looked down into Tilly's upturned face; then, as if making a decision, she said, 'We'll wrap you up, lass; you'll be riding all the way, you can't come to much harm. Come on, get on your feet.'

Tilly got on her feet, and Biddy bundled her into her coat and hat, and over her shoulders she placed her own shawl. A minute later when Tilly went to follow Phyllis out of the door she turned and, putting out her hand, she placed it on Biddy's chest, and Biddy, putting her own hand over it, said below her breath, 'Take whatever comes, lass, grab it with both hands; he's not just takin' the trouble to send for you to say it's a cold day.'

Tilly was not a little puzzled by Biddy's advice. Hadn't she warned her against accepting a room from Simon? Of course she couldn't mean the master was offering her anything like that, that was silly, but why had she said take what comes and grab it with both hands? Perhaps she was referring to money. But she hadn't done anything to be rewarded with money. Anyway, she'd know when she saw him, she'd know why he wanted to see her when she got there. . . .

As she was helped up the steps and through the lobby into the big hall there arose from some place within her, that was almost forgotten, a thread of laughter, merry laughter, sardonic laughter. She had been almost thrown out of the back door last year and here she was arriving in a coach. And being shown in through the front door! But her reception, she noted immediately, was anything but pleasant, because Mr Pike, who had always been civil to her, looked at her now with a face lacking even the slightest warmth. As for Mrs Lucas, who was standing at the bottom of the stairs, well, as Katie would have said, vinegar was sweet.

That there was little semblance left of the Tilly Trotter who had once worked in this house was evident when she came to a stop in the middle of the hall and, slowly pulling the shawl from around her shoulders, handed it to Mr Pike.

That the man was amazed by her brazen gesture she was well aware, and the thread of laughter widened in her as she stared at him for a moment ignoring the fact that Mrs Lucas was waiting and that Phyllis was looking at her open-mouthed. Yet as she looked at the butler, whose existence in comparison with those people living in the rows was one of high luxury, she found herself thinking the most odd thought. He wasn't alive. None of them here were alive, for they really knew nothing about life, not life as it was lived by those who grovelled in the bowels of the earth. That occupation made you savour life, life on the surface of the earth. Even if you only had skimmed milk and a crust and a few taties for your diet, you relished life in a way that these people knew nothing about.

Although her legs were wobbling beneath her long faded skirt, there came into her a strength that made her walk steadily towards Mrs Lucas and say, 'I understand the master wishes to see me?'

Mrs Lucas opened her mouth, then closed it again, turned and floated up the staircase without having to resort to holding the banister, as Tilly found she herself had to do before she was halfway to the landing

Then they were crossing the gallery and going down the wide west corridor. Presently Mrs Lucas paused, cast one glance in Tilly's direction before knocking on a door, then opened it and stood aside while Tilly passed her. She had not announced her in one way or the other but she stood long enough to hear her master, who was sitting in the long basket-chair in front of a blazing fire, exclaim loudly, 'Hello, Trotter. Well! hello.'

It was, as she said to them all in the kitchen a few minutes later, as if he were greeting an equal. She had never heard the likes of it, and it didn't portend good. Mark her words, it didn't portend good.

'Sit down. Sit down. Take off your coat. Simes, take Trotter's coat and hat. Sit down. Sit down.'

Just as she knew that she herself had changed during the past year, so she now recognised that the master had also changed, but within a shorter time, for his voice and manner now were different from those she had recognised in the dark; but then she told herself, he must have been changing since the time the mistress left him. In any case, there was one thing certain, he had changed.

After she was seated in the big chair opposite to him, he looked at her for a full minute before turning to the footman and saying, 'Leave us. Oh and by the way, tell Mrs Lucas to have tea sent up, a good tea, sandwiches, cake . . .'

'Yes, sir.'

When the door had closed on the footman, Mark leant forward and asked quietly, 'How are you, Trotter?'

'Quite well, sir.'

'Well, you don't look quite well. You were thin before, you're like a rake now.'

She laughed gently, then said, 'So I'm told, sir. Mrs Drew says she'll never be short of a clothes prop.'

He smiled widely, then said, 'You're staying with the Drews?'

'Yes, sir.'

'A bit crowded, isn't it?'

'Yes, 'tis a bit crowded. But they're good people; I'm happy there.'

She drew in a long breath then looked towards the fire, and she remained silent waiting for him to speak again. When he did it was to ask her a question. 'Did you ever think we'd see daylight, Trotter?'

'No, sir.'

'Nor me either.' And now his voice became a mutter as he ended, 'And I've wished more than once since that I hadn't.'

'Aw no, sir, no! don't say that.'

He turned his face towards her now and, his mouth smiling, he said, 'Can you remember all that transpired down there, Trotter?'

'Now I can, but at first when . . . when I was in hospital I couldn't call anything to mind except the blackness.'

'Yes, I think that was the hardest to bear, the blackness. You know the mine's finished, Trotter, flooded out?'

'So they tell me, sir.'

'And you know something else, Trotter?'

'No, sir.'

'I'm not sorry.' Again he looked towards the fire when he went on speaking: 'I must have been only half conscious most of the time but I remember you vividly. You talked to me like a mother.' His eyes came towards her again. 'You held me when I was yelling my head off, and God! how I yelled. That pain. Anyway, there's one thing certain, Trotter, I'll never own a mine again.'

'Oh. When the water goes down, sir, you could start it up.'

'Not me, Trotter, not me. I knew nothing about mines until I spent those days, and it was days, wasn't it? . . . three and a half days we were together down there. Well, that gave me a lifetime of experience of what men go through. No' – he shook his head slowly – 'I'm finished with mining. Let somebody else have it on their conscience but not me. I'm not strong enough to stand that kind of thing, I've got a weak stomach.' He laughed; then his face falling into lines that made him look almost like an old man, he sat staring at her, and she was so troubled by the sadness in his countenance that she wanted to extend her hand towards him, just as she had done in the darkness. But that would never do. No, that would never do.

'I sent for you, Trotter, for one or two reasons. First, because I wanted to see you and thank you for bringing me through that awful time.'

'Oh, sir, I didn't do . . .'

'Be quiet. Be quiet. I know what you did. But the other thing was, I wondered if you would be well enough to come to us over the holidays. I'm hoping to have the children here to see me. It might only be for two or three days but if you could. . . .'

'Oh, sir, yes; oh yes, sir, I would love that.' She moved forward on her chair and bent towards him eagerly as she said, 'Nothing would give me more pleasure, sir.'

'Good, good; that'll make me happy too. I'm longing to see them.'

'I can understand that, sir.'

'Of course we've got to take the weather into account, but I think we'll have a thaw and the roads will be clear. Ah' – he turned towards the door – 'here comes tea.'

Simes was entering the room carrying a large silver tray on which was set a silver tea service. He was followed by Amy Stiles. She was carrying a four-tiered cake stand on which there were plates of bread and butter, sandwiches and cakes. She set the stand down to the side of the table which was placed against the basket chair. She did not raise her eyes and look at Tilly, nor did Simes look at her, not even when the master said, 'That'll do; Trotter will see to me,' did they look in her direction.

When the door had closed on them, Mark, leaning towards her, said, 'Pretend you're back in the nursery and about to feed the five thousand.'

She smiled as she rose hastily to her feet, and after she had poured out the tea into the thin china cups she laid a napkin across the shawl that covered his legs, then handed him a small plate with one hand and extended the large plate of bread and butter towards him with the other. But he shook his head and said, 'I rarely eat at teatime,' and taking the bread plate from her, he poked his head towards her as he said softly, 'Tuck in.'

She wanted to act polite as her granny would have wished, but her stomach told her that politeness was stupid in this case, and so she tucked in. She had four pieces of bread and butter, she had three sandwiches and two pieces of cake, and as she ate she tried to do it delicately, not as her appetite bade her and gulp. She had never tasted food like this for months, and not even while she had worked in this house, for then the bread in the kitchen had been cut in collops. At one stage she became embarrassed that he didn't talk while she was eating but sat looking at her, and then he said, 'I hope you got all the things I sent you when in hospital?'

She swallowed deeply, staring at him, her mouth slightly agape; then the colour suffused her thin cheeks and she was about to say, 'Yes, thank you,' when he asked pointedly, 'You got the packages?'

She gulped again before she now said hesitantly, 'Yes thank you.'

'You didn't get them?'

She bowed her head, then turned and looked towards the window as she said, 'No, sir, I didn't get anything from you.'

'Bloody lot of thieves!'

It was strange to hear him swear, but in this moment he sounded very much like Sam when he was railing against the check weighman or the pit masters as a whole.

'Things go astray in a hospital, sir.'

'If my orders had been carried out, Trotter, these things would not have gone astray. I ordered special food to be sent four times, it was supposed to have been delivered to you.'

She watched him grind his teeth, then droop his head towards his chest as he said, 'Things are not right in this house. This is what happens when there's no mistress to take charge.'

As she stared at him she could have said – 'Things were happening like this when the mistress was here, sir,' but she doubted if he would have believed it.

'Well' – his head bobbed on his shoulder now – 'someone will pay for this, you mark my words.'

'Please, please, sir, I . . . I don't want to cause trouble. You see I've got to face this. They didn't like me when I was here, except Mr Leyburn and Phyllis, Phyllis Coates. The rumours from the village had followed me, about . . . about me being a witch, and things like that. They resented me, and at the same time, although it's hard to believe, sir, they were a bit afraid of me, and . . . and once or twice I played on that with Ada Tennant – she's the scullery maid you know.' She smiled now and for the first time she asked him a direct question, 'Do I look like a witch, sir?'

She saw his shoulders move, and then he began to chuckle before surprising her with his next remark. 'Yes, yes, you do, Trotter, you look very much like a witch, but a kind witch, a benevolent witch.'

'Oh, sir!'

'You charmed my children anyway into some semblance of order, especially when the rip went. Well now, to get back to the question of the children. I would like you to get the rooms prepared upstairs. I asked Mrs Lucas this morning if anything had been done up there of late and she had to admit that there hadn't. She put it down to the fact that they had all been very busy and concerned about me.' He pulled a slight face. 'I can smell an excuse a mile off. Yet' – he sighed now – 'I've got to admit we're very understaffed; for the size of this house we're very understaffed. You know, Trotter, in my father's time you couldn't move for maids and menservants, you were tripping over them. Ah well, those days are gone. Now' – he leaned back in the chair – 'when do you think you'll be fit to start?'

'Oh, any time, sir.'

'Well, I wouldn't say any time; by the look of you I think you are in need of a few more days' rest. Would you like to come here and take it? Your room is still vacant, I imagine, upstairs.'

'Oh no, sir, no, sir.' The words came at a rush. 'No; I'd better not come before I'm needed.'

He made no immediate answer, but stared at her for a long moment before saying, 'Someone of your disposition, Trotter, will always be needed. . . . Well, say three days' time?'

'Yes, sir.'

'In the meantime, by the look of you I think you need feeding up. Ring that bell there, will you?' He pointed to a thick twisted rope with tassels which was hanging to the side of the fireplace, and as she pulled it twice, which was the signal that he needed attention, she imagined she heard the clanging of the bell in the kitchen and the reluctant scurrying towards the stairs.

When Simes came into the room, Mark turned to him and said, 'I had chicken for lunch, I hardly touched it; tell cook to pack it up. And also the remains of the pressed tongue and a couple of jars of preserves. And tell Pike that I need a bottle of burgundy. When was the last baking done?'

'I . . . I wouldn't know, sir.'

'You're below stairs and you don't know when the cook was baking! Couldn't you smell it, man?'

'I . . . I think yesterday, sir.'

'Then tell her to send up a couple of loaves and cakes too, and bacon, a couple of pounds of it . . . the best end.'

'Yes, s . . . ir.' The words were spaced now, and when Simes was almost out of the door his master stopped him with, 'Wait! I want them packed in a hamper and brought up here. I wish to inspect them, you understand?'

Again the man said, 'Yes, sir.' But now the words were clipped and a slight agitation showed in his manner.

Tilly was sitting now on the edge of her chair. She was embarrassed; he was meaning all this food for her to take away with her. She should refuse it. But no, she wouldn't. She could see it all spread out on that bare wooden table; she could see the gleam in the eyes of the youngsters, especially when they saw the cakes. But mingled with her embarrassment was a certain bewilderment, she was puzzled by his manner. All the time she had been in this house before she had never heard him speak to the servants as he was doing today. But then she had never heard him talk as he was talking now. As she had thought earlier, he was a different man from the master she had respected, and an altogether different man from the one she had come to know down in the darkness. There was a roughness about him, and a hardly suppressed anger.

Her eyes resting on the foot of the chair where the cover, instead of being supported by the toes of two feet, dropped smoothly over the edge, she thought sadly that it was because of his feet he was fighting inside of himself, because of his feet he was taking it out of the staff, likely because there was nobody else to take it out on. None of his own people were with him. That was sad. Why didn't the mistress come back? She was no woman to leave him like this alone. Granted she was poorly, but her presence would have been a comfort to him.

'What are you thinking, Trotter? You're miles away.'

Caught off her guard, she turned her eyes quickly from the foot of the chair and said, 'Oh, something that me granny used to say.'

'What was it?'

What did her granny say? Her granny had so many sayings. 'Well, she used to say, when one door shuts another one opens.'

'And you think one has opened for you?'

She smiled brightly now, knowing she could say in truth, 'Yes, sir. This time last week the future looked pretty black, no work, nothing, and now I'm to have my old job back, well, just for a short while. But ... but I'm very grateful. And yes, as me granny would have said, the door has opened for me, sir.'

His face was straight and his eyes looked blank as he said now, 'The people in the rows are all out of work, what are they doing?'

'Travellin' the road, sir, looking for jobs. Sam, he was one of your hewers, perhaps you won't remember him, but he was the one that Mr Rosier sacked because he was learning to read.'

'Oh yes, yes, I remember him all right.'

'Well, he's got work in a candle factory. It's nothin' compared to the mine but ... but it's something. The fear among them is of being turned out on to the road and. ...' Her eyes widened, her mouth fell into a slight gape – she had forgotten for a moment to whom the cottages belonged. When she closed her mouth and gulped he reminded her of the very words. He gave a slightly mirthless laugh as he said, 'You forgot for the moment, Trotter, didn't you, you were talking to the landlord?'

Her head was down and she said, 'Yes, yes, I did, sir.'

'Well, you can tell them they're safe for a time, until the place is sold. In any case, whoever takes over might start the mine up again.' He made a jerking movement now and brought himself up straight in the chair and, leaning well forward towards her, he said, 'Don't pass that on, Trotter, I mean about anybody taking the place over.'

'No, sir, I won't.'

'You give them the assurance that they're not going to be turned out but ... but the fact that I may eventually sell the place, well that slipped out, you understand?'

'Oh yes, sir; yes, sir; I'll say nothing about that.'

'Ah! at last.' He turned and looked to where Simes was entering the room carrying a weighty hamper, and he said to him, 'Place it down there,' pointing to the floor between the basket chair and Tilly's feet; then without looking at the man, he said, 'Tell Leyburn to have the coach round in ... well, what shall we say?' He looked towards the window. 'It's getting dark, say fifteen minutes' time. Then you return and take this hamper downstairs and place it in the coach.' He paused now, then looking up quickly into Simes's face, he said, 'You heard what I said, Simes, didn't you? Place ... it ... in ... the ... coach.'

The man's face was red, his manner definitely troubled.

The door closed again. 'Well now,' he said, 'take what's left on that stand, Trotter, and put it in the hamper.'

'Oh, sir, there's enough.'

'Do as I tell you, girl.'

She did as he told her, and then she closed the lid and, rising from her knees, she looked down at him as she said softly, 'Thank you, sir. I'm grateful, so grateful.'

When he held out his hand she placed hers in it, and as he shook it gently he said, 'If I remember, we prepared to die like this, didn't we, Trotter?'

There was a lump in her throat. 'Yes, sir; we did that.'

'You're a good girl, Trotter.'

'Oh, sir.' She shook her head, holding back the tears; then turning quickly, she picked up her hat and coat and after she had placed the hat squarely on her head and buttoned up the coat to the neck she sat down once again on the edge of the chair waiting, and he, quiet now, sat looking at her.

She was so young, so thin, so poorly clad, but there was something about her face that was ageless; it was a kind of knowledge in the back of her eyes. It was the eyes that gave off the witch impression, he supposed. They were deep brown yet clear like pebbles that had been constantly washed by the sea, no impurity in them. She could have been his daughter born between Harry and Matthew. She intensified the longing he had to see his children, to hold Jessie Ann in his arms again. The anger that had subsided during this last hour or so rose for a moment and he cried inside, 'Damn! Blast her to hell! She's cruel, cruel.' Why hadn't she come back? Any woman worth her salt knowing the predicament he was in would have returned, if only to lie on her chaise-longue again. He had the dreadful feeling he was going to cry. He blinked and turned a thankful glance as the door opened and Simes came in once more.

Tilly was on her feet now. 'Good-bye, sir,' she said, 'and thank you so much. I'll ... I'll be here on Monday.'

'Good, good. Thank you, Trotter. I'll have the coach sent for you.'

She wanted to say, 'There's no need, sir, I can walk'; instead, she remained silent and inclined her head by way of acknowledging his kindness. Then she went out, followed by Simes carrying the hamper.

There was no one in the hall, Biddy's shawl was lying across the back of a carved hall chair standing between the windows. She picked it up and placed it around her shoulders. There was no butler to open the door, and she noted that Simes had to place the heavy hamper on the floor before he undid the latch of the front door. Then so hard did he push it back that it hit the wall with a resounding bang.

Fred Leyburn was standing on the gravel drive awaiting her approach. He had taken the hamper from Simes and placed it inside the coach, and now he held out his hand and assisted her up the step, and as he did so, he murmured, 'Be careful, madam,' and when from under her lashes she looked at him, he winked broadly at her, which made her almost fall on to the seat. She had a most inordinate desire to laugh, yet she knew it wouldn't remain ordinary laughter but would be the kind of laughter that finished up with her crying.

A door had opened just a little bit; she somehow sensed it could swing wide, and if it did, as Mrs Drew had advised, she was going to take whatever came through it and grab it with both hands.

৩ 3 ৩

'It's a bloody conspiracy.'

'Don't you dare use that language in my presence, Mark Sopwith!'

'Well, it is. If you could travel the road why couldn't the children?'

'Because as I told you both Luke and Jessie Ann have developed whooping cough.'

'Well, in that case I say again, Matthew and John would be well out of it.'

'Doctor Fellows advised strongly against it. Anyway, you have Harry coming for the holidays, you won't be alone.'

'Harry is a grown-up man, I want my children around me. . . . She's done this on purpose, hasn't she, just to spite me?'

'Don't be so childish, Mark. Really! you have become impossible. She was very concerned for you.'

'Huh! she's shown it. If she was concerned she would have been back here.'

'She's in no state to see to an invalid.'

'She wouldn't be expected to see to me, and well you know it; but she should be here.'

'What! and countenance your mistress?'

'Hell's flames, woman!' He tossed his head from one side to the other; then grabbing a book from the table he flung it across the room, bawling, 'I've no mistress! It was finished long before she got wind of it.'

Jane Forefoot-Meadows stood with her hand gripping the black velvet bow pinned to the top of her plum velvet dress. That she was shocked and not a little frightened was evident, and she stood speechless staring at her son-in-law while he, his head bowed, muttered now, 'I'm sorry, I'm sorry, only I'm so damned lonely here, Mother-in-law.' He lifted his head now and looked at her and asked quietly, 'Have you any idea what my life is like? The contrast is too much to take at once, a house buzzing with children's voices and a complaint every time I open the door about one or other of them being up to their tricks, then an almost empty house; well, empty of every person that mattered to me. That was bad enough but I was able to get out, go to work, ride, move' – his voice was rising again – 'but now!' He turned his hand palm upwards and held it out towards the bottom of the long chair. 'I tell you, Mother-in-law, sometimes I feel I'll go mad.'

'Doesn't anyone visit you?' Her voice was soft now, her tone sympathetic.

'One or two, the men; but they always come alone, they never bring their wives. Sometimes I want to laugh, but most times' – his head drooped – 'I just curse.'

'I've noticed that in the short time I've been with you. Yes, I've noticed that.' Her voice was astringent again. 'You never used to use such language.'

He looked up at her, and with a twisted smile on his face he said, 'Yes, I did, but not in front of you or the children.' And now he put out his hand. 'Forgive me. I . . . I appreciate what you've done in coming yourself, I do really.'

She came and sat beside him and asked, 'When is Harry coming?'

'The day after tomorrow I think. He was here the first two or three days after they found me but I didn't know much about it. It was no use him staying; he couldn't do anything and he had accepted an invitation at the end of term to go to France with a friend of his. But by his last letter he should be here two or three days before Christmas.'

'That'll be nice; you won't be alone.'

'No, I won't be alone.'

They sat in silence for a few minutes, and then she said, 'Doctor Fellows is looking into the business of – ' She stopped embarrassed, and he prompted, 'Yes? Tell me. About the feet?' She wetted her lips and inclined her head; then said, 'Yes. But he thinks it might be six months or more; what I mean is, they can't do very much until the wounds are . . . well, healed.'

'Yes, I understand.'

'There is a man in Scarborough who has been fitted with a complete leg' – she was nodding at him now, warming to her theme – 'and no one would ever believe it, you can't tell which is the real and which is the artificial one. Of course, in your case it will be slightly more difficult because. . . .'

'Yes, yes, Mother-in-law,' he interrupted her, closing his eyes tightly.

'Oh. Oh well, I was only trying to tell you.'

'I know. I know.' He nodded slowly.

There came a tap on the door and after he had called, 'Come in,' the opening door revealed Tilly, but she stopped when she saw Mrs Forefoot-Meadows.

'Come along in. Come along in, Trotter,' Mark called to her. 'I've disappointing news for you. Mrs Forefoot-Meadows has just come to tell me that Jessie Ann and Luke have caught the whooping cough, and so, of course, none of them will be able to travel.'

'Oh!' Her face registered her disappointment. 'Oh, I am sorry.'

'This is Trotter, Mother-in-law.' He turned to Jane Forefoot-Meadows. 'You may remember, she was the children's nurse.'

If Jane Forefoot-Meadows did remember she showed no recognition, she merely inclined her head and said, 'Oh yes.'

'She is also the young woman who was incarcerated with me down below; she was the one who kept me sane during those three and a half eternities we spent together.' He turned and smiled at Tilly, but Tilly did not answer his smile; she was looking at Mrs Forefoot-Meadows and Mrs Forefoot-Meadows at her.

Again Mrs Forefoot-Meadows said, 'Oh yes,' and on this Tilly turned and took her leave. But she had not reached the door when Mark, twisting his body round in the chair, called to her, 'I'll send for you later, Trotter; stay put until I call you.'

She inclined her head and went out, then stood on the landing looking first one way then the other. Nothing was straightforward, nothing turned out as you expected. The door wasn't opening after all. She let out a long shuddering breath and went towards the stairs that led to the nursery floor.

It was almost twenty-four hours later when Mark sent for her. Except for the time it took her to go down the stairs and empty the slops, she had remained in the nursery quarters. Her meals had been brought up to her, though reluctantly it would seem from the attitude of the bearer, whether it was Ada Tennant or Maggie Short, neither of the girls had a word to say to her, they even scurried from her presence as if they were indeed expecting a curse to be put upon them.

It was Simes who summoned her to the floor below. Both his manner and his voice were offensive. He had thrust open the schoolroom door as if expecting to find her at a disadvantage in some way; then jerking his head at her in much the same way as Mrs Lucas did, he said, 'You're wanted down below,' and stood staring at her as she rose from the schoolroom table and closed the book she was reading. He watched her as she went to the rack and replaced the book on the shelf. This was another thing that made her different and feared, she could read, not only headlines from a newspaper but apparently books like those in the library down below.

She did not turn immediately from the bookshelf, she knew he was standing watching her, but when she did confront him, her back straight, her voice firm and, she imagined, in a good imitation of Mrs Ross, she said, 'Very well, thank you.' The thank you was a dismissal, and it must have brought his lips tight together for he went out banging the door after him.

Her back no longer straight, she leant over the table and looked down at her hands pressed flat on it and asked of them why they should all hate her so, she had done nothing to bring it about. But there was one thing certain, she would never be able to do anything to make them change their attitude towards her.

When she entered Mark's room he was again sitting in the long basket-chair opposite the blazing fire, and he smiled at her; but it was a thin smile expressing weariness, and when she stood at the foot of the chair and looked at him, he said slowly, 'Come and sit down,' indicating with a lift of his hand a chair by his side.

When she was seated he said, 'Yesterday you looked almost as disappointed as I was.'

'I was, sir, very disappointed.'

'My mother-in-law has promised me faithfully that, weather permitting, she'll bring at least one of them on her next trip this way.'

'That'll be nice.'

He laid his head back against the cushion now and his voice was merely a mutter as he said, 'But that won't be for some time; the roads will get worse before they're better.'

She nodded. 'She's a very brave lady to have made the journey, her being so – ' She stopped, she had almost said 'old'; and now he turned his face towards her and smiled widely as he said, 'You nearly said old, didn't you? My! my! Trotter, you must not even think of that term with regard to my mother-in-law, else all her paint and powder will be wasted. But nevertheless, I've got to agree with you, for her age, which I won't mention, it was very brave of her to make

the journey and without her maid. Yes, without her maid. And now about you.'
She moved uneasily on the chair.
'What will you do if you go back to . . . the Drews?'
'Look for some work, sir. That's all I can do.'
'What will you say if I offer you a post here?'
Her eyes widened for a moment and then, her lids drooping, she moved her head slowly as she answered, "Twould be no use, sir; they wouldn't accept me, them down below, the staff.'
'Because of the witch business?'
'I suppose so, sir. There's something about me they don't like.' She lifted her hand in a gesture that implied she couldn't understand the reason.
'Bloody ignorant fools!' he said; then added, 'But what if I was to say to you you'd have a position of authority over them, as Price had. Oh, I knew all about Price's authority, she even dominated Mrs Lucas, didn't she? Well, let me put it to you like this. Simes sees to my wants. Now between you and me' – his voice fell to a whisper and he leant his head towards her – 'I don't care for Simes; he's a subservient individual. You know what subservient means, Trotter?'
She paused thinking. Mr Burgess had used that word, she had heard him explain its meaning to the children. She couldn't remember the word he had put in its place but she knew the meaning of it. She was smiling as she said, 'A crawler, sir.'
As his laugh rang out, her smile widened into what could only be described as a grin, and for a moment she felt utterly happy she had said something to make him laugh. Now if she could only remember some of the things that were said in the Drews' kitchen and caused roars. But he was talking about her position. . . . Her position. She became astounded as she listened to him.
'I had a nurse at the beginning. I didn't like her either. She talked and acted like a sergeant-major and she treated me as if I were still in binders and of the same age mentally. And I cannot talk to Simes – you can't talk to somebody you don't like – but I can talk to you, Trotter. It's strange this. I asked myself last night why it was I could talk to you, but I couldn't find the answer, for after all you haven't much to say. Now, have you?'
'Well, 'tisn't my place, sir.'
'No, Trotter, it isn't your place.' He sighed. 'Haven't we gone through this before? I remember faintly discussing place with you down there. Perhaps I'm mistaken. Anyway, what would you say if I asked you to forget your place and speak first for a change. Tell me what you think, about anything' – he spread his arms wide – 'this, that or the other, just so the time will pass.'
She stared at him for a moment before she said, 'Have you thought about engaging Mr Burgess again?'
'Burgess? Now why would I want to engage Burgess? I think I'm past the learning stage. I know my letters, at least I think I do.' He made a slight face at her, and she smiled as she answered, "Twas for conversation, sir; Mr Burgess talks well. I used to like to listen to him talking to the children, he made the simplest things sound . . . well, interestin' like. I could have listened to him for hours. He gave me books to read and. . . .'
'Burgess gave you books to read. . . . And you read them?'

'Some of them, sir. Others were beyond me. The first one ... well, I can't understand it yet.'

'What was the title?'

The title. She thought a moment, then said, '*Can ... did ... de.*'

'*Candide*. My God! he never gave you that. Voltaire's *Candide*? Oh, really!'

'Well, he said it was a great adventure and when I told him I couldn't understand it, he said he didn't expect me to, not yet, only if I'd read it once a month for twenty years.'

Again Mark put his head back and laughed, saying now, 'The old fool.'

'I liked him.' Her voice had a flat note to it. 'He was very kind to me and I learned things from him.'

'I'm sorry Trotter.' His voice was flat too now. 'That remark was meant in a most kindly way. Burgess, I'm sure, is a very wise man. . . . So you'd like me to engage him merely to talk?'

'Well, not only to talk, sir; perhaps he could look after you. He's not all that old; well, what I mean is not too old to work; he can't be seventy.'

Mark stared at her. Not too old to work, he can't be seventy. Strange, but he felt he was learning from this girl as she must have learned from old Burgess. 'You might have hit on something there, Trotter,' he said, 'I'll think about it. But now back to you. How about you taking on the position of nurse-cum-matron-cum-dictator of the first floor?'

She half rose from the chair but his hand on her knee pressed her down again and when she began, 'They wouldn't have it, sir, they'd. . . .' he interrupted, 'To hell with them, Trotter! Am I master here or not?'

'Oh yes, sir.'

'Well, if I say you're in charge of me and of this room and of all that goes on above the kitchen level, then that's how things will be. So what do you say?'

'Oh! sir, I ... I can't say anything. It's just too big, too much.'

'Too big, you say? Well, do you think you're big enough to tackle it, and them?' He flung his hand outwards towards the door.

Their glances held, she felt her back straightening, her chin tucking in. The door had opened. Was she going through it? Automatically she placed one hand on top of the other, palm upwards in her lap, very much as she had seen Mrs Lucas do when she was going to lay down the law, and now her face unsmiling but her eyes bright, she said, 'I'll be grateful to accept the post, sir.'

'Done! Done, Trotter. Well, if nothing else we'll have some excitement in the house during the next few days. What do you say?'

His words almost took the stiffness from her back and lifted her hands from her lap. Yes, indeed there would be excitement. They would lead her a hell of a life; they'd make things unbearable for her. . . . But only if she let them. Yes, only if she let them. And with the master behind her, well, she couldn't fail. Or could she? Could she bear the hostility that would rise up from the kitchen quarters and the servants' hall like black suffocating vapour from a midden bog?

When his hand suddenly came on hers she started visibly, and then her eyelids blinked rapidly as he went on, 'When a girl who was entrapped in darkness had the courage not to show her fear but to give her attention to someone who was in dire need of it at the time and to go on doing it for days, well, I would think she would have enough courage to face a few mean-minded people. What do you say?'

She swallowed deeply before answering. 'Aye, sir; you would think so.'

They now smiled at each other. Then briskly, he said, 'You'll have to have a uniform and decent clothes. You'll go into Shields tomorrow or wherever Mrs Lucas deals and fit yourself out. And by the way, go now and tell her I wish to see her. . . . You afraid?'

'No, sir.' She rose to her feet, paused for a moment to look down on him, then walked from the room, her brisk step denying the tremor inside her.

As he watched the door close behind her he lay back and his body slumped into the pillows and he closed his eyes. The days wouldn't be so long from now on; part of the loneliness would lift. Her very presence took him out of himself, and what was more, he was going to enjoy the war that was impending.

Of a sudden a deep, almost shameful sadness enveloped him. His mental state must be very low if the only thing he could find of interest was friction within his staff. As if in denial, he reached out and picked up a book from the table and began to read, and as he did so he thought wryly that his choice of literature would meet with the approval of Mr Burgess.

4

'I'm not standing for it, it's gone too far. My God! when you come to think of it, I knew from the first time I clapped eyes on her there was something weird about her. She's a witch I tell you, she's a witch.'

'Don't be silly, Cook. . . .'

'And don't you tell me I'm silly, Phyllis Coates. You admitted it yourself last night there was something very strange the way she's got round the master.'

'Aye, I did, but that isn't to say she's a witch.'

'Well, then, you explain to me how a slip of a lass who was brought up livin' from hand to mouth in a cottage on this very estate an spent most of her days digging or sawing wood, how other has she got the power to entertain a man like the master, an' not only him but now Master Harry? You tell me, Phyllis Coates. Why, if she were an educated person you might be able to understand it, but she's an ignorant little slut who's never been further than Shields in her life. Now you explain to me where she gets her powers from.'

'She's not ignorant, Cook, she can read and write better' – her voice dropped – 'than Mrs Lucas, so Fred says.'

'Aye, and what was the cost of her readin' and writin', ruination of the parson's wife an' him an' all. And don't forget about the farmer, him on our very door so to speak, and the fiasco on his weddin' night all through her. And now Master Harry walking with her in the grounds.'

'Someone talking about me?'

The cook, Phyllis, and Maggie Short who was standing stoning raisins at the table, all started and turned towards the kitchen door leading into the yard.

During the period between the death of his mother and the remarriage of his father, Harry Sopwith had been in the habit of running wild about the place, but all this had been put a stop to with the advent of Eileen. And now this was the second time in four days he had come into the house through the kitchen. He was changed was Master Harry, they all said so, free and easy, sort of gay. It was as if he were pleased to find his stepmother gone from the house.

He said again, 'Did I hear my name mentioned, taken in vain?' He was looking from one to the other; then, his eyes coming to rest on the cook, he said, 'Well, Cook?'

Looking back into the long, tanned face of the young man, Cook saw this as an opportunity to make her stand and for her grievances to be expressed in the proper quarters, and so she said, 'Aye, you did hear your name mentioned, Master Harry, but not taken in vain.' Then remembering how she had mentioned his name, she side-stepped the issue by saying, 'We were glad to see you back an' so happy like in spite of the tragedy that has befallen the house, and – 'now her fat head wagged on her fat neck and, her lips forming a tight rosebud, she spat out, 'And I say tragedy in more ways than one.'

'Yes?' He inclined his head towards her.

'Aye, Master Harry. I might as well come clean 'cos things have got to such a pitch we can't go on like this, none of us can.' She looked from one to the other. ''Tis that Tilly Trotter, Master Harry.'

'Trotter? What's she got to do with tragedy except that she was in it, very much up to the neck so to speak?'

''Tisn't that tragedy I'm referrin' to, 'tis the trouble she's caused since she's come into the house. It was a peaceful house afore she stepped into it. It began the day she came to look after the children, but then we came back to normal like once she was gone. But now she's back an' life's unbearable, Master Harry.'

The tolerant smile slipped from the young man's face and he asked, 'In what way, Cook?'

'Well – ' She looked from Phyllis Coates to Maggie Short as if for support, then said lamely, ''Tisn't right, she shouldn't be in the position she's got, not over us. From Mr Pike downwards we all say the same, 'tisn't right. She's even topping Mrs Lucas.'

'In what way? Explain yourself.'

'Well' – she tossed her head – 'she sends down orders through Maggie Short there' – she jerked her head in the direction of the kitchen maid – 'or Ada Tennant who's in the scullery.' Her head moved in the other direction now. 'She even gives orders to Mr Pike for them outside. Well, it's not to be tolerated, Master Harry, oh no! We've got our heads together an' I'll tell you this much' – she paused now – 'we . . . we want it put to the master' – again she paused – 'either she goes or we all go. There, that's how we feel, from top to bottom that's how we feel.'

'Oh, those are strong words, Cook.'

At this point Mrs Lucas came through the green-baized door and the cook turned eagerly towards her, almost shouting down the length of the room now. 'I've been tellin' Master Harry about that 'un up there.' Her head jerked towards the ceiling. 'I've told him if the master doesn't get rid of her he'll have to get rid of us, it's one or t'other, isn't it, Mrs Lucas?'

The housekeeper came to a stop at the top of the table and, looking at the cook, she said, 'It is my place, Cook, to say what the staff have decided or not decided, but' – she now turned her head slowly and looked at Harry – 'I must say this, Master Harry, things are not right in the house and there's got to be changes or else . . . well, there'll be trouble. You can't run an establishment with resentment like what is filling this house at the present moment.'

'Why haven't you put this to my father if you feel so strongly about it, Mrs Lucas?'

'I . . . I intend to; it's got to be settled.'

'Settled?' He bent his head slightly towards her. 'Which means I understand from the cook that if Trotter doesn't go you will all go?'

Mrs Lucas's tight frame gave a slight shudder that brought her head wagging and she said, 'Well, yes, something along those lines because I . . . I am at the end of my tether. I'm the housekeeper but I'm not given my position. It . . . it was bad enough when Miss Price was here, but . . . but she was a lady compared with the person upstairs.'

Harry's eyes narrowed as he looked at Mrs Lucas and his voice was quiet and very like his father's as he said, 'I have been here four days now, Mrs Lucas, and most of the time Trotter seems to have been tending my father, seeing to his needs and the business of the rooms. The only time, to my knowledge, that I've known her even come downstairs was when she took the air in the garden yesterday, and except for the twice I've been out riding I've been in the house most of the time. I don't see what you're getting at.'

Mrs Lucas looked at the cook and the cook looked at Mrs Lucas, then they looked at Maggie Short, but when the eyes turned on Phyllis Coates she had her head bowed and her eyes cast towards the floor, and Harry looked from one to the other and he broke the silence by saying, 'I'll inform my father of the situation.'

'Thank you, Master Harry.' Mrs Lucas's voice sounded prim.

Harry now walked up the kitchen past Maggie Short and Phyllis Coates, who both dipped their knees, and through the green-baized door into the hall and up the stairs.

Why did they hate the girl? There was nothing about her to dislike that he could see; in fact, he had never seen his father so light-hearted even when he had been able to get about. Yet his father had changed, he was a different man, nervy, he talked louder than he used to, and he was impatient most of the time. Well, that was all to be expected. My God! it must be dreadful to have no feet.

Tilly was in the dressing-room when she heard Harry enter the bedroom and she remained there busying herself with sorting the linen and choosing a shirt and cravat which the master would wear on the morrow. She liked the feel of all his clothes, especially his underwear; as she had discovered down below, the fine wool felt almost like silk.

Their voices came to her muted, then rising and falling, and she did not pay much attention until she heard Mark say, 'I'm sorry about Parliament, it will be beyond me'; then Harry's answer, 'That's all right, I was never keen on it anyway. But I'll be grateful for another year up there. You can bring it down to a hundred, I can manage on that.'

'No, we'll keep it to a hundred and fifty.'

'Is there no hope at all of the mine being reopened?'

'None whatever I should say, well, not without a lot of money being spent on it. And you know that's an impossibility for me now, it will take me all my time to support Eileen and the children from my investments, and these, as you know, fluctuate. Should they go down . . . well, I'm afraid this place will sink with them.'

'How many have you employed here now, Father?'

'Oh, about a dozen inside and out. It's nothing I suppose, but they all need feeding and clothing and by some of the bills Mrs Lucas presented me with last week they must be eating their heads off down there. Still, what can you do? I don't suppose it could be run on less.' There was a long pause; then as Tilly went to close a drawer her hands became still as she heard Master Harry say, 'Where's Trotter, next door?'

'No, I thought she went upstairs. Yes, she went up there. Listen.'

She, too, listened to the faint footsteps going across the nursery floor and wondered for a moment who it could be. Then Harry's voice brought her head jerking towards the half-open door as he said, 'How do you find her?'

'What do you mean?'

'I mean, how do you find Trotter? Is she quarrelsome, throwing her weight about, anything like that?'

'Don't be silly. What are you getting at? She's the best thing that's come into my life since this happened. Oh' – there followed a laugh now – 'you've been hearing the witch story.'

'Witch story?'

'Yes, some of them think she's a witch. Can you believe it? Ignorance, you know, Harry, can be really terrifying, for if there was anyone less like a witch than that girl it would be hard to find.'

'No, I hadn't heard the witch story. So they think she's a witch, do they? Good heavens! Likely that's what it's all about.'

'What what's all about?'

'They want rid of her downstairs.'

'They want what!'

'Mrs Lucas and the cook, I think they're going to present you with an ultimatum, either she goes or they do.'

In the silence that followed Tilly's imagination couldn't conjure up any picture of the reaction these words had on the master until she heard his voice filling the room like a bawl now: 'My God! an ultimatum? Either they or she? The bloody craven upstarts!'

'Now, now, don't excite yourself.'

'Excite myself? God! I wish I were on my feet. I'd give them ultimatum. Anyway, I can do it from here.'

'Now! now! now! Father. Now please don't get so excited, you'll only make yourself ill.'

'Shut up! Shut up! I'm not an invalid. I'm handicapped but that's all. Anyway, you can tell them to come up and present their ultimatum.'

'What do you intend to do?'

'Take them at their word. They go, every damn one of them who won't take orders from Trotter . . . they go.'

'But you can't do that, Father, you can't leave the house without a staff.'

'I can leave the house without a staff of that kind; and perhaps you don't know it but there are people roundabout here crying out for work.'

'But they won't be trained to this kind of work.'

'Look, Harry, Trotter wasn't trained. She was an ordinary girl, she had one advantage, she could read and write, but you know something, she's better than any of those damn nurses I had. And as for Simes, well she could wipe her feet on Simes. What's more, she's intelligent. I've thought these last few days, given the chance she could be something, that girl. Old Burgess set her off reading. No, no, it was the parson's wife. But he took her deep into it, Voltaire as ever was. Can you believe it, Voltaire? She admits she doesn't understand it but she will one day I'm sure. But as for that ignorant lot, ultimatum! Well, let them bring their ultimatum. You tell Lucas I want to see her.'

'I would . . . I would rest on it, Father, if I were you. The Christmas holidays are on us and it would only make things very unpleasant.'

'But aren't they already unpleasant?'

'Well, think it over. Let them come to you.'

'Get me a drink will you, Harry? The decanter's in the cupboard in the dressing-room.'

Tilly opened her mouth wide, then closed it and turned swiftly to stand with her back to the drawer, her hands outstretched at each side of it. And that was how Harry saw her when he entered the room. When she swiftly put her fingers to her lips he gave a slight nod, went to the cupboard, took out the tray with the decanter and a glass on it, and returned to the bedroom.

A few minutes later, excusing himself, he went into the dressing-room and closed the door; but finding the room empty, he went out into the corridor before making his way to the nursery floor; and as if she had been waiting for him Tilly faced him as he entered the schoolroom.

Smiling at her, he said, 'They say listeners never hear any good of themselves, but that wasn't true in this case, was it, Trotter?'

'I'm . . . I'm sorry, Master Harry, I'd no intention of listening but . . . but when you mentioned my name, well, I couldn't get out of the room.'

'I understand. Well, anyway, you now know about the ultimatum.'

'It's better that I go, Master Harry.'

'Oh no, no, Trotter, I don't think so. I . . . well, I agree with my father, there's changes needed in the house, and outside too. Just before I met you in the garden yesterday I had come across both Pilby and Summers fast asleep in the greenhouse. I know it is winter and the ground is too hard to dig but from what I could see during my walk, there were a thousand and one things they could have been doing; the gardens are very neglected. Yes, I think there are changes needed both inside and outside the house, but it is making the change that is going to be awkward. My father thinks he could re-staff from the men and women who are out of work at the mine.'

'Aye, yes, he could do that.' Her eyes widened and an eager note came into her voice. 'I don't want to see anybody pushed out of a job, Master Harry, but I can tell you this much, he could do that and save himself a deal of money into the bargain, because most of them would just work for their food and shelter.'

'Oh' – his face stiffened – 'that would never be allowed, we're not starting a new slave trade.'

'I . . . I wasn't meaning to annoy, Master Harry, but what I say is true. With all the master's workmen and their families, the main concern is food. Yet' – her voice sank – 'after saying all that I feel it would be better if I went.'

'My father wouldn't hear of it. But don't worry, something will work out. It's strange how such trifles are overcome.'

. . . Such trifles.

At half past three the following afternoon Tilly was hurrying back from a visit to the Drews.

Early that morning the master had given her half a sovereign to buy herself a present for Christmas, and she had taken it to Biddy, and Biddy had held her in her arms, and Katie had fallen on her neck, and the youngsters had cried, and she had cried with them.

She had not stayed more than fifteen minutes because she was eager to get back to her duties, and in spite of the bitter winds the whole Drew family had insisted on setting her to the end of the row, and their cries of 'Merry Christmas, Tilly!' as she ran along the road into the deepening gloom had warmed her.

She was taking the short cut behind the lodge at the back gates of the estate when she stumbled into Frank Summers, a small basket of eggs in one hand and a rough parcel from which protruded a side of bacon in the other. They both stopped and stared at each other. It was she who spoke first. 'I . . . I advise you to take those back, Mr Summers,' she said.

There was a pause before he answered; then, 'Mind your own bloody business you!' he growled, 'else I'll give it to you where it hurts most, right atween your eyes. I've had enough of you. The lot of us have. You! You young scut!'

He put down the basket and parcel in front of the door and began to advance on her, and she cried at him, 'don't you dare! Don't you dare lay a finger on me! If you do you'll know about it. Now I'm warnin' you.'

But even as she spoke she backed from him and rounded the corner of the Lodge towards the drive, the while he slowly advanced on her, muttering, 'You dirty sneaking young runt you! Puttin' Master Harry on to us yesterda'!'

'I did no such thing.'

'Who else then?'

'Perhaps he's finding things out for himself.' She was still moving slowly backwards.

'You're a menace. You know that? You're a menace.'

'An' you an' the rest of you are a lot of thieves. You've been robbin' the master for years. You've been stuffin' things in there' – she flung out her arm now – 'all summer. You're as bad as them in the house, chargin' the master double for everything with their share-outs once a month. You should be ashamed of yourself, the lot of yous.'

'Shut your mouth, you sneaking little witch! The bits we take nobody would miss.'

'Bits!' She was yelling back at him now. 'Dozens of eggs at one go; and pigs . . . I know, I've seen you at it afore. And they're picked up for the market, aren't they? And the fruit from the greenhouses. For two pins I'd go back right there and tell the master everything.'

'You do, me dear, you do, an' you take it from me you won't be able to see out of your eyes or walk for weeks. This is one you haven't got frightened, witch or no witch. . . . Look, I'm not afeared to grab you.'

As his hands came on her she screamed and tore at his face with her fingers. But it was all over in a moment because she seemed to be torn from him and thrust into the long grass, and as she saw a whip descend across his shoulders she held her hand tightly over her mouth.

When she scrambled to her feet Summers was standing bent against the wall of the lodge holding his hand to his neck.

'Go on! Get away and pack up whatever belongs to you and get off this land as from today!'

'You . . . you didn't employ me.' Summers was walking backwards now, still holding his neck. ''Tis only the master can sack me!' and Harry followed him, saying, 'Well, I'm acting for the master, and – ' He now looked towards the parcel and the basket lying at the lodge door and ended, 'Give me the key of the lodge.'

'I haven't got it.'

Harry turned his head and looked towards Tilly. She did not speak but bent down and groped in the grass. After a moment she found the stone and took from under it the key and handed it to him.

Opening the door of the lodge, Harry went inside. On the bench in the scullery there were three empty fruit skips and, leaning against the wall under the bench, was a sack filled up to its gaping top with potatoes.

Turning to Tilly, he said, 'Bring those packages in, Trotter'; and when she entered the scullery, he said, 'Put them on the bench there and take up the empty ones.'

She did this and went outside again where Summers was standing some distance away scowling darkly. When Harry said to him, 'Get back to your quarters and stay there until I come,' the man moved his head slowly and ground his teeth before turning away.

Harry now looked at Tilly, saying quietly, 'Throw those skips into the grass. Whoever is going to pick that stuff up' – he nodded towards the window – 'will come before dark surely. . . . Can you lead a horse?'

'I . . . I haven't done so yet, Master Harry.'

'Well, come.' He led the way on to the drive, saying, 'He's gentle. Just take the lead, walk by his side, and take him to Leyburn. No, on second thoughts, I'll tie him up along the drive.'

'But . . . but what if there's more than one of them, Master Harry?'

'Don't worry; I'm not going to do anything brave, I'm just going to see who picks the stuff up. But I don't think it'll be any of the miners or those really in need, not if, as you say, this has been going on for a long time.'

She lowered her head as she muttered now, 'I've . . . I've wanted to speak about it but I knew it would only cause trouble.'

'You say inside is as bad too?'

'Worse, if anything, Master Harry. The bills could be lessened by half, I know that.'

'Are they all in it?'

'Aye, yes.'

'Good Lord!' Her jerked his head. 'How does it work?'

'They dish it out according to their positions.'

'And you? How did you come off when you looked after the children?'

Her head was bent again. 'They allotted me coppers, I didn't want it but . . . but they had enough against me so I took it to keep the peace.'

'Well, well, we live and learn. I know there's always bound to be rake-offs, but I thought it would only be the butler with the wine, you know, or the housekeeper getting a little percentage back from the tradesmen. But you think everything has been doubled?'

She didn't answer for a while, but then moved her head in an uncertain movement, saying now, 'Well, I don't know what the bills were but it seemed a lot of money to me that was doled out from Cook's book.'

'Cook's book?' There was a high enquiry in his voice now.

'Well, she was over the kitchen staff and . . . and. . . . Oh, I feel terrible, Master Harry, saying all this.'

'Well, you're only confirming what I already overheard from the road. And apart from that, I think I came just in time because that man was vicious, he could have done you an injury; and apparently' – now he poked his head towards her – 'he isn't afraid of witches.'

She didn't smile, she was sick to the pit of her stomach. Mr Pike, Simes, Mrs Lucas, the cook, Maggie Short, Ada Tennant, Amy Stiles, Phyllis Coates – Oh aye – Phyllis. What would happen to Phyllis? And Fred, Fred Leyburn. And then the outside men. She didn't care what happened to Summers, nor yet to Pilby, but Mr Hillman . . . well, he had his cottage, and his wife wasn't in the best of health either. She had at one time been one of the laundry maids but she'd had to give it up when the daily ones came in. . . . It was Christmas and they'd all be out of work. She'd be putting them out of work. Oh no, she couldn't take the blame for that.

'Go along now; but don't say anything to my father.'

She turned away and went up the drive and into the house by the side door, and when she reached her room on the nursery floor she lit the candle and sat down for a moment on the side of the bed. She was still in her outdoor clothes, but she was cold right to the heart of her. What was it about her that seemed to invite trouble? Was she so different from other girls? No, not that she could see. The only difference was that she could read and write a bit; but as yet her writing wasn't up to much. These two accomplishments were the only difference that divided her from the rest of youth because she was sure her feelings were just like those of other girls of her age: Katie, for instance, although she was younger; Maggie Short in the kitchen. There now came a doubt in her mind. Did they lie awake at night thinking of love? Not by anybody. Oh no not by anybody, just by one person. But no matter what they thought, people didn't react to them like they reacted to herself. And it wasn't only women who were against her, it was men too. They either loved her or hated her, there was no in between, no friendliness. That's what she wanted. If she couldn't have love, then friendliness was the next best thing, and at this moment that seemed as remote from her as the nightly desire and dream that Simon Bentwood was laying his head on her breast.

She rose from the bed and took off her coat and hat before putting on her bibbed apron and her white linen cuffs; smoothed her hair back, then adjusted her starched cap on top of it and, ready, she went down to the next floor.

❧ 5 ❦

The Christmas holidays came and went, as did New Year, and there was no jollification in the house. The staff were perturbed; since the dismissal of Summers they had been waiting daily for a call to the master's room; but no such call had come. It was as if the master was ignoring the whole affair, and soon there were heard murmurs amongst them that Frank Summers deserved all he got, doing a bit on the side like that. And apparently not just a bit, by what John Hillman let out, because both Pilby and Hillman had been in on it. Nobody else had known about it, not even Leyburn because his work mostly kept him to the yard. But that the master was annoyed about something was evident in the fact that this year there had been no Christmas gifts sent down to the servants' hall, and no message to Mr Pike to take a bottle or two from the cellar. But that hadn't stopped him, of course. Then again, they thought this omission could have been because there was no mistress in the house and it was usually the mistress who remembered these kinds of things.

So with time passing and Mr Harry now gone, their anxiety disappeared, although the perplexity still remained, and there was resurrected the feeling against – that one, because again, hadn't she been the cause of trouble? If she hadn't sneaked on Frank Summers he'd still be here, wouldn't he? So what was going to be done about her? Nobody was safe as long as she stayed.

Then out of the blue the call came down to the kitchen. The master had summoned Mr Pike, and Pike came back downstairs on legs that were feeling decidedly weak, and he, summoning Mrs Lucas, the cook, and Simes, announced, 'The master wants to see you all.'

On this Mrs Lucas demanded, 'Why wasn't I informed if the master wanted to see any member of the female staff?'

And to this Pike replied wearily, 'What you forget, woman, is that I am really in charge of the house, but I've let you take the lead for years, it's saved trouble. And now let me tell you, I think we're all in for trouble.'

Tilly opened the door to them and she could have been an automatic hinge on it for all the notice any of them took of her for their eyes went directly to the basket-chair and the man sitting upright in it.

They stood in line at the foot of the chair and Mark looked at them: the tall, thin, weary-looking Pike, the narrow-faced Simes, Mrs Lucas looking like a small tightly stuffed model of a human being, and the woman Brackett, the cook, looking as if she had sampled every dish she had ever cooked in her life. Strange, he had only seen her twice in as many years but she seemed to have doubled her size. His eyes slid from her to Trotter who was going into the dressing-room, and when the door closed on her he turned his attention to the group before him, and it was to them as a group that he spoke.

'I have been waiting,' he said, 'for you coming to see me, because I understand that you have a proposition to put before me. Is that so, Mr Pike?' His voice was quiet, his tone even, and there was about his manner a casual air that deceived them all; yet not quite in Mr Pike's case, and he, knowing he should be spokesman, was finding difficulty in answering his master, and he blinked and he shuffled his feet on the carpet, rubbed his hands together as if he were washing them, then said, 'Well, sir, it's . . . it's. . . .'

'Yes, go on.'

Mr Pike now switched his eyes to the side and to where Mrs Lucas, who was looking at him, as also was Jane Brackett, and the cook's irritation made evident by the sudden movement of her hips told the housekeeper that if she wasn't careful Jane Brackett would get in before her, and so she, looking at her master, said, 'He finds it difficult, sir, as . . . as we all do, to speak . . . to speak about this matter.'

'What matter?'

'Well –' Mrs Lucas proved she had a body inside her uniform because it stretched and her neck craned round to the dressing-room door, and now her voice dropping a number of tones, it came over just above a whisper as she said, 'Trotter, sir.'

'Trotter!' Mark's voice sounded high with surprise. 'What about Trotter?'

'Well, sir. . . .'

It appeared that the housekeeper was in the same difficulty as the butler, and this being evident Jane Brackett could see the whole interview coming to nothing, or at least going against them, so it was she who broke in. 'Begging your pardon, master, it isn't my place I know, 'tis Mr Pike's or Mrs Lucas's here to put it to you, but . . . but it's got to be said and we all think alike, sir, from the top to the bottom.' She now looked at Mr Pike standing at one side of Mrs Lucas and at Simes on her other side, then continued, 'Trotter is a bad influence like. There's been no peace in the house since she's come, and what's more . . . well, as Mrs Lucas here will tell you' – the rolls of fat on her neck indicated the housekeeper as she jerked her head – 'nobody's got their place any more. You see, master, as you know, you don't have to be told I'm sure of that, you have your place on a staff and it gets your bile when someone like the likes of her start throwing their weight about and giving orders.'

'Trotter throwing her weight about? That surprises me, Cook. She has always appeared very diffident to me, rather shy.'

'Oh! master' – she was nodding at him – 'people can be taken in. We know what we know, don't we?' She looked from one to the other again. 'It . . . it was the same when she was on the nursery floor, nothing went right in the house, she seemed to brew trouble, and . . . and now it's worse.'

'Really!' He hitched himself slightly up in the chair; then leaning forward and his manner definitely expressing sympathy and his voice low, he said, 'And what do you suggest I should do?'

Jane Brackett felt exuberant. There now, why hadn't they done this before? And she dared to move so much out of her place as to take a step nearer the foot of the chair and, her voice low now, she said, 'Get rid of her, master.'

'Get rid of her?'

'Yes, master.'

'But what if I can't.' He didn't say won't, but as if appealing to her he used the word can't, which emboldened her now to say, 'Well then, master, I'm afraid you're in for trouble. Well, what I mean is, begging your pardon, we said it afore Christmas but we let the holidays go by, but you see . . . well' – she attempted to straighten her front shoulders – 'it's either her or us. You'll lose your staff, master, if you don't get rid of her, and . . . and we've proved ourselves, we've been with you for years, Mr Pike here the longest, since a lad he's been in your family, and I've served you well for the last ten years, master, and. . . .'

'Yes, yes, you have, Cook, yes, indeed, you have served me well for the last ten years.' He was now leaning back against the pillows. 'But you haven't served me as well as you've served yourself, Cook, have you?'

Her face changed colour. She didn't speak, no one spoke, nor moved, and now he lifted his eyes from one to the other before he said, 'You've all served yourselves well, haven't you? How much have you made out of *your* little book, Mrs Lucas?'

'S . . . sir!'

'And you, I understand, Cook, have a special book for your fiddling. Summers wasn't in it, *you* ran your racket, didn't you?' His voice hadn't risen but his manner had changed and the words that he was speaking were dropping like pointed icicles on their heads. 'Now your proposition is that I get rid of Trotter or you go. Well now, for your information I am keeping Trotter, so what does that tell you?'

Still no one spoke.

'You, Simes, and you, Mrs Lucas, and you, Brackett, will take a week's notice as from today. I will allow you a month's pay in lieu of further notice. As for you, Pike, I'm going to give you a choice, you served not only my father but also my grandfather, but although it is an understood thing that the butler has his perks, it is also understood that they don't amount to robbery. Now you may go with the rest or you may stay. You needn't answer now, you can fight that out when you get downstairs. In the meantime, there remain four other members of the indoor staff: those who wish to stay you will send up to me; after they have been you will bid Leyburn, Pilby, and Hillman to come to me. That is all.'

'Tisn't right.'

'What isn't right, Simes?'

'To ... to be thrown out like this.'

'But you don't care for your position, Simes.'

'I've ... I've never said ...'

'No, you've never said but your attitude when you thought I was at your mercy was at times nothing short of callous. You can leave me now, all of you; and I think, Simes, you had better help Mrs Lucas out, she needs your assistance.'

Pike and Simes with Mrs Lucas between them made for the door, but Jane Brackett remained staring at him, her mouth open to speak; but no words came, and she didn't move until Mark's voice, at the pitch of a shout now, cried, 'Leave me, woman!'

She left, wobbling, he thought, like a fat bull at a cattle show.

It was some minutes before Tilly made her appearance in the room. Her face was ashen white, her head was bowed, and so he cried at her, 'Don't let your conscience on this matter bring you low, Trotter, you didn't start this business. Now by what Harry worked out for me, the household expenses can be cut by half, and that's something to be considered at this time, that is providing you're successful in arranging what we talked about yesterday.... Lift your head.'

She lifted her head, then said, 'They'll be out of work, sir, I can't help feeling sorry....'

'Did they feel sorry for you? They would have had you thrown out and never turned a hair. That woman, that cook, she's vicious. My God! to think one has been served by such as her.' He turned his head to the side. 'You just don't know what goes on in your own house. Anyway, remember what you once said to me.' He smiled slowly. 'It seems so far away now, like a dream, but I remember you saying, when one door shuts another one opens. Well, this afternoon take the coach and carry out what was decided on yesterday.... Well! come on, look pleased, girl.'

'I am pleased, sir.' Her voice was soft, but she could have added, 'I'm afraid too because the cook, Mrs Lucas, and Simes now have joined the villagers.'

The Drews' kitchen smelt of wet clothes, sweat and the fumes that come from banked-down coal dust. There was no blazing fire today, the free coal was finished and the only way to keep some sort of a fire going was to rake the pit heap.

The kitchen was crowded, all the family were indoors with the exception of Sam.

They had greeted her, each in his own particular way, the older boys with jerks of their heads and a smile which expressed their liking, but the girls, Katie and Peg and Fanny, crowded round her and their welcome was none the less warm because she had come empty-handed. And this fact was brought into the open by Jimmy suddenly saying, 'You brought nowt the day, Tilly?'

There was the sound of a crack as Biddy's hand contacted her son's ear, and when he cried, 'Oh, ma!' she yelled at him, 'And I'll oh ma you if you don't keep your mouth shut. That's the only thing about you that grows, your mouth.' While the others laughed, Tilly put her hand out and drew Jimmy towards her side and, smiling down at him, she said, 'I haven't come empty-handed.'

She was aware of the eyes all on her now and of some slanting from her towards the door and the coach outside. They still couldn't get used to her coming to visit them in a coach and she was aware that the older ones were trying not to imagine there was something fishy behind the privilege afforded her.

Now they were waiting, and she savoured their waiting; then putting her hands out impulsively and grabbing Biddy, she pulled her down to a chair, saying, 'You'd better sit down before you fall down when you hear me news.'

Like a troop advancing to a central point, they all came slowly towards her, but she continued to share her glance between Biddy and Katie who was standing at her mother's side, and slowly she said, 'Can you cook, Mrs Biddy Drew?'

Biddy closed her eyes for a moment and turned her head to the side; then looking at Tilly again, she said, 'Yes, ma'am; given the ingredients, I'm not a bad hand at cooking.'

'Good. You're engaged. Miss Drew' – she now looked at Katie – 'would you care to assist your mother in the kitchen? I'm aware that you are no hand at cookin' but there's hope for you, you could learn.'

'Eeh! Tilly, what you gettin' at?'

'Aye' – Biddy's face was straight now – 'what you gettin' at, lass? Come on, don't keep us in the dark.'

Tilly straightened her shoulders and looked around them with tenderness, and she said quietly, 'You've all got jobs if you want them.'

'All of us?' Biddy pulled herself to her feet.

'Aye, and not only you but one or two of the men down the row, the Waters and Mr McCann, but they'll only be on part time. . . .'

'Eeh! My God! jobs. You mean it, Tilly?'

'Where's this to be, Tilly, I mean the jobs for the men, Tilly?'

'Listen. Listen, and . . . and it mightn't suit all of you, at least not the older ones, but . . . well – ' She now said, 'Can I sit down?'

'Out of the way!' Biddy swept two of the boys from the front of the form, and Tilly, sitting down, began from the beginning, filling in the parts that Biddy or Katie knew nothing about which was the hate that had been directed towards her in the house, and also the fiddling that had grown out of all proportion both in the house and in the grounds, and then she ended, 'It wasn't really me, it was the master who thought of you.'

'I'll believe that when they give me wings.' It was Alec speaking and she turned to him and said, 'It's right, Alec.'

'With a little push from you.' Katie accompanied this by digging Tilly in the side playfully with her fist.

She went on talking while they gazed at her open-mouthed, and she ended, 'Ada Tennant's staying, she's the scullery maid, and Phyllis Coates, the first housemaid, she's staying, but Amy Stiles . . . well, I think she wanted to stay but she was frightened of the cook and so she's going. So you, Peg, would be under Phyllis. As for the men . . . well now, there's a point here. The master, I think, is up against it in more ways than one as the mine's finished, an' as I see it he's still got to support the mistress and children, although they're staying with her mother, so in all cases the wages won't be anything like you got in the pit. But what you will get is your food, good food, the men an' all, and that's something.'

Biddy now dropped her head back on her shoulders and looked up towards the ceiling and what she said was 'Something? It's everything, lass. Oh, thanks be to God in Heaven!' and her head coming slowly down, she added 'And to you, Tilly Trotter. It was a lucky day for us when our Katie stumbled across you.'

Katie smiled and again punched Tilly, and she, turning and looking at Alec who was the eldest there, said, 'Well now, Alec, there's you and Arthur and young Jimmy here' – she pressed the boy to her side – 'what would you feel like working outside, I mean digging and clearing and seeing to the vegetables and things like that? There's little livestock, only hens and pigs, but there's piles of land that used to be cultivated for vegetables and now it's all overgrown, and ... and as I put it to the master, not only is there enough space to grow stuff to feed the whole household but, just like they've been doing on the side, it could go to market and help to pay your wages.'

'Lass' – Biddy gripped hold of Tilly's arm – 'as long as we can eat through this winter we'll work like Trojans, because what more is needed if you have food, heat and shelter?'

'Will Sam see it that way, Mrs Drew?'

'Oh aye, lass, Sam'll see it that way, I can promise you. And so will the Waters and McCann and any other that could get work for their food.'

'But their jobs mightn't last all that long. Over the winter months perhaps. And yet I don't know.' She looked over their heads towards the smouldering fire and said, 'All that land there, a couple of horses and a plough.'

'And it used to be under plough. There used to be a farm at this end of the estate an' all at one time, so I'm told.'

'Oh, speaking of farms, that reminds me. Not that the farmer was here, but the young lad, Steve, he came on Sunday expecting you to be here and was asking how you were.'

'You'll have to look out for him, Tilly.' It was Alec laughing and nodding towards her now, and she looked at him solemnly as she said, 'He's just a friend, a childhood friend'; and under the warning glance from his mother, Alec said, 'Aye. Aye.'

Biddy now, to the surprise of her entire family, turned her body sharply round and, dropping her head on to the table, began to cry. Such was the amazement of all her brood that no one moved for a moment. They had never seen their mother cry, not one of them could remember ever seeing her shedding a tear, not even when their father died. They had heard her making strange noises in the bed that night, but they hadn't actually seen her cry.

'Aw, Ma! Ma!' The protest came from all of them and she lifted her head and said, "Tis all right, you cry when you're happy, and aw, lass' – she turned to Tilly – 'the sight of you this day and what you've brought us ... well, I'll never be able to thank you, lass.'

Tilly herself felt the rising of tears in her throat now. It was wonderful to be liked, to be loved, and she felt that Mrs Drew loved her like she did each one of her children. She rose to her feet now, saying, 'I'll have to be getting back.'

It was as she went to the door that Katie said softly, 'If that lad calls again what shall I tell him?'

'Oh' – Tilly turned to her – 'just say I'm all right and thank him for calling.'

'He was askin' did he think he could call up at the house now that you're settled there in a good position, and I said I didn't know but when I saw you I would ask you.'

'Come on. Come on, our Katie, let Tilly get away. It wouldn't do for him to go up there. You don't want him up there, Tilly, do you?'

Tilly looked at Biddy and said, 'Well, it could be awkward.'

'Aye, I'm sure it would. Well, I'll deal with him kindly when he next comes.'

'Thanks. Ta-rah.' She spread her smile over them, and they all answered, 'Ta-rah! Tilly. Ta-rah.'

Biddy stopped them all from following her into the road, but as Tilly went towards the coach and Fred Leyburn, who was standing flapping his arms about himself to keep himself warm, Biddy followed her, and at the step she whispered, 'You'll let me know when, lass?'

Smiling now, Tilly said, 'Oh dear, I forgot. On Saturday afternoon; they'll be gone by then.'

'Well and good, lass.'

Biddy stood back. The wind, taking her apron, threatened to lift it over her head, and she pressed it down with her hands and remained standing so until the coach rolled away past the end of the muddy row.

PART FOUR

And The
Bewitched

1

The early months of 1840 were to Tilly like time spent in a new world. All her long life she was to look back upon them as a form of awakening, for it was during these months that she learned to take on responsibility. She learned the sweet taste of deference, but above all she learned what it was to be a constant companion to a man, a gentleman. There was also bred in her a new fear, or rather the resurrection of the old one, for most of the work that the Drew boys and Mr Waters and Mr McCann had done outside in the way of planting had on two occasions been completely trampled to ground level.

It was after the second devastation that the master had ordered the setting of man-traps. As Sam had said to her, he hated the very name of man-traps and the men who laid them, and also he hated the men who ordered their laying; yet after seeing their efforts reduced to nothing he had been forced to consider another side to the business, and in anger he himself had helped to set them up and put a notice on both lodge gates to the effect that the grounds were trapped.

The destruction in the garden had definitely been the work of a number of men, and Tilly didn't know if they came from the village or from Jarrow, which was Jane Brackett's home. But she had a suspicion, as they all had, that the raids had been planned in Jarrow, for the cook had been known to say that if it was the last thing she did she'd bring 'that 'un' down, and not only her but the lot of them.

But today was bright, a high wind was scudding the clouds; it had been blowing for days as if in answer to Tilly's prayers to harden the roads, because if the master was to be disappointed this time he wouldn't be able to contain himself. There were times of late when his frustration had burst forth in temper and he had stormed at Mr Burgess and everybody who came near him, including herself; not that she minded, nor did Mr Burgess. Mr Burgess was wonderful with him. His half-daily visits when he helped to bathe him and talk to him had brought a new interest into his life.

For herself she had discovered something afresh about Mr Burgess. He liked to gossip, and that he brought the news of births, deaths and scandals to the master's ears she was well aware, particularly, she thought, about the scandals because often when she was entering the room Burgess would change the conversation and in a way that wouldn't have deceived a child.

The house, she had felt for weeks, was growing happy. It was cleaner than she had ever seen it. And even at this early time of the year the gardens were looking different. Paths had been weeded, hedges cut, ground that hadn't seen the light of day for years had been cleared. John Hillman was working for his money these days, but he was seeing that all those under him did the same, and the result was pleasing, so much so that Mark had talked of getting a wheel-chair to take him round the grounds, for he couldn't see himself ever being able to stand on false feet which would enable him to use crutches.

So on this bright morning Tilly, excitement and not a little apprehension filling her, was making a tour of the house to see that everything was in order for the arrival of Mrs Forefoot-Meadows and the children. She was as excited about the children coming as was the master.

All the furniture in the dining-room was glowing, the epergne in the centre of the table sprayed out daffodils, and the silver on the long mahogany sideboard gleamed; and in the drawing-room the fire was blazing in the grate, the lace drapes at the long windows had all been washed, the heavy velvet curtains and pelmets had been taken down and brushed, even the tops of the oil paintings surrounding the walls had been dusted. Tilly was satisfied there wasn't a speck of dirt anywhere.

In the hall a big blue vase of ferns banked the great newel post at the bottom of the stairs; the red stair-carpet that was worn in parts had been taken up and relaid and the effect, Tilly thought, was almost like new.

On through the house she went. The nursery floor was in readiness, the room that she had once occupied was now given over to Katie, whose work it would be to tend to the children during their three days' stay in the house. Her own room now was at the other side of the dressing-room, and she still couldn't get used to the difference. A feather bed, a huge wardrobe with full-length mirrors for doors, a wash-hand-stand with her own bowl and jug and a slop bucket so pretty that she hated to pour dirty water into it.

She stood now in front of the mirror. It wasn't often she had time to stand and appraise herself, but when she did she was always surprised at the reflection. She was eighteen but she looked older. Perhaps it was her uniform, a beautiful uniform, grey alpaca. The waist clung to her like a skin. The skirt wasn't very full; they had wanted to put another panel in it but she had said no. That would, she had thought, be aping the ladies, and she felt she had stepped out of her place enough without her dress causing comment. She was wearing drawers now for the first time in her life, and also boned stays. She didn't mind the drawers but the stays she found cumbersome; yet she wore them because there were what was called suspenders hanging from the bottom and these kept up her white cotton stockings better than garters.

Her cap was different too; this one didn't cover all her hair but sat on the top of it, as she laughingly thought to herself, like a starched crown.

She moved closer to the mirror and touched the skin of her face. Her com-plexion wasn't bad. She knew she was being mealy-mouthed, but she couldn't say, it's lovely, 'cos as her granny would have said, never believe what the mirror tells you 'cos you only see what you want to see.

She now fastened the top button of her dress, smoothed her hands down over her hips, then went out into the corridor, turned into the dressing-room and there paused for a moment to see that everything was in order, then went in to the bedroom.

Mr Burgess was sitting by the cane chair and his head was back and he was laughing, and the master was laughing too. His face was flushed, his eyes were bright, and he was looking different this morning, younger. He had taken pains to brush his unruly hair flat across the top of his head. He was wearing a white silk shirt with a ruffle. He had also, she noticed, forced himself to put on trousers, which she considered was a big step forward, for he mostly spent his days in his nightshirt and dressing-gown. However, the small cage this morning was across the bottom of the chair with a rug covering it, but his dress and the way he was sitting gave the impression of wholeness.

'Well, Trotter, done your rounds?'

'Yes, sir.'

'Everything in order?'

'As far as I can see, yes, sir.'

'And the meals? As much as I enjoy roast beef, roast lamb, meat puddings and such I don't think they will satisfy my mother-in-law's palate. Have you seen the cook?'

'Yes, sir; we discussed the meals last night.'

'And what did you hatch up?'

'Well, sir, Mrs Drew thought of starting with white soup, and then a bit of boiled salmon with sauce, and the main course to be roast chicken with carrots and mashed turnips and other vegetables; then she was making a choice of puddings, cabinet pudding or rhubarb tart and special custard with eggs, I mean made with eggs' – she laughed – 'and fruit – she could have a choice – and then there's cheeses.'

Mark turned now and looked at Mr Burgess, saying, 'What do you think of that, Burgess?'

'It sounds very appetising, sir, very appetising indeed, in fact it's causing my juices to rise.' As he spoke he got to his feet and now looked at Tilly, saying, 'I'm sure Mrs Forefoot-Meadows will be pleased.'

She did not answer, except that her eyes smiled at him.

Mr Burgess now turned to Mark, saying, 'I will leave you now, sir, if I may, but I shall be here in the morning and share your pleasure in seeing the children once again.'

'Thank you, Burgess, I'm sure they'll be delighted to see you. And if I'm not mistaken they will wish they were back under your care.'

'I would wish that too, sir, but – ' he shrugged his shoulders and spread out his hands. 'C'est la vie, telle quelle . . . telle quelle.'

'Yes, indeed, indeed.'

Mr Burgess went out and Mark, turning to Tilly, said, 'I don't think I've felt so excited about anything since the night Harry was born. And isn't it a bit of luck that he'll be here the day after tomorrow. He'll have one day among them anyway.' He turned his head away and looked towards the window, saying now with deep bitterness, 'Three days! Damnable!'

Sensing his changing mood, she went quickly towards the chair and, straightening the cover that had slipped slightly from the cage, she said brightly, 'They'll likely make so much narration, sir, that you'll be glad to see the back of them.'

His head came round to her sharply and his voice seemed to be censoring the stupidity of her remark when he said, 'Yes, as glad as I would be to see the back of you, Trotter.'

She stood silent now looking at him as she often did when she thought it was better not to give any answer to his remarks.

'If Mr Burgess had remained a little longer he would have said that that remark of yours was stupid, trite. Do you understand that?'

'All I understand is, sir, that I was aiming to lighten your despair with regard to the children.'

His expression altered as he stared at her: there had been spirit in the answer that wouldn't have been there a few months ago. He didn't object to it, in fact he liked it for he was catching a glimpse of the emerging woman that lay beneath the yes, sir, no, sir, attitude of hers. His voice quiet now, he asked, 'If you had four children taken away from you what would you do, Trotter?'

He watched her think a moment before answering, 'As ... as I've never had children I cannot tell to what depth my feelings would go. I can just judge on the reactions of Mrs Drew to her family. But I'm not as strong as Mrs Drew so I think I might go mad. Then again, sir, it's a question that is difficult to answer because if I had four children why should they be taken away?' She felt the blood rushing to her face and her eyes widened as she stared at him; and now his voice ominously quiet, he said, 'Go on, finish.'

When she didn't speak he supplied the meaning to her words, saying, 'You were about to tell me that you would never do anything that would bring about losing your children, was that it?'

She remained mute.

'Well, my answer to that, Trotter, is, you have a long way to go yet and a lot to learn about human nature, and also a great deal to learn about the penalties for sin. Some sentences are out of all proportion to the crime. ... What's that?' He turned quickly and, raising himself on his hands to look over the broad sill of the window, his whole expression changing, he cried, 'It's the coach! It's them. Go on down. Go on down.'

She turned from him now and ran out of the room and across the landing and down the stairs. Pike was already waiting; both doors were thrown wide open and there, on the drive, the coach had come to a standstill.

It was her place, she knew, to stand at the top of the steps and welcome Mrs Forefoot-Meadows in, as she had seen Mrs Lucas do, but she so much forgot herself she ran down the steps and it seemed that before she reached the bottom they were around her shouting, 'Hello! Trotter. Hello! Trotter.' Even Matthew was smiling.

'Enough! Enough! Behave yourselves.' The voice of their grandmother did not immediately quell their boisterous enthusiasm, but they left Tilly and raced up the steps and into the house; and Tilly, looking at Mrs Forefoot-Meadows, said, 'I hope you had a good journey, madam?'

The surprise of being greeted by this girl seemed to have struck Jane Forefoot-Meadows dumb because she looked from her and up the steps to where Pike was standing; then turning from her without even the acknowledgment of a nod, she swept up to the terrace and passed Pike, saying as she did so, 'What's this? What's this?'

'I hope you had a pleasant jour. ...'

'Never mind about the journey, where's Mrs Lucas?'

'She's no longer here, madam.'

'No longer here!' As she unloosened her cape she looked about her, saying, 'And Simes?'

'He's no longer in the master's service either, madam.'

'What's going on here?' At the bottom of the stairs she stopped and again she looked around the hall. The difference in the house was already striking her, yet she couldn't put an actual finger on it.

When a moment or so later she entered Mark's room she put both hands up to her ears, crying, 'Stop it! Stop that noise this instant!' and again the laughter and chatter subsided.

Going towards the chair now, where Mark had Jessie Ann cradled in one arm and John in the other, while the two older boys sat halfway down on either side, she did not ask after her son-in-law's health but said, 'What's this I've come across? No housekeeper, no footman, and that girl!'

'It's a long story, Mother-in-law, a long, long story, and you'll hear about it all in good time; but first, get off your feet.'

'I've been off my feet for hours, my bones are stiff. . . . Stop making that racket, John, and speak correctly. Haven't I told you?'

'Y . . . yes, Gramama.'

Mark looked at his small son who no longer seemed so small; not one of his children seemed small now, they had all grown in their different ways. But John's speech was worse than when he had been at home, he was actually stammering now.

'Leave your father alone and get away all of you up to the nursery, and get out of your travelling clothes and don't come downstairs until I give you leave. Away with you now.'

Mark bit on his lip as Jessie Ann and John slid from his arms; then Jessie Ann, looking towards the cage, said, 'Are your feet still sore, Papa?'

Mark did not take his glance from her and he continued to smile at her as he said, 'Yes; yes, they're still sore, my dear.'

'Perhaps you want your toe-nails cut, mine stick in me and Willy Nilly digs the scissors in and cuts them off. It hurts . . .'

'Who's Willy Nilly?'

It was his mother-in-law who answered now, saying, 'Williams, their nurse. Go on, children, do as you're bid.'

And they went scrambling and laughing out of the room, and the noise was like music in his ears, it was as if they had never been away. Yet they had been away and the change in all of them was evident, at least in their growth.

'Well now, what's this? The house is all topsy-turvy.'

'No, Mother-in-law, the house is no longer topsy-turvy. The house, I am pleased to say, is being run as it should have been for years.'

Her plucked eyebrows moved upwards, the wrinkles around her eyes stretched themselves, and she said one word, 'Indeed!'

'Yes, indeed. Sit yourself down and I'll give you all my news. I'm sure you'd like to hear it before you give me yours.'

Flinging off her dust-coat, she sat down and she made no comment whatever until Mark had finished outlining the story of the changeover, and then she said, 'Pit folk in the house?'

'Yes, as I said; and outside too and doing splendidly.'

'It can't work.'

'But it does.' His voice was high. 'And I'm going to tell you something more, at one-third of the cost.'

'A third!' She pulled her bony chin into the sagging flesh of her neck that formed a ridge around the high collar of her dress.

'Yes, a third; and from what I gather the whole house is cleaner, and from what I see' – he pointed to the window – 'the grounds have been unearthed in all quarters. Then there is the food. The bills have gone down in a remarkable way, for everybody, I understand, eats well, including myself.'

'That girl, do you know she was at the bottom of the steps when I got out of the carriage, leaving Pike at the door?'

'Perhaps she wanted to greet you.'

'Don't be ridiculous, Mark; she doesn't know her place.'

His face and voice lost its pleasantness now as he said sharply, 'She knows her place all right. She's running this house, and what's more she's seeing to me.'

She almost made to rise; then her mouth opened and closed again on his words 'She's a better nurse than that big battleship who tended me. . . .'

'It isn't right, it isn't decent, she's . . .'

'Oh, the decencies are seen to by Burgess.'

'Burgess . . . you mean the tutor?'

'Yes, the tutor. He comes in every day and sees to the main decencies, so have no fear, my dear Mother-in-law, the proprieties are being observed.'

'I don't like it.' She rose to her feet. 'Neither will Eileen.'

'God in Heaven!' It was as if he had been startled by the remark so quickly did he bounce up from the back of the chair. 'What's Eileen got to do with it, I ask you?'

'She is still your wife.'

'Then if she's my wife she should be here. What do you think I've felt like all these bloody months being left . . .'

'I will not have you swearing in my presence, Mark.'

'I'll swear where I bloody well like, Mother-in-law, and if it doesn't suit you, you know what you can do. But don't you come here talking about morality or improprieties that would shock my wife, for I won't have it. Her place is here with my children. Three days she has allowed me! My God! if I take it into my head I'll keep them for good and let her fight it out.'

'Don't agitate yourself so, Mark, and don't talk nonsense. The children's place is with their mother.'

'And her place is here!'

'You should have thought about that some long time ago. Anyway, I have things to discuss with you, but the time is not now, I am tired after my journey. You don't seem to appreciate, Mark, the trial that journey is to me.'

He drew in a number of deep breaths before lowering his head, when he muttered, 'I do, I do; and I appreciate the effort you make.' Then lifting his head, his voice still quiet, he said, 'But can you appreciate what it is like for me to be tied to this chair, to this room? I've asked myself more and more of late, is it worth going on.'

'Don't talk nonsense! I won't stay and listen to such weak prattle; I shall join you later.'

As she stormed out he couldn't but marvel at her spirit; no one knew her right age but she couldn't be far from seventy. Had she passed some of it on to her daughter things might have been different. He lay back in his chair and looked towards the cage covering the stumps of his legs. If only he had been left with even one foot. He pulled himself up straight on the chair; he must make an effort and try this wooden leg business.

For two days the house had been alive with scampering feet and laughter. No longer were the children kept to the nursery floor; even Jane Forefoot-Meadows found it impossible to confine them, for as soon as her back was turned they were down in their father's room or out in the grounds, or following Tilly around the house. They had at first viewed with surprise the change in the staff, particularly in the kitchen. They had accepted Katie in the nursery, but who was this little girl no older than Jessie Ann and not as big who was working in the kitchen? And there was no fat woman cooking there now but a tall woman with a big bony face.

During their first encounter Matthew had enquired imperiously of Biddy, 'What is your name?' and she had answered, 'Biddy, master. What is yours?'

And without hesitation he had said, 'Matthew.'

'Well, how are you, Master Matthew?'

'I am very well, thank you.' The conversation wasn't going as he imagined it should, and he had turned and looked at his brothers and Jessie Ann, and they had all burst out laughing, and it was Jessie Ann who said, 'What are you making for our tea, Mrs Biddy?'

And Biddy had delighted her by bending down and whispering, 'Fairy cakes, miss, with cream on their wings.'

As Biddy put it to Tilly later, the house was alive with life, and at seven o'clock on the evening of the second day when the life was filling the nursery with laughter it brought Mark's head round towards the dressing-room door, calling, 'What's going on up there, Trotter?'

Tilly came into the bedroom and, pushing the table and his half-eaten supper away, she said, 'I think they're havin' a bit carry-on.'

'Carry-on!' He was still looking upwards. 'It must be something to cause those gales of laughter. Go on up and see what it is.'

She smiled at him, saying, 'They'll want to come down if I go up, sir.'

'And what harm is there in that?' he demanded, poking his face towards her. 'Their grandmother is at her supper and she's likely to be there for another hour if I know her. Go on up.'

She only just stopped herself from actually running out of the room because she realised that was a habit she must get out of; but once on the landing she ran along the corridor and up the stairs and burst into the nursery, there to see Katie sitting on the mat before the nursery fire holding Jessie Ann while they both rocked with laughter. Luke was sitting at the nursery table, his arms spread out over it, his head between them, and Matthew was standing in front of John saying, 'Say the other one. Say the other one.'

'What is it?' Tilly looked from one to the other but they just spluttered, until Katie, getting to her feet now and drying her eyes, said, ''Twas Master John, Tilly, he . . . he was saying a piece of poetry.'

'It's all about us.' Jessie Ann came towards her, yelling, 'It has our names in it, Trotter, even Papa's.'

'And is it that funny?'

It was Matthew who answered, 'Yes; yes, it is, Trotter. Go on, John, say it again for Trotter. Go on.'

And John, his face one huge grin, took up his stance with feet planted slightly apart, hands joined behind his back, and began, stammering almost with each word:

'Ma . . . Matthew, Mark, Luke and. . . .
John, Hold the . . . cuddy till I get on.
If it k . . . kicks pull it . . . its tail
If it p . . . piddles hold the p . . . pail.'

Again they were doubled up, John as well now. He was on his knees and trying to stand on his head while the other children rolled in agonies of laughter, and Katie, her hand across her mouth, looked at Tilly and muttered, 'They didn't learn it here, believe me. One of the gardeners at their granny's. An' that isn't all. The fellow must be from these parts 'cos they know "When I was a laddie" – she nodded – 'you know, "When I was a laddie and lived with me granny".'

'Never!' Tilly was biting down hard on her lip now. And then she muttered in an aside, 'But that isn't as bad as Matthew, Mark. I had me ears boxed once for singing it.' She now turned from Katie, saying, 'Quiet! Now quiet! Listen.' They were all standing round her now, and she looked from one to the other. 'I'll take you downstairs to your papa if you promise to leave the minute I bid you, because your grandmama will come up immediately her supper is done. Promise?'

'Yes, Trotter. Yes, Trotter.'

As they made for the door she cried at them, 'Put your dressing-gowns on,' and they all scampered out of the schoolroom and into their rooms leaving Tilly and Katie looking at each other, both with their hands over their mouths now, then Tilly said, 'He . . . the master, he heard the laughter.'

'Can you hear as plain as that down there?'

'Yes, when the noise is so loud.'

'We'll have to be careful. . . . It's lovely havin' bairns in the house, isn't it?'

'Yes, Katie, lovely. But I'll tell you something, they're different bairns to those I met at first. Eeh! they were demons, especially that Matthew.'

'Aye' – the smile slid from Katie's face – 'he's a bit bossy is Master Matthew, wants his own way, wants to rule the roost.'

'That's nothing; you haven't had a frog put in your bed or bowls of porridge splashed all over the table.'

'Is that what you had?'

'Oh yes, and more.'

The children came back into the room now, crying in loud whispers, 'Come on. Come on, Trotter.'

Taking John's and Jessie's hands, she ran them out of the room, but stopped at the top of the stairs, warning them, 'Now, go quietly, tiptoe, because if your grandmother hears you she'll be up like a shot.'

They nodded at her; then in exaggerated steps went quietly down the stairs, along the corridor and into their father's room; but there they almost threw themselves on him, chattering and laughing, until Mark quietened them, saying in mock sternness, 'I haven't sent for you to have fun but to enquire what was making the noise and disturbing my supper.'

They pushed at each other now, sniggering and giggling; then Luke said, 'It was John, Papa, he was saying a funny rhyme; but it's about us.'

Oh dear me! Tilly groaned to herself. That's one thing she should have done, she should have told them not to repeat that one.

Again Matthew was taking charge. Pulling his young brother to the side of the basket-chair, he said, 'Perform for Papa. Perform for Papa. Go on.'

And John performed for Papa; but there was no great burst of laughter at the end because they were all looking at their father's face. His eyes were wide, his nose was twitching, his lips were slightly pursed. Was he vexed? He looked over their heads towards Tilly and he said one word, 'Katie?'

'No, no, sir; they didn't learn it here.' Oh dear, he wasn't going to laugh.

When his face began to crumple, the children scrambled towards him, but he put his hand up in a warning gesture, crying now, 'Laugh if you dare. One sound out of you and up the stairs you fly, because don't forget, the dining-room is below here, and who is in the dining-room?'

'Grandmama.' They all said the word together.

'Yes, Grandmama.'

He looked at his small son whose face was bright with the fact that he had entertained them, but what had really made that coarse rhyme funny was the child's stammer. It had worsened considerably during his absence from the house.

'He knows a song, Papa, about Grandmama.'

'About Grandmama?'

'Yes, Papa.' They all started to giggle now; then Luke said, 'We all know it, Papa, but John sings it the best. Go on, John. Sing "When I was a laddie".'

John seemed only too eager to please and, taking up his stance again, he began to sing now and he hardly stammered at all as, his face one big smile, he gaily went into the song:

> 'When I was a laddie i lived with me granny,
> And many a hammering she give . . . me,
> But now I'm a m . . . man I can hammer me granny,
> And it serves her right for hammering me.'

He finished the last line with a rush and when Mark, unable to contain himself, lay back against the cushions, his hand tight against his mouth and his eyes now gleaming with tears of laughter, they fell upon him, all the while smothering their own laughter.

Pressing them from him, Mark said, 'Who's . . . who's been teaching you these rhymes . . . your nurse?'

'No, Papa; it's Brigwell, one of the gardeners.'

'Old Brigwell?'

'Yes, Papa.' They all nodded at him.

'Oh, may he be forgiven! But he won't be should your grandmama hear of any of these rhymes.'

'Oh, we don't let her hear,' said Luke. 'We sing altogether, in the stables. Don't we, Matthew?'

Mark looked at the boy whose fair head was no longer covered in curls. He couldn't believe he was almost twelve years old, yet he looked older, and when Matthew, said, 'Shall we all sing it for you, Papa? It sounds very jolly when we sing it altogether,' he moved his lips one over the other before saying, 'Yes, yes; I should like to hear you sing it all together. But –' He raised his hand and wagged his finger before pointing it towards the carpet, saying 'Don't forget who's below.'

Scrambling now, they all stood in line at the foot of the basket-chair, with Tilly who was already there, and it looked as if she, too, was about to perform. And she could have joined them, so happy did she feel inside, for she had never seen the master so light-hearted for months, in fact never at all, for his face now was looking like that of a young man; and so when they started her lips too moved in unison with theirs.

> 'When I was a laddie I lived with me granny,
> And many a hammering she give me,
> But now I'm a man. . . .'

It was at this point that the door opened quietly and only Mark saw the visitor, and as the children were singing the words 'I can hammer me granny' he raised his hand slightly as if to warn them. but they were oblivious of the intruder, because the sound being made by their combined voices, although muted, was taking up all their attention. They finished the last line, 'And serve her right for hammering me.'

'*What . . . is . . . this! What did I hear?*'

The children turned really startled, and it was Jessie Ann who piped, 'Just singing a little song for Papa, Grandmama.'

'I heard what you were singing: hitting your granny' – it would appear that she couldn't allow her tongue to use the word hammering – 'And it serves her right for hitting you. Where on earth have you learned such a thing?' She was towering over them, and now her glance lifted to Tilly. 'You have taught them this?'

'No, ma'am.'

'Then it's that person up above. Mark, you must. . . .'

'Hold your hand! Hold your hand! Good-night, children. Good-night. Come and say good-night to me.'

They now scrambled to the couch and each placed his lips against his cheek before being hustled out of the room by Tilly.

'That girl . . . !'

'That girl's got nothing to do with this issue, Mother-in-law. No one here taught the children the rhymes.'

'Vulgarity!'

'Yes, indeed, vulgarity. But they didn't learn it here.'

'I don't believe you . . .'

'Believe me or not.' His tone was sharp. 'You'll have to go back to your own home to find out the person who brings a little merriment into their existence, and you'll find it in your valued old retainer, none other than Brigwell.'

'Brigwell! I don't believe it.'

'Believe it or not, Brigwell taught them that little ditty. And more. You don't know the half of it.'

'Brigwell has been in our family . . . well as' – she tossed her head – 'as long as I have.'

'Yes, and likely he found it very dull.'

'Mark!'

'What do you know what goes on in people's minds, what they do in their spare time? You've lived behind a moat in your pseudo-castle since you were a girl.'

He stopped abruptly and they stared at each other; then she said, with deep indignation in her tone, 'I am beginning to see another side to Eileen's existence in this house for you talk like a. . . .'

'Like a what?'

'A man who has stepped down from his class.'

After a moment longer, and while continuing to stare at her, he laid his head back against the cushions and let out a mirthless laugh; then almost childishly he made use of her words by saying, 'Oh, if only I could step down from anywhere at this moment, what I would not give.'

'I can well understand that, but your manner certainly doesn't beg sympathy.'

'Who is begging sympathy?' He was again glaring at her.

'Oh, Mark!' She tossed her head now, the artificial coils in her hair bouncing as if they would jump away from her scalp; and then her whole manner changing, she said, 'I had hoped to have a quiet talk with you tonight about . . . about a private matter, but I can see you're not in the mood, so I will leave it until tomorrow.'

'I won't be in any better mood tomorrow, Mother-in-law, so sit yourself down and get started on your private conversation.'

He sounded weary and his tone took the edge off the bluntness of his words, and after a moment she seated herself in the chair to the side of the fire and opposite him; then arranging the three overskirts of her gaberdine dress, she placed her two long narrow feet together, joined her hands in her lap, then said, ''Tis difficult to know where to begin when touching on your private life.'

He did not help by word or sign, but waited.

'Eileen wishes me to assure you that, as sorry as she is for your predicament, there is no possibility of her returning here. That being so, she wishes to be fair to you and offers you a legal separation, and you could settle on her a sum, a moderate sum. . . .'

There was another pause while she waited now for some response to her words, but when none came her hands moved from her lap and, as if she had just put on her gown, she adjusted the row of small silk bows leading from the neck to the waist; and there her fingers became still as she said, 'She thinks it would be to your advantage.'

Again Mark made no answer. But during the last few minutes while he had been listening to his mother-in-law his body had stiffened, and he had the impression that his toes were pushing past the cage and against the shawl covering it. His feet began to pain him and the pain now spread up his legs until it reached his waist, and there it took the form of a wire band constricting him.

'Now please, Mark, don't be angry. She is thinking of your interests too.'

'Be damned, she is! Legal separation! Do you know something? She's a fool. A legal separation would be a judicial separation and in such a case I could claim custody of the children.'

'No!'

'Oh yes, Mother-in-law, yes.... My god! a moderate sum, when I'm having to beggar myself to pay her what I do. It's a wonder she hasn't thought of divorce; but perhaps she has and has found out that a woman can't divorce her husband for infidelity only. Now Mother-in-law –' He pulled himself further down the chair and leant towards her until he was almost within an arm's length of her as he cried, 'You can go back and tell my dear wife that if she's not careful I shall yell it out aloud in court that she never allowed me her bed after John was born, and that the invalid business was a put-up game; very much so, because my children informed me only this morning that Mama goes out walking now; Mama goes out driving now; Mama went to the theatre last week. And too, Mr Swinburne took Mama all round the picture gallery; and Mr Swinburne took Matthew and Luke and Mama to a musical afternoon.... Mama has suddenly got the use of her legs, hasn't she, Mother-in-law? Oh –' Slowly he eased himself back on to his cushions; then looking at the blanched face of his mother-in-law, he said, 'You go back and tell your daughter I'll strike a bargain with her. If she returns my children to me without any fuss I'll increase her personal allowance, but if she doesn't I can, as I've said, apply for a judicial separation, in which case the law will give me custody of my own children.'

Jane Forefoot-Meadows was on her feet now, her face diffused with a natural colour. She cried at him, 'She will never let you have the children! Make up your mind to that.'

'She mightn't have any choice. Anyway, I have them now, Mother-in-law' – his voice was ominously quiet – 'possession is nine points of the law. What if I decide to keep them with me?'

'She'll fight you. She'll bring up your constant infidelities which amounted to cruelty. Yes, cruelty! That's what she can charge you with. Just you wait and see.'

Speechless now, he watched her flounce round and sail out of the room, and as the door banged to behind her he gripped hold of each side of the chair and actually shook it in a spasm of anger while with his head down on his chest he brought out, 'Damn and blast you and her to hell's flames!'

The next morning there was an argument between Mark and Jane Forefoot-Meadows with regard to the counting of time. She had arrived on the Monday afternoon and she said she was going to leave on the Thursday morning.

To this he had replied coolly, 'The children were to stay with me three days and they either stay with me three full days, returning on the Friday morning, or they do not return to Waterford Place at all.'

That he was utterly in earnest Jane Forefoot-Meadows realised. Nevertheless she did not comply with this demand without protest, and in no small voice.

Katie was downstairs collecting the children's lunch, and Tilly, hearing the noise from above combating even Mrs Forefoot-Meadow's voice from the master's bedroom, hurried up to the nursery floor and when she pushed open the schoolroom door it was to find Matthew and Luke rolling on the floor, their battle being egged on with cries from Jessie Ann and John.

Having separated them, she held them apart. Luke appeared to be on the verge of tears but Matthew's face was merely dark with anger.

'Now what is this all about?' Tilly demanded. 'Fancy wasting your time fighting. What's come over both of you? What I should do is knock your heads together. Don't you know that your father can hear you down below?'

'We . . . we can hear Grand . . . Grandmama yelling,' John stammered.

Tilly turned a warm affectionate glance on the small boy and he laughed back at her; then loosening her hold on the two boys, she said, 'There now, make it up. But why on earth are you fighting anyway?'

'It was 'cos of you, Trotter,' Jessie Ann put in pertly.

'Me?' She looked from one to the other of the boys, and while Matthew stared back at her, Luke hung his head and Jessie Ann went on, 'Luke said he was going to marry you when he grows up and Matthew said he wasn't 'cos he's going to marry you himself.'

She should have laughed, she should have pulled them into her arms and said, 'You silly billies,' but as she looked at them the old fear erupted in her. Men, they either loved her or hated her, but whichever line they took it led to trouble, now even trouble among children.

She was saved from making any comment to the boys by Katie entering the room carrying a laden tray, and as she lowered it on to the table she turned quickly to Tilly, saying, 'Anything wrong, lass?'

'No, no; they were just having a bit of carry-on and I came up to see what it was all about.'

'They were fighting,' put in the ever informative Jessie Ann. 'Matthew and Luke, they were fighting about who's going to marry Trotter.'

Katie was on the point of bursting out laughing when the look on Tilly's face prevented her; but being Katie she had to see the funny side of it, and so, pulling the cloth from over the covered dishes, she said, 'Eeh! well, I think they'll have to take their turn 'cos there's three of our lads are after her an' all.'

'Don't say that!' When the side of Matthew's hand came sharply across Katie's arm she winced and cried 'Here now! None of that,' and Tilly, grabbing Matthew by the shoulder, shook him as she demanded of him, 'Say you're sorry to Drew.'

'I shan't.'

She straightened up. 'Oh then, well you shan't, but don't you come fussing around me or expect me to tell your father what a fine fellow you are.' She turned on her heel now and marched out of the room, but she had just reached the top of the nursery stairs when Matthew caught up with her and, grabbing her apron, he pulled her to a stop. His face was scarlet, his lips were trembling, his round grey eyes were bright, and when he muttered, 'I'm . . . I'm sorry, Trotter,' she, too, felt a moisture in her eyes. It was something for the great Master Matthew to say he was sorry; he had certainly changed. When she put her arm around his shoulder she found herself suddenly hugged to him, and she stroked his hair, saying, 'There, there now.'

When he looked up to her the moisture had deepened in his eyes and was lingering on his fair lashes, and his voice sounded tight as he said, 'I don't want to go back with Grandmama, Trotter; none of us do.'

'But you'll have to.'

'But why can't we stay here? You could look after us, and Drew, and I wouldn't mind going to school from here as long as I could come back. Can't . . . can't you persuade father to keep us?'

'It . . . it doesn't seem to lie with your father, Matthew, it's your mother who has to be persuaded to come back. You understand?'

He moved his head slowly and lowered his eyes as he said, 'Yes, yes, of course.' Then his head jerking upwards, he blinked at her as he now brought out rapidly, 'I . . . I meant what I said, I won't let Luke marry you, I'll . . . I'll marry you when I grow up. I . . . I know it isn't the right thing for a gentleman to marry a menial but it's different with you because you can read and write. You'll let me marry you, won't you, Trotter?'

'But I'm nearly twice your age, Master Matthew.'

'Oh, I know that and I don't mind, because you'd be able to look after me better, being older. And anyway, you're not really twice, only six years, and if I know you'll marry me it would be something to look forward to because the holidays are very boring at grandmama's.'

'Well; just as you say then, Master Matthew.'

'Oh, thank you, Trotter, thank you. You know what, Trotter?' His voice sank to a whisper. 'A boy at school told me he had once kissed a girl right on the mouth, but I didn't believe him because I know that you cannot kiss anyone on the mouth until you are married. Can you, Trotter?'

'Er' – she gulped in her throat – 'no. That's right, Master Matthew, that's right.' He now smiled at her and she gulped again before saying, 'Go along and get your dinner and . . . and tell Drew that you're sorry.'

'Yes, Trotter, yes.' He backed two steps from her, then turned and ran into the schoolroom, while she stood at the top of the stairs not knowing whether to laugh or cry. You can't kiss anyone on the mouth until you are married. Who'd have thought that went on in Matthew's head, him of all people, the terror, the little upstart that he was, or had been. Growing changed people; it was changing herself, and with the change came wants, just starting in that eleven-year-old boy, but galloping in herself now.

She hurried down the staircase and to her duties.

2

The children had been gone a week and Master Harry had left yesterday, not for the university but for France again. From what Tilly had overheard in conversation between him and his father, his friend who was half French had a sister and for most holidays, the sister and her parents returned to a castle in France, a chateau they called it. The master had explained that to her last night; he had talked about his son in snatches all the evening. 'He wasn't always gay like this, you know, Trotter,' he had said; 'he was a very solemn child and a more solemn youth. I am glad he has these friends in France because it has shown me another side of him. He is quite the man of the world, don't you think, Trotter?'

'Yes, sir, he's a very nice young gentleman, Master Harry, very likeable.'

'Yes, indeed, very likeable. I wonder if he'll marry this French girl. Her name is Yvette. Nice name for a daughter-in-law, Yvette. . . . Do you miss the children, Trotter?'

'Oh yes, sir, yes, sir, very much. The house is so quiet without them.'

'Yes, it is. Everyone seems to have deserted us at once, even Burgess.'

'His cold was very heavy, sir. I think it was wise of him to stay in bed for a few days, colds can be catchin'.'

'He lives entirely alone, doesn't he?'

'Yes, sir.'

'That must be very trying. I'd hate that, to live entirely alone.'

'I . . . I don't think he minds so much, sir, he . . . he kind of loses himself in books.' She smiled now. 'He has hardly anything in his house but books, just the bare necessities and books.'

'You have been there?'

'Yes, sir, I . . . I have been a number of times, but . . . but I went on my half-day on Sunday.'

'How does he manage to cook for himself?'

'Oh, his wants are very few, I think; he . . . he mainly lives on porridge and milk most times, and a little mutton now and again.'

'Really! Does he have a meal when he's here?'

'Well' – she turned her head slightly to the side – 'he sometimes has a snack in the kitchen, sir.'

'In future, Trotter, see that he has a good meal on each of his visits. And I think it would be a kindness if you slipped along and took him something hot now that he's unwell, or send one of them from downstairs.'

'I would very much like to take him something, sir. It . . . it wouldn't take me long, I could be there and back within the hour.'

'Well, do that, do that. And you needn't hurry; you've hardly been out of doors for days.' He paused before he ended, 'Do you find it tiresome to be tied to this room and me?'

'Tire-some!' Her lips lingered over the word; then she shook her head and her smile widened as she said, 'Oh no, sir, no; there's nothing I would like to do better. It has been like a – ' She looked to the side, then lowered her head, and he said, 'Been like a what?'

'A kind of new life to me, like the things Mr Burgess used to talk about, bringing one alive.'

'Looking after me has been like that to you?'

'Yes, sir.'

He stared at her for a long moment before he said quietly, 'You don't ask much from life, do you, Trotter?'

'Only peace, sir.'

'Peace!' The word was high, and he repeated it, even louder now and on a laugh, 'Peace! At your age, girl! 'Tisn't peace you want at your age, it's excitement, laughter, joy.'

She returned his stare. He seemed to be forgetting her position, and not only hers but also that of the very young who had at one time worked for him. There had been very little excitement, laughter and joy for those who had had to tear a living out of the earth, whether above or below it. What she had meant to convey to him by saying she wanted peace was the peace wherein she could work without fear, without having to fight against the waves of resentment.

'Why are you looking so stiff-faced? Have I said something to annoy you?'

Again she didn't answer him, at least not immediately, because masters or mistresses didn't trouble whom they annoyed. In her class, servants were there to suffer annoyance. He was in a way placing her in an awkward situation. As the saying went, she was neither fish, fowl, nor good raw meat. At times she didn't know where she stood with him, as servant, or nurse, or confidante, especially when he talked to her about the children and his son, Harry, and even his mother-in-law; although one person he never mentioned was his wife.

She said flatly now, 'What I meant, sir, was all I desired was to work in peace, and . . . and out of that could come a bit of laughter now and again, but as for excitement and joy, well – ' Her voice sank low in her throat as she ended, 'It doesn't come to everybody, sir.'

His eyes held hers now as he asked, 'Don't you want it to come to you, Trotter?'

And she dared to answer, 'What one wants and what one gets are two different things, sir. I . . . I haven't as yet seen much excitement and joy among the people I know, except on fair days when some of them get drunk. All they seem to do most of the time is work and. . . .'

She was startled by the movement that he made. Swinging out his arm, he almost knocked over the jug of fruit juice standing on the table with a glass beside it. Only her own quick movement stopped it from tumbling to the floor, and after she had steadied it she stood back from the long chair and looked at him in astonishment, for his look was almost ferocious as he cried, 'What is in your mind, Trotter, and in the minds of most of your class is that you are the only people who suffer indignities, the only people that joy doesn't touch, the only people who haven't any chance of excitement, these you make yourself believe are prerogatives of the upper class. Now am I right?'

She dared to answer him but in a very small voice, 'Well, aren't they, sir?'

'No, they are not, Trotter; money, position, titles, none of these bring happiness. Excitement perhaps when one has the money to run an estate and shoot, or money enough to seek big game, that kind of excitement, but joy, real happiness, is no more the prerogative of the rich than it is of the poor, it is something that is within you. Yes, yes, of course' – he jerked his head up and down as if answering some remark of hers now – 'I know what you're thinking: you don't go hungry when you've got money, you can be sick in comfort, like me' – he now spread his arms wide – 'my money and position enables me to have someone like you to wait on me hand and foot – foot! that's saying something – whereas if I were a poor man I wouldn't be able to enjoy these privileges. Granted, granted, but if I were a poor man, Trotter, I wouldn't be weighed down with responsibilities, I wouldn't be afraid of public censure, I wouldn't have to conform to patterns that are against the grain; I wouldn't have to keep up a way of life I can't afford, I wouldn't have a thousand and one things that irk me; and if I were poor I wouldn't have to lie here, Trotter, thinking about ways and means of how I'm going to carry on now that the mine is no longer working.'

He turned his head away and pressed his lips tightly together, and, her voice soft and contrite, she said, 'I'm sorry, sir. I'm sorry I've upset you.'

'You haven't upset me' – he was looking at her again – 'I'm just trying to explain something to you.'

'I . . . I know, sir, and I understand.'

'You do?'

'Yes, sir. I . . . I haven't the words to explain how I understand but . . . but I do.'

He let out a long breath and slumped against his cushions, then smiled ruefully, saying, 'Well, if that's the case we're getting some place, and at the beginning of this conversation, if I remember rightly, you were about to go some place.'

She answered his smile now by saying, 'Yes, sir, to Mr Burgess.'

'Well, get yourself away before the sun goes down. Enjoy your walk, and give him my best respects. Tell him I miss his conversation and' – he brought his head forward towards her – 'his tidbits.'

'I'll do that, sir, and I . . . I won't be long.'

'Take your time, but get back before dark.'

'Oh yes, sir, I'll be back before dark.'

When the door closed on her he screwed his eyes up tight as if trying to blot out the mental picture of her, then muttered to himself, 'Oh! Trotter. Tilly Trotter. Tilly Trotter.'

Mr Burgess was delighted to see her.

'What have I done to deserve such kindness, I'll never be able to eat all that.' He pointed to the cold chicken, the meat pie, the bread, cheese, and slab of butter, among other things, on the table, and she answered, 'Well, if you don't you'll never be able to get out of that chair. And just look at your fire, it's almost dead. I thought you said there was a boy brought your kindlin' and coal in?'

'I... I did, he does, but he hasn't been for the last two days, he mustn't be well himself, it's these bitter winds. Do you know there was frost on the window pane this morning and here we are at the end of April? I long for the summer.'

'You'll never see it if you don't look after yourself.' She bustled about the room and he smiled at her as he said, 'You'd make a marvellous mother, Trotter; you're just like a hen, be it a little tall.'

'Oh, Mr Burgess!' She flapped her hand at him. 'I don't take that as a compliment.'

'Well, you should because the master thinks you're a wonderful hen.'

'Mr Burgess!' Her tone was indignant even while she suppressed a smile, then she added, 'I don't feel like a hen.'

'No, my dear, I'm sure you don't; you're more like a peacock. Given the right clothes you could outdo any peacock.'

'Tut! tut!' She turned away from him. 'I think your cold's addled your head. Anyway, hens, peacocks and the rest of the farmyard, if you don't make yourself eat I'll ask the master if I can send one of the girls over to see to you, and you won't like that, will you?'

He aroused himself in the chair, saying, 'No, Trotter, I wouldn't like that. I can't abide people fussing around me and moving my' – he paused – 'things.'

Seeing that the main things in the room were books, and that these were scattered everywhere, she could imagine his reaction if anyone were to attempt to tidy him up; but she was genuinely concerned for him, and so for the next half-hour she brought in a stack of wood and coal, she emptied slops, she filled cans with fresh water from the well, and when she had finished she washed her hands in the tin dish standing on a small table at the end of the room, and as she dried them she looked towards the window and said, 'It looks as if it could rain and the twilight's setting in, so I'll have to be off, but you'll promise me, won't you' – she went up the room and stood in front of him – 'that you'll eat everything that is in that cupboard?' She pointed towards the old press from which she'd had to take books to make way for the food. 'And if I can't get over tomorrow I'll be here the next day.'

Mr Burgess didn't speak, but he held out his hand to her, and when she took it he said quietly, 'You bring happiness to so many people, Trotter.'

Her face had no answering softness in it when she replied, 'And trouble an' all, it would seem, Mr Burgess.'

'Don't you worry about the trouble, my dear; people bring trouble on themselves, it's their thinking that creates the trouble. You go on as you are and one day you'll come into your own. Yes, you will.' He moved his head slowly up and down. 'I have a strong premonition about many things and I've always had one about you, one day you'll come into your own.'

His words, said with such deep sincerity, brought a lump to her throat and she turned from him and, getting into her coat, she buttoned it up to the neck, then put on her hat which was the same straw one that she had worn for years. Finally, picking up the basket, she said, 'Now take care, won't you?' and he answered, 'Yes, my dear, I'll take care. And thank the master for me and tell him I'll soon be on duty again.'

'He'll be glad to hear that, he misses you.'

'And I him. Yes, I him. I find him a very interesting man.'

They stared at each other for a moment longer; then again she said, 'Good-bye, Mr Burgess' and he answered, 'Good-bye, my dear,' and she went out.

The air had turned even colder and it caught at her breath, and the twilight, threatening to be short tonight, made her hurry her step.

Mr Burgess's cottage was situated up a narrow lane at the end of which were two roads, one that would eventually take you into Shields, the other into Jarrow. Along one side of the Shields road was a high bank which led on to common land. At the far side was some woodland running along the top of what was almost a small gorge. Once through the wood you came on the estate. She had come from the house by this route and she was returning the same way.

Inside the wood it was dim, even dark in parts, but this didn't frighten her. No darkness frightened her now since she had experienced the total blackness of the mine; even night-time seemed light to her now.

She was emerging from the wood and was passing the last big tree close to the edge of the gorge when her heart seemed to leap into her throat and bring her breathing to choking point as a man stepped from the side of the tree and blocked her path. For a full minute neither of them moved, but they stared at each other; and as she looked into the face of Hal McGrath a scream tore up through her but found no escape past the constriction in her throat.

'Aye, well, so here we are, eh?'

Her lips fell apart. She took a step to the side, and slowly he did the same.

'Didn't expect to see me the day, did you, *Mistress* Trotter, 'cos a mistress I hear you are now up at the big house? Done well for yourself, haven't you?'

Still no words came.

'Been easy in yer mind lately, haven't you, since I was well outa the way? An' things've been happenin' up there, haven't they? By! from what I hear they have that. You know what they're sayin' back in the village? They're sayin' that no ordinary lass could have brought about what you've brought about. Got rid of the whole caboodle you did, and put your own crew in, an' now your sail's full of wind you're away. . . . Well, haven't you anythin' to say to me after all this time? No, not a word?'

He pulled his head back from her now as if to survey her better, then went on, 'You've changed, thickened out a bit. You needed that, but I don't know whether I'm gona like the woman better than the lass. Anyway, we'll see, eh?' . . . . On these last words his hands came out like the snapping wires of a hawser and when they gripped her arms she found her voice and she screamed at him, 'You leave go of me, Hal McGrath. It's no girl you're dealin' with now. Leave go of me!' Being unable to use her arms she used her feet; but her skirt impeded the blows and only caused him to laugh. Then he swung her round as if she had been a paper bag and, pulling her clear of the dim wood, he thrust her against the bole of the tree, and holding her there, he growled, 'That's better. I can see what I'm doin' here, eh? I can see what I'm doin'.'

When she again used her feet he leaned his body at an angle towards her. Then his jovial manner changing and his face close to hers, he hissed at her through his clenched teeth, 'God Almighty! but I've dreamed of this night after night, day after day. Me belly wrenched with sickness, me arms nearly torn out of their sockets, sea-boots in me arse, I still dreamed of this minute, and now it's come an' I'm going to have me payment, an' there's nobody on God's earth gona stop me. Do you hear that, Tilly Trotter?' He brought her shoulders from the tree now and with a quick jerk banged her head back against it. Then as she gasped and cried out, he said, 'That's only the beginning 'cos I've never known a minute's luck or peace since me thoughts settled on you. I thought it was the money at first, but it wasn't, that was only part.' Now to her horror he gripped her throat with one hand and like an iron band he held it to the tree, and as her hands tore at his face and her feet kicked at his shins he did not seem to notice. With his other hand he ripped her coat from her back, with one twisting pull he tore the front of it open and the buttons flew like bullets from the cloth; and now his hand was on the bodice of her print dress, and when the cotton was rent his fist was inside her body shirt tearing it from her bare flesh.

It was when his fingers dug into her breast that the scream tore through her body but found no escape; and then gathering her last remaining strength she did what she had done once before, she brought up her knee with as much viciousness as she was able to his groin. Instantly his grip sprang from her throat and he was standing away from her bent forward, his two hands clutching at the bottom of his belly.

Filled with terror as she was, she hadn't the strength to run for a moment, and in the gasping pause she took in the fact that he was standing on the very edge of the steep bank. She also knew that in another moment or two he would recover and then God help her, for if she did run he would catch her. How she forced herself to put her hands on him she never knew but she ran at him and the impetus nearly took her over the side at the same time as it toppled him backwards, his arms now wide and the curses flowing from his mouth, and in the instant she turned to run she heard him scream. It was a high, thin scream, not like something that would come from his throat at all. She remained still, turned about again and looked down. His body was at a strange angle. He was on his back, he had fallen among an outcrop of rock and his middle seemed heaved up. For a moment she saw him in a position similar to that in which the master had lain. When he made no movement she put her hand to her mouth and whimpered, 'Oh no! God, don't say that.'

The next minute, holding her tattered clothes about her, she scrambled down the steep bank; then her approach to him slow, her step cautious in case the whole thing were a trick, she paused within an arm's length of him. His eyes were closed. Then slowly they opened and he groaned. When she saw him try to move she turned quickly away, but his voice stopped her as he growled, 'Me back. I'm stuck. Give me a hand.'

When she shook her head he closed his eyes again; and now his words slower and with what she detected might be panic in them, he muttered, 'Then get somebody. Don't leave me here, you bitch, with the night comin' on. D'ya hear? D'ya hear?'

She knew his eyes were following her as she climbed the bank. Once on top she began to run.

It was almost dark when she reached the house. She had seen no one at all.

Letting herself in through the still-room door, she came into the corridor, and there halted. There was the muted sound of laughter coming from the servants' hall. It was around the time of the day they stopped to partake of a drink of beer or tea, and a bite.

On tiptoe now, she stumbled up the back stairway, and like an intruder she slunk through the green baize door and across the gallery. And it was as she made her way past Mark's bedroom to go to her own room that his voice came loudly from the room saying, 'Out there, is that you, Trotter?' Then louder, 'Trotter!'

She now leaned against the wall to the side of the door, and when his voice came again, demanding, 'Who is it out there?' she knew there was nothing for it but she must put in an appearance or else he would undoubtedly ring the bell to the kitchen.

When she opened the door and moved slowly into the room he drew himself up on the chair, exclaiming, 'God above! What . . . what has happened to you?'

'Hal McGrath. He was waiting for me outside the wood.'

'Good God! look at you. What has he done? Come . . . come here. Sit down. Sit down!'

His hand going out now and gripping her wrist, he muttered, 'What happened?' then added, 'Never mind. First of all, go and take a glass of brandy.' And when she shook her head he commanded, 'Go along, girl! It will stop that trembling.'

In the dressing-room a minute later, after pouring herself out a small amount of the brandy she sipped on it, choked and started to cough; and it was some time before she could control it and go back into the bedroom.

His impatience showing in his voice now, he said, 'Well! Come, tell me.' And she told him all there was to tell, but when she finished, 'He's . . . he's hurt his back, he . . . he can't move. Somebody will have to be told,' he interrupted quickly, saying, 'Somebody will have to be told? Have some sense, girl. The best thing that can happen is that he be left there and let's hope the night will finish him off because that man is a danger to you. Go now and change your things. And listen. Don't mention this to anybody, not a soul. Do you hear? . . . Did anyone see you come in in this state?'

'No, sir.'

'Good. Now look; go into my closet and clean up as much as you can because if any of the staff see you in that predicament they might blame me. What's more, never try to tiptoe past my door, my ear has become attuned to your step, even on the carpets.' His voice had now taken on a light note, doubtless to cheer her, but she couldn't move her face into a smile. . . .

Having washed, she put on an overall she kept to cover her uniform when cleaning the closet out. She took this precaution just in case she should see someone when making the short distance between this and her own room. And again she was fortunate. So, as no one but the master knew what had happened to her, why should she be worrying now in case Hal McGrath should die out there. She wanted him dead, didn't she? Yes, oh yes; but she didn't want his death on her conscience. If only she could tell someone. Who? Biddy? But the master had warned her to keep silent . . . yet, oh dear God, she didn't know what to do.

She got the answer when a tap came on the door and Katie came quietly into the room, saying, 'Tilly, that lad's come again, Steve. He wants to see you. He was here just after you left. You all right? You look peaky.'

'I . . . I feel a bit bilious.'

'Well, it must have been the duck 'cos my stomach felt a bit squeezy after me dinner. It takes some getting used to, rich food, after hard tack for years.' She smiled broadly, then said in a whisper, 'Are you comin' down?'

Tilly nodded, adding, 'I'll be there in a minute tell him.'

'Aye. Aye, all right, Tilly.'

A few minutes later she went down the corridor but not on tiptoe. In the kitchen she looked about her and Biddy, jerking her head towards the yard, said, 'He wouldn't come in, he just said he wanted to have a word with you.'

They exchanged glances and she went out.

The yard was lit by the candle lantern hanging from a bracket and its light seemed to have drained all the colour from Steve's thin face and he began straightaway without his usual greeting of 'Hello, Tilly.'

'He's back, our Hal,' he said. 'He came in last night. There he was this mornin' when I came off me shift. I could have died. He knew I'd come and tell you, an' he threaten'd to do me in. Me ma kept me in the house all mornin'. She took the ladder away from the attic so I couldn't get down, and then when she did let me out he'd been gone for hours. I . . . I came as quick as I could, Tilly, I. . . .'

She put her hand on his arm and said, 'I know, Steve. I've . . . I've met him.'

'You what! And you're still whole? Eeh! Tilly, the things he said he would do to you. And he was solid and sober when he said them, that made it worse. Eeh! Tilly' – he shook his head 'what did he say? How did you get . . . ?'

She now pulled him away from the light of the lantern and into the darkness of the high wall that bordered the gardens, and her voice a whisper now, she told him briefly what had happened. After she finished he didn't speak for some time; then he said, 'You think his back's gone?'

'Well, he couldn't move, Steve. And . . . and he might die, and I don't want him on me conscience.'

'You're daft, Tilly, you're daft. You don't know what you're sayin'. I'll tell you somethin' and it's the truth. It's either you or him. He's not right in the head, not where you're concerned he's not; an' he never will be as long as he breathes. He'll do for you either way. If in some way he were to marry you he'd still do for you, he'd beat the daylights out of you. You've got into him somehow. I don't understand it, I only know that you come atween him an' his wits, so the best thing to do is . . . is leave him there.'

'No, no, Steve. Neither of us could stand it if we left him there to die. I hope he dies, but . . . but not that way, not without something being done, so go and see if he's managed to get up. If not, well, you know what to do, tell your da, and they'll come and fetch him.'

When he shook his head slowly she said, 'Please, Steve, please, for my sake.'

'I won't be doing it for your sake, Tilly, don't you see – it's like signing your death warrant, an' me own an' all, for he'll cripple me altogether one of these days. He's not going back to sea an' he'll hound you, you won't know a minute's peace. Aw Christ! Why was he born?' He became quiet for a moment, then said,

'Go on in.' He pushed at her roughly. 'Go on in, you're shiverin'. It'll be all right. Go on in.'

'You'll go? Promise me you'll go, Steve.'

'Aye, all right, I'll go.'

'Thanks, Steve, thanks.'

He made no answer and she watched the dark blur of him turn away into the night.

❧ 3 ❦

It was the following afternoon when the news reached the Manor, Sam brought it. He had been into Shields to the corn chandler's. All the news of the town and the villages about sifted through the corn chandler's and, like chaff wafted on the wind, it spread. Of course a dead man found in a gully wasn't all that exciting, not for Shields anyway, sailors were always being found up alleyways bashed and stark naked. The waterfront had its own excitements where killings were concerned. But this fellow had just come off a boat in the Tyne the day before yesterday, and he had been found early on this morning lying in a gully, a knife through his ribs. The general opinion was that the poor bugger would have been best off had he stayed at sea. But that was life.

Had he been in a fight? Nobody knew, only that he was lying on his face. It looked as if he had fallen down a steep bank and on to his own knife because his initials, they said, were on the handle of the knife.

But why would he have his knife out if he wasn't fighting? Well, as far as could be gathered there was no sign on his body that he had been in a fight, black eyes or bruises, nothing like that, just a few scratches on his face where apparently the brambles had caught him.

Sam gave the news to Katie and Katie took it into her mother, and Biddy stared at her open-mouthed until Katie said, 'What is it, Ma, are you sick?' and Biddy answered, 'No, it's just come as a bit of surprise, that's all, because he was the fellow who used to torment Tilly, an' for him to die like that and near the grounds an' all.'

'Aye, he was, and she for one'll be pleased at the news. I'll go and tell her.'

She met Tilly in the corridor, outside the master's room.

Staring at Katie, Tilly opened her mouth twice before she could whisper, 'Dead? He's dead?'

'Aye; as I said. Fell on his knife, so Sam says! Dead as a door nail, so you'll have no more trouble from him. What's the matter? Eeh! you're not gona pass out, are you? Some folks do with relief – it's like shock,' she was speaking in a soft hiss.

'I've ... I've got to go and see to the ... the master.'

'Aye. Aye, Tilly, but I thought you'd like to know.'

'Yes; thanks. Thanks, Katie, ta.'

Tilly turned away and went back into the room where Mark was waiting for her. His eyes narrowing, he looked at her as he said sharply, 'Well, what is it? You've ... you've had news?'

She went and stood by his side, and now she wrung her hands as she gabbled, 'They've ... they've found him, but believe me ... believe me, sir, not as I left him. When I left him he was lying on his back over the outcrop. News has come that he was on his face with' – she gulped in her throat and wetted her lips before she brought out in a thin whisper, 'with a knife atween his ribs.'

'A knife?'

'Aye, yes, sir.'

'A knife.' He chewed on his lip a moment. Then he said, 'Somebody must have been there after you, somebody who hated him even more than you did.'

'Yes, sir.'

'Have you any idea?'

She lowered her eyes. 'His ... his brother, he came last night. I asked him to go and find him because ... because I couldn't have his death on me conscience and ... and I thought he might die in the night. He, Steve ... he promised to go and ... and. ...'

'Well, it seems evident that he did go and all I can say is he's done you a very good turn.'

'But if they were to find out he'd ... he'd swing.'

'Very likely' – his voice was cool sounding – 'but we shall see what transpires. And, Trotter.' He reached out and gripped her hand and, pulling her nearer to him, he looked up into her face as he said, 'You're rid of him. That's one fear less in your life. And it's been your chief fear, hasn't it?'

'Yes, sir. But now I'm afeared for Steve.'

'Well, why should they suspect him? Only you and I know about this matter, so who's to accuse the brother of killing him? Now come.' He shook her hand. 'You wont be implicated in any way.'

'I ... I don't know so much, sir. Steve said that Hal had threatened to beat him up if he came and warned me. And anyway, the mother locked Steve up in the attic, and when he went out, Hal McGrath, they would know he was goin' lookin' for me.'

'Well, let them say what they like; you've never been away from my side for a week and I'd swear to this on all the Bibles in Christendom. Forget that you visited Mr Burgess, forget that you've ever left me for a moment. Your friends downstairs will forget it too if it comes to the push.' His voice trailed away and his eyes held hers, and when with a break in her voice she said, 'I'd die if anything should happen to Steve through me,' his grip tightened on her fingers and, his words coming from deep in his throat, he said, 'And I should die, Tilly Trotter, if anything should happen to you.'

As they stared at each other her mind started to gallop. *Oh, no! No! No! Not that door.* She didn't want that kind of door to open. But yet, hadn't she known it had been pushing ajar for a long time now?

*

No one came to the Manor enquiring for Miss Matilda Trotter to ask her questions about her movements on a certain day because at the inquest it was brought out that the man, after leaving his ship, had spent most of the evening in a tavern on the waterfront and had left there at a very late hour. His parents admitted that he had arrived home in the early hours of the morning and yes, he was under the influence of drink. But although they insisted that he had slept the drink off before he left the house the next day, the coroner took little account of this. But what he did take into account was that there had been no sign of a struggle. There were bruises on the man's back where he must have hit the boulders as he fell before rolling on to his face and his knife. Why he should have a knife in his hand would remain a mystery; but the knife was his own and his parents had confirmed this. A verdict of accidental death was returned.

On the day of the inquest the village waited. What would the McGraths do? They wouldn't take this lying down, would they? Would Big McGrath go to the Manor and haul that Trotter piece out? because if she hadn't actually done it she had certainly put her curse on Hal. And that last night of his life he had come through the village shouting her name. The whole village had heard him.

But Big McGrath did nothing because his wife said, 'No! no more,' because if he opened his mouth against that one now he would lose another son.

McGrath had gaped at his wife as if she had lost her senses when she said simply, 'Stevie did it. Anyway, Hal would have swung in any case because he meant to do for that accursed bitch.'

'I don't believe it,' Big McGrath had said, 'not Stevie; he wouldn't have the guts.'

'He had the guts, although he nearly threw them up in the gorge in the middle of the night – that's where I found him.'

'But why . . . why his brother?' He spoke now as if he had been unaware of the animosity between his sons.

'Two reasons,' said his wife. 'Hal has knocked him from dog to devil since he was a bairn. The other, he's caught, like Hal himsel' was, in the traps of that witch. An' that, I would say, was the main reason.'

'God Almighty! and we're to sit here and do nowt?'

'Aye,' she said. 'But God and the devil have a way of fighting things out. Bide your time. Bide your time and join your prayers to all the others who have suffered at her hands an' her day will come. You'll see, her day will come. God speed it and grant I'll be there.'

∽ 4 ∾

Summer came and it brought the children for a full week. The house once again rang with laughter and the big event at that time was the master racing them along the broad drive in his new acquisition, an iron-rimmed wheel-chair. The only fly in the ointment of that particular week for Mark, and definitely for Tilly, was the presence of Mrs Forefoot-Meadows, accompanied this time by her maid, Miss Phillips, who could have been twin to Miss Mabel Price.

After they departed the house once again fell into its familiar pattern, and the master became morose and seemingly more demanding as the days went on. There were times when nothing was right. These came generally after his failure to adjust to the wooden stump and false foot for his left leg. The apparatus was leather-capped, as was the smaller artificial foot to adjust to the right ankle. Yet he had more success with the leg that extended to the knee than with the foot attached to his ankle; the bones here were so sensitive that the slightest pressure caused the water to spring to his eyes and his nails to dig into whatever he was holding at the time, which more often than not was Tilly's arm.

Always he apologised for this; and one time he unbuttoned the cuff of her sleeve and, pushing it up, he looked at the blue marks his nails had caused. For a moment she imagined he was going to put his lips to them, and so she had pulled her arm away, saying, "Tis nothing, sir. 'Tis nothing.'

There was no fear in her life now. The village could have been on another planet. It was so long ago since she had passed through it, she had even forgotten what it looked like. And those about her bore her no resentment, much the reverse. She was given respect and her wishes were adhered to in every possible way. Yet she was not happy, for deep inside her she knew that sooner or later a question would be put to her, and if she said 'No', what then? And should she say 'Yes'. . . . But she couldn't say 'Yes'. She couldn't give herself to somebody she didn't love. Yet she had a feeling for him, a strong feeling but different from that she still carried for Simon.

At times when she couldn't imagine herself living any kind of life but that which she was living now she would ask herself why not, because this present way of living would lead nowhere. She knew what happened to serving girls who gave in to masters. Oh yes, she knew that well enough. Yet she no longer felt a serving girl, and that was strange. Well, not so strange, she told herself, because it wasn't every servant girl who could discuss books. And then again he wasn't like an ordinary master. There were times when she felt she knew him better than any wife would know her husband, certainly better than his own wife did, for she knew she had spent more time with him in one month than his wife had spent with him in years, at least in the years after she had taken to her couch. So what was going to come of it? She didn't know. Then one night the opportunity was given to her to find out.

It was two days before Christmas, 1840. The house was warm and there was a gaiety prevailing in it, even without the children being present. Bunches of holly were hanging here and there. There was a mistletoe bough hanging in the hall where a huge fire was blazing in the iron basket on the great open hearth. The drawing-room was ablaze with light. All the lamps were lit in the house because the master was expecting company. Mr John Tolman and his lady, Mr Stanley Fieldman and his lady, and Mr Albert Cragg and his lady were coming to dinner.

Mark was dressed in a new blue velvet dinner-jacket and a cream silk shirt and cravat. Mr Burgess had trimmed his hair to just above the top of his collar. A few minutes before he was ready to be carried downstairs by Fred Leyburn and John Hillman he said to Tilly, 'Well! and how do I look? The caterpillar emerging from the chrysalis. But a very late emergence, therefore a very old butterfly.'

She smiled widely at him, saying, 'You look very handsome, sir.'

'Thank you, Trotter. And you, you look very . . . very charming. Grey suits you, but . . . but I would take that apron off.'

She looked down at the small dainty lawn apron hemmed by a tiny frill that had taken her hours to sew, and she said, 'You don't like it, sir?'

'It's all right in its place but not for tonight. You are acting in the role of housekeeper, aren't you?'

'Yes, sir.'

'Do you know what is expected of you?'

'Yes, sir. I'm to take the ladies into . . . madam's room' – she had paused before uttering the word madam – 'and assist them off with their cloaks, and . . . and wait in the dressing-room in case they call me. And to be on hand during the evening should . . . they need to come upstairs.'

'You have been well primed. Who told you of this procedure? I just meant you to help them off with their cloaks when they came up. . . .'

'I understand it's what Mrs Lucas used to do, sir.'

'Oh, I see. Well, I shall leave that part to you. Now tell Leyburn that I am ready. . . .'

Ten minutes later he was ensconced in the wheel-chair in the drawing-room, and when the butler came in to tend the fire, he said, 'Everything in order, Pike?'

'Yes, sir. I think the table is as you wish it, and Cook has carried out your orders as regards the main course. The turkey is a fine bird, sir, together with the braised tongue.'

'Good. Good.'

'And Miss Trotter wrote out a menu for the cook to cover the rest of the meal: Soup for the first course, sir, then crimped cod and oyster sauce, followed by pork cutlets in tomato sauce; then, as I said, the turkey and tongue, sir. This will be followed by cheesecake and nesselrobe pudding, and, of course, the cheeses; we have a very fine ripe Stilton, sir.'

'Sounds excellent, Pike, excellent.' Mark had turned the chair towards the fire;

he could not let the old man see that he was amused. Now that he knew Trotter was in favour, Pike never missed an opportunity to sing her praises, if unobtrusively. And it was quite some time ago off his own bat, that Pike had appended the miss to Trotter. It was what Trotter had once referred to as crawling, yet there were times when he felt sorry for the man, for he had aged visibly since most of the old staff were dismissed and he had elected to stay on, and his legs seemed hardly able to carry him. What would happen to him should he retire him now he didn't know, for he had known no other home but this house since he was a boy. Oh! why concern himself about such things at this moment. Tonight he was entertaining friends for the first time in more than two years, and there would be women at his table.

It was odd when he came to think about it but it wasn't he who had suggested the get-together; it was Cragg on his last visit who had said, 'Isn't it about time you had some company?' and he had gladly fallen in with the suggestion.

When he heard the carriages draw up outside he wheeled himself into the hall, there to welcome his guests. 'Delighted to see you, delighted to see you. Hello, Joan. Hello, my dear Olive. Why Bernice, such a long time since we last met.'

'Wonderful to see you, Mark.'

'You're looking so well, Mark.'

'My dear Mark, how lovely to be here again.'

'Will you come this way, madam?'

After a moment the ladies turned and followed the tall, slim, grey-clad figure. Their silken skirts making sounds like the ebbing waves on a beach, they swept up the staircase, across the gallery and into the wide corridor where Tilly, after opening the door leading into what was once Eileen's sitting-room, stood aside and allowed them to enter.

The room was softly lit by the light from two pink-shaded oil lamps and a glowing fire, and it showed up the gold embroidery on the chaise-longue, and the deep rose velvet upholstery of the Louis-Seize. Added light was given by the candelabra arranged at each end of the long dressing-table, and between them lay the powder boxes and toilet water ready to hand.

One after the other she helped the three women off with their cloaks, and one after the other she hung the velvet and fur-trimmed garments in the wardrobe, conscious all the while that the women were eyeing her, one of them through the long cheval mirror, another from where she sat in front of the dressing-table; the third, a very stout madam, stood looking at her without any pretext whatsoever.

Tilly wetted her lips, swallowed her spittle, then said, 'If the ladies should require me I shall be in the adjoining room.'

Had she said the right thing or the wrong thing, for now all three of them were looking at her directly? And then she did the unforgivable, she forgot her place to such an extent that she didn't bend her knee. Of late, she had been out of the habit of doing so, and when she did remember it was too late, she was already entering the dressing-room.

Closing the door behind her, she stood with her back to it and let out a long-drawn breath, then closed her eyes tightly, and as she stood thus the muted voices came to her, words indistinguishable at first, but then snatches here and there.

'I told you, didn't I?'

'It was evident, Albert said.'

'Nonsense!'

'You were right, Bernice.'

'Nonsense!'

'Not after Myton; he would never stoop. Educating her . . . Nonsense!'

'Stanley says it's impossible to educate the peasantry.'

'Queer stories.'

'Odd looking altogether . . . shapeless.'

One of them laughed, a high laugh; then a voice said, 'Well, what are we here for?' and another answered, in a quite ordinary tone, 'What indeed! Let us go down.'

'*Girl!*'

She paused a moment, then turned and opened the door. The three women were standing close together, that is as close as their billowing skirts would allow, and it was the stout one who, with a lazy gesture, waved her hand towards the door. Following the silent command, Tilly opened it and stood aside, and they all three floated past her, leaving behind them a beautiful smell of perfume.

After closing this door, too, she stood with her back to it. And now she asked herself why she should feel so angry, was it because they had been talking about her? Yet when she tried to recall the disjointed sentences she found she was unable to do so. But the impression remained strong and disturbing: they *had* been talking about her, and she imagined that if she were not the main reason, she was certainly part of the reason why they were here tonight.

'Aw, don't be daft.' She pulled herself from the door and went to sit down on a chair, but stopped herself as she thought, No, it wouldn't be right, not in this room; and so, going out, she went into the master's room and there, sitting down, she asked herself why it was one instinctively disliked some people. Those three, for instance, she felt she hated them. It was the way they had looked at her, as if she were of no more account than an animal. Less, for the class were known to care for their horses and their hounds. Biddy was saying the other day that there were good gentry and bad. In some of their houses you were in luck, in others you were like muck. Biddy came out with some funny sayings. Which reminded her, she'd better get downstairs.

A few minutes later she was in the kitchen.

Here there was bustle and excitement: Mr Pike and Phyllis were serving in the dining-room, but waiting on them were Peg and Katie, and running back and forward in the kitchen was Ada Tennant and young Fanny, while supervising them all was Biddy.

'How's it going?' She was standing by Biddy's side.

'All right from this end, lass. Everything was done to a turn. But my God! that puddin', it has me worried. I only hope it tastes as good as all the stuff that's gone into it. The cheesecake's all right and the rest, but oh' – she glanced at Tilly – 'this is more up my street, not fancy puddings,' and she continued stacking the small sausages round the base of the bird. Lastly, she poured a glazed sauce over its breastbone, and standing back, she looked at it with her head on one side as she said, 'We could get through that quite nicely worsels, eh Tilly?' Then, 'There now, Peg; put the cover on, and in you go with it. Steady! Don't spill the juice. And you, Katie, get the vegetables in.'

She now went up the kitchen and took from the round oven the silver vegetable dishes, saying, 'They're not that hot, you can handle them. There you are.' She placed four on a tray that was large enough to cause Katie to have to spread her arms wide in order to carry it.

Returning to the table, she said, 'Once the main course is in I always think it's easy going after that.'

'You'll be glad to get off your legs.'

'Aye, I will. It's been a long day, but an important one.' She nodded at Tilly. 'You see, I've never cooked a dinner like this for the gentry afore, not for a proper do. It's different sending bits and pieces upstairs. Everything had to be right for this, hadn't it?'

'And you got it right. I knew you would.'

'You look tired, lass. Anything wrong?'

'No, nothing.'

'What are they like, the ladies?'

It suddenly sprang to Tilly's mind to answer, 'Bitches!' but instead, she said, 'If they hadn't their fine clothes on they'd look like ordinary women.'

At this Biddy put her head back and laughed, then slanting her eyes towards Tilly, she said, 'You're learnin', lass. Aye you're learnin'. Put me in mind of what me granda used to say, so me mother told me, when she used to come back from her place at the castle and talked about the ladies and gentlemen there. He used to say, "Aye; aye, lass; but just remember they've got to gan to the closet like ye and me." '

Tilly pressed her lips together, then said, 'How right you are.'

After a moment Biddy asked, 'Where's your apron, I thought you were goin' to wear it, the one that you made?'

'The master didn't like it; he . . . he told me to take it off.'

Biddy was looking squarely at her now. 'Why?'

'I don't know. I . . . I suppose he just didn't like it.'

Biddy turned from her and, reaching out, gently lifted up the elaborate iced pudding reposing on a shallow cut-glass dish, the base of which was surrounded by coloured crystallised flowers, and she gently shook her head but made no further remark, and Tilly, divining her thoughts, turned away. . . .

The dinner lasted about an hour and a half. Snatches of talk and laughter seeped into the hall, but later, after the company had retired to the drawing-room the laughter and talk became louder, the scent of cigar smoke filled the house, and the air seemed filled with jollity. Definitely so in the servants' hall, where they were all tucking into the remains of the feast.

Tilly had had a tray brought upstairs so that she could be on hand if the ladies should require her. She had forgotten to show them the way to the closet, but none of them seemed to have been in need of it so far. It was eleven o'clock and she'd been up from six that morning and now, right or wrong, she was sitting in the armchair, her head nodding, when she heard the chatter outside on the landing.

She was on her feet when the door opened and the three women came into the room. Passing her as if she were non-existent, they flopped down here and there on the chairs. Then one laughing said, 'I need the closet,' and another answered, 'Me, too; but I'll have to wait until I get home and get out of me stays.'

'Do you think you'll last, Bernice?'

'Well, if I don't ... pop goes the weasel!'

Standing at the far end of the room, beside the door leading into the dressing-room, Tilly could hardly believe her ears. They were coarse these women, yet they were ladies, in fact two of them were daughters of men with titles. They had acted like great dames a few hours ago, now, full of wine and food, they were talking no better than those they employed; in fact, there were some ordinary folk who didn't discuss such things, personal things.

'Me cloak, girl!'

She walked swiftly across the room and, taking a cloak down from the wardrobe, she tentatively held it out to the woman. 'That isn't mine. Don't be stupid, girl! The brown velvet.'

She brought the brown velvet and helped the owner into it. Then taking another cloak from the wardrobe, she stood with it in her hand looking towards the two women, and one of them said, quite civilly, 'That's mine.' Then they were all ready to go and, laughing and chatting, they went from the room without a glance in her direction. And yet, strangely, she knew they were as aware of her as she was of them. Snatches of their conversation came to her as she followed them down the corridor.

'Did you see his face when Albert mentioned Agnes's new bull?'

''Twas naughty of Albert, and Mark was mad.'

'What d'you think of the other?'

'Don't really know. Could be.'

'I thought I'd have the vapours when Stanley grumbled about his feet and the gout.'

''Twasn't intentional, 'twasn't.'

'God! I want the closet.'

Tilly didn't know if she were supposed to follow them downstairs and help to see them out, but she didn't go. Mr Pike was there, that would suffice. The bull they were referring to was likely Lady Myton's new lover, and this must have displeased the master. They were as she had dubbed them at first, bitches, three bitches.

The door could hardly have closed on them when the master ordered to be carried upstairs, and when she saw his face she knew he was in a temper.

The men carried him past her and into the closet; afterwards they sat him in a chair beside the bed. When they had gone he called to her in the dressing-room, his voice imperious, 'Trotter! Trotter!'

'Yes, sir?' She stood in front of him and when he looked up at her without speaking she said, 'Have you had a good evening, sir?'

'No, Trotter,' he replied, 'I have not, as you say, had a good evening.' He spaced the words. 'How many friends can you expect to have in life, can you tell me?'

'No, sir.'

'If you have two, you are damned lucky, but I don't think I have one, not a true friend. A man who was a true friend would control his wife, at least her tongue, when in company. Trotter, those three ladies came tonight to find out something. Have you any idea what it was?'

She stared unblinking at him as she said, 'No, sir,' knowing now that she could truthfully have said, 'Yes, sir.'

'That's just as well. Here, pull this shirt off me.' He tore at his cravat, and when she had stripped him down to the waist he said as he always did now, 'I can manage.' She had already laid his nightshirt on the bed. There was no nightcap beside it, for he was strange in that he didn't like nightcaps. And yet most gentlemen wore nightcaps, so she understood. Perhaps it was because he had never powdered his hair or worn a wig. But then lots of gentlemen didn't wear wigs today or powdered. Even so, she would have thought they all wore nightcaps.

'Get yourself to bed, you must be tired.'

'Yes, sir. Good-night, sir.'

'Good-night, Trotter. By the way' – he paused – 'it was an excellent meal, I've never tasted better. Tell Cook that.'

'I will, sir. She'll be very pleased.'

In her room, she sat for a while in the chair by the side of the bed. She was feeling sad inside, sad for herself, but more sad for him: he hadn't enjoyed the evening, yet everybody else in the house had. Of course, she couldn't speak for the guests.

She rose slowly and undressed and got into bed.

She did not know how long she had been asleep but the crash woke her, bringing her sitting upright and wide awake all in a moment. The noise had come from the room beyond the closet and the dressing-room. Had . . . had he fallen? Had he tried to get out of bed and knocked something over?

She was out of the door, along the corridor and into the bedroom before she had even given herself the answer to the question, and there before her, showing up faintly in the glow of the night candle in the red glass bowl, was the over-turned side table, the water carafe not broken but half empty now as it lay on its side, and a glass that had snapped clean in two. Also spread about the floor were a number of books and as far away as the fire, lying on the rug, was the square brass travelling clock.

'What is it? What is it?' She had gone round to the other side of the bed. He was lying back now on his pillows, his face twisted. 'I . . . I had an accident, the table toppled.'

'Don't worry. Don't worry, I'll soon clear it up.'

He roused himself, saying, 'The glass, mind your feet.'

'Yes, yes, all right. Just lie still.'

She lit the candles; then taking one, she hurried through the dressing-room and into the closet. As she was picking up the pail and cloth there was a tap on the door. When she opened it, there stood Katie and Ada Tennant. For some time now they had been sleeping up on the nursery floor, while Biddy, Peg, and Fanny went to the back lodge which was now their home.

'What ... what's happened? We heard the crash.'

'It's all right. He ... the master upset the table, the side table.'

'Is there anything I can do, Tilly?'

'No, no, Katie. Get back to bed.' She now looked at Ada Tennant who was hanging on to Katie's arm. She seemed frightened. She was a silly girl, vacant in some way, and her mind, what little she had, was open to all impressions. And so she reassured her now, saying, 'It's all right, Ada, nothing's happened. Go on back to bed.'

As Ada nodded her plump face at her, the thought came to her that in a few years time she would look like Mrs Brackett, because like her, she was always eating.

When the girls had gone she closed the door, then went swiftly through the dressing-room and into the bedroom. He was lying as she had left him, his head back, his eyes closed.

After picking up the debris from the floor and sopping up the water from the carpet, she took the pail and the broken glass into the closet and left it there. She would deal with that in the morning. All she had to do now was to fill the carafe again and give him a clean glass.

He was sitting propped up against the pillows when she returned to the bedroom and, going to him, she said, 'Is ... is there anything more I can do for you, sir?'

His eyes were wide open and he continued to stare at her, and then he said slowly, 'Yes, Trotter; sit down here beside me.' He patted the side of the bed.

'But, sir.'

'Trotter, please.'

Her hand went instinctively now to the front of her nightdress. She hadn't even got her dressing-gown on. She said softly, 'Will you excuse me a moment, sir, while I get me dressing-gown?'

'No, Trotter, I wouldn't excuse you a moment. Just sit down as you are.'

Slowly she obeyed him.

'Give me your hand.'

She gave him her hand, and when he took it he turned it over until her palm was upright. Then he placed his other hand on top of it and, his voice now like a low rumble in his throat, he said, 'During these past months I've been very lonely, Trotter, but never so much as tonight ... downstairs.'

Her surprise overcame her feeling of apprehension for a moment and she managed to bring out, 'They ... they are your friends, sir.'

'No, Trotter, no; I have no friends. I am going to tell you something, Trotter. Those men who were here tonight all have mistresses. Two are kept in Newcastle and one in Durham. One of those gentlemen has lost count of the number of mistresses he has had. And their wives know of these kept women, yet they live an apparently normal life. But me, I had one affair, not my first I admit, but the only one during the time of my second marriage, and what happens? I lose my wife and my children, and because my wife leaves me I am shunned. Had she chosen to stay, my escapade would merely have been a talking and a laughing point among my so-called friends. Can you understand it, Trotter?'

She made no answer. She couldn't. She knew what he had said was true, but the unfairness of it provided her with no words of consolation.

'I sound full of self-pity, don't I?'

'No, sir.'

'Well, what do I sound like to you?'

This she could answer without taking time to consider. 'Somebody lonely, sir.'

'Somebody lonely.' He repeated her words. 'How right you are, Trotter. Somebody lonely. But it does nothing to help a man's ego to admit that he's lonely. You know what an ego is?'

'No, sir.'

'Well, it is . . . it's his pride, it's that thing inside of him which tells him he's a great I am. Both big and small men are born with it. Strange' – he gave a huh! of a laugh here – 'but the smaller the man the bigger the ego. You see, the small man's got to fight to prove himself. But here am I, neither big nor small, and my ego has dropped to rock bottom. It must have, to make me act as I have done tonight in order to bring you to me.'

He turned now and looked at the righted table and he said, 'I upset that lot purposely because I wanted you here near me.' He did not turn his head now and look at her, but feeling her hand stiffen in his, he said, 'Don't . . . don't be afraid of me, Trotter.'

'I'm not, sir.'

'You're not?'

'No, sir.'

'Then why did you shrink from me?'

'I didn't shrink; I . . . I was only surprised, sir.'

'And shocked?'

'No, sir, not shocked.'

'You know what I'm asking of you, Trotter?'

She looked down to where their clasped hands lay on the padded eiderdown and she moved her head once as she said, 'Yes, sir.'

'And –' His voice scarcely a whisper now, he asked, 'are you willing?'

Her head was still down as she answered him bluntly, 'No, sir.'

When his fingers withdrew from hers she raised her eyes and looked at him and said, 'I'm . . . I'm sorry, sir. I . . . I would do anything for you, anything but . . . but . . .'

'Lie with me?'

Again her head was down.

'You . . . you don't like me?'

'Oh yes; yes, sir.' She instinctively put out her hand towards his now; then withdrew it as she went on, 'Oh yes, sir, I like you. I like you very much, sir.'

'But not enough to comfort me?'

'It wouldn't be right, sir. And . . . and it would alter things.'

'In what way?'

'It . . . it wouldn't be the same, me going around the house, I –' She turned and looked across the dimly lighted room now and it was some seconds before she could find words to express her feelings, and then she said, 'I . . . I wouldn't be able to keep my head up.'

Again he made a small sound like a laugh in his throat, then said, 'That is what is known as working-class morality.'

'What, sir?'

'It doesn't matter, Trotter. But tell me, have ... have you ever loved anyone?' He watched her chest expand underneath the cotton nightdress, he saw her neck jerk as she swallowed deeply, and when he insisted, 'Have you?' she said 'Yes.'

'And he? Does he love you?'

'I ... I think he does in a way, sir.'

'In a way? What do you mean in a way?'

'Well, it would be no use, sir, 'twouldn't be right.'

'Oh! Trotter. Trotter!' The sound of his laughter was more defined now and he shook his head as he said, 'You're unfortunate, Trotter. It would appear that you only arouse the love of married men. I suppose he is married?'

'Yes, sir.'

'Is it the farmer?'

When she actually started, he said, 'Oh, don't be upset; I'm sure your secret must be suspected by a number of people for it isn't every bridegroom that leaves his bride on his wedding night to go to the assistance of a beautiful young girl. Nor does a man take her into his house in spite of his wife's protests. By the way I'm just guessing at the last. When I found you living in the outhouse I thought something was amiss in the farmer's household for you to have returned to the ruins of the cottage. ... So, Trotter, you're in love with a man who can never mean anything to you. What are you going to do? Spend your life fighting against frustration until you're a wizened old maid?'

'No, sir.' Her voice was clear now. 'I shall marry. Some day I shall marry and have a family.'

He peered at her now through the lamplight and her answer seemed to deflate him still further, for he lay back on his pillows and sighed.

'I'm sorry, sir.' Her voice conveyed her feelings.

'It's all right, Trotter, it's all right. But stay. Would ... would you do something for me? It's not going to hurt you in any way. But it'll bring ... well, it'll bring to life a sort of fancy I've had of late.'

'Anything I can, sir.'

'Well then, lay yourself on top of this bed with your head on the pillow facing me.'

'Sir!' She was on her feet now, her hands joined together at her waist, and he said, 'It is nothing much to ask. I won't hurt you in any way, I'll be under the clothes and you'll be on top of them. I just want to see you lying there.'

He watched her head slowly droop until her chin was on her chest. He watched her turn slowly and walk round the foot of the bed and to the other side. He watched her pull her nightdress up slightly and her bare knee touch the coverlet. Then after resting on her elbow, she lay straight down. He watched her stretch out her hand and push her nightdress well down over her knees. And now they were lying, their faces opposite to each other.

When he lifted his hand and gently touched her cheek, Tilly closed her eyes and told herself loudly in her head not to cry, because if she cried it would be the undoing of her, for pity for him would swamp her and she would no longer lie on top of the bedclothes.

'You're very beautiful, Trotter. You know that?'

She made no answer.

'I'm going to tell you something. I dislike your name very much, I hate it every time I've got to say it, it's a harsh name, Trotter. Your name is Tilly and Tilly sounds so nice, gay, warm. A Tilly, I feel, could be no other than nice. I think of you as Tilly.'

'Oh, sir.'

His fingers now were moving round her eye sockets as he said, 'You've got the strangest eyes, Trotter, they're so clear and deep. That's why people take you for a witch.'

Again she said, 'Oh, sir.'

'And you know, I don't think they're far wrong. I was thinking the other day it's a good job that you hadn't been born into the class because you would have played havoc there. There would have been no peace for any man who set eyes on you.'

She had to speak or cry, and so she said, 'That isn't right, sir. Some people . . . some men dislike me wholeheartedly.'

'It's only because they want you.'

'No, sir. No, sir. 'Tis something in me. Women dislike me too. That's the hardest to bear, women dislikin' me.'

After a moment his hand left her face and he lay looking at her. Her eyes were shaded now, and he let his own travel down her shape underneath the cheap nightdress.

Then of a sudden they both turned their heads and looked up towards the ceiling as the sound of a door closing came to them, and when she rose quickly to her elbow she looked at him and he at her, and now he said, 'All right, my dear, and thank you.'

She slipped from the bed and made for the dressing-room door, but as she turned and looked backwards she saw he was lying on his side staring towards her. Swiftly she went into the room now, then through into the closet, and there, sitting down, she bent forward and dropped her face into her hands. Her whole body was shivering while her mind was chattering at her. Another minute or so and I would have. The pity of it, the pity of it. And him the master. 'Tisn't right. If only I could. But no, no, 'twouldn't be right. And as I said, I couldn't hold me head up. And he knows about Simon. Well, if he's twigged, how many more? His wife? Oh yes, his wife. But what's going to happen now? How can I go on knowing what he wants, and he's so nice, so kind? I do like him. Yes, I do, I do.

She got to her feet now, her mind saying harshly, 'Get to bed! For God's sake! get to bed.'

She had to go out of the closet door to get to her room, and she had just stepped into the passage when she came face to face with Ada Tennant. Ada was holding a candlestick; she held it above her head and peered at Tilly. She had a coat on over her nightdress and Tilly, remembering her position, said sternly, 'Where have you been?'

'Just down to kitchen, I was hungry. Me belly grumbles in the night. I've just had a shive.'

Ada now turned her gaze on Tilly. Tilly wasn't wearing anything over her nightdress and she dared to say, 'You've been with the master? You've had to see to the master all this time? and Tilly said rapidly, 'No, no, of course not. I've just been to the closet.'

'Oh. Oh aye. Thought I heard him talkin' as I passed goin' down. Must have been dreamin'.' She now turned away and went towards the end of the corridor and the stairs leading to the attic, and Tilly went into her room where, almost throwing herself into bed, she lay stiffly staring up into the darkness. It only needed Ada Tennant to put two and two together, and as simple as she was, she wasn't past doing that, and it would be all over the place that she was serving the master in more ways than one. Swinging herself about, she turned on to her stomach and tried to squash the thought that had sprung into her mind: she wished she could serve him in more ways than one, and except for the fact that she might be landed with a bairn she would, yes, she would, because where would this feeling for Simon ever get her?

Gone now was the idea that if she followed such a course she wouldn't be able to hold her head up again.

∞ 5 ∞

Routine can become tedious, but often it signifies a time of peace. From the night of the bed incident a new relationship came to life between Mark and Tilly. No reference was made to the incident, nor did his manner towards her alter in any way. But on her part, she had found difficulty for days afterwards in being her natural self. Soon, however, she took the cue from him and life went on smoothly, too smoothly.

Then one morning the smoothness was ruffled. Like the surface of the sea before a storm, all had been calm, but following the slight ruffle came a wind, and it churned up the waves so fiercely that at one point Tilly thought she would drown.

She was entering the kitchen when Peg came hurrying towards her, saying, 'Steve, the lad, is at the back door askin' for you, Tilly.'

Endeavouring to hide her impatience, she said, 'Thanks, Peg. I'll see to him,' and went down to the kitchen, past Biddy who turned her bent back from the stove, raised her eyebrows and shook her head but said nothing.

Steve had grown within the last year or so. He was now almost eighteen but he looked older; it was his solemn countenance that went a long way towards putting at least two years on him. He greeted her as usual: 'Hello, Tilly.'

'Hello, Steve,' she said. 'How are you?'

He did not answer her question but asked, 'Can I talk to you like, away from here?'

She turned for a moment and looked back into the kitchen, then said, 'Well, I'm on duty; but I can give you five minutes or so.'

She was surprised when he closed his eyes for a moment as he tossed his head upwards; then he was walking by her side and through the archway, and into the shelter of the high stone wall which had been bordered at one time by a rough hedge, but now the land was all cleared and showed a neat path and low-trimmed box hedges.

She was again surprised by his manner when he stopped abruptly and said, 'I've come to ask you something.'

She didn't say, 'Well, what is it?' she just waited a while, looking into his face; and so he went on, 'I feel I've got to speak out and get me say in afore he gets over his pretended sorrow and comes lookin' for you.'

'What are you talking about?'

'You know what I'm talkin' about.'

'I don't, Steve.' She shook her head impatiently.

'Well, first of all I don't care what they say about you and . . . and him. . . .' He pointed in the direction of the top of the wall and the house beyond.

'What do you mean?' Her chin came into her neck now as she felt her body stretching upwards.

'Aw' – he lowered his head and shook it – 'you know what I mean.'

'I don't know what you mean, Steve McGrath.'

'Well, you should do if you've got your wits about you. Ask yourself, which lass of your standin' is taken into a big house like that and put in charge and runnin' it like a mistress? They say you don't get chances like that for doin' nowt.'

'Well, I got my chance for doing nowt.' Her voice was loud, and, realising this, she turned her head first to one side, then to the other, and pressed her fingers over her lips for a moment.

'You mean there's nothin'?' His tone was contrite now.'

'I don't see why I should bother even to answer you.'

'Aw, I'm sorry.' He looked to the side, then kicked at a pebble on the path. 'It's the village; they seem to have nobody to talk about but you. It's funny.'

'I don't think it's funny.'

'You know what I mean. Well, anyway' – he now drew himself up and said, 'I'll come to the point, I've been beatin' about the bush for as long as I can remember. I . . . I want to marry you, Tilly. I . . . I want to know if I can start courtin' you? I'll soon be on the face workin' and I'll earn enough to keep us. . . .'

She was looking at the ground. She, however, did not kick at a pebble but remained perfectly still for a moment with one lifted palm outwards before her face. It was this action which had stopped him talking.

There was a long silence before he said softly, 'I'll wait as long as you like.'

'It's no use, Steve. I . . . I don't think of you in that way.'

"Cos I'm a year younger?'

'No, it's got nothing to do with that, I . . . I just think of you . . . well, as a brother.'

'I don't want you to think of me as a brother, I never have.'

'I know.'

'You know?'

'Well, of course, I know, and . . . and I've tried to put you off. You can't say I haven't.'

'You won't put me off, Tilly, not until you go and marry somebody else.'

'Steve' – she put her hand gently on his arm now – 'please don't wait for me 'cos it can never be, not . . . not with you. As much as I like you, it can't þe, Steve.'

He lowered his head now as he said, 'Things happen; you might be glad of me one day.'

'I'll . . . I'll always be glad of you, of your friendship, Steve, but . . . but not as anything else.'

She watched his face crumple as if he were going to cry, and what he said now startled her.

'I killed our Hal for you, Tilly.'

'Don't say that!' The hoarse whisper came from deep in her throat, and she repeated again, 'Don't say it. I told you to go and help him . . . oh my God! Anyway, if you did it you didn't do it for me, you did it because you hated him.'

His head came up with a jerk as he said, 'I hated him because of what he did to you, and what I did to him I did for you. What's more, they know that I did it, at least me ma does. But she won't give me away because she'd lose another one, an' me pay packet an' all.'

The bitter irony of his words saddened her, and for a moment she wanted to put her arms about him and hold him and tell him how grateful she was for what he had done because inside she was grateful, but she knew what the result of that would be, so she said, 'Oh, Steve, I'm sorry. I'm sorry, and I would do anything for you, but . . . but that. Try to look upon me as a friend, Steve. There's good lasses about. Katie, you know, she's always talkin' about you, she likes you a lot, she's a nice lass.'

'Aw. Shut up Tilly! it's like tellin' a thirsty bloke to chew sand.'

There was silence again between them until she said, 'I've got to go, Steve, I'm . . . I'm sorry.'

'I'll wait.'

'Please, please, Steve, don't, it's useless.'

'Aye well, I can't feel worse off than I am now, but I thought I'd get the first one in afore the farmer comes gallopin' over.'

She stared at him, her brows meeting. 'What do you mean, the farmer comes galloping over? I've never seen Si . . . Mr Bentwood for months. And what makes you think he'll come galloping over here?' Her voice was stiff, as was her face now.

'Well, he's a widower now, isn't he?'

'What!'

He stared at her. 'You didn't know that she, his wife, was dead?'

Her mouth opened to let in a long draught of air and she shook her head slowly before saying, 'When?'

'Four . . . no, six weeks gone. And you didn't know?'

'Well, why should I?' She was finding it difficult to speak now. 'We get no one . . . no one from the village here.'

'But surely somebody in the house?'

She looked away to the side as she thought, Yes, surely somebody in the house. The master, he was bound to know that the farmer's wife had died. Yet why should he? Then there was Mr Burgess, he knew all the gossip of the countryside, he surely would have spoken of it. Her gaze flicked from side to side as if searching for an answer; then she said, 'I've . . . I've got to go. Goodbye, Steve. I'm . . . I'm sorry.'

'Tilly.'

She refused to answer the plea in his voice and, turning hurriedly away, went through the arch and over the courtyard and into the kitchen; and there met Phyllis who was coming through the green-baize door and who in a loud whisper said, 'I . . . I was just comin' for you; there's company.'

'Company? Who?'

'Mr Rosier has just been shown up.'

His feelings were such that Mark would have welcomed the company of any man that morning, with the exception of the one who now stood before him.

'Well, how do I find you?'

'You find me very well.' Mark did not look towards Mr Burgess and say, 'Give the gentleman a seat,' but Mr Burgess, of his own accord, proffered the visitor a chair before he himself left the room.

'I should have called before but I have been busy.'

It was now more than a year since the mine disaster, and so whatever had prompted Rosier's presence here today wasn't out of compassion or sympathy. . . . But why ask the road he knew?

'How are things?'

'As you see' – Mark waved his hand in an arc which encompassed the room – 'most comfortable. Everything I need.'

'Yes, yes.' Rosier now patted his knee; then jerking his small body up from the chair, he flicked his coat tails to the side before saying, 'I was never much use at small talk – don't believe in it anyway – I think you know why I'm here today.'

Mark remained quiet, just staring at the man.

'It's like this, Sopwith, there's not a damn thing been done to your pit since the water took over. Now if you leave it like that much longer it will be too late to save anything.'

'I wasn't aware that I'd given the impression I wanted to save anything.'

'Don't be a fool, man.' Rosier screwed his buttocks hard on the chair now, and both his face and his voice showed impatience as he said, 'And don't let's spar. And I'm not going to talk light because you're no invalid. Let's speak man to man, you're in a hell of a mess.'

'I beg your pardon!'

'You heard what I said all right, you're in a hell of a mess. You haven't got the money to put that place in order and, as it is, nobody but a fool would take it on.'

'I would never have classed you in that category, Rosier.'

'Ah, don't fiddle-faddle, you know what I mean. The place needs money spent on it, even when it's pumped dry, and that'll take the devil of a lot of doing. But you know, you've always been behind the times. Now you've got to admit that.

Why, you're one of the few pits that's been running solely on horses for years. You thought you could go it alone. All pits are joining up their wagonways, some going straight to the ports. Look what's happening across the river. Seghill has become dissatisfied with the Cramlington wagonway and is building its own line to Howdon.'

'Go on. Go on.'

'Aye, I'm going on. Now, as I proposed to you when I last spoke about sharing, the wagonway between us would have been of great benefit, we could have joined up with the main line going to the river....'

'Great benefit to whom?'

'Now don't take that lord almighty tack, Sopwith. If you had taken my offer on a fifty-fifty basis we would have both benefited, now your place is hardly worth the ground it stands on.'

'Then why are you here?'

'Because I'm a man who takes risks, a gambler at heart, I suppose.

'And you're willing to gamble on something that's not worth the ground it stands on? Oh, who do you think you're talking to, Rosier? Now – ' He put his hand up to check a further flow from the visitor, saying, 'Wait! That mine has been in our family for generations, before rolley ways or wagonways were thought of when the ponies and horses carried the coal on their backs, and it's going to remain in our family. Dry or wet, working or still, it's going to remain there. Have I made myself clear?'

Rosier was on his feet now wagging his bullet head from side to side. 'You're a bloody fool, Sopwith,' he said 'That's what you are. You're sinking. All about you you're sinking, your house, your land. It might as well have been flooded with the pit for all the use it's going to be to you when you haven't got the money to keep it going. I can promise you twenty-five per cent of what I'll get out of that hole in a couple of years' time, enough to keep you safe here for the rest of your days.'

Mark reached out and grabbed at the bell rope to the side of the fireplace; then his hand releasing that, he picked up the bell on the side table and rang it violently.

Before Pike's stiff legs were halfway up the stairs, Mr Burgess had entered the room.

'Kindly show this gentleman out, Burgess.'

Mr Burgess lowered his head and stood aside for the visitor to leave, but Rosier remained standing staring at Mark, and what he said now was, 'Your days are done; you and your kind's time has passed. Things are happening out there. Iron is coming into its own; steam is giving horses a kick in the arse, you'll see. You'll see. You and your horses carrying the coal out on your wooden tracks! God! you're as dead as last century.'

When he turned he almost knocked Mr Burgess over; in fact, if it hadn't been for the support of the door the man would have fallen.

Pike was at the top of the stairs to meet the visitor, but he, too, was thrust aside.

Tilly held her breath for a moment as she watched Mr Pike support himself against the balustrade; then she hurried towards the bedroom.

Mr Burgess was leaning over the chair as she entered the room and he was saying, 'Are you all right, sir?' and for answer Mark said, 'No, I'm not all right, Burgess; who could be all right after that?'

Burgess straightened up and, his voice quiet now, he said, 'Pigs are supposed to be intelligent, sir, and one can believe this, but on no account will they ever be capable of fitting into civilised society.'

'Oh, Burgess!' Mark put his head down for a moment; then looking up at Tilly, he said, 'Bring me a glass of something, not milk or soup.'

She smiled at him before hurrying to the dressing-room.

A few minutes later, after he had sipped at the glass of brandy she had brought him, he looked from her to Mr Burgess and said quietly, 'He's right you know, he's right in one way, I belong to the last century.'

'Nonsense!'

He smiled at Burgess; then said to Tilly, 'I don't suppose we'll have another visit from him, but leave word, Trotter, that he has not to be admitted to this house again, on any account.'

'Yes, sir.'

She left the room, went downstairs, and gave the order to Mr Pike, who said, 'Well, that's good news, for nothing would please me better than to show that gentleman the door before he got over the step.'

Returning upstairs again, she went immediately into the dressing-room and there she waited until she heard Burgess take his leave. There was something she wanted to ask the master, at least there were two things she wanted to ask him; the first one was if she could have this afternoon off. When she thought of what this might lead to she put her hand to her breast as if to still the quickened beating of her heart. She knew why Simon hadn't come to see her since his wife had died, for the simple reason it wouldn't be proper and no matter how forthright he might appear she knew he cared about people's opinion of him. But there was nothing to stop her visiting him to offer her condolences. Oh, she tossed her head at the thought – she was acting like a hypocrite, thinking like a hypocrite. She was glad she was dead. She was, she was. No. No. She mustn't think like that. Well, what other way could she think? Simon was now free and she loved Simon ... and he loved her. She had known this for years, even perhaps before he knew it.

She went into the room now and, standing a little distance from Mark, she said, 'Could I ask a favour of you, sir?'

'Yes, Trotter, anything. You know that I will grant you anything within my power.'

'May ... may I have this afternoon off, sir?'

When he put his head back and laughed she smiled widely. After the rumpus of that meeting it was good to hear him laugh.

'Of course, Trotter, you may have the afternoon off. I think we should arrange that you have more afternoons off, you spend too much time in the house and' – he paused – 'and in this room.'

'Oh, I don't mind that, sir.'

'I'm glad you don't, Trotter. Are you thinking of going into Shields or taking a trip into Newcastle?'

'No, sir, neither.'

'Oh.' He waited, his face full of enquiry, and now she put her second question to him. 'Did you know, sir, that Farmer Bentwood's wife had died?'

His eyes held hers, but even before that her face had flushed with the question she had put to him, for she was remembering the confession of her feelings on a certain night some months ago.

'Yes, yes, I knew, Trotter.'

She could now feel her face stretching in amazement. When she found her voice she wanted to demand, 'And why didn't you tell me?' but the thought came to her, How did he know? Someone must have told him. Such a thing wouldn't be of any interest to the viewer or the agent who sometimes called about the mine; perhaps it was Mr Tolman or Mr Cragg. And then she knew who had brought the news, Mr Burgess. Her voice was quiet when she said, 'Does . . . did anyone else know, sir, that she had died?'

'Yes, Trotter, Burgess.'

'Oh.'

'You may wonder why he didn't mention it to you?'

'Yes, sir.'

'Well, it's because I told him not to.'

Her face again stretched; then he was going on, 'I had my reasons, Trotter, very good reasons. If Farmer Bentwood wants you he'll come for you, that's how I see it. If I loved someone and I knew they were available I would make it my business to go to them and tell them how I felt.'

'It . . . it wouldn't have been right, sir, if . . . she's only been gone a short while.'

'Almost six weeks, Trotter.'

His eyes had never left her face. 'As for not being right, that's damn nonsense. I needn't ask if he's written to you because, had he, you wouldn't be showing so much surprise and agitation now.'

When she bowed her head, he said, 'Wouldn't it be better if you were to wait . . . in fact, I think it would be better if you were to postpone your visit. Give him time to – ' When he stopped abruptly she raised her head and looked at him, and he shrugged his shoulders.

They looked at each other for a moment in silence, then she said, 'May I still have the afternoon off, sir?'

'Yes, Trotter.'

'Thank you, sir. I . . . I shall see to your lunch first.'

As she turned away, he lifted himself up from the chair by his arms as if to follow her or speak; then dropping back, he turned his head and looked over the wide sill and out of the window, and he thought, If she goes, what then? . . . Dear God! Let's hope Burgess is right.

'I am going on an errand,' she said to Biddy.

'You'll be blown away, lass.'

'Doesn't matter, the sun's shining.'

'Won't be for long.' Katie had come in through the back door on a gale of wind and thrusting her thick buttocks out, she pressed the door closed, saying, 'Phew! that was a narrow escape. A slate came off the roof and almost slid past me nose. Boy! one of those could cut you in two. . . . Where you goin' Tilly?'

'I'm just going on an errand.'

'Oh.' Katie knew when to stop asking questions, but she added, 'Well, if I were you I'd put a scarf round me hat else you'll be leap-frogging across the fields after it.'

'Stop your chattin',' her mother said to her now. 'Get about your business and let Tilly get away. . . . Make the best of your walk, lass; you don't get out enough.'

'I will.' She nodded at Biddy, then went out and with the wind at her back she had to stop herself from running.

She was well away from the house when her desire to run was frustrated by the wind now being in her face, and she had to battle against it, holding her hat on with one hand and keeping the front of her skirt down with the other.

She took the road along the bridle path and past the cottage. Here, she stopped for a moment, her back to the wind, and gazed at the charred walls. The tangled grass had grown up almost to – the ground floor window-sill. It seemed a long lifetime away since she had lived there, so much had happened to her, yet she hadn't moved more than two miles away from it. She cut through Billings Flat; then to avoid the village she climbed the steep bank, went through the rock-strewn field and so on to the fell proper. Coming to a low stone wall, she sat on top of it and as she threw her legs over she scattered a few sheep sheltering on the other side. As they ran from her she laughed out loud. It was good to be out in the air and the wind. She had the desire to run again, but now she was approaching the farmland and she might meet up with Randy Simmons or Billy Young or Ally Taylor.

She saw none of the hands until she reached the farmyard proper, and it was Randy Simmons she saw first. He was coming out of the byre directing a heifer by prodding its rump with a sharp stick, and he became still as he stared at her while the animal galloped away to the end of the yard. And he didn't move until Bill Young shouted, 'Where's this 'un off to?' Then he, too, stopped after he had brought the animal to a halt, and from each end of the yard they looked at her.

Turning her back to the wind, she was now facing Bill Young and she called, 'Is . . . is Mr Bentwood about?'

Pushing the animal forward now, Bill Young came up to her and stared at her for a moment before saying, 'Well, no, no, he's not, Tilly.'

'Tell you where you'll find him.'

She turned now in the direction of Randy Simmons and waited for him to speak again, and after a moment of staring at her, he thumbed over his shoulder, saying, 'Workin' in the bottom field in barn down there.'

'Thank you.' She turned away from them. She was facing the wind again and she heard Bill Young's voice raised and Randy Simmon's answer him, but she couldn't make out what they said.

She went up the road and through a gate into a field. Once inside, she had to skirt it as it had been freshly ploughed up. Then she was in a grass meadow, and down in the dip at the very end of it lay the barn.

She was running now, letting the wind carry her right to the very doors. They were closed but not locked. She pushed against one and it gave way almost a foot, and then it stuck. As she went to squeeze through the narrow aperture her hat caught against the edge of the closed door and pushed it over her eyes. When she pushed it back she was through the door but could go no further for to her amazement she was standing within a few inches of the flanks of a horse, and when it lifted its back leg and struck the rough stone floor she gasped and pressed herself against the inside of the door, then moved along it.

Why had he brought his horse in here? Was he using it as a stable now? Had he got more horses? She blinked in the dimness and peered about her. Then her eyes became wide and fixed, her whole body frozen. She had stepped into her dream of Simon and herself loving, but now the dream was a waking nightmare. She was looking at him. He was naked except for a pair of white linings, and these hung loose. His body was twisted round and he was supporting himself on one knee. As he grabbed for his coat and pulled it in front of him the woman on the straw raised herself on her elbow. She was completely naked. She had been laughing, but now her face took on a look of haughty surprise. Yet she made no move to cover herself. But when she exclaimed in a high tone that could have indicated that a servant had come into a room unannounced, 'Really! that girl,' there erupted from Tilly a long-drawn-out moan; and now she was squeezing through the door again, and once more her hat was tilted over her eyes. Again she was running and when the wind lifted her skirt up almost around her waist, she paid no attention to it.

She was going through the meadow gate, and when of habit she turned to close it she saw him standing outside the barn she didn't stop to close the gate, nor did she skirt the field, but she ran straight across the furrows, then tumbled over the wall and ran and ran, and didn't stop until she reached the dimness of Billings Flat. There, leaning for support against a tree, she put her arms around it, unheeding now when her hat fell to the ground, and she moaned aloud making unintelligible sounds, for her mind, as yet, was not presenting her with words which would translate her feelings, for it was filled with a picture, a number of pictures. She saw herself standing before the master and he saying, 'Wait until he comes for you. . . .' He had known. He had known what was going on. And with the same woman, too, who had ruined his life. And the picture of Randy Simmons telling her where she would find his master and the jumbled words when Bill Young must have gone for him, knowing what she would find. And what had she found?

The picture expanded. It covered the tree trunk; it spread over the copse, up the bank, getting wider and wider, the two forms filling it, the man like a baby with his mouth to the breast, the contorted limbs, and then the woman sitting up shameless.

Nowhere in the picture did she see Simon's face clearly, because in this moment she knew she never wanted to see his face again.

Easing herself from the tree, she picked up her hat, then leant her back against the bole. Why wasn't she crying? Her whole being inside was torn to ribbons so why wasn't she crying? She wasn't crying because she mustn't cry. She had to go back and face them all. Mrs Drew would be kind, and Katie and Peg. She mustn't have kindness at this moment, she couldn't bear kindness. Ever since her granny had gone she had longed for kindness; kindness had meant everything to her; but kindness now would break her. What she wanted now was somebody to fight with, to argue with. That was strange, because she had never wanted to fight in her life, nor argue, but she had the desire now to strike at someone and, as if that person was herself, the fool that was in her, the romantic silly fool, a girl, even a child, she took her doubled fist and drove it into her chest, and such was the force of the blow, it brought her shoulders hunching forward.

After a moment she put on her hat, straightened her coat, wiped her wet soil-covered boots by twisting her feet this way and that on the grass, rubbed the mud from the bottom of her skirt; then, her walk slow now, she made her way back to the house.

'You haven't been long, lass,' said Biddy, looking at her closely, 'Would you like a cup of tea?'

'No, thanks.'

'The wind's chewed you, you looked peaked.'

'Yes, it's strong. I'll just go up.'

'I'll send you a tray up, lass.'

The words had followed her down the kitchen, and without turning, she said, 'Thanks. Ta,' and went through the hall and up the main staircase, across the gallery, down the landing, and into her room.

She went to flop down on the bed but stopped herself. It was as if a voice, very like her granny's, said, 'Don't sit down; you're not strong enough to stand it,' so she took off her things, tidied her hair, put on her uniform, and was about to leave the room and go about her duties when Katie knocked on the door and, not waiting for an invitation to enter, opened it, bent down and picked the tray up from the carpet; then coming further in, she placed it on the little table under the window, saying, 'I buttered the scones. Me ma's just made them fresh. Look' – she turned her head to the side – 'is owt wrong with you, Tilly?',

'No.'

'Aw, you can't kid me. Can't you tell me?'

'No, no, Katie. Perhaps some other time.'

'Is it that Steve lad?'

'Steve? Oh no! No!'

'All right, I'll leave you, but by the way, he, the master, he rang.' She jerked her head backwards. 'An' Mr Pike was down in the cellar and Phyllis was across in the stables, so me ma sent me up. Oh Lord! he scared the daylights out of me, Tilly. Eeh I think you're wonderful the way you manage him. The way he looks at you, you feel like a plate of glass.'

'What did he want?'

'Oh, he just wanted some letters taking out to catch the coach. . . .Sure you're all right?'

'Yes, Katie, thanks.'

'I'll be seein' you then.'

'Yes, aye, Katie.'

She remained standing while she drank the tea, but she didn't eat any of Biddy's scones; then taking in a long shuddering breath, she went out and along the corridor and into his room, prepared for the questioning. But the wind was taken completely out of her sails when, after staring at her for some seconds, he made no mention of her having been out, or of the purpose of her errand, but, as if she had just a moment before left the room, he said, 'I think I'll go down into the drawing-room tonight, Trotter. You know, at one time I used to play the piano. There's nothing wrong with my hands, is there?' He held them both out and turned them back to front a number of times. 'I don't see why I shouldn't have a hobby, do you?'

'No, sir.'

'Then tell Leyburn that he'll be needed. And also I think I'll dine downstairs tonight. Yes, yes, I will. It'll be a change. See to it, will you, Trotter?'

'Yes, sir.'

She stood outside the door for a moment, her lips held tightly between the thumb and the joint of her first finger. He knew, he knew what she would find. . . . Yet how could he have known? And why hadn't he said something? Why? because it was likely too delicate a matter for him to bring up. The woman who had been his mistress now finding her amusement with his tenant. Oh, she was sick, sick. She wished she was miles away. Nothing good ever came her way; nor would it as long as she remained here. She wished it was bedtime for now she wanted to cry. Oh, how she wanted to cry.

It was as if he was doing it on purpose, it was well past ten and he was still downstairs. They had brought him down at five o'clock and he had played the piano, and every now and again some of them had crept into the hall and listened outside the drawing-room door; and they all said he played 'Lovely.'

He dined at seven o'clock. Afterwards he again went into the drawing-room but now he played at patience.

Not until half-past ten did he give the order to be taken upstairs and then straight into the closet where he stayed for almost another half-hour.

When he appeared in the bedroom he was changed and ready for bed.

The house was quiet now; the lights were out except for those night-lights in the gallery and in the corridor.

The bedclothes were turned back, his night table was set, the fire banked down; and she was now standing some distance from the bed, as she always did, saying, 'Have you got everything you require, sir?' and to this he didn't answer as usual, 'Yes, thank you, Trotter,' but said, 'No, no, I haven't; and I'm very tired. And I've made this night last out as long as twenty.' And when her eyes widened slightly, he said, 'As soon as you came in that door this afternoon you expected to be met by a battery of questions, and what would have been the result? Well, from the look on your face I judged that most surely you would have broken down; and then the whole household would have been aware of your private business. Well now, they're all in bed . . . we hope. Anyway' – he jerked his head upwards – 'there's only the two maids upstairs, and they should be asleep by now, so come – ' He held out his hand and, his voice dropping to a gentle softness, he said, 'Sit down here near me and tell me what happened.'

She couldn't move, she could hardly breathe, the avalanche was rising in her, but she mustn't, she mustn't cry; they likely weren't asleep up there, they would hear her.

'Come.'

She was moving towards him now and the touch of his hand drained the last strength from her.

'Did you see him?'

Her head was hanging; she was looking down on to the brown velvet of his dressing-gown and to where her hand lay in his on top of his knees.

'Tell me. What happened? What did he say?'

Still she couldn't speak.

It seemed a long while before he said, 'He told you he was having an affair with Lady Myton, didn't he?'

When she moved her head from side to side, he said, 'Then what happened? You must have found something out?' There was an impatient note in his voice now.

She lifted her face to his. She was gulping in her throat now, the lump there was choking her.

When the tears seemed to spring from every pore in her body and the constriction in her throat was like a knife tearing at her gullet, his arms came about her and he pulled her towards him and smothered her crying in his shoulder, saying, 'There, there, my dear. There, there! no one is worth such tears. Ssh! Ssh! Ssh! Come' his voice was a whisper – 'you don't want to waken the whole house, and after my long, long night of keeping them all at bay.'

Long after her paroxysm had passed he held her to him; then when at last she raised her head he took a large white handkerchief and gently wiped her face, and she said, 'Oh, sir, I'm . . . I'm sorry.'

'Don't be sorry for crying; you wouldn't be a woman if you didn't cry. My father had a saying about ladies who cried, he said – tears were from a woman's weak kidney.'

She did not respond to this with a smile and he, making a little movement with his head, said, 'And this is no time to joke. I will ask you just one more question, perhaps two. First, did you talk to him?'

'No.'

He drew back from her now, saying, 'Then why?'

'Because –' She now drew in a shuddering breath, lowered her gaze for a moment, then lifted her head and looking at him, straight in the face, she said, 'I was directed to . . . to the barn. I saw him there.'

'Oh my God!' He turned his head to the side and said quietly, 'Both of them?'

'Yes, sir.'

'Why did you go to the barn?'

'I . . . I was directed there.'

'Who directed you?'

'One of his men, a man called Randy Simmons.'

'Cruel swine! Well now, it's over.' He put his finger under her chin and pushed her head upwards. 'You remember what you said about being able to hold your head up? Well, you go on doing just that. But I'll ask you another question and then we won't mention the subject again. . . . If he were to come tomorrow and beg your forgiveness would you take him?'

She looked at him steadily for a moment before she said, 'No, sir, not after today, I . . . I couldn't.'

After a short silence, he said, 'Odd, isn't it; we both have suffered through the one lady. You can see she has practically ruined my life, but that needn't be so in your case, in fact it could be the making of you. Put it behind you, Tilly. You're worthy of something better than the farmer. I've always known that. Go now, go to bed and sleep, and start a new life tomorrow.'

She rose from where she had been kneeling by the side of his chair and, drawing in a deep breath, she stood straight, before saying, 'Good-night, sir.'

'Good-night, my dear.'

As she went out of the door he knew he had missed an opportunity; he could have kept her with him tonight. But he didn't want it that way. There was time enough now.

᪐ 6 ᪐

When eventually he took Tilly she came to him like a mother to a sick child.

It should happen that about three weeks later a tragedy enveloped Mark and spread over the whole house. It came in the form of two letters. Both Mr Burgess and Tilly were in the room at the time he opened them. The first he slit open with a paper knife; he was always meticulous about the way he opened his mail. He often looked at the postmark and the stamp before opening a letter. Now, taking the letter from the envelope, he leaned back in his chair and began to read, and the first line brought him sitting upright. His brows gathered into a deep line above his nose and his lips fell apart for the words he had just read were:

It is with great sorrow that I write this, I being Harry's chaplain since first he came to the university. His death will be a loss to many.

He seemed to have stopped breathing, and such was the expression on his face that both Tilly and Mr Burgess stood still and stared at him. Then he was tearing at the other long envelope with his fingers, and when he pulled out the single sheet of paper his hand was already crushing the bottom of it.

My dear Sir,

It is with the deepest regret that I have to inform you that your son, Harry, was knocked down and killed instantaneously yesterday morning by a runaway dray horse in Petty Cury. This news must come as a great and grievous shock to you, as indeed it has to all of us here at the college. Believe me, sir, you have our deepest sympathy.

A coroner's inquest has already been held, at which a verdict of accidental death was returned, and I shall now await your instructions as to the disposal of your son's mortal remains and of his personal effects.

I send you these most unhappy tidings by the mail coach. If you will reply likewise, I shall personally ensure that your wishes are carried out to the letter and as swiftly as possible.

Again may I offer you and your family my deepest sympathy in your great and grievous bereavement.

I am, my dear sir,
Yours very truly,
W. R. Pritchard
Dean.

He lay back and looked at the two faces before him. His mouth opened and closed several times; then he moved his head slowly from side to side and when he did speak it was a drawn-out whispered syllable. 'N . . . o!'

'You have had distressing news, sir?' Mr Burgess was bending over him and for answer Mark lifted the sheet of paper from his knees and handed it to him.

When Mr Burgess had read it he looked at Tilly and she whispered, 'What is it?'

'Master Harry.'

'Oh no!'

He now handed the letter to her, and when she had read it she gripped the front of her bodice with one hand and, her lips quivering, she stared at Mark. His head was up and tightly pressed against the back of the chair, his eyes directed towards the ceiling. He was so still that for a moment she thought he'd had a seizure; but as she made to go to him his head snapped forward, his shoulders with it, and his knees came up, and now he was gripping them with his hands.

Silently they stood one on each side of him until he made a jerking movement with his head and muttered, 'Leave me.' And on this they went from the room.

It was a week later when the coffin arrived. It lay in state in the library for a day before being taken to the cemetery.

The funeral was a quiet affair. Mark sitting alone in the first carriage followed the hearse. Behind him came another carriage holding his mother-in-law, together with Matthew and Luke; following this were various carriages bearing male members of different families. The only mourners on foot were the male members of the staff, and these were made up mostly of the Drew family.

Both Mark and Mrs Forefoot-Meadows sat in their carriages and watched the coffin being lowered into the ground. Mark, being alone, could cry and he cried as he had never cried in his life before. And in this moment he felt alone as he had never felt alone in his life before. He already knew the feeling of loneliness, but this was a different sort of aloneness: his first-born had gone, just apparently when they were beginning to know each other. After his second marriage the boy had been unfriendly, only returning to his old self when Eileen had gone from the house. The last time they had spoken together the boy, or the young man, the young man that he had become, had spoken to him of his affection for the sister of his friend, which explained his frequent visits to France, and he had confessed that he thought his affection was being returned. So now another young heart would also be pining.

When he returned from the cemetery the mourners, realising his predicament, didn't censure the fact that he wasn't present at the meal laid for them in the dining-room and presided over by Mrs Forefoot-Meadows.

After receiving the usual condolences Mark had ordered that he be taken straight upstairs, and once there he told both Tilly and Mr Burgess that he did not wish to be disturbed, and that he would ring when he needed them. He even refused to see his mother-in-law until the following morning which, needless to say, annoyed Mrs Forefoot-Meadows.

When they did meet they seemed, at least for a time, as if they had nothing to say to each other. Mark sat stiffly in his chair, his eyes directed towards the window, while Jane Forefoot-Meadows sat as stiffly in hers as if waiting for him to open the conversation, and when he did it was abruptly. Turning his head towards her, he almost growled, 'My son is dead, my first-born, and she hadn't even the decency to come to his funeral. What was she afraid of, I'd have her chained up?'

'She is not well. The journey would have been too much, and. . . .'

'From all I hear she's still well enough to take jaunts. You may have your informants here who take the news back to Scarborough; well, it's amazing how my friends are desirous of bringing the news from Scarborough to here.'

'There is life in Scarborough, things to do, entertainments. There was nothing such here.'

'God in Heaven!' He threw his head up. 'The times I've tried to get her off that couch and into a coach and go to the city, to a concert or a play, but no, she was always indisposed, too ill. Hell's flames! when I think of the game she played, how she deceived me. . . .'

'Oh, Mark! Mark! think. I shouldn't bring that word into the conversation if I were you.'

'Look, Mother-in-law –' He now bent towards her and, his voice quiet, he said, 'There are various forms of defection and the worst of them isn't having a mistress.'

'Perhaps we don't see eye to eye on this matter, nor do I think did Eileen. And while we're on the subject of news going backwards and forwards I am not going to beat about the bush with what I am about to say, and that is, you should get rid of that girl.'

'What girl? Trotter?'

'Which other girl is there who looks after you?'

'Will you give me one good reason why I should get rid of Trotter?'

'I could give you several but the main one is your name is being coupled with her.'

'Oh! my name is being coupled with her? Will you go on and describe in which way?'

'Don't be silly, Mark; you don't need me to put it into words.'

'Oh yes, I do, Mother-in-law. Oh yes, I do. Trotter acts in the capacity of my nurse, also as housekeeper, and she does both very well. . . .'

'You should have a male nurse, you know that.'

'I have one, Burgess; but I also like to have a woman about me to attend to the niceties of life, my life such as it is. Now the main capacity you are referring to is the part of mistress. Well, there, I must disappoint you for as yet she hasn't taken up that position.'

When he broke off and they stared at each other, Jane Forefoot-Meadows realised from the look of him that he was speaking the truth; but then he added, 'I hate to receive any favour that I haven't really earned, so please tell my wife that I will do my best to see that Trotter complies with the main duty in future.'

'I ... I was only putting you on your guard.'

'Thank you for your concern.'

'People will talk, the girl is young and ... and ....'

'Yes, Mother-in-law, what were you going to say, beautiful?'

'No, I wasn't.'

'Then what?'

'Oh, it doesn't matter. Only personally, I don't like the girl; there ... there is something about her. And what's more, she doesn't know her place.'

'Has she been rude to you?'

'No, she hasn't, she scarcely opens her mouth.'

'Is that to be held against her?'

'There is a way to be silent and a way not to be silent. The look of the girl. Anyway, I would advise you, Mark, and I do this in all sincerity, I would advise you to get rid of her.'

'And in all sincerity, Mother-in-law, I must tell you, and you can also convey the message to my wife, that I have no intention of getting rid of Trotter, ever. If she leaves this house it will be of her own wish because she has been of more help and comfort to me than anyone in my life before. Now you tell that word for word to my wife. And also tell her I shall never forgive her to my dying day for not being present with me at this time. I knew well enough that she was never fond of Harry, in fact she disliked him, but out of respect and as a matter of courtesy she should have been at my side today. In the eyes of the whole county I am being treated like a leper; not one of them will believe that she has left me simply because of the Myton affair. I am sure they think I was a monster to her. What else would have kept her away at this time?'

It was some moments before Jane Forefoot-Meadows spoke again, and then, her voice small, she said, 'She sent her condolences; you had her letter.'

'Oh yes, I had her condolences, I had her letter, a letter that was so formal she must have copied it from a book headed: Appropriate letters to be sent to the relations of the deceased. There is such a book, I have read it and laughed over it.'

There followed another silence before she spoke. 'You must remember that she brought the boys from school out of respect.'

When he closed his eyes and made no answer, she went on, 'Speaking of the boys; there is *a* little matter I think I must bring up. Matthew has had to be moved to another school.'

'Why?' His enquiry was sharp.

'Because he apparently didn't like the school he was at, and he misbehaved. This ... this other establishment is very expensive and ... and ....'

'You want me to foot the bill?'

'Well, Eileen would be grateful if you ....'

'Tell Eileen from me she is getting all I am able to give her. If she can't afford to keep the children, send them back home; they'll live much cheaper here, schools included.'

She stared at him, her eyes hard now, before she said, 'You should have sold the mine when you had the chance.'

'What do you know about the mine and me getting the chance? Oh. Oh, your informant of all my doings. I wonder who it is.'

'It is public knowledge that Mr Rosier is willing to buy.'

'And, Mother-in-law, let it be public knowledge to the effect that my mine will lie there and rot, which it is doing now admittedly, before I sell it to Rosier or any of his kin.'

'You're being foolish. What good is it as it stands now? You haven't the money to. . . .'

'No, I haven't the money to set it going again, but I am bloody well sure it's not going to be set in working order by Rosier. I hate the fellow and all he stands for.'

'You are a very trying man, you know that?'

Mark looked at his mother-in-law. She had now risen to her feet. He was about to make some tart retort, but checked it as he thought yet again that she was an old woman and she had made this long journey to be at his side at this particular time, yet he knew deep in his heart that were the journey twice as long and twice as hard she would have tackled it rather than let her daughter come back to him. The possessive mother had her daughter to herself once again. What he did say was, 'Thank you for coming, Mother-in-law.'

And to this she answered, 'It was as little as I could do'; and when she added, 'I am very sorry for you, Mark,' he was surprised at the sincerity of her tone. Then quite astonished when she added, 'Would . . . would it be any help to you if I left the boys for another week or so? You could send them back in the care of Leyburn. I . . . I would explain to Eileen.'

He stared at her for a full minute before saying, 'That's very kind of you, but . . . but no, take them back with you, there . . . there would be no pleasure, no joy for them here at the moment. He couldn't add that he didn't want to see his sons at this particular time. He couldn't really understand the feeling himself but their boisterousness, which they wouldn't be able to subdue for as yet death had no real meaning for them, and even their voices, muted as they would be coming from above, would rub salt into the wound that was gaping wide at this moment.

'I understand but I thought it might help you.'

'I am very grateful and will always be grateful for your suggestion.'

'Well now, I . . . I must be away. Phillips has packed. I shall send her for the boys, they will likely be in the nursery. You will, of course, wish to see them?'

'Oh yes, yes, of course.'

'Good-bye, Mark.'

'Good-bye, Mother-in-law. And again please accept my thanks for coming.'

She inclined her head towards him and walked out.

After a moment, during which he lay back in the chair and closed his eyes tightly, while at the same time gnawing on his lip, he leaned forward and pulled the bell rope. . . .

Five minutes later Tilly showed the boys into the room, then left them. They stood one each side of Mark's chair and he, looking from one face to the other, smiled at them. Matthew, he noticed, had since he had last seen him changed the more. He was taller and his fair hair seemed to have darkened somewhat, but it was his eyes that showed the biggest change. Where they had looked merry and mischievous, devilish in fact at times, there was now in their depths a look that puzzled him; in an older person he would have named it misery, not untinged with fear, but Matthew was a spirited boy, so the look must have another explanation. Luke, for instance, had hardly changed at all, his round dark eyes were bright, and his mouth still had the appearance of constantly hovering on a smile. But as different as they looked, they were both of one mind, and this they confirmed within a few minutes. After greeting them he went on to say that he hoped they would have a good return journey, and he thanked them for coming. But before he had finished speaking Matthew put in, 'Papa.'

'Yes, Matthew?'

'I . . . I should like to ask you something. We . . . we would both like to ask you something, wouldn't we, Luke?' And to this Luke nodded and said firmly, 'Yes, Papa.'

'What is it you would like to ask me?'

'We . . . we would like to return home.'

Again Mark closed his eyes, and now he lowered his head as he said, 'I'm afraid that doesn't rest with me entirely, Matthew; it is for your mama to decide. If you could persuade her to return and. . . .'

'She . . . she won't listen to us, Papa. If . . . if you could talk to her, write, and I promise you if you let us come back I wouldn't cause any trouble, I mean not to the servants, I'd be good, we'd both be good, wouldn't we, Luke?'

Again Luke nodded and said, 'Yes, Papa, we would be good.'

Mark swallowed deeply and as he tried to find words to answer his sons, Matthew started again: 'We've . . . we've talked it over with Trotter. Trotter would like us to come back and . . . and we promised her, too, we wouldn't get up to any tricks. And . . . and I'll go to school from here, Papa. I could go into Newcastle.'

Mark now put his hand gently on Matthew's shoulder and he said, 'I'm sorry, my dear boy, very sorry. There is nothing I would like better than to have you all back home, but as I said, it . . . it depends on your mama. If you can persuade her, all well and good. You see, to run a house like this is difficult at any time, but when there are children, four in fact, well it needs. . . .'

Oh dear, dear, the boy was going to cry, the tough devil-may-care Matthew. He mustn't, he mustn't; he just couldn't bear it if the child cried. 'Now, now! We are not little boy,s any more, are we?' He put his hands on both their shoulders and he forced himself to smile as he said, 'I'll make it my business to see that you spend all your next holiday here, and in the meantime I shall write to your mama and talk things over with her.'

He watched Matthew blink rapidly and swallow deeply before saying, 'Thank you, Papa.'

And Luke, now smiling, said, 'Oh, thank you, Papa. And Jessie Ann and John would love to be back too.' And bending forward, he whispered almost in Mark's ear, 'They are like suet dumplings.'

'Suet dumplings?' Mark raised his eyebrows in enquiry and Luke, his smile broader now, nodded, saying, 'All of them at Grandmama's, Grandpapa, Phillips, all the servants, suet dumplings. That's what Brigwell calls them. Sometimes he says they are stodgy pud.'

Mark looked into the bright face and thought, He'll get by, he'll ride the storms out; but what about Matthew? Matthew wouldn't sit and ride the storm out, he would fight it, even when full of fear he would fight it.

'Go now,' he said, 'and be good boys; and we'll meet very shortly.'

'Good-bye, Papa.'

'Good-bye, Papa. You will write to Mama, won't you?'

'Yes, Matthew, I'll write to your mama. Good-bye, my dears.'

When the door closed on the children he turned his chair towards the broad window-sill and, leaning forward, rested his arm along it and laid his head down in the crook of it.

After eight hours during which he hadn't rung, Tilly ventured to tap on the door. When she opened it she saw him sitting in the dark by the window gazing out into the starlit night. He didn't turn at her approach and when, her voice soft, she said, 'I have brought you a hot drink, sir,' his head made the slightest movement of dissent. The room being lit only by the reflection from the landing through the open doorway, she now put the tray down and lit the candle in the night-light; then after closing the door, she returned to his side, and there she put her hand gently on his shoulder.

The touch brought him round to her and, looking up into her face in the dim light, he said, 'Why? Can you understand it, Trotter? Why him of all people, on the verge of life, to be killed by a dray horse?'

She was unable to answer his why, and after a moment he said, 'We were just getting to know each other. I now feel buried under a load of guilt because I neglected him for years. There were the others. He must have felt it because . . . well, you saw how he was, bright, jolly, that was because they were no longer here. Nor was she.'

All Tilly could do was to go hurriedly into the dressing-room, pour out a glass of brandy, bring it back to the tray, then pour it into the hot milk. He was partial to brandy and hot milk. When she handed him the glass in the silver holder he said, 'Thanks, Trotter,' then added, 'Go to bed; it's been a long day.'

She hesitated now, saying, 'I'm . . . I'm not tired; I'll stay with you a while, sir.'

'Not tonight, Trotter. Thank you all the same. Good-night.'

'Good-night, sir.'

The days moved into weeks and the master showed no further inclination to be taken downstairs. He seemed to have lost interest in most things. Mr Burgess told him of a new author he had come across by the name of William Makepeace Thackeray who had written a book called *The Yellowplush Correspondence*. It was very good reading and would the master like to pursue it? The master thanked him and said 'Yes, yes, sometime, Burgess.'

The master's lethargy was worrying the whole household. Biddy demanded what was the use of cooking for him, it was a waste of good food; not that anything that was returned from the first floor was ever wasted. But then, as she pointed out, workers, like hens, could do on roughage, but she didn't see the point of stuffing them with food made from butter, eggs and cream.

On the evening of the day she said to Tilly, 'Can't you think of anything, lass, that will bring him out of himself?' they were sitting, as they sometimes did last thing at night, in the kitchen. The house was quiet, the others had all gone to their beds. The fires were banked down. The lamps turned low, with the exception of the main one in the kitchen. And now Biddy rose and, going to it, lifted up the tall glass funnel, turned the flame down low, nipped at the black edge of the wick with her finger and thumb, rubbed her fingers on the seat of her dark serge skirt, then said, 'Well?' and to this Tilly answered briefly, 'Yes?'

'Well then, what you going to do about it?'

'What do you think I should do?'

Biddy replaced the glass shade before saying, ''Tisn't for me to guide you. I haven't got your mind, or heart. *You* know how *you* feel . . . and the whole house knows how *he* feels. Whichever way you look at it it's a big step. But, it could be in the right direction for you in the long run.'

'Lots of folks think it's already happened, Mrs Forefoot-Meadows most of all. She wanted to get rid of me.'

'Well, that being the case, if you were to live up to the name you haven't earned, that would potch her, for he'd never let you go. And that, lass' – she turned now and looked straight at Tilly – 'is what you've got to face up to, there'd be no other man for you, no respectable marriage.'

They stared at each other for a moment, then Tilly rose slowly to her feet and without saying anything further went from the kitchen.

Up in her room she washed herself down in warm water from head to foot, using the scented soap from the master's closet. She put on, for the first time, a new nightdress. It was made of a piece of fine lawn that she had come across when looking through one of the boxes up in the loft. There were a lot of boxes up there holding old gowns, and one had lengths of material in it, and she had felt no compunction in taking the smallest piece of lawn which measured about four yards. It had provided occupation for her hands over the months and the final herring-boning of the front had pleased her mightily.

She now smoothed it down over her knees. Then looking at her hands, she held them out under the lamp. They had grown soft, there were now no dark lines under her nails; the rim of flesh bordering the nails was no longer broken. The backs of her hands were almost as white as the fronts. She now put her hand up to her head. She washed her hair every week, and every night, that is if she wasn't too tired, she brushed it well before plaiting it.

She now pulled the plaits to the front of her shoulders. They reached to below her breasts and felt silky to the touch. She was clean and smelt sweet. Her body was ready but she had her mind to deal with. What she was aiming to do was likely to alter her whole life, as Biddy had hinted. What if she had a bairn? Well, what if she had a bairn? She wouldn't be the first. And if it were his, and it would be no other's, he wasn't a man to throw off his responsibilities.

But before that eventuality came about, if it did, did she really want to do this just in order to give him comfort? Or was there any other reason? Yes, there was another reason, but her mind would not allow her to dwell on it, it was too private. Apart from that, did she like him enough to do this off her own bat?

She looked down at the palms of her hands again and nodded towards them. Yes, oh yes, she liked him enough. . . .

The dressing-gown round her, a candle in her hand, she now tiptoed out of the room, along the landing and into the dressing-room. There was a clock on the mantelpiece and it said the time was twenty minutes to twelve. Would he be asleep? Well, if he was she wouldn't waken him.

Opening the communicating door, she stepped quietly into the room. It was in complete darkness except for the light from her own candle. She lifted it high above her head, and it showed him propped up on his pillows, his eyes wide and staring at her. His face looked pale in the light, his hair showing no grey at the temples looked black. He pulled himself slightly upwards and said, 'Trotter. . . . What is it?'

'I . . . I have come to keep you company, sir.'

He was sitting bolt upright now, and after a moment his head drooped forward and he ran his fingers through his hair muttering as he did so, 'Oh, Tilly! Tilly!' When he slowly raised his head and looked at her again, he said, 'You're sorry for me?'

'It isn't only that, sir.'

'No? You really mean that?'

'Yes.'

He held out his hand now and when she placed hers in it he said, 'On top of the clothes or underneath?'

She was pleased to hear a slight jocular note in the question and, turning slightly from him, she placed the candlestick on the side table, then deliberately with her free hand she turned the covers back and, taking her other hand from his hold, she turned her back on him, dropped her dressing-gown to the floor, sat on the edge of the bed, and slowly lifted her feet up and got under the bedclothes. And now sitting side by side with him, she turned her head slightly towards him but didn't look at him as she said, 'You think me overbold?'

'Oh, Tilly! Tilly! Oh, my dear.'

She was in his arms now and so quickly had he grasped her that they both fell back on to the pillows. And then they became still.

'Oh, Tilly. Tilly.' His fingers came up and touched her chin. 'I never thought, never dreamed you'd make the first move yourself. I . . . I thought I'd have to cajole you, manoeuvre you, and doubtless I would have at some future date even when my need of you wasn't as great as at this moment. Thank you, thank you, my dear one, for coming to me.'

His fingers now moved up and followed the bone formation of her face and his eyes followed his hand, and when his fingers touched her lids, he said, 'You have the strangest, the most beautiful eyes I've ever seen in a woman. Do you know that, Tilly?'

There was an audible sound of her swallowing her spittle before she said, 'No, sir.'

'Don't call me sir any more, Tilly. . . . Do you hear?'

She was looking at him now.

'Don't call me sir any more, at least not when we're together, like this, and at other times omit it as often as, what shall we say, decorum allows. My name as you know is Mark. Say it, Tilly, Mark.'

'I . . . I couldn't. If I . . .' She gave the smallest of laughs here and repeated 'No, I couldn't, sir.'

'Tilly, Tilly Trotter, this is an order, you will in future, give me my name. How can you love someone you call sir . . . Tilly – ' He waited for a moment. Then, his voice thick and from deep in his throat, he asked, 'Do you care for me, just . . . just a little?'

She did not hesitate. 'Yes. Oh yes, yes I care for you.'

'Thank you, my dear. Thank you. Now I'm going to tell you something, Tilly, and you must believe me. . . . It's just this. I love you. Do you hear? I love you. The feeling I have for you I have never experienced in my life before, not for my first wife or my second wife, or for my children. From the first time I became aware of you I think I knew I was going to be bewitched.' When she gave a slight movement he pulled her tightly to him and murmured, 'The day I offered you the post in the nursery I had the feeling then because I just wanted to keep looking at you, and I wanted you to look at me. I didn't recognise it as love, but that's what it was, Tilly, love. I love you. . . . I love you. . . . Oh Tilly, I love you.'

When she shivered within his embrace, his voice changing now, he said, 'You know what you're about to do? It may have consequences and I may not be able to give you my protection, except in a monetary way. You understand that?'

She eased herself slightly back from him till she could see his face half reflected in the candlelight and she said, 'I understand very little at this moment. All I know is that I want to make you happy.'

'Tilly, my dear, my dear. Oh, you're like a gift from the gods. Do you know that? You, so young and beautiful, I . . . I find it hard to believe you're here. Tell me, does . . . does my condition not repel you?'

'You . . . you mean, the accident, your feet?'

'Just that.'

'Aw . . . w!' The common exclamation had a sort of trill to it, and then she added quietly, 'Not a bit. Not a bit. To me you're a wonderful man, all over.'

And a moment later she proved her words, for when the stump of his leg gently eased itself between hers, she did not shrink either outwardly or inwardly, but now of her own accord she put her arms about him and when his mouth covered hers and his hand moved down over her hips and she responded to him he moaned his joy, and it was in this moment that her love for him was born.

TILLY TROTTER
WED

Author's Note

With regard to some of the details in the second part of this book, I feel I owe a debt of gratitude to T. R. Fehrenbach and Sue Flanagan.

Having read two histories of the USA, I was led to *Lone Star* (New York, Macmillan, 1968) and *Comanches* (London, George Allen & Unwin, 1975) and from then on became lost in admiration for Mr Fehrenbach's knowledge of the Indians in the early history of Texas. But his scholarship made me pause and caused me to ask myself how I dare attempt to write about a place I had not even visited.

When I had the urge to move for once out of my milieu, I chose Texas. Why, I don't know. And it wasn't until I was advised to read the above books that the audaciousness of my effort opened up before me and I hesitated whether to continue with my story. Only the fact that I was in no way attempting to emulate, even as a faint shadow, the scholarship in these books but was merely imbibing the flavour for a background to a novel allowed me to go ahead.

Apart from the facts I have gained from these books, my personal interest in Texas has been aroused and my education certainly furthered.

From Sue Flanagan's work I received great help too. The wonderful photographs in her book, *Sam Houston's Texas* (Austin, University of Texas Press, 1964), and the information attached, I found invaluable.

Finally, I may say I have tried within my capacity to keep to facts, but like most authors of novels I may have resorted now and again to a little licence; so should this be noted by a Texan I beg his forbearance, for after all I am merely a teller of tales.

Catherine Cookson,
March 1980.

PART ONE

Back to the Beginning

1

'She should leave the house, and now!'

'You can't turf her out just like that, Jessie Ann, she's entitled to stay until after the funeral; and there's every possibility, naturally, she'll be mentioned in the will.'

'Naturally, you say!'

'Yes, naturally, because she's acted as a wife to Father for years.'

'She's acted as the creature who's kept us away from our birthright for years.'

'Y . . . you, you . . . talk like a penny magazine, Jessie Ann.'

Mrs Jessie Ann Cartwright, one time Jessie Ann Sopwith, rounded on her nineteen-year-old brother, crying, 'Don't talk to me like that, John! I won't be spoken to in that fashion.'

As the young man opened his mouth to stammer out a reply his elder brother sat down heavily on a chair, put his hands to his head and said, 'God! I wish this was over. And I wish you, Jessie Ann, would stop bickering and acting like a matronly bitch.'

At this the young Mrs Cartwright swelled so much inside her black taffeta that the silk rustled, and her indignation was such that she found it impossible to speak. And now John, as always aiming to smooth matters, approached his sister, saying, 'Luke didn't mean that, we . . . we are all t . . . tensed up. And . . . and you know, Jessie Ann, y . . . you . . . you used to be as fond of Tro . . . Trotter as any of us, so what's made you so b . . . bitter?'

'Don't be stupid!' Jessie Ann thrust out her hand towards him as if pushing him aside. 'You know as well as I do we'd have all returned home four years ago when Mother died if it hadn't been for her.'

'Oh. Oh, be fair.' Luke was on his feet now, pointing towards her. 'We all had the chance to come back.'

'Yes, on terms that we accept her status in the household, she who had been a maid, a nursery maid, and then assumed the position of mistress.'

'Well, she was mistress, his mistress, and mistress of the house. And for my part I think she did it very well because what you seem to forget, Jessie Ann, is that after Father had the accident in the mine and lost his feet he became a different person altogether, and as the years went on a most trying individual, and if it hadn't been for Trotter, God only knows what would have happened to him.'

As their sister stared at them the two young men returned her look, but not with her hostility; then John put in softly, 'Sh . . . she had a lot to p . . . put up with, had Trotter, she was in a very difficult position and . . . and what you forget, Jessie Ann, is that s . . . she didn't marry him and she could have. He told Luke and me here, di . . . didn't he Luke? that he had tried to per . . . persuade her, so I think that's very much in her favour.'

'She's got you two besotted, like she had Father. Well, she didn't have that effect on Matthew or me.'

'I . . . I wouldn't be too sure of that if I were you.'

She now jerked her plump chin towards Luke. 'Well, I am sure of it. Matthew went to America when he got the chance because he couldn't stand the situation.'

'No, he couldn't stand the situation, but not for the reason that you imagine.'

'What do you mean?'

'Well, partly I mean that he couldn't stand the set-up in Scarborough any longer, and Mama's whining and then Grandma's domination after her going.'

'Oh, how dare you, Luke!'

'I dare, Jessie Ann, because it's the truth. And when the invitation came from Uncle Alvero for Matthew to go and try his hand out there he jumped at it. And with Grandfather dying and leaving him pretty warm there was nothing to stop him, so there you have it.'

Jessie Ann's taffeta rustled again and John, after walking towards the blazing fire whose flames were illuminating the room on this dark January afternoon, bent forward, holding out his hands to the warmth as he said, 'Th . . . that's always puzzled me about Matthew, no . . . not Grandfather le . . . leaving him all that money but that he didn't offer to help Father. He could have reopened the mine and go . . . got things working again.'

'Flogging a dead horse.'

John turned his head and glanced at Luke. 'You . . . you think so?'

'Yes, yes, of course. In any case, I think he did offer but Father would have none of it.'

'Did he tell you?'

'No; you know Matthew, tight as a drum and off like a cannon if one probed too deeply. No, but it was something Father said.'

'I think he should have made an effort to come for the funeral.'

'What are you talking about, Jessie Ann?' There was a note of weary impatience in Luke's voice now. 'Word can't possibly have reached him yet that Father is dead.'

'He knew months ago that he was fading. I informed him myself; I told him he had better come.' And Jessie Ann nodded from one to the other now.

'Oh!' The two brothers emitted the word simultaneously.

'Yes.' She kept nodding, and her fair curls hanging beneath her black lace cap bobbed up and down as if they were wired. 'He's the heir and he should be here; I told him so.'

'Yes, I suppose you're right in one way.' Luke hunched his shoulders. 'But then, what is there here for him if he has no intention of reopening the mine? After all these years of lying under water, the thought of that task I should imagine would keep anyone in America. I know it would me.'

'But there's the estate.'

Luke now shook his head as he stared at his sister. 'Estate! What is it after all?

A farm, half a dozen houses, two lodges, a few cottages and seven hundred acres; that's all that's left; there's no shooting or fishing. Oh, I think he's doing the wise thing in staying. . . .'

'Well, will you tell me what's going to happen to it?'

'Yes, I will, Jessie Ann.' He bowed his head deeply towards her. 'After the will is read I'll tell you. But then, of course, there won't be any need, will there, for you will know too by then?'

'Oh!' Jessie Ann bounced from her chair, her short plump body bristling as she glared at the young army officer, the second of her three brothers and the one whom she disliked most heartily.

Returning her look and reciprocating her feelings, Luke said, 'Be funny if in some way Father has managed to leave the whole damn lot to Trotter, wouldn't it, Jessie Ann? Then, of course, you would have some reason for venting your spleen on her, whereas as things stand now Trotter, in my opinion, is deserving of our gratitude.'

The two young men both watched their sister now hold her hands palm upwards against her waist, not in the front of it but slightly to the side. It was a stance, dating from her nursery days, which she always assumed whenever she was about to deliver some piece of news which she hoped would startle them. And now the young matron succeeded in doing just that as she gave the reason for her heightened animosity towards her one-time nurse. 'Gratitude!' she said. 'Well, I hope that you are prepared to shower it on her abundantly when she presents you with a half-brother or sister, or perhaps both, in . . . in five months' time.' She now savoured the look of astonishment on the faces before her; then inclining her head first to one, then the other, she turned slowly about and went from the room, whilst Luke and John Sopwith turned and gazed at each other for a moment, and while both of them attempted to speak they changed their minds and, turning about, they walked towards the fire and, their hands on the high marble mantelshelf, they stared into it.

2

Tilly Trotter stood in the library of Highfield Manor looking down on to the face of the man whom she had served for the last twelve years as wife, mother, nurse and mistress. That she had no legal claim to the word wife made no difference for she knew she had been as a wife to this man. The thick grey hair parted in the middle came down to the top of his cheekbones. The face, which in the last three days had assumed a smoothness of youth denying his fifty-seven years, was now shadowed with the blue hue of decay.

She looked at the hands folded on his breast. She had loved those hands. They had been gentle, always gentle; at the height of his passion they had still remained gentle. She could feel them even now combing through the thick abundance of her hair. He had liked to do that, spreading it all over the pillows; then, like an artist, his fingers tracing the bone formation of her face while his deep voice murmured, 'Tilly! Tilly! my Tilly Trotter, my beautiful wonderful Tilly Trotter.'

He had disliked the name Trotter yet he had called her by such since he had taken her into his service as a nursemaid when she was sixteen, after the McGraths and the mad vindictive villagers had burned down her granny's cottage and brought on her death.

Immediately after the fire Simon Bentwood, the tenant farmer on the estate, had taken her and her granny to his home, only for her to be confronted there with the further vindictiveness of his new wife, and when her granny died within a few days she herself had refused his invitation to stay on at the farm, even while her heart, full of young love for him, wanted only to be near him.

Destitute, she had taken up her abode in an outhouse behind the burnt-out shell of the cottage; and it was there that Mark Sopwith, the owner of the cottage, because it too was on his estate, found her and offered her the post of nursemaid to his children.

She had been both thankful and yet feared to accept the situation because she knew that her reputation as a witch had gone before her. The tragedies that she had inadvertently created had, through the village family of McGraths, stamped her as being possessed of supernatural powers; but she knew that anyone less like a witch than herself would be hard to find, for she had never wished bad on anyone in her life, except perhaps Hal McGrath who had been determined to marry her, even if it had meant raping her first, and all this because he imagined that there was stolen money hidden somewhere in the cottage in which her grandparents had lived all their married life.

That her fame had gone before her she soon found out, for the majority of the staff at the Manor both feared and hated her; and it was when the man, lying dead here now, had been indiscreet enough to have an affair with a newcomer in the vicinity, Lady Agnes Myton, that his wife had made this an excuse to leave the invalid couch where she had for so long taken refuge from the obligations of married life and return to her mother at Waterford Place near Scarborough, taking with her her four children, and that the housekeeper, in her turn, then took the greatest pleasure in turfing 'the witch' out.

Tilly often wondered what she would have done if it hadn't been for the Drews, a pit family, most of the members of which, both male and female, worked in Mark Sopwith's drift mine. Biddy Drew had taken her in when there was hardly space for the ten people already packed into two rooms.

Looking back now Tilly saw the events in her life as pieces in a jigsaw all dropping into place and leading to her sojourn in the mine – that nightmare period of her life, which reached its climax when she was caught in the flood with, of all people, the owner, Mark Sopwith himself. The result of those three and a half days in the blackness was that he lost both feet and she herself narrowly escaped death.

From the time he called her back to the household to be his nurse she had sensed what his ultimate aim was, and when he finally invited her into his bed she had refused, even while knowing that the love she bore Simon Bentwood was hopeless.

That what she imagined to be undying love could be killed at one blow she was to learn on the day she heard of the death of Simon's wife, actually weeks after the woman's passing. She had flown to him, only to find him in the barn with the very lady who had ruined her master, and she as naked as the day she was born.

Although her love died at the sight, the death throes stayed with her for some time, right until the night she voluntarily gave herself to the man she was now gazing at through misted eyes.

Her fingers gently touching the discoloured cheek, she whispered, 'Oh Mark! Mark! what am I going to do without you?' When her hand left his face she placed it on the slight mound of her stomach. He had been determined to live to see the child. The very day before he died, he had written to his solicitor to tell him that he wished him to call as soon as possible.

She didn't know what he had put in the letter, she only knew that he had written it after she had promised to marry him. But she wondered now why she hadn't given in to his repeated request before. And yet she did know why. After his wife left him his friends had shied off for a time; then the notoriety attached to his name when he took herself as mistress did not improve matters, and so, had she consented to marry him she would have been looked upon as a scheming wench, and his position in the county would have been worsened because she would not have been accepted.

This particular fact wouldn't have troubled Mark, but it would have troubled her. Isolated as he was, he needed friends. He could protest as much as he liked to her that she was all he wanted from life, but she knew he needed other company.

Not even the companionship of the children for the short periods, two or three times a year, they were allowed to visit, nor the daily companionship of Mr Burgess the one-time children's tutor, she knew, had been enough; he had needed contact with the outside world. Sometimes she thought that he'd had ideas of starting up the mine again. She guessed that when Matthew came into his grandfather's money he had been tempted to accept his son's offer to reopen it, but it was about this time that his heart began to trouble him and the doctor advised against all stress. And so the mine remained as it was, flooded, except in those roads where the water had seeped away naturally.

Over the years she wondered why she hadn't become pregnant; his loving passion had been such that she should have been surrounded by a brood. Then one morning she had woken up to realise with amazement what was causing the strange feeling that couldn't be placed under the category of illness yet was making her feel so unwell. When she broke the news to him he had laughed until his sides ached, then held her tightly as he said, 'That's what you have always wanted, isn't it? And now you'll have to marry me.' And he had added, in a strangely sombre note as if he knew his future, 'And once that is done I'll die happy for then, Tilly Trotter, I'll know that Tilly Sopwith will live in some sort of security to the end of her days.'

She bent now and placed her lips against the blue lifeless forehead. It was the last time she would touch him, the last time she would see him, for in a short while they would be screwing him down. She turned blindly away, the pain in her heart not sharp and piercing as it had been when she found him dead in his chair, but dull now and so heavy that it forced its way into her limbs and all she desired to do was to drop where she stood and sleep, preferably the everlasting sleep with him.

She went out of the library, through the hall and upstairs, conscious as she did so that the family were in hot discussion in the drawing-room.

Up to four years ago two of the boys and the girl had seemed to accept her position in the household, but not Matthew. Matthew had never countenanced her position, in fact his manner towards her had at times reverted back to that of the insolent little boy she had first encountered up in the nursery.

She hadn't been surprised at Jessie Ann's changed attitude towards her. At the time of her mother's death Jessie Ann was seventeen, and she had wished to return to this house, to act as its mistress, but her father had told her that although he would love to have her back, have them all back, the house already had a mistress, and if she returned she would have to accept the situation. It was from that time that Jessie Ann's open hate of her was born. But Luke and John had taken the situation as a natural event. John had come home, but Luke had gone into the army. Then there was Matthew. Although he had not acted towards her with the same open hostility as his sister, his manner at times had hovered between aloofness and sarcastic jesting. She was always glad when Matthew's visits ended and more than glad when, after leaving university three years ago, he had gone to America.

Slowly now she went up the stairs, across the gallery, down the broad corridor and into the bedroom, the master's bedroom, their bedroom. Everything was neat and tidy. She looked at the bed in which she would never again sleep. Then she walked into the dressing-room, and from there entered the closet. She sluiced her face in cold water, and as she stood drying herself she looked into the mirror. There was no colour in her cheeks, her eyes lay deep in their sockets and appeared black instead of their usual dark brown. Her wide full-lipped mouth looked tremulous. She was thirty years old. Did she look it? No, not really. Mark had always said she had stayed at twenty. Well, that, she knew, had been a loving exaggeration. Yet she was aware she had the kind of bone formation that would fight age, and she supposed she must look upon this as compensation for her unfashionable figure, for even with the years neither her bust nor her hips had developed. Her body, because of its slimness, had at one time worried her, imagining she was deprived of womanly grace. But Mark had viewed her lack of flesh as something beautiful.

And then there was her height. She was too tall for a woman, having grown to almost five foot ten inches.

But what did it matter now how she looked? She was carrying a child, Mark's child; in a few months she would be a mother. In the meantime her stomach would swell and, with it, her breasts and her hips. She would at last have flesh on her. When it was too late she would have flesh on her because, whereas a few weeks ago she was delighting in her condition, now it had become a burden and the old fears were rising in her again. What would she do if they didn't let her stay here? She doubted very much if Miss Jessie Ann would countenance her presence in the house one moment longer than was necessary. She had talked her future over with Mr Burgess and he had said she must go to him. It was kind of him but what would life be like in that book-strewn little cottage?

There was another thing she now regretted, and that was since becoming Mark's mistress she had refused to take a wage, for that had appeared to her as being too much like payment for her services. Moreover, she knew that it had taken him all his time to pay an allotment to his wife and keep his children at school, and still pay the expenses of running this large establishment. Of course, with regard to the latter she had some long time ago halved these expenses when she had got rid of the thieving staff and brought in the Drew family.

Biddy Drew was still down in the kitchen there, and Katie, now promoted to house-parlour-maid, could do the work of two young women. Then there was Peg, who in the last few years had been married and widowed. She had become a sort of female butler, seeing to the door and the dining-room. Young Fanny, of the same calibre, now twenty-one, was doing the work of both scullery and kitchen-maids. Sam had returned to the pit, and was followed by Alec, and both were married now. But Bill, Arthur and Jimmy still worked in the grounds and between them kept the place spruce. The men slept in the rooms above the stables, and the four women of the Drew family lived in the North Lodge, which after a two-roomed hovel of the pit row appeared like a palace to them.

Tilly had no fear that the Drews would be dismissed; they kept the place running smoothly. Of course, there was no butler now and no footman, but Fred Leyburn still saw to the coach and the horses and the yard in general. But Phyllis Coates, who had been first housemaid and who had married Fred Leyburn ten years ago, had no more time for work inside the house for she had filled one of the cottages on the estate with eight children.

Together with herself, the entire staff only numbered nine and, as Mark had often pointed out, must be the smallest staff running a manor house such as this in the county.

Tilly now went out of the closet and along the corridor into what was still known as her room but which, until the past few days, she had only used when the family was visiting. Sitting near the window she looked out into the lowering sky, and as she did so there came a tap on the door and she turned and said, 'Come in,' and was surprised to see Biddy Drew with a tray in her hands. It was usually Katie who brought her tea up.

Having placed the tray on the table, Biddy proceeded to pour the tea out from a small silver teapot, saying as she did so, 'Sitting in the gloaming, lass, 'll do you no good, you should light your lamp. Here, drink that. And look, I've brought you some sandwiches. You've got to eat because, whether you like it or not, you've got to go on, and if you don't want to damage what's inside you through starvation you'll make yourself eat.'

'I've got no appetite, Biddy, I don't feel like eating.'

'I know that, lass; but we've all got to do things we don't want to do.' She now sat down on the edge of the window seat opposite to Tilly and asked quietly, 'Have you heard anything more?'

Tilly shook her head. 'No,' she said, 'and I don't suppose I shall until tomorrow after the funeral.'

'She's turned into a little madam, that one, hasn't she? My God! a proper little upstart if I've ever seen one, you wouldn't credit it, knowin' what a canny bairn she was. Marrying into that family I suppose has given her ideas. Dolman Cartwright, my God! what a name. She's bad enough now, but when the old fellow dies and she becomes Lady Dolman Cartwright there'll be no holdin' her.' Biddy's tone changed as she said quietly, 'She's determined to have you out, lass. Katie heard them going at it in the drawing-room. The lads are for you, but not her.'

'I know that, Biddy; but the house, the estate isn't hers, it will go naturally to Matthew. The only thing is, I don't know who'll be in charge until he comes home, likely Luke. But then he's got to return to his regiment. That only leaves John, and I doubt if he'll leave university to look after the place. So we are left with Miss Jessie Ann, aren't we, Biddy?'

'Well, she won't be able to stay here and see to things.'

'Oh, I don't know, she will if she has to. Anyway, she could engage a house-keeper.'

Biddy got to her feet. 'Never on your life! she wouldn't dare.'

'Oh, she would, Biddy, and she can. And she'd be within her right.'

'My God!' Biddy stamped down the room and came back again before she said, 'After all you've done: you kept the master from going barmy; you've run this house like nobody else could. The place is a credit to you.'

'I've had a little help.' Tilly gave a weak smile.

'Aye, I suppose so; but you were the instigation of the help in the first place. If it hadn't been for you gettin' us here this place would have been like a ghost house. Aye, my God! the things that happen in life. 'Tisn't fair. All your young days you had your bellyful of one an' another, then although you may have been happy with him and I'm not sayin' you weren't he wasn't an easy man to get on with; I know you had your work cut out at times to pacify him and then for this to happen. You should have married him.' She brought out the last words on a low growl. 'I told you years ago. I said the door was opening for you and you should grab everything inside it. But what do you do? Leave it until it's too late. You're daft. Do you know that, Tilly? You're daft. One side of you is business-like and this makes for a good manager, but the other side, the bigger side, is soft, as soft as clarts. . . . You should have married him years ago.'

Tilly sighed and closed her eyes for a moment, then said, 'Hindsight, Biddy, hindsight; we realise, on looking back, the things we should have done. But I didn't, did I? So I've got to face up to what's coming.'

'Drink your tea.' Biddy's voice was soft now. 'And you needn't bother comin' down if you don't want to, I've got the dinner all mapped out: vermicelli soup, then rissoles 'n patties; and the main dish is what you ordered, leg of mutton and a curried rabbit 'n boiled rice; an' there's plum puddin' and apple fritters for puddin', whatever they choose. There's no Stilton left, just the Bondon cheeses. Anyway, if they get that lot down them they won't starve. Eeh my! it amazes me where they put it. You would have thought there'd been thirty around the turkey yesterday instead of three of them, and they even scoffed the whole lot of chestnuts. As for the partridges, as I said to Katie, hawks couldn't have cleaned the bones better. Mind you, I think it's Master John that gollops the most. By!

that lad can stow it away, you'd think he was workin' double shift instead of lying about all day. Yet of the lot, I think I like him the best, him and his poor stammer. Aw well, I'll get down. Don't worry your head about anything, I'll see it all goes smoothly. She'll have no need to complain.'

'Thanks, Biddy. I'll be down later.'

'Aye now, that'll be wise, company is what you need now. Ta-rah, lass. Try not to fret.' She nodded twice and then went out.

The door had hardly closed when it was opened again and Katie, pushing past her mother, said in a whisper, ''Tis Miss Jessie . . . I mean Mrs Cartwright. She wants to see you, Tilly, down in the mornin'-room.'

Tilly rose slowly to her feet before she said, 'Very well. Thank you, Katie. I'll be down in a minute.'

After the door was closed she still remained standing. The temporary mistress of the house had sent for her, she should be scurrying to obey the order; but it was years since she had scurried and she had no intention of doing so now.

Slowly she walked to the mirror and smoothed her hair back. She no longer wore a cap, nor yet a uniform; her dress today was the darkest one she had, a plum-coloured corded velvet. It had been Mark's last Christmas present to her, together with a small brooch designed in the shape of a single spray of lily of the valley, made up of fourteen small diamonds set in gold, which had once belonged to his mother. It was the only piece he had retained from the last case of jewellery that had been brought from the bank and which he had been forced to dispose of two years ago to offset losses from his shares.

It was a full five minutes later when she opened the morning-room door without knocking, and this impertinent gesture was not overlooked by the young matron who was sitting in the leather chair to the side of the fireplace.

'You wished to see me, Mrs Cartwright?'

'Yes, Trotter, otherwise I wouldn't have sent for you.' She stared up at the tall stiff figure. 'I shall come to the point. I have no need to tell you that your position in this house is an embarrassment.'

'To whom, Mrs Cartwright?'

'Don't be impertinent, Trotter, and remember to whom you are speaking.'

'I do remember, and I wish it could be otherwise because the person who is addressing me as you are doing has no relation whatever to the young lady I once knew.'

Jessie Ann Cartwright's face became suffused with colour, but even so the redness did not indicate to the full the temper that was raging within her. This menial talking like a lady! the result of old Burgess's coaching over the years. She had the desire to stand up and slap her face; and yet at the same time she couldn't explain why she was feeling so vehement towards her one-time nurse. It wasn't only that she had alienated her father away from the rest of his family, even though that was a great part of the reason. No, if they had all been able to return here after their mother died she herself would not have been in such a hurry to marry and get away from the domineering influence of her grandmother. Not that she disliked Cartwright, but marriage was such a trial in more ways than one, and living with her husband's people was almost as frustrating as life had been under the domination of both her mother and her grandmother.

She swallowed deeply before saying, 'I have no wish to bandy words with you, Trotter, I merely brought you here to tell you that from now on I shall be taking charge of the house, and I shall thank you to keep to the nursery quarters until after my father's funeral.'

Tilly stared down into the round almost childish plump face, and she forced herself to keep her voice steady as she replied, 'I am sorry, Mrs Cartwright, that I won't be able to comply with your order; I intend to carry out my duties as housekeeper until your father's will is read, then I shall know his wishes. I may also inform you, Mrs Cartwright, that over the past four years your father tried to persuade me to marry him. I had my own reasons for refusing, but at this moment I am very, very sorry I made such a foolish mistake. However, even if I had been in the position of mistress of this house I should have hoped I would have had the courtesy to hide my feelings whatever they were concerning you.' Her chin jerked slightly upwards as she ended, 'If you will excuse me, Mrs Cartwright, I shall go about my duties. Dinner will be served at seven o'clock, as usual.'

Tilly had reached the door when Jessie Ann Cartwright's voice, in a most unladylike screech, cried, 'Trotter!'

'Yes, Mrs Cartwright?'

'How dare you! How dare you!'

Tilly stared across the room at the small bristling young matron before saying quietly, 'I dare, Mrs Cartwright. Having played the part of nurse, mother, wife and mistress to your father for twelve years, I dare.'

Jessie Ann Cartwright was actually thrusting her hands under the black lace cap and gripping handsful of her fair hair when the door leading from the morning-room into the dining-room opened and she turned, startled, to see John entering the room. He came in quietly smiling, saying, 'Sorry. S . . . s . . . sorry, Jessie Ann, but I just happened to be next door. W . . . well, I was on the point of c . . . coming in here when y . . . you started on her. By! I'll say she can hold her own can Tro . . . Trotter. She had you on the floor there, Jessie Ann.'

'Shut up you! Of all the fools on this earth, you're one. Shut up! you gormless idiot.'

John's countenance, from expressing slight amusement, took on a stiffness and his voice was no longer that of the fool of the family, as he was often called because of his desire to amuse and mostly through his stammer. But his stammer now very pronounced, he said, 'I s . . . say with Tro . . . Trotter, don't speak to me like that, Jessie Ann. It's y . . . you who forget yourself. If I've never witnessed the l . . . lack of breeding in an approach to a s . . . servant, then I've just heard it n . . . now. You are a li . . . little upstart, Jessie Ann. And why you don't like Tro . . . Trotter is because she's a beautiful woman with a pr . . . presence. Yes, that's what she's g . . . got, a presence. And you'll never have a pr . . . presence, Jessie Ann, not because you're too sm . . . small and p . . . plump, but because you have no dig . . . dig . . . dignity. And now there you have it. I've been wanting to say this to you for a lo . . . long time, so don't think I'll come and apologise because if you w . . . wait for that you'll wait a long time.'

And now to Jessie Ann's amazement she watched her brother who was only two years younger than herself but whom she had always treated as a stupid boy march out of the room.

To say that she was astonished was putting it mildly. John had turned on her. All her life she had used her youngest brother as a whipping block while at the same time feeling that nothing she could do or say to him would change his affection for her. But now he had turned on her, and all through that woman.

Her face crinkled, her eyes screwed up into slits and, turning to the fireplace, she beat her soft white fists against the marble mantelpiece while the tears of frustration and temper ran down her cheeks. Oh, she wished it was tomorrow. Just wait until tomorrow; she would then personally see that woman go out of the door. She would. *She would.*

It said something for the nature of John that he looked for an opportunity to get Tilly alone, but it wasn't until after dinner when his sister had cornered Luke in the drawing-room and was waging a private battle with him, over what he didn't know and at the moment didn't care, that when crossing the gallery he espied Tilly leaving her room and making her way towards the nursery staircase. Hurrying after her, he caught up with her at the bottom of the stairs and as he took the lamp from her hand he said, 'L... let me carry it for you, Trotter.'

She offered him no resistance, nor did she speak; but he, having set the lamp down on the old nursery table, looked around the room and said, 'Hasn't altered a b... bit. C... could have been yesterday, don't you think, Tr... Trotter?'

His evident concern for her made it impossible for her to give him any answer, and she bowed her head and swallowed deeply.

Coming close to her, he put his hand on her shoulder as he said, 'Don't be upset Tr... Trotter, I know how you feel. Jessie Ann is behaving ab... ab... abominably.' His mouth had opened wide on the word, and he closed his eyes and wagged his head a number of times before managing to bring out, 'C... c... come and sit down. Is it too cold for you?' He looked towards the empty hearth. 'There used to be a blazing f... f... fire there.'

When Tilly sat down in the wooden chair near the table he too took a seat, opposite to her, and said softly, 'I remember the early days, Trotter. I... I can look back right to the first time I s... saw you. You came into the b... bedroom and you hung over me. Your face hasn't altered a bit since then. Was it the f... first night or the s... second night that Matthew put the fr... frog in your bed and you came back and p... pushed it down his shirt?' He now put his head back and laughed. 'I can hear him screaming yet. He was a de... devil, wasn't he?'

'Yes, he was a devil.' She didn't add 'Master John' and she couldn't say 'John', but aiming to stop herself from breaking down she brought the conversation on to a less emotional plane by asking, 'Are you happy at Cambridge?'

'Yes and no, Tr... Trotter.' He turned round and looked about him before going on to say, 'I... I'm not one of the booky s... sort, you know, Trotter, not intellectual at all. You know wh... what I'd like to be? I'd like to be a f... f... farmer.'

'Would you really?' She smiled gently at him.

'Yes, Trotter. I like the country. C... can't stand the towns. Yet you know, it's funny, when I go to London to dine with Luke. Oh' – he pulled a long face at her – 'L... Luke dines very well and in the most unusual places.' He winked his eye now and she was forced to smile at him. 'And he stands all the expenses. I'm mostly b... broke and everything is so expensive up there. Do you know what a c... cabby charges from the Eastern Counties Railway to Le... Leicester Square?'

She shook her head at him.

'Two sh... sh... shillings and fourpence.' He bowed his head deeply. 'You could almost buy a h... horse in Newcastle for that.' Again he had his head back and was laughing. Then looking at her once more, he said, 'No one can help liking London, Trotter; there are so m... m... many marvellous things to s... see. Last year Luke took me to the Exhibition of Industry. It was s... s... simply amazing. All the nations had sent their products: chemicals, machinery, cloth, and... and art – sculpture. It was amazing. Luke is very g... good to me, Trotter.'

'I'm sure he is.'

'Of course he has the money to do it with because Grandfather left him at t... t... tidy sum. But he was very measly to m... me, was Grandfather. And you know why, Trotter?'

'No.'

'Well –' His head went down now, his eyes closed tightly and he had to open his mouth wide before he could bring out, 'Just because he c... couldn't stand to hear me st... stammer. He imagined I must be wr... wr... wrong in the head.'

She put her hand across the table and placed it on top of his as she said, 'Your head's in the right place, John, as is your heart, and that's the main thing.'

'Thank you, Trotter. You... you were always so k... kind. That's why Father l... loved you I suppose. And he did love you.'

'Yes, he loved me. 'Again guiding him from the painful subject, she said, 'Are you going straight back to Cambridge?'

'No, Trotter. Although term begins on the thirteenth I'm... I'm going up to London with Luke.' He smiled now as he said, 'And I'm afraid that Luke will not c... continue in mourning because, after all, we... we didn't know F... Father very well, did we?'

'No, you didn't.'

There followed a slight pause before he said now, 'L... Luke likes the gay life. He goes to the th... th... theatre regularly, and to exhibitions. But mostly to the theatre, the one called the Adelphi, and another in Covent Garden. Th... that's where the fruit market is. Oh, and so many more. And all the sights you... see there, Trotter, you wouldn't believe. Newcastle? Well, Newcastle is like a vi... village compared with London.'

'Oh, I can't believe that.'

''Tis, Trotter, 't... 'tis. At the theatre, oh, the ladies! They don't go to see the pl... plays you know, Trotter.'

'No?'

'No, they go to outsh... shine each other in their dress and jewellery. And the gentlemen are as bad. Oh, the... the powder. I feel v... very much the boy from the country because, as you see, I don't p... powder my hair.' He now grinned widely and ended, 'I couldn't afford to p... pay the tax, one pound three shillings and sixpence tax, oh no!'

She found herself smiling. He was so likeable, even lovable, different from all the others. Luke was all right, but so taken up with himself and the army; and Jessie Ann, well, there was only one word for Mrs Dolman Cartwright, and that was spiteful. She was a spiteful little vixen. Whoever would have thought she would have turned out as she had done.... And Matthew, the new master of the estate? She had always felt a little uneasy in Matthew's company. His manner towards her, although not offensive, had held a quality to which she could put no name. On his visits she had often caught him looking at her with an expression on his face very like that on his father's when he was angry; and no doubt he was angry at the position she had come to hold in his father's life and esteem.

The nursery door opened suddenly and they both turned their faces towards it and breathed easier when they saw that the visitor was Luke. Moving towards them, he said, 'I thought I'd find you here.' He was nodding at his brother now and he added, 'The sparks are flying downstairs and you'd better show yourself. I'm sorry, Trotter.' He brought his gaze kindly on to Tilly and she, rising to her feet, merely inclined her head towards him, then watched them both leave the room.

The door closed, she sat down again and looked about her. Perhaps this was to be the last night she would sit in this room. Unless Mark had made provision that she stay on as the housekeeper until Matthew returned from abroad Jessie Ann would have her out of the door quicker than the old housekeeper had pushed her out years ago. Strange how things repeated themselves.

How would she take to living in a little house of only four rooms, three of which were strewn with books, and sleeping in the loft under the eaves? Well – she straightened her shoulders – it was no use asking herself such questions, for it was no use planning until tomorrow. But she knew one thing, and the thought brought bitterness on to her tongue, if she was turned out the village would celebrate.

Although she hadn't been near the village for years she knew that they were aware of everything that transpired in the Manor House; they had always made it their business to find out what the witch was up to. The word no longer frightened her because Mark had used it so often, his beautiful witch he had called her. She had never felt like a witch, beautiful or otherwise, and not since Hal McGrath's death had she wished bad on anyone, yet she knew if it lay with some of the villagers their wishes would bring her so low that she would be face down in the mud and they dancing on her. There was evil in people. Some picked it up from their parents, its growth fostered by listening to their superstitious chatter, their jealous venom, while others were born with evil in them. Hal McGrath had been such a one. And the old cook, that overflowing receptacle of gluttony, had been another. And both had tainted those with whom they came in contact. As Mr Burgess said, one advanced through education to reason and one retreated through ignorance to evil. He was so right. At least she was convinced she herself had advanced through education to reason. And yet she couldn't reason out the fact why it was some people loved her on sight, whereas others could hate her with an equal passion.

ॐ 3 ॐ

The breath issued like puffs of white smoke from the horses' nostrils, seeming to mingle with the black plumes dancing on their tossing heads before thinning in the still biting air.

Tilly stood at the bedroom window, one hand held tightly across her throat, not to stop any flow of tears – these she had spent during the long sleepless nights – but in order to quell the long moan that was bent on escaping and which, she felt, given rein, would increase into a wail similar to those vented by the Irish women in Rosier's pit cottages at the news that yet another of their men had been taken by the coal.

The hearse was standing opposite the front door and behind it to the left and reaching to the end of the house and round into the courtyard was a row of carriages, the blinds of the windows drawn, the horses black-draped. To the right, where the drive wound its way for almost half a mile before reaching the main road and for as far as the eye could see, were more carriages. These were already occupied and were being arranged along the verge in some form of precedence to follow those that were to hold the relatives and associates of the deceased.

At the head of each pair of horses stood a groom, black streamers hanging limply from his high hat.

The whole scene was a picture of black and white. The frost had not lifted, and the only break in the black-garbed figures were the faces, some very white, some pink, some florid red. All the hands were covered in black gloves.

The coffin was being borne down the steps towards the hearse, and as Tilly's eyes followed it her mind did not whimper, 'Good-bye, Mark'; because she knew that in that elaborate box there lay only his crippled body; his spirit was strong about her in this room where he had lived, where they had both lived for the last twelve years. A short while ago she had thought she would be happy if when having to leave this house she could take this room with her, but she was wise enough to know that once she was gone from the place time would erase the essence of it until it became merely a faint imprint on her mind, and with the fading the pain in her heart would ease. In this moment she longed for the power to leap years ahead into age, deep age with which would have come tranquillity, for age surely earned tranquillity.

The thought conjured up her grandmother and grandfather, who had acted like parents to her from she was five years old. Loving, caring, tender parents, too tender, too loving, for their care hadn't prepared her for the onslaught of animosity that had attacked her from all sides since she was fifteen and was with her to this day for there, going down the steps now, was the epitome of it, Jessie Ann. She couldn't associate her with the fancified name of Mrs Dolman Cartwright. She didn't look a Mrs Dolman Cartwright. Even in her elaborate black she looked fussy, plump, a little matron who as yet had acquired no knowledge of what was expected of a real matron, a real mistress.

She was followed by Luke and John. They stood at the bottom of the steps while the hearse moved slowly forward, then they entered the first carriage. When this moved on there came a second carriage, and a third. Fourteen carriages passed by the window before the courtyard was cleared and those waiting on the drive could join the cortège. Half the county seemed to have come to pay its respects. And all the mourners were male, with the exception of Mrs Dolman Cartwright.

That Jessie Ann had insisted on attending her father's funeral was, Tilly knew, merely in order to give point to her position. There had, years previously, been a great deal of talk when their grandmother had attended her grandson's funeral. Gentlewomen did not attend funerals whether the deceased be male or female, it was unseemly.

When the last carriage passed from view Tilly turned her face from the window and brought her eyes to rest on the big four-poster bed. She walked slowly towards it and placed her hand gently on the near-side pillow, and her fingers stroked it as she murmured 'Mark. Mark.'

She had half turned away from the bed when she stopped again and looked down on the square bedside table. It was this very table he had knocked flying one night when, in the depths of his loneliness, he had used its crashing noise and the breaking of the water glass and the spilling of the carafe to bring her scurrying from her bed to him. Yet that night she had refused him, for, young and silly as she was, she had imagined her heart was still with the farmer, Simon Bentwood. She'd had a lot to learn, and Dear . . . Dear Mark . . . Dearest . . . Dearest Mark had taught her.

It would be two hours before those invited would return to the Manor to gorge themselves on hot soup, warm fresh bread and the cold victuals laid out in the dining-room: hams, pressed tongue, boiled capons, roast ducks, pasties, pies and an assortment of sweetmeats and cheeses. She had seen to the last of the preparations this morning and it was all finished before Mrs Dolman Cartwright put in an appearance and, as Tilly had expected, found something to criticise, not only something but the whole layout.

'There should have been a hot meal ready for the mourners. See to it!' she had said, and Tilly had enraged the little lady still further by answering quietly, 'This is what I have ordered and like this it will stay.' She had no need to reiterate what she had said earlier: 'I consider myself mistress here until this afternoon; then we shall see who it is who will legally take over,' because the look in her eyes was speaking plainly for her.

She went slowly from the room, along the wide corridor, across the gallery and down the shallow stairs into the hall. The whole house was dark and gloom-filled, the drawn blinds shutting out the meagre light of the sombre day. Only in the kitchen were the windows bare of heavy black drapes.

Biddy, as usual, was at the table. She was preparing the meal for the staff, a plain roast with suet pudding, but she stopped and, wiping her hands on her apron, turned to Tilly and, like a mother addressing a daughter, she said, inclining her head towards the stove, 'I've made a fresh pot of tea and if I were you I'd lace it with a drop of whisky, 'cos I fear you're going to need it, lass.'

'Yes, I think you're right, Biddy. Yes – ' Tilly nodded her head in small jerks – 'I feel I'm going to need it.'

A few minutes later, sitting on the short wooden settle placed at right angles to the corner of the great open hearth, she sipped at the whisky-laced tea and stared towards the hanging spit from which was suspended a sirloin of beef, the fat dripping slowly into the iron receptacle below. Automatically she leant forward and, gripping the iron handle, turned the spit, after which she sat back and looked at Biddy Drew, the woman who had been as a mother to her and whom she loved as a mother, and she said, 'I'm not only anxious about myself, Biddy, but I'm now worried about you all because if that little madam takes over she'll take it out on you, merely because I was a means of bringing you here.'

'Don't you worry yourself about that, lass. With the steady wage we've had all these years and nowt to do with it except buy our Sunday best we won't starve. We'll manage until the lasses get set on some place, an' the lads an' all.'

'But it's the lodge, you've made it such a comfortable home, and the girls love it.'

'Aye, I know that, and I admit it'll be a wrench if we have to go. There's no doubt about that. But God tempers the wind to the shorn lamb, and we'll find some place; as long as you've got the money in your pocket you can always rent. And as I said to the lads last night, they've had it easy for a long time now and their characters must be gettin' soft, there's nothin' like trouble and turmoil for pickin' out the men from the lads.'

'Aw, Biddy!' Tilly closed her eyes and turned her head to the side as she said, 'The lads and all of you have worked like Trojans in this place. In the ordinary way it would have taken twice their number to keep it as it is; they've put their whole heart and soul into it, they couldn't have done more if the place had belonged to them.'

'Aye, yes, I suppose they have worked. We've all worked because we were grateful.' Biddy's voice sank as her hand came out and gripped Tilly's knee. 'God! lass, you'll never know how grateful we were to be taken out of that stinkin' hole and brought here, never! I'm not a prayin' woman 'cos I suppose up till you appeared there was little to thank Him for, but there's never a day gone by these past years but I've said to Him 'Thank you for creating Tilly Trotter'. . . .Aw, lass . . . lass, don't. I didn't mean to make you cry. . . . Aw, don't give over.'

Tilly got abruptly to her feet and, swallowing deeply and her lids blinking rapidly, she said, 'And I don't want to cry, Biddy, not now, not today . . . I'm . . . I'm going to put a coat on and walk round the grounds, blow the cobwebs away.' She smiled now, and Biddy nodded at her but said nothing; not until Tilly had gone from the room, when she looked upwards and whispered half aloud, 'Make it right for her, please. Do that, don't let her be downed again.'

$$\mathit{co}\mathit{D}\quad 4 \quad \mathit{G}\mathit{o}$$

Mr Blandford's buttocks were poised on the edge of a Louis XVI chair and as he read each name from the parchment in front of him he rocked forward bringing the back legs of the chair off the carpet. He was a nervous man, by nature retiring, that's why he always left the business of the court proceedings to the junior partners in Blandford, Coleman and Stocks. Even dealing with wills affected him, especially, as now, the reading of them to relatives, because almost never did he face a family group without encountering dissension, animosity, and even venom, causing his left eyelid to twitch and the flesh to wriggle on his bones as if bent on leaving its support.

Today, he was finding, was no exception; in fact, there was a mixed tension in the room. Such was his nervous system that it picked up the separate emotions and anxieties from those sitting to the right facing him. These were all members of the staff, while the small group of three to the left of him represented the immediate family. He had no doubt in his mind that it was from his late client's daughter that the vexatious vapour was emanating, while interest . . . keen, yet remaining merely interest, were the feelings being expressed by the sons.

In a seat by herself in front of the staff sat the young woman who had for some years held a precarious position in this house. That she could have been its legal mistress any time during the past four years he was well aware, for Mr Mark Sopwith had made no secret of this when he made his last will two years ago. That he had perhaps intended to alter it was more than a surmise, but his message had come too late. He had himself answered the letter from Mr Sopwith which had said he required his presence here at the Manor as soon as was conveniently possible. But on his arrival it was to find the master of the house dead.

He had already read the usual preliminary statements about being of sound mind and such, and had delivered the fact that the estate would go to his eldest son, Matthew George Sopwith, who was now residing in America. And here he paused, wetted his lips, rocked twice backwards and forwards on the chair before proceeding in a voice devoid of emotion or even inflexion as he read, 'I have very little money to leave any of my children but this can be of no great concern to them as I understand their grandparents have left them considerable amounts of money, that is with the exception of my youngest son, John, and to him I leave my three per cent consols due to mature in 1853.' Here Mr Blandford paused and the twitching of his eyelid increased as he looked at the plump young figure in black who was staring at him as if he were to be held personally responsible for her being omitted from sharing in any part of the estate. As for her older brother his reaction was to purse his lips. He could not see what expression was on the youngest son's face because he had his head lowered. He liked that young man, he was the nicest of the family.

He took a deep breath, rocked himself once again as if preparing himself for another effort, then continued. 'To Matilda Trotter, who has acted, not only as my nurse, but as my wife for many years and brought me great comfort, I should like to be able to say I leave all my possessions including my estate because she has earned it, and if I could have been successful in persuading her to become my wife, which attempt I have made many times, things would have been much more straightforward at this moment, but because she did not wish to embarrass my family, a matter which I may say did not trouble me, she would not consent to such an arrangement, so, therefore, to my dearest Tilly all I can leave her is two sets of shares, five hundred East Indian stock and five hundred in Palmer Brothers and Company, Jarrow shipyard, hoping that they will both rise to procure security for her in later life. . . .'

When the daughter of the house made a quick movement on her chair, which caused her younger brother to imagine she was falling and to put out his hand to steady her, all other eyes in the room turned towards her. But Mr Blandford only allowed his glance to pass over her for her bristling indignation was causing his nerves to jangle. Clearing his throat once more and again bringing the back legs of the chair from the carpet, he went on, 'Now to my staff, an odd assortment, having been miners, both men and women, all their lives with no domestic experience until they came into my home, from which time they have worked like no others, I leave each the sum of ten pounds, and moreover because my dear Tilly wished it, I bequeath to Mrs Bridget Drew the North Lodge, together with an acre of land taking up three sides of it and excluding the drive. And I would trust that my son, Matthew, would be happy to keep them all employed, together with my dear Tilly in her capacity of housekeeper. Lastly, to Mr Herbert Vincent Burgess I bequeath fifty books of his choice from the library; and to Fred Leyburn, my coachman, the sum of £30.

Signed this 14th day of March, 1851.
Mark John Henry Sopwith.'

Tilly was the first to rise to her feet and, turning round, she put out her hand and helped Biddy up, because that woman seemed too stunned at the moment to move. The rest followed, Katie, Peg, Fanny, Bill, Arthur, and Jimmy Drew, and lastly Fred Leyburn. . . .

Luke and John were now standing in front of the table looking down at Mr Blandford who was busily and fussily arranging his papers, and it was Luke who said, 'Thank you, sir.'

Mr Blandford did not answer him but looked past the young men to where their sister was still sitting, her back straight, her hands gripped tightly on her lap, and what he said now was, 'I don't make wills, I merely take down my clients' wishes. The late Mr Sopwith, I may say, was most insistent that his should be expressed in his own words.'

'I understand, sir, and . . . and I think my father was . . . well, he was very fair. And it's true my sister and I don't really need money. Of course' – he gave a shaky laugh – 'it's questionable that one can have too much.'

"'Tis, 'tis' – the solicitor nodded at him – 'it's questionable, but it's no good thing. Speaking from experience, 'tis no good thing.'

'No, sir, perhaps you're right. But I'm glad my father thought of John.' He turned now to his brother.

John, his face pink-hued, said, 'V . . . very good of F . . . Father. . . . S . . . sur . . . surprised. 'Twas very thoughtful of him.'

'Yes, yes, indeed.' The solicitor was nodding at him. Then rising from his rocking seat, he took up his case and moved from behind the table and paused for a moment in front of Jessie Ann and suffered her malignant gaze on him as he said, 'Good-day, madam.'

She gave him no answer, merely stared unblinking at him; but as Luke escorted him from the room she turned her head slowly in their direction until the door had closed behind them. Only then did she get to her feet and, like an army sergeant who had been maddened by some indiscipline, began to march up and down the room.

As she passed John for the third time he dared to commiserate with her, although he really did not know why she should need sympathy. 'I'm s . . . sorry, Jessie A. . . .'

'Shut up will you! Shut up!'

Stung to retort, his mouth was wide open in an effort to bring out the words when the door opened and Luke entered the room again to face the brunt of his sister's fury.

'It's damnable, damnable! Not even to be mentioned. Did you know anything about these bonds? That woman! That . . . !'

'Oh, give over, Jessie Ann; anyone would think you were on the stage acting a part. Lord! you don't need the money, it's as Father said.'

'That isn't the point.'

'What is then? You tell me.' His voice was flat, cool; it was the soldier speaking now, not her brother, and for a moment she was nonplussed. Her mouth worked, her nose twitched before she brought out, 'The point is, he put that woman before us, his own flesh and blood.'

'And . . . and wh . . . what had we done for him? I ask you.' John pointed his finger directly at his sister. 'Don't you dare tell me to s . . . shut up again because if you. . . . do I won't be answerable for my re . . . re . . . reactions.'

There was a quiet smile on Luke's face now as he looked at his younger brother, a smile which seemed to say, Good for you, and it made Jessie Ann pause but did nothing to direct her temper away from its objective, for now she cried, 'She's not staying here!'

'Father's wishes were that Matthew keep her on as his housekeeper.'

'But, my dear Luke, Matthew is not here, is he? And we have to act for him in his absence. Now it should be you who takes over, but you are returning to your regiment tomorrow, aren't you? And John here' – she thumbed towards her brother – 'is going up to London with you for a time, so I am the only one free to take charge and I'm going to tell you something now. One thing I was certain of in the will was that Father couldn't leave the estate away from Matthew, and as I knew he couldn't get here in time I wrote to him and told him that I'd be pleased to keep things going until he arrived to take charge himself.'

'You little bitch!' Luke's words were brought out on a laugh half-filled with admiration at the duplicity and foresight of his sister; then more soberly he added, 'You do hate her, don't you?'

'Well, if I haven't made that evident by now I've underestimated your intelligence, brother.'

'I ... I d ... don't think she'll want to stay anyway.'

'She's not going to get the chance, conniving hussy! And anyway, she made quite sure she was going to have some place to go to, getting Father to leave the North Lodge to the cook. Really! it's fantastic when you think of it. That's an excellent lodge, better than the main one.'

'Oh really!' Luke thumped his forehead now with the palm of his hand. 'Give me a war any day in the week.' Then he turned towards John who was looking at Jessie Ann and was saying with hardly a stammer to his words, 'You know something, Jessie Ann, you'll 1 ... live to regret this day. Trotter will come out on top, you'll s ... see. I've ... I've got a feeling about Trotter, she's different.'

'Oh!' – Jessie Ann waved her hand at him now – 'don't come the witch business, grow up.'

'Well, witch or n ... no witch, there's something in Trotter, an attraction. I can understand Father. . . .'

It was on the point of Jessie Ann's tongue to cry again, 'Shut up!' but thinking better of it, she stared from one to the other of her brothers, her plump breasts swelling with her temper; then she turned from them both and stalked out of the room; and John, looking at Luke, said, ''Tis all because she's je ... jealous, insanely jealous because Tro ... Trotter's beautiful. She is. Don't you think so, Luke? F ... Father thought her beautiful, and sometimes I thought Matthew did too, in spite of the way he w ... went on.'

Luke didn't answer for a moment, and when he did his voice had a thoughtful note to it as he said, 'Yes, I think Matthew did too.'

'You will leave the house immediately. You will take nothing with you but what belongs to you personally.'

'Thank you. Is that all, Mrs Cartwright?'

'That is all.' It was as much as Jessie Ann could bring out without allowing herself to scream or stamp her feet.

Again Tilly said, 'Thank you.' Then after a slight pause, she added, 'And may I wish you, Mrs Cartwright, all that you deserve in the life ahead of you.'

For a moment Tilly had the satisfaction of seeing the little madam look startled, there was the same expression in her eyes as used to be in those of the half-witted scullery maid Ada Tennant when she'd had occasion to speak to her sharply. But whereas Ada's look would cause her to smile inwardly, the expression in Jessie Ann's eyes was too much akin to that she had seen so often on the faces of the villagers to cause her any amusement, had she felt like being amused at this moment.

She went out of the morning-room, across the hall and into the kitchen. There, they were waiting for her, and she looked from one to the other, saying in a voice from which she tried to withhold a tremor, 'It's as I expected, my marching orders, and right now.'

'Oh my God!' When Biddy sank down on to a chair, Tilly put her hand on her shoulder as she said, 'Don't worry, I'll not starve. Nor will mine.' She now patted her stomach gently. 'And for the present I'll be well housed. And I couldn't have a better companion than Mr Burgess, could I?' There was now a break in her voice and no one answered her.

'The bloody unfairness of it!'

'She's a little sod.'

'I won't want to work for her long.'

At this Tilly, looking from one to the other, said, 'Stay put all of you. When Master Matthew comes home things may be different.'

'I don't know so much,' said Jimmy. 'As I remember him, he was a bit of a hard 'un; had very little to say, snooty like.'

Nobody contradicted this, not even Tilly, but what she said now was, 'Come and help me get packed, Katie; and as I won't be allowed to use the carriage, will you see that my things go on the wagon, Arthur?'

She did not wait for Arthur to reply but hurried from them up the kitchen, through the green-baized door into the hall, and as she was crossing it, Luke and John came out of the drawing-room, and when they met at the bottom of the stairs they looked at each other. And it was John who spoke first, saying, 'I'm . . . I'm so s . . . sorry, Trotter.'

'It's all right. It's all right.'

'Me too. Me too, Trotter.'

She looked at Luke now, and he added, 'When Matthew comes home he might see things differently.'

She gave no verbal answer to this but made a small movement with her head, and when they stood aside to allow her to pass, she went up the stairs, past the bedroom, past the dressing-room, past the closet and into her own room. There, turning her face to the door, she pressed it into her hands, but she didn't cry. . . .

Half an hour later she was ready dressed but not in black. She wore a plum-coloured melton cloth coat with a fur collar and a matching velour hat with a feather curling round the brim, and as she walked across the gallery and down the stairs again she could have been the lady of the house going out on a visit.

She did not go to the kitchen again but walked straight across the hall and through the front door and down the steps to where Arthur was waiting with the wagon. Fred Leyburn, she knew, would gladly have driven her in the carriage, as he had done during the past years, but now he had his position to think about and that depended on his new mistress.

Arthur helped her up on to the front seat of the wagon, called, 'Hie-up there!' to the horse, and they were off.

As they rumbled slowly along the drive towards the main gates there rose from the deep sadness of her heart a thread of wry humour which said, 'At least, this time of being thrown out you're not leaving by the back drive.'

Arthur had already lit the side lamps and before their journey ended, two miles along the main road and another quarter mile up a rutted lane, the winter twilight had dropped suddenly into night, and so it was dark when the wagon pulled up at the small gate which opened into the equally small garden of Mr Burgess's cottage.

Before she had alighted the old man had opened the door. A blanket around his shoulders and nodding his head at her, he cried, 'I expected you. I expected you, my dear.'

She did not answer him, merely took his outstretched hand; then with her other hand pressed him back into the room towards the fire.

After Arthur had brought in two bass hampers, a bass bag, a wooden box and a hat box, she turned to him and, her voice thick and her words hesitant, she said, 'Thanks, Arthur. I'll . . . I'll be seeing you.'

He stared at her for a moment, then said, 'We'll be waitin' for you, Tilly.'

Before turning towards the door he nodded to the old man, saying, 'Ta-rah, Mr Burgess'; at the door, he looked at Tilly again and, his voice husky now, he said, 'It isn't the end, Tilly. You'll see your day, you will, you will that,' and, nodding confirmation to his words, he turned about and mounted the wagon.

Having closed the door, she bowed her head and paused for a moment before going towards the fire; and there she stood near the man who had taught her all she knew, with the exception of love. And yet in a way he had taught her that too because, as he often said, there were many kinds of love, and whichever one you were experiencing lessened your need for the others.

The first part of his particular philosophy she could agree with. There were, she knew, many kinds of love, but that one kind lessened the intensity of the main one wasn't true, for no other feeling she had as yet experienced had lessened the love that had grown within her for Mark Sopwith. Perhaps Mr Burgess had never known the love of a woman, the only love he had ever spoken of was his love of literature; and it was evident in this room and right through the cottage.

She had lost count of the times she had arranged his books on the stout shelves she'd had one of the boys erect for him round the walls of the main room, but every time she returned to visit him there they were, strewn on the floor, on the table, and on the couch Mark had allowed her to take down from the attic rooms and bring here for his comfort.

He had dropped the blanket from his shoulders and was now taking her coat from her, saying, 'Look, I have set the tea. Aren't I clever?' He pointed to the side of the fireplace to a round table covered with a white lace cloth and holding crockery and a teapot and milk jug. 'And I've kept the muffins in the tin; we'll have them toasted. You must be frozen, sit down, my dear.' But as he went to press her into a chair she took his hands and said quietly, 'You sit down; I'll see to things.'

'No, no.'

'Yes, please let me; it will ease my mind.'

Readily, he allowed himself to be persuaded, and sat watching her as she took off her outdoor things, then busied herself between the table and the open grate where the kettle was boiling on the hob, and not until she was seated opposite to him and had handed him his cup of tea did he say, 'Well?' and she answered, 'Her little ladyship took great delight in turning me out.'

He looked down into his cup and slowly stirred the spoon round it as he said, 'I want to say I cannot believe it of her, yet as a child I detected a slyness in her, a vanity; but because she was so small, so petite, one said to oneself, she is but a child. Yet in later years as she grew I watched her during her visits to the house, and she could not bear the fact that her father could care for any other female but the one he had created. Tell me, how did he leave you, the master?'

'As far as I can gather, provided for. He had bequeathed me two lots of shares, five hundred in each.'

'Oh, good, good, my dear. I'm so glad. What are they?'

'One lot is in Palmer's shipyard in Jarrow and the other is some kind of East Indian stock. I don't know really what that entails.'

'Oh, but that's fine, fine.' He nodded at her. 'I'm so glad. They will keep you in good stead. Was there any other stock mentioned?'

'Only some consols to John.'

'Really!' He nodded his head. 'Did you know he was in very bad straits? Did he ever mention that he was selling his bonds and such in order to keep the house going?'

Her eyes widened slightly as she answered, 'No; he . . . he never discussed money with me, nor I with him.'

'Well, I'm afraid he would soon have had to, my dear. I think he intended to write to Matthew for help.'

'Really!'

'Yes. I gathered so much when we talked about finance, as we often did you know, among other things, and very often about your dear self, because he so admired the way you ran the house, and on a mere pittance too, and the comfort you brought him just with your presence. No, no; please, don't cry, my dear.'

'No, no, I'm not. I'm not.' And she mustn't cry, not yet, not until she was in the room above the rafters upstairs when she could smother her moans in the feather tick. She prayed that tonight the wind would rise to such an extent that Mr Burgess wouldn't hear her crying for, once alone, she would be unable to contain her agony.

She stretched her eyes, opened her mouth wide, and then said, 'And he didn't forget you.'

'Me? What . . . what could he leave me?'

'Fifty books. Your own choice from the library.'

His two hands were raised in the air and his head went back on his shoulders as if he were witnessing manna dropping from heaven, for nothing could have pleased him more on this earth. Looking at her again, he repeated softly, 'Fifty?'

'Yes; and of your own choice.'

'Dear, dear. The thoughtful man. Oh, he was kind. In so many ways he was kind.'

He became silent for a moment while savouring the joy of adding to his enormous collection of what he thought of as gems because every book he possessed was dear to him. Then leaning forward, the white silken quiff of his hair falling between his brows, he put his hand out towards her and, his fingers touching hers, he said, 'I'm so happy to have you with me, so happy to have you with me, Tilly.'

She made no answer for a moment; then said, 'What when the baby comes?'

'Oh that!' He moved his head from side to side and, his face crinkling into a wide smile, he answered her, as he was wont to do at times, in poetical language,

'I shall be born again. Its first cry will stimulate my mind, and the touch of its hand will rejuvenate this old body, and I will see in it a new receptacle into which I'll pour a minute grain of wisdom from the crucible of my life pounded by the pestle of my seventy-odd years.'

'Oh! Mr Burgess.' She now gripped his hand between both hers as she said, 'What would I have done without you all these years?'

'Being you, you would have managed very well, my dear.'

'Oh no, no. Years ago I was thrust into a different world, into a different class, and I viewed it as a servant because I was a servant; but when Mark took me into his life it was you who took my mind in hand, as it were. From our first meeting in the nursery when you realised I could read and write and you loaned me Voltaire's *Candide* – you remember? – and I told you I couldn't understand a word of it, and I didn't until years later, you took me under your wing. And now I can almost say with Candide's old woman, "So you see, I'm a woman of experience." '

Mr Burgess smiled appreciatively. 'Yes, Trotter, my dear, you have grown into a woman of experience. But I hope I don't end up like Candide's old tutor, Doctor Pangloss.' Then leaning forward again, he said, 'The word tutor reminds me I am very greedy for my inheritance. When may I collect the books?'

'At any time I should think, but I wouldn't venture out, not until we have a fine day. I'll arrange for Arthur to come and take you and bring back your treasures.'

'Thank you, my dear. . . . Well now' – he leaned back – 'shall I start preparing some supper?'

'No, no.' She made play of keeping him in his seat by flapping her hand gently at him. 'Leave that to me.' And to this he answered, 'Just as you wish, my dear. Just as you wish.' Then bending to his side, he picked up a book from the floor, put his hand down the side of the couch to recover his spectacles, placed them on the end of his nose, and lost himself in the main love of his life.

And Tilly, after unpacking the bass bag into which Biddy had put enough food to see them over the next two days, set out a meal. When it was over and she had cleared away, she humped the two hampers and the boxes upstairs to the room under the eaves, and there she unpacked her things.

An hour later she saw the old man to his room, then cleared the books from the floor, banked down the fire, and once again mounted the stairs.

The attic was freezing cold but she did not scramble out of her clothes, and when finally she crept between the sheets and sank into the feather bed it smelt musty and damp, even though Katie had been over twice during the last few days and aired the sheets, and placed the hot cinder pan on the tick, just in case the bed should be needed for the present emergency.

Her knees drawn up, and lying on her side, her hands pinned tight under her oxters, she waited for the avalanche to overtake her. But strangely it didn't. It was as if all her tears had solidified to form a mountain that was now resting on top of her stomach pressing down on the child.

'Mark.' She said his name aloud; then again, 'Mark,' louder now. And she saw it winging away across the countryside over the frozen earth and dropping down through the loose black mould until it reached the wood of the coffin; then, forcing its way through, touched his lips and he became alive again. And there he was, his head on the pillow beside her, his eyes looking into hers through the lamplight, and his voice murmuring, 'You're beautiful, Tilly Trotter. You know that? You're beautiful.'

◉ 5 ◉

January slipped out on ice-laden roads, the frost so heavy that even at midday it settled on the brows and the eyelashes of humans and brought the cattle to a premature stillness of death.

Tilly spent most of her time sawing wood to keep the fire going. It was as if she were back in her childhood and early girlhood, only now she found no joy in the exercise.

When February brought the snow up to the window-sills she was cut off from all contact with those at the Manor for over a week, and she knew that if Mr Burgess had been left on his own he would never have survived this period. Living, as he had, the scholastic life, he paid little attention to the needs of the body, and the blankets he would have heaped on himself instead of braving the elements to fetch in wood would not have been sufficient to keep out the piercing merciless cold; added to which he would not have bothered about meals, except to make porridge and drink tea. So she told herself that at least one good thing had come out of her present situation.

Her stomach seemed to be rising daily; her body was noticing her weight. Physically she was feeling well enough, that is if she didn't take into account the misery in her heart and the perpetual cold, because the little house, its surroundings being bare of trees, was open to the weather on its four sides, and although the walls were fifteen inches thick they and the stone floor did not tend to engender warmth.

After the sun had shone for two days the thaw set in and there was movement on the roads once more; but not by horse or carriage, merely by those on foot. But they had to walk through drifts still halfway up their thighs.

When Arthur eventually managed to make his way to the cottage it was with the added burden of a bulky sack across his shoulders, and after he had thumped on the door and Tilly had opened it to him, he slid his burden from his back and pushed it into her arms before kicking the snow from his high boots and shaking it from the tails of his coat.

'Why! Arthur, what made you come out weather like this?'

'Mam thought you would be starving. I'd better take me boots off, they're sodden.'

'No, no; come inside, you'll freeze.' She reached out her hand and gripped his arm and pulled him over the threshold, where he stood stamping his feet on the matting as he looked across the room to where Mr Burgess was sitting, his chair pulled close up to the hearth; and he called to him, saying simply, 'Snifter.'

'Yes, yes, indeed, Arthur, 'tis a snifter as you say; and a long, long snifter it's been. Do you think we've seen the end of it?'

'Not by a long chalk, Mr Burgess, not by a long chalk. The sky's laden with it again.'

'Come over to the fire.' Tilly beckoned him further into the room, but he hesitated, saying, 'I'm mucky, Tilly; I'll mess up the floor.'

'Well, it won't be the first time it's been messed up. Sit yourself down, Arthur.' There was a command in her voice. 'I'll make you a drink.'

She put the sack on the table, then looked at him and said, 'How did you manage to get this out?'

'She's gone, Tilly. Madam God Almighty went just afore the heavy fall. I tried to get in to tell you afore but I had to turn back. You'll never guess what.'

'Matthew's come?'

'Oh no! no! not Master Matthew but Master John. He came back from Scarborough; he had gone on there to get away from her; he had only been gone a week or so. Apparently he had had a letter from Master Matthew, it had been sent on to him from here, saying he'd like him to look after things until he could get back, never mentioned his sister. Of course, you would likely know that Master Luke couldn't do anything about it, him being in the army. Anyway, the young 'un was simply over the moon. Katie said she heard him letting the young madam havin't hot and strong with hardly a flicker to his tongue. Oh, and how she went on. An' you know what? She was goin' to have her husband down and her sister-in-law, and she wasn't going to take any notice of the letter Master John had until, so Katie said, the solicitor had been informed. Well, Master John said he had, and that he was coming out to confirm things like. Eeh! me ma did laugh. As she said, the little madam went round the house as if she had been stung in the backside by a bee. I didn't know she hadn't a proper home of her own, Tilly, but lived with her in-laws, and that was why she wanted to play the madam back at the house. . . . Did you know that, Tilly?'

'Yes, I knew she lived with her . . . her husband's people.'

'It makes things clear, doesn't it?' Arthur looked towards Mr Burgess. 'I mean, why she wanted to stay on here.'

Mr Burgess smiled widely as he nodded and said, 'Yes, it certainly makes things clear. In-laws are noted for their inability to hand over power to either their sons or their daughters. Man's ego is not entirely man's alone, woman has a share of it, and with her she used it as a weapon.'

'Aye. Aye.' Arthur nodded at the old man, his face slightly blank, being unable, as usual, to follow his way of talking and reasoning, yet at the same time aware that the old man was in entire agreement with what he himself had been saying. He turned now and, looking at Tilly, said, 'Me ma wants to know how you're feelin', Tilly.'

'Oh, tell her I'm very well. Here –' She handed him a bowl of hot soup and a shive of bread, saying, 'Get off your feet and drink that.'

Arthur lowered his stubby form down on to the wooden stool at the other side of the hearth, and as he gulped at the soup and chewed on the crusty bread he talked, giving snippets about the goings on during the past weeks in the house. And then, as he reached forward and put the bowl down on the corner of the table, he said, 'You could be coming back now, Tilly. Me ma says there could be every chance of you coming back.'

She was standing some way behind Mr Burgess's chair and she made a quick jerking movement with her head towards Arthur as she answered, 'Oh, I don't think that will be possible, Arthur; it would only cause more dissent among the family, and there's been enough of that already.'

Arthur, holding her gaze and taking the message indicated by her shaking head rather than what she had said, nodded at her as he got to his feet, muttering, 'Aye. Aye, I suppose you're right, Tilly. I suppose you're right. Well, I'll be off, Mr Burgess.' He bent stiffly forward, and Mr Burgess, as if coming out of a doze, said, 'Oh. Oh, yes, Arthur. It's been very nice seeing you. Give my regards to your mother.'

'I . . . I will, Mr Burgess. Yes, I will.'

Tilly walked with him to the door and when, pulling his cap tight down about his ears and turning the collar of his coat up to meet it, he said, 'Sorry, Tilly. I put me foot in it somehow, didn't I?' she answered, 'It's all right, Arthur.' Her voice was low. 'I think he would worry if he thought he was going to be left on his own. He's . . . he's a sick man, and he knows it. No matter if I had the opportunity of returning, I couldn't do it at present. In any case, I don't think it would be wise for me to go back there, not under the circumstances.' Her hand went involuntarily to her stomach, and he lowered his eyes from hers as he said, 'Perhaps you're right, Tilly. Perhaps you're right. But . . . but we miss you. Me ma misses you a lot. The house isn't the same. The work's bein' done but, as me ma said yesterday, not with good grace. You know – ' His straight lips slipped into a wide smile and he added, 'I remember what me da used to say. I was only a little bairn at the time, but he created a very strange picture in me mind about God and the devil 'cos he used to say if he had the option of working for God who would say, 'Well done, thou good and faithful servant,' or the devil who'd slap him on the back and say, 'By lad! you've done a good job there,' he knew for which one he'd work.'

As he went to turn away from her on a laugh he turned as quickly again towards her, his hand across his mouth, saying, 'Not that I'm likin' you to the devil, Tilly.'

She was smiling widely herself now as she said, 'Well, if you're not, Arthur, you're having a very good try.'

'Aw, Tilly!' He flapped his hand towards her. 'So long. I'll see you again soon, that's if that holds up.' He pointed away into the distance to where the sky seemed to be hovering just above the hills.

She watched him until he had gone some way down the road before going in and closing the door. Oh, it was nice to see one of them again. Each one of the Drews seemed to belong to her, like a member of her family, the only family she had.

When she turned towards the fire and Mr Burgess, he was sitting up straight in his chair. Putting his hand out towards her, he said, 'Come here, my dear.'

And when she stood in front of him, he blinked up at her through his watery eyes as he said, 'Now you must not consider me. If Master John asks you to go back you must do so. I'm all right. I'm not in my dotage yet and it's about time I took a hand in looking after myself.'

'Yes, it is.' She nodded her head towards him; then leaning forward, she pulled the shawl around his shoulders before pressing him back in the chair and adding, 'So get yourself well and on to your feet and trotting round again, and then we'll talk about where I'm going to go.'

'Oh, Trotter.' His head drooped towards his chest and there was a break in his voice as he murmured, 'I don't deserve you. I don't. I'm a selfish old man. I've been selfish all my life. All I've thought about are these.' He waved his hand slackly over the books on the little table to his side. 'You can say I've given them my life, and what use are they to me now? Inanimate things. All my life I have called them my companions but do they speak to me now and bring me comfort? All the knowledge I have garnered from them is not going to help me to die in peace. All they say to me is, don't go yet, enjoy me more. In the night they talk to me, Trotter, and ask what will happen to us when you're gone? Don't go, they say; we can keep you happy for years yet. And when I tell them I cannot stay much longer, they look at me blankly and not one of them says, 'Here, take my hand for comfort.' There is only you, Trotter, who has ever held out a hand to me in comfort. The master, he was good and kind to me, but his goodness was of the mind, while yours comes from the heart.'

'Oh, my dear! My dear!' They were the only words she could speak as she pressed the white head against her waist. Presently releasing her hold on him, she dropped down on to her knees by his side and, gripping his blue-veined hands, she said, 'You're not going to die for a long time. You're going to get better; you're going to be the first to hear my child cry. You're going to nurse him . . . her . . . whatever, on your knee while I get on with my work. And another thing' – she shook the hands within her grasp – 'your books have been your true friends, don't desert them now.'

'My dear, dear, Trotter.' The tears were welling from the corner of his eyes and dropping slowly down the furrows of his cheeks. 'I once prophesied that you'd come into your own, didn't I?'

When she nodded at him he said, 'Well, I shall repeat that. One day you'll be a lady in your own right, Tilly Trotter. You are indeed a lady now, and that is true; but one day you'll be a lady in your own right.'

↩ 6 ↪

There was the promise of spring, the sun was shining and the air had lost its bitterness, although the snow still lay in brown-capped moulds against the hedges and the sides of the roads and there was time yet for other falls. Tilly remembered that two years ago they had been snowed up all over the Easter, but today was bright and warm and Mr Burgess was on his feet walking about the room, picking up this book and that and looking as if the spring was also bringing renewed life into his old bones.

She turned from putting the last of the logs from the wicker basket on to the fire and saw him standing gazing out of the window. 'Good to see the sun,' she said.

'Yes, yes, isn't it, my dear, the life-giving sun. And it has brought the children out.'

'Children?' She came to his side and, looking through one of the small panes, she saw three boys coming down the road. They were jumping and pushing each other and Mr Burgess remarked, 'Like lambs, the spring has got into their legs.'

She smiled as she turned away, went back to the fireplace, picked up the wicker basket and went down the room, through the small scullery, took her cloak from behind the door and went into the yard.

There were only two small outhouses and they were placed at the bottom of the yard. One was a closet which had a modern touch in that it had a wooden seat with a hole which was placed directly above the bucket. The other was a woodshed, only large enough to hold a sawing block and with space for a single stack of logs around its walls. The walls were now two-thirds bare and they told her that before long she must get them covered again, because soon she would not be able to hump wood or saw. Arthur was kind but it was only at odd times he could get away, apart from his monthly leave.

She had half filled her skip when her body became still, and it was still bent when she turned her head and cocked her ear towards the door. And now she felt the colour draining from her face, in fact seeming to drain from her whole body as the word floated over the cottage towards her: 'Witch! Witch!'

Aw no! not again. She closed her eyes for a moment before hurrying towards the back of the house. But she hesitated at the door, then went swiftly round the side, there to see the three young boys standing on the roadway. They had their eyes riveted on the front door, and so they did not at first notice her as she stood between the corner of the cottage and the privet hedge that marked the boundary of the small piece of adjoining land, and she listened to them chanting:

'Witch, witch, witch,
Come out without a stitch;
Tis time you learned
You're going to be burned,
Witch, witch, witch.'

The two smaller boys had snowballs in their hands and they pelted them towards the door. It was the biggest of the three who, finding a large stone in the snow, threw it with perfect aim towards the window.

At the sound of the breaking glass she ran forward and the boys, expecting the front door to open, were for the moment petrified at the sight of her, for they saw an extremely tall creature flying towards them, her head hooded and the sides of her black cloak spread wide.

The biggest boy was the first to turn and run, but the other two, springing out of their fear-filled, almost petrified state, turned to each other as they made to scamper away, and so collided. As they stumbled, Tilly's hands grabbed at their collars; and it would have been no surprise if they had there and then died from fright.

Her arms were thin but still extremely strong, the result of the saw bench and the manual work she had undertaken in the mine, and so she shook them, staring as she did so from one face to the other.

It was the bigger one who found his tongue, and he spluttered, "Twa... 'twasn't me, missis. I... I never broke your window. 'Twas Billy.'

'What is your name?'

'T... Taylor, missis.'

'Where are you from?' But need she ask, for she knew the answer before he spluttered, 'Th... the village.'

'And you?' She now shook the smaller boy until his head wobbled on his shoulders. 'What is your name?'

'Pear... Pearson, missis, Tommy Pearson.'

Pearson. There was only one Pearson in the village, at least there had been only one twelve years ago, and his name was Tom Pearson and he'd been a friend to her.

'Is your father called Tom?' she demanded.

'Yes, missis.'

'Well now' – she bent her head over him – 'you are to go back now and tell him what you have done. Do you hear me?'

'Ye... yes, missis.'

'I shall know whether you have or not. You understand?'

'Yes, missis.'

'Tell him he has to give you a good thrashing.'

The 'Yes, missis' did not come as promptly now but the boy gulped, then muttered on a whisper, 'Aye. Yes, missis.'

'As for you' – she now shook the other boy – 'tell me this: Who sent you along here? Who told you to come?'

'Billy McGrath, him.' He jerked his head backwards as his arm swung outwards towards the boy standing some way down the road, and Tilly lifted her head and stared over the distance. A McGrath... a McGrath again, the son of one of the remaining brothers. It couldn't be Steve's boy because Steve had left the district years ago, and Steve, too, had been her friend. The trouble with Steve had been he'd wanted to be more than a friend, as Hal had. That was the reason he had killed Hal; well, part of it, for he had been bullied and ill-treated by his elder brother from when he was a child. And now here was another generation of McGraths starting on her. Surely it wasn't going to begin all over again. Aw no!

As if in answer to her question, the young McGrath yelled now as he danced from one side of the road to the other, 'Witch! Witch! you're an old witch an' a murderer. You killed me Uncle Hal, you did, you did. But me granny'll get you. She says she will an' she will. Witch! Witch!'

It was on the last 'witch' delivered by the boy at the pitch of his lungs that the rider came round the bend in the road and reined up behind him, and the boy turned and jumped into the ditch, and there stood looking up at the man on the horse.

'What's your game, boy?'

'Getting at the witch, Mr Bentwood.'

The rider lifted his eyes and looked along the road to where Tilly still stood holding the younger boys by their collars and, taking in the scene, he bent down towards the young McGrath and, his whip cracking over the lad's head, he said, 'Now get back, you young scoundrel, to where you belong, and if I catch you along this road again I'll skin you. Do you hear me? And tell that to your father, and your granny. Understand?'

The boy made no answer but he sidled along the ditch away from the rider as Simon Bentwood walked his horse towards Tilly.

Tilly did not raise her head, but she looked at the boys and she said, 'Remember what I told you!' and on this she brought their heads together with a crack that could have been much harder had she cared. Then releasing them and pushing them from her, she watched them turn and run down the road, their palms to their foreheads, before she herself looked up at the man on the horse. And what she said now was, 'I am quite capable, Mr Bentwood, of managing my own affairs. I will thank you not to take any part in this.'

'Aw, Tilly!' He put the whip into the hand that was holding the reins, then shaded his eyes for a moment with his free palm, and when he looked at her again it was some seconds before he said, 'Can't you let bygones be bygones, for after all there's neither of us turned out to be a saint?'

What he said was quite true. He had had an affair with a married woman, and she had had an affair with a married man. It could be said that she was worse than him, for her affair had lasted for twelve years whereas his had quickly fizzled out. The man-crazy Lady Myton had tired of him, and that, she understood, hadn't been long after the day she had found them naked in the barn together.

She had often wondered why that discovery should have hit her so hard. Perhaps it was the shattering of an ideal, a dream, her first love. And he had been her first love, for she had loved Simon Bentwood from the moment she had set eyes on him when she was five years old. On the day he broke the news that he was going to be married and that he wished her to come and dance at his wedding she told herself her heart was broken. But she had been given proof on his wedding night that she still meant something to him, for on that night he left his bride and came to her rescue and saved her from being raped by Hal McGrath. When the McGraths burned down her granny's cottage and he took both her and her granny into the shelter of his home, her love for him increased, if that were possible, and this had not escaped his wife.

When he later found out that he had married the wrong woman he had wanted to set her up in a house in Shields, but she was having none of that. She had even preferred working down the mine rather than being known as his kept woman.

She was already established on the staff in the Manor when she heard of his wife's death and was amazed to know that this had happened some weeks previously. The reason for his nonappearance she had put down to his sense of decency. But no sense of decency had needed to be considered on her part when she decided to go and commiserate with him on his loss, while at the same time knowing that she was a hypocrite and was only hoping that she would be strong enough to contain her joy. But what did she find when she reached the farm? She found him in the act of love, or so called, with the very lady who had been the means of ruining the master.

It was because of Mark's affair with Lady Myton that his wife had left him and taken their four children with her, leaving him as desolate as Simon Bentwood had left her. Yet it wasn't desolate, until she had gone willingly to the master's bed that she realised, as Mr Burgess was so apt at quoting, there were so many different kinds of love.

Looking up at the figure on the horse she noted how changed he was from the man she had known. There was the suspicion of jowls to his broad face meeting the flesh of his neck pressing upwards out of his high collar; only the top button of his riding coat fastened, and the gap in his waistcoat from which his stomach protruded and seemed to rest on the saddle in front of him were all evidence of the physical change in him. Even his eyes were not the same. They lay in pouches of flesh and were slightly bloodshot.

She thought, with amazement, he was only forty years old, and then he was remarking on the change in her. Bending from the saddle and looking down into her face he said, 'You've changed, I can see that. You know, we've never been so close for over twelve years.'

'We all change with the years.' Her tone was as cold as the air.

'Oh yes, yes' – he patted his stomach – 'I'm not the man I was. Is that what you're meaning?'

'My words had no special meaning, I was merely making a statement, an obvious statement.'

'Huh!' his chin jerked upwards – 'we do speak correctly, don't we? Of course, you've been mixing with the gentry for a long time and naturally it rubs off. And then, you have your private tutor.' He turned his head quickly in the direction of the cottage, where Mr Burgess could be seen standing.

When she did not take umbrage at his remark but returned his gaze, saying quietly, 'Yes, I have been very fortunate. It does not fall to everyone's lot to meet two such men,' he jerked at the reins and caused the horse to rear before he brought out on a growl, 'Oh for God's sake, Tilly, come off your high horse, be yourself, your memory's short.'

Her voice was now as angry as his as she glared up at him and replied, 'No, my memory isn't short, Simon Bentwood, it's very long. And looking back down it, I have nothing to thank you for.'

'No? Well, let me tell you, Tilly, that's where you're mistaken. I kept you and your grandparents alive for years with the sovereign brought them every month. The stolen money had run out long afore that. But there's more let me tell you. My marriage might have got off to a good start if it hadn't been for seeing to you, like the bloody fool I was. And anyway, what have you done that you can hold your head up while I should bow mine? That affair with her ladyship was over and done with as quick as she finished it with your fancy man. She liked variety, did her ladyship, but even so she didn't cause half the scandal in the county that you did when you went to bed with Sopwith. And you're still managing to set fire to scandal, for after twelve years what has he left you? A bellyful, and thrown out on your backside into the bargain, because the family hates your guts. And another thing I'll tell you, although I chased that little beggar of a McGrath away, it isn't the last you'll hear of them because old Ma McGrath wanted to build a bonfire the day they knew you had been shown the door. And if I know her she's not finished with you yet, and when they start on you again, the villagers as a whole, because you spell bad luck for the lot of them, who will you run to this time, eh?'

Her eyes were steady, her voice equally so, as she gazed back into his unfuriated face and said quietly, 'Not you, Simon, never you.

Again he pulled the horse into a rearing position; but then, all anger seeming to seep from him, he brought the animal once more to a standstill and, his voice now holding a deep sadness, he spoke her name.

'Tilly! aw Tilly!' he said; then leaning forward, he added, 'I'd give anything – do you hear? – anything in this wide world to put the clock back.'

A tinge of pity threaded her thinking and caused her to pause and change the tart reply that was on her tongue, and what she said now was, 'That's impossible, Simon, and you know it.'

'Could we be friends, Tilly?'

'No, Simon' – she shook her head slowly – 'not again.'

He turned his body in the saddle and, leaning towards the horse's head, he stroked its neck twice before saying, 'When the child comes, what then, who's to see to you?'

'Myself Simon. Always myself.'

'You'll find it hard; you're a lone woman and the whole place is agen you.'

'The world is wide, I won't remain here always, just as long as Mr Burgess needs me.'

Again he was bending over the horse's neck, and stroking it, and he said, 'I'd be good to you, Tilly. I would take it and bring it up as my own.'

The swift angry retort 'You bring up Mark's child as your own, never!' stopped at her lips; then she bowed her head. And her tight lips and her attitude must have given him hope, because he was leaning well out of the saddle towards her when she raised her eyes to him and said, 'Thank you, Simon, but I have no intention of marrying.'

'You might change your mind.'

'I don't think so.'

'You know something, Tilly?' His voice had lost its softness again. 'I could have been married twelve times over during these last years. But I waited, aye, I waited, hoping for this moment. I felt sure something would happen sooner or later, and it has, And you know something, Tilly? I'm going on waitin'. I was going to finish by saying you'll need me afore I need you, but that would be wrong. I've always needed you, and I always will, and I'll be here when you whistle.' He gave a wry twisted smile now as, changing the last word of the song, he said, 'Whistle an' I'll come to ye, me lass. Remember that, Tilly, you've just got to whistle. Get up there!' He brought his heels sharply into the horse's belly, and it kicked up the snow-covered stones in the road before going into a trot.

She did not stay and watch him ride away but turned swiftly and went up the path, round the corner and to the woodshed again, and there she finished filling the skip before returning to the house.

But as soon as she came into the room she dropped the skip and hurried towards the couch where Mr Burgess was sitting, his hand in a bowl of warm water.

'Aw no! you're cut.'

'Just a splinter, just a splinter. It's all right. I put some salt in the water, it's cleansed.'

She looked at the towel on the seat beside him, saying, 'It's bled a lot.'

'Just a little. It's stopped now.'

'The devil!'

'Village boys, were they?'

'Yes, one of the McGraths, a new generation.'

'And the rider was the farmer?'

'Yes.'

'Come to rescue you?' He raised his wrinkled lids and smiled up at her.

'You could say that.'

'Did he get a flea in his ear?'

'Yes, you could say that too.'

'He wants you to marry him and save you disgrace?'

She patted his shoulder and nodded, 'Right again.' She left him and went to the end of the room and picked up the skip of logs, and as she placed them near the fireside he said soberly, 'I wish you were back in the Manor, you're not safe here. I wonder why Master John hasn't called?'

Master John called the very next day. He, too, came on horseback and when Tilly heard the sound of the horse's hooves on the road she hurried to the window and stood to one side looking out from behind the lace curtains. Upon ascertaining that it wasn't Simon Bentwood, she drew in a long relieving breath and, turning to Mr Burgess who was dozing before the fire, she said, 'It's Master John; he must have heard you yesterday.'

From the open door she watched the young man tying the horse to the gatepost, and she went over the step to greet him, saying, 'How nice to see you.'

Coming swiftly forward, he held out his hands and his mouth opened wide before he could bring out, 'And ... and you, Trotter.'

She said formally now, 'It's a lovely day, isn't it?'

'Tis, Trotter, 'tis. ... Ah! there you are, Mr Bur ... Burgess.' He was crossing the room now and when he took the old man's outstretched hand he added, 'You're looking very well, ve ... very well.'

'I am feeling very well, thanks to my good nurse.' Mr Burgess inclined his head towards Tilly and she, looking at John, said, 'What can I get you to drink?'

'What have you? Brandy, sherry, p ... p ... port, liq ... liqueur?'

She flapped her hand at him playfully. 'Bring it down to tea or soup and you can have your choice.'

'Tea then, Tro ... Trotter. Thank you very much.'

'Do sit down. ... Here, give me your coat.'

He handed her his coat and hat and riding crop and when he was seated opposite the old man, Mr Burgess said, 'Your visit portends good news I hope?'

'Oh well.' John turned his head first one way, then another, and his eyes came to rest on Tilly, where she was coming from the delf rack with a tea-tray in her hands, and he flushed slightly as he said, 'No ... not really. N ... n ... nothing I'm afraid that can ... can be of any help at the mo ... moment, but I thought it b ... b ... better to ... to come and explain.'

She laid the tray on the table, then stood looking at him; and he, addressing her slowly now, said, 'When Jessie Ann left I wa ... wanted you to come back to the house, and I told her this was one of the fir ... first things I was going to do. It was th ... then she' – his mouth now opened wide and he closed his eyes and his head bobbed before he brought out the next words on a rush – 'informed me that she had already wr ... written to Matthew telling him what she had do ... done, so I was, well, sort of stum ... stumped, Trotter. You understand?'

She inclined her head towards him and waited, and he glanced at Mr Burgess before returning his gaze to her and going on, 'I wrote immediately to Matthew and explained the situation and str ... str ... stressed your – ' he blinked rapidly now and, his mouth once again open wide, he said, 'Con ... condition, and only yesterday I got a reply from him, in which he states he's c ... c ... coming home. He should be back about August or September because Uncle – ' Again he glanced at Mr Burgess, explaining now, 'He is not really our uncle because he is ... is ... was my grandmother's half-brother and the youngest of the f ... f ... family.' He laughed now, his mouth stretching wide illuminating his pleasant features as he ended, 'I do ... don't know what relationship that makes us to him b ... b ... but having n ... no children of his own, he addresses us as nephews. Matthew seems to l ... l ... like him very much, he says he's a fine man. I don't really think that Matthew wants to leave Texas but anyway he is c ... coming back.'

'Texas? Texas!' Mr Burgess nodded his head now. 'What a state for Matthew to choose to live in! It has been called the state of adventurers, and a slave state; everybody seems to want it and nobody seems to want it. After the tragedy of the Alamo and the massacres that followed you'd have thought politicians both Mexican, American and British would have allowed it to remain an independent republic. We wanted it to remain independent – ' he nooded from John to Tilly

now – 'oh yes, it was to our benefit those days that she should remain independent. Now Master John' – he leant towards the young man – 'I'm going to ask
you something, the same question that I asked your brother not all those many
years ago in the schoolroom. What was the Alamo?'

John cast a laughing glance now towards Tilly, then said, 'I . . . I think it was
a mission chapel, sir, in which the American soldiers took refuge in the w . . .
w . . . war against the Mex . . . Mex . . . Mexicans.'

'Yes, yes, you're right. But you know what the answer Master Luke gave me
to that question when I asked him what the Alamo was, eh?'

'I have no idea, s . . . sir.'

'He said it was a river that ran into the Mississippi. Can you imagine that?'

'Yes, yes; I can w . . . well imagine that, sir. Luke was never v . . . very strong
on history. When I saw him last I said I hoped he has a g . . . g . . . good sergeant
when he is due to go to India and a g . . . g . . . guide book.'

They all laughed; then Tilly, stirring the tea in the teapot with a long-handled
spoon, asked, 'Are you home for good, Master John?'

'It . . . it all depends, Tr . . . Trotter. I . . . I hope so but I cannot say anything
def . . . definite until Matthew comes. I have a strong f . . . f . . . feeling he might
want to return to America. If that is so I . . . I would be pleased to stay and se . . .
see to things.' He turned his head now and looked at Mr Burgess as he ended,
'I di . . . didn't really enjoy university life, sir. I'm s . . . s . . . sorry.'

Tilly handed the two men their tea and when presently the conversation
became general and Mr Burgess's head began to nod, John made a signal towards
Tilly and, rising softly from the seat, he picked up his hat and coat and tiptoed
towards the door, and she followed him.

Outside on the path, she asked a question that had been in her mind since
John had mentioned the letter he had received from his brother. 'Did Matthew
make any reference to me, John?'

The young man struck at the top of his leather gaiters with his crop before
saying, 'No, Trotter. I explained things to him but he m . . . m . . . made no ref . . .
reference in his reply. You see' – he looked at her shyly – 'I asked him if I c . . .
could take you back in the position of housekeeper because th . . . the place needs
a housekeeper, Trotter. B . . . Biddy is very good, and K . . . K . . . Katie and the
rest, but there is no gui . . . guiding hand. I wish he had mentioned it.'

'Don't worry, John.' She put her hand out and touched his sleeve. 'I'm sure
Biddy won't let things slide. As for me, well, I'm all right here.'

His face flushing slightly now and his stammer more pronounced, he said, 'It
isn't the . . . the pl . . . pl . . . place for a ba . . . baby to be born, Trotter.'

'Many have been born in worse places than this, John.'

'Yes, undou . . . dou . . . doubtedly, but what I'm thinking is the ch . . . child
will be my half-brother or s . . . s . . . sister.'

'It's nice of you to look at it in that way. You are so kind, John, I wish there
were more like you.'

'St . . . stammer or no?' He was laughing now.

'St . . . stammer or no.'

'I worry about the st . . . stammer, Trotter.' He again struck his gaiters. 'No
young l . . . l . . . lady is going to p . . . p . . . put up with me.'

'Nonsense! nonsense! You've got a fine figure and you have a face to go with it. When the right one comes along how you speak won't trouble her.'

'Not even when I have to say I ... I lo ... love you?'

She looked at him sadly for a moment. That was one of his most endearing points, he could make a joke of his affliction, even while it hurt him, even tore at him as now when presenting him with a bleak and loveless future. She wanted to put her arms around him and say, 'I love you,' for she did, like a mother, because she was the first one to have shown him love even while smacking his bottom.

Copying his light mood, she leant towards him now and gripping his arm tightly, said, 'They're positive in the village that I'm a witch, and your father at times said I was too, and sometimes I believe it myself. I believe that if I wish for a thing hard enough it'll come true, and so, from now on, I'm going to conjure up the image of the young lady who is going to throw her heart at your feet.'

'Oh, Tro ... Trotter!' His mouth wide open, his head back, he gulped and said again, 'Tro ... Trotter you're a pr ... pr ... priceless gem. I've always underst ... st ... stood why Father loved you. Good-bye, Tr ... Trotter, I'll keep you in ... formed. I'll p ... p ... pop over often from now on.'

'Good-bye, John.' She watched him mount the horse and answered his wave before turning to go back into the cottage.

Mr Burgess was fast asleep now, his head resting against the high padded arm of the couch. Softly, she made her way up the stairs and when she reached the bedroom under the eaves she sat on the side of the low bed and after taking in a deep breath she dropped her head forward into her hands and the tears spurted through her fingers. She had experienced loneliness before, but never like this. Within the last few minutes it had become intensified, the result of that kind young man bringing the essence of the house with him, the house which had become to her as home, and the feeling brought from her the plea, Mark! Mark! what am I going to do?

༺༄ 7 ༄༻

Tilly's baby was born at five minutes past midnight on the 27th of June, 1853. It was a boy, and when Biddy held him up by the feet and smacked his blood-stained buttocks he yelled, as any boy would, and when Katie stumbled up the steep stairs with a dish of water in her hands, her mother cried at her, 'It's a lad! Here, put that down and take him while I see to her.'

Peering down through the lamplight on to the sweat-streaming face of the young woman she thought of and loved as if she were of her own flesh, she said softly, 'Look lass, you've got a son, and he's a whopper. Lie still, you're all right.'

Tilly touched her son's face, then closed her eyes and only now when she let out a long weary breath did her stomach subside, its walls seeming to touch her backbone. She was tired, so very tired. It had been a long struggle, thirty-six hours in fact, but she had a son. She and Mark had a son. 'Oh, Mark! Mark! I wonder if you know.'

'What do you say, lass?'

'Do you think he knows, Biddy?'

'Who, lass?'

'Mark . . . the master.'

'He'll know all right, lass. He'll know. Now I'm just gona tidy you up, then off you go to sleep because if I know anything you need it. An' that fellow there's gona be at you afore you know where you are.'

'Thank you, Biddy. Thank you.' There was no strength in the clasp of her hand now. . . .

The daylight was coming through the small window and in the light she could see Biddy holding the child out towards her. She took it into her arms and when it nuzzled her breast Biddy said, 'Now you know you're a mother, lass.'

She looked down on her son and was surprised to see that he had hair, and more surprised still to see that his face was an almost exact replica of his father's every feature in miniature. She gazed in wonder at the small hand kneading her breast. It was broad, the fingers square. She laughed as she looked up at Biddy, saying now, 'If he doesn't change there won't be much trouble in identifying the father.'

'No; you've said it. Even Katie remarked on it right away.'

'Will he change much?'

'Oh, he'll change, they all do, yet at the same time remain the same, if you know what I mean.'

'No, I don't' – Tilly laughed gently – 'but I follow you.'

'Master John's been along.'

'So early?'

'Well, it's on seven o'clock now.'

'How are they managing up there?'

'Oh, we've got it all arranged. He said we had to see to you, so I've fixed everything. Arthur's trotting us back and forward in the wagon. Then in a few day's time when you're feeling more like yourself Phyllis's girl, Betty, she's coming over to stay with you until you're nearly on your feet. She's a sensible lass.'

'But I thought she was over at the Redheads?'

'She left when her bond was up. Couldn't stand the cook. Sixteen hours a day was a bit too much for her, for anybody, but for a ten-year-old, well her legs were swollen as big as a porker's hock. Master John said I can take her on and start her in the kitchen. . . .'

It was later that day Tilly heard a knock on the door and when, later, Biddy came upstairs but didn't mention who had called, she asked, 'Who was that at the door?'

'Oh, just some lass. Got the wrong house I think.'

'Wrong house? Someone starting service?'

'No, no.' Biddy was busying herself at the wash-hand-stand tucked into the corner under the sloping roof. 'Gentry, I'd say; come on her horse.'

'Who was she looking for?'

'Somebody . . . oh, somebody of the name of Smith.'

Tilly's brows came together. 'Smith? There's no Smith round here, not that the gentry would visit. And they wouldn't be living in a cottage like this, would they? Now who was it, Biddy?'

Biddy turned to her. 'I've told you. As true as I'm standing here it was a young girl on a horse, but she had come to the wrong house. You don't believe me?'

'It's very strange.' Tilly shook her head.

'There's lots of strange things happen in the world and that to me isn't one of them. She's just a lass, or a lady if you must have it, who mistook a house. Likely she was visiting a dependant or some such. I hope that when I'm in my dotage you'll come and visit me at the lodge.'

'Oh, shut up.' Tilly turned her head to the side and Biddy, making use of one of her boys' jocular retorts, said, 'I would if I had a shop, a music hall, or a coal mine.'

All Tilly could reply to this was a huh! accompanied by a shake of her head with closed eyes, which she opened quickly at the sound of a heavy tread at the bottom of the stairs. They looked at each other, and Tilly said, 'Go and give him a hand, Biddy, he'll break his neck one of these times.'

'The quicker you're downstairs the better, lass.' Biddy jerked her head. 'This is the third time since last night an' I'm puffed out helping him through that hole in the floor.'

As Tilly watched Biddy lower herself gingerly on to her knees and extend a hand through the open hatchway from which the stairs descended, she marvelled at the compensations life offered one; for every two enemies she had she had a friend, and as Mr Burgess was always quoting, one ounce of good outweighed a pound of evil. If only that ounce of good would outweigh the void inside her, fill it up and take away this great sense of loneliness, for even the child as yet had not entered the void.

What if it never filled the void; what if time would offer no replacement? Time erased all pain, they said.

'There you are, my dear.' Mr Burgess was bending over her, smiling down on them both, and as he so often did he seemed to pick up her thoughts, for he said, 'You'll never be lonely again. He'll bring love into your life. You'll see.'

$$\text{8}$$

The child was three months old. He was a lusty infant, good-tempered, crying only when he was hungry, when it was more of a whine than a cry. He gurgled at every face that hung above him, particularly that of Mr Burgess whose sparse beard had an attraction for his fingers.

The old man seemed to have lost the new life that came in with the spring and he now spent most of his mornings in bed and his afternoons dozing by the fire.

Tilly had to keep the clothes basket, which served as a cradle for the baby, well out of his way, for in his sudden spurts towards his books on the shelves he was apt to stumble over anything in front of him that was not any higher than his knees.

Sometimes she could go almost a week without seeing anyone other than Mr Burgess, the child, and a quick visit from Arthur bringing some dainties from the kitchen. But on this particular day she had three visitors.

The first one came in the morning and he was Tom Pearson. When she opened the door to him she could not hide her surprise. She had not seen anyone from the village, except the children, for years. The Manor had protected her like a fortress. And she had no need to go through the village ever; whenever she went into Shields, or as far away as Newcastle, she went by coach along the main road.

'Mr Pearson!'

'Aye, Tilly. It is a long time since we met.'

'Yes, yes, it is.' She did not invite him in because Mr Burgess was still asleep, but she stepped towards him, drawing the door closed behind her, and as she did so he said, 'You'll be wondering why I'm here, or why I haven't come afore.'

She was puzzled for a moment until he added, 'My young 'un . . . I only heard yesterday of what he got up to some months back. He let slip something and I whacked the rest out of him. I'm sorry, Tilly.'

'Oh, it's all right, Mr Pearson. I should say I'm used to it by now, but somehow I feel I'll never get used to it.'

'Tisn't likely. So unfair. I've said that all along, 'tis so unfair. But they're ignorant an' they breed ignorance. That young McGrath is a chip off the old block, and I've warned my Tommy that if I catch him runnin' round with him again I'll take the skin off him. Anyway, how are you, Tilly?'

'I'm very well, thank you, Mr Pearson.'

'An' . . . an' the bairn, can I ask after it?'

'Yes, and thank you. And he's very well too.'

'I'm glad to hear that.' He sighed now. 'Bairns . . . well, they're a blessin' and a curse, all in the same breath. My eldest, Bobby, he's heading for America next week.'

'Really!'

'Aye. All happened through gettin' into conversation with some fellow on the quay at Newcastle last year. The fellow was off to join his brother, who was working in some factory picking up money like nuggets he said. I'll believe that when I see it, but you can't stop them once they get something in their head like that.'

'Well perhaps he will make his fortune and then send for you.'

'Not me, Tilly, not me; I'm past pipe dreams, me. And I can't get his mother hardly over the doorstep, never mind America. She's even afeared of the few horses and carriages an' the like in the village.'

Tilly merely nodded now. She had heard years ago that Mrs Pearson was afraid of anything that moved on the roads, and that she wouldn't even let the children have a cat or a dog in the house in case they came to harm.

'Well, I just thought I'd come and tell you, Tilly, it was none of my doings or with my knowledge he came along pesterin' you.'

'No, I'm sure of that, Mr Pearson.'

'And while I'm at it I can tell you that I'm sorry for your plight.'

'There's no need, Mr Pearson, I'm quite comfortable.'

'But it can't be the same, lass, not like up there.' He jerked his head and his hand at the same time in the direction in which the Manor lay. She made no answer to this, and so, after shuffling his feet on the rough path, he said, 'I'll be off then, Tilly; an' good luck always in whatever you do.'

'Thank you, Mr Pearson. And thank you for coming.'

'Aye. Aye.' He bobbed his head at her, then went marching off down the road.

He'd always been for her, had Mr Pearson. She remembered the couple of rabbits he had left outside in the shed before the cottage was burned down. At first she had thought Steve had put them there. . . . Steve. She didn't know what had happened to Steve; she only hoped he was happy and had found a nice girl and settled down. He should have married Katie. Katie had liked him, more than liked him.

The second visitor was more surprising still. The baby had come to the end of its midday meal and was lying contentedly in her arms, its pink cheek against her warm breast, when she heard the sound of a horse being brought to a stop. Quickly she put the child in the basket, covered her breast, buttoned up her blouse, then went to the window, there to see a young lady walking towards the front door.

She let her knock before she went and opened it, and she stared at the young person who stared at her, and they both showed surprise. It was the visitor who spoke first. 'I . . . I must have made a mistake again, but . . . but they told me that this was the cottage, a . . . a Mr Burgess's cottage.'

'Yes, that's right. Do you wish to see him? He's not very well at present.'

'No! no!' The young lady shook her head so vigorously that the feather in her velour hat bobbed up and down.

When she did not go on to explain whom she wished to see, Tilly's eyes narrowed as she stared at her. She could be pretty. She had a round heart-shaped face and warm brown eyes; her lips, although wide, were well shaped, but the face missed prettiness because of its expression. She guessed that the girl was around eighteen years old but the look on her face, given off by the expression of her eyes and the drooping corners of the mouth, was that of someone deeply aggrieved, not angry, but hurt. She was speaking now, her words hesitant, 'I . . . I don't know what to say but . . . but perhaps it is your mother I am looking for.'

'My mother?' Tilly's gaze narrowed even more now. She repeated, 'My mother? My mother has been dead for many years.'

'Someone called Trotter, a Tilly Trotter.'

'Well, you have found Tilly Trotter because that is my name. Why do you want to see me?'

'You!' The girl seemed for a moment as if she was about to step backwards; then shaking her head, she said, 'I'm sorry; they must have been mistaken.'

'Who are they?'

'Oh, well, it's hard to explain.'

Tilly's voice was stiff now as she said, 'Well, try. I would like to understand why you wish to see me. And who sent you here?'

'No . . . no one sent me here, but I heard them talking. It was the maids.'

'Whose maids?'

'My grandmama's and aunt's. My grandmama is Mrs McGill of Felton Hall, and I am Anna McGill.'

'Felton Hall?' Tilly's eyes now opened wide. Felton Hall was all of eight or nine miles away, beyond Fellburn, beyond Gateshead. She had heard, as everyone in the county had, of Felton Hall because Mrs McGill's only son and his wife had been lost at sea last year. This girl must be their daughter.

She said quietly, 'And what had your grandmother's maids to say about me?'

The girl now hung her head as she said, 'There . . . there must be a mistake, I must have misunderstood them. I . . . I suppose it was because I . . . I felt so desperate, I became stupid and . . . and clutched at any straw.'

Tilly continued to look at the now bowed head for some seconds before she said, 'Please come in.' When the girl hesitated, she said again, 'Please.'

Once inside the room and the door closed, Tilly moved her forward with a motion of her hand to the easy chair set to the right of the fireplace. Mr Burgess was not in his usual place on the couch, not having yet risen from bed.

Seating herself on the couch opposite the girl, Tilly said, 'Why are you in need of help and why did you think that I would be able to afford you that help?'

Unblinking, the young girl stared at Tilly; then slowly her hands, going up to her neck, swung aside the white silk scarf that almost reached one ear, and as she unfolded it she exposed the deep purple stain running from the lobe of the left ear, under the chin and almost to the middle of it, then spread downwards until it disappeared into the collar of her riding jacket, and as she turned her head slightly so she showed where it covered her neck right up to the hair line. Her voice almost a whisper now, she said, 'It . . . it goes down to the top of my breast and halfway across my shoulders. I . . . I cannot wear an evening gown or . . . or go out like . . . like other young people.'

Tilly looked into the eyes before her. She seemed to draw the sorrow into herself and in this moment and for the only time in her life she wished that she was a witch and had the power to erase the hideous birthmark. It was no use offering polite platitudes to this girl whose face had aged well beyond her years.

She watched the girl winding the scarf about her neck again and listened to the murmur of her voice as she said, 'It wasn't so bad when I lived in Norfolk. I met so few people there. I had a private tutor and I rarely went out beyond the grounds. My parents did not entertain and they took their holidays alone. But now, this last year coming to live with Grandmama, there is so much going on, so much activity, coming and going, she says I should accept it. What cannot be cured must be endured is her slogan. One night she made me come downstairs in an evening gown, my shoulder bare. Everyone was embarrassed, except her. That . . . that was the night I tried to jump out of the window. My Aunt Susan caught me. She understands, my aunt, but not my grandmama, and so when I heard this maid talking about – ' She shook her head now and bowed it deep on her chest.

'About me being a witch?'

The head was slowly raised and the eyes looked into hers for a moment before she said, 'Yes; but . . . but you're not, are you?'

'No, I am not.'

'I can see that; no witch could look like you.'

'What was the name of the maid who said I was a witch?'

'Short, I think, Maggie Short.'

'It would be.' She smiled at the girl now. 'You see, I was the means of getting her aunt, who was cook at the Manor, dismissed because of her thieving, and apparently she and her niece, Maggie, still follow my career, hoping for my complete downfall. . . . What did you expect me to do for you?'

'I don't know. Touch me perhaps and it would disappear.'

'I take you to be an intelligent girl; you know that couldn't happen.'

'Yes, one part of me knows but the other part, the painful part, keeps hoping for miracles, or just one miracle. They . . . they said it would fade with the years, but it seems to get deeper.'

'You know what I think?'

'No.'

'I think in part your grandmother is right. Oh please!' She lifted her hand against the look on the girl's face. 'I don't mean that you should wear evening dress and expose your shoulders, but there is no need to cover up your neck. You see, a moment ago when your head was level all I saw of the mark was the stain coming from your ear down on to your neck, I didn't see it under your chin because you've got quite a broad jaw-line. You could wear clothes, at least daytime clothes, that would almost cover up the defect, a boned lace collar, a starched frill, so many things.'

'Do you think so? I mean, you don't notice it so much if I keep my head level or slightly forward?'

'Yes, that's what I mean. And you must smile more. You're very pretty, you know.'

'Oh no! My . . . my mother said that I was un. . . .' She stopped and turned her head away, and Tilly now put in, 'I don't know what your mother said but I'm telling you you are very pretty. You also have a very good figure, and have some way to develop yet I imagine. How old are you?'

'Eighteen ... and a half,' she added as if giving a weight to her maturity. Then as if taking her mind off herself she looked about her and said, 'I've never seen so many books except in the library at home, and then they were mostly in glass cases. These look very used.' She smiled faintly now.

'Yes, my friend Mr Burgess, who was tutor at the Manor for some years, is a great reader. At the moment he's in bed. He doesn't rise very early because he's getting old and isn't too well, but I'm sure he would have been very pleased to meet you. He's a highly intelligent and amusing man, also a very discerning one.... Would you care to come again?'

'Oh ... yes ... yes.' The words were drawn out. 'So kind of you. I ... I've never felt so good, I mean ... well, so happy – and no, that isn't the word – comforted perhaps is a better word ... before, ever.'

Tilly rose to her feet now, saying, 'Well, shall we do things in the proper manner? Would you care to come for tea on Saturday, Miss McGill?'

'I ... I should be delighted, Miss ... Mrs Trotter.' The hesitation had come as the girl glanced down on the sleeping baby whose presence until now she had pointedly ignored.

'You were right first time, it is Miss Trotter.'

They were both walking towards the door when the young girl turned sharply towards her and asked, 'Would you do something for me? Would you touch my neck, put your fingers on it?'

The brightness went out of Tilly's face and her voice was stiff as she said, 'No, I will not touch your neck, Miss McGill, for I have no power in my hands, the only power I have is in my mind. And that's no more than the power you have in yours. What I can do you can do equally; the only way I can help you is to suggest that you tell yourself to face up to this affliction, adopting an attitude of confidence. Tell yourself that you are a whole woman and that some day you will meet a gentleman who will take you for what you are. Tell yourself that some day you'll meet a man who will put his lips to that stain. Believe this and it will come about.'

The girl now said simply, 'Thank you.' Beyond the door she turned and, looking at Tilly once more, she said, 'I'll never forget this day. As long as I live I'll remember it. Good-bye.'

'Good-bye,' said Tilly.

When she entered the room again she leant with her back against the door and, looking upwards, she murmured, 'Poor soul! Poor soul!' To be afflicted so in youth. Yet that stain would not be erased when that girl's youth stepped into maturity, that stain would be there until the day she died. Would she ever find a man big enough to bear with it? Men were strange creatures. Not so often afflicted with illness themselves, rarely did they bear such in women except through compassion. But that girl needed more than compassion, she needed love, because by the sound of it she had never known it....

It was around teatime when John rode up, and he almost ran up the path in his excitement, opening the door even as he knocked on it.

Tilly hadn't heard the horse because she was in the back room settling Mr Burgess down to his tea in bed, for he had shown a disinclination to get up at all today.

John hurried in towards her, saying, 'M . . . M . . . Matthew is c . . . c . . . coming. He should be l . . . l . . . landing next week. I received his mail only this afternoon. Oh, I am so looking f . . . f . . . forward to s . . . s . . . seeing him. Once he's here we'll g . . . g . . . get everything fixed up and you'll come back.'

She now held out her hand, palm upwards towards him for some seconds before she said, 'I think I've told you before, John, I couldn't possibly leave Mr Burgess.' Her voice sank low. 'He's not well at all. He's fading; slowly but surely he's fading. He could last a few months or perhaps a year, but . . . but no matter how long I must stay with him.'

'Matthew w . . . w . . . would have him up at the house.'

'He wouldn't want to go, he's lived here too long. There's a thing, you know, about dying in your own bed.'

'Oh, Tr . . . Trotter, that was half the f . . . f . . . fun, half the pleasure in Matthew c . . . c . . . coming back that you would once again be over w . . . w . . . with us at the house.'

'John' – she pressed him gently down into the seat opposite her – 'you make all these plans but you know I shouldn't have to point out to you it's Matthew who is head of the house and his ideas, if I remember Matthew aright' – she now turned her head to the side and slanted her eyes at him – 'never ran along the same lines as yours, or Luke's, or, thank goodness, his sister's. No, I think we had better wait until he is home and settled before we start planning. Do you know' – she shook her head from side to side – 'this has been a day of events, you are the third visitor I've had. I wonder who'll be next?'

'Who . . . who were the others?'

'Mr Pearson, you know from the village. He's the painter and odd jobber.'

'Oh yes, yes, I remember. May I ask wh . . . wh . . . what he wanted? You don't often have v . . . v . . . visitors from the vill . . . vill . . . village.'

When she had finished telling him the reason for Tom Pearson's visit he nodded his head and said, 'He seems an honourable man.'

'Yes, he is, he is.'

'And your other v . . . v . . . visitor?'

'Oh' – she shook her head slowly at him – 'here lies a tale. It was a young lady, a beautiful young lady.'

Now why had she said that? Well, she supposed the girl could look beautiful, at least full-faced and at the right side.

As she watched him now put his head back, his mouth wide as he endeavoured to repeat her words, a beautiful young lady, there crept into her brain an idea. But once it had become an idea it no longer crept, but leapt into a scheme, and she could again hear his voice saying, 'No young lady is going to put up with me.' And she saw the girl with sadness imprinted on her face by the handicap that she must bear alone for all her days, and so, leaning forward, she said, 'Will you do something for me, John?'

'Anything, Tr . . . Tr . . . Trotter. You know that, anything.' 'Will you come to tea on Saturday?'

'Tea?'

'Yes, to tea to meet the young lady I've just mentioned.'

'Oh.' His face fell. 'No, no, Tr . . . Trotter, don't ask me. You know wh . . . what I'm like with strangers. I'm b . . . b . . . bad enough with you and you put me at my ease more than anybody else that I know of.'

She leant forward and caught hold of his hand, saying now, 'Be quiet for a moment and listen. If you saw someone in great distress and they were very lonely and you knew that by even looking at them, smiling at them, you could alleviate that loneliness, what would you do, walk away?'

'I . . . I don't f . . . f . . . follow you, Trotter.'

'Well, it's like this, John. This young lady has a handicap. She is beautiful.' And she had no doubt that when Miss McGill came to see her on Saturday she would look beautiful.

'Beautiful with a ha . . . ha . . . handicap? Is she a cripple?'

'No; her body as far as I can see is perfect. Her features are good; she has lovely eyes and lovely hair.'

'B . . . b . . . but she has a h . . . handicap?' He now lowered his head and looked at her from under his eyebrows and he said, 'Don't t . . . t . . . tell me, Tro . . . Trotter that she st . . . st . . . stammers.'

She burst out laughing at this, and shook her head; then raising her hand to his ear, to his amazement she began to trace her finger along his jawbone, then down over his throat to the top of his collar, and when her finger stopped there she said, 'She has a birthmark; it is about there where I've drawn with my finger. Apparently she has always been made aware of it until now she is a sad and lost young girl. And you know why she came here today?'

He shook his head.

'She heard one of the maids who used to be at the Manor telling another maid about a witch by the name of Trotter.'

'Aw no! Aw no! How awful for you.'

'But how much worse for her when she was so desperate she had to come in search of this witch.'

'And you ha . . . have asked her b . . . b . . . back to tea?'

'Yes; and I would like you to come and help me prove to her that people will not spurn her because of her birthmark.'

'But she'll want a fellow, a m . . . man who can talk to her, Trotter. I'm not the one to do it. T . . . t . . . talking of handicaps, I have m . . . m . . . my own and I would exchange it for hers any day in the w . . . w . . . week.'

'Well, I hope that you'll tell her that some day.'

'Oh, Trotter.'

'Please, John. I don't think I've asked anything of you before, have I?'

He stared at her blankly. Then smiling ruefully, he said, 'G . . . G . . . God help the poor girl if she's expecting a s . . . s . . . saviour in me. I'll not be able to get one w . . . w . . . word out, you'll see.'

'Yes, I'll see.'

And Tilly saw, but not until she had given up hope of seeing either of them for it had poured hard since early morning, and now at half-past three in the afternoon she'd had to light the lamp. Looking towards Mr Burgess, who was dressed in his well-worn velvet jacket that she had brushed and sponged down yet again for this occasion, she said, 'It won't surprise me if neither of them turns up.'

'Give them time, especially the young lady; as you say, she's got all of eight miles to come through this.'

It was John who arrived first, and his relief was evident when he knew he was to be the only visitor. But he had hardly taken off his wet cloak and said, 'I've taken B . . . B . . . Bobtail round the b . . . b . . . back, it's more sheltered there,' when Tilly, glancing out of the window, said, 'And you'd better put your cloak on again, John, and go and take Miss McGill's horse to keep Bobtail company. Good gracious, she looks drenched.'

'Oh! Tro . . . Trotter.' He almost grabbed the cloak from her and he put it on as he went down the path.

She watched from the open doorway as he took the reins from the young girl's hands without saying a word and then led the horse around the side of the house.

When the girl came into the room she looked quite strained and said immediately, 'The young man, who is he?'

'A friend of mine; he just happened to pop in. Here, let me have your coat and your hat, you're drenched.'

'I . . . I shouldn't have come, I mean if there had been any way to let you know. Oh dear! my hair.' As she pulled the long pin out of her velour hat the coil of her hair became unloosened and fell on to her shoulder, and she had her hands above her head pinning it back into place when John came hurriedly through the door, only to stop and stand with his hand behind his back holding the iron ring of the latch staring at the girl.

She, patting her hair into place now, looked from one to the other, saying, 'I'm . . . I'm afraid I mustn't stay long, my . . . my horse is very wet, and . . . and I have no cover.'

'I've s . . . s . . . seen to that; I took some s . . . s . . . sacks' – he was looking at Tilly now 'from the w . . . w . . . woodshed, Tr . . . Tr . . . Trotter, and put over them both.'

'That was sensible. Come along now, both of you.' She went to turn away, but then said, 'Oh dear me, I'm forgetting my duty. This is Mr John Sopwith. . . . Miss Anna McGill.'

'How do you do?' The girl inclined her head towards him, and he, bowing slightly from the shoulders, answered, 'a pl . . . pleasure to meet you.' Then they all turned towards the voice coming from the fireplace, saying, 'And I am Herbert Vincent Burgess and nobody cares a hoot that I'm dying for my tea, and that my horse is champing on its bit in the bedroom waiting to gallop me to London Town, there to have supper with a man called Johnson and his friend Boswell, and from where in the morning I shall set sail for France, there to have breakfast with Voltaire; and the following day I shall return to the City, although I have refused my Lord Chesterfield's invitation because, do you know, his lackeys expect to be tipped as you leave his house. . . .'

'Oh! be quiet. Be quiet.' Tilly laughingly pushed him gently. 'Behave yourself, will you? Nobody understands a word you say.'

'I do.'

Tilly turned amazed to see the girl smiling widely, and when Mr Burgess held out his hand to her, saying, 'At last, at last. Come here, my dear. A soul mate at last, at last. Would you believe it, Trotter?'

They all started to laugh, and when young William, unused to the strange noise, let out a high gurgle the laughter mounted and there was nothing for it but that Tilly should pick the baby up to be admired and cooed over. The ice was broken.

An hour later, from the window she watched John leading the horses on to the road, then helping Miss McGill to mount, before taking his place at her side and riding off, not in the direction of home but towards Gateshead.

She was still watching from the window when Mr Burgess's voice, tired-sounding now, brought her swiftly round as he said, 'They'll be married in a year or so, thanks to your witchery.'

PART TWO

❧ The Homecoming ❧

1

They had finished dinner, they had drunk their port and smoked their cigars and were now making their way towards the library, not the drawing-room as one would have expected, for since his return Matthew had shown an open aversion to sitting in the drawing-room in the evenings.

The library was a long room with a plaster-panelled ceiling. The circular motifs in the triangles had long since lost their colour of rose and grey, taking their tones from the smoke that every now and again billowed out from the open hearth whenever a gust of wind roared down the chimney.

Matthew coughed and blinked his eyes before pointing to the fireplace, saying, 'When was that last swept?'

'Couldn't s . . . say, Matthew, b . . . b . . . but it doesn't often smoke. It's the wind, it's a howler tonight.'

'It's a howler every night if you ask me.' Matthew now seated himself in the leather chair and, stretching out a leg, thrust the end of a burning log further on to the iron fire basket, then lay back and looked about him.

The room was as he remembered it, and as he had pictured it so many times over the past few years, yet it was different, though not smaller, not shrunken as houses and places kept alive by memory alone appeared when viewed in reality. If anything it seemed larger, but that likely was due to comparing it with the homestead.

He couldn't exactly put his finger on the change, not just in the room or the rest of the house, but even in the land outside and the people on it everything was alien to him. It was as if in leaving America he had left home, and over the past days he had asked himself many times why he had come back. It wasn't an enormous estate he had to manage, and there was no industry connected with it that would need looking into. It might have been different if the mine had been working. . . . The mine. He'd go there tomorrow; he'd have to do something, this stagnation would drive him mad.

He started slightly when John, picking up his thoughts, said, 'You're . . . you're finding everything ch . . . ch . . . changed, Matthew. You d . . . d . . . didn't w . . . ant to come back, did you?'

'No, you're right there, John, I didn't want to come back. And there's nothing to be done here, the place is dead.'

'Yes, r . . . r . . . round here, but not in the towns. You were in N . . . N . . . Newcastle today, there's plenty g . . . g . . . going on there. Now you c . . . can't say there isn't.'

'Yes, there appears to be plenty going on but' – he leant forward now and looked into the fire – 'it seems to me that all the enterprises, shipping, factories, mines, the whole lot could be put into a teacup.' He turned now and held both hands out towards John, saying, 'You see, for the last three years I've been used to space, admitted mostly empty space, thousands of miles of it, but when you did get into a township the activity... well, it was incredible. In Newcastle today I had the impression that everybody was marking time, whereas in a similar town over there, although there are no towns similar to Newcastle, I admit, with regard to buildings, but the difference is those in America are making time, they're using it to the full. It's a different world, John. No talking, no explaining can give you the picture of it, you've got to be there.... Oh, let's have a drink.' He put out his hand to pull the bell rope to the side of the fireplace, but stopped, and his square face taking on an almost pugnacious look he said, 'I hate ringing for women. If I'm to stay here there'll have to be menservants again. No house can be expected to run efficiently without a butler and a footman, the very least.'

John got to his feet, saying now and almost as irritably as Matthew had spoken, 'I'll b... b... bring the tr... tray; and the house has been r... r... run very well for years without menservants. Anyway, father c... c... couldn't afford them and we wouldn't have had the c... c... comfort we have had, had it not been for Tr... Tr... Trotter.'

There, he had said her name again. Well, a man should speak as he found, and Matthew was unfair to Trotter. He wasn't in the house twenty-four hours before he had said, 'Look, I don't want to hear anymore about Trotter. As for having her back, no! definitely not.'

The brothers stared at each other. Matthew, his head pressed against the high back of the leather chair, looked steadily up into the thin long sensitive face above him. The black hair lying smooth across the high dome of his brother's head was in sharp contrast to his own fair matt. He'd had his cut and trimmed quite close a week ago but already it was aiming to become a busby again, and he ran his fingers through it as he said, 'Dear, dear; I fear that if Father hadn't fallen on his face his youngest son might have; after all, what does eleven years matter when one is in love?'

'Matthew!' John's shocked indignation came over in the name that was spoken without a tremor. 'How dare you! Tr... Tr... Trotter's been like a m... m... mother to me.... Damn you! M... M... Matthew. D... D... Damn you!'

Matthew was on his feet now holding John by the shoulders. 'I'm sorry. Really I am. It's only that she's... well, she's disrupted so many lives.'

John was gulping in his throat now, the colour was seeping back into his face which a moment before had looked blanched, but his tone remained stiff as he said, 'I... I don't agree with y... you. You c... c... couldn't blame her for what F... F... Father did in the first place. And I think she was a k... k... kind of saviour to Father. He would have gone insane without her.'

'Perhaps you're right.' Matthew turned towards the chair again. 'Anyway, don't let it raise an issue between us. Look.' He turned his head towards John now. 'Tomorrow I'm going to the mine; I have an idea I might open it again.'

'Open up the m... m... mine! It would take a small fortune.'

'Well, I've got a small fortune, a couple of small fortunes.'

'Does that m... m... mean you're g... g... going to stay, I mean settle here?'

'Oh, I don't know about that; Uncle wants me back there. In the meantime, getting the old mine going again would give me something to exercise my wits, otherwise I'll become like the rest of them around here, riding, drinking, whoring. Not that I'd mind the latter.'

'Oh, Matthew!'

'Oh, Matthew!' He mimicked John, then said, 'You're too good to be true you know, brother.'

'I'm n... n... not too good to be t... t... true. You don't know anything about me really. B... B... But I think, there's a lim... limit; one must draw the l... line.'

'And where would you draw the line?' Matthew was grinning at him now.

'Oh, you! You!' John pushed out his fist towards him. 'You're im... po... po... possible.'

'Are you going to get that tray or have I to ring for a female?'

As John went out of the room, his head moving from side to side, Matthew settled deep into the chair. Presently, thrusting his foot out towards the end of the log from where the resin was dripping on to the iron dog, he muttered between his teeth, 'Trotter! Trotter!'

'Well, he's on his last legs I think, lass.'

'Yes, it won't be long now.'

'Now, lass, you mustn't grieve.' Biddy put her hand on Tilly's shoulder. 'He's an old man and by all accounts he's enjoyed his life. All he seemed to want was his books, an' he's had them. And he's been lucky to have you an' all to see to him.'

'I've been very lucky to have him, Biddy.'

'Aye well, six and two three's, if you look at it like that. And you've got a roof over your head for life if you want it. It was as little as he could do to leave it to you, not that I think it's a fit settin' for you but it'll do in the meantime. I get a bit mad at times.' Biddy went now and picked up the long black coat from a chair and as Tilly helped her into it she said, 'Your place is over yonder, an' your child's place an' all. Eeh!' She shook her head. 'I can't make him out. He comes back from that pit, glar up to the eyes, lookin' worse than my lot ever did. They say he goes into places where none of the others'll venture. And yet he's so bloody high-handed. The master never acted like he does: gentlemen take it as their right to have the whip hand but at times he speaks to you as if you were dirt 'neath his feet, then the next minutes he goes outside and hobnobs with the lads, talks to them as if they were equals. One minute he's playin' the lord and master, the next it seems to me he doesn't know his place. Now Master John, he's a different kettle of fish altogether. He even tried to apologise for t'other one, said that in America they live differently. Well, I could understand it if he remained the same with everybody, but with the lasses and me he's as snotty as a polis. ... But I say, lass' – she thrust her head towards Tilly – 'what do you think of Master John an' the miss he's hooked on to?'

'I think they're both very lucky.'

'Aye, an' I think you're right. I've only seen her once, that was from a distance, she looked bonny. She was in the yard lookin' in the stables. He didn't bring her into the house but, as Katie said, he likely didn't want her to encounter Master Matthew 'cos that bloke's got a thing against women. I'd like to bet he had an affair out there that went wrong.'

'I shouldn't wonder, Biddy.'

'Oh, what am I keepin' jabbering on about, you've got your hands full.' She pinned on her hat now, wound the long woollen scarf around her neck, pulled on a matching pair of gloves, then said, 'I'll be off then, lass. Katie or Peg'll look in this afternoon. You know, that's funny' – she turned from the door and stabbed her finger into Tilly's chest – 'he knows I come along, he's seen our Arthur fetch me. He's even passed us on the road on his horse. An' twice or more Katie's said that he's watched her going down the drive. She was sure he followed her one time to see in which direction she went. Now, he knows we come here an' he's never said, "Stop." Aw! he's a funny fellow. Well, bye-bye, lass. You say the doctor'll be along the day?'

'Yes, Biddy; he promised to look in.'

'Well, there's nothing he can do, but it's nice to know he takes such pains. He's different to old Kemp. Bye-bye again, lass.'

'Bye-bye, Biddy. Mind how you go. If Arthur isn't at the crossroads you wait for him; don't attempt to walk all the way.'

'Aye, aye; don't worry.'

When Biddy was lost to sight, Tilly shut the door on the icy wind and, going towards the clothes basket set near the fireplace, she bent down and took her son's face between her palms and shook it gently, and he gurgled at her and grabbed at her wrist. He was in his fifth month and thriving. He was so bonny awake or asleep, he brought a thrill to her heart. She put a small linen sugar bag into his mouth and he sucked on one end while grabbing the other in his small fists.

She now went to the hob and stirred the pan of mutton broth that was simmering there. She didn't feel like eating and it was no use putting any out for Mr Burgess, he hadn't touched food for two days now, he no longer required it. She pulled the pan to the side, dusted her hands one against the other, then went down the kitchen and into the bedroom.

The old man was lying propped up against his pillows. He did not turn his head when she came into the room but, sensing her presence, his fingers moved, and when she took his hand he murmured, 'Trotter. Dear Trotter.'

She put out her other hand and pulled up the chair close to the bed. She did not speak, and when he turned his eyes towards her and smiled at her she felt a constriction in her throat.

'Time's running out, my dear.'

She made no reply.

'Been a very fortunate man. I . . . I must tell you something, Trotter.'

She waited, saying nothing; but when he told her in words scarcely above a whisper the lump in her throat expanded until she felt she would choke, for what he said was, 'I have loved you, Trotter; like all the others I have loved you, but more like he did in so many different ways. When he died, his hands in yours, I thought, if only I could be so . . . so fortunate. There is no God, Trotter, it would be utterly childish to imagine there is, there is only thought and the power of thought, and my thought has arranged it so I get my wish.'

The last word was scarcely audible and she could no longer see the expression on his face for her eyes were so blinded with tears as soundlessly she cried, and brokenly she whispered. 'Thank you for coming into my life.'

The parson's wife had taught her to read and write, but she could never have imbued her with the knowledge that this old man had, for to her he had been the storehouse of all knowledge. There was no subject on which he couldn't talk, yet he was so humble he considered himself ignorant. Once he had said to her, 'Like Socrates, I can say I haven't any knowledge to boast of but I am a little above other men because I am quite aware of my ignorance and I do not think that I know what I do not know, but what I do not know I make it my poor business to try and find out.'

She had been fortunate, she knew, in having been the companion of a gentleman for twelve years, yet it wasn't he who had taught her to think. But he had taught her to love, and that was a different thing; he had taught her that the act of love wasn't merely a physical thing, its pleasure being halved without the assistance of the mind. But it was Mr Burgess, this old man breathing his last here now, who had taught her how to use her mind. Right from the beginning he had warned her that once your mind took you below the surface of mundane things, you would never again know real peace because the mind was an adventure, it led you into strange places and was forever asking why, and as the world outside could not give you true answers, you were forever groping and searching through your spirit for the truth.

She remembered being shocked when he had first said to her there was no such thing as a God. There were gods, all kinds of gods, and different men brought up in different spheres created these beings in accordance with the environment about them. As for Christianity, he likened it to a slave driver with a whip and this whip had many thongs called denominations and all made up of fear that had the power to thrust souls into everlasting flames, flames that would sear them for all eternity. Who, he had asked her, would not profess a belief in this particular God who, if he withheld his forgiveness of your sins, could cast you into this everlasting hell. Why! he had told her, had he not begun to think for himself he, too, would have believed in this God, for he did not relish pain, either in this world or the next. Such ideas had now ceased to shock her.

She still could not see him when she felt him lifting her hand to his cheek, and she leant forward, resting her other forearm on the bedside; and she remained like this until her arm became cramped.

It was some time later when her tears had stopped and her vision had cleared that she gently withdrew her fingers from his hand and, bending over him, she put her lips to his brow although she knew he could no longer feel them.

Dear, dear, Mr Burgess. Dear, dear friend. The eyes that were looking straight into hers were smiling at her. Slowly she closed the lids and when she went to cross his arms on his breast she hesitated, as in death so in life. He did not believe in any cross and wherever his spirit was winging to now it would certainly not be to a hell. If there was a God, and she, too, had her doubts, oh yes, grave doubts, but should there be such a being He would at this moment be taking into account all the good that this man had done in his life. True, she had only known him for fifteen years but during that time his one aim in life had been to help people, help them to help themselves. He had certainly helped her to help herself. His going would leave a void in her life that would never be filled.

But as she drew the sheet up over his face she experienced for a fleeting moment a strange sense of joy. She imagined that they were there, both of them, talking and laughing as they had done so often, Mark and the tutor of his children.

She would cry no more for his passing.

⮜ 2 ⮞

It was a very small cortège that attended the funeral. Arthur, Jimmy, and Bill Drew and Fred Leyburn carried out the oak coffin, and when they had placed it in the hearse and the driver had urged his horse a few yards along the lane, Matthew and John Sopwith entered their coach; behind that, the four men got into the second coach, if it could be called such. It was merely a covered vehicle used mostly for carrying stores from the town and occasionally pigs' carcases and vegetables to it. But today it was very welcome to the men for the wind was cutting and the sky was low, its leaden colour portending snow.

Biddy, standing beside Tilly at the window, said softly, 'He'll be lucky if he's underground afore the snow comes, I can smell it in the air. Come on, lass; no use standing here any longer.'

Biddy turned from the window but Tilly remained looking out on to the narrow empty lane. The joyous feeling she had experienced at the moment of his passing had not remained with her; there was on her now a deep sadness. She felt alone again, as she had done at Mark's passing. Biddy's voice came to her from the fireplace, saying, 'I didn't expect his lordship to show up. Is that the first time you've seen him?'

For a moment Tilly didn't answer, then as if having just heard the question, she said, 'Yes, yes, the first time,' and she recalled now the surprise, even shock, she had experienced when not a half hour ago he had stood in this room facing her. There was nothing remaining of the Matthew she remembered; the boy, the youth, the young man, had always carried an air of arrogance, but this had deepened, widened, as his body had done. She had imagined him to be taller; perhaps it was his growing so broad that had taken off his height. His shoulders were thick, seeming to strain the Melton cloth of his greatcoat. His face was broad, his eyes more deep set, and his hair, the hair that had been golden and inclined to curl, now looked like a thick unruly matt. It was cut in the most odd way; she had understood Biddy's description of his hair when she had likened it to that cut under a pot pie basin, for his neck was bare of hair, and none of it she imagined was more than two inches long. She could not believe that he was only twenty-five, he could be taken for a man of thirty-five; and his voice and manner gave the impression of maturity, hard maturity.

He had stared at her unblinking for almost a minute before speaking, and then it wasn't to give her any kind of greeting, he simply said, 'We all have to die sometime, and the old fellow had a good run for his money.'

His words, so unfeeling, so out of place, brought sweeping through her that rare feeling of anger, and it was as much as she could do not to turn on him, even order him out. John, on the other hand, had been courtesy and kindness itself and his stammer, bringing with it the balm of oil, said, 'I'll m ... m ... miss the old man, Tr ... Tr ... Trotter, b ... b ... but not as much as y ... y ... you will; and he w ... was very f ... f ... fond of you.'

She had not answered John, she had not opened her lips while the two men were in the room; not even when the men were carrying the coffin out did she speak, nor yet show any emotion, for tears shed in front of Master Matthew would, she felt, have certainly evoked some derisive or sarcastic remark.

She understood fully now Biddy's inability to get on with her new master; but then, of course, hadn't he always been difficult right from the beginning? And Biddy had expressed a hope that now she might return to the Manor. Never! Not under him.

She went towards the table. Biddy had covered it with a white cloth and set out the tea things.

'We'll have a cup of tea, lass,' she said, 'an' a bite. There'll be nobody coming back here. The lads will go straight to the kitchen, Katie will have set a meal for them. But anyway I'll be back meself by then to see to things. Sit down and get off your feet, it's over.'

After they had been sitting at the table in silence for some minutes, Biddy asked quietly, 'What are you going to do with yourself, lass? Stay here?'

'Yes, Biddy. I can't see me doing anything else, not until he's a little older.' She turned and glanced at the child and he laughed at her and made a gurgle in his throat. Then she added, 'That's if they'll let me be.'

'Oh, they'll let you be all right. That's one thing I don't think he'd stand for. If not him, then Master John wouldn't. I can see that lad down in the village with a horse whip if you had any trouble from that quarter again.'

'As long as there's a McGrath in the village I'll always have trouble, Biddy.'

'Well, there's not many of 'em left; there's only her, and the son.'

'And his children.'

'Aye yes; and his children. Bairns are worse than grown-ups sometimes. Anyway, don't worry about that.'

There was a silence until Biddy proffered the question, and tentatively, 'What would you say if he asked you to come back?'

'He won't, and I wouldn't.' Tilly's voice was sharp. 'So don't bank on that, Biddy.'

'No, you're right, lass, he won't and you wouldn't. But anyway, this is your own house now and you've got your own income. An' if you're gettin' rid of some of these books you could make it nice.'

Tilly nodded, then said, 'I'll make it nice but I won't get rid of his books; I'll put them up at the end of the loft.'

'He never came for those fifty that he was left, Tilly.'

'No.'

'I suppose they're yours now, as he's left everything to you.'

'It could be said they are, but I'll not claim them.'

Biddy gave a huh! before she said, 'He'd likely make a court case of it if you tried, he's that kind of a young bugger. You know, it's hard to believe he's still a young fella; he looks older than my Henry and he's almost kicking forty.'

Tilly made no comment on this, but she wondered in an aside how life in America could change anyone so much, externally that is, for inwardly she sensed he was the same as he had always been, arrogant, bumptious, spoilt. He had to be top-dog, master of all he surveyed or else somebody suffered.

In the beginning it was the nursemaids, then it would have been her, but he didn't get off with it; the boarding school seemed to have tamed him for a time but only for a time, for the young man who had visited his father on rare occasions had been what her granny would have called an upstart. And yet this description would not have been accurate because he had not risen from nothing, he had been born into the class. There was a difference.

A week had passed; snow had come and disappeared again leaving the roads slushy. But if this wind kept up and the temperature kept dropping as it had done since noon, there'd be a hard frost tonight and tomorrow the roads would be like glass.

Having told herself that the best antidote against loneliness was work, she had for the past days carried the maxim to the extreme, for from dawn till dusk, stopping only to feed the child and tend to a light meal for herself, she had carried the hundreds of books up the steep ladder to the room above; then crawled to where the eaves met the floor and began the stacking of what she imagined would be close on two thousand volumes.

She had decided she would still keep the end of the loft as her bedroom and clear the main room downstairs entirely of books and turn what had been Mr Burgess's bedroom into a study. With this in mind she had sorted out the books she intended to keep downstairs and which she told herself she would peruse during the coming months, for once the cottage was straight there would only be the child to see to, and she must occupy her spare time with some undertaking. And what better than reading and learning. Mr Burgess would be happy to think that she was going to further his coaching. Yet even as she planned her future she experienced a sense of dismay that such activity practised without someone to share it, to discuss her progress with, would become stale.

She hadn't seen anyone from the house for four days, which was unusual, and she wondered if the feeling of loneliness on her would increase. She wondered, too, why the child, loved as it was, should leave room in her being for the need for other people. The fact that it was so created in her a feeling of guilt.

She looked towards him. He was sleeping peacefully in his basket. The fire was bright in the open hearth. She had re-arranged the room, washed all the curtains and covers, brought in all but one of the six rugs that had been shared between her own bedroom and Mr Burgess's, and placed them at intervals over the stone floor, so that there was now an air of comfort about the room.

She had changed from her working clothes into the soft plum-coloured cord dress that Mark had liked to see her in and that Mr Burgess had always remarked on. This changing of her clothes in the middle of the day had become a habit picked up when she had first begun to dine with Mark in the upstairs room. Before her close association she had always worn a kind of uniform, but on the day that she first ate with him, he said, 'You will change each day for dinner, Tilly.' And she had liked the idea and adopted it until it had become a pattern of life.

A change in the wind brought a grumble and growl down the chimney. She went to the fireplace and, taking some logs from the skip, she went to put them on the bank of red-hot ashes but paused for a moment. It was a lovely fire for the griddle pan, she could make some griddle cakes. But then, why bother? she hated cooking for herself alone. And anyway she had changed. Tomorrow morning she'd bake some bread.

She placed the logs on the fire, dusted her hands and went to pick up the child; then, her back bent, she turned her head towards the door. There was someone knocking. It must be someone on foot, she hadn't heard a horse or cart.

When she opened the door she stared at the man who was staring at her. 'May I come in?'

She stood aside and watched him walk into the room, stop and look about him for a moment, then walk on towards the fire, and there he stood between the table and the couch.

She hadn't moved but two steps from the door.

'I have come to apologise; John said I was rude to you the other day.'

She continued to stare at him, giving him no answer until, hunching his shoulders upwards, he exclaimed, 'Well! what can I say except that my stay in America hasn't improved my manners . . . ?' He looked from side to side now, saying, 'May I sit down?'

She moved slowly towards him and, pointing to the chair opposite the couch, she said, 'Yes, certainly.'

He didn't immediately take the seat, but with a gesture of exaggerated courtesy he extended his hand towards the couch and when she had seated herself on it, he sat in the chair opposite, facing her now and also the child where, at the end of the couch near the fire, it was lying still asleep in the basket.

Tilly returned his unblinking stare until she became embarrassed. Turning her head to the side, she said, 'I have known you long enough, Matthew, to realise that you didn't consider your manner towards me the other day as warranting an apology. Will you come to the point and tell me the reason for your visit?'

He smiled now and the movement of his features altered his whole face, the arrogant look going, the coldness seeping from the eyes. He became attractive, even handsome, and the smile slipped into laughter as he said, 'That is the Trotter I remember, straight to the point, no beating about the bush. Now, me lad, let's get things straight. You put a frog in my bed, I put a frog down your shirt.'

Her head jerked back and he nodded at her, saying, 'Oh, yes, yes; John is always saying Trotter has done a lot of good in her time, but I say that Trotter has done one or two not so good things in her time, things that have repercussions to this day, such as nightmares.'

Her lips moved soundlessly on the word, and then she repeated aloud, 'Nightmares?'

'Yes, Miss Trotter, nightmares. I experienced the first one at boarding school. Raised the dormitory screaming my head off because I was being smothered in slime with all the frogs crawling over me.'

She shook her head, her face straight, her eyes troubled now.

'The boys nearly jumped for the windows, they thought there was a fire. But that was nothing to the bunkhouse in Texas. They were tough lads those, but when I scream, I scream, and to a man they sprang for their guns; they thought it was a raid on their horses. Imagine ten men in their linings rushing out into the night. And it was the first time they'd had their clothes off in months!'

She looked at him. His head was back, he was laughing loudly. The concern seeped from her eyes. She said stiffly, 'You're exaggerating.'

He brought his head forward and stared at her for a moment before he said soberly now, 'Yes, perhaps a little, but it's true about the nightmares. I've had nightmares, Trotter, ever since you put that frog down my shirt and always, always about frogs; big ones, little ones, gigantic ones, all crawling over me, smothering me.'

'No!' She shook her head and pressed herself back against the couch. 'Don't say I've caused you to have nightmares.'

'But it's true, you did.'

She swallowed deeply, wetted her lips. 'Then I could have had nightmares, because it was you who put the frog in my bed.'

'Yes, I give you that, but then you were a young woman, sixteen years old, and I was but a boy of ten, a sensitive boy.'

Again she jerked her head to the side while keeping her eyes on him, and she repeated, 'Sensitive?' and she knew she sounded like Biddy when she said, 'If you were a sensitive child, then pigskin is made of silk.'

He laughed again, but quietly now while he continued to look at her; then he asked, 'Why do you think I was such a little devil?'

'I think you were born like that.'

'Nobody is born like that, Trotter. I thought you would have learned that much with all the wisdom you've imbibed from Mr Burgess. It is environment that makes us what we are. I saw my mother for five minutes a day, no longer, living in the same house day after day, year after year. Even before she took to her couch I can't remember seeing her for any length of time. I can't remember being held in her arms. I can't remember feeling loved. None of us did, but I was her first-born. I resented the others even while knowing that she gave to them no more than to me. If I'd been brought up in the home of your Biddy, who is apparently so fond of you, and you of her, I would I am sure have emerged a much happier person. I would not have had any cause to force myself on people's notice. And I did that by playing tricks on nursemaids, so that my father would come and threaten to thrash me. He never did. I longed for him to thrash me because then I would have known I meant something at least to him. I loved my father. Do you know that, Trotter?'

She paused before she said, 'My answer to that is, you had a very odd way of showing it. You left him lonely for years before he died when it was in your power to come and see him.'

'He didn't want me, Trotter, all he wanted was you, and he had you.'

'And that's why you . . . you hated me?'

'Who said I hated you?'

'You showed it in every possible way during your brief visits, and I don't find that your sojourn abroad has softened your attitude.'

He looked down towards his hands which were now placed on each knee, and he said quietly, 'I'm sorry that you should think that way. But you are right, in part that is, I did hate you. As for my attitude towards you not having altered, I'm . . . I'm afraid I would have to do a lot of explaining before I could make you understand, and it has nothing to do with my sojourn abroad. Yet again that isn't true. Oh' – he now tossed his head – 'this is not the time for delving into the whys and wherefores of one's reactions; the only thing I will say' – he looked straight at her now, one corner of his mouth lifted in an ironic smile – 'that no man, English, Irish, Scotch, Welsh, or any other for that matter, who spends three years in any state of America, or in Texas, particularly in Texas, could remain unchanged or, let me add, retain his refinement. America is another world. Although the majority of the people you meet have hailed from here, one generation is enough to change them into practically different species. They tear at life to make a living, or, like a few, scheme to make it. They are different, and I suppose some of the difference has rubbed off on me. It has undoubtedly shown in my irritation, as John informs me.' He rose now and took two steps towards the fireplace as he added, 'The pace of life is so slow here, even the horses seem slower.' He laughed on the last words and looked at her over his shoulder. 'I was in the hunt the other day. There we were, lolloping over hedges and gates, pushing our way through woods, hollering and yelling; yet I had the strange fancy that we were all standing still for I could see the vast, vast plains, no sight before the horse's head for miles and miles and miles. There's no world beyond the plains. Like the sky, they go on for ever. What they call a township is merely a meteor dropped from the heavens. Oh dear, dear.' He drooped his head now and laughed. 'Shades of Mr Burgess. That's how he used to go on, isn't it?'

He turned his back to the fire now and stared at her, and as he did so the child in the basket awoke, coughed and spluttered a little, and the sound brought Tilly from her seat. Bending down, she lifted up her son and held him upright in her arms, supporting him with her hand on his back, so that his face was on a level with Matthew's.

For a moment she thought he was going to turn away; she could see the muscles of his jaw pressed tight against the skin. She waited for him to speak, to acknowledge the child, and he did so.

'My half-brother?'

'Yes.'

'You were a long time in bringing it about.'

She knew the colour was suffusing her face. She turned the child now and pressed its head against her neck, and he said on a defensive tone, 'Well, you were, weren't you? And it's a pity you didn't leave it a little longer because he won't be recognised other than as a bastard.'

Her lips were tight-pressed for a moment before she could bring herself to say, 'I chose to have him as a bastard. I could have married your father years ago. I wish I had now. Oh! how I wish I had. And then my son would have had his rightful place, and you wouldn't be standing here daring to insult me.'

'Aw, Trotter!' His voice and manner had changed so dramatically that as he swung round and reached up to the high mantelpiece above the fireplace and gripped the edge of it, she felt for a moment she was dealing with the young boy in the nursery, and there flashed across her mind a picture of him standing at the top of the nursery landing telling her he didn't want to go back to boarding school. And she remembered the reason why they were standing there. He'd had a fight with Luke as to who was to marry her when they grew up. And he had told her that a boy at school had said he had kissed a girl on the lips. She could see his face now as he had appealed to her. 'You cannot kiss anyone on the mouth until you are married. Can you, Trotter?'

She stared at his broad shoulders, his head hanging forward, the odd cut of his hair, and it came to her that the great Matthew was a very unhappy man. He had been an unhappy boy but that she suspected was nothing to his present state.

When he turned slowly to her his voice was low and his question had a plea in it. 'Will you come back? That's the reason for my visit today. You may have what rooms you like, and ... and you can run the house as you did before.'

A lightness came into her body. There was nothing at the moment she would have welcomed more than to be back in the house. Coming down in the morning into the kitchen, talking to Biddy about the day's menus, writing down what stores she needed, going from room to room seeing that everything was in order; then some part of the day, winter or summer, walking in the garden, not solely for pleasure, yet it was a pleasure to see the work that the boys were doing, and she never stinted in telling them of her pleasure.

Why was she hesitating? She stared into the face of the man before her. There was no arrogance on his countenance now. The scowl, the ever present scowl that gave one the impression of ugliness, was no longer present. Again she saw the baby, but with more knowledge of him now that he had told her the cause of his actions when young. So why, why was she hesitating?

She seemed to surprise herself as she said, 'It's very kind of you but I'm ... I'm afraid I can't accept.'

Her head drooped forward and stayed bent in the silence that followed her refusal, until he said, 'Why?'

'There ... there are, I suppose, a number of reasons. First your sister, Mrs. ...'

'Oh, Jessie Ann.' He threw the name off as if with scorn. 'She is a little bitch. She always was, she always will be. I went to Scarborough before I came on home. She acted like a fishwife, solely because I had put John in charge.'

'Well, what do you expect her reactions to be if you engage me?'

'Hell's flames!' He flung one arm wide now and walked past her and round the table. 'The Manor is my house, I own it, I can do what I like with it, engage whom I like to run it. Jessie Ann has no say in my life. Anyway, we never got on together. And look!' The arrogance was back in both his face and his actions for, thrusting his arm out, he pointed his finger at her now, saying, 'If you don't take my offer I'll bring in male staff, a butler, a footman, the lot, and your Drew family won't like that, will they? Both inside and out they run the place as if they had been born there, owned it, as if they were. . .'

'Concerned for its welfare.'

'Oh – ' He turned his head on to his shoulder and, his voice dropping, he muttered, 'Why are we always at loggerheads? Can't we call a truce? What is past is past, I am willing to forget it.'

'That is very noble of you.'

'Don't be sarcastic with me, Trotter.' The voice and the look was that of the master speaking to the servant, and now her voice and look was that of an equal as she almost barked back at him, 'And don't you take that tone with me. You have no control over me whatsoever, I am an independent person. This is my house, small and humble as it is, it is mine. I've enough money to keep me for the rest of my days and to educate my son as I think fit.'

'Don't be too sure of that; you only have shares, they've been known to flop.'

'Well, say they do; I still have my hands left and, what is more, my head. Now you've had the answer to the question you came to ask me so I'll thank you if you will leave.'

He stood, one hand gripping the front of his cravat, staring at her, glaring at her.

He looked like a man who at any moment could lash out with his fist. For an instant she had the impression he was one of the villagers, a working man, untutored, no grain of a gentleman in him.

As he snapped his gaze from her there seemed to be an audible click, so sharp was the movement, and, grabbing up his cloak and hat, he went to the door. There he turned and his lips hardly moved as he said, 'You'll need me before I need you, Trotter.' On this he went out, banging the door behind him with such force that the child jumped in her arms and his face crumpled and, what was most unusual, he began to whimper, then cry loudly.

Dropping on to the chair, she rocked him backwards and forwards. Her eyes closed, her mouth open, she took in small gulps of air. A feeling of fear that she hadn't experienced for a long time was sweeping through her. It wasn't the kind of fear engendered by the villagers; she couldn't put a name to it, she only knew that she was afraid, afraid of him. And then she asked herself, Why? He could do nothing to her. Of course he could dismiss all the Drews and get in a male staff but he couldn't put Biddy out of the lodge; that was her property now. Yet the fear somehow wasn't connected with the Drews; it was an unexplainable fear. . . . Yet was it so unexplainable? The answer that thought brought to her was: madness, sheer madness.

◈ 3 ◈

Tilly had never made use of a carrier cart since she had taken up residence in the Manor and she was loth to start now for she would have to rub shoulders with the villagers, that's if they allowed themselves to get near enough to touch her shoulder; and so for her visits into the town to replenish her cupboard, she had to rely on Arthur taking the cart into Shields. Even that trip had become hazardous, not for herself, but for the child, because the weather was cruelly cold.

There was only a week to Christmas and she felt she must do some shopping, not for presents but for necessities; the only presents she had to give were to the Drews. She had been knitting scarves, mufflers and gloves for weeks past now, and she had made a fine shawl for Biddy. She had also decided to give herself a Christmas box. She was going to buy the material to make a warm winter dress, as well as more flannel for petticoats for the child.

She had arranged yesterday with Katie for her to sneak out, and that was the word that Katie used, in order that she could look after the baby for two hours or so. Arthur was to bring her on the cart, and then pick herself up and take her into Shields, where he would leave her while he went and collected the weekly supply of fodder for the horses. She would later meet him at the top of the Mill Dam bank and return home.

She was ready except for putting her hat on when she heard the stamping of the horse on the road and glanced out of the window in passing, then took one step back and became still. It wasn't Arthur with the cart, it was Simon Bentwood. She nipped hard down on her lip and allowed him to knock on the door before she opened it. He was smiling at her, his arm extended towards her and from his hand was dangling a medium-sized goose.

'I thought it might do for your Christmas dinner, Tilly.'

She looked at him sadly now and, shaking her head, said, 'Thank you, Simon, but I can't accept it.'

'Why can't you?'

'Because I can't take presents from you.'

''Tis merely a gift like from one neighbour to another.'

She turned her head away and looked down towards the step for a moment, then said, 'We both know, Simon, that it is no ordinary gift. If . . . if I accepted it you . . . you would think. . . . Oh well!' – she spread out her hands – 'it doesn't need any explaining. I appreciate your kindness, Simon, and I hold no bitterness towards you now, but . . . but I cannot take anything from you.'

His face was stiff, his lids half lowered. He looked down at the bird dangling from his hand; then he hit it almost savagely with his crop as he said, 'You can't stop me from trying to get things back as they once were, and you've no intention of going up there again.' His head jerked to the side. 'You refused to go back so what do you intend to do, spend the rest of your life in this little hole?'

How did he know that she had refused to go back to the Manor? She had, of course, told Biddy and she would, of course, have told Katie and Katie would have told ... on and on, until it reached Fred Leyburn and then the two part-time outside men that Matthew had engaged lately.

'You can't mean to remain on your own for the rest of your life, Tilly, you're not made that way. And you won't be allowed to, men being what they are. I made one mistake, but as I said afore I'm not the only one, am I? We both could forgive and forget. I'd look after you, Tilly.'

'I'm quite capable of looking after myself, Simon. And Simon, listen to me, I want to make this final, I shall never marry you, Simon, loneliness or necessity would never drive me to marry you. I have known one man. I looked upon him as my husband, I hope he suffices me.'

'Suffices you, did you say? Huh!' His face was one large sneer now. 'By what I hear you're going to run through the family. One man sufficing you? They're never off your doorstep. Huh! Do you know your name's like clarts, a whore could claim more respect than you round here. I could make you into a decent woman.'

The blood had drained from her face and she felt as if it was draining from her whole body, her legs were weak. She put out her hand and supported herself against the stanchion of the door, but she kept her head up and her gaze steady on him as she answered, 'If my name is like clarts then our names are well matched; you've had to come down in the social scale since Lady Myton, for I understand you're quite at home in the Shields brothels.'

She thought for a moment he was going to strike her. It was strange but there was the same look on his face as had been on Matthew's a few weeks ago when he had stood by the table and glared at her as if he could kill her. That Simon might actually have hit her, or at least grabbed hold of her, she was sure except at that moment the cart came into view round the bend in the road and Arthur, jumping down from the high front seat, came smiling towards them, only to jump to the side as Simon flinging round from Tilly went striding past him, the goose swinging from his hand.

'Something wrong, lass?'

She had pushed the door wide open and was leaning against it.

'Here! has he done owt to you?' He had his hand on her shoulder whilst looking back to where Simon was mounting his horse; then he exclaimed on a high note, 'God! he's thrown the bird into the thicket, he's as mad as a hatter. What's happened, Tilly?'

She walked away from him and, sitting down by the fire, she said on a shaky laugh, 'He ... he brought a proposal of marriage, Arthur.'

'Oh. Huh! Oh, I see. Well, I've heard of rejected suitors but I've never imagined one as mad as he looks. Are you sure you're all right, lass?' His face was serious now.

'No, Arthur, quite candidly I don't feel all right; encounters like that rather shake you.' She looked towards the doorway. 'Where's Katie?'

'Well' – he pulled off his cap and scratched his head – 'she couldn't get away. The master's going round like a bear with a sore skull. He had me mam in this mornin' tellin' her he was implementin', that was the word he used, implementin' the staff. He told her to send the lasses over and prepare the other rooms above the stables. We don't fancy anybody next door to us now 'cos as you know, Tilly, we've been there since Katie and Peg went down to the lodge. . . . Anyway, just afore I came out he ordered Fred to get the coach ready 'cos he's off somewhere. I laughingly said to Fred it might be to pick up the butler and such, as if he would, but as he said you'd just get the throw-outs at this time of the year. Anyway, the butlers are generally recommended men. Anyhow, Katie can't get away so there's nowt for it, lass, but you'll have to wrap the young 'un up if you want to come along of us. 'Tisn't all that cold the day, in fact it's pleasanter than it's been for weeks; and you've had it out afore in the cart.'

'Yes, yes, of course. I'll . . . I'll wrap him up well.'

'You can take the basket an' all. Put it in the back at your feet. He'd be better in there than on your knee.'

'That's a good idea, Arthur. And I can put an extra blanket over the top.' She turned to him now, saying on a weary laugh, 'I'll have to leave the basket in the cart while I go shopping, so don't forget to lift it out before you start loading up.'

'I'm not daft, Tilly. Here! give him to me and get your hat on.'

Whilst Arthur carried the basket and the child out to the cart Tilly stood pinning her hat on; then she banked down the fire and placed the iron screen in front of it. But before she went towards the door she stood with her hands on the table and, looking down at them, a familiar thought came back into her mind, for she told herself she wished she was old. Oh, how she wished she was old, so old that this thing that she possessed that drew men to her would have withered and died as if it had never been and the shell of her would at last know peace. . . .

The ride was pleasant, smooth in parts, that was until they reached Shields, and there the traffic had defied the wind to harden the surface of the mud roads. But in the main shopping centre of King Street was a pavement and there Arthur put Tilly down with the baby in her arms, together with her bass shopping bag, and as he placed the latter in her hand he said, 'Now don't pack that too full 'cos he's enough for you to hump.'

'Don't worry, Arthur. Remember what you once said? I've got arms like steel bands.'

'Aye, that was once upon a time but they've softened a lot since then. Well, I'll see you in an hour, eh?'

'Thanks, Arthur.'

Although the streets were crowded she had no difficulty in making her purchases, and she was able to rest in the drapery shop on one of the many seats provided for the customers while the assistant unrolled bale after bale very anxious to please her, knowing that here was a customer who didn't want a rough serge or a moleskin, nor yet cheap prints, but a good cord velvet – she had already purchased five yards of the finest flannel. The assistant was puzzled by her. She certainly had money to spend and she spoke well but although her speech was correct it was interspersed with ordinary words; she looked like a lady, yet her dress wasn't fine enough, and then again she was carrying her own baby and she hadn't arrived by carriage. The street was full of them passing by but there wasn't one standing outside the shop. Moreover, she carried a bass bag and no real lady would carry a common bass bag.

'Eight yards, madam? Thank you, madam. And you would wish for a good lining, madam? Certainly, madam. Certainly, madam.'

Tilly looked at her watch. It was almost twenty minutes to three; she had plenty of time to take a quick walk round the market. She liked the market, it was an exciting place. It was strange but she'd always preferred Shields to the city of Newcastle. Although Newcastle had more in the cultural line to offer, such as galleries, not to mention very fine shops with huge plate-glass windows and in which you could stand and gaze for hours, she still preferred Shields. Perhaps it was because of its sea front and the wild waters of the North Sea so near. Whatever it was she preferred it, and she wished she could visit the town more often. Lately, she had been toying with the idea of a pony and trap; she had sufficient money to buy both, and the pony could graze on the common land.

The shop assistant showed her to the door where he condescended to place the handle of the bass bag over her forearm, and so she smiled at him as she thanked him even as she thought, That's what I'll do as soon as the year turns, I'll get a pony and trap. Why haven't I done it before?

As the shop assistant was bowing her out he still held the door open to allow a man to enter; but the man stopped, and Tilly stopped, and both said, 'Why! hello.' And both were surprised.

'What are you doing here, Fred?'

She did not mean why was he entering a draper's shop but why was he in Shields. She had understood from Arthur that he was taking his master into Newcastle, yet she remembered that there had been no place mentioned.

Fred Leyburn, smiling at her broadly, said, 'I don't need to ask you what you've been doing, Tilly, been buying the shop it looks like. Where are you off to?'

'I'm just going to walk round the market and then meet Arthur at the corner, he'll be there at three o'clock.'

'Well, wait a minute, I'll walk with you; I just want some thread for Phyllis.' He turned to the assistant who was still holding the door open and, handing him a piece of paper around which was tied a few brown threads, he said, 'Could you get me two bobbins of that, please?'

'Certainly, sir.'

As the assistant went back into the shop, Fred, bending towards the child, said, 'Hello there, Big Willy. How you gettin' on?' And the baby laughed at him and grabbed at his finger and Tilly said, 'Have you come in on your own? I thought you were. . . .'

'Me! on my own?' he cut her off. 'Me life's not me own these days, lass. I'm here, there and everywhere, like a cat on hot bricks. No, the master's gone to see some solicitor bloke with offices just down the street. He said he'd be half an hour, so I haven't stabled the coach, I've left a runner hanging on to it at the end of the market. Of course if his nibs knew I'd done that I'd likely get the sack. Eeh! Tilly, I'm tellin' you, that fellow doesn't know where he is half his time. He's not here afore he's there, and he's not there afore he's back here again. . . . Oh, ta.' He turned to the assistant who was handing him a small paper bag. 'How much?'

'Twopence, sir.'

'There, and thanks.'

As they walked into the street Fred said, 'Shall I carry the bairn for you, Tilly?' and she answered, 'No, but you can take this bag, Fred.'

'You say Arthur's just at the other end of the street?'

'Yes.'

'Well, after a quick walk round I'll see you to him 'cos you've got enough to hump with that 'un.' He thumbed towards the child, and Tilly, laughing said, 'Yes, this 'un's no light weight.'

They had entered the market square now, Fred walking a little in front of Tilly wending his way between the fish stalls, the meat stalls, the hawkers' baskets and the people milling all around them.

When above the usual cries of the market there arose some shrill screams, Fred turned to Tilly and, pulling a face, said, 'Look out! Look out! We'd better keep clear; there's a fight going on ahead. Oh my!' He caught hold of her arm as the people before them, most of them laughing and jeering, backed away from the combatants. But when Fred went to turn Tilly about and make their escape they were checked by the throng behind them who, although not wanting to be brought into the fight, were still interested in the progress of the two women who were tearing at each other's hair, while a man and a boy tried to separate them. The boy had a stout stick in his hand and he was belaying the buttocks of one of the women with it. When at last the viragoes were parted and only their screaming filled the air, Fred remarked, 'Tight as drums. They've started well afore Christmas those two. Come on, let's get out of here.'

Being unable to go back, he now led her towards a gap between two stalls, and it was just as they neared the opening that the larger of the two women turned about. Over the distance of a few yards she stared at Tilly; then grabbing at the shoulder of the boy by her side, she cried, 'Bloody well look at that! This is a day of bad luck all round I'll say. No wonder that whore stole me purse. An' after me standin' her a drink an' all, 'cos look at that, will you! Will you look at that!'

A number of people had gathered in the opening between the two stalls and before Fred could pull Tilly forward Mrs McGrath was upon her, screaming now, 'The bloody witch who killed me son!' Even as she spoke she grabbed the stick from the boy's hand and seemingly in one movement struck out at Tilly's head. Instinctively as Tilly jerked her head away, Fred's arm came upwards to ward off the blow, but too late, it missed both Tilly's head and his arm and caught the child across the forehead.

The cry that went up from all sides drowned that of the child's scream, and when its blood ran over Tilly's hand she, too, screamed. 'Oh my God!'

'She's knocked the bairn's brains out.'

'Eeh! where's the polis? They're never here when they're wanted.'

'She's as drunk as a noodle, but why had she to go and do that? The poor bairn.'

'Oh my God! My God!' Tilly was trying to quench the blood flowing from the gash in the child's brow. There was so much blood that she didn't know exactly where the cut was.

'Here, give him to me. There's an apothecary along the street, he'll do something.' Fred grabbed the child from her arms now and pushed his way through the crowd. Once clear, he ran down the main street, Tilly at his side holding a sodden handkerchief to the child's brow.

The apothecary said, 'Dear! dear!' as he swabbed the child's forehead. Then looking at Tilly, he said, 'There's very little I can do, you must see a doctor. At a pinch I could cauterize it; then again the cut is much too long and it requires stitching. Look, I will bandage it up temporarily but I think you must get him to a doctor as soon as possible.'

'Which . . . which is the nearest one?'

'Oh . . . let me see. He scratched his forehead, then said, 'It isn't the nearest one you want but the best one. Now there's a Doctor Simpson. He lives in Prudhoe Street, that's just before you get to Westoe. It's a tidy step but I know he's used to stitching people up.'

'Thank you. Thank you. How much do I owe you?'

'Nothing, nothing, my dear, nothing. I only hope the little man is no worse for this accident.'

Accident. Accident. Those McGraths, they'd be the death of her and her child; nothing they ever did was an accident. Oh God! Oh God! where was it going to end?

Fred picked up the child once more and they hurried out, and in the street he said, 'I'll take you to Arthur and he'll run you along, Tilly, 'cos I'll have to get back to his nibs. He'll be playing hell as it is, leaving the coach in charge of a runner and him but a lad.'

'Yes, yes, Fred. And thank you, thank you. I don't know what I would have done if you hadn't been there. Oh that woman!'

'You'd likely not gone into the market at all.'

'Oh yes, I would; I intended to go round. He's quiet, is he all right?'

'Aye, he's all right. Don't worry.'

'In the name of God!' The long drawn out exclamation came from Arthur as he saw them hurrying towards him, the child lying limp in Fred's arms, the bandage heavily blood-stained and both he and Tilly bespattered with blood.

After Fred had explained briefly what had happened, Arthur looked at Tilly and, shaking his head, said, 'Eeh! them McGraths. They're devils. Males and females, they're devils. Eeh! By! wait until our Sam and Henry hear of this, they'll deal with the buggers, her an' all. Oh aye, her an' all.'

All Tilly said was, 'Hurry! Arthur. Please hurry.' Then as they moved away she looked down from the cart on Fred, saying again, 'Thank you, Fred. Thank you.'

The cart gone, Fred now took to his heels and ran back the length of King Street, across the market and towards the Mill Dam end, there to see his master mounting the carriage, definitely intent on driving it back himself and, as Fred said later, it was only the sight of the blood on him that stopped him from taking the horses off at a gallop.

'What's happened to you? Been in a fight? Well, it looks as if someone has given you what I would like to give you this minute. Don't you ever dare leave my coach in charge of a boy again, because I promise you it'll be the last time you handle it.'

'Sir, it's . . . it's Miss Trotter.'

'What! What did you say?' Matthew's hands slackened on the reins.

'I . . . I met her while shoppin'. She . . . she was carryin' the child. She . . . she wanted to . . . to. . . .'

'Yes! man. What's happened to her?' Matthew had got down from the box now and was standing facing Fred.

'It isn't her, sir, it's the child. She was carrying the boy an' she met up with Mrs . . . Mrs McGrath. The woman was fightin', and then she saw Tilly . . . Miss Trotter, and she went for her with a big stick.' His hands made an involuntary motion as if measuring the size of the stick. 'But it missed her and struck the bairn's head open.

'No! Where are they?' The words were quiet, flat sounding.

'I took him to the apothecary's but he advised a doctor and so Arthur . . . Drew, sir, he was in the town collecting stores and I . . . I asked him to take her along.'

'Which doctor, man? Which doctor?'

'Someone near Westoe, Prudhoe Street, a Doctor Simpson.'

'Get up. Let's get off. Go there.'

As Fred scrambled up on to the box, Matthew entered the coach. McGrath. McGraths, those were the people that hated her. One of them who had wanted her had died, stabbed. He remembered his grandmother coming back with some tales about that being the second man who had died through her. His grandmother had never liked her. But then very few women would. Yet the women of that Drew family adored her. She seemed to court tragedy. What was it about her? Oh God! need he ask? He knew what it was about her; only too well did he know what it was about her. He wished she had never been born; or having been born, she hadn't come to dwell on the estate and enchant his father, because that's what she had done, enchanted him.

He put his head out of the carriage window, saying, 'Can't you make them move?'

'Too much traffic, sir.'

'Aren't there any short cuts?'

'Not to Westoe, sir. . . .'

Fred had no difficulty in finding Doctor Simpson's house in Prudhoe Street because there was the cart standing outside the iron gate and sitting in it rocking the child was Tilly.

When Matthew reached the tail board he began without any leading up, 'Why are you sitting there?'

Tilly showed no surprise at seeing him, she simply answered, 'He's not in, he's not expected for another half-hour.'

'Come out of that.'

'He's . . . he's quiet; as long as I rock him he's quiet.'

'Look, give him here!' He almost grabbed the child from her arms, then said, 'Come!' and with that he marched towards the small iron gate, which Arthur, as quickly, jumped to open, then strode up the pathway leading to the front door, to the side of which was a brass plate with a simple statement on it: Arnold P. Simpson, Physician and Surgeon.

'Ring the bell!' He had glanced over his shoulder at Tilly and when she obeyed his command and the door was eventually opened, he stepped forward, almost thrusting the maid aside, saying, 'You have a waiting-room?'

'Doctor ain't in, won't be for. . . .' The girl looked from Matthew to Tilly, then said, 'Aye, there's a waitin'-room, but it's for specials like.'

'Then may I inform you that we are' – he thrust his head forward over the child – 'specials like. Take us to this room immediately.'

The girl went hastily across the narrow hall and opened a door, then watched the gentleman place the child in the woman's arms before turning and saying, 'Fetch a dish of cold water and some hand towels.'

'Eeh! can't do that, mistress wouldn't have it.'

'Is your mistress at home?'

'No, sir, she be out visitin'.'

'Then, my girl, you bring me that water and hand towels or else I shall get them myself. Now away with you!'

When he turned to Tilly he smiled gently at her as he said, mocking himself, 'Terrible man. Terrible man.'

She looked at him but could say nothing, and now he bent over her and his voice was unusually gentle as he said, 'Don't worry. Children are very resilient and, you know, a little blood goes a long way. One thing you must be thankful for, the blow did not touch his eyes.'

Yes, she should be thankful for that. At first she really had thought he had been blinded.

When the maid returned with a bowl of cold water and two towels, she deposited them on a side table, then scampered from the room, and he remarked again with a smile, 'She thinks I'm the devil. Now let's see the damage.'

She was hesitant in unwinding the blood-soaked bandage, and so he, taking it from her fingers, slowly unwound it to reveal the gash still oozing blood, but not so heavily now. The cut went across the middle of the forehead, extending from the outer corner of the child's left eye to a point above the middle of his right eye. Dipping the end of a towel in the water, he gently sponged the blood away from the surface of the brow. Then he dipped the whole huckaback towel in the water and wrung it out before folding it into a narrow length and placing it over the child's brow, saying, 'There, that should quell the bleeding; and it will be ready for him to start on when he comes . . . when he comes.'

He now opened his coat and took out his watch from his waistcoat pocket, saying, 'It is almost four o'clock.' Then standing and looking around the sparsely furnished and dimly lit room, he said, 'If that girl has any sense she'd tell the cook or whoever is in charge to bring you some refreshment. I'll. . . .'

'Please! Please, don't trouble anyone; I'm . . . I'm perfectly all right.'

As she finished speaking there was a slight commotion in the hall and the sound of a chattering voice; then the door opened and the doctor entered. He was a small squat man with a bald head and his appearance would have shattered all preconceived ideas of doctors or surgeons except that his manner was brusque. 'What's this?' he demanded. 'What's this?'

'The child has been hurt, sir.'

The small man looked at the larger one and seemed to take him in at one glance. This was the fellow who had demanded waiting room, water and towels. Evidently a gentleman and one who was used to throwing his weight about.

'Well, let me have a look at the patient.' He took the wet towel from the child's brow, then said, 'H'mm! h'mm! Nasty but fortunate, very fortunate. Another fraction and it would have got his eyes. How did this happen?' He looked from one to the other, but it was Tilly who answered, 'In the market; a drunken woman aimed a staff at me. It missed and hit the child.'

'A drunken woman in the market is nothing new. Locked up half of them; chained up some of them. Wild cats, fish wives, trollops.' The words came out in staccato fashion as he went to the end of the room, opened a glass-fronted cabinet and took out a small box of implements. Then coming back towards them, he looked at Tilly, saying, 'You'd better let your husband hold him, he'll have more stomach for this.'

She opened her mouth twice to speak while the colour seeped temporarily back into her pallid face, and it was Matthew who answered stiffly, 'She is not my wife, she is a Miss Trotter, an old friend of my family. My coachman happened to find her in distress.'

'Oh!' The doctor blinked first at Matthew and then at Tilly, and again he said 'Oh! Well it makes no difference to the stitching, does it? You can still hold the child I suppose.'

Tilly, getting to her feet, placed the baby into Matthew's outstretched arms, and why she should shudder at the contact with him she didn't know, but shudder she did.

'There you are, little fellow. Now we'll put this on first to take some of the sting away. It won't stop you from howling, but you'll have forgotten all about it in a few minutes' time. Although you'll remember it later on because you're going to have a scar here for life. If you're ever lost they'll be able to find you all right.'

Tilly was standing facing the long window that looked on to what appeared to be a back garden and she closed her eyes when the child gave a sharp cry and continued to cry for what seemed an endless time, and she kept them closed until she heard the brusque voice say, 'There, that's done. It took more than I thought. Now a nice little bandage round that and you can face the world again.'

The bandaging done, he now turned to Tilly and said quietly, 'Let him rest for the next few days. No jogging up and down.' He gave her a demonstration. 'No chit-chat, pretty boying, just let him be quiet. He has sustained a shock and that will take time to heal, as well as the cut. Anyway, bring him to me in a week's time. Have you far to go?'

'Quite a way.'

'She . . . she will be here when required, sir.'

The doctor looked at the broad individual with the granite face as he thought to himself, Yes, if he says she'll be here she'll be here. One of those: I speak, you obey. Well, it took all types to make the world go round. He was tired and hungry, and he'd had a day of it. He had drawn splintered bones together, he had stitched up the throat of an unsuccessful suicide, and lastly he had just over an hour ago pushed a man's guts back, and put enough stitches in him to hold a feather tick together. But even so the fellow would likely die, having been at sea three days with part of a spar stuck in his belly.

'Good-day to you.'

'Good-day, doctor. Thank you very much.'

'Good-day, sir, I too thank you.'

He nodded from the man to the woman and blinked at them as he thought, Funny couple this, not man and wife, yet he shows the concern of a husband and she the reserved indifference of a wife. Looking at Matthew, he said, 'I did not get your name, sir.'

'I didn't give it to you, sir, but it is Sopwith, Matthew Sopwith of Highfield Manor. You can send your bill there.'

Sopwith? Oh yes, yes. Now he had the picture clear and bright in his mind. This was the son come back from abroad. Blandford had mentioned something about them. Senior had a mistress who had been a maid or something. Oh yes, yes. Well, well, he could understand it now; she was a beautiful woman. He could also understand the gentleman's concern for the child, his half-brother. Yes, yes. And he had put his foot in it, hadn't he, thinking they were husband and wife? Dear! Dear! 'Good-day to you.'

'Good-day to you. . . .'

Tilly did not protest when Matthew insisted that she get into the coach for all she wanted to do was to get home. . . .

Not until she felt Fred pulling the horses round to enter the gates of the Manor did she speak, and then quickly she said, 'I'll . . . I'll get off here, I can find my way.'

'Don't talk nonsense!'

'Please, I insist.'

'Go on insisting.'

She remained stiff in the seat for a moment until he bent towards her, peering at her in the dim gleam from the carriage lamps as he said, 'Look, Trotter; forget your feeling towards me, at least for the present, the child needs care. You heard what the doctor said. And you yourself need care after the shock you've had. Now you can't look after yourself and the child properly back in that cottage. The weather is vile. Let's be practical; you've got to go out for kindling, what happens if you take ill, who is going to see to the child then? It would have to come here if that happened, wouldn't it?'

She couldn't say, Why should it? And he was right, for what would happen to it if she took ill? She felt tired, weary. Again she had the desire to lay her head down somewhere and cry, but that had become too much of a pattern lately and had to be resisted.

When she remained quiet he said, 'That's it then, that's settled. There's one thing certain, it will be as good as a Christmas present to your friends, the

Drews; they'll have rooms prepared for you in the shake of a lamb's tail.'

She knew that he was smiling and she knew that what he said was right. Of a sudden there was no protest in her, she had the feeling that she was going to float away . . . she was floating away.

She had never before really fainted in her life. As a young girl she had told herself that fainting was the prerogative of ladies and that they usually did it in church or in their drawing-rooms. Even when McGrath and the others had put her in the stocks and pelted her with rotten fruit she hadn't actually fainted.

She opened her eyes to find Biddy bending over her, saying, 'There now. There now.'

'Bring some brandy.' She couldn't see Matthew's face but she recognised his voice and for a moment she wondered where she was. Then she remembered the child and, aiming to rise, said, 'Willy.'

'He's all right. He's all right. He's warmly tucked up and asleep. Don't worry.'

As she closed her eyes again she had the feeling it wasn't Biddy he had asked to fetch the brandy. A moment later when Biddy said, 'Can you raise yourself, lass, and take this drink?' she looked from her to John, who was holding the glass in his hand, and when he said, 'Poor, Tr . . . Trotter,' there was so much kindness in his voice that she had to press her lids tightly closed again to stop herself from crying. She had never felt so weak or so tired, not even when the child was being born; it must be the shock and the knowledge that the McGraths were on her horizon again. Yes, yes, that was it, the McGraths were on her horizon again.

She choked on the brandy and when John said, 'Dr . . . Dr . . . Drink it all up, Trotter, it'll d . . . d . . . do you good,' she drank it. Then she made to rise, saying, 'I'm all right now.'

'Stay where you are, there's nothing to rush for.' Matthew was standing at the back of the couch now looking down on her. 'As Biddy said, the child is all right. Your room will be ready for you in a little while, then you can retire to bed and have a meal there.'

'Thank you, but no.' She pressed Biddy gently aside and, swinging her feet from the couch, she managed to sit upright in spite of still feeling she needed some support. 'I cannot put you to this trouble, and there is no need.'

'Whist! now. Do what the master says and be sensible.' Biddy's tone sounded almost like her master's at the moment. 'The child needs attention, and you an' all. Go tomorrow if you must, but for the night, you stay put.'

'B . . . B . . . Biddy's right, Trotter. B . . . B . . . Be a good girl now.'

As John backed from her she wanted to smile at him.

Be a good girl now. He was a sweet creature was John. If only some of it had rubbed off on to his older brother.

She turned her head and saw them both going from the room, and when the door had closed on them Biddy, pulling a foot stool up to the couch, sat in front of her and, taking her hands, gripped them tight, saying, 'You have some sense, lass, if not for your own sake then for the child's. You're back here, so stay.' She leaned forward until her face was almost touching Tilly's and she whispered, 'From what I gather he'll be off to the Americas again shortly. He's like a cat on hot bricks; he can't find enough to occupy him here. Even since he's taken on opening the pit he's still looking for something to use his energy on. I've never seen a creature so full of unrest, he's never still a minute, so it's my belief he won't be here much longer. He'll leave Master John in charge and then things will run as before. And then the way things are going I'll be surprised if Master John and Miss McGill don't make a match of it. She thinks highly of you that girl. Katie heard her speaking of you to Master John, and his nibs was there an' all. He didn't say a word, Katie said, although I'll give him this 'cos she said he was very nice to the lass. I suppose you've noticed she's got a birthmark? Aye, well, we've all got things to bear. She's got a nice nature and she's sweet on Master John, you can see that, anybody with half an eye can see that. So now, you take my advice. I've never given it you wrong since we met, now have I?'

'No, Biddy.'

'Then, lass' – Biddy's voice dropped to a soft whisper – 'do this for me, stay on. And it's Christmas and we could have a lovely time because I'll not know a minute's peace if you're back there on your own and the sky outside there laden with snow, and if it falls like it did last year we won't be able to get through to you for days, perhaps not for weeks. It's happened afore, it could happen again. I worry over you, lass, just as if you were me own; in fact' – she looked downwards now – 'I feel guilty at times 'cos I think of you more than I do me own.'

'Oh, Biddy. Biddy. Do you know something?' Tilly was smiling faintly now, 'You shouldn't be in ordinary service, it is the diplomatic service you should have gone into.'

'And what kind of service may I ask is that?'

'Well, it's for people who have the powers of persuasion.'

The door opened and Katie came stealthily into the room. 'It's all ready, the fire's burning nicely, bed warmer in, and Peg's got your tray all set.'

'Oh dear me!' Tilly drooped her head and Katie, looking at her mother, said, 'What's wrong now? Starting to be contrary again, is she?'

'Less of your cheek,' said Biddy, getting to her feet; 'and get about your business.'

Instead of Katie going about her business she came up to Tilly and, dropping on to her hunkers in a fashion they had both used whilst working side by side down the pit, she said with a grin, 'Eeh! it's like old times, isn't it, Tilly? And we'll have some Christmas jollification an' all that, eh? I wasn't going to decorate our hall but I'll do it the morrow. I'll get the lads to bring some holly in. And I wonder if his nibs will let us do something to the main hall now 'cos he said we hadn't to bother. Didn't he, Ma?'

'Yes, he did,' said Biddy nodding; 'but now, there's a bairn in the house an' that makes the Christmas, a bairn, so go ahead and decorate the main hall an' all, and put some holly in the dining-room.'

'And what about some mistletoe?' said Katie, now smiling broadly. 'Master John might take a nibble at Miss McGill. That would be good to see. But I can't see his nibs kissing anybody, can you, Ma? That would turn them to vinegar right off.'

'Look.' Biddy pointed her finger at her chattering daughter whom, although only a year younger than Tilly, she still treated as a girl. 'What did I tell you? Get yourself away about your business afore I skelp your lug for you, and you'd need some vinegar to put on that!'

Katie went out laughing and Biddy remarked, 'That 'un'll never change: chatter, chatter, chatter. 'Tis well she hasn't married, she'd drive a man to drink. Come on, lass; let's get you upstairs.'

As if Tilly was a real invalid, Biddy helped her up from the couch, but as they made their way towards the drawing-room door Tilly stopped and said, 'Where are they putting me?'

'In your old room of course.'

She remained staring at Biddy. Which old room? The room that she and Mark had shared or the one at the end of the corridor that she had rarely used?

And Biddy added bluntly, 'The one you started with.'

Tilly turned away and, unaided now, walked across the hall and up the broad stairs, over the gallery and down the long corridor. She did not even glance towards the main bedroom but went on past it, past the dressing-room, past the closet and into the end room, and as she entered it she knew that she had come back and to stay; but at the same time that strange fear mounted in her again, the fear that she was afraid to put a name to, the fear that wasn't connected with either the McGraths or the villagers.

PART THREE

❧ The Child ❧

1

She had fallen into the routine of the house as if she had never left it. Christmas had been a gay affair, although the Christmas dinner was the only time she had allowed herself to sit in the dining-room and eat. From the day following her entry back into the house she had refused Matthew's order that she must eat with him. It was only on John's plea that Miss McGill would feel a little out of place, there being one lady and two men, that she consented to have her Christmas dinner in the dining-room instead of in the servants' hall. She had also said firmly that if she were to stay then she must make her rooms, as in the early days, on the nursery floor for now she had a child to see to.

Matthew raised no objection to this, and things went smoothly between them until the second week of the New Year when, returning from the town late one afternoon he called her into the library, and there without any preamble he said, 'I am sure you'll be pleased to learn that the McGrath woman will shortly get her deserts.'

'What do you mean?' She peered at him through narrowed lids.

'Well, what I've just said.' He nodded towards her. 'The matter has been in the hands of my solicitor since shortly after the incident. She is to appear in court the day after tomorrow. Leyburn will testify, as will you yourself.'

'*No! No!*' Her voice was loud. 'I won't. I won't go into court again! You should not have done this.'

'Not have done it? She could have killed the child and you say I shouldn't have done it!'

'Yes; I repeat you shouldn't have done it, it's none of your business.'

'Trotter!' His voice was low and his tone cold. 'I don't want to remind you again that the child is my half-brother. There is the question of blood, I have an interest in him, he will carry that woman's mark to his grave.'

'He is my child, you have no claim on him, none whatever. And I would like you to get that firmly in your head: *You have no claim on him.* What is more, you have no right to do this.' She choked and hunched her shoulders up around her neck; then she bent her head forward and placed her hand on her brow as she said, 'You don't understand. Even if she had murdered him I ... I could not have gone into court. I have been in a court. I was accused in a court of being a witch and of being the instigation of causing a man's death. The scene has never left me. You may have nightmares about frogs but' – she swung her head from side to side – 'there are periods when I'm back in that courtroom night after night.'

She now raised her head, and they stared at each other; then, her voice soft, her tone flat, she said, 'I . . . I appreciate your concern, I do really, but believe me I don't want this matter to go to court. She was drunk else she would never have done what she did, as bad as she is. And . . . and another thing, that family has known enough trouble inadvertently through me. If . . . if that woman were sent to prison I . . . I wouldn't know a moment's rest. And I can tell you this, if that family were to suffer again through me it would cause such bad feeling in the village I would be afraid to move out of these gates. One of her sons died in . . . in strange circumstances.' She lowered her eyes now. 'I . . . I was held responsible for it, although the matter never came to court. The youngest son, who incidentally was different from all the rest and . . . and was kind to me, he left home never to return. A third son went into the army and was killed. She has one son left now and one grandson.'

As her head drooped again a silence fell between them until he said, 'It will be as you wish. I . . . I imagined that you would have liked retribution, but I can see that I was wrong.'

He walked now the length of the room towards the window, and there he stood looking out for some moments before he said, 'There was another matter I wanted to speak about. In about two weeks' time I would like you to prepare a small dinner party. It will be for six. Just an ordinary affair, nothing too elaborate. The guests will be Mr and Mrs Rosier and a Miss Alicia Bennett, Mrs Rosier's cousin. And then, of course, John and Anna and. . . .'

'The Rosiers?' The name escaped her.

He turned now and walked back towards her, saying, 'Yes, the Rosiers. He is going into partnership with me in the mine.'

'Partnership!. . . . Your father. . . .'

The change in him startled her for he almost yelled at her now, 'What my father did and what I want to do are two entirely different things. My father had a personal prejudice against the Rosiers. I have no feelings for them one way or the other, but I need his expertise. He knows all about mines, I unfortunately don't as yet. And if I return to America . . . I should say, when I return to America, John will be left in charge, and he knows less than nothing about mining. I am putting a great deal of money into this concern, and Mr Rosier has enough faith in the project to add more to it. Moreover, he has the experience to pick men with the ability not only to manage but to work the mine. . . .'

'Yes, and drive them like slaves and house them in hovels, and dismiss them at a moment's notice if they dare attempt to read and write, put them on to the road in effect.'

'That was some years ago' – his tone had altered now – 'things have improved.'

'Oh no they haven't, not by what I hear.'

'The Drews still keep you supplied with pit news then?'

When she didn't reply he said, 'By all accounts my father wasn't any better an employer than Mr Rosier. He allowed you to work in his mine, didn't he? And the little girl who was killed beside you in the fall, how old was she? And speaking of cottages, I was through his row yesterday, and although they have become more dilapidated with the years there is still evidence of what they would have been when inhabited; and let me tell you this, some of the roughnecks I met in America would have preferred to sleep outside in the open and braved the elements and wild animals rather than bunk down into those hovels. . . .

'So – ' he moved nearer to her until she was only an arm's length from him and, looking straight into her face, he said, 'If you would be kind enough, Trotter, to oblige me by arranging, as I said, a small dinner party for the twenty-eighth? Thank you.'

She was left standing, her hands tightly gripped in front of her waist.

Why was it he always seemed to put her in the wrong? And why was it she always had the desire to go against him, argue with him? And it wasn't her place. But what was her place? As her granny would have said, she was neither fish, fowl, nor good red meat. Left to herself she felt as if she were mistress of the house, but in his presence she became a servant. Yet the odd thing was he never treated her as such, rather, more as an equal.

But this Rosier business. Well, she supposed he was right in all he had said: he had no knowledge of mines and if he was going back to America he'd have to leave someone in charge. She wished he were going back tomorrow. Oh yes, tomorrow. The sooner the better.

It was a blustery day towards the end of April when the wind seemed to be trying to obliterate the sun by sending scudding clouds across the sky. Tilly was in the nursery; she had the child in her arms and was standing before the window pointing upwards, saying, 'Look! birdie. . . . Look! Willy, birdie.'

But the child didn't follow her pointing finger, he made an unintelligible sound and stroked her cheek with his plump hand, and she stared into his eyes, large soft brown eyes; then she traced her finger above the jagged scar running across his brow. It hadn't faded as the doctor had said it would, it still showed as a narrow red weal; and on each visit he still assured her that as the child grew older the weal would flatten; he would always carry a scar but it would be hardly noticeable in later life as his skin grew tougher.

The doctor had insisted that she take the child to him every month. He would look into the child's eyes and mutter, but make no comment other than to say jocularly, 'He's a healthy little beggar, is our Willy.'

The nursery door opened and John peeped round into the room, saying, c . . . c . . . can I have a . . . w . . . word with you, Trotter?'

'Yes, of course.'

'I know I sh . . . sh . . . shouldn't disturb you in your r . . . r . . . rest time but I w . . . w . . . wanted you to be the f . . . first to know.'

She smiled at him as she seated herself at the corner of the nursery table and pointed to the seat opposite. She knew exactly what news he was about to divulge but she waited, saying nothing.

'Tr . . . Trotter – ' he blinked his eyes, screwed them up tight, then opened his mouth wide before he brought out, 'I . . . I don't know whether y . . . y . . . you've s . . . s . . . seen it or not, but I'm in lo . . . lo . . . love with Anna.'

'Well, I had noticed something different about you.' She now burst out laughing, and he put his head down and covered his eyes with his hands for a moment before he said, 'I'm going to her gr . . . gr . . . grandmama today to ask p . . . per . . . mission to marry her.'

'Oh, I'm so glad, John, so glad.' She put her free hand across the table towards him, and he said, 'I th ... thought you ... might be, and I know you like Anna. She ... she ... she dotes on you. But I'm r ... rather ... wor ... worried, her gr ... grand ... grandmama is a very stiff old girl.'

'Oh, you'll soften her up, never fear, John. You'll soften her up.'

'I'm n ... not so sure, in some ... some ways she p ... puts me in mind of my gr ... grandmama. You remember, sh ... she ... she didn't like me just because I ... I stammered.'

'Well, she wasn't a nice person and very few people liked her.'

'You kn ... know, Trotter, it w ... was you who brought us together. We'll never forget that, never.' He moved his head slowly as he looked at her, then said, 'And now I must g ... go and f ... f ... find Matthew. He went out r ... r ... riding about an hour ago, but I don't know whether he's gone to the m ... m ... mine or gone riding with Miss ... Miss Bennett.' He rose to his feet and bending towards her said in a mock whisper, 'Wouldn't it be f ... f ... funny if we had a d ... double engagement, Trotter? Wouldn't it?'

She made no answer but watched him walk to the door, and as he opened it she said, 'Is Matthew thinking about going back to America shortly?'

There was a broad grin on his face as he answered, 'Never heard a w ... w ... word of it recently, not s ... s ... since he met the d ... divine Alicia. She scares me a b ... b ... bit. I think Matthew has met his m ... m ... match. What do you think?'

She didn't say what she thought, she just shook her head and he went out. She rose and placed the child on the rug before walking to the window again and looking out. Well, there was one thing certain, if the divine Alicia became mistress of this house she herself would once again pack her bundle and depart.

Later that day John and Anna came running through the house like two children, calling, 'Trotter! Trotter!' and after being directed to the servants' hall they stood before her, and she held out her hands to both of them and said, 'I'm so glad.'

It was Anna who spoke first. Her voice full of meaning, she said, 'Thank you, Trotter.'

John, leaning towards her, his eyes sparkling with happiness, exclaimed on a laugh, 'W ... W ... Wouldn't believe it, Trotter. I n ... n ... nearly fainted, her gr ... grandmama k ... k ... kissed me.'

Tilly watched them lean against each other. Then John turned towards Biddy, and she came forward and said, 'I'm happy for you, sir. I'm happy for you both. I'll make the grandest spread for you in the county on the day it happens.'

'Thank you, B. ... Biddy.'

'Oh, thank you, Biddy.'

Katie now came forward and dipped her knee to the young girl, and Fanny, Peg and Betty followed.

'Ha ... have a drink at d ... d ... dinnertime to us.' John nodded from one to the other. 'Will you br ... br ... bring a bottle up, Trotter?'

'Yes, I'll do that.'

As the two of them turned hand in hand and ran from the room the girls all put their hands over their mouths to still their laughter, and Biddy said, 'There's two that'll make it.'

It was Katie who turned to her mother now and said, 'An' I wonder if the master will make it with Miss Bennett. What do you think?'

Biddy's answer was abrupt. 'I'm not paid for thinkin', I'm paid for workin', and so are you. Now you've finished your tea get on with it.' And as Katie's hand went out to the last cake left on a plate her mother slapped the hand aside, saying, 'Go on, leave that alone; you're always stuffin' your kite. You never see green cheese but your mouth waters.'

'Aw, Ma, you!' Katie replied and pushed Fanny before her.

As Biddy turned and walked towards the door leading to the kitchen she said, 'What's your idea about him and the horse-mad heifer?'

Tilly paused before answering, 'I haven't really thought about it,' at the same time reminding herself that very little passed Biddy's nose. 'If he wants her, he'll have her, I suppose; he's that kind of man.'

'I wish he'd get himself off back to the Americas, that's what I wish.'

As Tilly now walked up the kitchen she answered quietly without looking in Biddy's direction, 'You're not the only one, Biddy. You're not the only one.'

↊ 2 ↋

The engagement party was being held in honour of Willy's forthcoming birthday too. The day had been very hot and the evening promised no relief until the moon should come up.

The preparations in the house during the past two weeks had been on from early morning until late at night. John and Anna had wanted a small private engagement party, but Matthew had shouted them down, saying that as he was the first of the three to put the halter round his neck, it must be done at least with a little ostentation, not too much, but just a little.

The meal was to consist of a cold buffet supper, and concerning this Matthew had annoyed not only Biddy but Tilly also, for apart from the cold game, porks, sirloins and hams, and the pastries and cakes, the roasting and baking of which Biddy had perfected over the years, he had ordered from a Newcastle firm a large iced three-tiered cake that was to be the centre of the main table, as well as trays of fancy tit-bits.

Then at the last moment, only two days ago in fact, he had informed Tilly that he was engaging six male servants from Newcastle, one to act as butler, two as first and second footman, and three as wine waiters. There was also to be a quartet to provide music.

When she had shown her surprise and open displeasure at the engaging of the male staff, he had turned on her, saying, 'I do it to relieve you of the responsibility of the staff on that evening. You manage the household, in fact act as its mistress, so I want you to put on your best dress and help receive the guests . . . as its mistress.'

She recalled the scene, the open quarrel that ensued when she cried at him 'Oh no! No! Do you wish to humiliate me? You have given me the list of guests, and in it I notice three names, supposed friends of your father, the Fieldmans, the Tolmans and the Craggs. I remember just how their wives considered me the last time they were in this house. To them I was merely a servant, and rightly so, but there are ways and ways of treating a servant. Apart from Miss Bennett I don't know any of the other names on the guest list, but I know those three ladies. There is a name for them. I remember applying it to them all those years ago, it still remains vivid in my mind, and that name is bitch. They were three bitches then, so imagine their reaction to me if I should be in the hall to receive them, as you say, mistress of the house. . . . Oh, you know the correct procedure better than most, so why are you set on subjecting me to this humiliation? Anyway, the rightful people on this occasion to receive the guests are John and Anna. And my part, I can assure you, will be that of the housekeeper, because after all that is what I am, the housekeeper, and I would thank you to remember that and not embarrass me with such ridiculous suggestions.'

'God!' He had gripped his unruly hair with both hands and swung round from her as he exclaimed, 'Of all the bloody aggravating women on this earth, Trotter, you'd be hard to beat! All right' – he had turned to her again – 'you want to be a housekeeper, from now on I'll see that you are treated as a housekeeper.'

She had glared at him, returning a look similar to that in his eyes and stretching her neck upwards and so, outreaching his height, she had said, 'Very good, sir,' then turned and walked out of the drawing-room. But as she went to close the door she had paused for a second as his muttered oath came to her, saying, 'Damn and blast you!'

That night she had hardly slept, and the next morning John had come to her and said without any lead up, 'Now, Trotter, you are to c . . . c . . . come to the p . . . p . . . party, M . . . M . . . Matthew is furious, like a b . . . bear with a sore skull.' And he had put his head on one side as he added, 'I . . . I don't know how it is, Trotter, b . . . b . . . but you know you g . . . g . . . get under his skin . . . skin more than anyone else I know. I c . . . c . . . can't understand it, you who are s . . . s . . . so good and tactful with everybody, but you s . . . s . . . seem to an . . . annoy him. Why? Why, Trotter?'

'I don't mean to, John; but I don't think he's ever forgiven me for being your father's mistress.'

'Oh, I th . . . think he has, Trotter; in fact, I know he's v . . . v . . . very concerned for you and li . . . li . . . little Willy. He's very f . . . f . . . fond of Willy, as we all are, and as he said the party c . . . c . . . could be a celebration f . . . f . . . for his first birthday too. Oh, come on.' He put his hand on her arm. 'After all, Tr . . . Trotter, both Anna and I know that y . . . you m . . . made our engagement possible.'

'Don't worry.' She smiled at him. 'Just leave it, we'll see.'

'You m . . . m . . . must, Trotter.'

'All right, all right.'

'Good! Good!'

John went out of the room, down the stairs taking them two at a time, almost upsetting Katie who was carrying a tray of dishes from the morning-room. As he steadied her and the tray, he said, 'M ... M ... Matthew. M ... M ... Master Matthew, has he gone?'

'No, he's still in there, Master John.'

John entered the morning-room almost at a run, to see his brother standing looking out of the window on to the side lawn, and he said immediately, 'I've s ... s ... seen her. She'll c ... c ... come as the f ... family. You kn ... know, Matthew, you are too rough with p ... p ... people and Trotter is a s ... s ... sensitive p ... person.'

'*Sensitive! ... Sensitive!*' Matthew swung round from the window. 'When she decides she's not going to do anything she's about as sensitive as a long-horned bull.'

John laughed at this, then said, 'Well, I would have f ... f ... felt awful if she just t ... took up the position of a s ... s ... servant to ... tomorrow night. You see I cannot help it, Matthew, b ... but I feel she is something sp ... sp ... special in a way, and both Anna and I owe her so much. You s ... s ... see, Anna went to her in the first place thinking she was a wi ... witch and that she might be able to remove the b ... b ... birthmark. And you know, I ... I somehow think she is a bi ... bit of a witch because ... because. ...'

'Don't say that word, and don't couple it with her! Do you hear me? Don't ever couple it with her!'

'Oh, Ma ... Matthew, I'm s ... s ... sorry but I didn't m ... m ... mean it in a n ... n ... nasty way, you know that, it was a s ... sort of a com ... compliment.'

'There's no compliment in being called a witch. I know of places in America where people bow their heads when that word is used, some in shame, some in sorrow; those in shame because their ancestors were not ignorant scum but class people, who would have been known as gentry here, and it was mainly they and the clergy who condemned innocent people to be hung and just from hearsay.'

'Oh.' The syllable sounded placating but lacked a note of interest. 'They were as b ... bad as they w ... w ... were here then?'

'Worse, I should say. There was a time towards the end of the sixteen hundreds when people in Massachusetts, and other states too, went crazy in witch hunts. Some young clergyman wrote a book about an old woman in Boston who had been executed for being a witch. The story goes that the book got into the hands of three silly girls and they accused someone of being a witch, and to save her own neck the victim implicated others. It got so bad that there were special courts appointed to try the supposed witches. The frightened victims confessed to all kinds of things, saying that some travelled on broomsticks and held conversations with the devil. Those who dared raise their voice against the courts were immediately accused of being the devil's tongue. Some of the victims were hanged and one man, so I heard from a descendant of his, was pressed to death. I tell you, John' – Matthew pointed at his brother, his voice harsh, and his face red – 'although it's a long time since a witch was burnt in this country the fear still prevails. You've only to go back to what happened to Trotter because she danced with the parson's wife. You won't remember it, except by hearsay, but they put her in the stocks. And when the parson's wife accidentally killed one of Trotter's persecutors they burned down her grandmother's cottage. Although the rubble has all been cleared away the foundations still remain as a grim reminder at the east end of the estate.'

'I d ... d ... didn't understand. I never meant. ...'

'Oh, I know you didn't.' Matthew made a conciliatory movement with his hand. 'I never thought much about witchcraft myself until I went to America. I knew people here referred to Trotter as a witch, but to me then the word simply meant somebody bewitching as she undoubtedly was. But when I came across two families who, I understood, had hated each other for more than a hundred years and was told the reason why, well, since then, the very word is anathema to me, because hatred caused the death, supposedly accidental, of the son of one house and kept the daughter of the other house separated. They had fallen in love. The result was, one grew into a sour old maid and the other was killed. And this all came about through the word witch. And the sour old maid happens to be Uncle's daughter.'

'Oh! Oh! R ... really? I'm sorry, Ma ... Matthew. I understand how you f ... f ... feel so strongly about it. R ... R ... Rest ass ... assured I'll n ... never apply that name to Trotter again. In fact, I d ... d ... don't think I'll ever use it again in ... in ... in any way.'

Matthew drew in a long breath, lowered his head and shook it from side to side before saying, 'You must think me odd at times, John, a little crazy, but living over there has changed my views on everything and everyone. There's a rawness about it that ... that finds its counterpart inside me. When I left England for the first time I felt capable of holding my own with anyone, gentry or commoner. Well, I found I could hold my own with the so-called gentry, they were no different as I said from what they are over here, except perhaps a little more ruthless, for they have more to gain and more to lose; but it was the common man, the ordinary fellow who stands up to you and tells you that he's as good as you, boy. They don't do it in so many words, it's by looks and actions, it's more of what they leave out than what they put into their attitude towards you that brings you down. What you value they laugh at, they spit at; oh yes, literally. It turns your stomach at first, because everybody spits; no matter where they are, who they are, they spit. They chew tobacco and spit. I found it so nauseating that I actually wanted to vomit at times. Really, I did.' He nodded his head now as he smiled at John. 'Then you get used to it. You have to. In fact, at times you're even tempted to copy them instead of swallowing, especially if you're smoking a pipe. Good lord!' He laughed now as he put his arm around John's shoulders, saying, 'I have gone on, haven't I? America, first lesson, from witches to spit!'

'It was in ... inter ... interesting. I wish you would talk more, Matthew. You've told me v ... v ... very little about Uncle; I don't even know what he looks like, this uncle. I only hope he doesn't t ... t ... take after Gr ... Gr ... Grandmama. He was her half-bro ... brother, wasn't he?'

'Yes, but I can assure you there's nothing of Grandmama in Alvero Portes, except perhaps his determination to have his own way; but unlike Grandmama, he tempers this with a great deal of tact. Anyway, we'll talk about him later; but now, to get back to the present and my bone of contention, namely Trotter. You succeeded where I failed, and when I come to think of it, you always did have a better effect on her than I had. Well now, I think you'd better go and carry out your charm in the kitchen because the wind there I fear is against me. If they had any sense they'd know they couldn't cope with everything tomorrow and that I was thinking of them, when I ordered the additional staff.'

'N . . . n . . . no, you weren't.' John pushed Matthew none too playfully now in the shoulder. 'Y . . . you know you weren't. Os . . . os . . . ostentation you said, a bit, not too much. Are you ins . . . ins . . . insisting on them wearing s . . . s . . . satin breeches and g . . . gaiters?'

'No, kilts like the Scots in order to placate your future wife's grandmother who, I understand, hails from over the Border.'

'Oh.' John put his head back and let out a free peal of laughter, and they were both laughing when they crossed the hall and picked up their tall hats and coats and went out of the door and to the stables.

A few minutes later, as Tilly watched them both riding down the drive, she thought how unlike their temperaments were. If only Matthew had been born with a little of John's kindness and softness. But what about the other way? Yes, she supposed it would have helped John if in his turn he'd had a little more self-assurance; but not so much that it amounted to bombast.

She repeated the word to herself, bombast. But could that word be correctly applied to Matthew? What did it mean? She was thinking in the way of Mr Burgess as she said to herself: Stuffing, padding, loud assertiveness, over-stressed eloquent phrasing. Well no, bombast was the wrong word, there was no padding about him, he was too forthright. . . . Loud assertiveness? Yes; he yelled more often than not, especially when he was angry. And of course, he did assert himself, but not with high-falutin phrases. . . . Oh, why on earth was she standing here dissecting his character? Didn't she get enough of him when they were face to face? She was becoming daily more irritated by his very presence. And then the party tomorrow. He had taken as much trouble over if as if it was to celebrate his own engagement. Hm! Perhaps it was, too. Well, the sooner the better. She turned from the window and went about her duties.

As Biddy remarked later to Katie, 'She's going round lookin' like I feel, as if the only thing that would ease her would be to slap somebody's lug.'

It was many a year since the house had known such gaiety, and the almost full moon and the soft night together seemed to lend enchantment to the whole affair.

At ten o'clock Matthew's eloquent but brief speech, followed by the drinking of the health of the happy couple, was over and most of the guests had dispersed into the grounds, which gave Matthew the idea to have the quartet brought from the gallery on to the terrace. The young people were dancing on the sunken lawn; and not only the young, for the wine seemed to have loosened the stiffness in the legs of their parents and many were showing their paces, dancing not only the minuet, but the schottische, and even the faster polka.

The waiters, too, were kept busy, moving among the guests handing plates of sweetmeats and even more substantial cuts; and it was nothing to see a velvet-coated gentleman gnawing at a chicken leg, or another holding his head back as he dangled a slice of sirloin above his gaping mouth.

The lamps on the terrace and the lights from the house assisting the moon showed the scene up almost as if it were being enacted in daylight. Tilly was standing just within the open window of the morning-room at the end of the terrace. The shadow cast by the cypress tree fell across the window and so hid the expression on her face, a mixture of anger and disdain as she looked down on the scene. Her eyes were focused on a small group of women.

Those three! She felt that she had jumped back thirteen years. As on that night years ago Mrs Tolman, Mrs Fieldman and Mrs Cragg and their parties had all arrived together, and just as on that night they had made a point of speaking about her as if she weren't present, so they had done tonight but with a difference. On the previous occasion when they had discussed her they had not been certain of her position in the house, but tonight they were, and as if prior to their arrival they had together decided what form their attitude towards her was to be, they had all stared boldly at her as they stood side by side like three ravens: one was dressed in blue taffeta, one in dark green silk, and the other in black lace, and the colours combined were like the sheen on a raven's back. What was more, they had pointedly ignored John's introduction of her, and his 'Miss Trotter, a friend of the family' brought a sound like a hoot from Mrs Bernice Cragg. But the final insult was when Alice Tolman, the eldest of the four Tolman girls, who, although being twenty-eight years old and plain, was of a pleasant nature, had stopped to speak to her, for it was then her mother sailed towards them and, without looking at either of them, said, 'You should know your place, Alice, even if others forget theirs.'

She should never, never have allowed herself to be persuaded to act as hostess tonight. She looked down at her dress. It was pretty, simple but pretty, made of yellow cotton with a pale blue forget-me-not sprig. She had purchased it in Newcastle at the last moment. The bodice was close fitting and the skirt not entirely fashionable, for it wasn't over full; the neck was square but not low enough to show the dip between her small breasts. The sleeves were elbow length with an attached loose frill that came half way down her forearms. Her hair, swept upwards from the back and the sides, made her appear even taller than she was. She wore neither powder nor rouge and therefore in comparison with most of the ladies present looked a tall, willowy pale thing.

All the Drews had exclaimed aloud when they saw her. But then they would, wouldn't they? They were like her family and real families never decried their own. But Anna, too, had said she looked nice, only she had used the word beautiful. And John had endorsed her remark. Matthew had said nothing, he had merely looked her up and down. But he had said nothing.

He had, she noticed, been drinking heavily during the evening. They all had, the noise from the garden proclaimed this, and the merriment had, in some quarters, turned to vulgarity, fathers chasing young girls who weren't their daughters, men guzzling meat like market-day yokels. In fact, the whole scene had now taken on the appearance of a fairground. She turned into the darkened room and peered at the clock on the mantelpiece. Ten minutes to twelve. She was tired, weary. She wished she could go to bed, but this she wouldn't be able to do until the last of the guests had gone, and as yet no one had shown any sign of leaving.

She made her way out of the room into the hall and as she went past the foot of the stairs on her way to the kitchen she was almost knocked on to her back by one of the Fieldman boys chasing Miss Phoebe Cragg. Neither stopped to apologise, and she stood for a moment watching them racing out of the front door and down the steps on to the drive.

When she reached the kitchen it was to see Biddy still busy at the table packing plates with pies and tarts and handing them to the girls, who in turn would take them out the back way to supply the waiters, who had set up a long table, near the end of the terrace.

Without looking up, Biddy said, 'They've gone through the fancy tit-bits an' now they're startin' on the real food.'

'Will you have enough?'

'I should say so; we've baked two hundred pasties and a hundred big tarts in the last four days. But I can tell you something, Tilly, I'm droppin' on me feet.'

'Yes, I know you are, Biddy; I wish you'd let me help.'

'What!' Biddy turned and looked at her and smiled wearily now, saying, 'Your place is in there. Get yourself back. How's things goin'?'

'Oh, very well I should say.'

'Aye, by the sound of it I should say that an' all. As Katie said, it's more like a harvest do than an engagement party. It'll surprise me if the rabbits don't start breedin' after this.'

'Oh' Tilly managed to laugh – ''tisn't as bad as that. They're all very jolly, wine jolly, mostly.'

'Aye, well, when drink's in wits are out, as they say. An' when the men reach that stage it's no use warnin' the lasses to keep their eyes open and their skirts down. As the saying goes, there's no difference atween a lord and a lout when they are both without a clout.'

'Oh Biddy!' Again Tilly laughed; then she added, 'I'll slip up and see how Willy is. He was as sound as a top an hour ago but the narration might have woken him up.'

As Biddy turned away to hand two plates to Peg, she said, 'You're not enjoyin' it, are you?'

Tilly half turned now and looked at her, but Biddy was busily filling more plates and she answered, 'About as much as you are.' Then she went out; but she did not go into the hall, she took the back stairs and entered the gallery from a side door, and as she crossed it to go up the corridor Matthew came out of his father's room accompanied by Alicia Bennett.

Her pause was hardly perceivable, only long enough to glance at them, and as Matthew went to speak she was already some steps away from them.

Inside, she was ablaze. How dare he take that woman in there! Whatever he wanted to do with her, why didn't he take her to his own room?

She reached the night nursery and stood for a moment looking down on the sleeping child. She was gripping the side of the cot as much in anger as for support as her thoughts reminded her that after all it was his room. Every room in the house was his room; that's what she kept forgetting. He was the master here, Mark was dead, and she herself had no position other than that of house-keeper.

She sat down on the low nursing chair near the banked-down fire which, in spite of the heat, was always kept alight, and she asked herself what was the matter with her? She felt so unhappy, so lost. She had felt unhappy after Mark died, but then the companionship of Mr Burgess and the waiting time whilst she was carrying the child she saw now as a time of peace. Even in her loneliness there was a certain kind of happiness, but she had never known a moment's happiness since she had come back into this house.

Pulling a small table towards her, she leant her arms on it and dropped her head on to them. . . .

She jumped with a start when a hand came on her shoulder, then gasped as she looked up into Katie's face.

'Eeh! I'm sorry to wake you, Tilly, but we wondered where you were. They've nearly all gone.'

'*What!*'

'Well, it's half past two.'

'*No!* Oh dear, dear!' She rose to her feet. 'I . . . I must have fallen asleep.'

'Well, it'll do you good. An' that's what I want to do, fall asleep, I'm nearly droppin' on me feet.'

'You say they've nearly all gone?'

'Aye; the Rosiers have just left, and the Tolmans and the Craggs, at least the old 'uns of that lot have. But some of the young uns are hangin' on, especially the fellows who came on horseback. One went off with a lass up afront of him. I don't know who he was but all of them on the drive were splittin' their sides.'

'What about Mrs McGill?'

'Oh, she went off about an hour ago, and the aunt an' all. I liked her. She spoke to me, they both did. They're sort of gentry, good gentry those two, not like some of them there the night. Coo! the Bull an' Pen on a Saturday night is nothin' to some of the things I saw goin' on. Lordy . . . !'

'What about Miss Anna?'

'Oh, she went along of them, and Master John, he rode aside the carriage. A lot of the young 'uns ran alongside as they went down the drive, cheerin' and laughin'. That was nice.'

'I'll come down.'

'Me ma's dead beat.'

'I should think she would be. You must make her lie in tomorrow morning; I can see to things here.'

'Oh, I doubt if she'll stand for that.'

Before leaving the nursery, they both went and looked at the child. He was lying with his thumb in his mouth and Katie said, 'When he looks like that I could eat him.'

They went quietly out and down the stairs on to the main landing. The house was strangely still now.

In the kitchen Biddy was sitting with her feet up on a cracket and, turning and looking towards Tilly, she said, 'I thought you were lost, lass.'

'I'm sorry; I fell asleep.'

'Nowt to be sorry for. Anyway, it's all over except payin' the bill. An' I bet this's cost him a pretty penny the night.'

'The waiters . . . ?'

'Oh, they went off in the brake with the band about fifteen minutes ago. And you know something?' She turned her head and looked up at Tilly. 'They were for taking the remainder of the stuff that was left outside. Aye, they were. . . . Aw, I told them where to go to. By! I did. They said it was the rule. Well, I said to them, there's a first time for everything an' this is the first time your rule's gona be broken, an' I hope it won't be the last. . . . Five bob a night each and all they could eat . . . and drink, and then they wanted to take the foodstuff. My! some people get their livin' easy.'

'Come on. Get off to bed. And you an' all, Katie. I'll see to things here.'

Biddy got slowly to her feet, saying, 'Yes, lass, I think I will. We've cleared up as much as we can, we'll do the rest in the mornin'. But look, how are we gona get down the drive without bumping into somebody? There's still young 'uns kickin' about in the garden.'

'Go round by the orchard and the water garden.'

'Oh, I don't like that way,' Katie put in now; 'it's dark round there, you've got to go under them cypresses.' And when Fanny and Peg endorsed this by saying together, 'Me neither,' Tilly said, 'Well, go and ask Arthur to go with you, or one of the others can leave the stables now the carriages are nearly all gone. Anyway, Fred may still be about; he's nearly sure to be.'

'Oh, don't bother them; they've had enough on their plates the night.' Biddy flapped her hand towards the girls, saying, 'Don't worry; there's none of the young sparks going to break you in.'

'Oh, Ma! The things you say. She's awful, isn't she, Tilly?'

Tilly smiled at Fanny as she said now, 'Come on, I'll walk with you, I could do with a breath of air.'

Biddy gave one last look around the kitchen; then motioning to her daughters, she waved them out of the door before following them; and when in the yard she stood and looked up towards the moonlit sky, she said, 'Well, if he had paid to have a night like this he couldn't have got better value for his money, could he now?'

'You're right there, Biddy.' Tilly smiled at her. 'It's a most beautiful night, almost like day. I don't remember ever seeing a brighter one. And it isn't a full moon yet.'

They met no one on their journey back to the lodge but they heard laughter and running footsteps here and there in the garden, and when Biddy remarked, 'Somebody's still loose. I hope he hurries up an catches her so we can settle down,' the girls smothered their giggles.

With the back of the lodge in sight Biddy said, 'Well, here we are. Thanks, lass. And good-night, or good-mornin'. See you later on.'

'Good-night, Biddy . . . Good-night, Katie. Good-night, Peg. Good-night, Fanny.'

'Good-night, Tilly. Good-night, Tilly. Good-night, Tilly. Good-night, Tilly.'

The whispered farewells over, Tilly turned slowly and made her way back to the cypress walk.

There were no sounds coming from the garden now; that was until she had almost reached the end of the walk. Then she was startled by the sound of laughter, and it brought her to a dead stop for she recognised that laugh, and she knew that if she continued on for the next few yards she would come up with the owner of that voice and his companion, and so, taking two cautious steps to the side, she stood in the deep shadow of a cypress tree. Then again she was startled by the fact that whoever was on the other path had also stopped, for now the laughter seemed to be almost in her ear.

Then the woman's voice came to her, saying, 'You know something? You are drunk, Matthew Sopwith, you are drunk'; and Matthew's voice answered on a throaty laugh, 'And you are not a kick in the backside from it, Miss Bennett, not a kick in the backside from it.'

Alicia Bennett's laughter now joined his, and Tilly had the impression that they were leaning against each other.

Now Alicia Bennett was saying, 'Why were you so mad a while back? Come on, tell me, why were you so mad?'

'I wasn't mad.'

'Oh-yes-you-were. And all because I wanted to see the nursery floor.'

'Well, as I told you, it's private up there.'

'*Private? Housekeeper's quarters, private! When were housekeeper's apartments private?* No servants' quarters are private. I know what it was, you didn't want me to see the child, did you? Is anything wrong with it? Two heads? Has it two heads? Or water on the brain? I once saw a child with water on the brain. It was so big they propped its head up in a cage.'

'Don't be silly, water on the brain! You have water on the brain. I don't care if you see the child; anybody can see the child. Anyway, forget about it. Come on.'

'No, listen. Stop it. I want to know something. Why do you have that one as your housekeeper?'

'Why shouldn't I have her as my housekeeper?'

'Oh, you know as well as I do. . . .'

'Look, I don't want to discuss this with you, Alicia. Anyway, I want a drink, come on.'

'It's the talk of the county.'

There followed a pause.

'What's the talk of the county?'

The tone of Matthew's voice now caused Tilly to press her hand tightly over her mouth.

'You know as well as I do: your father's mistress, now your housekeeper. As my pa always says, have your fun on the side but should there be results keep them on the side too.'

There was a longer pause now before Matthew's voice came thick and fuddled: 'Well, your pa should know what he's talkin' about as he's done a lot of work on the side, hasn't he, Alicia? His sidelines run right through his four farms, an' away beyond, so I understand. I've only one little half-brother but you must have enough to fill a workhouse, 'cos that's where they go, don't they, the maids with their bellies full?'

Now Alicia Bennett's voice came harsh, the words spitting, 'That isn't funny; I don't find you amusing. You're acting like a swine.'

'Only because you, my dear Alicia, are acting like some cheap hussy.'

'Cheap hussy, am I? Huh!' She gave a short laugh now before saying on a high sarcastic note, 'Oh, do please forgive me, Matthew, for daring to criticise your father's whore, I. . . .'

There followed the sound of a ringing slap, a gasp, then a long-drawn-out 'O . . . h!' Then Alicia Bennett's voice, deep and sober-sounding, came through the thicket of the trees like barbed prongs, saying, 'You shouldn't have done that, Matthew Sopwith. That was no slap, that was a blow. You are the first man who has ever dared lift his hand to me. You'll be sorry. You mark my words.'

Tilly stood as if she had become rooted to the spot. She heard one set of footsteps running into the distance but she dare not move because she knew that Matthew would be still standing where Alicia Bennett had left him. Then she almost cried out aloud as the trunk of the cypress which she was facing began to shake, and she knew that he had hold of it and that his hands were within an arm's length of her face. And when, as if he were speaking to her, his voice came on a groan, saying, 'Christ Almighty!' she closed her eyes tightly and gripped her mouth until the pressure hurt.

When at last she heard him move from the tree, she held her breath wondering if he would turn at the end of the path and come down the cypress walk. And when he did just that she prayed, 'Oh God! don't let him see me.'

When he came abreast of her his head was down, his chin almost on his breast, and his walk was not that of a drunken man, but rather that of an old one.

Presently his footsteps faded away in the distance, and she came from out of the shadows.

She didn't run back to the house, she walked slowly, but her whole body was shaking, and she was asking herself the question that she had asked a number of times in her life, Was it starting again?

 3

By lunchtime the following day the house was back to normal, at least as far as clearing up was concerned; but there seemed to be a tension running through every member of the household. Katie, Peg, Fanny and Betty all grumbled about the mess left by the hired waiters; Biddy hadn't a civil word for anyone; the men outside hadn't been able to go to bed until the last horse had gone from the stable, and that had been nearly four o'clock; the master himself, Arthur said, mustn't have slept at all because he was dressed and out on his horse by seven, and he must have harnessed the animal himself.

The only one who seemed happy was John, and it was around one o'clock in the afternoon that Tilly met him as she went through the main gates. He was riding back from having paid a brief visit to the mine. He stopped and, looking down at her, said, 'You off for a w . . . w . . . walk, Trotter?'

'I'm going to the cottage.'

'Oh, that's a l . . . long tr . . . tr . . . trail. Why don't you t . . . t . . . take the trap?'

'I want to walk.'

'Oh, yes. Well I . . . I understand. I, too, f . . . felt I had to g . . . g . . . get out this morning after the r . . . rumpus of l . . . last night. Went off won . . . won . . . wonderfully, didn't it?'

'Yes, it did, John; a great success.'

'It was d . . . d . . . dawn before the l . . . last ones left and I slept late. Then Arthur t . . . t . . . told me that Ma . . . Matthew had been up and gone since s . . . s . . . seven, so I've just b . . . been along to see him, and he's l . . . l . . . like a bear with a sore scalp. I don't think he r . . . really cares much for parties and such. Being in America has ch . . . changed his taste about many things. Did you know he was in a p . . . p . . . paddy, Trotter?'

'No.'

'Well, something or some . . . somebody has upset him. I asked him if he was c . . . c . . . coming back to dinner and he said no, he was going into New . . . New . . . Newcastle.' He bent further towards her and grinned now as he said, 'Likely had w . . . w . . . words with the Lady Alicia, eh?'

She swallowed deeply before she answered, 'Yes, likely.'

'Well, bye, Tr . . . Tr . . . Trotter. Have a nice w . . . w . . . walk.'

As he urged his horse on she turned away and went into the main road. John was in love. His world looked rosy.

But his brother wasn't the only one who couldn't bear the house today; she had been longing from early morning to get out of it, and now the nearer she came to the cottage the more she wished with all her heart that she was living in it again, just her and the child.

When she reached it the first thing she did was to open all the windows. Unless the fire was kept on the musty smell from the old books permeated the house. After taking off her light dust-coat and hat she sat on the couch near the empty fireplace and looked about her. There was nothing to stop her coming back here; she was independent, she didn't need to work. But what excuse could she give to him for leaving the house? Did she need to give him any excuse? Couldn't she just say she wished to return to the cottage? Then what would happen? She couldn't give herself an answer to this, but in her mind's eye she could see him stalking round the room yelling; she could see his face hovering above hers, his eyes fierce with a light that created an inward shaking in her. What was she to do? She must do something, and soon, because if she didn't it would be too late, and then she wouldn't be able to do anything about it. She didn't explain to herself what it was she'd be unable to do anything about, it was something she hadn't as yet had the courage to put into words because once she admitted it that would be the end of her and the beginning of something that couldn't be countenanced.

She rose to her feet. She was thirsty, she could do with a cup of tea. But it wasn't worth lighting the fire for that; the well water would be cool. She went through the room and the scullery and unlocked the back door, and taking the water bucket that was hanging from a hook in the ceiling, she went out to the well.

She took the wooden lid off the top of the well, attached the bucket to the chain, then allowed it to drop slowly down. It had a cool sound as it hit the water.

As she wound it back again and pulled the bucket on to the stone rim of the well she had the odd feeling that there was someone watching her, and, the old fear of the McGraths acting like a spring, she swung round and the bucket toppled back into the well again.

A man was standing by the corner of the cottage. He was staring at her with as much surprise on his face as was on hers. It took more than a moment for her to recognise him; the last time she had seen him he had appeared but a boy, he was eighteen years old and was pressing her to marry him. Almost his last words came back to her, 'I killed me brother for you, Tilly,' he had said. But there was hardly any resemblance in the Steve McGrath of thirteen years ago and this man. Yet it was he, but he seemed twice as tall, twice as broad, and there was no sullen, sad look about his face. It was a good-looking face, even a handsome one; but even if she hadn't been able to recognise him his left forearm held at that odd angle would have been evidence enough of his identity.

It was he who spoke first. 'Why, Tilly, I . . . I never expected to see you here.'

'Steve! Oh, you did give me a fright. The bucket's gone.' She looked down the well; then turned to him, laughing now, and he, coming up to her, smiled into her face before bending over and looking down to where the bucket was bobbing far below on the cool water.

'Have you got another bucket?'

'Yes, but not a special one; this is the one I used to keep for the water.'

'Well, let's see if we can get it up.'

She watched him as he wound down the chain, and when it was at its full stretch he began to manoeuvre it gently until of a sudden he gave it a jerk, then glanced at her, saying, 'Got it!'

When the bucket was once more standing on the stone surround he took it off the hook; then lifting it up, he said, 'I could do with a drink of this myself.'

'Well, it's cheap.' She laughed at him before turning away and walking towards the cottage.

A minute later, after they had both drunk a mugful of the ice-cold water, she said, 'Sit down, won't you, Steve. Oh, I'm still amazed. I can't believe it's you. You know, you have changed.'

He was about to sit himself on the couch when he turned and glanced at her as he said, 'Can't say the same for you, Tilly.'

She blinked and flushed slightly, then said, 'Where've you been all this time, and what are you doing back here now?'

'I . . . I was looking for a cottage and I understood this one was empty.'

'Really? Well, you see' – she spread her hands wide – 'it isn't empty, but it's mine.'

'It's yours, Tilly?'

'Yes. Oh, it's a long story, but you remember Mr Burgess?'

'Oh yes, I remember Mr Burgess.'

'Well, I' – she looked downwards for a moment – 'when I left the house, I came and lived with Mr Burgess for a time and he bequeathed it to me.'

'You're living here then?'

'No, no; I'm housekeeper back at the Manor.' Her words were spaced and it was he who blinked his eyes now and looked away as he said, 'Oh aye. Aye, I see.' Then more brightly, 'But you still own this?'

'Yes.'

'Are you thinking of selling it?'

'No, no; I don't think I'd ever sell it, it's got a sentimental value for me.'

'Would ... would you let it then?'

She stared at him. 'You'd want to take it? But ... but are you working round here? What about your mother?' Even the word brought a tightening of her stomach muscles.

His voice as he answered her was grim. 'Answering your last question, Tilly, I want nothing to do with me mother, or our George. They don't know I'm back and it'll make no difference when they do. I haven't seen them since I left home thirteen years ago. Anyway, I'm now engaged at the Sopwith and Rosier mine as under-manager.'

'Under-manager!' the words came out on a high surprised note and he nodded, a pleased expression on his face. 'Aye. Would you believe it, the pitman an under-manager? It's a long story. I suppose you could say I've been lucky. When I left here I want on the road for a time, then landed up at a Durham pit and I lodged with a Mr Ransome. He was a deputy, and his wife was a canny body, they made me feel at home. Well, it was the only real home life I'd ever experienced and Mr Ransome was very taken up with his job, and he had a ready listener in me, so just listenin' to him I learned more things in a year than I would have done in a lifetime otherwise, I mean about the workings of the pit. Well, he got me so interested that I started to study an' for once I found no opposition to the fact that I could read and write. Well, after a lot of night work, burning the midnight oil ... and candles' – he laughed – 'I got me deputy's ticket. And I thought that was the end, but it was only the beginning. I went on from there, and last year I passed for under-manager and when I heard they were wantin' one here I applied, and with a little push from Mr Ransome and Mr Burrows, the manager, I was accepted. At first I was hesitant about coming so near the village an' me mother again, but it was the only post going. And you've got to be an under-manager afore you can become a manager. So there you have it, Tilly.'

'Oh, Steve, I'm so glad for you. And nobody deserves success more than you do.' She now hesitated before asking a very touchy question and when it did come out she tried to make it sound ordinary, conversational. 'Are you married, Steve?'

He looked straight at her for a second before he said quietly, 'No, Tilly, I'm not married.'

'Oh.' She lowered her gaze from his. 'You know I have a son now, Steve?'

'Aye' – he nodded at her – 'I heard you had, Tilly. I hope he's in good fettle, I mean I hope he's fully recovered. I also heard what happened to him because of me mother, and how you stopped the case and her going along the line.'

She ignored the last and said, 'Yes, he's fully recovered, well, at least' – she shook her head in small movements before she said – 'I've still got to take him to the doctor's every month. I think it's in case his eyes become affected.'

'Eeh!' He now got to his feet and walked towards the table, his back towards her as he said, 'The things our family have done to you, it's unbelievable.' Then turning abruptly towards her again, he asked pointedly now, 'What made you go back there, I mean after' – there was an embarrassed silence before he ended – 'after you left?'

She returned his questioning look as she said, 'It happened the day he was struck. It was fortunate that Mr Matthew was in town and . . . and he saw us to a doctor; then I think the shock had been a little too much for me and I collapsed, and it was natural I suppose that he took me back to the Manor, and just as natural that I should take up my old post again.'

'Oh.' His chin jerked upwards on the word. 'He's a funny fellow, isn't he?'

'Who?'

'Mr Matthew, quite a lad. Perhaps that's the wrong word. I don't mean with the women, though I don't know anything about him in that line, but he's not bothered about getting himself mucked up, he'll crawl with you side by side and talk to you man to man. Then when he's above ground he's like a different being, closes up like a clam, as if you might take advantage like.'

'You've worked with him?'

'I've been down two or three times along of Mr Rowland when he was showing me the layout. They say he's got a temper like a fiend, an' I can well imagine it. I wouldn't like to cross him.' He smiled wryly now.

'Well, by the size you've grow into, Steve, I think you'd be able to hold your own.' She smiled and he lowered his head as he said, 'Aye, all the years I lived around here I seemed to be stunted in all ways, but once I got away I sprouted. I think Mrs Ransome's good food and care helped more than a bit. But well now, about this place.' He now moved his hand widely, taking in the room. 'Will you let it to me, Tilly?'

She rose from the settle, considered a moment, then said, 'I don't see why not, Steve. It'll save me having to send someone along every week to keep it aired. Have . . . have you any furniture?'

'No, not a stick.'

'Would you like to take it as it is?'

'Oh, that would be grand, Tilly, grand.'

'There'd be one stipulation. The loft bedroom upstairs is half full of books, I'd want them left as they are. They are Mr Burgess's and he valued them greatly, and I do too.'

'Nothing'll be touched, Tilly. It's fine and comfortable looking as it is. You have my word for it, nothing'll be touched, except I might be glad to read some of them books.'   ·

'You'll be very welcome to do that, and I'm sure he'll be pleased to know that they are being put to use again.'

'Then that's settled. How much will you want a week?'

'Oh, I don't know.' She shook her head. 'I really don't want anything. Let's say rent free for old time's sake.'

'Ah no, Tilly. No, no. If it's a business deal it's a business deal. What about three shillings a week, how's that?'

'Oh, if that'll suit you it'll suit me.'

'Well, we'll shake on it.' He held out his hand, and she hesitated a moment before she put hers into it. His grip was firm and warm.

She had to withdraw her fingers from his and she turned from him, saying, 'I'll leave the key with you then, Steve; I've got to go now.'

'Aye. Aye.' He followed her to the door, where on a laugh he said, 'By, life's funny. When I came off that road I never thought that within the next hour I'd have a home of me own, your home. It makes me glad to be back, Tilly.'

Outside the door she turned to him and out of politeness she said, 'It's nice to see you back, Steve. Good-bye now.'

'Good-bye, Tilly. We'll be knocking into each other I've no doubt.'

She looked over her shoulder at him as she answered, 'Yes, yes, of course, Steve.'

She was well out of sight of the cottage when she stopped. Nice to see him back. Was it? No! No! The Steve of thirteen years ago had altered physically, but the Steve underneath she could see through the light in his eyes was still the same Steve, and because he hadn't married she knew he had brought back with him all the old complications.

Yet need they be complications? He could offer her a way out. She liked him, you couldn't help but like him, and he'd always been so kind to her; and he would continue to be kind to her, no matter what happened. Yes, here was a way out, a loophole, an escape from that fear that must soon take shape and spring upon her; it was in the atmosphere; it pervaded the air. Up till last night she had imagined she could ward it off, fight it with a manner of aloofness, call up propriety to her aid, but after hearing the sound of that blow in her defence when she was called a whore, she knew that neither aloofness nor propriety would be strong enough to withstand the onslaught of the fear when it did take shape and gave voice.

Perhaps God had sent Steve at this opportune time to save her.

෨෧ 4 ෨෧

'What's this I hear, Trotter?'

'What do you hear?' She had just descended the front steps to the drive and at the sight of her he had dismounted from his horse, slapping it on the rump as he did so and sending it towards the yard.

'That you have let your cottage.'

'That's right.'

'I hope you know what you've done.'

'Yes, I think I do.'

'He's a McGrath.'

'I know that too, but he's a good McGrath, the only good McGrath. He's been a friend of mine since childhood.'

'Really! Suppose his parents start visiting him?'

'For my part they're welcome to, as I shan't be there. But I doubt if he'll welcome any visit from them seeing that he cut adrift some years ago.'

'You know he's to be my under-manager?'

'Yes, he told me so, and I think he'll be a very good one.'

'That remains to be seen.' He now struck the top of his leather boot with his crop as he said, 'What if you at one time should wish to return to the cottage?'

'I can't see that offering any problem, I could give him notice.'

They stared at each other like two combatants waiting for the other to thrust and he made the final move when he said, 'By what I recollect from one and another you may not need to give him notice.'

She felt herself rearing inside but she warned herself to keep calm, and when she spoke her words came without a tremor as she said, 'That could be quite possible, and if it should happen it could realise his long-felt wish.'

She did not step back from him but her shoulders receded and her chin drew into her neck pulling her head slightly to the side for a moment as he again struck his leather gaiter with his whip. Then after staring at her, he passed her and went up the steps towards the door. Strangely, as one would have expected from the look on his face, he did not run up them, or even hurry, but he took each step slowly and firmly, and he had passed through the doors and into the hall before she herself felt able to move; then she went on towards the lower garden and the greenhouses, there to see what fruit was available for dessert.

Twenty minutes later when she returned to the house by the kitchen Biddy met her at the door, saying, 'There's hell going on in the library. That Mr Rosier's there, and it's who can shout the loudest. You can hear them all over the house. Peg says it's about Master Matthew hitting that Miss Bennett. I can't believe that, can you? He's got a temper I know, but he's a gentleman at bottom an' he's gone on her, at least he was. There was all the signs of it, wasn't there? Out gallopin' the countryside together!'

Tilly put the skip of fruit on the table and she surprised Biddy by making no comment at all but instead hurried up the kitchen, along the passage and into the hall. But after closing the door she went no further. She stood with her back pressed to it as she watched the library door burst open and Mr Rosier come stalking out, crying as he did so, 'If it wasn't that we are linked in business I'd have you up. Begod! I would. And her father might yet, so don't think you're out of the wood. There's such a thing as defamation of character.'

'Go to hell! And take Bennett with you, and his bastards. They could fill it up. Tell him so from me.'

Tilly watched Mr Rosier turn back towards the door and, his voice lower now but his words deep and telling, brought the particular fear that she kept buried in the dungeon of her mind tearing up through her being, bringing her hands to cover her ears but unable to shut out his voice as he said, 'You talk of a man's bastards, you of all people! Thou shalt not covet thy neighbour's wife or . . . thy father's whore. Alicia wasn't blind.'

Although she wasn't aware of pressing her back against the green-baized door and so opening it, she was vitally aware of Matthew standing like a stone image and as speechless.

When she managed to get round the door and into the passage, there was Biddy standing, and that she had heard every word was evident, because her face at this moment was so stretched all the furrows and wrinkles in her skin were smoothed out.

When Tilly gasped and put her hand to her throat Biddy made no move towards her; not until Tilly closed her eyes and drooped her head forward did her hand come on to her shoulder. But she said nothing to her, just turned, went into the kitchen and, looking towards where Betty Leyburn was chopping up vegetables at the long table, said to her, 'Go and see if Peg wants any help upstairs.'

'Me, Mrs Drew?'

'Aye, who else? There's nobody here but you, is there? Go on; get yourself away. Go out the back and up the side stairs.'

When the girl was gone, Biddy pulled Tilly from the door against which she was pressed and led her down the kitchen, and having sat her down in a chair she dragged the end of the form from under the table and seated herself before saying, 'Aw, lass, is this true?'

'Oh, Biddy.' Tilly's head drooped further. 'I don't know. I don't know.'

'Aw, you're bound to know, if it's got outside an' roundabout, you're bound to know.'

Tilly's head now jerked upwards and she said stiffly, 'He's never said a word to me along those lines, not one word.'

'Yet you know he wants you?'

Her head went down again, but she remained quiet, and Biddy let out a deep-drawn sigh as she said, 'God above! what a state of affairs. How long have you known?'

'I . . . I don't really know. Truthfully I don't really know.'

'What brought it all out, I mean why did the Rosier man come this morning?'

Tilly, turning her head, now muttered, 'Because Matthew did strike Miss Bennett. It was after I left you. I heard them on the other side of the walk and I hid amongst the trees. Apparently she had wanted to go up into the nursery and he wouldn't take her, and . . . and so she taunted him and he struck her. They were both drunk.'

'Well, the blow must have sobered her up, lass, an' she's put two and two together. Now where do you go from here?'

'Don't ask me, Biddy. But if I hadn't let the cottage to Steve, I'd go there this very day.'

'Well, as far as I can see that wouldn't make much difference, you'd be more open to him there than you are here. Tell me something, how do you feel about him?'

'Again I say I . . . I don't know, Biddy, and that's the truth. I wish I did know.'

'Father, then son. 'Tisn't right, lass. 'Tisn't right.'

'I know that, Biddy, I know that, nobody better.'

'And the child his half-brother. It's a complication, lass. If ever there was one it's a complication. There's only one thing to be thankful for now, as far as I can see, an' that is that you didn't marry the father, for from the little I've seen of this one's character if he does a thing he does it, he wants to go the whole hog. I can't see him havin' you on the side and. . . .'

'Oh Biddy! Biddy!' Tilly ground the words out as she got to her feet. 'Don't suggest such things.'

'Don't suggest such things, you say? Well, it looks to me that the time's almost past for sayin' such things when the stage is set for action.'

'Oh . . . dear . . . God!' Tilly brought the words out on a long shuddering breath, and Biddy repeated them, saying, 'Aye, oh dear God!' Then she asked, 'Did he see you out there? Did he know you heard?'

'No; the last he saw of me was I was going into the garden. Yet' – she moved her head with a jerk 'that was some time ago.'

'Well, get into the garden again because it's my bet he'll come rampaging through here. He knows we've all got ears like cuddys' lugs, and as long as he thinks that you haven't got the gist of what's in his mind you've got time to pull yourself together and by! lass, you'll need to pull yourself together.'

As if she was a child again obeying an order, Tilly went from the kitchen, across the yard, under the arch and into the garden, and she came to a stop by the high stone wall, just where she had stood all those years ago when Steve had said to her 'Will you marry me, Tilly?'

Steve. There was an escape route, and the sooner she took it the better.

When she returned some time later to the house she did not see Matthew nor, as Biddy had prophesied, had he come rampaging through the house looking for her, but he had left the yard, apparently bent on going to the mine. What Biddy said to her straightaway was, 'Young Betty brought the bairn down, he was screaming his head off, he had bumped into something. . . . Now, now, it's all right, he hasn't cut himself or anything, just a little bump on the head. I put some butter on it. You're takin' him in the morrow, aren't you? Well, I'd ask them to have a good look at his eyes. That's not the first time in the last few days he's bumped into something. Now, now, don't go off like a divil in a gale of wind.'

But Tilly was running across the hall and up the stairs. When she reached the nursery floor it was to see Betty bouncing the child on her knee, and the child laughing. Grabbing him up into her arms, she looked at the small bump in the middle of his forehead a little above the scar, and Betty said, 'He went into the leg of the table, Miss Tilly. It wasn't my fault.'

'It's all right. It's all right. Don't worry.' She glanced at the girl. 'Bring me his grey coat and bonnet, we're going out for a walk. . . .'

Half an hour later, carrying the child, she turned off the coach road on to the lane leading to the cottage. Coming upon a fallen tree, she sat down on the trunk and asked herself if she knew what she was doing. And whether it was fair to Steve. She could give him only affection, a respectful affection, for he would never be able to touch the burning want in her. It appeared that only a Sopwith could allay that feeling in her. Oh dear, dear God! She stood up, moved the child from one arm to another, then went on, and it wasn't until she came in sight of the cottage that she said to herself in Biddy's colloquial way, 'You must be up the pole. It's three o'clock in the afternoon, under-manager or not he's a workman, he'll be at the pit.'

But there were shifts, and managers and under-managers rarely worked in shifts. As she expected, the door was locked. She put the child down on the grass to the side of the path, then looked through the window. The room was tidy. She could see that the fire had been banked down, and right opposite to her in the middle of the table was a jar full of wild flowers. It was the sight of these that made her straighten up, turn her back to the window and, resting her buttocks against the window-sill, bow her head down. There was something nice, something good in Steve. It wasn't fair to make a fool of him. Nor could she now ask him to leave the cottage. What was she to do?

The child had turned on to his hands and knees and was crawling over the grass; then when he was almost opposite to her he lumbered to his feet and, swaying, he held out his arms to her, saying, 'Mama, Mama.'

Swiftly she gathered him up and pressed him tightly to her, and as swiftly she left the cottage, went back down the lane and on to the coach road again, there to see not a hundred yards from her Matthew and John.

It was John who turned and cried, 'Why, Tr ... Tr ... Trotter!' Then they both reined their horses until she came abreast of them, and after a moment they dismounted and it was John who said, 'Wh ... Wh ... What are you doing out here?'

'I've been to the cottage.'

'Oh, I ... I thought you had l ... l ... let it to the ... the under-manager?'

'Yes, I have, but he's an old friend of mine, I just wanted to see how he was faring.'

She was walking by John's side. Matthew, leading his horse, was walking between the two animals and because of their bobbing heads and the fact that he didn't turn and look at her she couldn't see the expression on his face as he said, 'Very good fellow, McGrath. I think he'll turn out to be valuable. As you remarked the other day, the only good one of that particular bunch.'

She stared past John and over the horse's back; her eyes were wide, her mouth slightly open. If he had said to her, 'You are to go ahead and marry this man,' he couldn't have made it any plainer. It was evident in this moment that he wanted to be out of this situation as much as she did. Well now, at last she knew where she stood.

It was a full minute later when she said to John, 'Do please mount.'

'N ... no, Trotter; we ... we can't leave you w ... w ... walking along with that heavy b ... bundle.' He poked the child in the chest gently with his fingers. 'It ... tell you wh ... what I'll do, I'll ... I'll ride him home. He'll ... he'll like that, f ... f ... first ride on a horse.'

'No! No!' She stepped to the side, but he pulled the horse to a standstill and mounted, then held out his arms, saying, 'All right, Trotter, I w ... w ... won't drop him.'

Matthew, too, had stopped. He was looking across at her now and she couldn't fathom the expression on his face, in fact it seemed utterly expressionless, just blank. But when John laughingly looked down on her, saying, 'W . . . w . . . would you f . . . feel he was safer w . . . w . . . with Matthew?' she immediately handed her son up to him and he, seating the child on the front of the saddle, cradled him firmly with one arm, while jerking the reins with the other, and he moved forward leaving an empty space between herself and Matthew.

When she turned to follow John, Matthew did not mount his horse but led it forward and walked by her side; and they never uttered one word for the remainder of the journey, nor did he look at her when, having reached the house steps, they parted, he going on towards the stables and she reaching up to take the child from John.

It was, she felt, the end of something that had not yet begun.

⟡ 5 ⟡

She had other things on her mind when she returned from Shields after seeing the doctor the following day, for she had been given a letter to take to a Dr Davidson at the Newcastle Infirmary in four days' time. Apparently Doctor Simpson was not entirely satisfied about the child's sight. He had assured her there was really nothing to worry about but that this particular Dr Davidson had had a great deal of experience with regard to eyesight and that perhaps all the child would need in the future would be spectacles.

There was a feeling of unrest in the house, not, as Biddy said, that you could put the blame down to his nibs rampaging, but quite the reverse, for during the last few days he hadn't appeared as his natural self at all; in fact the house had hardly seen him. If he wasn't at the mine he was away in the city, where he had been from early morning yesterday until late last night. And she didn't voice what she was thinking: What do men want to spend all day in Newcastle for? for she would have answered herself by saying, 'Well, what do young bucks like him go to the city for in any case, their kind of business doesn't need a board room.'

But this morning he hadn't gone to the mine, and he hadn't gone to Newcastle, he had come down to breakfast and was now closeted with John in the morning-room, and at this moment John was gazing at him sadly as he was saying, 'B . . . B . . . But why do you w . . . want to go back so s . . . s . . . soon? Anyway, Matthew I don't think I'm ca . . . ca . . . capable of man . . . managing the mine on my own.'

'You won't have to manage on your own, you'll have two good men, Rowland and the new one, McGrath; he . . . he shows to be very promising.'

'But . . . but . . . but what has happened b . . . b . . . between you and Mr Ro . . .

Ro ... Rosier that he w ... w ... wants to sell out now? He was so k ... keen, it was he who p ... p ... put you on to opening it. There must be a se ... se ... serious reason.'

'There is.'

'Well, I f ... f ... feel I'm enti ... enti ... entitled to know what it is.'

'I struck Alicia on the night of your engagement party.'

'Y ... Y ... *You what!*'

'You heard me, John, I struck Alicia, if you can call slapping her face striking her. She was bent on finding out all about Trotter, and when I wouldn't go along with her she insulted her. My only excuse is that I was drunk, and so was she. The blow must have sobered her up.'

'G ... G ... God! that's why she t ... t ... turned down Pl ... Pl ... Platt's Walk when she saw me c ... c ... coming the other day. I w ... w ... waved to her but she ... she galloped off. Oh my G ... God! Matthew, that was an awful thing t ... t ... to do. I thought you liked her ... well m ... m ... more than liked her.'

'I liked her but I didn't more than like her, John, and I never had any intention of letting the liking grow; nor did I give her to understand this. That, I fear, is what piqued her.'

'Aw' – John wagged his head from side to side – 'and I imagined it was a l ... l ... lovely party. So did Anna.'

'It was a lovely party. That incident was private. ...'

'And it's having it ... it ... its repercussions' – John was nodding his head grimly at Matthew now – 'and driving you off b ... b ... back to America.'

'I intended to go in any case.'

'But not so s ... s ... soon. Oh, w ... w ... wait a little longer, say three m ... months until I g ... g ... get more used to it.'

'You'll never be more used to the mine, John, until you have to take full responsibility. The thing to do is to get married and bring Anna here. You could both be very happy here.'

'I ... I have n ... n ... no doubt of that, Matthew, b ... b ... but I'd be happier if I knew that you were ... were ... were about, at least at the m ... mine. You can manage m ... m ... men, you ... you've got a w ... w ... way with you that ... that I'll never acquire.'

Matthew smiled weakly as he said, 'I shout more, but men can see through that. If they respect you they'll work for you, and you're highly respected.'

'Oh! Matthew.' John now walked towards his brother and, putting his hands on his shoulders, he looked into his face and like a young boy, that he really was at heart, he pleaded, 'M ... M ... Must you go? Must you go, Matthew?'

'I must, John. Yes, I must.'

'The f ... f ... fourth of July, it's like tomorrow, just over f ... f ... four weeks. There's something I don't quite understand, I wouldn't have thought that thi ... thi ... this business with Ro ... Rosier would have m ... m ... made you turn tail, more like stand up and f ... f ... fight him when he's b ... backing out.'

'Don't try, John. As for him backing out, it isn't like that. If it meant a fight and I couldn't afford to buy him out and wanted him to stick to his contract then I likely would have stayed, but as it is I want him out and I can afford to pay the damned exorbitant percentage he's asking. So now' – he put out his hand and ruffled John's straight hair – 'what we've got to do, boyo, is to get you to that mine every day, and not just on the top but down below. Your training is going to be intensive during the next few weeks.'

'Have ... have you t ... t ... told Trotter?'

Matthew turned away now and went towards the mantelpiece and lifting up a long-stemmed wooden pipe, he bent down and knocked out the dottle into the empty grate before he said briefly, 'No.'

'She's g ... g ... going to be very upset.'

'I don't think so.'

'Oh, she w ... will be.'

Matthew now turned and smiled wryly at his brother as he said, 'It would be nice to think so, but I think she will be as relieved as many others when I depart from these shores.'

'You have a very p ... p ... poor opinion of yourself, Matthew. You. ...'

'On the contrary' – Matthew's voice took on its customary arrogant tone – 'I've a very high opinion of myself, let me tell you, John; in fact, inside I don't think there's anyone to come up to me. Of course, outside' – he pulled a wry face now – 'things are a little different. Men don't see me with my eyes ... nor do women. I'll have to do something about the latter.'

'Oh! Matthew.' John was laughing now but sadly as he said, 'You're a c ... c ... case, L ... L ... Luke always s ... said there was only one of you and it would have been dis ... disastrous had there been twins and. ...' Of a sudden John stopped and, his head bowed, he added softly, 'Oh, M ... Matthew, I'm g ... g ... going to m ... miss you. You don't know how m ... m ... much I love you.'

Swiftly now Matthew went to his brother and put his arms about him, and they clung together for a moment before Matthew, thrusting him away, turned and went hastily from the room.

⤜ 6 ⤛

It was five o'clock in the afternoon. They had both returned from the mine dirty and almost wet through for their capes hadn't succeeded in keeping out the heavy rain. It had rained for the past two days, the heat of the earlier June days being but a faint memory now; the roads were like bogs, the sky low, promising more rain to come.

They dismounted and after handing their horses to Fred Leyburn John said, 'I ... w ... want a bath, hot, steaming. I'll t ... t ... toss you for which one gets prepared first.'

At the top of the steps, Matthew turned and, thrusting his hand into his breeches' pocket, pulled out a coin, saying, 'Tails,' and they were entering the hall as he flicked the coin; then lifting the palm of his hand up quickly from the back of his other hand, he said, 'You win.'

'Good. W . . . W . . . Why is it you don't mind being wet, Matthew?'

'I suppose it was because I was dry, so dry during those three years over there when at times I would have given half my life to stand in the rain.'

Peg was in the hall to meet them. She took their sodden cloaks and hats from them, and as John dashed towards the stairs, crying, 'Hot . . . w . . . water, Peg. Hot w . . . water,' she said, ''Tis all ready, sir, 'tis all ready. It'll be up in your room in a minute.'

It was something in her voice that made Matthew turn and look her full in the face. It was evident that she had been crying; her eyes were red, her lashes still wet. His voice holding a hearty tone, he said, 'Ho! ho! what's this, isn't there enough water outside?'

She blinked now and, her head drooping further, the tears ran down her cheeks which made him ask, his tone more sympathetic now, 'What is it, girl? What's happened? Are you in trouble? Your mother?'

'Not me, sir, nor mam, 'tis the child.'

'What! What's happened to the child?'

'Tilly . . . Miss Tilly, she took him to Newcastle to see the eye man. He says the child is to go blind.'

He screwed up his face, his eyes narrowing and his lips moving silently on the word blind.

'Miss Tilly's in a state, she's. . . .'

He did not wait to hear what more she had to say but, taking the stairs two at a time, he ran across the gallery, along the corridor and up to the nursery floor where he thrust open the schoolroom door, only to find the room empty. He remained standing now and looking from one door to the other; he had not been up on this floor since she had taken possession of it. His eyes became focused on the second door to the left of him. That had been her room when she first came here.

Quickly he walked towards it, but gently now he turned the handle and pushed it open. She was lying on the bed, her back to him, her arm round the child. She did not move, likely thinking it was one of the Drews, but when he placed his hand on her shoulder she swung round as if she had been stung, and lay staring up at him.

There was no sign of tears on her face, there was no colour in it; it was even no longer fleshly pale, it was more the colour of a piece of bleached lint. Her eyes were dark pools of pain, her mouth was slightly open, her lips trembling. He took his hand from her and, bending over her, he lifted the child up and, taking it to the window, looked into its eyes.

The child smiled at him and grabbed at his face.

'What did he say?' He was still looking at the child as he asked the question, but when she didn't answer he turned his head towards her.

She was sitting on the edge of the bed now, her body bent forward, and, her voice low, she answered, 'He said he didn't think there was much could be done. The . . . the sight of the left eye is already gone. Spectacles may help for a short time with the other but he doesn't. . . .' Her voice choked and when she turned her body round and buried her face in the pillow he quickly went to the bed and laid the child down again; then coming round the foot of it he dropped on to his knees by her side and, putting his arm around her shoulder, he brought her towards him, looking into her face as he said, 'Don't . . . don't cry like that.'

When her head drooped further and the tears flowed down her cheeks he implored, 'Please, please, Trotter, don't, it will be the undoing of me. Don't.'

When there erupted from her throat a strangled cry, he closed his own eyes tightly and brought his teeth clamping down on his lower lip and what he said now was, 'You should have let me prosecute that woman.'

Her breath was choking her, the tears seemed to be oozing out of every pore in her body. If the restriction in her throat didn't ease she would die. Oh, if she could only die this minute and take the child with her.

'Tilly! Tilly! Oh my God! Tilly.' His arms were about her. He was sitting on the side of the bed now beside her. It was even more difficult to get her breath because her head was pressed tight into his neck, and he was talking, talking, talking. Now his hands were in her hair, lifting her face up towards him. She couldn't see him, she could only hear him, hear him repeating her name, 'Oh Tilly! Tilly!' His father had said it like that, 'Oh Tilly! Tilly!' She must get away, push him off, this was wrong, she was going to marry Steve. Steve would be her salvation. But she didn't want salvation; she wanted two things at this moment, she wanted her child to be able to see and she wanted this man's arms around her. She wanted to feel his lips forever on her face as they were now. But it was wrong, wrong, in all ways it was wrong. And she was so much older than he but she looked so much younger; he wasn't a young man, he had never been a young man. He was strong, determined; she would be safe with him, wherever she went she would be safe with him. And he was still talking, talking, talking.

Now he was wiping her eyes and her face with his handkerchief and whispering all the while, 'Oh, my love! My love! You know, don't you, you've always known? When I hated you I loved you; when I knew you had given Father a child I think I would have murdered you if I had been near you. Now I love the child' – he glanced towards it – 'but I don't love you as I love the child. What feeling I have for you is past love, Tilly, it's like a rage, a mad consuming rage; it has grown with the years, it's been like a malignant disease. I've feared at times I would die of it, and if I don't have you, Tilly, I will die of it in the end. But I know that before I do I'll make so many people miserable. That's me; if I'm not happy I make other people unhappy too, I hate suffering alone. I have the power to make people miserable; I can be one big bloody swine. I know myself, Tilly. There is something in me that is mean. I knew this when I was a boy. You knew it too, didn't you? Yet, once you put the weight of your love on the scales I could become a saint, at least a lovable, generous individual. Oh my dearest, dearest, Tilly.'

His lips were moving over hers gently, gently backward and forward. Then he was talking again, talking, talking. 'The effect you have on a man, the effect you've always had on me. I even loved my nightmares because you gave them to me, Trotter. Trotter. From the first moment you stepped on to this floor you had me, all of me, the good, the bad, the rotten. Oh Tilly! my Tilly! I adore you. If God was a woman then you would be my God, you are my God . . . my God, the only God I want. Oh my dearest, don't push me away, please.'

'Matthew.' His name came out as if it were weighed down with lead; then again, 'Matthew, we mustn't, we can't.'

'We can and we will. Do you hear me, Tilly Trotter?' He was holding her face between his hands now. 'We can and we will. We must come together; there will be no meaning in my life if we don't. You were in it from the beginning. I wasn't born until I was ten and that was the moment I saw you bending over me in the bed across the landing there.' He pointed his arm backwards. 'And from that moment until now I've never known any release from you. When you went to Father I went to hell.'

'But . . . but it doesn't seem right, clean. . . . I can't. . . .'

'Don't say that!' His voice was harsh now. 'There is nothing unclean about it. It was only by chance you went to Father and more out of pity and compassion I guess than anything else, and of course his need for you, for what man being near you wouldn't want you. I don't blame Father now, I don't blame you, but you were mine before you were Father's. Tell me, look me straight in the face. Come on, lift your lids, Tilly Trotter, and look into my eyes and tell me that you don't love me.'

She lifted her lids and she looked into his eyes and what she said was, 'Oh Matthew! Matthew!' and then she was in his arms once more; and now the fear in her was gone and in its place was a feeling akin to anguish, and when she returned his kiss with a fierceness that his father had never evoked in her she knew that at this age of thirty-two she was for the first time really experiencing young love, not the kind of love she'd had for Simon Bentwood, nor that tender love she'd had for Mark Sopwith, but the love that should come to every woman in her youth. And she was in her youth again and the six years between them was as nothing.

When their lips parted and they looked at each other she knew she'd remember the expression on his face until the day she died. It was such that would be seen on the look of a man given freedom after years of confinement. There was such a light of love in his eyes that she bowed her head against it.

'We'll be married before we sail for America.'

'What!' Her head jerked up.

'I'm due to sail on the fourth of next month.'

'But . . . but, Matthew. . . .'

'No buts. No buts.' He put two fingers on her lips.

She moved slightly away from him. 'But yes, I must; there is your position, the county.'

'Damn and blast the county!'

'Oh Matthew!' She shook her head slowly. 'You can damn and blast the county as much as you like but . . . but you would never live this down.'

When she turned her head away he cried at her, 'Oh no! no! not another situation like with Father, not for me and you, oh no! no! You marry me, Tilly. I want you for mine, I want to own you, yes, own you. You are to be mine legally.

Now get that into your head, you are to be mine, to belong to me. And what do I care for the county? Blast the county to hell and all in it! Even if we were staying here, but we're not, we're going to America where nobody will know anything about us or him.' He thumbed towards the child. 'I have married a widow with a young child. That's all that need be known. Anyway, I wonder why you put so much stock on the damn county, what do you care for the county? Look' – he got hold of her hands – 'I know you are thinking only of me, as you thought of Father when you refused to marry him, but I'm not having you other than as a wife, and I mean to have you as a wife if I've got to drag you to the church, or even to a registry office, anywhere we can be signed and sealed before sailing. *Now, is that clear. . . . Trotter?'*

She smiled wanly at him now as she said, 'Yes, Master Matthew.'

'Oh my dear, dear Tilly.' Gently now he drew her towards him as he said, 'You know I've never liked the name Trotter or even Tilly; I think from the day we are married I shall call you Matilda. It has a good homespun sound, Matilda. It will deny that you are beautiful and alluring, and no other man will be very interested in anyone called Matilda Sopwith.'

Her smile was wider now as she said, 'Then the day you call me Matilda I shall call you Matt.'

'Good! Good! I like that. . . . Oh my love. Oh my love.'

They were enfolded again tightly, her face lost in his, when the door burst open and Katie almost left the ground in amazed surprise which brought from her the high exclamation of 'Oh my God!'

As she made to dash from the room Matthew sprang from the bed and pulled her forcedly back, then pushed her towards Tilly, saying, 'You are the first to know, Katie Drew, that your friend has promised to become my wife.'

'Wh. . . . What!'

Tilly had to bow her head against the look of utter incredulity on Katie's face and her stammer that sounded so much like John's.

'Yes, wh . . . what! And now, Katie Drew, you may go downstairs and tell your dear mama the news, and anyone else you come across. You may also tell them that on the fourth of July you are sailing with your master and mistress to America as nursemaid to the young William there.' Again he thumbed towards the child, and when Katie's mouth opened again to say, 'What!' he checked her with a finger wagging in her face, saying, 'And get out of the habit of that syllabic silly What! and replace it with pardon. Now go.'

Katie backed from him, she backed from them both until she reached the open door, and there all she could say after looking from one to the other was, 'Eeh!'

When the door had closed on her they gazed at each other and Tilly asked, quietly now, 'You meant that, you weren't joking, you'll take her with us?'

'Yes, of course. You'll want someone to help look after the child, and I'll want my wife to myself now and then.' Again he was cupping her face and she turned and looked down towards the boy, who was lying quite peaceably sucking his thumb, and the joy going from her face, she muttered, 'Blind. How will he bear it?'

His voice was soft, his tone compassionate as he said, 'He'll become used to it and he'll always have us. But' – he squeezed her face tightly now – 'these eye men can work miracles today, they put lenses in spectacles that can enlarge a spot as if the wearer were looking through a telescope. Look, I'll go tomorrow and see him. We'll have the best advice in the country. Don't worry; as long as he has partial sight of one eye he'll be all right.' And now he paused and staring into her misted eyes, he said, 'Do you love me, Tilly? Really love me? I feel you do but I want to hear you say it aloud. I've made you say it in the night; I've made you say, "Matthew, Matthew, I love you." And at those times when we've been going at each other's throats, part of me has been crying, "Say it, Tilly. Oh, say you love me." And now I want to hear it from your lips.'

It was she who put her hands out now and, covering his rough bristled coal-dust and rain-smeared face, said gently, 'I love you, Matthew Sopwith. I love you. I don't know when it began, I only know I feel for you as I've felt for no other, not even your father.'

'Tilly! Tilly!' There was a break in his voice and he drew her to her feet, and now as he held her close her slim body seemed to sink into his and she knew that for good or ill she'd always want it to remain there.

❦ 7 ❧

Biddy couldn't believe it; Katie couldn't believe it; none of the Drew family could believe it; and least of all could Tilly believe that she was to be married and would be going to America, to that strange wild, new country.

But the villagers said they could believe it for anything that was a sin before God could be attributed to that witch. Some of the more godly even went as far as persuading the parson to go and see her. He came but he was confronted by Matthew, and his exit from the house was much more hurried than his entry. As he later said to his housekeeper, he did not blame the woman so much as the man, because well-born he might have been, but he had certainly not grown into a gentleman.

Did the county believe it? Oh yes, the Tolmans, the Fieldmans, and the Craggs all said they had known about it all along, since he had first come home in fact; they knew that that piece, having lost the father and thereby her place in the house would leave no stone unturned until she could regain it. And what would be the best way to do that? To entangle the son in her snares. It was a disgrace, obscene. Oh yes, gentlemen had married servants before today, they all said, they were well aware of this, but the father and son to share a mistress, well! that was something different. It was just as well they were leaving the district; if not, the place would become too hot for both of them.

And they were leaving that young stammerer in charge of the mine. Well! they knew what would happen to that now it was deprived of Mr Rosier's expert advice and control. Mr Rosier had shown himself to be a man of high morals; immediately he had heard about this scandalous affair he had cut adrift from all connection with the Sopwiths. . . . Really! the things that happened.

When the last words were also reiterated in the village, it was Tom Pearson who brought censure upon himself by ending it with, 'They've been unfortunate, they've been found out. If all the things that happened, not only among the county lot, but in this very village were aired the devil would be declared headman.'

Tom Pearson, the parson again confided in his housekeeper, wasn't a good influence in the village; he would have to arrange that the man got very few orders for painting or odd jobs for this might induce him to seek a habitation further afield.

No one knew what Steve McGrath thought or had said about the scandalous affair, but it was known that his mother had visited him at the cottage and when he wouldn't allow her entry she, like her grandson, had thrown a brick through the window.

When lastly it was rumoured that Trotter's child was going blind few, if any, attributed any blame to Mrs McGrath except to say that God had a strange way of dealing out punishment, and who was to blame Him for the instruments He chose.

Although no one mentioned the villagers or any member of the county to Tilly she was well aware of the seething hostility surrounding her and she knew that she would never have survived it if Matthew had decided to stay on here.

They were to be married by special licence on the third of July and were to sail from Liverpool on the evening of the fourth. It had been arranged that Katie, accompanied by Arthur, would take the child and travel to Liverpool on the morning of the wedding, there to await Matthew's and Tilly's arrival.

The marriage was to take place in Newcastle attended only by John, Luke and Biddy; and following this, the couple would board the train and so begin their journey.

So there was to be a farewell family party on the Saturday evening. Biddy had suggested that the master, and Mr John and Mr Luke should be present, but Tilly had said no, it was just for those who for years she had considered her family, together with Phyllis and Fred and Sam and Alec and their families, because it was not only a farewell to her but also a farewell to Katie.

That Katie was the envy of her sisters was plain to be seen, but that she herself was also fearful of the journey and of the new life ahead of her was equally evident, for as she said to her mother as she stood by the table laden with the fare they had been cooking for the last two days: 'What if I don't like it, Ma?'

'You can always come home, lass. They'll see to it. You can always come home.'

'Yet I wouldn't want to leave her.'

'Well, what you've got to remember, our Katie, is that she's got a husband and as yet you haven't, so if the place doesn't suit you or you don't suit it, come back to where you belong.'

'I'm all excited inside, Ma.'

'I'm all sad inside, lass.'

For the first time that Katie could remember, her mother enfolded her in her arms and so warming was her mother's embrace that she began to cry and said, 'I don't know whether I want to go or not, Ma.'

Biddy pushed her away, saying, 'You're goin'. Your bags are packed, your ticket's got, and, who knows, you might find a lad out there who'll take a fancy to your face.'

'Oh, our Ma! . . . I'm going to miss you, our Ma.'

'And I'll miss you, lass. And I'll miss her an' all because she's been like one of me own. You know that.'

'Aye, I do. Sometimes I've thought you even think more of her than you do of any of us.'

Biddy didn't answer this; instead, she said, 'I'd be happy to know that she's got you with her because there'll be times when she'll need a friend and comforter.'

'Oh, I can't see that, Ma, not having him.'

'Aye, me girl, it's just because she does have him for, as I see it, he's gona be no easy packet is Master Matthew. Jealous as sin he'll be of her, you mark my words, an', like the devil, he'll hold on to what he's got; and she being who she is, 'cos she's of a proud nature, there'll come times I'm sure when he'll hold the reins too tightly and she won't like the bit in her mouth. Then the skull and hair'll fly.'

'Oh, Ma, you sound doleful.'

'No, no, I'm not, lass' – Biddy shook her head – 'but I've been through life an' I've seen a bit an' it's taught me to read a character, an' as I said, there'll come a time when she may need you.'

'Aye, well, I hope you're wrong there, Ma, in that particular way anyhow. Oh! there's the carriage.' She ran to the kitchen door and craned out her neck. 'It will be Master Luke. I wonder what he thought about it all when he heard. By! I bet he got a gliff.'

The three brothers were seated in the drawing-room. There had been very little talk during the journey from Newcastle and no mention at all of why Luke had been asked to get leave, and so John, aiming to ease what he imagined to be a rather embarrassing situation, said, 'That uniform's s . . . s . . . so smart, L . . . Luke, that I think . . . think I'll join up myself.'

'Good idea; they can do with fellows like you in the cookhouse.'

'Oh you!' John tossed his head.

There followed another short silence; then when they both looked at Matthew where he was standing with his back to the fire, he, looking back at his brothers, said briefly, 'Well! out with it.'

'Out with what?'

'Don't hedge, you know why you're here. Didn't my letter surprise you?'

'No.' Luke pursed his lips, then moved his head from side to side before repeating, 'No; why should I be surprised about something I've known all my life?'

Both John and Matthew stared at him now.

'She turned you crazy the first time you set eyes on her, she did the same to me. She didn't affect John there' – he turned and laughed at his younger brother now – 'he wasn't old enough, but you remember the incident when we came from Grandmama's that time and I said I was going to marry her when I grew up . . . you do remember that, don't you?'

'Yes, I remember it.'

'Well then, you know what happened, you nearly knocked the daylights out of me. She had to come up and separate us.'

Matthew lowered his head and gave a short laugh.

'I used to envy you,' said Luke now, 'because you were bigger than me and therefore, I thought, she would show you that much more affection.'

Matthew smiled across at Luke as he asked, 'Do you envy me now?'

'No, no, I don't, Matthew.' Luke's tone and expression were so solemn that the brothers stared at him as he went on, 'I wouldn't want to love anyone like you do, Matthew. I'm all against self-torture. Your kind of love is. . . .'

'Is what?' The question was flat.

Luke now got to his feet and, pulling his tunic down round his hips, he shook his head slowly, saying, 'You know, I can't find a word to explain it. Don't be mad at me. Come on, don't look like that, but . . . but your feelings have always been so intense, Matthew, where she's concerned, as if she had. . . .'

'Don't say it, Luke. Don't say it.'

'What was I going to say?'

'Bewitched me.'

'Yes, I suppose I was, but there's no harm in that. In a way I wish I could find some woman who would bewitch me. They love me and leave me and I get a bit pipped about it, but I don't suffer any agony. Yes, that's the word.' He pointed to Matthew now as he laughed, 'That's the word to describe your love, agony.'

'Oh, don't be so bloody silly, Luke! The feeling I have for Tilly is anything but agony.'

'Well, I'm glad to hear it at last, I'm glad to hear it.' Luke walked across to Matthew now and, thumping him in the shoulder, said, 'Where is she anyway? And you know something?' He poked his long face towards his brother. 'I'll tell you a secret, I've always wanted to kiss her and now I'm going to do just that; and you stay there, big fellow, you stay there.'

He pushed Matthew hard in the shoulder, almost overbalancing him into the fire; then laughing, he went hurrying down the room, calling, 'Trotter! Where are you, Trotter?'

As Matthew now made to follow Luke, John pulled at his arm, saying quietly, 'L . . . L . . . Let him g . . . go, Matthew. L . . . L . . . Let him go.'

'But why is he acting like this, he's being almost insulting?'

Now it was John who poked his face forward and said, 'D . . . D . . . Don't you know?'

'No. I don't.'

'Well, I'd b . . . b . . . better tell you, big . . . big . . . big brother, he's j . . . jealous.'

'Don't be silly.'

'I'm not. He has l . . . lots of women has L . . . Luke. They all trip . . . trip over themselves f . . . for him; but he's never found one like Tro . . . Trotter . . . he's jealous.'

'Huh!' Matthew's eyes crinkled in laughter now and again he said, 'Huh!' then putting his arm around John's shoulder, he pressed him close, saying, 'You know, besides being the best of our particular bunch, you're also the wisest.'

৩৩ 8 ৩৩

'Matthew George Sopwith, wilt thou have this woman to thy wedded wife, to live together after God's ordinance in the holy estate of Matrimony? Wilt thou love her, comfort her, honour, and keep her, in sickness and in health; and, forsaking all other, keep thee only unto her, as long as ye both shall live?'

'I will.'

'Matilda Trotter, wilt thou have this man to thy wedded husband, to live together after God's ordinance in the holy estate of Matrimony? Wilt thou obey him, and serve him, love, honour, and keep him, in sickness and in health; and forsaking all other, keep thee only unto him, so long as ye both shall live?'

'I will.'

She couldn't believe it was happening, it was so unreal. She was cold, yet she was sweating. Was she really standing here being married to Matthew? Her hand was in his and he was saying:

'I Matthew take thee Matilda to my wedded wife, to have and to hold from this day forward, for better for worse, for richer for poorer, in sickness and in health, to love and to cherish, till death do us part, according to God's holy ordinance; and thereto I plight thee my troth.'

'I Matilda take thee Matthew to my wedded husband, to have and to hold from this day forward, for better for worse, for richer for poorer, in sickness and in health, to love, cherish, and to obey, till death do us part, according to God's holy ordinance; and thereto I give thee my troth.'

'With this ring I thee wed, with my body I thee worship, and with all my worldly goods I thee endow: In the name of the Father, and of the Son, and of the Holy Ghost. Amen.'

Not until later in the vestry did the full impact of the ceremony and realisation of its meaning affect her. The ring was on her finger. She was married, married to Matthew. She was no longer Tilly Trotter, she was Mrs Matilda Sopwith. She felt faint. His lips were on hers, his eyes looking deep into hers. She heard John laugh and Luke say, 'It's my privilege to kiss the bride'; and she wasn't really aware that he kissed her hard on the lips.

John's face was now hovering close to hers. He looked at her for some seconds before placing his lips against her cheek, saying softly and without any stammer, 'Now I've got a sister whom I can love.'

The word sister brought back the scene of a week ago when Jessie Ann had descended on the house merely to tell her brother what she thought of him and to order him not to go through with this thing that was almost sacrilegious in her eyes and, she had added, in those of everyone else.

She hadn't come face to face with Jessie Ann, she had only heard her voice and seen Matthew escorting her almost forcibly to her carriage. Oh, she was glad she was leaving and going to America to a new life. Oh she was. And she was happy, so happy she couldn't believe it. But she wouldn't be able to let that happiness have full rein until she saw the shores of this country receding from view; then, and then only, she knew she would feel free because then no one would know about her except Matthew, her beloved Matthew. And he was her beloved Matthew. She felt no shame now in her love for him. Nor did she feel guilt for the part she had played in his father's life.

And then there was Katie. Katie would be a comfort. She would never feel that she had lost all the Drew family as long as she had Katie. . . . And her child. Well, he would grow up in a new country, free; even if his sight was impaired there would be no one to shout after him 'Witch's spawn!' She was leaving this country without one regret. Well, perhaps just one. She wished she hadn't to carry the memory of the look on Steve McGrath's face. They had met only once after the news of her impending marriage had set the village and the district aflame. She had met him on the main road and they had stopped and stared at each other; and as she looked into his face she had longed for words that would bring him some kind of comfort, for the look in his eyes had been the same as on that day when, a boy, he had asked her to marry him.

There had been no lead up to their brief conversation. 'Do you still want to stay in the cottage, Steve?' she had asked him quietly, and after a moment he had answered, 'Why not? One place is just the same as another.'

As she nodded at him and made to move away he had added, 'In spite of what I feel, Tilly, I still wish you happiness,' and to this she had muttered, 'Thanks Steve, thanks. That's . . . that's kind of you. . . .'

She was outside in the street. Matthew had helped Biddy up into the carriage, and when he turned to her, after a moment's pause he put his arms about her and almost lifted her in. Then Luke entered and John climbed on the box beside Fred Leyburn, and Matthew cried, 'To breakfast!' and seated himself beside Tilly.

His hand gripping hers, he looked across at Luke, asking now, 'How long have we got before the train goes?'

'Oh.' Luke glanced at his watch. 'An hour and a half, ample time.'

Following this there was silence except for the rumbling of the wheels over the cobbles. Nor was there much merriment at the breakfast except that which was supplied by John. His stammer much in evidence again, he kept up an almost one-sided jocular conversation during the meal.

Little over an hour later they were all standing under the awning of the station. The train was in, the engine noisily puffing out steam, their personal luggage was on the rack, and now the actual moment of parting had arrived.

When Biddy and Tilly put their arms about each other there were no words spoken. Their eyes were wet and their throats were full. Then Luke was kissing her again, a soft kiss now, his face straight, his eyes thoughtful, and what he said was, 'Be good to him, Trotter.'

Next came John and what he said was, 'I'll ha ... have a w ... w ... wife shortly, Trotter, b ... b ... but I'll never have a fr ... friend like you.' He touched her cheek gently with his fingers, then turned her round towards where Matthew was waiting; and Matthew, silently now and soberly, lifted her up the high step and into the compartment. Then he was saying good-bye to his brothers.

At one moment he was holding both their hands, then they stood close, their arms about each other's shoulders like triplets, and like triplets about to be severed there was pain on each face.

And lastly, Matthew stood before Biddy and, bending over her, he put his lips to her wrinkled face and what he said to her under his breath was, 'Look after the house and all in it, for who knows, we may be back some day. ...'

They hung out of the window until those on the platform were lost by the curve of the rails and the steam from the engine, and then for the first time they were really alone.

Sitting close now, their fingers linked tightly, they looked at each other; but it was some moments before any words came. Gently withdrawing his hands from hers, he put them up to her head and there slowly pulled out the pins from her hat and laid them on the seat opposite; then putting his fingers into her hair he brought her face close to his and his gaze was soft and his voice tender as he said, 'You're beautiful, Mrs Matilda Sopwith, and you're mine. At last you're mine, all mine for life.'

Mrs Sopwith. Tilly Trotter was no more. She had turned into Matilda Sopwith and she knew that Matilda Sopwith would be loved as Tilly Trotter had never been, and that as Matilda Sopwith she would love as Tilly Trotter had never loved. She put her arms about his neck and all she could find to say was, 'Oh, Matthew! Matthew!'

PART FOUR

⟋ Tilly Trotter Wed ⟍

৩ 1 ৩

As Matthew helped Tilly down the gangway at Galveston she prayed silently
and fervently that she wouldn't be called upon ever in her life again to board
any kind of boat.

The crossing of the Atlantic had been such that during it she had longed to
be back anywhere in England, even in the village, anywhere but on the heaving,
rolling, stomach-erupting sea. That she had got over her bout of seasickness
within the first week hadn't helped for there were the cramped quarters to
contend with, and Katie who was in a bad state for the whole of the following
two weeks of the journey; and then the child. At one time he had been so ill she
thought she was going to lose him.

One thing the journey did teach her was that the heat of love, rising from no
matter what depth of passion, could be cooled by the physical weaknesses of
the body. Constant retching and the efforts of will it took to attend to Katie
and the child caused her to ask herself more than once why she had done this
mad thing. To marry a man six years her junior and follow him across the world
would have been test enough for a young girl with an adventurous spirit, but
she was no longer a young girl, she was thirty-three years old with the responsibility of a handicapped child and an almost equal responsibility for Katie who,
from a tough little woman when on land had, from first setting foot on the ship,
disintegrated into a bundle of nerves, and the ship was then still in dock.

That Matthew experienced no seasickness, in fact seemed to enjoy every minute
of the voyage, did not help in the least; nor did the fact that he did all he could
to alleviate their sufferings; his very heartiness became an irritation.

But now it was all over. They were on dry land, standing amidst smiling faces,
black faces, brown faces, white faces, most of the latter seeming to be bearded.
There was bustle and talk all about her, deep guttural laughter, hand-shaking,
people being met, all except them apparently.

Matthew was looking about him. He turned to her and smiled, saying, 'They'll
be here somewhere. Look; stay there, sit on that trunk.' He pressed her down.
'I'll be back in a minute.'

As she watched him making his way among the throng, she felt a sudden
pride rise in her and with it an onrush of love that the sea seemed to have
washed away. He was a fine, upstanding figure of a man, handsome, and he
looked older than his years, for which she was glad. She turned to Katie who
was sitting on the trunk beside her holding the child in her arms whilst staring
about her in bewilderment, and she said, 'We'll soon be home.' It sounded so
natural to say, 'We'll soon be home.'

When Katie, bringing her white peaked face towards her, said, 'Aye, well, thank God for that,' she laughed out aloud, which brought the eyes of two strange-looking black men upon her. They were carrying big hessian-wrapped bales on their shoulders and they twisted their heads towards her, pausing for a second before going on.

Her hand still over her mouth, she looked at Katie and said, 'You sounded just as if we were back in the kitchen.'

'Aye, well, I've got to say it, Tilly, I wish I was at this minute.'

'Oh, it's going to be all right.'

'You think so?' There was a tinge of fear in the question, and Tilly, her face straight now, said, 'Of course it is.'

Katie moved her head to gaze beyond the child's face towards the end of the quay, then turned it slowly to take in the buildings, some that looked like warehouses, others squat-shaped huts, and what she said was, 'Everything looks odd. An' the faces, some of them would scare the daylights out of you.'

Tilly now leaned towards her and muttered, 'You're in a different country, Katie,' and Katie, nodding her head now, replied tartly, 'There'll be no need to keep tellin' me that, I've got eyes.' Then lowering her glance, she spoke under her breath, saying, 'There's a fellow just to your right starin' at us. He's comin' this way.'

Tilly turned her head sharply and saw coming towards them a tall, gangling young man wearing a wide hat that looked as if it was about to fall off the back of his head, or perhaps it had been pushed there to show off an abundance of red curly hair. He wore an open-necked shirt, tight breeches that disappeared below the knee into high leather boots. His face was long and clean-shaven, his open mouth showed a set of big teeth, from which one only seemed to be missing. This left a gap in the middle of the lower set through which now he seemed to whistle as he scrutinized Tilly. After a moment he walked behind her and looked at the name on the trunk; then he rounded the remaining pile of luggage before stepping in front of her again, saying, 'Doug Scott, ma'am.'

Tilly slid to her feet as she said, 'How . . . how do you do?'

'I'm fine, ma'am. Where is he?'

'He's. . . . Well' – she moved her head – 'I think he must be looking for you, Mr Scott.'

'Doug, ma'am, if you don't mind, Doug.' He grinned widely at her.

Tilly swallowed, made a motion with her head but said nothing, until Mr Doug Scott turned his attention to Katie and the child, when she put in quickly, 'This is my friend, Miss Katie Drew, and my son, Willy.'

'Son?' Doug Scott's eyes were narrowed now as he stared at Tilly. 'You are Matt's missis, aren't you?'

'Yes; yes, I am.'

'Oh!'

She smiled at his perplexity and repeated what they had arranged to answer in just such circumstances. 'I was a widow when I married Mr Sopwith.'

'O . . . h. Oh yes, ma'am. Yes. Yes.'

'Doug! Why Doug!'

At the sound of his name Doug Scott swung round. Then they were striding towards each other, Doug Scott and Matthew, their hands outstretched, then shaking and thumping each other, as Tilly thought, like long-lost brothers. When they came towards her Doug was saying, 'Bloody axle broke just passing through Hempstead. Should have been in yesterday by rights. God! was I sweatin'. Heard the boat was sighted. Anyway, got two fresh horses from Lob Curtis. Boy! was he pleased to know you're comin'. An' the girls. But their noses are put out now you've got yourself a spicy piece.'

Matthew was smiling widely. He looked relaxed and happy as he put his arm round Tilly's shoulders, saying, 'You've met this bloke already. He's the only articulate ranger in the whole of the frontier.'

'What do you mean, articulate, you little islander?'

Matthew again hugged Tilly to him as he said, 'He's the only Texan I've ever met who never stops talking. I've told you, haven't I? You can sit for days with some of them and they never open their mouths, but not our Doug here.'

'Aw, don't make me out to be a blatherer. Come on with you, I've got you rooms in the tavern a little way out. You'll be more comfortable there for the night. It'll be like barbecue night at the hotel here, so many comin' in and none leavin'; we'll soon won't be able to move.' He laughed at his own joke. Then beckoning a tall negro towards him, he said, 'Give a hand here,' then added, 'You take the ladies on, Matt; the buggy's at the end of the row. Diego is drivin'. See you in a few minutes.'

The buggy was like a cab that was a common sight in Newcastle, only it was bigger and was driven by two horses, not big strapping-looking animals but more like the horses that had been used down the pit, not the ponies but the ones who pulled the wagon sets. Yet these looked thinner and unlovely beasts. Matthew had told her that this was horse country, that most of the wealth had lain in horses and cattle until the gold rush started; and then in some cases a horse had become as precious as the gold dust itself.

During the voyage Matthew had talked endlessly about this country. He had tried to take her mind off the heaving seas by telling her about the ranchers, the homesteaders, and the Indian tribes. He hadn't dwelt much on the Indians, just to give them names, strange sounding names like Tonkawas and Wichitas, and some that he called the Comanche. The Indians, she understood, were people who lived by hunting the buffalo, the deer, and such animals, and the ranchers lived by trading horses and cattle called shorthorns, while the homesteaders were what she surmised to be like English farmers. They ploughed the land, grew corn, they built their own houses and lived mostly by means of the exchange of goods. But nothing he had told her had fitted in with anything she had seen so far. But hadn't she just landed! She chastised herself.

'Hello, Diego. Hello there. How are you?'

The half-breed Mexican Indian smiled widely at Matthew; but Matthew did not extend his hand, nor did the man seem to expect it, but that he was delighted to see Matthew was evident.

'Wel . . . come back, boss-two.'

'Good to see you, Diego. How is Big Maria and Ki?'

'Good, very good. Ki shoot well . . . own gun now. Eight years old.'

'Oh, that's good, that's good. . . . This is my wife, Diego, and my stepson.'

The man gazed at Tilly for a moment; then slowly touched the brim of what she took to be a bowler hat, which was set ludicrously on top of his long straight black hair, and what he said was, 'Good'; then turning his gaze on to Katie and the child, he looked them over before repeating 'Good,' before once again letting his eyes rest on Tilly. Now he spoke in a strange tongue while he moved his hands over his face, then swept one hand down the length of his body, and his actions caused Matthew to laugh and say, 'I will tell her, she will be very pleased,' and turning, he said, 'Ah, there comes Boss Scott. Give him a hand, Diego.'

The man turned away but he did not hurry towards Doug Scott and the negro who were holding the luggage, his step was slow if not stately, and as Matthew helped Tilly up into the buggy he said, 'Diego's a character. He's a half-breed, he speaks mostly Mexican. He paid you a fine compliment, he said you were beautiful like the land beyond the plains where it towers high.'

As she sank down on to the hide-covered straight-backed seat she made a slight face at him, saying, 'And that's a compliment?'

'Indeed! Indeed!' He turned now and, taking the child from Katie's arms, he lifted it on to Tilly's lap; then putting his hands under Katie's oxters, he said, 'Up you go! and take that frightened look off your face, nobody's going to eat you, not yet at any rate.'

Presently the sound of thumping coming from the back of the buggy caused both Tilly and Katie to look round. The luggage was being stacked, but now Doug Scott's voice drowned the noise as he shouted, 'Great sport next week. 'Tis all arranged, a bear hunt. Lob Curtis, Peter Ingersoll, the Purdies.'

'Quiet, man! Quiet!' That was Matthew's voice, and both Katie and Tilly now exchanged glances as Katie's lips silently formed the word bears.

Tilly said, 'Well, there's bound to be wild animals here, it's a big country.'

'But bears! Tilly.'

'Aw, for goodness sake, stop worrying, Katie. Look, we haven't got there yet.' There was a note of impatience in her voice now. 'There'll be plenty of time to start worrying when there's something to worry about.'

'Aye, perhaps you're right. But somehow I don't think that'll be very far ahead.' Katie sounded so like her mother as she made this terse remark that Tilly knew a moment of home-sickness while at the same time seeming to take into herself the dread that Katie had expressed, and she recalled the words she had said to Matthew on the last night of the voyage, 'What if I don't turn out to be made of pioneer material?'

They were on the road again, bumping and jostling. At times they were thrown from one end of the seat to the other. What seemed to make things worse for Tilly was being alone in the buggy with Katie and the child, no longer having Matthew's support. He was riding alongside Doug Scott. From time to time she caught sight of them galloping away into the distance; then Matthew would turn about and ride back to the window, laughing in on her, nodding and gesticulating. He was happy as she had never seen him happy. This was a different Matthew; he seemed to be one with the people and the surrounding countryside.

For a time the buggy rolled along smoothly and she had time to look out at the landscape. It was nice in parts, tree-lined slopes, the thin line of a river far away; but as yet she had seen no houses since leaving the tavern.

... And the tavern, so called, she had seen as merely a large wooden hut. Every part of it was wood, the walls, the floor, the furniture; and all rough hewn, no polish on anything. The bed was a wooden platform set in the middle of four posts but, unlike a four-poster bed, it had no canopy and no drapes. Still, she had slept well, and she had eaten well; the food had been roughly served, but there had been plenty of it.

It had been their first night in a real bed and they had loved and laughed, and she had gone to sleep in his arms.

She awoke to find herself alone; and when she did see him he was fully dressed and had already been outside with the men.

She discovered that he had enormous energy. It seemed that he must always be up and doing; and she understood now the sense of frustration he must have felt during the time he had spent at home.

Home. He spoke of this place for which they were bound as home. When she had asked him how far it was he had said, 'Oh, we'll be home by tomorrow nightfall at the latest.'

They had already made two stops, one at Houston, then at a place called Hempstead. They had made another short stop between these two places at a kind of crossroads, where Matthew had walked her around and pointed into the empty distance naming places, San Antonio away to the left, Huntsville to the right, and vaguely somewhere in between the place for which they were making. And all the time referring to a man named Sam Houston. Then, of course, the river that they were travelling beside was the Brazos. One day soon, he promised, he'd take her to the falls of Brazos where there was a trading post; and oh, she would enjoy seeing Indians bringing in the pelts, and listening to the subsequent bargaining, mostly by signs, which he had demonstrated.

She had gazed at him in amazement as he talked. He spoke like a man who was walking on land that he owned. She also knew that he had become lost in himself, that he wasn't so much explaining to her but telling himself of its wonders, its charm. She had, since landing in this country, become aware of yet another facet of his character, a new facet, and with the awareness had come the knowledge that she really knew very little about this husband of hers. He appeared as strange to her now as the land about her; but one thing was evident, he was at one with this land, it was as if he had been born here, reared here, for he obviously loved it. She was already realising too that, with the exception of Houston, what the men referred to as towns were little more than villages; in fact the village at home was bigger and certainly looked more substantial, the houses being brick and stone built.

At the last wayside tavern where they had stopped she had listened to the garrulous Mr Scott talking about places which all seemed to be preceded by the word Fort: Fort Worth, Fort Belknap, Fort Phantom Hill, and when he seemed about to enlarge on the fact by saying they had rounded the beggars up there, she knew that the only reason why he stopped was because of some signal he had received from Matthew, who at the time had his back to her.

She knew there had to be forts to protect people from the Indians. She had learned from Matthew all about the Indians and their raids on the settlers, but all this, she understood, took place in a distant part of the country. Anyway, the rangers saw to it that the Indians toed the line. These were Matthew's words, this was Matthew's explanation. But strangely from the very moment they landed and had met up with Mr Scott, she'd had the strong feeling that Matthew's statements were not quite accurate, but that he made them light in order to alleviate any fears that the true situation might arouse in her. She felt that she wouldn't have to be long in Mr Scott's company for the true state of affairs to be made clear, absolutely clear.

The distance before the next stop was comparatively short, and at Washington-on-the-Brazos she sat at a table in what for the first time she considered a real house, but again one made entirely of wood, yet artistically so this time. It was a private house owned by a Mr Rankin. He was a small, spare-framed man, whose wife seemed to have been cut out of the same mould. They had two sons. The family had a chandler's store in the town which the father and the eldest son appeared to run, but the younger one's business seemed to be with horses, and the conversation at the dinner table revolved generally around horses, particularly mustangs.

Although the men talked and the mother listened she knew that the family were all covertly weighing her up. Their greetings to her had been friendly but not effusive as they had been towards Matthew, yet even that had been expressed in handshakes and slapping on backs accompanied by very few words.

No one asked her any questions. They had merely nodded at Matthew's explanation of the child's presence; Katie they took for granted, she was a nursemaid.

They, too, had servants, many more than a house of this size would have entailed had it been in England: one Mexican waited on table, with another hovering in the background, while earlier in the yard she had seen three negro slaves.

She had yet to take in the fact that people who kept slaves could be nice, friendly creatures. Years ago the parson's wife had talked about slaves and the hard cruel people who owned them, but as yet she had seen no sign of cruelty, but as yet, too, she told herself she had barely set foot on this land; then wryly she thought, she might barely have set foot but her back and buttocks were feeling as if they had been bumping along these roads for years.

She noticed with this family too that the men either talked a lot or they talked little, that there seemed to be no happy medium.

The meal over, they sat on the verandah and watched the night creeping into the great expanse of sky, but it was as much as Tilly could do to remain seated in the slat-back wooden chair and not run to the closet, which even in this house was an exposed hut at the end of the yard. All her life she had seen men spitting. The roadways and pavements of Shields, and Jarrow and Newcastle were covered with sputum and the fireplaces of the poor were often tattooed with it, but to hear the constant pinging aimed into an iron receptacle set between the chairs became almost too much to bear, especially on top of a meal of pork, but the three Rankin men sucked at their pipes, coughed, then spat until the sound almost created a nauseating melody in her head.

Matthew was smoking, but like his father he didn't spit, except into a handkerchief, and for this she was thankful.

Making the child an excuse to leave the company, she rose to her feet. Matthew, too, rose, and smiled and nodded towards her before resuming his seat.

As she walked along the verandah to go into the house she heard the young son laugh as he said, 'Long spanker there, Matthew man. A horse like that and . . . ' She passed out of earshot, but when, on her way along another corridor towards their room, she saw through an open door Katie sitting at the end of a table with Doug Scott, and the two of them laughing, she had an overwhelming urge to join them. But here she recognised another obstacle facing her in this free country, there was status to be considered. As Matthew had said laughingly, although they wouldn't have it said they were more class conscious here than they were in England, for here there were more divisions of class. There were the slaves at the bottom of the grades, then the half-castes, which could be Mexican Indians or Mexican whites or even Indian whites; and there were the homesteaders, the majority of them respectable but others who were slackers; then there were the whites who set the standards, the tradesmen, the bankers, the lawyers. It was from these came the offshoots, the politicians and, one mustn't forget, the army. Some of the officers were class, mainly those, Matthew had added, who had come over from England; but a number of them were mere mercenaries, no better than the men they controlled, the majority of whom were scum who had merely joined up to escape punishment of one kind or another, not realising that life in the so-called forts was a punishment alone to outdo all others.

He had spoken of this so lightly, much as Mr Burgess would have done in giving a history lesson, like something that had happened in some bygone time. The only difference was the bygone time was now and she was experiencing the happening.

Katie, glimpsing her, got to her feet as she said, 'Do you want me, Ti . . . ma'am?'

'No, no,' she called back; 'it's all right,' and Katie resumed her seat.

That was another thing; she must be ma'am now all the time to Katie, and she smiled to herself as she recalled the difficulty Katie had in remembering this form of address.

The child was asleep. He had kicked the clothes down to the bottom of the rocking cradle. She had been surprised when first shown the cradle; then Mrs Rankin had informed her that she had three married daughters and a number of grandchildren. Willy had the fingers of one hand in his hair as if he were scratching his head, his other small fist was doubled under his chin. He looked funny, amusing and beautiful. Whenever she looked at him like this she always wanted to gather him into her arms and press him into her, he was so precious and so loving. If only his eyes. . . . She shook her head. She mustn't start whining about this, she had got to face up to it, and help him to meet it too. He could still see out of one eye. They could but hope he would continue to do so until he was old enough to be fitted with spectacles.

She turned now quickly from the crib as the door opened and Matthew entered, and moved swiftly towards her. With his arm about her, he stood looking down with her on the sleeping child. She found it strange that he should care so much for the child, that there was no trace of jealousy in him, it was as if the child were his own.

When they turned from the cot he peered at her in the fading light, and taking her face between his hands, he said, 'They like you,' then jerking his chin upwards as if in annoyance at an inane remark, he repeated, 'They like you. What I mean is, you've knocked them flat on their faces.'

She opened her eyes wide as she lowered her head while still looking at him, and she said, 'It wasn't apparent to me.'

'Because they don't talk? You can't go by that; it's something one detects in their manner, in their look. You've got to wait a couple of years before they speak to you.'

'Well, that's something to look forward to.'

'Oh, darling! Darling!' He pulled her into his arms and they kissed and clung tightly together; then after a moment, as he released her, she asked, 'How much further, really?'

'If we make good time, no hitches, we should be there by noon tomorrow.'

She looked at him soberly now as she said, 'I'm a bit scared, Matthew.'

'Of the country?'

'No.'

'The Indians?'

'No, no; although' – she nodded – 'I wouldn't want to meet any Indians. No, it's meeting your uncle and his daughter. You said he looked upon you as a sort of son. Well, he may not like his son having taken a wife.'

'Nonsense! Nonsense! He's a fine man, a most understanding man. About most things that is. One thing I've never fathomed about him is the fact that he doesn't seem to understand his own daughter; nor for that matter does his daughter understand him, although I must admit she's got a point. Oh yes, yes; she's got a point.'

She waited but he did not go on to explain what the point was.

'Anyway, come on; they're talking about a barbecue they're putting on in a fortnight's time.'

'A barbecue. What's a barbecue?'

'Oh, well, now' – he scratched his head – 'it's a cross between a county ball and a barn dance, somewhere in the middle.'

'Oh, I'll have to see this.'

'Yes, you'll have to see this.' He again pulled her into his arms. 'And they'll all want to see you because you'll be the belle of the ball. There's been nothing like you around here for a long, long time. I'll lay my last dollar on that.'

She looked at him in silence now. He was so proud of her; yet she knew it to be a strange pride, one of possession. And he endorsed this as he now said, 'I've always believed that if you want a thing badly enough you'll get it in the end, yet there were times when I doubted it, but not any more. Tilly Trotter that was, you're mine, mine!' His lips pressed so hard against hers that the kiss became painful, but she endured it.

✑ 2 ✑

They seemed to have left the tree-lined country miles and miles behind them. They had passed dwellings, poor makeshift affairs, but each passing had always been greeted with wavings and calls from both sides. At one such place they had stopped for Tilly and Katie to get out to stretch their legs and the men to water the horses in a brook nearby. The family had stood gaping at her: the woman of indeterminable age, a girl of about twelve, and two small children, their sex hidden under long skirts. Neither the woman nor the children spoke, they just gaped at her as if she were a mirage dropped from the sky.

What had simply amazed Tilly and sent her mind questioning was the sight of a man running from a far field accompanied by a small boy who could have been no more than seven years old, for both of them were carrying guns. The man hailed Doug Scott enthusiastically and nodded in a friendly fashion towards Matthew, but when he looked at her it was some moments before he spoke, and then he said, 'How-do, ma'am?'

The boy with the gun slung across his shoulders stared at her, his mouth partly open, his eyes wide and smiling.

She wanted to say to the boy, 'Why are you carrying a gun?' but then she asked herself, why not? At home young boys shot rabbits. Yes, but not a boy as small as this one. And another thing, from the condition of his boots and his hands it was evident that he had been working in the fields.

She turned to Matthew, but Matthew was now preparing to leave and he called to her, 'Come along'; then to the family he said, 'Good-day.'

All nodded towards him, and she, looking at the woman, said, 'Good-bye.' Still the woman didn't speak, she merely inclined her head towards her.

The poverty, the almost squalid poverty of the family depressed her. It was Katie who voiced her thoughts, saying, 'I've never seen anybody as poorly off as that, not even in the pit row. I thought we had reached bottom there. And that little lad. Did you see he was carrying a gun? Why was that now, do you think?'

Tilly shook her head as she answered, 'Likely for game. There's a tremendous amount around; you saw for yourself a way back.'

'Aye, but there's no trees here for them to live among. Would it be to shoot them Indians do you think?' It was a fear-tinged question and Tilly was quick to respond, 'Oh no, of course not. The rangers see to them. In any case, they're miles away, two hundred, three hundred, four hundred. So Matthew says.'

'Well, that's something to be thankful for.'

They smiled at each other. Then Katie put a question to Tilly that she couldn't answer. What she said was, 'Do you see how they treat Diego? Mr Scott speaks to him all right and, of course, the boss, but them we just left, and them last night took no notice of him. Is it because he looks a bit like an Indian?'

Tilly considered for a moment before she said, 'Well, Katie, we've got to face it, it's likely the servant question over again. She finished this on a laugh, and Katie, laughing with her, said 'Aye, you could be right. Although I wouldn't have thought we would have come across anything like that out here where everything's so rough.'

Yes, where everything was so rough. The land was rough. Beautiful, yes, but rough and dangerous. They had spoken again of bears last night. And the people. Even those one expected to show some refinement had a roughness about them. Oh, she wished she was settled in to the new home. She wished she knew what was facing her. She had a strange, even a weird feeling of premonition hanging over her. Well, she would soon know. Less than a couple of hours now and she would know.

She saw the homestead when still some way off. It was what she termed the railings she saw first surrounding what appeared to be a large farm. She was leaning her head slightly out of the window and through the dust from the galloping horses' hooves she saw Matthew and Doug Scott riding ahead. They were shouting as they rode, their voices coming back to her in an unintelligible sound. Diego was yelling too, and his cry she made out to be, 'Hi-hi! . . . Hi-hi!'

Then the buggy was rolling between the high fences and into a big open space, and the horses suddenly seeming to skid to a stop brought her, Katie, and the child into a heap on the seat.

They were disentangling themselves when the door was pulled open and Matthew, his face alight, said, 'Come.'

Tilly straightened her hat, took a handkerchief swiftly around her face, and pulled down the skirt of her long blue coat before holding out her hand to him.

Then they were in the compound and he was leading her towards the tall grey-haired man who was standing at the bottom of a set of steps that led to the long verandah fronting the wooden house, which appeared quite imposing in its style.

'Well, Uncle, here we are.'

Matthew still kept hold of her hand as he held out his other to Alvero Portes, and the man, taking it, gripped it hard as he said simply, 'Welcome home, Matthew. Welcome home.' Then turning his attention to Tilly, he looked her up and down; and she returned his gaze, and as she did so she knew immediately that this man resented her presence. Even when he smiled at her and said, 'And welcome to your wife,' that innate knowledge which she possessed that had not been born of experience but which she had inherited from some ancestor who had been wise in knowing told her that a smile, no matter how oiled, could not hide the truth that lay deep in the eyes.

'Come in, come in; you must be tired. Oh.' He paused and looked towards where Katie was standing with the child in her arms and he said, 'Ah, your stepson. I was prepared; I got your mail yesterday.' He did not give any more attention to the child but turned and went up the steps, and Matthew, gripping her hand tightly, drew her with him, and thus she entered the house.

The house itself was a surprise. The door from the verandah led into a large room, which she guessed to be thirty feet or more long and two-thirds of its length wide. To the far right of her a table was set out for a meal, the glass on it glinting in the shaded dimness of the room. To the left of her in the end wall was a stone fireplace, the open area being almost concealed by a huge jug of dried grasses. At right angles to the fireplace was a couch covered with various animal skins lying loosely on it. There were a number of chairs in the room, one large and hide-covered; the others she took to be wooden chairs, but with one noticeable difference from those she had seen beforehand, these were all polished.

There were three doors in the room, one by which she had entered, one almost opposite leading into a passageway, the third at the end of the room where the dining-table was. The whole atmosphere gave off a sense of comfort touching on elegance. This last was created by, of all things, a diamond-paned china cabinet standing to the right of the doorway that led into the corridor. There were four windows giving on to the verandah, which shaded the light that would otherwise have penetrated the room.

'Isn't it a lovely room?' Matthew threw his arm out in a wide sweep, and she nodded at him, smiling as she said, 'Yes, indeed it is.'

'Never mind about admiring the room. Take your wife to your quarters; I'm sure she needs to freshen up after her little jaunt.' Laughter accompanied the last words and the sound was high, unexpected coming from the full-lipped wide mouth.

As Matthew led Tilly towards the corridor Katie was about to follow with the child in her arms when for a moment she imagined that the tall man was going to stop her passage for he made a movement with his hand, then checked it. Following this he inclined his head slightly towards her: it was permission that she could cross the room and follow her mistress.

The apartments were two rooms at the end of the corridor. The bedroom was comfortably furnished, the window looking out on to an open space where a number of horses were standing as if asleep. The other room was a kind of dressing-room-cum-study; in it was a wash-hand-stand holding a jug and basin, and clean white towels hung from a rack beside it.

As she took off her coat and hat she let out a long sigh which brought Matthew to come and stand in front of her, and there was a note of slight anxiety in his voice as he said, 'Well, this is it. What do you think?'

She did not return his smile as she answered, 'I think it's too early to say.'

'Oh, Matilda! You're going to like it, you must, it's going to be our home.'

'Always? In this house with . . . with your uncle?'

'Don't you like him?'

She turned her head slightly to the side. 'I've hardly met him. I glimpsed a tall, aristocratic man who was delighted to have you back but would have preferred you to have come alone.'

'Oh now! Now!' He wagged his finger in her face. 'If you've only glimpsed him for a moment, as you say, how can you make that out? Be fair. I'd wait a little while before you pass judgment on him. He's a fine man. He has his faults, haven't we all, but you'll come to like and respect him. You'll see.'

'Where is his daughter?'

'Oh, she's likely in the dog run.'

'*The what!*' She screwed up her face at him, and he now said, 'Oh, that isn't as bad as it sounds. It was the original house built here years ago, it's a kind of log hut with an open runway going through it. Anyway, we'll see it all later on.'

'But why does she live there?'

'Oh, it's a long story and interesting, and I'll tell you about it later. . . . Come now.'

'Wait.' She pushed him gently aside. 'I must see to Katie and the child; I'd forgotten.'

'Oh yes, yes, of course.'

Tilly opened the door to see Katie, her face straight, standing holding the child, and she took the boy into her arms, saying, 'I'm sorry. I'm sorry, Katie. We'll get settled shortly.' She now turned towards Matthew. 'What . . . what about Katie and a room for the nursery?'

He stood looking at her for a moment gnawing on his lip, a look of perplexity on his face; then going past them, he said, 'Just wait a moment, I'll see Uncle.'

'Come in and sit down.' Tilly motioned Katie into the room, and Katie came in but she didn't sit down. Looking at Tilly, she said, 'He wasn't going to let me across the room.'

'What do you mean?'

'That man, his uncle, he was for making me go round the back, wherever that is.'

'Oh no!'

'Oh aye, Tilly, I saw it in his face: What is the meaning of this! Wrong door, tradesmen's entrance. You know what it was like back home.'

Tilly bowed her head for a moment before she said, 'It's all going to be so different from back home, Katie; we've both got to understand that.'

'Oh, I understand it, never fear. Don't worry about me.' Katie smiled at her now, but it was a tight smile. 'Only you can't help noticin' things, an' some of them pip you. You know what I mean?'

'Yes, I know what you mean.' They looked at each other and nodded, and they both knew that the servant-mistress association was going to be much more difficult in this home than it had been at the Manor. . . .

They had taken the child's dust-covered outer clothes off, washed his hands and face; Tilly had also freshened herself with a wash and told Katie to do the same; following this, they sat waiting for another five minutes before Tilly, rising impatiently to her feet, said, 'I'll go and see what's happening.'

Leaving the room, she went along the corridor and through the open door that led into the main room. There was no one in the room except a Mexican, who looked very like Diego. He had been attending to the table and he glanced towards her and in stilted English said, 'Ma'am, I . . . I Emilio.'

'Hello, Emilio.' She inclined her head towards him, and he bowed slightly before turning and walking towards the door beyond the table.

Alone, she could now hear voices coming from beyond the fireplace end of the room. There was no door there, just a heavy embroidered curtain hanging on the wall. She had earlier taken it to be a piece of tapestry but now she realised that there must be a room beyond. She was nearing it when she stopped as the old man's voice came to her, saying, 'As I said, I'm not against you marrying, my dear boy, but a widow with a child! You say her husband was a gentleman?'

'Yes.' The syllable was curt.

'Landed?'

'Yes, the owner of an estate, and a mine.'

'Did he leave her well off?'

'She has an income.'

'It must have happened very quickly.'

'No, not at all, Uncle. I've been in love with her for years.'

'As a married woman?' There was a shocked note in the question.

'Yes, as a married woman; and before.'

'You must have been a mere boy. How long was she married?'

'Oh, I don't know, two or three years, five perhaps.'

'Well, I'm sorry to say it, Matthew, but she doesn't on first appearance seem to be the type that will settle for this kind of life; she is dressed and certainly looks like a town woman.'

'You don't know anything about her as yet, Uncle. She's had a strange life, a hard life in some ways. She. . . .'

'Hard? But you said she was married to a gentleman?'

There was a silence now and during it Tilly turned away, but as she did so Matthew's voice came to her, saying, 'And he was a gentleman, very much so. I . . . I shall tell you about him some day perhaps. In the meantime, Uncle, as I asked earlier, can you tell me where I can house the child and the maid?'

When she returned to the room at the end of the corridor she paused before opening the door and drew in a long shuddering breath, she mustn't let Katie see she was upset.

On entering the room, she said, 'He's talking to his uncle; they must be arranging something.'

'What's the matter?' Katie got to her feet; 'you look white.'

'I feel white; it's been a long journey.'

'Aye, you could say that.'

Of a sudden Tilly put out her hands and grabbed those of the dumpy young woman facing her, and her voice had a break in it as she said, 'Oh! Katie, I'm glad you came with me, and never more than at this minute.'

Within an hour the space with the dormer windows under the roof had been cleared by four negroes, one a man with white hair, another in his middle years, the other two in their early twenties.

While this was being done, Matthew escorted Tilly around the homestead, and she made the acquaintance of Luisa Portes.

They had left the house by the door at the end of the main room, walked across some duck boards and into a room that Tilly took to be a kitchen, for it was fully equipped with all that was needed in a kitchen including a table and a wood oven stove, besides rows of pans and kitchen utensils hanging on one wall and a rough-hewn dresser flanking the opposite one.

Emilio was in the kitchen. He was grinding meat through an iron sieve bolted to the corner of the table, and he stopped his work and smiled at them, but waited for Matthew to speak. 'Good to see you again, Emilio,' Matthew said.

'And you, young boss.'

'How are the children?'

'Very well, thrivin' ... that is right? thrivin'?'

'Yes' – Matthew laughed now – 'that is right, thriving. ... Where is Miss Luisa?'

'In quarter.' The man jerked his head backwards.

'Thank you.' Matthew took her arm now and led her out of another door where there was another set of duck boards leading to a door opposite, but he didn't take her through this door; instead, stepping off the boards on to the rough ground, he guided her to the front of the house and on to yet another layer of duck boards. These fronted a doorless space, through which she could see to the far end and out to where a tree was growing.

When she glanced at him enquiringly he said, speaking under his breath now, 'This is called a dog run. It was at one time used for sheltering the animals; it also serves another purpose, it forms an air tunnel in high summer, and you need it, I can tell you.'

Tilly followed him into the open space which had two doors on either side and when he tapped on one of them it was opened almost immediately and Tilly found herself looking down on a woman whose age puzzled her at the moment. The woman was small and sturdily built; she was wearing a long faded serge skirt and a striped blouse over which was a fine fur-skin waistcoat. Her hair was drawn tightly back from her forehead; it was black without a trace of grey in it. Her face appeared square owing to the width of her jaw, her skin had a warm olive tint and her eyes lying in deep hollows appeared black, but a fiery black.

'Hello, Luisa.'

The woman looked from Matthew to Tilly and into her eyes for some seconds before answering Matthew's greeting, saying simply, 'Hello.' Then standing aside, she allowed them to enter the room.

Tilly had no time to take in more than a fleeting impression of the room but that was enough to tell her that the place looked comfortless, even stark in its furnishing, which was so utterly in contrast to that in the big room across the yard.

When Matthew said, 'My wife, Luisa,' Tilly held out her hand, saying, 'I'm very pleased to meet you.'

It was with some hesitation that Tilly's hand was taken. She was surprised at the hard firmness of the grip; then she was more surprised, even startled when the woman gave a laugh and, looking her up and down, she said, 'You'd be anything but a welcome surprise to him.'

'Come, come, Luisa.' Matthew caught hold of her arm. 'Don't tell me things haven't improved; you promised you would try.'

'I promised no such thing.' Luisa withdrew her arm with a jerk from Matthew's hold. 'And as for improving, you know that's an impossibility; things don't improve with him, they only get worse. Oh ... oh' – she now shook her head from side to side – 'this isn't done I know.' She was looking at Tilly now. 'One should be polite and greet the guests, but as you're going to live here you might as well know how things stand from the start. So I can tell you I hate that man across there and always will. I cook for him, and that's as far as it goes. I don't enter his house, but you' – there was a suspicion, just a suspicion of a smile on her face now as she added, 'you're in a different position, you'll be living under his roof and you'll make up your mind for yourself. And I can tell you this right away, if he decides to put on a good face for you now that he has partly lost his adopted son to you' – she jerked her head towards Matthew – 'you'll find me in the wrong. My attitude you'll put down to that of a crabbed old maid. Well, so be it, time will tell. Anyway, I'm glad to see you. It's good to see another woman's face about the place, a white woman's, and if things get too hot for you over in the ... palace, then you'll always be welcome to use this' – she made a flicking movement with her hand – 'as a fort.'

'Thank you.' Tilly smiled at the woman and she knew immediately that she was going to like her, she did like her, whereas she doubted if she would like her father.

'I'll take you at your word,' she said; and with her next words she didn't consider if she was vexing or pleasing Matthew, but she added, 'And I'll bring the baby and my friend too.' She made a 'Huh!' sound in her throat now as she ended, 'She's supposed to be nursemaid to the child but we've been friends for many years.'

As she ended she cast a glance at Matthew. He was looking at her quizzically but he said nothing.

'Sit down and have a drink. What is it for you, the same as usual?'

'Yes, Luisa, the same as usual.'

'And you? By the way, what must I call you?'

'Ti ... Matilda.'

'Matilda. Well, Matilda, what's your drink? I can offer you one of three, Spanish wine, brandy or whisky.'

'I'll have the wine, please.' Tilly watched the small woman go to a cupboard in the wall and take out two bottles and three glasses, and when she had poured out the drinks she handed Tilly the wine, and as she gave Matthew the glass of brandy she said briefly, 'Bear hunt next week. Far better if they joined the rangers; ten bears ain't half as troublesome as one Indian. Mack's out you know.'

'Where?'

'Waco, beyond the falls, bloody Comanches. It's been quiet for too long. More families have settled up there now and that's drawing the bloody barbarians out again.'

'Which group is he riding with?'

'O'Toole's.'

'O'Toole's? When did they leave?'

'The day before yesterday. And – ' she nodded now, a sneer on her face and in her voice as she said, 'You won't believe it, you know what that Jefferson Davis has gone and done?' She waited while Matthew stared at her. 'Supplied the army with camels. Huh! Huh! did you ever hear anything like it? Camels! If he spent the money on reinforcing the rangers instead on humpty-backed camels we'd likely get somewhere. They make me bloody mad these politicians.' On this she lifted the glass to her mouth and threw her drink off in one gulp; then banging the glass down on a rough wooden table to her side, she said, 'Forts, forts, forts! They'll soon have as many bloody forts as they have buffalo; they're springing up all over the damn place.'

'Well, as I see it, Luisa, that isn't a bad thing.'

'New one up river, near the Brazos Reservation, Fort Belknap. But they opened that before you left, didn't they? Then the fellows tell me there's another one below Brazos Reservation, Phantom Hill they call that one. Oh my God! we won't see the wood for the trees shortly. Another drink?' She looked from one to the other, and Matthew, getting to his feet, said, 'No thanks, not at the moment, Luisa; we're just going round the rest of the standing.'

At the door, Luisa looked up into Tilly's face as she said quietly, 'If you're going to stay, make him' – she now thumbed towards Matthew – 'build you a house outside.'

'I'll . . . I'll see he does that.'

'Don't wait too long.'

'I won't.'

'Come on. Come on.' Matthew gave her arm a sharp tug that caused her almost to jump off the step on to the duck board and to reprimand him, not actually in the words but in the tone that she gave to them as she said, 'Please, Matthew, careful.'

He was walking a little ahead of her as he remarked coolly now, 'You won't have to listen . . . at least you won't have to believe all that Luisa says.'

'Then I shouldn't insist on us having a home of our own?'

'Not yet at any rate.'

'And this talk of Indians and raids, you haven't told me any of this, Matthew; you indicated all this happened miles away.'

He slowed up and walked by her side now, his head slightly bent, and his voice was low but had a forced patient note to it as he said, 'This is a new country, there's always skirmishes. Most of the Indians have become friendly but there are some who won't toe the line. They've got to be made to fall into place, the place allotted to them by the state. So' – he turned and looked at her – 'there'll always be skirmishes but, as I've already told you, they take place hundreds of miles away.'

'Well, why does everyone seem to carry a gun? I noticed guns on each side of the fireplace in your uncle's room and one standing near the door. There was that little boy we passed, he had a gun while he was working in the fields.'

'It was at one time a necessary form of protection, now it has become a habit. That's all.'

They were nearing the long low row of huts now and she stopped and said to him quietly, 'As you are well aware, Matthew, I am no child, so it would be better if you did not treat me as such. If there is danger I would like to know about it, so . . . so that I, too, may become prepared.'

His face slid into a slow smile now and he said, 'Very well, Mrs Sopwith, when we have time to ourselves I shall put you into the picture; what is more, I shall teach you to shoot and to ride, and then' – he chuckled – 'you can be my bodyguard. . . .'

'Well! ... Hie!'

They both turned to see coming towards them a short-built man who appeared to be so thin his body seemed to be lost within the breeches and heavy coat he was wearing.

'Hello there, Rod.'

Tilly again watched Matthew shaking hands as if he were greeting a long-lost brother; then turning to her, he said, 'This is Rod Tyler, one of the best horse-breakers in Texas.'

'Go on with you! ... How do you do, ma'am?. ...Welcome.'

'Thank you.' She was smiling at the man, who she guessed to be in his mid-thirties, but then again it was difficult to tell the ages of the people she had met in this strange wild land. He had a pleasant face, handsome in a way. His eyes were merry and they seemed to infect his voice and laugh.

They were walking towards the bunkhouse now and Matthew said, 'I hear Mack's gone out.'

'Aye, the silly old fool. We nearly had an up-'n-downer for it, but I let him have it as he knows that district better than me.'

'Are you on your own then but for Doug?'

'No; Pete Ford and Andy O'Brien have stopped along the way. You remember them?'

'Oh yes, I remember them, and they'll remember me. Remember the nightmare?'

As Rod Tyler was going through the doorway he turned and threw his head back and let out a roar of a laugh as he thumped Matthew on the back, saying, 'Do I remember your nightmare! we thought the horse maniacs had certainly come to say hello. Boy! did you cause a stir that night. God! I'll say.'

Laughing, they entered the bunkhouse which Tilly saw was just that, a long room that held ten narrow cots, and running down the middle were two tables end to end with long forms underneath them. But at one end of the house a door led into what apparently was an extra room, a kitchen she surmised; at the other end a stove dominated the wall with a black pipe going up to the ceiling and through it.

'Well, this is home from home, ma'am.' Rod Tyler grinned widely as he waved his arm from one side to the other. 'And there's many worse I can tell you.' And looking at Tilly, he said, 'We'll make you a hash one night, ma'am, after a hunt. You've never tasted anything like our hash, especially when Doug Scott's got a hand in it.'

'Where's Doug, by the way?'

'He's gone off to the bottom corral with Pete and Andy. We brought in a couple of herds last week but it's gettin' a bit too dry ... and too cold for them down there, they'd be better up here.'

The room was stuffy, there was a strong smell, a mixture of sweat and smoke and the odd odour that comes from hides and leather, and Tilly was glad when she got out into the air again.

As they stood in the doorway of the bunkhouse Rod Tyler, looking at Matthew, said, 'Good to see you back.' Then turning his glance on Tilly, he added, 'And with such a spankin' lady. ... You ride, ma'am?'

'No, I'm afraid I don't.'

'I'm soon going to cure that failing.' Matthew nodded at Rod Tyler, and he, nodding back, said, 'Pick you one of the best out.'

Tilly, laughing now, put in, 'You may, but it'll be another job to get me on its back.'

'We'll do that, ma'am, never fear, ma'am. What do you say, eh, Matt?'

It was strange to hear Matthew being called Matt. She had said jokingly that she would call him Matt if he called her Matilda but she had found it didn't come natural, so he was always Matthew to her; but only at odd times did she revert to Tilly to him.

They were now making their way to the far corner of the compound towards a small huddle of huts, four in all, and Matthew, stopping before the first hut, leant slightly forward as he called, 'Hie there! You in there, Ma One?'

Almost immediately the rickety door was pulled open and the aperture was filled with the figure of a large old negro woman; her face one big smile, she said, 'Ah! young boss come back. Welcome. Welcome, young boss.'

'How are you, Ma One?'

'As best the good Lord sends.'

'Then you couldn't be better.'

"S'right, young boss. 'S'right.'

'This is my wife, Ma One.'

'Yes, I see your wife. Tall, great lady. Ah yes! Ah yes! Fine great lady, ma'am.'

All Tilly could add to this stilted conversation was the equally and formally stilted words of, 'How do you do?' and to this the old negress answered, 'Aw, do fine, ma'am, do fine.'

'One, all right, Ma?'

'One all right, boss, One all right.'

'And Two, Three and Four?'

'Two all right, boss, but Three 'n Four' – she laughed now, her huge breasts wobbling as she said, 'They'll never be all right till they reach great age, young never all right. But Three, He better this past time for boss Tyler let him ride.'

'Oh, good, good; I'm glad of that.'

'You find Miss Luisa good, boss?'

'Yes, Ma One, in fine fettle.'

'I keep her well, in fine fettle, look after her well.' The smile had slid from her face and she was nodding her head slowly; and Matthew nodded back at her, saying, 'I know you do, Ma One, and she is very grateful.'

The old woman nodded her head even more slowly now and when Matthew said, 'We are making the rounds, we'll go and see the boys,' the old woman laughed. 'All in stable make tallow,' she said.

They smiled at each other now and without more ado Matthew turned Tilly about and led her along by the side of the wire fence towards a row of well-built wooden huts, and as they went she, looking straight ahead, said, 'Why on earth do you call the negroes by numbers?'

'Oh, Uncle apparently did this years ago when he bought them and it's stuck.'

'Bought them?'

'Yes, bought them, they're slaves.'

'Slaves?' She drew him to a stop, then pulled the collar of her coat tighter around her neck as she looked at him for a moment before saying, 'Do you condone slavery, Matthew?'

He paused and his face had that straight look that spoke of mixed feelings, and what he said was, 'No, I don't condone slavery, dear. In England I would abhor it, but here I accept it as an economical fact; they were first imported as labour for the plantations.'

'Imported?' She stared steadily at him, and he repeated, 'Yes, imported, like goods, but not as carefully handled as goods I must admit; yet in many cases they were a much more valuable cargo.'

'It's terrible.'

'Well, you're not alone in thinking like that, dear, but one thing I ask of you, don't express your opinions with regard to the slaves or even the half-breeds such as Diego or Emilio in front of Uncle, for you'll be on very swampy ground here and you'll find yourself sinking under his arguments.' He smiled, adding, 'On the importation of slaves, on the keeping in their place of half-castes, and on the absolute extermination of all Indians, Uncle holds himself as an authority.'

She shivered slightly and again tucked her collar tight under her chin before saying, 'You're very fond of him, aren't you?'

'Yes, I'm fond of him, but I'm not blind to his defects nor do I adhere to his opinions, nor keep his petty laws; but again, in spite of all this, I must say I am fond of him And you'll grow to be fond of him too when you get to know him.'

'His daughter knows him and she's not fond of him.'

His face darkened slightly and again he turned her about and walked her forward, saying now, 'Whatever is between them is a family matter. I've told you I'll explain it to you later, at least my particular knowledge of it.'

They now entered the first block of the stables where three negroes were working. A tall spare-framed old negro with white hair was stirring an obnoxious-smelling liquid in an iron pot over a wood-burning stove. He straightened up immediately, as did the other two men, and they stood in a rough line as they smiled at Matthew.

Touching his forehead, the old man said, 'Hello, young boss.'

Matthew answered his greeting with, 'Hello, One,' then he nodded at the other two, saying, 'Hello there. . . . How are things?'

'Things good, boss, things good.'

Tilly stared at the ebony faces. Apart from the old man, the other two looked to be at least in their thirties. She learned later that they were not related to him.

As Tilly looked at them she was overwhelmed by a feeling of sadness: an old man and two men in their prime named by numbers and referred to as boys. In some ways the very numbers robbed them of their manhood. They were looking at her and nodding their heads and she had to force herself to smile at them. She was glad when a few minutes later they left the stable, but outside she saw the fourth negro. He was coming from the direction of the dog run. She told herself she'd never get used to calling the house a dog run, it was too akin to a dog kennel, but this negro did not make his way towards them, in fact Tilly thought he went out of his way to avoid them, and when she remarked on this Matthew said, 'Yes, very likely you're right; he's a sour one is Four, and that's been brought about by kindness, Luisa's kindness. He's her houseboy and she made the mistake of teaching him to read.'

'You think then it's a mistake for any human being to be able to read and understand words?'

'Now! now! now! don't get on your old high horse, Tilly Trotter.' He was tweaking her nose now. 'In this case, yes, because the others accept their lot, but the little knowledge he has gained has made him uneasy, groping. It has also prevented him from doing the one thing he wants to do, ride.'

'Why?'

'Well! . . . Oh dear me, it's such a tangled story; it's to do with Luisa. If she'd only be reasonable and go back and live in the house and act as a daughter should, Uncle would give her the earth, literally all this earth that he owns, and that's a few hundred square miles of it, not to mention his other assets, two banks and a factory, et cetera, et cetera. Well, since she won't act normally, he, being the man he is, takes it out on anyone she favours, so Four has a rough time of it. But strangely, the solution lies in the boy's own hands, he could ask for a transfer to the stables or other work, then once he left Luisa and the dog run, Uncle would see that he had a ride now and again; but it seems a toss up between learning to read or riding.'

'And loyalty to Luisa I should imagine.'

'Yes, that must be so. Still, that's the situation. I can't alter it, I have tried, and I would advise you, my dear, not to attempt it. Yet' – his head jerked – 'after having said that I would say that if you could bring Luisa back into the house Uncle would deck you out in jewels, I'm sure of that.'

'I've never had a taste for jewellery.' Quickly changing the conversation now she added, 'Those houses or huts outside the compound, who lives there?'

'Oh, Diego and his wife Big Maria. They have one child, Ki. Emilio lives there also with his two children, a boy and girl. His wife died about three years ago. She, too, was called Maria; there was Big Maria and Little Maria.'

'They look better houses than those inside the compound, quite big in fact for two families.'

'There are really four houses over there and they built them themselves. Two of them are empty.'

'Are we going over to see them?'

'No, not now; we'd better go in to dinner. And, darling' – he pulled her to a stop – 'you won't forget when answering Uncle's questions, and he'll be firing them at you, there's no doubt about that, that you are a widow of an English gentleman named Trotter?'

She answered him quietly, saying, 'I won't forget, but would it be so terrible if he did find out the true facts?'

He looked down towards the hard dry earth and moved a loose pebble with the toe of his boot as he said, 'I would rather he didn't know.' Then raising his eyes to her face, he added softly, 'This is a new life we're starting, you and I, and I don't want anything to mar it, and nothing or no one to come between us, and if anyone should try – ' His lips went into a twisted smile now and he pulled her arm tight into his waist as they went forward and he ended, 'Remember what I did to Luke in the nursery all those years ago when he dared to say he was going to marry you?' and she answered, 'Yes, I remember. But does the no one include your uncle?'

'Uncle! Don't be silly, dearest, Uncle would be the last person who'd attempt any such thing.'

'But just say he did.'

'Now, now, Matilda; stop it. The question will never arise. And I hate to hear you voicing such opinions before the dust is off your shoes. Really! what's come over you?'

They stopped at the foot of the verandah face to face, a silence between them, until she said, 'It could be called intuition.'

He was about to speak when there was a sudden high neighing of a horse, and the mass of horses in the corral began to move and stamp. At the same moment Alvero Portes appeared at the top of the steps, a gun in his hand, and he didn't look down on them or speak but peered through narrowed lids away to the right to where a thin cloud of dust blurred the skyline. After staring at it for a full minute, he placed his gun by the side of the verandah post and came down the steps towards them smiling. But Tilly didn't answer his smile, she looked at Matthew with her mouth slightly agape and a deep question in her eyes.

∞ 3 ∞

The days passed into weeks and the weeks mounted to Christmas; and Christmas passed, a strange Christmas, made familiar only by the cold nights. Tilly was surprised at the intenseness of the cold after the heat of the day, it seemed a different cold from that which she had experienced in the North of England. The winters had been severe there and she always felt if you could stand those you could stand anything, but at times here when the wind was from the north, the cold was bone-chilling in the night.

Yet the days passed pleasantly enough and time did not hang heavy on her hands, except when Matthew was out riding with the men; and when their task was to round up a fresh batch of horses he could be away for three or four days at a time, then no matter how she occupied herself, the hours seemed to drag.

Willy took up most of her time. He was running all over the place now and it took a considerable amount of energy both on hers and Katie's part to keep him in check, and to keep him from under the feet of. . . . Uncle, because being able only to see out of one eye he blundered into things, and when he came up against a leg he was apt to cling on to it; and Uncle apparently wasn't overfond of children.

Uncle's first love in life, Tilly thought, was horses. The second, and she hated to admit this to herself, seemed to be Matthew. It was beginning to irk her that Matthew could hardly enter the house before the old man would claim his attention.

She thought of Alvero Portes as a very old man, yet he could only be in his early sixties.

She was sorry to have to admit to herself that she couldn't like the man, but she let this knowledge go no further than her own mind, for if she had expressed her feelings wholly on this matter to Matthew she knew that she would have both troubled and hurt him. She told herself often that if Uncle had been a different kind of man she would have loved every minute of her stay in this strange, wild, beautiful country.

One thing that was giving her delight was the fact that she could now ride a horse. She could actually keep on its back when it went into a gallop, and this seemed wonderful to her. Her prowess was due to the encouragement of Matthew and the patience of Rod Tyler, and not a little to the admiration and slight envy she had for Luisa in her handling of a horse, for Luisa was as expert a rider as anyone on the ranch.

Luisa seemed a different being when she sat astride a horse; the years fell from her, the hard look left her face, and her eyes lost their habitual expression of aggressive weariness and became alight with excitement.

Then there was the shooting. At first, Matthew had had his work cut out to get her to take a gun into her hand. He did not give the reason why it was important she should learn to shoot, treating it more as a game or an added accomplishment for her. It was Luisa who opened her eyes to the necessity for being able to use a gun. Only yesterday Luisa had said to her, 'Matthew treats you as some delicate town lady, someone to be protected from reality, and you're not a town lady, are you? Underneath you're as tough and as stubborn as they come, only he can't see it.'

Tilly hadn't known whether to laugh or to be slightly annoyed, but Luisa decided that she take up the former attitude and said, 'Come on with you; you're nearly twice as tall as me but we're near alike under the skin, at least we will be when you get that doting husband of yours to understand that he's brought you to live on the prairies. Mind, I'm not saying that it's everyone that can be attracted to the prairies for I've known women to turn and run from the sight of land going on to nowhere; and not only women either, this is no place for men with weak stomachs. If we could get Mack talking sometime he'd open your eyes for you. Of course I can't promise when that might be.' She laughed one of her rare laughs. 'He opens up about once every two years and then he's got to be drunk.'

Tilly had discovered that if Luisa had an affection for anyone on the ranch it was for Mack McNeill. Mack, like all the men she had met, seemed of indetermin-able age; he could be forty, forty-five or even fifty. He was tall, thin, bearded and walked with a slight limp.

She had said to Luisa, 'How long has Mack been here? And why is he part ranger and part cowboy?'

The conversation had taken place in the cookhouse, the hut that divided the main house from the dog run, and Luisa, punching some dough with her fist as if she had a spite against it, said, 'He rides when necessary. He knows the country right away into the Comancheria; he's a scout, as good as any Indian. The Comanches laugh at the soldiery but never at the rangers. I think he and O'Toole's rangers have been farther north than any of them yet. Up there the Comanches had it all to themselves at one time; they used to ride down from the high plateaus, usually in moonlight, and raid the small ranchsteaders. Years ago they had it all their own way because, give it to them, they can make their horses run swifter than flying birds, and they think nothing of coming three or four hundred miles to carry out a raid. It took time for the rangers to get their measure, but they did. When they invaded the prairies the rangers followed them back to the high plateaus where they imagined no white man could go. Anyway, most of the Indians are under control now, all except the damned Comanches, and if Houston hadn't been so bloody soft they would have been settled, too, long before now. But' – she stopped speaking for a moment and, taking up the lump of dough, she flung it into a great earthenware bowl, then motioned to Ma One who lifted it from the table and laid it down on the hearth before the wood fire, then she said abruptly, 'You were asking how long Mack had been here, the answer is always.'

Tilly repeated, 'Always?' and Luisa had made a deep obeisance with her head as she replied, 'That's what I said, always. This was his place before it was ours.'

'The ranch?'

'Yes, the ranch; not all of it as it stands now, just this house. Father came along. He saw the situation, he liked it, he bought it. Mack's father had died; Mack himself was riding on patrol most of the time, his mother was left here alone. They had previously come out with the idea of herding cattle, but that didn't work out, the cattle ranged too far and it meant men and horses for the round-up. In those days, too, when you got a few horses together if the Indian raiders didn't take them some marauding dirty whites did, so what he had he sold to Father and stayed on between times as a cowboy, because Father had money which could be turned into horses and men, and so they could go ranging for the cattle. But Father wasn't satisfied with ordinary scraggy longhorn cattle; it was shorthorns he wanted to breed, and horses.' She had now leant her hands on the table and stared down towards it as she repeated with a strange bitterness, 'Hundreds, hundreds and hundreds of horses, not just common mustangs either, oh no, not for him, thoroughbred Arabs, Mexican strains. Oh – ' She had suddenly swung round from the table, ending with, 'What does it matter, and why am I jabbering like this? You know something, Matilda, you make people talk, there's something about you that loosens a body's tongue like drink.' Then abruptly changing the subject again, she said, 'What about that house you're going to have built? It should be started by now, at least the planning, for the haulage of the timber and stuff will take weeks in itself; even if they bring it up the river. Get at him.' On this she had turned about and walked abruptly out of the room leaving Tilly nonplussed for a moment, until Ma One came to her side and, smiling broadly at her, said, 'Good 'vice, own house 'n fire, good 'vice.'

That was yesterday, and now she was looking for Matthew to put to him the good advice. Last night he had been in no mood for discussion, he had been out with the hands all day and when he came in was both tired and hungry. A steaming hip bath had not seemed to refresh him and he had appeared preoccupied about something.

This morning he had been closeted with Uncle in the study. This was the small book-lined room behind the multi-coloured curtain.

The break in the morning for coffee was always in the company of Uncle, and this morning after coffee they had gone to the enclosure where some horses were in the process of being broken in. She could never watch this, the taming of a high spirit, the final submission, that look of pain that was in the eyes of all animals once their spirit was broken left something inside her that was too akin to human humiliation to be borne; so she had excused herself, which she knew had annoyed Matthew as he was about to try his not unskilful hand at the breaking.

But now, two hours later, there were few hands about, and she didn't like to ask where he was for it would appear, she imagined, as if she were hanging on to his coat tails. And then she met Alvero. He was making his way towards the house, and she caught up with him at the bottom of the steps.

'I'm looking for Matthew, Uncle.'

'Oh!' He turned and smiled at her. 'Then you'd better mount your horse and go off at a gallop. You should pick him up somewhere between Boonville and Wheelock.'

She paused for a moment on the steps as she said, 'I didn't know he had gone out.'

'Oh, I must tell him to inform you of his movements in future.'

Her face became tight, her shoulders stiffened. They surveyed each other in silence for some seconds before both moved across the verandah and into the room, and there, looking at him fully again, she said, 'I cannot help but say it, Mr Portes, but I don't like your manner.'

'Oh, you don't, madam? Dear! dear! dear!' He turned from her and walked up the room towards the fire. And now taking his stand with his back to it, he folded his arms across his chest as he stared at her walking slowly towards him, and when she was again confronting him she knew a moment of fear, yet it was overridden by a wave of anger, justifiable anger such as she had never felt for a long time, and she knew that the cards, so to speak, were on the table between her and this man. Her voice was low and deep, her words clipped as she said, 'I have no doubt in my mind, Mr Portes, that you object to my presence here; I've been aware of it from the moment of my arrival.'

'Please be seated, Mrs Sopwith.' As she had given him his full title, now he was giving her hers. As he extended his hand towards a chair she replied, 'I prefer to stand while discussing this matter.'

'As you wish.'

She watched him stretch his thin neck up out of the soft white muffler that he was in the habit of wearing over the high collar of his coat, and his words startled her. 'Are you married to my nephew, Matilda?' he said.

She took in a long slow breath and held it for a moment before she replied, 'Yes, I am married to Matthew. How dare you suggest otherwise! And at this point I will remind you that he is not your nephew, the relationship between you is very, very slight. He is the grandson of your half-sister and the blood tie there is very thin.'

Alvero reached in his pocket for a handkerchief with which he wiped his lips and she saw that his tanned skin for the moment had lost its healthy hue and she realised that he was experiencing an anger that went far beyond her own. Of a sudden she felt in danger. Then in a voice that held a slight tremor, he said, 'Heredity has the power to repeat itself after generations, it only needs that thread to which you refer, and I instinctively know I am repeated in Matthew. He is every inch me under the skin.'

'Never! There is nothing of you in him. I should know, I've known him since he was a child.'

He put his head on one side now as he said, 'You speak like a mother,' and he repeated, 'You've known him since he was a child? You know what I think, Mat... il... da?' He split her name up and his voice held the last syllable as if it were a note before he added, 'I think you are a woman of mystery; you have a past, a past that Matthew does his best to hide. I have tried to probe but without avail; all I could gather from him was that your late husband was a gentleman, a mine owner by the name of Trotter. Well, it may surprise you that as far as can be ascertained by my agent in England, and he, I understand from his letter, has gone into the matter thoroughly, there is no such coal owner under the name of Trotter in the North of England, or in any other part of it.... What was your husband, Matilda?'

She felt slightly faint; the anger was seeping from her and the fear was replacing it. If this man ever discovered the truth life would be unbearable; he was a Catholic, a narrow-minded Catholic. On Sundays he held some kind of a service in his study; where he spent an hour alone with lighted candles, a standing crucifix, and a Bible. He had at one time, Matthew had told her, held a service for the Mexicans.

Aiming to keep her voice steady, she said, 'My husband was a coal owner; he was a gentleman as were his forebears. Tro... Trotter was his middle name.'

'Oh! Then may I ask what his surname was?'

'You may, but I won't give you the satisfaction of telling you; you can enquire of Matthew when he returns. And finally, Mr Portes, I shall inform you that one of the reasons I was searching for Matthew was to take up the matter of our home, and this conversation has now made it imperative that we have our own establishment as soon as possible. And should you, Mr Portes, decide to put any spoke in this particular wheel I shall express my desire, and strongly, to leave this place, if not to return to England then to establish ourselves in another part of the state; and I, knowing my husband, know what course he will choose. If I were penniless then there would be a problem, but as it is there is nothing to stop me leaving, and I can assure you, Mr Portes, that your supposed nephew will accompany me.... Do we understand each other?' Again she knew a moment's fear of danger. 'Perfectly, Mrs Sopwith, perfectly,' he said, his words coming from between his teeth.

How her legs carried her from the room she did not know. When she got into the bedroom she dropped on to the bed and buried her face in the pillow, and Katie, coming from the other room holding the child by the hand, paused for a moment before relinquishing the boy and running towards her. Putting her arm around her shoulder, she said, 'What is it? What is it, Tilly?'

After a moment Tilly, raising her wet face from the pillow, gasped as she muttered, 'He . . . he knows.'

'No! Oh God, no!'

'Not everything. Not everything' – she shook her head – 'but he's written to England to find out if there was a mine owner called Trotter. I'll have to get hold of Matthew before he tackles him.'

'What's he done it for? What's his game?'

'His game, Katie' – Tilly now wiped her eyes – 'his game is to separate Matthew and me. He wants him for himself, he's resented me from the minute I came here.'

'Aye, I guessed that much; but if the master's got to pick and choose I know which direction he'll throw his quoit.'

'Yes, I've told him as much, but how far it'll check him I don't know.' She now leaned forward and picked Willy up from the floor and held him in her arms, and she stroked his hair as he chatted at her. Then she said, 'You know, Katie, that man's bad, evil bad; there's something about him that's frightening. I can understand how Luisa feels. At one time, he must have done something to her that has created her hate of him. But her hate will be nothing compared with mine if he comes between Matthew and me. And he can you know, Katie, he can, even while we're together he can come between us.'

Katie stood staring at her shaking her head; and then she said, 'Pity the Indians don't get him.'

This pronouncement did not bring the retort, 'Oh, what an awful thing to say, Katie,' for she found herself endorsing it in her own mind.

It was almost two hours later when Matthew returned. He came riding towards the ranch with Doug Scott and Pete Ford.

She was standing at the gate, and the road from it led straight for some way until it forked off into two directions, one seemingly to the horizon, the other quickly lost in a jumble of foothills and low scrub. They came out of the foothills, the three of them galloping side by side, and they were still galloping when they passed her and brought their mounts up to a skidding stop in the middle of the yard.

Matthew was first to alight and he paused for a moment, stretched his body upwards, banged the sides of his tight hide trousers with his hands, then stamped one high-leather-booted foot on the ground as if to ease cramp, passed some laughing remark with Doug Scott, then turned and walked towards her.

Tilly hadn't moved from the gate, she wanted to be well out of earshot of anyone when she spoke to him; and she did not put her hands out to touch him as was usual after they'd been separated even for only a short while, but she held them tightly joined at her waist; and his first words told her that he sensed trouble. 'What is it?' he asked, and when she didn't answer immediately he closed his eyes and screwed up his lips before saying, 'Oh, don't tell me you and Uncle again?'

'He knows, Matthew.'

'Knows what?'

'Well, what is there to know?'

'How can he?'

'Because he's crafty and cute. He . . . he has sent to England to . . . to find out if there was a coal owner named Trotter.'

He actually took a step back from her before making a small movement with his head; then he said, 'No!' The word rumbled in his chest. 'You're mistaken.'

It was she who closed her eyes now and she sighed before she said, 'He told me he put his agent on to investigating.'

'The devil he did!' As he turned and looked towards the house, his dust-covered skin showed a tinge of red; then looking at her again, he said, 'You're not mistaken?'

'No!' She had shouted the word and now she put her hand tightly over her mouth and looked out away into the endless land beyond, and in this moment she longed to be gone from this place, back home, oh yes, in spite of everything, back home. And the intensity of her feeling almost made her give voice to the desire, but it was checked as he said, 'I'll put a stop to this.' He took her arm. 'Come on.' Yet he did not lead her towards the front of the house but round the side, saying as he went, 'I want to clean up before I see him, he's always so spruce he puts one at a disadvantage.'

It was the first time she had heard him say anything that could be taken as a condemnation, however slight, of the man.

On their way round to the back door she said, 'I'll get Diego to fill the bath.'

'No, that'll take too long,' he said; 'I'll go into the wash-house.'

'But the water's cold there.'

'Well' – he looked at her with a forced smile – 'it may clear my head and sharpen my wits, I feel they're going to need it. And send me some clean clothes over.' Stopping for a moment, he took her hand and pressed it tightly, saying, 'Don't worry. This will be the last time he'll interfere in our lives, I'll see to that. And I think you may be right about a place of our own.'

She returned the grip on her fingers, and he left her and went towards the wooden hut that had on its roof a tank with pipes leading from it that ran over the ground for almost half a mile until they reached the river. The tank was filled by a hand pump, an ingenious contraption, and a lever inside the hut released the water through a perforated tin plate and so formed a shower.

It took him no more than fifteen minutes to get undressed, have his wash, and get into his clean clothes; after which he did not immediately leave the wash-house but stood for a good five minutes more weighing up how he would approach the old man and tell him what he thought of his intrusion into Tilly's private life.

But as often happens things didn't work out as planned and it was Alvero Portes who took the initiative. He was sitting before the fire, a book on his lap, a glass of wine standing on a small table to his side, and he did not raise his head when the door opened and Matthew entered the room. He did not even raise it to look at him when Matthew took up a stand opposite him at the side of the fireplace, but he spoke to him, saying, 'I know exactly what you're going to say, Matthew: it was none of my business, why did I do it. To say the least, it was a most ungentlemanly action. You have heard your wife's side of the conversation we held and no doubt you are furious. Now you're going to hear mine. Sit down.'

'I prefer to stand, Uncle.'

Alvero now raised his head and smiled, saying, 'That's the attitude your wife took. Well, just as you please. To begin with. As you know, I have interests in London, shipping interests, and I have corresponded with my agent there for many years. We have never met but we have formed a sort of ... what you would call distant friendship, we end our letters by asking after each other's family. He even hopes we're having no trouble with the Indians. He has a great respect for Mr Houston. Of course, his is only one man's opinion, but I am not so foolish as to tell him that his respect in my opinion is misplaced. Anyway, our correspondence does not deal solely with business and so it was most natural for me to say that my nephew had returned bringing with him a wife, a lady who had been widowed, that she was a very beautiful lady.' He inclined his head now to the side and his eyes slanted upwards towards Matthew. 'And I went on to say that she came from good stock, that her late husband was of the landed gentry and a mine owner into the bargain.' He paused here, before adding, 'As yet, can you find anything wrong in that, Matthew?'

Matthew said nothing, he merely waited, no muscle on his face moving, his eyes intent on the old man.

Alvero now went on, 'Well, it should happen in the last mail I received a letter from Mr Willis stating briefly that he was glad to know that you were happily married, but to his knowledge there was no gentleman by the name of Trotter who owned a mine.'

'Why should he go to the trouble to find out?' The question was slow and the tone of it cold.

'There is an explanation for that too, Matthew. He is not only my agent but he is an agent for a number of mine owners in the north of the country who have their coal transported by sea to London ... Now does my explanation coincide with your wife's version?'

'No, because as you have told it to me it hasn't upset me, and I am sure it wouldn't have upset her stated in this way.'

'Well' – Alvero now rose slowly to his feet – 'I don't happen to be on trial, Matthew. I have told you how this incident came about; I can do no more. You must believe me or you must believe her.'

'Why did you speak of it at all?'

'Oh' – the old man shook his head – 'if I remember rightly it came up in the course of conversation. I am sorry if she has been troubled by it, but on the other hand if she has nothing to hide why should she be troubled? You said you have known her for many years?'

'Yes that is what I said.'

'And her husband was a coal owner?'

'Yes.' Matthew swallowed, jerked his chin upwards, then said, 'Yes, he was a coal owner.'

'Well then, that is all that can be said about it. My agent is wrong. I shall tell him so when next I write. In the meantime, let us forget about this trifling matter. What happened at Boonville?'

'Nothing much. The stock was mixed and Pete thought not worth bargaining over, they were in very rough shape, even the mustangs.'

'Oh. Well if Pete thought they were in bad shape, they were in bad shape. I'll go and have a word with him. I'll see you at dinner.' He now lifted up his glass, drained it, replaced the glass on the table then walked slowly down the room; but he did not go through the main door, he went towards the end of the room where the dining-table was set for the meal, and he paused and looked at it before reaching out his hand and moving a silver cruet further into the middle of the table; then slowly made his way out.

Matthew stood for a while looking towards the far door; then lifting his gaze, he looked about the room as if seeing it for the first time: the roughness of the wooden wall vying with the elegance of the china cabinet, the silver on the dining-table, and these in turn looking incongruous against the array of animal skins, the heads dangling over the back of the couch as if gasping for breath.

There was a pain in his chest. It was just such that could be created either by a broken friendship or by the knowledge that one's father was a liar. And there was the point. In a way he had come to look upon this old man not as an uncle but as a father, one to replace the man he had rejected in England, the man who had for a time created a hate in him because he had taken to himself a particular young girl. For a moment he thought as a woman might think: men were ruthless, all men were ruthless, and he now saw his uncle as Tilly saw him, and he shuddered. If the old man had failed in his attempt to divide them, then he was just as likely to try again. . . . And what if he should divulge the other business, his own personal private business? Immediately he shut off his thinking and hurried from the room, and his body, from being cool, became hot with the thought that instead of saying to Tilly, 'I believe you, he's up to something,' he must say, 'You must go careful with him. If we mean to live with him we must placate him.'

God! he felt sick.

℮℮ 4 ℮℮

It was June. The earth was like a volcano; so great was its heat Tilly would not have been surprised if it had erupted and burst into flames. There was no colour in the sky and no movement outside or inside the ranch. It was as if everyone else was asleep or dead. All that is except Luisa. Tilly was sitting beside her in the dog run. The open space did not create a breeze, nor could you say it was cool, it was only less hot than outside.

The constant motion of Luisa's rocking chair was getting on Tilly's nerves, and her voice, rapid and moving from one subject to the other, told her that something was amiss; but it was no use asking for an explanation because Luisa rarely gave you a straightforward answer.

'Think this is hot! You should have been here in '49 when all that mad scum was rushing for gold, swarming across the country, all making for San Antonio; then from there across the Comanche Plains to the God-forsaken outpost of El Paso, and dying in their hundreds. They buried them where they dropped. It wasn't the Indians who killed them, you know. Oh no, it wasn't the Indians. Smallpox and the cholera got them; and it got the Indians too. Pity it didn't wipe the beggars off the map; had a good enough try at that, together with the measles and the goat's disease.'

'The goat's disease?' Tilly's voice was a limp enquiry.

'Yes, syphilis you know, syphilis. Men are no better than beasts. Beasts are better than men, any day. Funny but all the soldiery and the rangers and the Mexican troops, oh yes, the Mexican troops, they aimed to wipe the Indians off the face of the earth but 'twas the Spanish smallpox took over and nearly did it, nearly wiped them all off.'

'The smallpox did?'

'Aye, yes, the smallpox did; but that's some time ago. I ask myself why anyone wants to come and live here, I keep asking myself that, I've been doing it for years.'

'Couldn't you have gone away, I mean years ago?' Tilly's question was quiet.

'No, I couldn't.' Luisa turned on her as if she were answering a condemnation. 'I haven't a penny, I haven't any clothes but what I stand up in and my winter serge and skin coat.'

'But . . . but – ' Tilly now pulled herself upward in her chair and looked round at Luisa as she said, 'You mean you haven't got anything at all? Doesn't your father give . . . ?'

'No, he doesn't; but he would if I asked for it. He's just waiting for me to ask, but I wouldn't let him provide me even with a shroud, I've got that set aside, a white nightgown, and embroidered. Yet every penny, everything he has should belong to me, because it belonged to my mother. He has only his looks and his tongue and his so-called ancestry, but as soon as he got her he fastened up every penny. Then he murdered her. Yes, he did, he murdered her.'

'Oh no! No!' Tilly was shaking her head, her face screwed up in protest.

'Oh yes, he did. If you pull someone in front of you to save your own skin, that's murder. Oh, I could tell you things. He stops at nothing to get what he wants. You know, he's as mad as an Indian on the warpath 'cos your house is going up. And it's just as well it is, you're going to need it. Oh yes, you're going to need it.'

Tilly pulled herself to her feet, then rubbed her sweating palms down the sides of her print dress as she said, 'What is it, Luisa, what's troubling you? There's something on your mind?'

Luisa bowed her head and muttered, 'Can't tell you. Can't tell you.'

'Is it to do with me?'

'Sort of, yes; sort of, in a way.'

'Matthew!'

'Yes, yes, Matthew.' Now Luisa rose from the chair and, standing close to Tilly, she looked into her face as she said, 'It'll be up to you.'

'What will be up to me? I must know, Luisa.'

'Can't say.' Luisa turned her head away now. ''Tisn't for me to say, but I just want to put you on your guard, he's up to something. The thing is, he's danger-ous. He's lost me, and the thought that he's lost Matthew an' all must be unbearable to him. That's why he's done it.'

'Please, Luisa' – Tilly's voice was low, with a pleading note in it now – 'tell me what's facing us. Please.'

'You'll know soon enough, this time tomorrow when the wagon comes in.'

'Whose wagon? You don't mean something's going to happen to Matthew? Has he sent him and the others on a raid or something?' Her voice was rising high in her head now and Luisa was quick to answer.

'No, no; nothing like that, Matthew will be all right, he's with the others, and they'll all be back in the morning. But tonight I'd ask yourself how much your feeling for Matthew is worth.'

Tilly stood staring down at the shabby-looking little woman and she shook her head slowly but didn't ask any further questions because she knew that it would be useless. She had come to know Luisa's ways, and the more one probed the less likely one was to find out anything. She turned from her and took up a large straw hat from a hook on the wall and, putting it on, she went slowly out into the white light, and as slowly she walked past the cookhouse and towards the back door and into her room.

The child and Katie were upstairs and she knew that both were asleep. It had become the pattern of the day now to sleep if possible through the high heat. She went into the adjoining room and sluiced her face with tepid water, then sat down in front of the little dressing-table in the corner of the room and stared at herself. Her face was tanned, yet looked ashen; her eyes were red-rimmed; her hair, wet at the front, was sticking to her brow. She slanted her eyes towards the mirror as if not recognising the reflection in it. She knew there was hardly any resemblance to the woman who had left England just eleven months previously. She had hardened in lots of ways, both physically and mentally: she could ride and she could shoot; she had withstood the cold nights and now she was coping with intense heat; these had brought about physical change in her. The mental change went deeper and had come about through Alvero Portes's attitude towards her and her consequent fear of him, her acknowledged fear of him because she recognised he was a man it would be foolish not to fear, and fear made one wary, even sly.

Since she was sixteen she had known fear, the fear of the villagers, the fear of McGrath and his family; but the fear of Matthew's uncle put the other fears in the shade, yet at the same time created in her the strength with which to face it. It seemed to her that both she and the old man were fighting for a prize, the prize of Matthew. Yet he was already hers, avowedly hers; hardly a night passed but he made fresh vows. Once they were in that bed together the world was forgotten, their love and loving was something that could not be defined in words; yet with morning and the breakfast table there was the man, the tall Spanish-looking man, who was like a sword waiting to cleave them apart.

But what was this new thing hanging over them? Luisa had said, 'Ask yourself how much your feeling for Matthew is worth . . . ' So it was something to do with Matthew, something he had done when he was out here before. But what?

What could he have done that would make Luisa think it would have any effect on her feeling for him? She now bent her head deeply on to her chest and what she said was, 'Please God, don't let it be something that I couldn't countenance.'

❧ 5 ☙

The men returned around noon, dirty, sweaty, but, as usual, entering the ranch in a flurry, their faces and their shouting expressing their pleasure at being back.

For once Tilly was not in the compound waiting to meet Matthew but was up under the eaves looking out from the low window. She had sent Katie and the child over to the dog run; Luisa was always pleased to see them, in fact she seemed to unbend more with Katie than with herself.

She had been up here for the past two hours and now her chest was heaving with the heat from the roof.

An hour ago, from the side window, she had seen a small wagon train appear from out of the last hillocks and make its way towards Diego's and Emilio's house. The lead wagon was canvas-covered, barrel-shaped and fully flapped at the front; as for the man driving it, she could not tell from this distance if he were old or young, nor if the small woman by his side was old or young. The second wagon was covered too but more rudely; the third looked like the open carts used on the farms back home, with high wooden sides which were keeping in place a jumble of what looked like household furniture and utensils. She saw Emilio's children and Diego's boy come out and greet them. The children were jumping up and down by the side of the wagon. Mack McNeill had come into her view. He had stood in the open for a time, staring towards the wagons, before striding across to meet them.

She noticed what seemed to be an altercation going on between him and the man who had been driving the first wagon.

And now here were the men back, and Matthew was standing in the yard looking about him, looking for her. That he was perplexed, she had no doubt, for not only was she not in the yard but his uncle too was missing.

She watched Mack again coming into view. Because of his limp his tread was usually slow but now he was moving towards Matthew almost on the point of a hopping run. She watched him talking eagerly; and whatever he said made Matthew hunch his shoulders, then take off his soft felt hat and dash it against his legs before turning round and looking in the direction of the wagons now stationary in the distance; then slowly turning back towards Mack he put up his hand tightly against the side of his face and leant his head to one side. It seemed to be akin to the action of someone suffering severe earache. Almost immediately he swung round and looked towards the house, and as he seemed about to spring forward she saw Mack catch him by the arm and swing him about. It said something for the strength of those wiry arms that he could do this, for Matthew's body, always solid, had now toughened to a strength that could match that of any man on the ranch.

The cowhands had not moved from the compound and were joined now by Two, Three and Four, their black faces straight, their eyes wide.

Tilly now watched Mack gently guiding Matthew towards the ranch-house, and when they had disappeared inside, those in the yard, after a pause, resumed their normal business.

She rose stiffly from her cramped position on the floor and as she had been wont to do as a child, or even as a young girl, when upset or worried, she now pinned her hands under her oxters and rocked herself backward and forward, while asking herself, What was it? What had he done? But search as she might her mind gave her no answer; and she was afraid to know the answer, but she knew that once she met Matthew she would have the answer for he was bound to tell her what this all meant.

How long she walked up and down the room she didn't know, but she was brought to a stop by the muted sound of voices coming from below. Instantly she was out of the room and down the shallow stairs; but she came to a halt at the foot of them as she heard Matthew's voice saying, 'Why did you do this?'

'I tell you it is not of my making, my doing.'

'You're lying. Weeks ago you sent a message to José Cardenas through McCulloch's Indian scout.'

There was a pause before Alvero Portes's voice came to Tilly, saying now, 'Whoever informed you of that is possessed of a vivid imagination.'

'It is no imagination; how other are they here?'

'Apparently they decided on their own to return. Likely the longing of Leonilde to see you once more.'

'Don't say that. You know as well as I do it was by your order that they left never to return. What do you hope to gain by this? You're out to destroy my life, aren't you?'

'No, no, Matthew; never yours, never yours.' The words were uttered with deep feeling; and Matthew's voice, slow and bitter, now replied, 'If you spoil Matilda's you spoil mine; whatever hurts her hurts me doubly.'

'That you will be hurt more than she will be by this remains to be seen. The question is, will she be big enough to accept your little mistress and your child?'

The last words brought Tilly's mouth agape and her head drooping slowly; in fact, her whole body drooped with a sudden weakness, and she was about to slump on the stairs when she stiffened and remained poised for a moment. Then softly she made her way along the passage towards the back door.

There was no one in the back compound and she leant against the rough wood and plaster wall. So that was it, he'd had a mistress, a Mexican girl, and they'd had a child. Yet he had professed over and over again that he loved no one in his life but her, that she had been in him from when he could remember and would be there and be part of him until he died. . . . But he'd had a little, which she took to mean young, Mexican mistress and a child.

What about Mark and her? She had been his mistress for twelve years. Was it so different?

Yes, because Matthew had known about it, he had known everything about her, whereas she knew nothing of the life he had led until he returned to the Manor last year.

What was she going to do? His mistress and the child were on the doorstep so to speak, brought there by that old devil who was determined to wreck their marriage.

She brought herself from the wall and asked herself a question that had been prompted by Luisa: Would this make any difference to her feelings for Matthew? The answer didn't come immediately, but when it came it was a definite no. But having said that she knew she was filled with jealousy of this other person, this girl who had been in his life before her. Yet again that wasn't true; she was the one who had always been in his life, and if she hadn't become his father's mistress he would likely have shown his hand much sooner; perhaps years ago she would have become Mrs Matthew Sopwith. Even if not his wife, then his mistress, for who could tell how she would have reacted under his pressing charm.

She turned her head to the side to see Luisa coming towards her, and it was with an effort she pulled herself from the support of the wall. Luisa didn't speak but, taking her hand, she hurried her past the cookhouse and into the dog run, and when the sitting-room door was closed on them she faced Tilly and said, 'Well now, I can see you know. They're still at it in there. What are you going to do?'

It was some seconds before Tilly answered, 'I don't know, I . . . I still can't believe it somehow.'

'What can't you believe?' Luisa's voice was harsh. 'You're a grown woman; you've been married twice. You show me the man who says he went to a woman as she to him and I'll tell him he's a confounded liar. Look.' She pushed Tilly towards a chair, then seating herself in front of her, she placed her hands on her knees and leant forward. It was a manly gesture and her voice had almost the roughness of a man's as she said, 'When Matthew first came out here over four years gone he was dour and unhappy. Something had soured him, I don't know what. Leonilde was seventeen years old. She was working in the house.' She jerked her head sideways. 'She was a little thing, and bonny; hardly spoke a word of English, just Spanish. She was nearly all Spanish, hardly a trace of Indian. The Indian shows in her father José, and her brother Miguel. Well, it was summer and Matthew saw Leonilde flitting about and, the nights being hot, he flitted after her. But let me tell you this, he wasn't the only one. There was Emilio. He and his wife rowed over her. Then there was Andy O'Brien. You know' – she again jerked her head but towards the bunkhouse this time – 'he isn't permanent, he comes and goes, hot feet. She was seen with him more than once and with a dirty Mexican who was here but a short time, but mainly her eyes were on Matthew. And, of çourse, her father, who had an eye to the pesos, he pushed her, he could even hear wedding bells and see a nice little set-up for himself and his no-good son. Well, the top and bottom of it was she had a child, Josefina. But once that appeared Father saw what Cardenas was up to, and so he packs them off, undoubtedly paying them well. Now in the ordinary way their coming back wouldn't mean much because this kind of thing goes on all the time. Who bothers about Mexican Indians, they're there to be used, all women are there to be used. The Indians rape their captives, and that's the only merciful thing they do to them. The Mexicans rape their captives. And don't say the white man is any better. God no! The things I've seen. I tell you they're all alike where their wants are concerned, it is only their skins that are different. Language is no deterrent to that part of the business. Well – ' She now straightened her back, joined her hands together on top of her white apron and asked, 'What do you mean to do?' But without giving Tilly time to answer, she was again bending forward, her finger wagging now as she said, 'Do you know what I would do if I were in your place? But then you don't hate my father as much as I do.'

'Don't be too sure of that.' The reply came so quickly that it silenced Luisa for a moment; and then she said slowly, 'Well, that being so we could be of like mind and beat him at his own game.'

'What would you do?' Tilly's question was flat.

'Well, I would go over to the little Cardenas and I'd introduce myself, and I'd be nice to Leonilde; then I would take the child by the hand and bring it over here, up the front steps and into his very presence. And something more, I would indicate that I had known they were coming.'

Tilly moved her head slowly. 'No, no; I . . . I don't think I'd be able to do that, Luisa. And what would Matthew say anyway?'

'Well, it would take the wind out of their sails, and it would show that old devil straightaway whose side you were on. And if I'm any judge of men it would make Matthew become a better slave than either One, Two, Three or Four.'

As they stared at each other Tilly's mind raced. It would be a wonderful retaliation if only she could do it. Was she strong enough to carry it out? No, not on her own she wasn't; perhaps with Luisa by her side. She said, 'You know I know no Spanish, do . . . do they speak English?'

'No, very little, just a word here and there. Spanish yes, but little English. But I tell you what, I'll come and interpret for you. What do you say?' There was a look of devilish glee in Luisa's eyes that was almost frightening and for a moment longer Tilly hesitated, for she sensed that Luisa was anticipating a personal triumph through the failure of her father's plan. But what did it matter as long as she herself beat the man.

Getting to her feet, she said, 'Right. Right, Luisa. Let's go. . . .'

The Mexicans had unloaded the cart and taken the household goods into the last empty cabin when Tilly and Luisa arrived at the door. The two men, the young woman and the child were all in the room. It was strange, Tilly thought immediately, that the father looked very like Alvero Portes, with the same shaped features, the same stance; but the son wasn't half the size and, unlike that of his father, his body was podgy. The father was a man in his late fifties and the son appeared to be in his early thirties; but the young woman . . . the girl, for she still looked a girl, was small and dark complexioned . . . and beautiful, yet her face was utterly without expression. Looking into the eyes was like looking into a void.

And the child by her side? It was nothing like her except in its smallness, for it was tiny, with straight black Indian hair; its skin was dark; the eyes deep-set;

the upper lip was short, the mouth thin; the nose was like a brown button; and yet the whole combination of features presented a strange effect that went beyond beauty. Tilly found herself searching the face for some resemblance to Matthew, but there wasn't a feature she could recognise.

That they were all amazed to see Luisa and Tilly was clear, and it was Luisa who first spoke.

It seemed that her words were a greeting, for the two men bowed their heads towards her and answered briefly; and seconds later, the girl too inclined her head.

Now Luisa was talking and what she was saying was certainly having an impression on the father for he kept looking from her to Tilly.

When Luisa paused the man began to speak, his words seeming to tumble out of his mouth. He pointed first to his daughter and then to the child, and then out through the open door.

Again Luisa was speaking, but this time she had preceded her words with the man's name 'José Cardenas,' and she wagged her finger towards his face and her speech now was rapid as she pointed to the child, then to Tilly again. When she stopped and there was silence in the room, Tilly, speaking softly, asked, 'What are you saying?' and in clipped English now but without taking her eyes from the old man Luisa said, 'I told them that the big boss had sent for them in order that you should see the child and take it into your family.'

'What!'

'Be quiet! It's the best thing you can do if you want rid of them; if not you'll have them on your doorstep for the rest of your life here. Do you want that?' Her eyes had not moved from José Cardenas. 'Do you?'

'No, no. But to take the child, that's an admission. And Matthew....'

'Well, have it your own way. But as I said they'll be under your nose and Father'll make the most of it. Oh yes, mark my words, he'll make the most of it. You won't be able to stand it.'

'But I can't just walk out with the child.'

'Yes, you can; all this old devil wants is money. I might as well tell you he's as surprised as you are at this minute. He didn't know Matthew was married. It puts a different complexion on things; they're Catholics. Well, what do you say?'

Tilly gulped in her throat, paused for a long moment, then said, 'Go ahead.'

Luisa went ahead, and Tilly could not make out one word of what was being said except that Luisa and the old man repeated 'pesos' again and again. There was some kind of bargaining going on. Then for the first time the son spoke, only to be practically jumped on by Luisa who, swinging round to him, wagged her whole hand in his face, then pointed towards the doorway and, using both hands now, made a sweeping movement as if she was sending them all back along the road. This seemed to have an effect, at least on the father, for he spoke to his son now, and the man said nothing more but stood looking sullenly down towards his feet.

During all this the young girl had neither moved nor taken her eyes off Tilly, but when her father spoke to her she looked down on the child and seemingly without any qualms pushed her forward towards Luisa, who, taking the child's hands, smiled at her and spoke to her gently.

Her eyes wide, her lips apart, the child looked from Luisa to Tilly; and then she smiled, and the smile seemed to transform all her small features into a central light that shone out of her eyes, and when she held her hand upwards Tilly took it.

There was a great restriction in her throat; she had the greatest desire to draw the child to her. She turned and looked at the mother of the child. The vacant look had gone but there was no sign of regret on her face; in fact, Tilly had a momentary impression that she was glad to let the child go.

Outside, Luisa turned and once more began to speak in rapid Spanish, this time gesticulating between the wagons and the pieces of furniture in the cabin; then, the child between them, they moved across the open ground towards the main gate of the ranch; and as they went Luisa said, 'Tell Matthew, I want a hundred pesos. I'll take it to them; he mustn't see them at all. They'll be gone in the morning.'

'Oh! Luisa.'

'What?'

'I don't know what to say.'

'Well, don't bother; keep your spittle for the next few minutes, you're going to need it to loosen your tongue. Now I've gone as far as I can go, the rest is up to you. When you take her in there you'll be confronted by a very surprised man, if you ask me; but I know one thing, Father won't believe what he's seeing. Well you're on your own now. Shooting it out with the Indians is going to be nothing to it.'

As Luisa relinquished her hold on the child Tilly looked at her and she experienced a feeling of resentment for she knew that Luisa was enjoying this business, and that she had pushed her into something which in a way was going to alter their lives almost as much as a separation would have done. Yet no, no; a separation was unthinkable. But here she was saddled with a child, a half-caste child, and it had all happened within the space of minutes. Were the consequences ahead worth the triumph she would achieve over Alvero Portes?

She muttered, 'How . . . how old is she?'

'Oh, she . . . well, she'll be coming up for four, give a month or two.'

'What!' Tilly gazed down on the child. 'She looks no more than two, if that.'

'It's the way they're made. Some of them are like suet puddings, others like elves. It all depends which part they come from. Leonilde and her brother weren't from the same mother, that's for sure.' And on this Luisa walked away from her.

For a moment she stood looking at Luisa's back; and then she herself was walking towards the main gate.

The child caught her attention by saying 'Josefina'. Slowly she nodded down towards it and said, 'Yes, yes,' and the child started to skip by her side. And this action touched some chord in Tilly for she could see herself hitching and skipping whilst holding on to her grandmother's hand, and her grandmother chiding her, saying, 'Stop it! bairn; you'll wear your shoes out.' But this child was barefoot; its small brown feet were dust-covered, and its toes seemed to grip the ground with each step.

What had she done? What had she done? She would never be able to communicate with the little thing. Oh! Luisa. Luisa.

Once again all activity in the yard seemed to stop at the sight of the young boss's wife leading by the hand Leonilde's child and making straight for the ranch-house.

Mack stopped on his way to the corral. He was walking between two horses, his arms outstretched gripping their halters, and he stared at her open mouthed; as also did Doug Scott, and Numbers One and Three and Ma One who had come out to empty some slops. They all became still and she walked through them as if in a dream of the past with her old friends surrounding her, but they being without life.

When the child found difficulty in negotiating the steps to the verandah she bent down and whisked it up into her arms, and like this she entered the long room and came face to face with Alvero Portes and her husband.

Of the two, it was Matthew who showed the more astonishment. Alvero Portes was adept in hiding his true feelings, yet even he gaped at the woman before him, tall and slim, with the dark shabbily dressed bundle poised on her arm, and for a moment he might have been seeing an apparition, something that his mind told him could not possibly be there. But she was there and he could see in her eyes the light of battle, a battle indeed already won. His voice was unlike the suave tones he usually allowed to escape his lips as he said, 'What is the meaning of this? Why have you brought this child here?'

Tilly purposely raised her eyebrows and stretched her face questioningly before saying, 'Oh, am I mistaken? Was it not your intention that we should take the child?'

Alvero Portes forgot himself so far as to turn and look helplessly at Matthew; then he said, 'It was certainly not my intention, madam; and I would thank you to take her out of this room.'

'But she, I understand, is my husband's daughter.' She turned and looked straight at Matthew and she felt an overwhelming feeling of pity for him because her words had created a look on his face that she had never seen before. It was as if in this instant she was bringing him low, humiliating him. . . . But she was doing battle, and so she turned her attention again to the old man, saying now, 'You claim Matthew as your nephew, then this child is in some way related to you. Isn't that so?'

'How dare you?'

'I dare.' Her voice now was as harsh as his and she repeated, 'I dare, Mr Portes, because I am aware of your intention in bringing the child's mother back here.'

'I had nothing to do with their return.'

'You lie and you know you lie. I have known for some time of your intention.' Now she was lying and lying so well she could almost believe her own statements. 'In fact, I have been waiting for a small cavalcade to put in an appearance. Well now' – she turned her attention to Matthew, who was looking at her in the most odd way, but a recognisable odd way for there was something about his expression that touched on that of the children in the village when they had called her witch, and she inhaled deeply before she said in a tone she attempted to make airy, 'I shall need a hundred pesos to pay for the child. Your uncle was quite willing to pay them for coming and staying, so it is only right that we should pay them for going.'

'Madam, you have gone too far.'

'Then, sir, I feel I am level with you and your tactics.'

They stared at each other, and for a moment Alvero Portes seemed lost for words. Then pointing to the child, he said, 'That' – he did not even add the word child – 'cannot be allowed to remain under my roof.'

'I have no intention of allowing the child to stay under your roof, sir; nor are we staying under it. As from today we shall take up our abode in the new house.'

'It is unfinished, you can't.'

He was looking from her to Matthew now.

'There is one room habitable and the cooking range is in, we shall survive quite happily.' She now turned and looked at Matthew, and, her tone lowering, she said, 'Will you accompany me, Matthew, we have things to do?'

Not one word had he uttered during the whole scene, and even now he could say nothing. He glanced at Portes and for the first time he saw a break in the polished armour: the old man was shaking his head. It was a pleading gesture but he ignored it and, turning, he followed his wife out along the corridor and into their room.

Katie was there with Willy, and immediately Tilly put the child down on to the floor Willy went towards her; but when Josefina, in real fright at seeing this eager strange white face so close to hers, backed from him he grabbed at her. She struck out at him as she screamed, and when he joined his scream to hers pandemonium reigned for a moment until Katie, astonishment causing her mouth to gape, grabbed their hands and cried, 'Come on. Come on.' At the door she stopped and, looking from the child to Tilly, she said, 'It's all right to take her upstairs?'

'Yes, yes.'

The door closed on the cries of the children and she was left alone facing Matthew. . . .

Standing apart, they stared at each other, neither of them speaking or moving, and when his head drooped forward and he muttered her name she made no response, not until his hand came on to her arm, when as if she had been struck by a spark she jerked herself from him, saying, 'No, no; not yet.' And she backed from him before turning and going towards a chair that was placed near the window. Here she sat down and dropped her head on to her hand; and like this she stayed for a full minute fighting to dissolve the great lump of pain in her chest, the pain of jealousy. She was jealous of the fact that he had held the body of that slight dark beautiful girl in his arms, and that that holding had produced the child up above whilst here was she who had lain in his arms and experienced his loving night after night but as yet had shown no sign of producing visible evidence of it.

When the tears burst through her long-drawn-out moan he was at her side on his knees before her, his arms around her waist, his head buried in her lap, his voice muttering her name over and over. 'I'm sorry, my love, I'm sorry. Oh, Tilly darling, I'm sorry.'

It was some time before she found her voice. Her hands were on his head now stroking him. He still had his face buried in her lap and he did not raise it until she said, 'Why didn't you tell me?'

'I couldn't. And . . . and then at the time of its happening it seemed nothing. She . . . she was with others.' He lifted his head fully now. 'I'm not making excuses but it is true. Cardenas uses her. Then she is with child and he comes and says I'm responsible. It all happened in the first year I was here. Uncle paid him off and he left. I never saw the child until . . . until today. Tilly' – he was now gripping her hands – 'do you know what you've done, what you are doing?'

'Yes; it was either that or having her hanging over my head for the rest of our time here.'

'Did you know about it beforehand, really, for you didn't seem . . . ?'

'No, no, I knew nothing until yesterday. Luisa warned me something was coming and. . . .'

He knelt back from her. 'You've made this decision just today?'

'It was made for me, Luisa did it.'

He nodded his head slowly now. 'Luisa would; she was making her ammunition for someone else to fire.'

'Don't blame her; I . . . I think this is the right thing we are doing.'

He was holding her again, their faces close. 'You still love me?'

She nodded, 'Yes, but I'm experiencing jealousy for the first time.'

'Oh my dear, my dearest, that's ridiculous. Jealous of Leonilde? Oh, I tell you, she was just a. . . .'

She put her fingers on his lips now as she said softly, 'Don't say it, there is the child.'

'But Tilly' – he was now on his feet looking down at her – 'I don't really know whether it's mine or not, in fact I have my doubts. I looked at her. There's no resemblance; she's . . . she's real Mexican Indian.'

'I thought that too. But anyway, she's supposed to be yours, and your uncle played on the fact that she was yours, and he would have gone on using both the mother and the child as a weapon to come between us, and like dripping water wearing away a stone who knows? Only his tactics don't drip water, they drip acid and acid eats away quicker.'

He turned from her as he said, 'I've tried not to believe it of the old fellow but now, my God! this last proves what lengths he'll go to just. . . .'

'You might as well say it, just to keep you.'

He turned to her again and, coming back, he dropped on to his knees once more and, holding her to him, he said, 'You've been connected with every action in the whole of my life. The first woman I went with I did it not because the urge was on me, but in some roundabout way to spite my father and you. Every time I took a woman I imagined it was you.'

When he dropped his head on to her shoulder she stared straight before her. It was like a revelation. Why had she been so simple? She had imagined that that dark Mexican had been the first and now he spoke casually of the women he had had before her. But then his father too, what about Lady Myton and the others he had had?

It was the way of men.

It was in this instant as if she suddenly awakened to life. All she had gone through in her thirty-three years had taken place in the girl, but with Matthew's casual confession she had been turned into a woman, a woman who must go on loving, who couldn't help herself loving, even with the knowledge that she was last in a succession of women, even perhaps not the last. Oh no! Her mind rejected that thought. She had him and he had her and she would see that there were no more escapades.

If only they hadn't to carry the result of his latest with them, for how were they going to explain a Mexican Indian in their family when they returned home? What was she thinking about? She would never go home now.

⁊ **6** ⁊

They made the move to the unfinished house at the top of the slope which lay to the right of Luisa's dog run the day after they had acquired a new daughter. But they were no sooner settled in when Matthew who had hardly spoken to Tilly for most of the day made a sudden statement. He was going to find a homestead for them, preferably one already made with a suitable acreage of ground. It didn't matter he said, if it was back towards the south and Galveston or over to the west near San Antonio. He had talked the matter over openly with Mack, and Mack had agreed with him not only about the situation of a new home but about making a move as soon as possible.

Towards evening Mack came up to the house and for the first time during their acquaintance he talked openly and it became apparent to Tilly that he didn't like his employer any more than she did, and she guessed the reason he stayed on here was Luisa.

One thing he advised: they should not venture north-west any further than Fort Worth. Although there were lots of homesteaders settling around Dallas, it was still too near the Indian territory to be safe for, as he said, those beggars couldn't be trusted. The moon and fire water together could make them forget any treaty. And then there were the Comanches. They were a different proposition altogether, the Comanches, for at times they didn't need fire water or the moon to get the bloodlust up.

Then all thought of moving was shelved for a time when Alvero Portes became ill with a fever. At first it was thought he had caught cholera, and this caused slight pandemonium in the compound because many men were more scared of the cholera than they were of the Indians. And so it seemed to be with Pete Ford and Andy O'Brien, for they shouldered packs and left.

But Alvero Portes didn't have the cholera, nor yet the plague, it was some kind of intestinal disturbance that weakened him so much that at one time Matthew really thought the old man was about to die. Emilio and Diego between them did most of the nursing, Luisa never went near him.

Matthew visited him every day, but there was little conversation between them; what there was would follow the lines of:

'How are you?'

'Better.'

The next day. 'How are you?'

'It has returned.' This was with reference to the diarrhoea.

Another day. 'How are you?'

'Does it matter? I want to die.'

Then one day he looked at Matthew and said, 'Will you ask Luisa to visit me, please?'

It was on that day that Matthew really thought the old man was on his last legs, but when he took the message to Luisa she looked him straight in the face and said simply 'No!'

'He's dying, Luisa.'

'He's not dying; he won't die, it'll take more than a dose of diarrhoea to kill him. . . .'

Alvero Portes remained in bed for two months and after he finally did get up his recovery was slow. He spent his days sitting in the long room reading or looking out on to the compound and watching his horses being exercised.

When Luisa remarked with a sneer on the slowness of the convalescence to Tilly, Tilly repeated her words to Matthew. 'Luisa says he's spreading it out purposely to hold you here.'

At this Matthew didn't shake his head denying any such strategy on the old man's part, but what he said was, 'Then he's wasting his time. And yet if he is feeling well enough I don't know how he can sit there and look at his latest acquisition of horse flesh and not want to jump on its back, because as you know he lives horses.'

So the weeks passed into months. The house was finished and it was comfortable and she would have looked upon it as home if out of the window she didn't see the ranch in the near distance.

The house consisted of a living-room, an eating-room with a kitchen next to it, and two bedrooms on the ground floor with an indoor closet adjoining, and, above, a run-through room in the roof. This latter held two cots, Katie's bed, and also served as a makeshift play-cum-schoolroom.

Strangely, after their first tempestuous meeting the children got on extremely well together; in fact, where one was you'd always find the other.

The first two weeks had been very trying for the little girl cried each night for her mother, but it seemed as if she had taken naturally to Tilly being her new mother; and stranger still, Tilly had taken to her and had given her the same attention as she had bestowed on Willy. But with Matthew it was different. Matthew never consciously touched the child. Whenever, following Willy's actions and words, she would run towards him, saying 'Poppa! Poppa!' he didn't if he could help it put his hand on her. When Tilly said this was unfair to the child he replied he couldn't help it, that he had no feeling whatever that she belonged to him.

But here they were in November again. They had been here over a year now and during that time had received only three lots of mail from home. But on this day they were sitting before the fire, Tilly in the corner of a wooden settle that was padded with skins, Matthew in his favourite position on a bear rug on the floor, his back against her knees, his legs stretched out towards a rough stone hearth that supported a huge blazing cradle of wood. They were both reading their letters, and when she bent over to him he turned his face up to hers and they spoke simultaneously on a laugh, saying, 'They're married.'

He swung round and leant his elbow on the seat beside her as he said, 'Oh, I wish I'd been there. And it's almost three months ago. He looked at his letter again, saying, 'He sounds very happy, over the moon as it were.'

'And so he should be, Anna's a lovely girl. And she's very funny. Listen to this.' She read from her letter: 'The taffeta was so stiff with age it made an odd sound like moths beating their wings against the window pane, and as I went down the aisle I thought, Wouldn't it be funny if all the moths suddenly became alive and I took flight. And I wanted to giggle, but I coughed instead and Lord Bentley looked at me with concern. Fancy being given away by a Lord!'

Tilly looked laughingly at Matthew now, saying, 'She put that last bit in brackets.' Glancing at the letter again, she hooted with laughter as she read, 'He must have thought he was bestowing enough on us by his gesture because his wedding present was very mean. Lady Bentley said it had been in the family for years, it was an heirloom. Whatever its use I have yet to find out. It is not a vase because it has holes in the bottom; it is not a colander as it is not big enough. John thinks it is something that was used for a head cold: you put it over a bowl of boiling water, put your head in it and sniff.'

Tilly now leaned forward and dropped her own head towards Matthew's and as she laughed he brought himself up on to the seat beside her and, putting his arm around her, he said, 'Oh, it's good to see you laugh.'

As she dried her eyes she answered, 'It's good to laugh, and with you. You don't laugh enough, Matthew.'

His face straight, he said, 'No, perhaps not, dear. But we will, we will soon. Once away from here we will laugh till we split our sides.' He had yelled the last words; and now their heads were again together and they were laughing hilariously.

When he kissed her it was a long blood-stirring moment, and so it was with an effort that she disengaged herself from his arms, saying, 'Look, there's another three letters. And what did John say?'

He wrinkled his face at her, 'Oh, he's full of life and sounds quite important. Believe it or not, the mine is going well, no more trouble with water. He speaks of the under-manager being a good fellow. A Mr Steve McGrath. You remember, Mrs Sopwith?' He now rubbed his nose against hers. 'The gentleman to whom you let your cottage, the man you were going to marry to escape me.'

'Nonsense!' She pushed him away.

'It wasn't nonsense. Come on, own up, you were, weren't you?'

'Yes, yes, I was, Mr Sopwith.'

He looked at her in silence for a moment; then pulling her into his arms again, he pressed her tightly to him, saying now, 'I want to tell you something, I was for murdering him.'

'Don't be silly, you weren't.'

'Oh, yes I was. By accident you know, pushing him into a pothole down the pit, then holding him under.'

'Oh Matthew! The things you say.'

'It's true, I had such thoughts.'

Again she pushed at him, but this time she looked into his face and she knew that although he had spoken jokingly there was, nevertheless, a trace of truth in what he said, and she felt a tremor go through her as she realised that he would kill anyone who attempted to come between them, all that is except the man over there in the ranch-house.

Slowly now she opened the first of the three remaining letters, then said, 'This is Anna's handwriting but it's from Biddy,' and slowly she read the stilted paragraphs aloud: 'Dear Tilly, I hope this finds you well as it leaves me at present. Everything here is fine. Mistress Sopwith is a good mistress.'

She glanced up at Matthew, saying, 'Anna must have found it rather embarrassing to write that,' then went on, 'I miss you very much. I miss Katie an' all. There are two new helpers in the house but it isn't the same, pardon me saying so.' She turned to Matthew again. 'I wonder whom she was apologising to?' Then continued: 'Master John and his lady are well, thanks be to God. I hope this finds you as it leaves me at present. Ever your friend. Biddy Drew.'

There was a lump in Tilly's throat, and she bit on her lip before saying, 'Do you think we'll ever see them again?'

'Of course, of course. Why say such a thing? Of course we'll see them again. We'll go home for holidays and try to inveigle more of them to come out here.'

She had opened the next letter, and now she exclaimed on a high, excited tone, 'It's from Mrs Ross; you remember, the parson's wife back when I was a girl? Oh well, you won't remember her, but she was the one who first taught me to read and write . . . and dance. Oh yes, and dance.' Her face lost its smile, and she read the letter. It was short and telling: 'Dear Tilly, I am sorry to give you the news that my dear husband died some six months ago and I have returned to my family. I have had no news of you for some time but I trust that all is well with you. The last I heard of you was through a relative, who understood you were working in the Manor as nurse to the master who had been hurt in an accident. I have heard since coming home that he has died. I hope you yourself are well and that you have progressed in your studies over the years. Perhaps we may meet one day. I think of you with fondest memories. Your sincere friend, Ellen Ross.'

She looked at Matthew as she said, 'It's like hearing of someone from the dead. Strange, I've hardly thought of her in years. Life is funny, isn't it?'

'Yes.' He nodded at her; then putting his arm gently around her, he added, 'And beautiful and exciting and filled with wonder.'

As their heads went together again, a knock came on the door and Matthew turned and called, 'Come in,' and Luisa entered.

It was very rarely she came over in the evening and Tilly got to her feet, saying, 'Something wrong, Luisa?'

'Well, I don't know. It could be if it comes this way. Doug's just come back. He met up with Peter Ingersoll, his Bert and Terry, and the Purdies. They'd been on a bear hunt. Got three, but a mother was wounded and she and her two cubs made off. It was bad light and they couldn't find her. She got into the foothills and the brush, so she might come this way. It's too far for her to make for the forest, I think, and her wounded, so I thought I'd tell you.'

'Thanks, Luisa. That's all we want, a wounded bear running loose, and with cubs into the bargain. If she gets into the stockade – God! give me an Indian any day, or a couple for that matter. What is she, do you know?'

'A black, and mighty big by what Peter Ingersoll said. And she's likely very hungry and wants to fill up before she beds down for the winter with the young ones.'

'Funny time to have cubs, isn't it?'

'No, not really. And they musn't be all that young. Anyway' – she grinned towards him – 'don't go outside and shake hands with her, she mightn't like it.'

'Come and sit down, you look cold.'

'I am. I tell you what.' She nodded towards Matthew. 'If she should come this way and you get her I want the skin; I'm badly in need of another bed hap.'

'Have a drink.'

'I won't say no.'

As Matthew was pouring out three glasses of brandy Luisa looked round the room, saying, 'My! you're cosy here. You know what I was thinking, if it's all the same to you I wouldn't mind taking it over when you're gone. The dog run gets a bit dreary at times.'

Tilly looked over the back of the settle towards Matthew. His eyes seemed to be waiting for her. He had forgotten during the last half-hour or so that they weren't settled here, and a minute later when Matthew handed Luisa her glass she looked up at him and said, 'I'll miss you, I'll miss you both. God! how I'll miss you.' Then she added, 'If only the old bugger would peg out.'

Human reactions were strange, Tilly thought, as she again glanced at Matthew because she knew he was as shocked as she was at the vehemence, at the cold brutality in Luisa's words, yet at the same time she knew that they, too, wished Alvero Portes dead. Then Luisa laughed, her strange forced laugh, and they joined in with her.

Katie couldn't sleep, she had a lot on her mind, she had fallen in love and was finding it a different feeling altogether from that which she had felt for Steve McGrath all those years ago. Anyway, she had known there was no hope for her with Steve, the only one for him was Tilly. When he had gone away she had quickly forgotten about him, and when he returned, a different Steve altogether, there had been less likelihood of him looking the side she was on for he was going up in the world; not that he was an upstart; and what was more he had turned out to be a handsome man, there was none of the dour, shy boy left in him. And now, of course, being the silly fool that she was, she told herself, she would go and throw her cap at another big fellow, a red-headed one this time whose very glance from under that big hat of his made her go hot and cold.

What was troubling her now was the fact that she might again be throwing her quoit on to a stone wall. Yet Doug Scott was always going out of his way to have a word with her, and he joked with her an' all. He had once put his hand on her shoulder and laughed at her and said, 'You're a plump little dump, aren't you?' The words themselves hadn't conveyed a compliment but the way he had said them had.

She was cold. Why did it get so cold at night? She brought her knees up to towards her chin, and as she did so Willy muttered in his sleep and gave a little sob.

She raised herself on her elbow. She hoped he wasn't going to have a nightmare, not tonight, and wake up the other one for it was enough to freeze you. When the sound was repeated and louder this time, she flung the bedclothes back from the bottom of the bed, grabbed up a fur-lined coat which Tilly had given her at Christmas, and, dragging it on, she made her way across the room towards the cots. She had no need of a light for the winter moon was illuminating the land, except when it was obliterated by scudding clouds.

It was as she passed the window that she saw in the distance a huddled form coming across the open space towards the house. Her mouth dropped open, her eyes widened. The next instant she was kneeling by the window ignoring Willy's crying and gaping at the thing that had now become a shadow as the moon was momentarily obliterated. When it next came into her view it was only a hundred yards from the house and she saw what she took to be a huge man bent slightly forward and making stealthily towards the house.

Indians! Indians! The scream that erupted from her brought the two children immediately awake and Willy also screaming at the pitch of his lungs.

'Indians! Indians!' She was scrambling down the steep stairs yelling as she went, 'Indians! Indians! Tilly! Indians!' She was about to bang her fist on the bedroom door when it was wrenched open and she was confronted by Matthew in his nightshirt, and he was almost knocked on to his back as she flung herself on him, crying 'Indians! Indians!'

'Shut up! woman. Shut up!' He was growling at her now. 'Where? What did you see?'

She bounced her head a number of times and swallowed deeply before she managed to bring out, 'I saw one coming towards the house, a big, big fellow in . . . in war paint.'

'Quiet! Come on.' It wasn't to her he was speaking but to Tilly now, and at a run they all went into the living-room. There he snatched up his gun from the side of the fireplace, where it had been resting in a clip; then throwing open the lid of a box on a rough side table he took out first one Colt revolver and handed it to Tilly, then a second one to Katie. When her hand refused to grasp it he growled slowly, 'Take it, woman. You'll likely be glad of it before the night's over. And listen.' He gripped her shoulder. 'If they should get near you use it on yourself. Do you hear?'

Katie could utter no word, for every pore of her plump body was oozing trembling sweat.

All this time Tilly hadn't spoken. Twice she had glanced upwards to where the children were still crying, and when Matthew pushed Katie towards her she gripped her arm and led her to the window and, having pressed her down to one side of it, she took up her position at the other.

Matthew had gone down the room to the second window, that was to the left of the door, and, standing to the side of it, his gun cocked, he peered out into the compound and waited.

There was no sound but he knew from the various horrific stories he had listened to that that was how they came at first, soundlessly. They would let all the horses out of the stockade, leaving some of their warriors to herd them, and their own horses would be held at the ready. When they'd finished their work they would mount with their captives behind them and race back to their base, which could be two, three, even four hundred miles away; they had been known to ride a hundred miles in a day stopping only to change their mounts. If it wasn't that, like every other man, woman and child who had settled in this state, he feared them he would have admired them simply for the magnificence of their horsemanship. It was said that they had more concern for their animals than they had for their own women. He had never been in an Indian raid or seen the devastating effects left by one but he had heard enough to make his blood run cold and to know that if it came to the push he himself would kill Tilly and the children rather than let them fall into the hands of any Indian, especially a Comanche.

He had been given to understand when he first came here that should there be any sign of trouble three shots would be fired: this would alert the whole ranch. Well, he had heard no shots, so they mustn't have made themselves felt down below. Perhaps their intention was to take this place first.

Suddenly he thought of the back door. Was it locked? He had never locked it. He hissed now, 'Go and lock the back door, Katie.'

When there was no movement from the window, he sprang across the room, through the kitchen and to the door, and thrust the bar across it, then stood for a second breathing deeply before running back again to the window.

The moon was bright now, and he could see no movement outside, no sign of anyone. He wondered if he should set off the alarm. It would mean opening the window, and the slightest creak could put them on their guard or be a signal for them to begin their attack.

As he hesitated there came the sound of movement from the end of the house where the meat store was. They were likely raiding that first. It was often their way. If the buffalo and deer were scarce and the winter hard many of those in the small camps died of starvation, even being reduced to eating their horses, which only anticipated death, because without horses they couldn't hunt.

The noise became louder. They were dragging the meat out. They had likely overturned one of the barrels; he had helped salt down three hogs yesterday.

When the dark hump came into view, his body stiffened; then he dropped onto one knee and gently slid open the window, rested the muzzle of his rifle on the sill and waited. A shadow crossed the moon but he could pick out a figure moving towards him, slowly lumbering, nothing like the stealthiness of an Indian.

Of a sudden, the cloud left the moon and there, not ten yards from the house, stood an enormous bear and at its feet a shoulder of hog, and gnawing at the shoulder was a cub.

Matthew almost laughed with relief, but his laughter was short-lived when the bear took a limping step forward and he could see that its right shoulder was badly shattered. A healthy bear was dangerous but a wounded bear was something else.

'It's the bear, Matthew. It's the bear.'

'Yes, I know. Be quiet.'

A decision had to be made: to shoot or not to shoot. If he didn't kill the beast outright it could charge. The door might hold but not the window, and the beast was now almost opposite the window where Tilly and Katie were standing. Anyway, if he missed, as he could easily do from this angle, the sound would bring the others out.

The report of his gun seemed to shatter the room, and the children upstairs screamed louder; but the bullet had found its target for the bear reared on its hind legs and gave a cry that was almost human, and the cub, leaving its meal, ran in agitated circles around its mother.

But the animal was far from finished. It began to lumber now straight towards the window, attracted perhaps by the glint of the moonlight on the glass and the shadows of the figures behind it.

Knowing that he couldn't get it within his sights from where he was standing, it took but a split second to whip the bar from the door, and then he was in the open facing the animal which had now turned towards him. When Matthew fired again his aim must have been erratic; he had been aiming for the beast's heart, but the bear was still lumbering towards him.

Again he reloaded and pulled the trigger, but the lock stuck and the animal was now not more than eight feet from him. For the first time in his life he experienced panic: he was aware of shouts coming from the ranch and knew that the men would be here in minutes, but by then it would be seconds too late. He also knew that Tilly was by his side and he wanted to scream at her 'Get away! Get away!' But he had no voice. As he went to thrust his arm towards her he heard the shots, and when he glanced at her he saw that she was holding the Colt in both hands and he imagined she had her eyes closed.

As he and the animal fell to the ground together he felt a breath-tearing pain rip down his arm; then he was smothered in a weight of stinking fur. It was in his mouth, wet, sticky, sweet. He couldn't breathe, he was finished. Not until the hot blood-smeared weight was dragged off him did he realise he was almost naked and covered with blood.

'Tilly! Tilly!'

'She's all right, Matt, she's all right.'

'Where is she? Where is she?'

'It's all right, she's indoors. It didn't touch her, she fell clear, but it got you. Boy! it got you. Still, you're lucky. By God! I'll say you are, you're lucky. She's the biggest I've seen in years. She is the one that got away . . . but not quite, not quite.' Doug Scott talked all the while he was settling him in a chair in the room.

Luisa, her hair tucked underneath a white cap, her feet in top boots into which were thrust the sides of her nightgown, and this only partially covered by her old fur coat, was attending to Tilly. She too, like Doug Scott, was talking all the time. 'There now. There now. Come on, say something. It's the shock. It isn't every day you kill a bear. Brave lass, you are that. And a good shot. I saw you, you held it steady. I would have smacked your chops for you if you hadn't after all the lessons I gave you. Here, drink this. And you Katie, stop your shaking.' She turned to where Katie was huddled up in the corner of the settle. 'You've got the house trembling. Anyway, what is it after all? Only a bear. But by God!

I thought for a moment they had come. Somehow, been expecting them for years. I didn't stop to think they'd been pushed back too far this time to make it.' On and on she prattled, and not until her father appeared on the scene did she stop.

Alvero Portes didn't enquire what had happened, he could see for himself, and his concern was solely for Matthew. 'Bring him down,' he said to Mack McNeill; 'there are proper medical dressings down there.'

'I'm all right.' Matthew didn't look at him as he spoke.

'You're not all right. With that tear from those claws you could lose your arm, so don't be foolish, come down. Bring him down.' He again looked at Mack who, looking back at his boss, said nonchalantly, 'I can't carry him; and if he doesn't want to come, boss, he doesn't want to come.'

On this Alvero cast his glance from Mack to Doug Scott, then on to Matthew, and he said, 'Well, when you lose your arm you'll remember my words.' And on this he turned and went out.

Pressing Doug aside with his good hand, Matthew walked over to the settle, and there, dropping into a seat Luisa held out for him, he took hold of Tilly's hands, saying, 'It's all right, my dear, it's all right. You were wonderful . . . wonderful.'

As she looked into Matthew's face, Tilly wasn't thinking, I saved your life, but, I killed that poor creature. It looked at me and knew what I was going to do. I have killed a creature.

Other people could go out on bear hunts; the Indians could raid a homestead and massacre the inhabitants; the army and the rangers could retaliate and massacre the tribes; it was all hearsay, like listening to a story, nothing became true until you did it yourself. She had taken up a gun and killed a creature. That she had saved her husband's life didn't weigh against the fact that it was her hand that had killed. Was there something wrong with her that she should think this way?

She waited for the answer, and when it came it said, No; the only thing that's wrong is that you are a misfit in this country, and always will be.

❧ 7 ❦

Matthew's arm healed slowly. Although the rip had been but a surface one, one claw alone having done the damage, it caused him a great deal of pain. The rough stitching carried out by Mack with the help of a hefty measure of whisky had left a zig-zag weal from below his shoulder to the inside of his wrist; and each day he made a point of exercising the arm, stretching it, bending it, twisting it behind his back even while he had to grit his teeth in the process. The pain would be spasmodic, and he described it to Tilly as being like an attack of toothache.

And toothache was another thing. At times Katie was reduced to tears with the pain of a diseased molar but on no account would she let anyone extract it. Once Doug almost succeeded. He had got the pincers into her mouth but, before they had touched the tooth, she had clamped down on them and let out a yell as if the offending molar had left its socket. Katie's toothache had become a topic for joking down in the bunkhouse.

Tilly herself kept well in health, as did the children. Josefina had fallen into the pattern of the house as if she had been born to it. She spoke in a mixture of Spanish and English; and in turn Tilly, too, was learning a deal of Spanish.

Since the night of the bear, as that episode was referred to, Tilly had felt a change in herself. She couldn't actually put a name to the change, she only knew how it affected her; and even then the explanation she gave to herself was not the one that had come as an answer to her question on that particular night, for in her heart she knew that she would have to get used to this country because it had become Matthew's country, so what she told herself was, that she felt nearer the earth somehow. Yet when she tried to analyse this, the meaning behind it escaped her.

Now she had her own home she was kept more busy than usual, for she did her own cooking, with only one help. His name was Manuel Huerte. He was a full-blooded Mexican and from the beginning of his service he made it plain that he would have nothing to do with Diego or Emilio; to him they were Indian. In addition to his own tongue he spoke Spanish quite well, and it was through him that Tilly progressed in the latter and so was able to talk more with Josefina, and coach Willy too.

Katie came from the living-room where she had left the children playing on the rug before the fire and, sniffing loudly, said, 'Me nose tells me something.'

'And what's that?' Tilly turned from the table.

'You're making a peach pie.'

She came and bent over the table and sniffed at the dish of fruit, saying, 'Eeh! I never thought those wizened pieces of chopped leather, 'cos that's all they looked like, would ever turn into that. Why didn't they dry fruit like that back home?'

'Yes, why didn't they? Why didn't they make ice like they do here? And why don't they use animal hides like they do here? By, we'll make a difference over there when we go back.' Tilly grinned at Katie, and Katie, her face straight now, said, 'Think we ever will, Tilly?'

'Yes, yes, of course. Matthew's promised to take us over once we're settled away from here.'

'Is that still on?'

'Yes, definitely. When the spring comes he's going on the lookout for a homestead.'

'Oh, that'll be grand. But . . . but about hands?'

'Oh, we'll be able to hire hands.'

'Would any of them leave here?'

Tilly kept her head down as she replied, 'I should think so; all except Mack. I don't think he would leave.'

'No, I don't suppose he would.' Katie's voice had a bright note to it now. 'But do you think Rod and Doug would move?'

Tilly still kept her head down. 'Oh yes. Yes, I think they would come with us; they're very fond of Matthew.'

'Aye. Aye, they are. . . . Well I'd better get back to the terrors.' She was making for the door when she turned and said, 'You know it's touchin', Tilly, to see how she' – she jerked her head back into the room – 'looks after Willy. She hates me to do anything for him. I had to slap her hands yesterday 'cos she pushed me. And I'm sure she was swearin' at me in that tongue of hers.' She laughed, and Tilly laughed with her as she said, 'The main thing is, they've taken to each other.'

'Aye. Aye, they have that.' As Katie went to turn away Tilly said, 'When I get this in the oven I'm going to slip down to see Luisa. She wasn't too good last night, she's got a heavy cold on her. If I'm not back within half an hour look to the oven, will you?'

'Aye. Aye, I'll do that.'

They nodded at each other.

A few minutes later Tilly, muffled to the eyes in a long skin coat and hood, hurried over the hard ridged ground. The sharp air caught at her throat and she tucked her chin into the collar of her coat; but she lifted her head before entering the open passageway and looked about her hoping she might catch a glimpse of Matthew for he'd be somewhere in the compound, if not there over in the corral. But the only one she saw was Rod Tyler struggling with a mettlesome horse as he aimed to get him into one of the sheds; horses that had been used to roaming the plains took badly to cover.

When she tapped on Luisa's sitting-room door and she heard her croaking voice say, 'Come in,' she wasn't all that surprised to see that she wasn't alone. Mack McNeill was standing to one side of the fireplace, and Luisa sat at the other side.

Tilly nodded to Mack, then to Luisa and said, 'How is it?'

'Doing nicely, I should say. It seems to have taken up its abode on my chest. Damn the thing!'

Tilly now looked at Mack and said, 'She should be in bed.'

'Aye; I told her that.' The remark was brief, after which Mack lapsed into his habitual silence. Except for the one time he had come to the house and talked of them moving, she hadn't heard him speak more than half a dozen words at a time. She had become used to the fact that this man could be in your company for two hours and not open his mouth. If he answered a question it was brief and to the point. However, one thing she was sure of, nothing ever escaped him. She had no doubt that even though he might already have been here half an hour or more yet when he answered her it was perhaps only the second time he had spoken.

She had seen him at times standing silently listening to Luisa's prattle, and when he left it would be without a word of good-bye, merely a lifting of his chin; yet she knew there was a strong affinity between them. She oftened wondered why Luisa hadn't married him. Perhaps the answer was he hadn't spared the words to ask her. She smiled to herself now as she wondered how he might pop the question were he ever to get round to it.

But this time he surprised her by speaking as he was about to make his departure. Looking towards Luisa, he jerked his head at her, then said, 'Aye well'; then nodded at Tilly before turning and going out.

The door had hardly closed on him when Luisa, also jerking her chin upwards, said, 'You get tired of his constant chatter.'

At this Tilly burst out laughing, saying, 'He doesn't get the chance, poor fellow. Anyway, it's as he said, you should be in bed, and not down here on your own either. Why don't you do as I ask and come up and let me look after you. It's warmer up there. That passageway of yours, as Katie says, would blow the hair off your legs.'

'Katie' – Luisa pursed her lips – 'do you know that Doug Scott's for courting her?'

'Well . . . I'm not quite blind, and I've got the idea she won't run from him.'

'You wouldn't mind then?'

'Why should I? I'd be delighted if she could get married.'

'You might have to find another helper.'

'I doubt it; she won't want to leave me, we've been friends for many years now.'

'You know, I think that's funny, you and her friends. You're like chalk and cheese.'

'Perhaps that's why we get on so well together. She's a good woman is Katie.'

'I'm not saying a word against her, but when the man bug gets you it can beat any friendship feelings.'

'I think Doug would come with us.'

'Aye, he might at that.'

At this point the door opened and Ma One came in, and hurriedly wobbled across the room to Luisa's side, saying, 'Better let on. Big boss slidin' along backway makin' for here while back. Then boss McNeill come, an' he did back off. But now he's on trail again. You see him? Or will I tell him no?'

Luisa had risen to her feet and she looked from Ma One to Tilly; then turning from them, she stared into the fire for a moment before swinging round again and looking at the old negress and saying, 'Let him come.'

'You know what you doin'?'

'I know what I'm doing, Ma.'

'Well, God d'rect you.'

On this she quickly wobbled out again, and Tilly, pulling her hood on to her head, said, 'I'll be off, Luisa. It's better if. . . .'

'No' – there was a plea in Luisa's voice – 'don't go. For two reasons, don't go. One, I don't want to be left alone with him; the other is, if he doesn't see you you might learn things that you'd never guess at and which I couldn't bring myself to tell you. Go in the bedroom there. He doesn't know you're here else he wouldn't have come.'

Tilly hesitated for a moment as she looked towards the outer door, then turning, she hurried into the bedroom.

The room was dead cold and she stood shivering as she glanced about it. It was the first time she had been in this room. It was as sparsely furnished as the rest of the house; the only feminine touch about it was a silver-backed brush and hand mirror on the rough wooden dressing-table, and a wooden-framed picture of a man. She moved nearer and picked it up. It showed a young, pleasant-faced man in a slouch hat, the brim turned upwards from his face. He was wearing a neckerchief very much like the mufflers pitmen wore on a Sunday back home. His hair looked to be fair; his eyes round and merry; it was a nice face.

At the sound of Alvero Portes's voice coming from the next room she quickly replaced the picture on the dressing-table and, moving nearer the door, her head to the side, she listened. And as she did so she had to tell herself that it was Alvero Portes who was speaking, yet she could not associate the soft, whining tone or the buttered words with the man, the austere man who usually spoke in precise correct English, and Spanish too, for he would nearly always address Diego or Emilio in Spanish.

'You are not well, Luisa,' he was saying; 'I am worried about you, my dear. Please, please, can't you let bygones be bygones. I promise you things will be entirely different.... You look ill, child.'

'I am not a child.'

'You will always be a child to me, Luisa.'

'If that is so then why did you try to turn me into a woman?'

There was a pause; then Alvero Portes's voice muttered, 'Oh, Luisa! Luisa! I suffer nightly because of my sins. I pray to God nightly to forgive me.'

'If I remember, you've always prayed to God but it didn't stop you, did it?'

'Luisa! listen to me. Please listen to me. I promise you that if you will come and live with me again I shall not lay a hand on you, I shall not come nearer than an arm's length to you, and I'll swear on Christ's crucifix.'

'Huh! don't make me laugh; I have a cold on me and it hurts my throat. There was a crucifix, remember, hanging above my bed, put there by yourself before you first crept into it. It was winter, remember? like it is now. "I'm cold, Luisa, warm me," you whined. And my mother downstairs needing to be warmed. I was twelve years old, remember? *Twelve years ... old*, and no one to run to, for I daren't tell Mother; she had enough to carry without that. Yet she found out, didn't she? So, you took pleasure in killing her and killing the man who was about to take me away from your dirty claws.'

'Luisa, Luisa, why keep recalling the past. And I didn't, I didn't kill her, not your mother. I didn't kill her.'

'You didn't? You only held her in front of you and let Eddie's bullet go into her. Don't tell me to disbelieve the things my eyes saw. It was no wonder afterwards I lost my mind. And I'm telling you this, Father, whenever your hand touches me again it will be the end of you, and the same verdict you managed to wangle will be repeated, self-defence. Self-defence.'

Tilly was leaning against the wall next to the door; she had her hands beneath her collar holding her neck. She was feeling sick and her mind kept repeating, Poor Luisa. Poor Luisa.

Now Luisa's voice came to her again, saying, 'Well, you've had your answer and I'll thank you to go.'

There was no immediate movement. Then Alvero Portes's voice came again, saying, 'You have turned into a hard woman, Luisa. What if I were to tell you that I am a sick man and my days are numbered?'

'I would answer to that, that you've got the number of days under your own control. That business a little while back with the diarrhoea, you might have fooled others but you didn't fool me. You took enough horse jollop to make you ill but not enough to kill you. And all in vain, because you've now lost Matthew as well as me. You had him beguiled for those first three years but when he brought a wife back with him you couldn't bear it. You've done everything in your power to break them up, haven't you?'

'Only because she's not right for him.'

Tilly's head lifted sharply as Alvero's voice, now more recognisable as his usual one, said, 'There is something about her; she's not what she appears.'

'You'd like to think so, wouldn't you? Perhaps she keeps one step ahead of you.'

'I didn't come here to talk about her but about us. Luisa, if you'd only believe that I'm in earnest. You are my daughter, I love you, you're all I've got. What I did I did out of love for you.'

'*Get out!* If you stay a minute longer I'll swear to you I'll leave this place.'

'Don't talk foolishly. Where would you go?' His voice held a scornful note now.

'The Purdies; Tessie Curtis; or the Ingersolls. Any of them would gladly house me. The only reason I haven't gone to them before is because I didn't want to shame you. Nor did I want one or other of the men to come and beat the daylights out of you, which they would have done years ago if they had known the true set-up here. But there is one on this ranch who does know it, so in case I call for his help you'd better make yourself scarce.'

Luisa's voice ceased, and there was no response now from her father, nor did any movement come from the room, but it was a good minute later when Tilly heard the door close.

She didn't go immediately and join Luisa; in fact she didn't move until Luisa opened the bedroom door and without even glancing at her turned back into the sitting-room and seated herself once more in her chair by the fire.

Slowly Tilly walked into the room, but she didn't face Luisa. Somehow she couldn't look at her; nor apparently could Luisa look at her, for her attention was turned to the fire as she said, 'Well, what do you make of that?'

'It's unbelievable.'

'Ah well, you can believe it. He didn't deny a word I said, did he?'

'Why haven't you left before?'

'Where would I go?' Luisa now swung sharply around 'Oh yes, I said I could go to the Curtises or the Ingersolls or the Purdies; but wherever I went what could I do? They would put me up for a few weeks, in fact tell me to stay as long as I like; but what use would I be to them? The mothers and the daughters do their own cooking and their men wouldn't tolerate a woman riding out with them. Of course' – she tossed her head now and her voice was scornful – 'I could have gone to one of the forts and been a laundry-woman and made a dollar on the side supplying the soldiery. They're always wanting laundry-women at the forts because there are not many wives there.'

'You could have married. I'm sure you could have married.' Tilly spoke quietly now with the thought of Mack in her mind, and her statement was answered on a laugh that had no mirth in it.

'Yes, if anybody had asked me.'

Tilly now took the seat opposite to Luisa and she brought her attention towards her as she said, 'You mean to say Mack hasn't?'

Luisa coughed, then rubbed her chest with the heel of her hand before nodding and repeating, 'Yes, that's what I mean to say, he hasn't.'

'He . . . he cares for you, Luisa; I'm sure he does.'

'Aye, some people are fond of dogs.'

'Oh, don't talk like that.' Tilly got to her feet abruptly and she walked completely around the table before coming to a stop again; and then she said, 'I've wanted to say this for some time, and I'm speaking for Matthew, too. We've both got money. I have interest from shares; I don't need it. If you won't take money from Matthew then take it from me. I can't bear to see you any longer going round like a. . . .'

'A squaw? Seventh wife of Big Chief Buffalo Horn?' Luisa laughed now, but it was a laugh without bitterness, and she put her hand out towards Tilly and, patting her arm, she said, 'Thanks. I'll think about it in a year or two's time when I've got to save me nakedness.'

'Oh, Luisa!' Tilly now dropped on to her hunkers in front of the small woman and, gripping her hands, she said, 'I thought I'd had a rough time of it in my young days, but looking back it was nothing compared to what you've been through.'

'How did you have a rough time if you married into the gentry?'

Tilly dropped her gaze away as she muttered, 'I didn't always live with the gentry. Well, perhaps some day I'll tell you about it.'

'Ah yes, I'd like to hear because I agree with him about one thing, you're not all you seem. I've known that from the beginning, from the day Matthew brought you in . . . I've always wanted to ask you, did you know Matthew's people? He didn't talk about them; I felt he hadn't much use for them.'

'Oh, I think he had, at least for his father.'

'He was all right then, his father?'

'Oh yes, yes; he was all right.' Tilly now got to her feet, saying, 'I'd better be getting back, I left a pie in the oven. I'll come down later. Is there anything you want, I mean in the food line?'

'No, No, thanks; Ma sees that I'm well stoked up. . . . And Tilly.'

'Yes Luisa?'

'Don't repeat to Matthew what you've heard this morning.'

Tilly didn't answer immediately, and so Luisa said, 'Please, because if he knew I don't think he'd go near him again or wish to speak to him. For the remainder of the short time you'll be here now, let things rest as they are.'

'What do you mean, the remainder of the short time?'

'Oh, I can smell change on the wind. I should say you'd be gone by spring. Matthew's been making discreet enquiries about homesteads.'

'It'll be for the best, Luisa; although I'll miss you.'

'And me you. Still' – she let out a long, slow breath – 'who knows what might happen before the spring. You know, it's always amused me the folks who have come in from the towns, the casuals. They get bored, they say, because nothing happens along the plains. Dear God!' She moved her head slowly now. 'There's more tragedy and comedy happening in one week than you'd get in a town in a month of Sundays. A few years back people could be hale and hearty one day and without their hair the next; and the lads who rode in yesterday say they're breaking out again, the Comanches. And after all, this isn't such a long ride away for them.'

'Oh don't talk like that, Luisa. I thought you laid great stock on the rangers and the army, and Matthew says we're hundreds of miles away from them, especially the Comanches.'

'Yes, yes; but as I've said before what's a hundred miles to a horse Indian. The only time you're safe from Indians in this country is when you're dead. People around here are getting too complacent. They imagine that the politicians have them all nicely railed off in their tipis, but you can never rail an Indian off anyway, what am I talking about? If they come I'll scream for you like Katie did about the bear. And by the way, I still think it's a mistake to have kept the cub, 'cos cubs grow up, and then what? Far better to have shot it.'

Tilly said nothing to this but went out. She knew that Luisa's chatter about Indians was in the way of an attempt to erase from her mind the conversation she had heard from the bedroom. She liked Luisa, she was very fond of her, but she didn't profess to understand her. She had a strange turn of mind; yet could you wonder at it after what she had gone through with that man? that aping aristocrat, that hypocrite, that praying Christian who had aimed to seduce his daughter when she was but twelve!

Had he succeeded?

∝ 8 ∾

The ranch had become like a camp divided against itself. More and more Alvero Portes had excluded Matthew from the rides. In the beginning he had made Matthew's lacerated arm the excuse, but now when Matthew went down to the compound he would often find that Rod and Mack or Mack and Doug and the black boy Three, together with spare hands, had gone out on a round up.

One day last week Matthew had returned to the house furious because five of the men had been sent off almost at a moment's notice on a branding trip, which meant rounding up the already branded shorthorns and marking their calves by splitting their ears in a special way.

Stamping up and down the room, Matthew had exploded, crying, 'He's testing my temper! He's using breaking-in tactics, but he'll find out I'm no horse.' Then stopping abruptly in front of her, his voice sank deep into his chest as he said on a note that almost sounded like one of sorrow, 'I've had to keep telling myself he's the same man I knew before I returned home, but now there is no comparison, he's as sly and devious as an Indian, and he's vicious. Yes' – he had nodded at her – 'he's vicious. You know, you aren't aware of this and I didn't mean to tell you, but likely Luisa would when she gets prattling, but he flogged Four last night.'

'Flogged him? Oh no! But why? What had he done . . .'

'Supposed to have caught him ill-treating a horse. Can you imagine it? All Four ever wants to do is to get on to a horse's back. I've half expected him to steal one before now and go off. No, it's my opinion, and Doug's also, that he found the boy with Eagle, and having reared the animal himself, he values it more than any other in the stable, and likely Four was just admiring it. It would be enough for Uncle to see him put his black hand on it: daring to touch his precious thoroughbred! But I'm sure that was merely an excuse for the thrashing; he happens to be Luisa's boy, so it was a way of getting at her.'

After a moment of resting her head against his arm, she said, 'Let's get away from here, Matthew, soon, please,' and he nodded slowly as he replied, 'Yes, you're right; we must get away from here, and as you say, soon, the sooner the better. . . .'

On this particular morning the sun was shining, the air was clear, the sky was high, the grass on the plains was rolling in green and yellow waves on a never ending sea.

The young horses in the stockade were kicking their heels and galloping here and there as if they had suddenly become aware of the power in their sinews. Willy and Josefina were playing in front of the house with the tethered bear cub now named Nippy; they also had a wooden horse with a real horse's tail nailed to its end and a similar mane on its roughly carved head.

For all her one-year advantage over Willy, Josefina was not as big as he, nor as strong, as was proven when she tried to dislodge him from the saddle of the wooden horse, and so she attempted to straddle Nippy; which caused Katie to remark to Tilly who was passing through the kitchen, 'They're at it again, those two; fighting to see who's cock-o'-the-walk.'

Tilly turned her head on her shoulder and laughed as she said, 'Well, as long as it remains fifty-fifty we needn't worry.'

'Here's the boss comin'.' Katie pointed out of the window, and Tilly, hurrying through the room, went to the door and opened it and awaited Matthew's arrival with some trepidation, for he hadn't been left the house more than half an hour. However, she could see by his face that he wasn't troubled, but even pleased about something.

He came into the room with his hand outstretched, saying, 'It's a letter from the Curtises. They're having a barbecue at the weekend; they would like us to go and stay the night.'

'Oh, that would be nice. But why are they having a barbecue at this time?'

'The letter says' – he pulled it out of the envelope and handed it to her – 'two visiting dignitaries. It could be Houston, it doesn't say. Anyway . . . visiting dignitaries will have their entourage with them, and you know Tessie has three redheads to get rid of; although I wouldn't like to be the one who'd tackle either Bett or Ranny or Flo, unless they like dray horses.'

'Oh! Matthew.' Tilly flapped her hand at him. 'They're nice girls.'

'So are buffalo cows.'

'Matthew!' She pulled a long face and they both laughed. Then becoming serious, she asked, 'Has *he* got an invitation?'

'Oh likely; there was a letter for him.'

'Who brought them?'

'Oh, three cowboys on the trail; they've been working for Lob Curtis. I left them down in the yard. I think they're asking to be taken on for a day or so.'

'Do you think that Tessie didn't mention the name of the dignitaries in case one is Houston and they knew that your uncle wouldn't accept?'

'Could be.'

'Why doesn't he like Mr Houston? I can't just think it's the senator's policies.'

'I think it's because Mr Houston has never stopped here on his travels. He's travelled for years over the State, I understand, but has never given this ranch the honour of being his headquarters or Uncle his host. But one of the reasons Uncle says he can't stand the man is because of his sojourn with the Indians when he was a young fellow. At one time he lived with them for three years, so to my mind he should know them more than most. Anyway' – he waltzed her round the room now – 'we go to a real party and for the first time I'll have a chance to show you off.' He stopped abruptly and, pulling a grave face, said, 'You will wear your very best gown, Mrs Sopwith, and every piece of jewellery you own for I'm determined to be the envy of every American, rough or smooth neck, at that gathering.'

'Yes, master.'

They now pressed close to each other, laughing as Matthew said, 'I'm glad you know your place at last.'

Her voice serious now, Tilly asked, 'What kind of people will I be expected to meet really, because this won't be any little barn dance, will it, not with Tessie sending out formal invitations?'

'Oh, a political group likely, and between the eating and drinking and the jigging there'll be a lot of serious discussion; and decisions will be taken in quiet corners of the garden, mostly about the slavery question. Strange–' He turned from her and walked up the room and, standing with his back to the fire now, he said, 'At one time back home I thought of going into politics because I felt I understood the situation, but here' – he shook his head – 'a man seems to be for one thing today and changes his mind tomorrow, just as they're accusing Houston of doing; and on this point I think I am with him and against the extension of black slavery, yet because of his stand he's been branded as a traitor. And, of course, he's wholeheartedly for the Indians. It's odd, you know, but I find myself with him in this too. Of course, as Rod pointed out to me when we were talking along these lines a few weeks ago, I've never seen the result of an Indian raid else I wouldn't talk such codswallop. He wouldn't have it that most of the raids were in retaliation for the Government reneguing on their promises. And you know' – he nodded towards her – 'It's shamemaking the way they've done this. Two years ago just before I returned home I was talking to one of the Indian agents. By the way, these are not Indians, they're white Americans who are supposed to look after the welfare of the Indians who are living in reserves. He was a decent enough man but he told me of some of the practices that the agents used to rob the Indians of the very food supplied by the Government for them. Oh' – he beat the top of his head with the palm of his hand – 'it's all beyond me.' Then opening his arms out to her, he said, 'All I'm concerned about is you. Come here.'

When she was standing within the circle of his arms, he put his head on one side and said, 'I've got some news that I'm sure will please you, Mrs Sopwith.'

She waited, saying nothing until he said, 'Aren't you going to ask what it is?'

'Yes, master. What is it?'

He jerked her so tightly to him that she cried out; and then he said, 'Mack tells me of a place going over Cameron way.'

'Is that near the Red River?' Tilly put in quickly.

'No! No! it's miles from there, two hundred miles or so. No, this ranch lies about fifty miles west as the crow flies, between Caldwell and Cameron, but we'll have to go Washington way and cross the Brazos there. And so we'll have to travel about a hundred miles. But you needn't worry, we'll be well outside the Comanche country. Anyway, there's enough soldier-manned forts dotted about to keep the peace; of that I'm sure. Mack says it's an excellent house and he thinks they must have marked out three or four thousand acres. It's good grassland too with wood in plenty quite near. It somehow seems the realisation of a dream because I've thought for a long time now I'd like to start a good beef breed, not just rangy Longhorns, but half and half, the Longhorns for the stamina and say a Scottish breed for their fat. This business of letting them range wild on the plains is all right when there's no alternative, but I can see an alternative. Things are moving fast; there's railroads beginning to extend all over the States and they'll come this way. It might be a few years but they'll come this way. We have the rivers but we want the rails. Just imagine if there was a railroad near at hand and the fellows hadn't to go on that death trail with the herds, because they lose at least a third of them in the dry season. But' – he spread his palm out wide – 'imagine an engine with countless wagons behind.'

She moved from him, saying primly now, 'Yes, yes, I do imagine it, and the poor cattle herded into them with no room to turn or squat. Yes, I imagine it.'

'Oh' He caught her by the shoulders, saying softly, 'Tilly! Tilly!' You're in a wild country; you've got to become hardened to these things else you're going to suffer. Cattle are bred for eating. You like your joint as well as anyone.'

She closed her eyes and drooped her head and said, 'Yes, yes, I know, don't stress the point, I know. Anyway, about the answer to Tessie's letter. I suppose it will have to be formal.'

'Yes, I suppose it will.'

'Well, I'll get down to it right away. Honestly it's funny when you come to think of it' – she was laughing now – 'anyone expecting you to be formal in this –' She wagged her fingers in front of her face and ended weakly, 'place. It seems as if we are back in the county.'

'They have their standards.' His face was straight as he answered her. 'And I think that if you were in the towns you'd find more snobbery and social awareness than ever you did back home. In England ancestors are taken for granted and you rarely speak of them, here they mention them on every possible occasion.

If you can discuss your great-great-grandmother what's-her-name, then you can claim distinction. . . . Go on and write your prettiest acceptance, and I'll see it is sent off later today. . . .'

Tilly wrote the letter of acceptance; then she told Katie she was going down to Luisa's to see if she had received a similar invitation; or perhaps, if it had been included with her father's, she would as yet know nothing of it.

She paused on the slope before entering the compound and looked over the land away in the direction she thought the house would lie, and she knew a rising excitement within her and a feeling that she wanted in this instant to mount a horse and gallop across the land to see this place for herself. In her mind's eye she imagined she saw what it was like, a two-storey house with a white-pillared verandah and steps leading down to a green lawn. Matthew had said it was good grassland, but she told herself that his idea of grass and hers were two different things.

Such was her feeling at the moment that she only stopped herself from running the rest of the way down to the dog run and Luisa.

It was as she entered the compound through a rough log gate that two men, coming out of the bunkhouse, stopped and looked towards her. They were strangers and she surmised they were two of the three new hands about whom Matthew had spoken. She returned their glances and smiled, and as she turned away one of them spoke, saying, ''Tisn't, is it?'

Feeling the question was aimed at her, she turned her head and looked at the man coming towards her. She didn't know him. He had a long face which was bearded on both sides of his cheeks and met his hair underneath the big slouch hat; he was roughly dressed, not unlike the rangers, in long tight trousers and short jacket; he also wore a pocketed leather belt. He was about three yards from her when he stopped and said, 'Can't be two of you.' His voice was unlike those of the other hands and she had to recall where she had heard it last; and when it came into her mind she screwed up her eyes as she stared at the man. The inflexion was northern, English northern.

'Miss Trotter?'

'Yes, I . . . I was Miss Trotter.'

'Oh aye, I forgot. Sorry. Dad wrote 'n told me. Only had one letter from him since I came over. Aw, I've got you on the wrong foot. You don't know me? Well, you wouldn't remember me with all this, would you?' He stroked both sides of his face. 'And three years out here changes a man. I'm Bobby Pearson, you know.'

'Oh! Oh, Mr Pearson's son? Oh yes; he told me that you were bound for America. Well! Well!' For a moment her voice had been pleasant as if she were pleased to see him, but it had only been for a moment for the import of his presence rushed at her with sickening awareness.

'It's a small world, ain't it?'

'Yes, yes, indeed. What . . . what are you doing?'

'Oh, me an' me mate's trekkin' across country, makin' for the mines really . . . gold mines. But as I said, there'll be nowt left by the time we get there. That doesn't worry me though. Live for the day, that's me. We could've been there weeks gone but we dithered; laid up in the bad weather. Eeh! by, it is funny comin' across you here an' talkin' like this. Don't think I passed the time of day with you back home but I saw you many a time when you went out in the carriage. Aye.' He nodded his head as if recalling the scene . . . 'Mr Sopwith, he here? But of course he will be.' He nodded, then looked around the compound, saying, 'Good set-up this, well stocked as far as I've seen. The big boss has set us on for the drive.'

'Oh! has he?' She brought her head forward and wet her lips, then said, 'Well, if that's the case we'll be seeing each other, Mr Pearson.'

'Aye, we likely will.' He backed a step from her, his head bobbing, his face wide with a smile. 'Can't help but bump into people here. Yet there's so much space outside, it's apt to scare the breeches off you at times. . . . Well, be seein' you.'

She inclined her head and turned swiftly away and went towards the dog run; but once in the open corridor she didn't knock on Luisa's living-room door, she paused for a moment, screwed up her eyes tight, then went straight through and out the back way. Here again she paused and put her hand out against the wooden wall for support. He would talk; that man was not like his father, he was a jabberer, he would talk, he would lay claim to knowing all about her. She could see him holding the floor as he described her life back in the Manor, and also the attitude of the villagers towards her. She must find Matthew and put him on his guard.

Where was he? As she turned about to go back through the run into the compound Emilio came out of Luisa's kitchen, and so she hurried towards him, saying, 'Young boss. Have you seen young boss?'

Grinning widely at her, Emilio thumbed over his shoulder, 'He in . . . ' he said.

'Oh, thank you.'

When she rushed into the kitchen, both Luisa and Matthew turned and looked at her. Luisa was preparing some food at the table and Matthew was standing munching a small cake. At the sight of her he gulped at the food in his mouth and swallowed deeply before placing the other half on the table, then putting out his hands, saying, 'Here. Here. What's the matter?'

She looked from him to Luisa for a moment; then as if suddenly making up her mind, she said, 'One of the men that came in this morning who brought the letter, I've just seen him.'

As she paused, he said, 'Yes, what about him?'

'He's . . . he's the son of Mr Pearson. You remember? Or perhaps you don't, but Mr Pearson, he was the odd-job man in the village. He . . . he was very kind to me, always took my part. The last time we met he told me that his son was going to America. Well' – she nodded over her shoulder now – 'he's here, one . . . one of the three men.' She cast her glance at Luisa now and, as if explaining her attitude, she said, 'He . . . he knows all about me, about us, and he's a loose-tongued man, I can tell you. He'll tell them everything, and your uncle 'She was looking at Matthew again, and now she paused and her head moved in one wide sweep as she ended, 'This will be all he needs.'

'Leave him to me. If he dares open his mouth he won't close it for a long time; I'll make that plain to him. 'As he marched towards the door she ran to him and caught his arm and said, 'Go careful, Matthew, be tactful, I mean, don't . . . don't get his back up. Ask him, rather than tell him, not to mention my name.'

He looked at her hard for a moment before turning from her and going out; and when the door was closed she leant against it and looked towards Luisa.

'Is it as bad as all that?' asked Luisa.

'It . . . it isn't to me, it never was, it's how people will look at it.'

'Look at what?'

Tilly bowed her head, 'Me being . . . named a witch, and . . . and living with Matthew's father as his mistress for twelve years.'

She raised her eyes to see Luisa staring at her with her mouth agape. She had moved from the table and her back was almost against the wood-stoked oven. Then her remark surprised Tilly, for what she said was, 'A witch? Dear God! how strange.'

She hadn't shown any feminine horror over the knowledge that she had been Matthew's father's mistress, nor was she showing horror with regard to the witch question, rather her expression was one of amazement.

It was at this point that their attention was wrenched from each other and to the window and to the sound of the cries coming from the compound. Suddenly Tilly put her hand to her mouth and let out a high cry before rushing to the door, with Luisa after her; and there they stood together for a moment as they watched Matthew and Bobby Pearson come staggering out of the bunkhouse, their fists flailing.

When Tilly went to run towards them, Luisa, gripping her arm, hissed, 'Be still for a minute.' And so she remained still while at the same time her body seemed set for a spring. The yard was now full of people. Rod Tyler, Mack and Doug Scott were circling the combatants. The new men were in the bunkhouse doorway. One, Two, Three and Four, and Ma One were outside the stables, and Diego and Emilio were at the bottom of the house steps. But at the top, on the verandah, stood Alvero Portes, a look of amazement mixed with disdain on his face. And not until he saw Matthew borne to the ground by the new hand and the pair of them rolling in the dust did he hurry down the steps and shout, 'McNeill! Stop them! Stop them this instant!'

Mack moved away a little from the circle and, looking towards his boss, made a gesture with his hand which plainly said, 'No.' But when he saw that Matthew had the younger man pinned by the throat and was almost throttling him and that the man on the ground had ceased to thrash his legs, he sprang forward. Immediately Doug Scott was at his side and together they hauled Matthew upwards on to his feet; and it took them all their time to hold him. One of the men now ran from the bunkhouse doorway and, going to Bobby Pearson raised his head from the ground. Rod Tyler, too, went to his side, saying, 'You all right?'

Pearson jerked his head and felt his neck; then looking towards where Matthew was glaring at him, he gasped, 'Bloody maniac!'

'Get out!'

Both Mack and Doug felt Matthew stiffen like a ramrod when Alvero Portes's voice, rising above the murmured hubbub, said, 'I engaged this man, I'll tell him when to go. Now what is this all about?' He looked towards Pearson for an answer and he, his voice a growl, cried, 'All because I was speakin' about his bloody wife, so-called.'

'Steady! Steady!' Doug's voice came as a hissing whisper to Matthew. 'You can't stop him talkin' now; he's spilled it already, anyway.'

And he was right, for Pearson, looking towards Alvero Portes, cried, 'I knew her from I was a bairn, lived in the same village. She was hounded 'cos she was a witch; she caused trouble wherever she stepped.' Again he felt his neck and with his other hand wiped the blood that was oozing from the top of his lip and soaking his beard. 'She was the means of two men being killed; then she goes whorin' up at the Manor and was his da's mistress for years. She had a bairn to him . . . aye, aye. . . .'

As Matthew's body heaved itself forward he almost dragged the struggling Mack and Doug to the ground; this brought Rod Tyler to their assistance, saying, 'Get him up to the house.'

As the men managed to turn Matthew about, Tilly, too, turned away. There was no need now for Luisa to restrain her, nor did she attempt to follow Matthew and the men, but she allowed Luisa to lead her along the dog run and into the living-room, and when Luisa pressed her gently into a chair she made no resistance, she just sat with her hands on her lap staring before her.

A moment later Luisa, handing her a good measure of brandy, said, 'Get that down you.' And she did as she was bid, she swallowed the brandy in two gulps.

When Luisa said quietly, 'Well, you've been through the mill and come out ground down, haven't you?' she bowed her head and the tears oozed from her lids, and Luisa put in quickly, 'Don't worry your head, I'm not censuring you, I'm only amazed at the witch bit.'

'I was never a witch, nor did any witch-like things.' Tilly's voice had a weary flat note to it; it was as if she had suddenly become very tired.

'I believe you. But what I'm amazed at is that you too have suffered through being a so-called witch; I'm like I am today, a frustrated spinster, through much the same thing.'

When Tilly blinked the tears from her eyes and they widened, Luisa said, 'Witchery is a dirty word in some areas.' Then turning, she pulled a chair up and sat down and, her knees almost touching Tilly's, she said, 'You know the photo back in my bedroom? Well, his name was Bailey and he lived in Massachusetts; at least he was born there, but then his father brought him here when he was about two years old. Well, it should so happen that my father lived in Massachusetts and his people had lived there too for some generations. They were as poor as slaves but as proud as Lucifer. Well, the Baileys were ordinary people and someone of that name had in the far, far past during a witchery time named a Portes as some kind of sorcerer. Anyway, one of Father's relatives was hanged. Now as far as I can gather there were dozens of people by the name of Bailey roundabout the countryside, not so many Portes. Anyway, we were here and I was eighteen before I heard a word about this. You see' – she bowed her head now – 'I was never allowed to talk to men, never allowed to be alone with a man for five minutes, even a ranch hand, and never, never was I allowed to ride out on my own, he was always with me.' She jerked her head towards the house. 'Well, during our rides we often passed a homestead this side of Wheelock. It was a poor place, and nearly always I saw a young man and a woman in the fields, and the young man would straighten his back and look in my direction, and I in his. Then one day Father was ill and I went riding on my own and in the direction of that homestead; and for the first time I met and talked with Eddie Bailey, and straightaway we both knew what had happened to us.

'During that week I escaped the house three times and rode towards Wheelock. At our third meeting he took me in his arms and kissed me. It was as quick as that. But Father soon got better and I became hard put to slip away; I don't think we met more than six times during the next twelve months. And Eddie knew better than to show his face here, for he had heard enough about Senor Portes' – her voice held a sneer on the Senor – 'to know that he'd be kicked off the place for no other reason but that he was a man who was interested in me.'

When she stopped and rose to her feet and went towards the fire, Tilly turned her head slowly and looked at her and she could hardly hear Luisa's voice as she went on, 'When I was eighteen something happened, it was inevitable, we loved each other, keen mad about each other, so I told my mother about Eddie and my mother told him. God above!' Her head drooped on to the back of her shoulders as if she were straining to say something; and she stayed like that for a moment before she went on, 'He acted like a madman, he became almost insane . . . not almost' – she now shook her head – 'he did go insane, and over the name Bailey. Then it all came out: Eddie could have been one of a thousand Baileys, but no, he was the Bailey, or a descendant of the Bailey who had been the instigation of that poor Portes ending with a rope round his neck.'

She turned now and looked at Tilly. 'It's funny,' she said, 'how little things stick in your mind. I remember, as I watched him raging up and down the room, dashing things off the table on to the floor, I remember thinking he could make those steps into a dance. Wasn't that silly?' She gave a small laugh, then went on, 'You don't know how silly it was because I stopped him dancing by saying, "I have got to marry Eddie Bailey because I am going to have his child."

'I thought he was about to kill me. I remember crouching on the floor and Mother leaning over me to protect me from him. I can see him now grabbing at her arm and flinging her aside. She was thin and small and she spun like a top across the room. And then he was bending over me; and I looked up at him and you know what I said, Tilly? I said, "You are a filthy, dirty bugger of a man!" It was the first time I'd sworn in my life, and I ended by yelling, "You lay a hand on me and I'll drive this knife into you!" and, you know, I had a knife in my hand. He had scattered the cutlery off the dining-table and the knife was there to my side, and I would have used it, I know before God I would have used it, because I knew he was going to grab me. But at that moment Mack came into the room. How long he had been there or what he had heard I don't know, but he saved me from killing him because I had the knife held like that' – she demonstrated – 'and pointing upwards at the bottom of his belly.

'I kept in my room for almost three days. Then Mother told me that Mack had got word to Eddie about the situation, and that he was prepared to come over and get me on the Friday. That was two days ahead when Father had arranged to ride out with the hands for a round-up.

'Well, Friday came.' Luisa now paused and slowly seated herself again in front of Tilly. 'Mother and I watched them all ride out of the compound. We saw the dust settle. Then we waited for Eddie coming. It was almost half an hour later when he galloped into the yard leading another horse. I was all ready with my bundle, I'd thrown some things into a sheet, and there I stood in that room' – she jerked her head again – 'my heart beating fit to burst. Eddie came in through the doorway and we looked at each other across the space. It was the first time he had seen my mother, and it was the first time she had seen him. He said, "Hello, ma'am," and she answered, "Hello, Mr Bailey". It was all so slow and easygoing, there was no need to hurry, we had four days to get away, so we thought. Eddie spoke a little to my mother and told her he'd always take good care of me, and she thanked him. The tears were running down her face. It was as he picked up my bundle from the floor that Father appeared in the archway leading to the corridor. There were no words to explain the feeling of terror I experienced even before he fired. The bullet caught Eddie in the chest just below his left shoulder. He staggered and fell on to his side. But he was no sooner on the ground than he drew his Colt, and as he did so Father went to fire again, and at this Mother rushed at him. He could have thrust her aside but he didn't, it all happened in a split second. She was pinned to his chest when the bullet from Eddie's gun hit her. Then father let blaze. He emptied the other five bullets into him.'

Tilly's mouth was open and it remained so for some time before she gasped, 'Oh, Luisa! Oh, Luisa dear!' When she put out her hand, Luisa said, 'It's all right, it's just a memory now, but I've told you because I don't want you to feel too bad about what that swine of an English fellow spilled.'

Tilly now asked gently, 'The baby? Your baby?'

'Oh, I lost it, and, you know, I don't remember losing it. I screamed for days, they told me, then I went quiet and hardly moved or spoke for two years. It was another four before I recovered, if I ever have.' She smiled a sad smile now. 'The awful thing about it is, I couldn't move away from this place when I did recover. Ma One became my mother in a way and Mack ... what has Mack become?' She shrugged her shoulders now. 'A prop to keep hold of.' She became thoughtful for a moment before saying, 'I said it was all a memory, but what still fills me with bitterness is the fact that evil men can be honoured for their actions, because in some quarters Father was upheld for having killed the man who had left me with a child. Some of the sanctimonious hypocrites, and there are a number along this line, and the Curtises are among them, so are the Purdies, they upheld Father's action. It was, they said, just exactly what they would have done in the same circumstances should one of their daughters have been deflowered. That's the word they used, deflowered. Yet the things that go on in some homesteads! But they rarely creep out because the name must be kept clean, except when a brother might get drunk and attack the fellow who is making eyes at his sister, whom he himself has already had. And you hear them talking about the sacredness of womanhood! Oh my God! they would have you think that these things only happen in the forts. . . . Anyway, my dear – ' She once more rose to her feet and, putting her hand on Tilly's shoulder, she said, 'This is the end of your sojourn at the Portes's ranch. Matthew was telling me that he's got a place in mind. You must ride out there and see it, and soon, because after this he'll make your life unbearable.'

Tilly, too, got slowly to her feet, saying, 'I don't know how I can face the men after what's happened.'

'Oh, they'll think what they think, you can't stop men thinking; and they being men, you'll lose their respect. But what do you care about that? You've got Matthew, and he's one in a thousand. And you're a lucky girl. Aye, you're lucky, for what he feels for you is something that doesn't happen to many women. He might become hard to live with as the years go on because in a way he's as possessive as my father and. . . .'

'Oh, don't say that.' Tilly's voice was loud now, and Luisa answered, 'Oh, don't get me wrong, I don't mean that he's like him in any other way, except that he'll never bear the thought of anyone else sharing you.'

Tilly moved her head slowly, saying now, 'Yes, yes, I know that only too well, for even now I've got to be careful in the affection I show to the children, especially Josefina. Poor Josefina.'

'Oh, she's not so poor, she's got a home now that she'd never had with her mother, because Leonilde's a little whore if ever there was one. . . . But now, now you'd better go up for I'm thinking Matthew might be needing more attention than the fellows can give him. I'll be up later. And tomorrow get yourselves off if possible to look at that place. I'll keep an eye on Katie and the children; they'll come to no harm.'

They went out of the room together and into the dog run and as they neared the end of it they both stopped, for there, as if he had been waiting for her, stood Alvero Portes.

The man's face looked grey under his tan and his eyes appeared black round balls lying in their sockets but looking fiercer than Tilly had yet seen them. She watched his thin neck swell, his Adam's apple jerking up and down behind the tight high collar of his blue serge coat; then he spoke directly to her. He did not shout but his precise tone and the way he threw the words from his mouth seemed to spray them far and wide over the compound and halt the men there.

'You unclean thing!' he said. 'A witch indeed! for only one such could enslave a man like my nephew, after having entrapped his father. You will leave this place. . . .'

His words were cut off now by Tilly's voice which was indeed a scream. 'How dare you! Just how dare you put the name unclean to me, you filthy, horrible man! You who raped your own child. You . . . *you* dare to call me unclean! *You!*' The saliva was actually running from the corners of her mouth, she was consumed by a rage that was so fierce she had no control over it; and when it prompted her to spring on this hypocrite she obeyed it. Her fingers clawing at his face, he was for a moment utterly taken off his guard, so much so that he staggered back, bringing up his forearm to protect himself. But what he would have done next had not Luisa, Ma One and Emilio pulled her from him is doubtful; likely he would have felled her to the ground; but just as a short while previously the men had had their hands full restraining Matthew, now the same was happening with Tilly. The veneer of this pseudo-lady that Mr Burgess and Mark, between them, had created was stripped away, revealing almost a wild woman. And in this moment Tilly was wild, her whole being was retaliating against the injustice meted out to her by the villagers, the McGraths in particular. She was once again on the ground fighting as if for her life against the weight of Hal McGrath; she was in the stocks being pelted; she was in the courtroom being exposed as a witness; she was holding her Granny in her arms after the cottage had been burned down; she was in the kitchen of the Manor being subjected to the taunts and hate of the majority of the staff; she was suffering the humiliation of being turned out of the house; she was being brought low by Miss Jessie Ann's disdain and for the second time being forced to leave the Manor; she was in the market place avoiding Mrs McGrath's stick that then blinded her child; she was standing stiff-faced and straight-backed under the sneers and insults of the ladies of the county; and finally, here she had to suffer the hate of this dirty lecherous old beast who dared to say that she was unclean.

She ceased struggling, then shook off the hands that were clinging to her, and stood gasping for breath. She was speaking again as she looked at the man who was standing holding a white handkerchief to his face and whose features had seemed to assume those of the devil, and, her voice loud once more, she cried at him, 'Witch, you say I am. All right, as a witch I'll say this to you: One day you'll wish for death, you'll be so alone you'll wish for death.' And on this she turned and, pushing Luisa and Ma One roughly aside, she marched out of the compound and up the hill and almost burst into the room.

Rod Tyler, Mack and Doug turned as one to look at her. Matthew was the last to turn towards her for he had been sitting in a chair, his head bent forward, but he immediately got to his feet when he saw her.

She was gripping the side of the table and looking past the men towards him and she said, 'You'd better be prepared to get out of here as soon as possible because I've just left my signature on his face.'

'What!' Matthew came haltingly towards her. He was gripping the arm that the bear had torn as if it were causing him intense pain. Standing in front of her, he said, 'What did you say?'

She had to take a tight hold on the table to steady herself but when she spoke each word was on a tremble. 'He . . . he told me to get out because I . . . I was unclean, and I don't know what came over me . . . oh, yes I do' – she now shook her head – 'I became inflamed with the injustice of it, one more piled on top of the others, and I . . . I told him what he was, a filthy old man.' She now turned her head and looked at the three men who were gazing at her, and when she caught the eye of Mack he bowed his head and she said to him, 'You know to what I am referring, don't you?' She didn't wait for an answer but, looking at Matthew again, she said, 'We . . . we must get away to . . . to that place, no matter what it is like.' Then glancing at Mack again, she asked, 'What's it really like, this place?'

'It's a fine place. You could make it as good as this any day; but it's fine as it stands, and they want out soon as possible.'

She nodded at him, then said, 'That settles it then,' and, releasing her hold on the table she went up the room and slumped into a chair.

Moving uneasily now, the men nodded towards Matthew, and it was Doug who said, 'You all right, Matt?' and Matthew answered, 'Yes, yes, I'm all right. Thanks.'

Without further words, one after the other filed out, and now Matthew, going to Tilly, looked down at her as he muttered, 'You actually hit him?' She lifted her head wearily and, her voice expressing her feelings, she said, 'No, I didn't hit him, I clawed at him. I drew blood and I hope he carries the marks for a long time.'

'Oh Tilly! Tilly!'

She gave a weary laugh. 'Very unladylike.'

'To hell with being ladylike! What I'm thinking is that I've caused you to suffer this, my dear.' He sat down near to her and, taking her hand, said, 'Nothing's gone right since we came here, but once we're on our own things will be different.'

She looked down at their joined hands. 'Rumours spread. Fifty miles here is equal to a mile at home! I'll be known as a tainted woman, father and son.' She raised her eyes to him and the pain in them made him stretch out his arms to her, only for him to wince, and at the sight of his twisted face she said, 'Your arm... your arm, has it broken open?'

'No, no.' He shook his head. 'It's just that I haven't used it, not in that way for some time.' He smiled wryly now.

She looked anxiously at him as she said, 'You'll be able to ride?'

'Of course. Of course. And we'll go first thing in the morning, taking Manuel with us. He's an intelligent fellow and he knows the countryside well. There's not a chance of any of the others coming with us, not at the moment anyway. But when we're settled I think Doug will join us. He was saying as much just before you came in. Of course as I've said before, I think it's Katie that is the attraction, but what matter, he's a good fellow is Doug.'

'How long will it take?'

'To get there? Well, I don't suppose the way we travel we'll do more than forty to fifty miles a day; two days on the road there and we'll be able to settle matters in a day, and no matter what it's like we'll take it for the present, then two days back. Well, we could be settled in eight or nine days.'

'I can't believe it.' She leant her head against him now and her words were low, scarcely above a whisper, as she asked, 'You wouldn't want to return home, would you?' She waited for his answer without looking at him, and when it came his words, too, were low as he said, 'Never to live there, Tilly. Somehow this is my country. For good or bad it's where I want to be. I feel at home here as I've never felt in any place before. I can't explain it to you; I knew when I first set foot in it I wanted to live here and die here. But listen, my darling.' He lifted up her chin and looked deep into her sad eyes. 'Don't worry any more because once settled on our own, our life could become ideal.'

He bowed his head towards her, and when he placed his lips gently on hers she murmured to herself, Ideal. Ideal. But the picture the words presented brought no glow to her mind.

✑ 9 ✑

She was amazed at the beauty of the land. They had ridden for the last half-hour through shoulder-high grass and had just emerged on the high bank of a river. She was so impressed with the sight that she could find no words with which to express her feelings, but, like Matthew, she sat gazing down on the slatey-blue water winding its way swiftly between golden banks that looked from this distance like sand-strewn beaches; and away in the near distance like a vivid painting lay a line of purple hills. She had never seen such vivid colouring. On the journey from Galveston to the ranch they had passed through fine country but this was different, this had the appearance of a mighty mural, in fact, she thought it looked too beautiful to be real.

'Wonderful!'

She turned her head and looked at Matthew and repeated 'Wonderful! Yes, wonderful!' Then she asked, 'Will . . . Will it be like this all the way?'

'No, I'm afraid not.' He shook his head. 'Over there' – he pointed to the right – 'the land is like an endless pancake except for a few cottonwood trees and grass.'

'It would be lovely to have a homestead here.'

'Not good for homestead, mistress.'

'No? Why?' She turned to Manuel.

'All hills, no pastures; hills no safe.'

'Oh.' She was about to ask, 'In what way not safe?' when Matthew said, 'Well, we'd better be pushing on; the light will soon be fading and we're some way from the trading post.'

For the next hour they rode by the river, and curiously the hills seemed to remain the same distance away throughout the journey. Suddenly from twisting and turning through hillocks large and small, the land fell into a great flat expanse of nothingness again, and there, not a hundred yards from the river bank, stood a substantial timber-built trading post. In front of it were small groups of people, some standing, some leaning against what looked like a stout single pole fence that did not surround the post, merely ran along in front for a short distance. Others were squatting on the ground. And tethered to the fence were a number of small horses.

They were the first real Indians that Tilly had seen and it appeared that she was the first kind of white woman they had seen for those who were sitting rose from the ground and those who were leaning stood straight and with unblinking stares they watched her and the white man dismount. They watched the Mexican take their horses; then, their heads slowly turning, their eyes followed the progress of the tall thin woman whose walk was unsteady and who had to be aided by the sturdy young man up the steps and into the post; and slowly they drew together and gathered round the open doorway.

'Hello there. Pleased to see ya. How do you do, ma'am? Hello there, Manuel.' The man had inserted himself between Tilly and Matthew and was shouting through the doorway, 'Didn't know you were coming this way again. Thought you had settled with Portes. Hello, sir. 'He had turned his attention to Matthew. 'What can I do for you?'

The tall, thin, middle-aged, clean-shaven man who spoke with a strong Scottish accent and, unlike his countrymen, was anything but dour, now brought forward two wooden chairs, one swinging from each hand. The first he placed with a thud just behind Tilly's knees and she found herself sitting down without the effort. Then she looked to where Matthew was now seated and telling their host why they were here, where they were bound for, and that they would like to be put up for the night.

Tilly said nothing, she merely looked about her, all the while trying not to sneeze or to put her hands to her buttocks in an effort to ease the pain. She had been in a trading post before but not one as well stocked as this. Against one wall was a rough wooden table and on it were stacked piles of skins which apparently had been graded into sets. Lying at right angles to it was a smaller bench on which was a jumble of pelts; on the other side of the room was a counter at the end of which was a pair of large brass scales and below them, on the floor, a weighing machine. In front of the counter was a row of sacks with their tops open, full, as far as she could guess, of grain or meal; and behind the counter were shelves holding an assortment of tins and bottles.

Against the other wall was set a line of tools: shovels, picks, hoes and ploughs. Behind this, high up on the wall, were a number of guns, large and small. The only two she could recognise were a Colt revolver and a German rifle. The latter type Matthew had already tried to get her to handle but she had found it difficult, cumbersome; the Colt he always said was for men, most useful when fighting on horseback. But what caught her eye and held it by its very incongruity in such a place was a glass case.

In this rough store it looked as much out of place as did the china cabinet in Alvero Portes's sitting-room. From this distance she could just make out that it held a number of trinkets, mostly strings of beads and cards studded with bright buttons.

'Well now, ma'am, have you viewed everything?'

Somewhat startled, her attention was brought to Mr Ian Mackintosh, for there could be only one such man to correspond with the name on the board at the door. 'You've had a good look round?'

'Yes; it's . . . it's fascinating.'

'That's the word, that's the word' – he wagged his hand at her – 'fascinating. Aye, Aye, that's the word. Everything about here is fascinating. But now I suppose you'd like to get the dust off you. Are you sleepin' in or out?' he said, turning to Matthew, and he, getting to his feet, asked, 'Have you accommodation?'

'That room there.'

He did not indicate the room by either a toss of his head or his thumb over his shoulder but with his heavy leather-booted foot which he scraped on the floor in a backward movement very like a horse pawing at the earth, then went on, 'Dollar a night, including bedding. Or you can use your own. Soap and towel provided.'

Tilly could see that Matthew was striving not to laugh outright and he spoke politely, saying, 'Thank you, Mr Mackintosh; we'll be pleased to take it.'

When Tilly was shown into the room she did not endorse Matthew's last remark, for it was quite bare except for three beds and a rough, a very rough hand-made wash-hand-stand with a tin dish and jug on it, a piece of blue soap in a saucer, and a towel that would have been used for taking hot dripping tins from the oven back in the Manor.

But once the door was closed she smiled at Matthew and, pointing to the three beds, she said in a whisper, 'Is it likely we'll have company?'

'I shouldn't be surprised. . . .'

She had taken off her hat and coat, washed her face and hands, and was now sitting on the edge of the bed watching Matthew sluicing the water over his head when she said, 'Oh, I am stiff, all I want to do at this moment is lie on my face.'

'Tomorrow will be better.'

'So you say. Well, I hope so. By the way, those Indians out there, are they all right?'

'What's that?' He turned towards her now, blowing into the towel.

'I said those Indians out there, are they all right? They look . . . well. . . .'

'Oh yes; you needn't worry about them, they're from the reserves. A number of them will be scouts.'

'Scouts?'

'Yes; they scout for the army; all the forts have their Indian scouts. They can pick up a trail like a bloodhound, they know all the signs.'

'You mean they lead the soldiers on to their own people?'

'Aw, Tilly.' He now drew a comb through his thick stubbly hair as he said, 'It's no use, it's hardly any use explaining, I really don't understand it myself. There are so many tribes and so many different camps inside a tribe and as far back as anybody can remember the tribes have been fighting each other, in places they've almost wiped each other out. I understand at one time there might be five thousand in one camp and that would be only one section of a tribe; and their rights and their laws would fill a hundred books. Someone some day will get down to it. I only hope it isn't a politician, because they will only hear one side of it. Anyway, let's go and see what our friend, Mr Ian Mackintosh, has to offer us in the way of supper.'

As she rose stiffly from the bed, she asked quietly, 'How is your arm?'

'Not as bad as I thought it would be; it's still strong enough to put round you.'

They stood close for a few moments looking at each other, until he said, 'I love you. Do you know that, woman? I love you. I love you more every day. I thought that when we married my feelings couldn't possibly grow stronger, they were so intense then, but now . . . well, it is strange but the intensity has taken on a kind of . . . ' He paused and turned his head away and she asked gently, 'Kind of what?'

'Fear.'

'Fear?'

'Yes, fear. I've never really known what it was to be afraid until now and I have this strange fear on me that I am . . . well, too happy where you are concerned; even with what happened back there and the irritations that he's forced upon me during the last few months, these should have been predominant in my mind, but no, they have been pressed down by this real kind of fear that –' again he bowed his head, but now she didn't speak she simply waited and when he looked at her again he ended, 'that I may lose you.'

'Aw, don't be silly, my dear.' She was now holding him tightly. 'You'll never lose me. Nothing or no one can separate us. If he didn't, and Josefina didn't, no one can, not now. The only thing that can separate us is death, and not even that because we're so joined, we're so one in every way that if I go first I'll wait for you. I know this inside myself.' She tapped her breast. 'Perhaps that really is the witch part of me . . . and you'll do the same. I feel that wherever we're meant to go after death we'll fight against it until we can go on together.'

'Oh, Tilly! Tilly, there's no one in the whole world like you, no one.' His voice had a catch in it; and now they hid their faces in each other's shoulder and remained still.

It was just after first light next morning when they left the trading post. Tilly was so stiff she didn't know how she rose from the bed, and when she stumbled and almost upset the single candle that was their only form of light Matthew caught her, and pressing her down on the bed again, he massaged her limbs, laughing at her as he did so. She had always been amazed at his good humour first thing in the morning, so different from his father's, for Mark's temper had been taciturn during the early part of the day.

They hoped to reach their destination in three hours' time, do what business had to be done and be back at the trading post this evening. In fact, Matthew had not only paid for their bed in advance but had paid for the entire room. They had been lucky last night to have the place to themselves, but as Mr Mackintosh had explained that was unusual.

The countryside had changed again. They were riding now among low hills, crossing streams, some small and some not so small. They were surprised, at least Tilly was when passing through a narrow gully, to see stationed on one of its heights a man in uniform with a gun at his side. Matthew and Manuel had also seen the man. They drew rein for a moment; then Manuel, turning to Tilly, smiled as he said, 'He's the soldiery, one of the new cavalry.'

'What's that?' Matthew asked.

'There are bands of cavalry about now, sent to fight the Indians.'

As they rode out of the gully, they came upon a company breaking camp. The situation was in a depression bordered on two sides by hills and Manuel, looking about him, spoke now in rapid Spanish, then turning to Matthew, he said, 'Good bed to die in.'

Before Matthew had time to make any retort a young man marched smartly up to them. By his uniform he looked to be an officer and he spoke as one in command in a rather high-falutin manner, saying, 'Captain Dixon at your service, sir. And may I enquire your destination?'

Matthew stared down at the man for a moment; then with a wry smile, he said, with not a little mimicry in his tone, 'Matthew Sopwith at your service, sir, and our destination, as I understand it, is about five miles from Cameron.'

'Oh yes; Cameron. Well, that's all right.' He now turned and looked up at Tilly and, bowing slightly, he greeted her with one word, 'Ma'am,' and she in return merely inclined her head towards him.

The officer again turned to Matthew and said, 'I'd be obliged if I could have a word with you, sir.'

Matthew glanced first at Tilly and then at Manuel before dismounting and walking away with the captain towards where the men were now standing by their horses.

Tilly gazed at the soldiers. Most of them looked young. They were all staring towards her except for a sergeant who now began to shout unintelligible orders.

Within a few minutes Matthew returned, the officer with him. After mounting his horse again he looked down into the clean-shaven face and said, 'I wish you good-day.'

The officer said nothing, he merely stepped back and saluted, then waited for them to ride on.

As they passed the group of soldiers the sergeant was still barking his orders at them, but it didn't stop the men from casting their glances in Tilly's direction, and when she smiled at them she was answered instantly by wide grins.

But they were hardly out of earshot of the men when she rode abreast of Matthew and said, 'What did he want to say to you?'

'Oh, nothing. It strikes me he's very young to the game and he wouldn't have much chance of keeping that rabble in hand if it wasn't for the sergeant.'

'Matthew' – the tone of her voice brought his head round – 'don't keep anything from me, please.'

He blinked his eyes, then wet his lips before he said, 'Well, I'll tell you what he said. He suggested that we didn't go back to the trading post tonight, he thought we should make for the fort.'

'Because of danger?'

'Oh no!' He shook his head. 'I happened to mention that we stayed at the trading post and he didn't think it was any fit place for a lady such as you.'

She stared at him for a while before she said, 'Honest?'

'Honest; why should I lie?'

Yes, why should he lie.

'Come on,' he said; 'let's put a move on. I want to see this place.' And at that he galloped ahead while she urged her horse after him and Manuel came up in the rear. Manuel, she had noticed, like most Mexicans, became part of the animal he sat on. She had heard it said that it was from the Mexicans the Indians first learned how to ride and were now so famous in their handling of horses that they had become known as the horse Indians and, besides, so infamous that the very name of them chilled the blood.

They neared the homestead about eleven o'clock. They stopped on a rise, the three of them in a row, and looked down on it, and Tilly's eyes brightened and her face went into a broad smile before she turned to Matthew and said, 'Oh, isn't it nice?'

The house was long and low, with a verandah running along its front. This was supported by stout pillars. It had a wood shingle roof, and one end of it was covered with creeper. On three sides there was a white railing and on the fourth a large stockade, but dominating the whole scene was an outsize barn. It was higher and wider than the house and the other outbuildings all put together.

She felt Matthew letting out a deep sigh and when she looked at him his eyes were waiting for hers and he said simply, 'It was made for us; and if the outside's anything to go by, the inside should be all right too.'

'That won't matter, I'll make it all right.' She smiled at him, then turned her head to Manuel and said simply, 'It looks good.'

'Good. Yes, good. Hans Meyer good man. Work along here one time... good man but no more.'

When he shook his head she said, 'He has gone?'

He now pointed towards the earth and she put in quietly, 'Dead?'

'Dead.'

She turned to Matthew saying, 'Did you know this?'

'No; I know as little about them as you do. But come, we'll soon find out.'

It was as if Frau Meyer were waiting for their approach for she met them outside the white railings and, extending her hand first to Matthew and then Tilly, she spoke with a strong German accent. 'You velcome, very velcome. You kom sooner than I expect.'

'You expected us?'

The small woman nodded at Matthew, her round face one bright smile as she said, 'Oh yes, I knew early tis morning.'

Both Matthew and Tilly looked at each other, and it was Tilly who asked now, 'But how?'

'Oh, scout on his way to fort, he told me of your presence and vy.'

Matthew gave a brief laugh now as he said, 'Quicker than smoke signals.'

'Yes, yes, quicker 'n smoke signals, but do to kom in. You are very velcome, very velcome.'

Tilly found the inside of the house as pleasing as the outside. The furniture was all wooden and hand-made but with a difference, for there was a touch of artistry about every piece in the room from the dresser to the row of wooden mugs arranged on a shelf to the side of the fireplace, very much like the pieces of brass that used to bedeck the mantelpiece in her granny's cottage. The floor-boards had been sand-scrubbed and were covered here and there with bright hand-made rugs.

Tilly saw that the room was both living-room and kitchen. There were two doors going off it that spoke of other rooms, and at one end a steep wooden staircase that led to the floor above.

'I have meal ready for you, I am sure you hungry... You vill eat?'

'Yes. Yes, thank you very much. It is so kind of you, but tell me.' Tilly now glanced at Matthew, who had seated himself in a rocking-chair and was looking silently about the room, evidently pleased with everything he saw. 'Are you really thinking of selling this place, your... your home?'

'Yes.' The answer was brief; and then she put in, 'Your name is?'

'Mrs Sopwith.'

'Me, I am Anna Meyer. And yes, I must sell, for my children I must sell. Big Hans, my husband, he die two years. Little Hans he is twelve years and not strong, never like big Hans and Berta. She is nine years. No life for small children. Be very strong to stand life here.'

'Have you no men, I mean hands around the place?' It was Matthew who asked the question now, and Frau Meyer turned to him and said, 'We had two, Johann Braun and Franz Klein. They very good ven big Hans was here but not so good ven he was gone. Then they leave like that' – she snapped her finger – 'to go to gold mine. Gold rush been on a long time and they don't go, but sudden they go like that.' Again she snapped her finger.

'They just walked out and left you?' Matthew's brows were puckered now, and she nodded at him and said, 'Yes, they valk out. Vanted double pay. I couldn't pay double pay. They say that ven they came back I'd be glad to pay double pay, place get in bad state, but I von't be bullied or frightened so I sell and take my children back to Germany. I have been here twenty year but it is not home. I long for home. I have sisters and brothers my children have not seen.'

'Did you build all this yourselves?'

'Yes, noting here when ve came. Big Hans and me ve vork all time. Ve make small huts first, not this.' She smiled now as she waved her hand. 'Then ve buy cattle, and horses, one, two and three, four, and on and on. Then ve build barn. Many hands to build barn but many hands come by this way in those days 'fore gold rush, and lots of help from good friends. Then last, 'fore my son is born twelve years since, ve build again.' She caved her hand. 'This vas not finished ven he kom, and he saw first light there.' She pointed to a space before the stove. 'But now' – she turned away and walked towards a table that was fully set for a meal – 'all is finished. Life is split ven man goes, power leaves your arm. But kom, you vill vant to refresh yourself 'fore you eat, and I vill call my Hans and Berta to the table.'

They ate a substantial meal, joined by Manuel and Frau Meyer's two children. Young Hans touched Tilly's heart immediately, for she had seen so many pale faces like his back in England and heard the same sharp cough. Then there was Berta. There was nothing wrong with Berta; she was a bright replica of her mother, her eyes laughing, her tongue chattering.

After the meal they made an inspection of the outbuildings and both Matthew and Tilly expressed their amazement at the size of the barn. It had looked big from outside but inside it appeared enormous. It was filled mostly with dried hay but there were also sacks of grain and animal feed, yet there was still room enough left to drive a cart and horse into it. There were four milking cows and three calves, and some chickens. Following this, they mounted their horses and rode round the extent of the land. In one corral there was a herd of crossed mustangs, and Matthew noticed straightaway that, as horseflesh went, they were of little account; but that didn't matter, the land was good and included in it there was a large stretch of woodland to the east. Its presence explained the extensive outbuildings and the well-built house.

Altogether he was delighted with the place and showed it. The only thing that remained now to be settled was the question of the price.

Back in the house, drinking strong black coffee, he looked at Anna Meyer and said, 'Well now, Mrs Meyer, what are you asking for your place?'

The little woman joined her hands together and rubbed one over the other as if washing them and she moved her head in small jerks before she said, 'Eight hundred dollars. No less, no less.'

He opened his mouth as he stared at her. Then he looked towards Tilly and shook his head, and Mrs Meyer, taking the action that her price was too high, began to talk rapidly, her words interspersed with German, as she went on to explain about all the work they had put in; there was the stock and the land they had cultivated, and then this house.

Matthew was smiling widely when he held up his hand and said, 'Please, I am not disagreeing with your price, I am only surprised at its moderation.'

'Oh!' Mrs Meyer now dropped on to a chair and her round face slid into a smile and it broadened as she listened to Matthew saying, 'I will add half to that and gladly.'

'Oh, tank you, tank you.' Mrs Meyer now rose to her feet and held out her hand towards Matthew; then looking at Tilly, she said, 'You satisfied?'

'Oh yes, yes.' Tilly nodded at her quickly. 'And I love the house.' She spread her arms wide. 'I haven't seen one I like better. Oh I noticed some more pretentious ones in Galveston but I am sure they weren't half as comfortable.'

Showing her pleasure in the brightness of her face, Anna Meyer now said, 'I have only seen Galveston once; but I have seen Mr Houston, that vas an honour ven he kom to Caldvell. All vent mad to see him.' She waved her hand in a circle, and at this Matthew asked, 'Who is your nearest neighbour? We passed a number of homesteads further along the trail.'

'That would be the Owens, and further on there are the McKnights. They are about five miles back. Oh, there are plenty of neighbours that vay back, scattered but plenty. Not so many that vay. Austin is over there.' She waved her hand to the side. 'And far beyond in that direction,' she swooped her arm round, 'to the Comanche country.'

'Do you . . . I mean have you had any Indian raids this far?'

Anna Meyer now put her head to one side and lifted her shoulders as she said, 'Not for some years. Too many forts and rangers; they good as Indians in fighting. They first kom in the third year, yes; but Big Hans and the three vaqueros fought them off. The only thing they did was to burn our prairie-schooner.'

'Prairie-schooner?' Tilly twisted up her face in enquiry and Anna Meyer laughed as she said, 'The vagon that ve kom in; ve call it prairie-schooner.'

'Oh! prairie-schooner.' Tilly looked at Matthew, and he repeated, 'prairie-schooner'; and they both laughed as he said, 'Good name for it, because they had to sail some rough seas, those wagons.'

'Yes, yes, rough seas.'

It was after Matthew and Tilly had spent some time doing another round of the outbuildings when they heard the boy and the mother talking. They were passing the open back door of the house and the boy was saying, 'We are really going, Mama?' and the answer came with what sounded like a deep, deep note of relief, 'Really going, my son. Really going.'

It was then that Tilly looked at Matthew and said, 'Such a lovely place, why are they so anxious to leave do you think?'

'Well, you heard what she said. And I can understand it: men don't work for a woman like they do for a man, at least not a timid little creature like she is. She's too kind, she'd be taken advantage of.'

A moment or so later, standing near the white railing, Tilly leaned her back against it and spread her arms along the top and looked up towards the sky as she said, 'I never thought I'd ever settle here because somehow I felt I wasn't cut to the mould. I didn't seem to fit in like any of the women I've met. I could be as strong as them in body but not in the spirit it takes to pioneer. I would have stayed . . . oh yes, because of you.'

She turned her head and glanced at Matthew, then went on, 'But now, here in this place, I've got a feeling I've come to the end of something, or to the beginning of something. For the first time since I stepped on to this soil I've got a feeling of peace in me, as if I'm on the point of beginning a new life.'

Matthew came and stood in front of her. He said nothing, but, taking her arms from the railings, he brought her hands together and to his chest and he pressed them there; then bending his head, he kissed them.

When the little girl came running up to them they both turned and beamed down on her, and she said, 'Mama says will you stay tonight?' Then looking from one to the other she pleaded, 'Please do stay. It will be lovely. And Hans will play on his whistle for you and I will dance. I know how to dance.' She lifted up her long print skirt and exposed her tiny ankles, then to their merriment she executed a few hopping dance steps.

Tilly looked at Matthew. His face was unsmiling now, it was as if he were considering, gravely considering. Then he turned to her, saying brightly, 'Well, what about it? There's no hurry really.'

Tilly paused for a moment as she thought of the children. But the children were with Katie, and so she said, 'Why not? Why not?'

So it was arranged that they stay the night; and just as all decisions bear fruit, so this one altered the course of their lives.

10

The evening was sweet and calm. They sat on the verandah, Frau Meyer and her two children, Matthew, Tilly and Manuel.

Manuel was good company; he amused the children and them all with imitating the cries and calls of birds and animals, pulling his long, lean face into various shapes in the process.

Hans played his whistle while Berta danced to it on the smooth boards of the verandah. The evening seemed perfect.

When the moon came up and a chill spread over the land they went indoors; all except Manuel, who had arranged a warm place to sleep in the barn.

Indoors they did not immediately disperse to bed, there was so much to talk about, so much, Tilly considered, to learn from this little woman whom she wouldn't see again after tomorrow morning, that it was a full hour before they began to say their good-nights. Both Matthew and Tilly had refused to take Frau Meyer's room whilst she slept on a palliasse in the living-room. His wife, Matthew lied loudly, was used to sleeping rough; not that sleeping on the floor of this comfortable room could be considered roughing it. . . .

It was all of half an hour later when they lay enfolded in each other's arms, talking in whispers about their plans for the future, that they heard the cry or rather the scream from outside. This was followed by the sound of a gunshot.

Almost as one they rolled out of the blankets and were on their feet. Matthew had been sleeping in his small clothes but Tilly had on a nightdress, and as she grabbed for a coat he rushed to the corner of the room where his pack and rifle lay, and he was already kneeling by the window when Frau Meyer scrambled down the ladder, the two children tumbling close behind her.

'Vat is it? Vat is it?' Then she added on a high cry, 'Oh no! Oh no!'

'Have you a gun?'

'Yes, yes.' She answered Matthew's words by running to a cupboard at the side of the mantelpiece and there she took out two guns and after thrusting one into her young son's hands, they both ran to the further window at the other side of the door.

'Is your back door barred?'

'Yes.'

'Your windows upstairs, are they open?'

'No, no.'

The questions and answers were thrown back and forward in whispers.

Tilly was kneeling on the floor at the other side of the window opposite to Matthew. She was holding the Colt revolver in her shaking hand, and Matthew didn't look at her as he said under his breath, 'It isn't a bear this time, so remember what I told you.'

Oh my God! My God! She did not say the words aloud but they kept revolving in her mind. The children and Katie, what would they do? Oh my God! don't let it be Indians. Please, please God, don't let it be Indians.

When the lighted brand flashed up past the window and on to the roof she knew it was Indians; and when another one flashed upwards Matthew said, 'They can't do any harm, there's no straw there.' Then again he added, 'Remember what I said.'

The next minute Tilly closed her eyes tightly against the unearthly scream. When she opened them again it was to see Indians, mad, excited, bloodlust Indians for the first time. She did not know how many, but the verandah seemed full of them; then they were battering at the door.

When she heard Matthew firing, she, too, pulled the trigger of the Colt, and she was amazed to see a man fall backwards below the end of the room as the whole window was burst in, and almost at the same time there came through it three terrifying creatures. She did not see Frau Meyer fall, she only heard a long high moan and the children screaming. Then Matthew fired again and one of the Indians grasped at his neck. As Matthew reloaded his gun; she too fired, then she knew a moment of agony as she saw young Hans clutch his chest. There was no time to think, Oh God! Oh God! what have I done? for the two demons were almost on top of them. The very sight of them was so terrifying that it paralysed her finger on the trigger. They were like devils out of hell; their heads were crowned with buffalo skulls, the horns giving them every appearance of devils. Their faces and bare trunks were painted, and round their necks hung strings of bones.

She saw the axe lifted and about to cleave Matthew's head in two, but as he lifted the gun, which he had been unable to load, to ward off the blow and fell the Indian, the axe cleaved through his shoulders and he fell on to his side. It was then that she fired again, but she didn't see the man fall for his companion had gripped her by the hair. He, too, had an axe in his hand but he didn't use it on her. As he pulled her forward she fell over Matthew and her face and night-dress were covered with his blood. As her hands sought for something to grip to check herself being dragged outside she found nothing to stay her progress. Her screams were ringing in her ears. The roots of her hair were being dragged from her head. She was on her knees now, then on her belly, and her hands still flailing for a hold found something. It was the stout leg of a cupboard and as she hung on to it for a moment her other hand passed over a known object. It was the Colt. How she brought her arms upwards she never knew, she only knew that she was firing at random, and after the third shot the hold on her hair was released. And when this happened she didn't pause to rest but jerked herself to her knees to see the fearful creature bending over double and holding his guts while he stared down at her. She watched his mouth open into one great gap. He now turned his great twisted painted face from her and looked at his two companions lying in contorted heaps on the floor among the rest; then he swung about and stumbled back to the window and fell through it on to the verandah.

Dragging herself to her feet, she walked backwards, the gun still in her hand. At the top of the room she almost fell over Matthew's bloody body and, like one sleep-walking she ignored it and looked out of the window and there she saw what appeared to her to be a strange sight, for standing clear in the moonlight were two other fearsome Indians and they were helping the wounded one down the steps. She watched them dragging him across to the railings where the horses were tethered.

The scene was as light as day for now the moon was assisted by the flames from the barn. She saw the two Indians now gesticulating towards the house again as if they were coming back, and she stood rigid for a moment until she saw them mount their horses and move off. And then there settled on the whole place a quiet, a peaceful quiet such as had enveloped it not more than half an hour ago.

Oh my God! Oh dear God! Oh my God! She must do something. But what? She was going to faint. In this moment she remembered telling herself many years ago that it was only ladies in church who fainted, but she was going to faint now. No! No! Matthew, Matthew. She found herself kneeling by him and she closed her eyes tightly for a moment and bowed her head over his arm that was almost cleaved from his body. Slowly she laid her ear to his chest, never expecting for a moment to hear a beat, but when she did, she became galvanised into life and, looking around wildly, she grabbed at the rough holland sheet in which they had lain such a short while ago and, tearing it into strips, she set about aiming to join the arm to the shoulder. When she saw this was hopeless she simply bound the strips tightly around his chest and the great bleeding gap. But when his life blood soaked the sheet immediately she quickly rolled a piece of the linen into a flattish ball and pressed it into the gap, then pushed the arm against it and bound it with the remainder of the sheeting. Then she straightened out his legs and put a pillow under his head; after which she bowed her body over his unconscious one and whispered, 'Don't go, Matthew. Don't go. Oh my love, don't go.'

Slowly now, she pulled herself to her feet and for the first time she looked about her. And again she felt she was going to faint, for now she was looking past the two dead Indians to the crumpled Frau Meyer, whose head looked like a bright red ball. Closing her eyes she muttered, 'Oh Christ Almighty! Why? Why?' When she opened them again she was looking at little Hans.

Well, perhaps he had died mercifully. She had heard that they took children as captives and of what happened to them. But to think that she had shot him. Where was Berta? And Manuel?

She heard herself screaming now, 'Berta! Manuel!' For the first time the door was opened. Throwing the bar aside, she rushed on to the verandah and down the steps; and there she stopped and now she knew that she was going to faint, she must faint to get away from this sight, and as she sank to the ground she kept crying, 'No! No! not to little Berta.' What kind of creature would knock the brains out of a child against a post?

As she came out of the black depths into consciousness she knew she was being carried and the first thing she did was to scream, until a voice said, 'There now, there now, you're all right.'

She tried to open her eyes but she couldn't, and the voice said, 'Lay her down here.'

Someone was holding her head now and someone was making her swallow a liquid which burnt her throat. She coughed, and gradually she looked upwards and she thought for a moment it was a dream, that she must have fallen asleep after looking at that captain this morning, because here he was again bending over her, calling her ma'am.

She hung on to the thought of it being a dream until she heard the voice say softly, 'We've got him out, sir, but he's almost burnt to a cinder.' And then she knew it was no dream, it was Manuel they were talking about; and once more she was screaming, but sitting up now screaming, 'Matthew! Matthew!'

'It's all right. It's all right, ma'am; they're seeing to him.'

She was staring into a rough-looking face now and she recognised the voice. It was the sergeant who had kept bellowing, and now she spoke to him in a voice that was a croak: 'My husband?'

'They've strapped him up, ma'am. We'll get him to a doctor as soon as possible. Do you think you're fit to ride?'

'Yes, yes.' She tried to struggle to her feet but had to lean on the sergeant's arm, and now she asked dully, 'The others?' for she had forgotten for a moment what she had seen, and the sergeant turned his eyes away from her as he asked, 'How many were there?'

'The mother, and her two children, then Manuel, our guide, and my husband. . . .'

He still kept his head turned away as he shook it and muttered, 'Well, ma'am, I'm sorry to say 'tis only you and your husband who are left.'

'Oh my God! My God!'

'Indeed! Indeed, my God! ma'am. Indeed! Indeed! But we'll get the maniacs, we'll get 'em, never fear. They're on the warpath all along the line, but they'll suffer for it. Aye ma'am, they'll suffer for it, 'cos so are we, so are we, we're on the warpath an' all. Oh ay.'

'Other places too?'

'Yes, other places too, ma'am. It's been a night of blood all right.'

'I . . . I must go to my husband.'

The sergeant now supported her up the steps and into the room. She was surprised to see no bodies on the floor, only Matthew, and she saw immediately that he was conscious for he looked at her for a moment but he had no power to speak.

'He's all right, ma'am, but he's lost a great deal of blood. We'll get him to the fort as soon as possible.'

'Home.' The word was a whisper and both the sergeant and the captain, who had now come on the scene, bent over him, and it was the captain who spoke, saying, 'You must see a doctor, we'll have to take you to the fort first.'

'Home.'

The captain now drew Tilly aside, saying, 'If his wound' isn't stitched up ma'am, he'll bleed to death. We can have him in the fort within an hour and a half. Do you agree with me?'

'Yes.' She nodded wearily.

'We'll have to carry him by sling, but once there they'll be able to provide a cart.'

'Thank you.'

She looked around the room, then closed her eyes tightly as the tears rained down her face. And now she spluttered, 'It was so peaceful, so beautiful,' and the captain replied, 'I have no doubt, ma'am, I have no doubt. But they have a habit of breaking the peace, in all ways they have a habit of breaking the peace. But I warned your husband this morning for there's been unrest all along the line. There were a number of raids last week, and once they start they go on until their lust is dry, or until we manage to finish them first. . . . Come, there is nothing you can do here.'

When he put his arm out towards her she raised her head and looked down at her blood-smeared coat and nightgown, and now she said simply, 'I must dress,' and he answered, 'Yes, of course, ma'am. Yes, of course,' and both he and the sergeant turned briskly about and went out.

She got into her clothes, all the while looking down on Matthew's dead white face and inert body. And as she did so she silently asked, 'Why should this happen to us? We could have gone back. I could have insisted. I should have insisted. But no, I seem fated to bring people to their deaths. Little Hans. But the Indians would have got him anyway, if we hadn't stayed, or he would have soon died from the disease that was eating him up. But why should it fall to me to shoot him? Oh God, why don't you give me an answer? Why am I plagued like this?'

The moon was still high when they placed Matthew in a canvas sling and four of the soldiers carried him out. Then, supporting her, the sergeant led her down the steps and lifted her bodily on to a horse, and when he spoke to one of the soldiers the man mounted and rode close to her, putting his hand out now and again to steady her in the saddle.

There was a numbness on her now and she had a great desire to sleep. Automatically she would turn from time to time to look back towards the men carrying the sling.

The tiredness lifted from her somewhat when, it seemed eons later, she passed through two big gates and into a stockade and what appeared to her a confused bustle of soldiers and civilians . . . and Indians.

Her eyes, wide now, focused on the Indians. They alone weren't moving about, they were in one corner of the stockade, and when the soldier assisted her down from the horse she turned and stared open-mouthed towards them as if as much in surprise at seeing women and children among them. Some of them were lying on the ground and some were standing, but they were all motionless.

When dully she turned to go towards the men with the sling two women came and, standing one on either side of her, moved her away towards some steps and up them into a room. This room, too, seemed packed. At one end were cot beds with people lying in them, their heads and arms bandaged. There were also men lying on the floor.

The women sat her in a chair and one of them said, 'Where are you hurt, my dear?' and she shook her head at them, then pointed to where the soldiers were carrying the sling into the room, and she said, 'My husband.' The words came out on a rasping sound.

Her throat was dry as if she had been swallowing sand and when one of the women said, 'Drink this,' she gulped at the water, then pushing the women aside, she now stumbled up to where they had laid Matthew on the floor. It was near a table on which a man was working. She noted he was wearing a rubber apron and that every part of him seemed covered in blood, even his face, and when he looked down towards the sling his voice was a growl as he said, 'What's it here now?'

As she went to say this was her husband who was very ill, the captain came to the table and drew the man to one side.

A few minutes later they lifted a still form off the table and put Matthew on to it.

The women were at her side again. One had a very soft voice and she said, 'Come, my dear. Come.'

'No! No!' Her old strength was back in her arms and she thrust them forcibly from her, much to their surprise, and watched the sheeting being unwound from Matthew's body. And when the man pulled the pad away and unwound the last binding and she looked on the great, gaping hole she closed her eyes tightly for a moment; then they sprang open again as the man said, 'I can do nothing with this; let's have it off.'

When she saw him lift the chopper, an ordinary chopper, it was as if the Indians had come back to finish the job they had started, and when it came down through the remainder of the bone and Matthew's arm fell to the ground she let out a high, piercing scream and went to rush forward, but there were arms about her and she was literally carried down the room. When she screamed again someone poured something down her throat and the soothing voice said, 'There now. There now, my dear. He couldn't feel it, he was unconscious.'

She was gulping on the liquid that was still being poured into her mouth. She prayed to God to make her faint again but He didn't answer her prayer, instead He made her vomit. The good meal that she had eaten the night before, the main dish of which had been roast hog, came bursting up; but when her retching was over they again poured something down her throat.

After a while she became quiet inside, but she fought against it because this was no time to sleep, she must be with Matthew. Matthew! Matthew! Oh, my love. My love. His father had lost both feet and now he had lost his arm.

Why God? Why?

She was lying on a bed when she awoke. The sun was streaming through a small square of window. She lay looking about her; the quietness was still on her, yet she was aware of all that had happened.

A door opened and a woman entered. She was tall and thin, almost as tall as herself she noted, and she recognised her voice when she spoke. 'There you are, my dear,' she said. 'Do you feel rested?'

Tilly stared up at her. There were questions in her mind, words in her mouth, but somehow she couldn't get them through her lips. When the hand came on her head and stroked her hair and the voice said, 'Your husband has regained consciousness,' she came up in the bed like a spring; but the woman held her by the shoulder, saying, 'Now, now, he's all right. He has lost a great deal of blood and he is very weak, but otherwise he's all right.'

'You are sure?'

'Yes, yes, I am sure. Now if you would like to refresh yourself you will find everything you need inside there.' She pointed to a door. 'When you're ready you might eat a little breakfast; and then you can go to him.'

'I . . . I couldn't eat, but . . . but I must see him.'

'You will see him, dear. Come.' She helped her from the bed, then again pointed to the door.

The room was a sort of closet, not unlike the one back in the nursery of the Manor. A bucket stood underneath a wooden framework on which was a round seat; there was a bench holding a basin and jug, also a table with a small mirror on it.

The table was opposite the lavatory seat and whilst she sat she looked at the face staring back at her. There was no recognition in the eyes. She seemed to be looking at an old woman, an eyeless old woman with great dark sockets where the pupils had been.

When she came out of the room the woman was waiting for her. She had put a tray on the foot of the bed and Tilly, looking at it, shook her head, then said, 'Thank you, but . . . but I couldn't eat anything.'

'Well, drink this coffee.'

She had merely sipped at the coffee when she said, 'Please, please, let me see him.'

The woman hesitated for a moment, then on a gentle sigh she said, 'Come along then.'

She remembered the room with the cot beds in it and the table at the end of it and, too, the man in the rubber apron, but she didn't remember the smell; it was a mixture of blood and sweat and singed hair.

The man was still at the table, but he had a clean apron on and his face was no longer spattered with blood. He glanced towards her but said nothing, and the woman turned her gently and led her to a cot at the end of the room. Now she was looking down on a man who had changed as much as she had in the last twelve hours.

Matthew had his eyes open. The colour of them was the only recognisable thing about him. She leant forward and her face hung above his for what seemed an interminable time, then gently she laid her lips against his. But there was no pressure from then. When she raised her head his lips moved and he whispered, 'Tilly.'

'Oh, my love.' Her words weren't even audible to herself, her throat was dry, she felt she was about to choke.

'Tilly.'

'Yes, my dear?'

'Home.'

'Yes, my dear, we're going home. Lie quiet now, we're going home.'

She slowly raised herself upwards and was about to turn to the woman at her side when the voice of the doctor rasped through the room, saying, 'Let the filthy buggers wait. If I had my way I'd burn the lot this minute right in the compound, there, and slowly. Aye, slowly.'

There were a number of people attending to the wounded and they all stopped what they were doing and looked towards the table. A man in uniform was speaking to the doctor. His voice was low so that what he said did not reach the listeners; but the doctor's reply to him did, and what he cried now was, 'Sanctions, treaties, what do they know, those sitting on their backsides down there? Tell them to come out here and they'll damn soon see what their actions and treaties are worth. . . . Sanctions and treaties!' He actually spat the last words.

Now the officer's voice was louder and stiff as he said, 'They need attention. Because they act like savages it doesn't mean we've got to retaliate in the same way. Shoot them, yes, but don't let them die in agony.'

'Oh, away with you! Don't talk such bloody claptrap to me! Die in agony, you said.' The doctor's hand holding an implement on which the sun glinted flashed in the air for a moment, then as he bent over the patient on the table he cried,

'Sometimes I wonder which side the bloody army's on. The rangers don't ask questions, they act.'

'You'll hear more about this.' The words were low and muttered, and the officer now turned abruptly and marched towards the door where a soldier smartly opened it, and his last words were not inaudible but plain for all to hear as he said, 'Drunken fool!'

When Tilly looked at the woman at her side who had her head bent low she paused for a long moment before she asked her, 'Who . . . who am I to see for a conveyance?'

The woman slowly raised her head and for the first time Tilly saw that she, too, looked old. Yet she was younger than herself. 'I'm sorry' she said; 'he's . . . he's worn out, my husband's worn out. Two days and nights he's been working with hardly a rest.'

A doctor's wife in this place, in this shambles of a place. She glanced now towards the still form on the bed. Matthew's eyes were closed. She herself was here in this shambles because of love for a man, and this girl, for she was little more than a girl, was here too because of love for her man. Love. Love was a chain that dragged you through pity and compassion to places like this.

The young woman had hold of her arm again and was leading her out of the room. And now she was in the stockade and seeing it really for the first time. A large space surrounded by a stout high wall of timbers, just below the top of which ran a platform and on it dotted here and there were soldiers. The stockade itself was buzzing with life and the incongruity that struck her immediately was that of a small group of children playing at one side and the group of Indians huddled in a corner at the other side. There were few of them standing now and when her glance stayed on them she could see the reason for the officer demanding the doctor's attention. Yet in this moment there was no pity in her for them because the sight of them was overshadowed by the picture of little Berta's hairless skull and spattered brains, and she saw them for a moment heaped on the bonfire that the doctor had envisaged.

The doctor's wife had taken her by the arm and she was now being shown into the colonel's office. The colonel was a short man with a beard and he rose from behind his desk and bowed towards her, then pointed to a seat and as if to waste no words, he came straight to the point, saying, 'It would be unwise for you to travel without an escort and I have no soldiers to spare at the moment. Moreover, your husband would be better resting for a few days, anyway until the countryside has settled down again.'

'How . . . how far have they got?' she asked.

He understood her question and answered it immediately by saying, 'I'm not sure. I have three patrols out: The one that brought you and your husband in yesterday reported four other homesteads ravished. You can consider yourself fortunate, for there were no other survivors, that is unless they took some prisoners.'

She said now, 'I . . . I have left my children with friends. I am very anxious to return.'

'You live, I understand, just beyond Boonville. Well, I don't think they will have got that far. But again, you never know, they are unpredictable. Years ago, they thought of them as being so far away on the plains that they could never reach San Antonio; but they reached it and passed it and made for Gonzales. And people in the border area were always prepared for them, and they weren't soft-footed new settlers, they were Americans born and bred. Both they and their forefathers had fought Mexicans and the Indians time and time again, yet what happened on that August day? Well, it's history and I suppose you've heard all about it so I've no need to go over it, but the point I'm making is we never underestimate the length an Indian, especially a horse Indian, a Comanche, can ride, and so you'll understand, Mrs Sopwith, that it would be very unwise for you to travel without a full escort until we're sure that it is safe for you to do so.'

'When . . . when will your men be riding that way?'

'None of my men patrol as far east as that but we could be having a company of rangers dropping in at any time, they brought in some wounded last night. Yet again, the way things are at present I doubt if you'd be able to travel in their company; the best we can do for your husband on such a journey is to loan you a flat wagon, and in his condition that would have to be driven carefully. I'm afraid you'll have to have patience, Mrs Sopwith.'

She stared at him for a moment before rising to her feet, and as he rose stiffly from his chair the door opened and a sergeant saluted, then stood to attention.

'Yes, what is it, sergeant?' The colonel and the other officer in the room were looking towards the sergeant and he said in a voice that held a strong Irish accent, "Tis Captain Collins's rangers have come away in, sir. They have six wounded with them and there's a Ranger McNeill who asks for a word with you, sir.'

Before the colonel had a chance to answer him Tilly swung round, crying now, 'Ranger McNeill? Michael McNeill?'

The sergeant still standing stiffly turned his head towards her saying, "Tis what he said his name was, ma'am.'

Tilly did not take leave of the colonel but turned and rushed to the door, and there she actually threw herself into the arms of Mack and he held her for a moment, embarrassment on his face as he looked over his shoulder at the three men standing within the open door. Then gently disengaging himself, he said, 'It's all right,' and looking at the colonel and saluting, he said, 'Ranger Michael McNeill, sir. I had leave of Captain Collins to speak with you, but now . . . ' he ended lamely. Then looking at Tilly again, he asked quietly, 'Matt, is he all right?'

She shook her head, but before she had time to answer him the colonel said, 'Tell Captain Collins I would like a word with him.'

'Yes, sir.' Mack saluted smartly and as he turned away Tilly hurried by his side, saying, 'Are they all right? You left them all right?'

'Yes, yes; but when Dan Collins called in soon after you left and told us of the trouble at this end I asked to join in.'

'Oh, Mack!' She clung to his arm now. 'I've never been so happy to see anyone in my life as I am you at this moment. Matt's in a bad way.' She shook her head, moving it wildly from side to side, saying, 'They came so quickly. It was a tomahawk. He . . . he brought it down on his shoulder, right through. They' – she gulped now on a mouthful of spittle before she could say – 'they took his arm off last night.'

Mack said nothing, he just continued to walk looking straight ahead. But then stopping abruptly, he said, 'Wait there a minute, I must see the captain. I'll be back. I'll be back.'

She stood where he had left her and watched him go towards a group of dust-covered riders who were busily feeding their horses, and he spoke to a tall man in a slouch hat. This man's clothes were grey with dust but this did not cover the dark stains on his shirt front, nor those on his trousers. She had heard of Dan Collins, he was famed as a ranger who rode as fast as any horse Indian and had followed the raiders into the very heart of the Comanche country up in the high plains where the Indians felt safe among the great herds of buffalo and mustang.

He now looked in her direction; then saying something to Mack, they turned together and came towards her.

'Ma'am' – he touched the front of the upturned brim of his hat – 'Mack tells me of your trouble. I'm sorry we can't escort you back to your home, ma'am; the best I can do for you is to release Mack and one other of my men to see you in safe passage.'

'I am very grateful.'

He inclined his head towards her, then said, 'It has been a bad night, we must soon be on our way. Excuse me, ma'am.' He now turned from her and in an undertone to Mack said, 'Take Len with you; he's had more than enough. I know he's got a flesh wound in his leg but he won't have it seen to. See what you can do for him when you get settled. . . . Good luck.'

They stared at each other for a moment until Mack said, 'You an all. Thanks, Dan. Be seeing you soon. I'll join up with you near the Falls, or with Bill's lot.'

'You might be more use back in the ranch, Mack. This thing isn't over by a long chalk. Now they've started others could break out.'

'We'll see.'

They nodded at each other; then Mack turned towards Tilly again and asked, 'Where is he, Matt?'

She pointed, and they went towards the long hut where the wounded lay.

That Mack was shocked at the sight of Matthew was evident in his face but not in his voice, for it was rough and brusque as he exclaimed, 'What d'you think you've been up to eh? You went out house huntin', so I understand.'

'Hello, Mack.' Matthew's voice was low, scarcely audible, as he added, 'Going home.'

'Going home.' Mack nodded at him. 'We'll have you in your own bed 'fore you know where you are.' He took two steps backwards from the cot nodding as he went, and when they were again outside the hut he looked at Tilly, saying kindly, 'Doesn't look too good.'

'No; he's lost an awful lot of blood.'

'Well' – he gave a twisted smile – 'broth made with bullock's blood will soon put that right. The main thing is to get him home. I'll go and see about this wagon.'

'Thank you, Mack.' She put her hand on his arm. 'Oh, I am grateful to God you are here, Mack, you'll never know . . .'

He grinned again, nodded, then marched off, his limp very much in evidence;

through tiredness she guessed, for after doing a day's work he must have ridden through the night with few stops on the way, for his clothes, too, had dark stains on them.

Just an hour later Matthew was carried in a sling to the wagon and laid gently on a bed of sacks and blankets with a buffer of boxes at one side and Tilly seated with her back against the wooden rail at the other.

Len Wilson was driving the wagon and Mack was riding by the side of it, two mustangs on leading reins behind him. As they passed through the gates the last face she looked at was that of the doctor's wife who seemed sorry to see her leave. She hadn't said good-bye to the doctor for she couldn't thank him for cutting off her husband's arm. Another doctor, she told herself, would have tried to stitch it together.

When the big gates were closed behind them and the wagon moved over the rough ground she pressed her side tightly against the sacks in an attempt to stop Matthew being jolted.

The sky was high and clear. The day was warm. For a time they passed through waving grass, then along a river bank where the wheels of the wagon almost touched the water to avoid the cottonwood trees that bordered the river to where it narrowed almost into a small stream.

When they had crossed the river Len Wilson and Mack lay on the bank and ducked their heads deeply into the flow. They then helped Tilly down from the cart, and she, too, lay on the river bank and ducked her head into the water. Afterwards she took a mugful of it back to the wagon and with a handkerchief she bathed Matthew's face, then wetted his lips with water from the water bottle.

As Mack was about to mount she said to him in an undertone, 'How long will it take us?'

'About another five hours. We'll cut quite a slice off the distance going this way; Len knows it like the back of his hand. It'll be rough in parts but it'll be better than the main trail, and we'll be less likely to meet anybody.'

They stared at each other for a moment; then he turned from her and mounted his horse, and once more they were moving on.

Matthew appeared to sleep most of the time; at least so Tilly thought, until he opened his eyes and said to her, 'How much further?'

She bent her head over him. 'Not much longer, dear. Not much longer. About an hour I should say. . . . How are you feeling?'

He didn't answer her question; instead he said, 'Tilly,' and to this she answered, 'Yes, dear?' She watched him moisten his dry lips and look away from her before he spoke again, and then his words were low and spaced as if attuned to each sway of the wagon. 'If . . . if anything . . . happens . . . to me . . . go straight . . . back . . . home.'

'Oh, my dear. My dear.' She placed her two fingers gently on his lips, and he made an impatient movement with his head as if aiming to push them aside and went on, 'Do as I ask. Take Willy and go, not Josefina. Don't take her.'

She made no answer to this but simply stared down at him. He had closed his eyes once more. . . . She did not expect him to love the child, but he did not even like her. Whatever happened, Josefina was going to become a problem. . . .

They had left the river and the twisting bone-shaking path, and now she recognised the country they were passing through. In a short time they'd be home. Her heart was heavy with dread, yet she told herself that once he was in bed and she was able to nurse him he would recover. Look at the different men she had seen walking about with one arm or those hobbling about on one leg and a crutch, many had lived for years and years. Once they were back she would get him well. She would have to put up with Alvero Portes until Matthew was able to be moved to a new home. Where that would be she didn't know. But there'd never be another house like Anna Meyer's. No, there'd never be a house like that again.

On the last thought new hope sprang in her, perhaps this terrible experience they had gone through would change Matthew's idea of living here for the rest of his days and he'd be only too glad to go back to England.

They were nearing the ranch; there in the distance was the first boundary fencing. As the wagon rumbled along the road she looked towards the corral and her eyes widened. There wasn't a horse in sight.

They had ridden for about another half-mile when she saw Mack come to the back of the wagon and tie the two mustangs to the back-board, and then before she could ask him what was wrong he was riding off again. Now standing up and swaying she reached over to Len Wilson and, touching his arm, she shouted, 'What is it? Something wrong?'

It was some seconds before he turned to her and said simply, 'Smoke.'

She repeated his word, 'Smoke?'

'Aye. It might be nothing but Mack thought he'd better go and see.'

Of a sudden she slumped down on to the floor of the wagon, her hands now joined tightly between her knees, her head bent towards them, and again she was saying, 'Oh no! no! they couldn't have been this far. Oh no! Willy! Oh Willy! And Katie. And the child, and Luisa.' She found herself going through all the names, and then she was jerked forward as the wagon was drawn to a halt.

Again she was standing upright, staring ahead now towards a smoke haze in the distance, and her voice was a mere whimper as she muttered, 'They couldn't. They couldn't have got this far.'

'They can go to hell an' back, ma'am, that lot, hell an' back. But it may be nothing, just a barn fire. Stay still now.' He put out his hand as she attempted to climb down from the wagon, and again she whimpered, 'My children!'

He said nothing, just sat staring ahead; and the minutes passed and went into five, then ten, then fifteen.

They had reached thirty when she saw Mack come riding back towards them. Then he was facing them. Under the dirt, the tan, and his beard, his face looked as grey as the dust on his clothes. Len Wilson and he exchanged glances.

Now he was looking at Tilly and saying quietly, ''Twill be better if you don't go in. Drive round the west side. Your house is still standing, why I don't know, the....' – his head drooped now – 'the rest is burned out.'

'The children?' She was gripping his shoulders, her hands like claws dug deep into his coat. 'The children!'

He kept his head down. 'There's no sign of 'em, ma'am, no sign of 'em.'

'Oh God! Oh God!' She rocked on her feet and Mack put his arm about her, saying now, 'They might've got away.'

She drew a long, long breath before she gasped, 'Katie! Luisa!'

'There's no sign of 'em either.' Again his head was drooped.

'They ... they could have taken them? They do awful things. ... Oh God Almighty! God Almighty!' Her hands were in her hair now as if attempting to pull it from the roots.

'Come on.' As he assisted her along the road he nodded to Len Wilson, and when Matthew's weak voice came from the wagon they all ignored it.

Near the main gate, as Mack was about to direct Len Wilson away from it and along a side path that would lead to the house, Tilly, pulling herself from Mack's arm, cried, 'No! No, I must find the children. They'll be in there somewhere, they'll be in there. . . .'

Mack gripped her arms and actually shook her as he said, 'They're not there. An' don't go in, I'm tellin' you, unless you want nightmares till the end of your days.'

They stared at each other, and then she whimpered, 'But my child and Josefina, they're ... they're just babies, babies.' She shook her head wildly.

'I know ma'am, I know, but I tell you they're not there. If they've taken 'em there'll be a chance of them comin' back. They' – he gulped before continuing – 'they don't often harm children.' He didn't add, 'If they behave themselves and don't cry,' but tried to reassure her by saying, 'They've been known to be very kind to children. And I promise you, you'll get them back. Believe me. Wherever they've gone the rangers'll follow, you'll get them back.'

She stared at him unbelieving. Then her body seemed to slump and, turning, she looked towards the gates and, noticing movement, she said, 'Somebody's there.'

'Yes, they're ... they're clearin' up. The Curtises and Ingersolls were lucky; but the Purdies got it, and the Rankins.'

'Are they ...?' She couldn't ask the question, but he answered it, saying, 'Yes, all but Mrs Purdie. She was under the floorboards. They found her afterwards. She's a bit burnt but she'll be all right.'

Huh Ha-ha! Under the floorboards; a bit burnt; like taties in the ashes. Her granny used to split them open and put dripping in ... split them open. Ha-ha! She put her hand over her mouth tightly, she was going to laugh. She must be going mad.

Mack was supporting her as they went up the rise towards the house, Len driving the wagon behind them.

She stood in front of the verandah and looked at it. It was intact; even the bear was there straining at the end of his chain coming to greet them. Why had they left the bear? She now asked the question of Mack. 'Why did they leave the bear?'

'I don't think they got up this far, they were disturbed. Smith's rangers group came along this way. That's likely what saved the house.'

'But ... but not my children, not my children. Matthew! Matthew!'

She turned to the wagon where Len Wilson and Mack were now easing Matthew gently forward, and as they lifted the inert body into the house she walked sidewards in front of them and drew them through the room and into the bedroom; and when they laid Matthew gently down he looked at Mack and said simply, 'They've been here?'

'Yes, Matthew.'

'The children?'

'Don't worry.' It was Tilly hanging over him now. 'They'll be all right.' Her voice was high and squeaky as if she were going to burst into song. 'Mack says they're all right. Mack says he'll get them. Don't worry. Let me get the blankets off and wash you, and I'll see to your arm and I'll . . .'

Matthew's hand came on her wrist and checked her hysterical flow of words, and she closed her eyes so tightly that her face became contorted. Her voice a little steadier now, she said, 'It's all right, it's all right.' But when she went to try to take the blankets from around him she looked up helplessly at Mack and said simply, 'Help me, please. . . .'

It was a full half-hour later when Matthew was settled comfortably in bed, and so she left him for a moment and went into the other room where she stood looking about her. She couldn't believe it, nothing had been disturbed. She looked towards the table. It was set for breakfast: there was Katie's place and the children's two fancy mugs; the bread-board with a knife lying across it; a pot of preserves; a round of butter with a pattern on the top which told her that one of the Ingersolls had called – Clara Ingersoll always brought something dainty.

Oh, Willy! Willy! Oh, my dearest Willy, my baby. . . . Josefina. Dear little Josefina. She was a girl . . . they did things to girls. She had never discussed Indian raids openly but she kept her ears open. They gelded young boys and they used young girls. Mack had said they were kind to children, at least the men were, but the women were cruel to them, especially to girls. She'd heard of the things they did to girls. . . . Oh my God! she musn't think. No, she musn't keep repeating the same thing, she must think of Matthew, he needed her.

She started to pace the room, her head bent forward, her brow in the palm of her hand. She hated this country, she'd always hated it since first putting her foot on it. She hated the people in it, not just the Indians. They were rough, coarse, some no better than animals. Alvero Portes . . . oh yes, there were men like Alvero Portes, men in the towns living in their grand houses, and ladies spending their time titivating themselves and entertaining the politicians, but in the main there were the people, just the people, and they were elemental, barbaric, and . . . and . . . oh, Mr Burgess would have been able to put names to them. There must be something odd about people who wanted to come and live on this terror-ridden plain.

She looked towards the fireplace where one rifle was still slung. She had the desire to take it up and clear this whole wide planet of people, people like Alvero Portes, people like . . . Bobby Pearson . . . and the Indians. Oh the Indians! Yes, she would do what the doctor said, burn them all on a great bonfire. . . .

Oh my God! what was the matter with her? Was she losing her reason? She must pull herself together; this was no time to go on talking like this, and she was talking, talking aloud. . . . She had to get Matthew well. What had she come out here for? Oh yes, to make him some gruel. Where did she keep the oatmeal? Her head was spinning. . . . What time was it?

She was about to look round to the clock when movement through the window caught her eye. There outside were five dark figures. The great scream rose to her throat but she stilled it by stuffing her knuckles into her mouth. Two of the figures were tiny, two were women and dumpy, the third was a man, a tall man. She staggered to the door and pulled it open and gazed with her mouth agape and her eyes stretched wide at the five mud-covered creatures staring at her. Then a great cry was riven up from her bowels and she jumped the three steps down to the ground, crying, 'Willy! Katie, No! no! it can't be.' She was hugging the two wet mud-covered children to her while Katie and Luisa stood looking down at her. It was Doug Scott who spoke first, and what he said sounded so ordinary, 'You all right, ma'am?'

She looked up at him with tears making furrows down her mud-spattered face. She had no power to speak but she made a deep obeisance with her head until he said, 'And Matt?'

And now she struggled to her feet and looked back towards the house, and it was Luisa who stated, 'He's hurt.'

'Yes.'

'Badly?' Luisa's voice had still the crisp, terse note to it; nothing might have happened.

'He's lost an arm and . . . and a lot of blood.'

'Well, let's get inside.'

Luisa went first. The children were still clinging to Tilly, and Katie was still standing gaping at her. Katie hadn't yet spoken, but now she fell forward into Tilly's arms and the sobs shook her whole body as she kept repeating, 'Oh, Tilly! Oh, Tilly! Oh, Tilly!'

Her distress brought Tilly to herself for a moment and she said, 'Come on, come on, get cleaned up'; then looking over her shoulder at Doug, she asked quietly, 'Have you been down there?'

For answer he gave a small motion of his head and at this Katie's crying became louder and she spluttered now, '"Tis terrible, 'tis terrible. Oh Tilly! Tilly!'

'Go inside now, and stop your crying!' It was Doug Scott speaking with unusual authority, no laughter about him now. 'Get yourself cleaned up, I'll be back shortly.' He now exchanged a glance with Tilly and turned round and went down the slope towards what was left of the ranch.

They were cleaned up. They'd all had a hot drink but no one could touch food. Nor had anyone told Tilly how they had escaped, and it wasn't until Luisa walked out and down the slope to where once had stood her home that Katie's tongue became loosened. She stood staring through the open door at the sturdy figure who looked most odd now, dressed as she was in one of Tilly's dresses that was much too long and had been looped at the waist and so tight for her bust she'd had to resort to a shawl. 'She's brave, she is,' she said.

'How did you manage to escape?' Tilly asked.

At this Katie bowed her head and muttered, 'Likely 'cos I was about to misbehave meself.'

'What!'

Katie raised her head a little now and said, 'I was just on goin' to bed when Doug came up on the quiet an' tapped on the window.' Her head drooped again. 'We got talkin' like and – ' her head drooped still further and her voice was scarcely audible as she muttered, 'I let him kiss me. 'Twas then we were both scared out of our wits, an' that was afore the Indians come, 'cos Luisa appeared on the scene and she went for Doug sayin' that he was sneakin' up here to do me harm an' take me good name an' that he wouldn't have done it if you and the master had been at home, and to get himself down there quick sharp an' – ' now Katie gulped and seemed to find breathing difficult as she added, ''Twas just at that moment that we heard the screams. Oh my God! Tilly, they chilled you to the bone them screams. An' Doug stood frozen like for a minute. Then there were more screams and shootin' an' firebrands flying. An' then he yelled at us to get the bairns, and both Luisa and me flew up the stairs and grabbed them. Then he hustled us across the back way through that grass, and I had no shoes on and I wanted to scream myself. On and on he pushed us until we came to the river bank. An' then I couldn't believe it for he was stickin' us all into a muddy hole in the bank. He tried one first and it wasn't big enough; then he pulled us to another. We had to crawl in on our hands and knees and the river was flowing into it. It was almost up to our waist at one time; I thought I would die with cold. And then when Willy began to cry, Doug tied his hands behind his back and took off his neckchief and put it round his mouth. I thought the poor bairn would suffocate. Josefina never opened her mouth. It was as if, well, she had been in this kind of thing afore. 'Twas weird like, Tilly, 'cos she didn't open her mouth or make one squeak. Nor did Luisa, but me – well, I couldn't help it, I was groanin' like a stuck pig 'cos I was covered with mud and water an' I was so freezin'. An' then' – her head bowed again – ''cos I couldn't stop, he . . . well, he slapped me face – ' she stared at Tilly now and her head bobbed as she said, 'he did, he slapped me face. Then he said something terrible to me that made me want to vomit. But it shut me up. You know what he said?'

Tilly didn't answer, and she gabbled on, 'I'll never forget it, not as long as I live, 'cos he hissed at me, "You'll have something to groan about if they get you, an' it'll shut your trap 'cos they'll cut off your breasts an' stuff 'em in your mouth." He did. I didn't believe it at the time, but it shut me up. But Tilly – ' again she was looking up into Tilly's face and now she spluttered tearfully, 'I can believe it after what I saw down there, I can believe it all right. Ma One, poor Ma One was split open, right open, Tilly, and there was this spear through her right into the ground, an' Diego an' Emilio an' all of them. Ee, but it was nothing to Mr Portes. They had him covered up on the ground when I saw him. He was covered up like the rest, what was left of him. One, Two and Four, an' poor Rod Tyler, too. But I heard Mack telling Doug what they'd done to Mr Portes. They had nailed him to the door and Mack said there wasn't a . . . some word like portrushun left on his body not from his nose to his toes. An' you know what? Luisa went to look at him, she did, she did. She pulled the sheet aside an' looked at him. And she never moved a muscle. She's brave but she's hard. . . . I wanna go home, Tilly. Oh, I wanna go home. I wanna go home, Tilly. I wanna. . . . '

'There now. There now. Don't cry. Don't cry.'

As she held Katie's face against her waist she thought: Not a protrusion left on his body. Dear God! Dear God! She hadn't liked the man, in fact she had hated him. And what had she said to him when she had last spoken to him?

One day you'll wish for death, you'll be so alone you'll wish for death. And he hadn't died alone. She could only pray to God that he had died well before they started slicing him.

'Oh, I wanna go home.'

'There now. There now. If you want to go so badly we'll see about sending you off.'

Katie's head came up quickly, saying now, 'But not without you. You want to go an' all, don't you?'

'Yes . . . yes, I want to go. There's nothing I want more at this moment than to get on a boat and go home. But I've got a husband, Katie; and in spite of everything he loves this place. And I married him and so where he goes I go.'

Gently now, Tilly disengaged herself from Katie's hold and, turning, she went towards the bedroom and the man who was tying her to this barbaric country.

ᕽᖇᑯ 11 ᕽᖇᑯ

A month had passed, all sign of the Indian raid had been cleared away, in fact a rough homestead had already been erected, but Luisa had not yet gone to live in it. At night she slept on a shaky-down in the living-room but most of her days were spent down in the ranch planning and discussing things with Doug and Mack.

Two days ago she had come back from Houston where she had been to see a solicitor with regard to her father's will. Before going she had said to Tilly, 'It wouldn't surprise me if he has left the whole bang lot to some forty-second cousin just to spite me.' But when she returned she said simply, 'I bought meself a frock and a coat because I am a very rich woman.'

The change in her fortune hadn't seemed to alter her except that now whenever she rode out with either Mack or Doug she was always accompanied by Three, for he had escaped the massacre. It had been imagined that the Comanches had taken him prisoner but he had returned a week later, saying that he had gone, as he did often at night, to the corral and had ridden one of the horses. Apparently Mack and Rod Tyler knew of these escapades, but this one had certainly saved his life, for he had just returned the horse to the corral when the advance party of Indians rode in and herded the animals out and back along the trail to the high plains to add still further to their massive stocks.

There was great talk about the new measures being taken against the Comanches. The authorities in headquarters were issuing orders for a real drive this time, but all this talk, in fact all the commotion that went on about the place seemed to be floating over Tilly's head; all she was concerned about was Matthew, because Matthew wasn't improving.

The doctor had called twice during the last week because he wasn't satisfied with the condition of the arm, and only yesterday he had taken Tilly aside and said, 'I am afraid the matter has now become serious. Septicaemia has set in. There is little one can do now but pray.' It seemed to be a favourite saying of his, he usually ended any conversation he had with her with the words, 'There is little one can do now but pray.' But now, for the first time, it made her think kindly of the doctor back in the fort; he wouldn't just have relied on prayer, he would have done something.

Yesterday she had said, 'Isn't there any medicine?' and he answered, 'I have used everything possible. But he is of a strong constitution, we can but hope . . . and pray.'

It was now one o'clock in the morning. The lamp was turned low. She had been sitting in a chair by Matthew's side for the past three hours and she must have dozed for she almost sprang to her feet with the touch of his hand on hers and she bent over him, saying, 'What is it, dear? Do you want a drink?'

'No, nothing, I . . . I just want to talk.'

'You'd far better rest, dear.'

'I've rested for a long time, Tilly. How many years have I been lying here?'

She gave a forced soft laugh, saying, 'Not a month, dear.'

'Every hour has been a year. Turn the lamp up so I can see your face.'

She turned up the lamp and sat facing him; then she took his hand again, and what he said now cut into her heart as if he had taken a knife and cleaved open her breast. 'I haven't much longer, dear,' he said.

'Please! Please! Matthew' – she closed her eyes tightly – 'I beg you, don't talk like that.'

'Look at me.'

She opened her eyes.

'We must face the inevitable, I know what is happening, nothing more can be done. This might be the last time we'll ever talk together.'

'Oh! Matthew. Matthew.'

'Please, darling, don't cry, just . . . listen to me. I'm not going to waste words telling you how much I love you, and how I have loved you since the first moment I set eyes on you, I've said it so many times before, you must be tired of hearing it. Nevertheless it is true. It is so true that you have become a sort of mania with me. I have been jealous of your very glance at another, even at the child. Oh yes' – he moved his head on the pillow – 'every soft glance you have bestowed on the child has been a dart in here.' He glanced wearily down towards his chest, then after a long pause, he went on, 'I know inside that I am not a good man because, had you ever said you would leave me, I know, and this is true, I would have killed you first; and if you were leaving me for anyone else I would have killed him too.'

When his chest heaved and he drew in a long breath she gripped his hand and said, 'Matthew, please, please, don't go on. You are tiring yourself.'

'No, no, Tilly darling; it's strange but I don't feel tired, I've got a sort of elation on me, a peaceful elation which really isn't me at all because I've never known peace. All my life I've been ravished with desire, desire for you. As I said, it became a mania, and although I have this feeling of quietude inside the mania still remains with me.' His fingers gripped hers now with an unusual strength and his eyes that were sunken in his head gleamed darkly as he gazed at her. And then he spoke again: 'I want you to promise me something. Will you promise me anything I ask, Tilly?'

It was some time before she could bring the words through her throat, and when she said, 'Yes, yes, darling, anything. But believe me, you are going to get well.' He shook her hand in a way that showed his irritation and, his voice changing, he said, 'You swear you'll promise me this?'

'Yes, yes, anything, darling; anything.'

'Then swear to me, swear to me that you will never marry again.'

Her head came forward, her eyes stretching wide. Her face dropped into pitying lines as she whispered, 'Oh, Matthew!'

'Promise me? I want to hear you say it.'

In this moment she could hear her granny's voice, saying, 'Peggy Richardson, poor Peggy Richardson, promising that mother of hers on her deathbed not to marry Billy Conway because he was a Catholic, and look at her now, a wizened nerve-tortured creature. Oh, the dying have a lot to answer for.' But here was her Matthew whom she loved with every fibre of her being asking for her to promise not to marry again. Well, would she ever? Never! Never! She brought his hand to her chest and, holding it tightly there, she said, 'I promise. Oh, I promise.'

'Say it. Say, Matthew I shall never marry again, I shall never put another man in your place.'

The words seemed hard in coming, she didn't know why because her heart was in the answer:

'Matthew, dearest, I shall never marry again, I shall never put another man in your place.'

His whole body seemed to sink further into the bed, he closed his eyes, the grip on her hand relaxed. Of a sudden she felt that she had just gone through some great travail, much worse than the first raid, or even the second, when she thought that the children were gone. Her body felt weak, her mind heavy with the pressure that was numbing thought. She looked at him. If he were to die, and yes, he would die, she knew that now, she had known it for days, well why not go with him?

And the children? Mark's child and Matthew's child. Whether he disowned it or not she thought of the child as his.

She lay back in the chair. She was so tired, so very, very tired . . .

She slept and it was Katie who woke her up as the first light was breaking. She must have been in the room some time for she had done something, she had covered Matthew's face with a sheet.

Tilly sat staring at the sheet. It was a white sheet; then suddenly it changed colour to blue, then to black, and it turned into a wooden box, a black box, and she saw it being lowered into a black hole, and in it was all that had been worth living for. She had lost this man's father by death, now she had lost him; everything she touched turned to death. And there was young Hans Meyer, and Hal McGrath. She had killed as many people as the Indians. She now saw the Indian. He was walking over the bed towards her, his face was all paint, yet she could see the wrinkles in his brow and his great nose and the gap of his mouth. But what was coming right for her was the buffalo head – the horns were pointing straight at her – but just before he neared her he stopped and they looked at each other again as they had done a short while back. Then he lifted his tomahawk and cleaved her on the head, and as it struck her she knew her wish was coming true and that she was going to join Matthew.

☙ 12 ❧

The sun was shining. For days now, she had been looking at it through the window, but it was the first time she had really noticed it. It was causing a heat haze to cover the ranch like a low canopy. There were houses down there again, low rambling ones and high ones. Had it ever been a smouldering waste? At times she was confused in her mind about the ranch, believing that nothing had ever happened to it except that the shape of the buildings now was different. Yet the dog run had gone and the bunkhouse, and Alvero Portes's palace. Why did she still think about Alvero Portes with sarcasm? He had died a terrible death, a death that was far beyond any payment due for what ill he had done in his lifetime. Even Christ hadn't suffered that kind of death. But then Christ hadn't known Indians. Some day she would go down the slope and see the new house, Luisa's house with all its new furniture, not rough made, Katie had said, but real furniture, some pieces like those which had been in the Manor.

She had watched the wagons coming and going for weeks now, first bringing the wood and the men who hammered and hammered. At first, the nails had gone through her head, all knocked in by the tomahawk, and the blood had run all over her face, and Katie and Luisa had wiped it away.

How many times had she fought the Indians? After one terrible fight she had woken up in Doug Scott's arms. He was holding her tightly and for a moment she thought it was Matthew and laid her cheek against his until he had spoken to her, and his voice was not Matthew's voice.

Another time she had crawled out of bed and got the gun. She had done it very quietly because she knew the Indians were all round watching her, and she had got it into her hands and was lying on the floor aiming it at the Indian who had jumped through the window. But this time it was Mack who foiled her aim. And after that they had tied her to the bed and let the Indians have their way with her. They were cruel, cruel; even the white people were cruel.

It had taken her a long time to recognise the faces about her. Even when she recognised them she still fought them when they kept pouring laudanum and aniseed into her.

She lay back against the pillow on the bed which was arranged so that she could see out of the window. She must have been a great trial to everybody during these past weeks... months. Had she been in this bed for nearly five months? She had been sick but once in her life before and now she felt she'd be sick for the rest of her life. She'd be tied to this bed for the rest of her life. There was nothing wrong with her limbs but she had no desire to move them; she had wished to die and she had died inside, for there was no feeling in her, not even for Willy, and this troubled her greatly. She could look at her son, into his beautiful eyes, one without sight and the other straining to see, she could feel his arms around her neck and hear his voice, saying, 'Mama! Mama! Get up Mama. Take me for a walk,' and be quite untouched by his plea or by the look on his face.

Josefina had the strange habit of tracing her fingers lightly over her jawbones as if she were feeling the texture of her skin, and she, too, would say, 'Mama! Mama!' but she'd make no request, she would just sit on the bed and look on her with those dark eyes filled with love. She knew they were filled with love, but she could not return the feeling in any way.

And then there was Katie. Katie, too, must have been ill. Although she hadn't taken to her bed she had lost her buoyancy; she did not chatter as she used to. The only one who appeared the same to her was Luisa. Luisa was brisk and stimulating; yet her stimulation could not probe the deadness within herself. If only she could feel again. Only yesterday she had heard Luisa say to Katie, 'I'd prefer her ravings to this dummy-like attitude. Something's got to be done, but what? It's gone past me. It'll likely take another raid to get her on her feet'; to which Katie's answer had been a groan: 'Oh, don't say that. Don't say that.'

And now here was Luisa coming into the room. She had some letters in her hand and she placed them on the bed, saying 'These should cheer you up, the mail's just come in.'

As Luisa pushed the letters under her fingers Tilly said, 'Read them to me.'

'I'll do no such thing; they're private letters, you read them yourself. Now come on. I'll open them for you and that's as far as I'll go. There you are!' She slit open the three letters and out of the first she lifted a sheet of paper which she pushed into Tilly's hand, saying, 'Get on with it. I'll come back later and listen to your news.'

Slowly Tilly raised the letter to her face and her eyes travelled down to the signature first. It was from John, and it began: 'Dearest Tilly, I don't know what to say, only that I am devastated, I cannot believe that Matthew has gone. I could never imagine Matthew dying; he seemed to be the epitome of life. Oh my dear Tilly, how sore your heart must be at this moment.

'I am sending this off immediately, and both Anna and I say, please come home, we want you, we need you. I cannot see to write any more, I feel heartbroken. We send our deepest love to you. Let me call myself your brother. John.'

John. John. Dear John. She wished she could see John. Oh, how she wished she could see John, to hear his voice, his stammer, his dear stammer. Come home, he said. Oh, she wanted to be home.

She saw herself rising from the bed, packing the cases, then taking the children by the hand and walking down the hill through the burning rubble of the ranch.... No, no; it was burning no longer. A new ranch had sprung up in its place and it was a better ranch. Under Luisa it would be a better place to live, but she would never live in it. No, she would pass through it, lift the children into the buggy and they would drive all the way to Galveston. . . . Oh, Galveston and the sea.

She dropped the letter on to the quilt and, putting her hands to each side of her hips, she pulled herself upwards; then looking down the bed where her toes made hills under the bedclothes she moved her feet.

If she could walk she could go home. Slowly she drew her knees upwards; then as slowly she twisted her body and let her feet drop to the floor, but when she made to stand she swayed and fell backwards on to the bed.

If you can walk you can go home.

She seemed to be reading the words in front of her eyes. Pulling herself upwards again she gripped the bedhead, then took in a long slow breath and looked about her. They had changed the room; naturally in placing the bed by the window they would have to. The little dressing-table was in the far corner. She looked towards it. Had she altered much? What little flesh she had seemed to have dropped from her bones and her skin felt dry, particularly her hair; her hair felt husky. She reached out and with the support of a chair, she made her way tentatively towards the dressing-table. Before it was a stool with an embroidered top. When she came within reach of it she leaned forward and placed her hands on it and rested for a moment before sitting down. Then she was looking into the mirror . . . staring into the mirror . . . gaping into the mirror.

Who was that woman in there? She even turned her eyes to the side to see if there was anyone behind her. But no; there was no one there but herself. Yet she could not recognise the face that was staring back at her. It was an old face, the skin drawn tight over the bones, no wrinkles, just taut skin. But what was that over her brow? It must be a trick of light. She glanced towards the window and looked back into the mirror again, and her hands went slowly up to her hair, her beautiful hair, the hair that Matthew loved. It was piled upwards on the top of her head. Katie dressed her hair every morning. She did it from behind the low bedhead, combing it off her brow. If she had thought at all about her hair it was to think that it wasn't so thick as usual. But then when one was sick your hair dropped out. But this wasn't her hair, her hair was a shining brown, in certain lights it shone with gold threads, but the hair that she was looking at was white, dead white.

As the door opened she turned her head from the mirror and Katie stood looking at her, her mouth wide open, her hands held up as if in horror. 'Oh, Tilly!' she said.

'My hair! Katie. My hair!'

'Yes, pet, yes.' Katie moved slowly towards her. 'It's . . . it's because of what you went through.'

'But . . . but it's white, Katie.'

'Yes, yes, Tilly, it's white. But . . . but it still looks good, lovely; in fact, I think it suits you better. . . .'

'O . . . h! Katie. Katie!' Something clicked inside her head, followed by a grating sound like that of a sluice gate, an unused sluice gate being lifted. The water gushed out on a high cry, it burst from her eyes, her nose, it spluttered out of her throat, even her kidneys were affected. She was swamped in water and so great was the noise she made as Katie held her that the children came running in from their play and stood at the bedroom door and joined their crying to hers.

Three, who was in the kitchen, taking in the situation, pelted down the hill as if competing in a race, and brought up Luisa. But when she entered the room she did not commiserate with Tilly; instead her face bright now, she said, 'Good! Good! At last. 'And although she, too, put her arms about Tilly her words weren't soothing. She did not say, 'There now. There now. Give over,' what she said was, 'Let it come. This is the best thing I've seen in weeks, months. Go on, get it out of you. The past is finished, let it flow away, you'll start again now. Katie – ' she looked at Katie whose face was close to hers and she said, 'Make a pot of strong tea and lace it with whisky.'

'Yes, ma'am, Yes, ma'am.' Katie, too, was crying but now she was smiling as she cried and Luisa, left alone with Tilly, drew her to her feet and guided her into a chair, and not until Tilly's crying seemed that it would never stop did she take a towel and, drying her face with it, say, 'Stop it! Now stop it! Enough is enough, you're clear, it's all washed out. You'll pick up your life and go on from here, and it'll be up to you to decide where you're going to spend it.'

☙ 13 ❧

It seemed they had been packing for days on end, yet there were only two trunks and four cases, and the cases were mostly taken up with the children's clothes and toys.

Katie had a separate trunk. She took a long time to pack it. She would put something in it, then take it out again, saying, 'Well, I won't need that back there.'

After she had said this for the third time in an hour Tilly, making an effort, gave Katie her full attention. It was difficult, she was finding, to force her mind to dwell on any subject for any length of time, but she couldn't help but notice that Katie had been acting strangely of late. First of all she had put it down to the shock she had sustained; although she hadn't gone under like herself, nevertheless she had suffered from it.

'What's wrong with you, Katie?' she now demanded.

'Wrong with me?' Katie turned towards her. 'Nothing! Nothing! Nothing that two or three boat journeys and a long bout of seasickness and a ride in a train won't cure.'

'You really want to go home?'

Katie paused and bent over her trunk before saying, 'Well now, what do you think? And imagine you turning up at the Manor without me. Can you hear me ma?'

'You've been acting strangely of late, more so since Christmas.'

Katie straightened her back and looked up at Tilly as she said softly, 'We've all been actin' strangely of late. I don't think there'll be any of us who'll ever act naturally in our lives again.'

'No . . . no, perhaps you're right.'

'I know I am.' She turned away and stood looking out of the window, not speaking, quiet. Very unlike herself. . . .

It came to the night before they were due to leave. Luisa had been hovering about them all day. Only once had she referred to their going. When she said, 'Like emigrating birds there's everything pulling you back and nothing'll make you stay, but I'm going to miss you, Tilly.'

Tilly had answered, 'And me you, Luisa. Oh yes, I'll miss you. But I must go.'

'Yes, I know that, you must go.'

And then Luisa had added, 'Is Katie of the same mind?' Somewhat surprised, Tilly had answered, 'Yes, yes, of course, as far as I know.' And to this Luisa had answered, 'As far as you know,' and had then gone out.

It was towards evening when Doug Scott appeared in the doorway. Katie was upstairs with the children and Tilly pointed this out. 'Katie's upstairs, Doug; I'll call her.'

'Tisn't Katie I've come to see this time, ma'am, 'tis you.'

'Well, come in, Doug.'

Doug came in. He took off his slouch hat and held it in his two hands. His fingers didn't fidget but remained still on the brim and he came to the point, saying, 'Don't know whether you know it or not, ma'am, but I've taken to Katie, think highly of her, very highly of her, and . . . and as I've sounded her, she thinks the same of me, so that being the case I've done me best to persuade her to stay put an' wed me. Make it double-like, for as you may know, Miss Luisa, she's going to wed Mack.'

At this Tilly's face showed her surprise, and Doug, now flapping his hat against his side, said, 'Oh, I seem to have let the cat out of the bag, but she would likely have told you before you left. Anyway, she's offered me head man under Mack and me own house, this one in fact if you'll excuse me sayin' it, ma'am, if I can get settled with Katie.'

Tilly's face was now straight and her voice stiff as she said, 'Well, what does Katie say about this?'

'All she says, ma'am, is that you need her; she came with you and she'll go back with you, and as you had only one child when you came but you're taking two back, you can't manage on your own.'

Tilly turned her head to the side and looked down the room. Her own sorrow had made her blind to the things that were happening under her nose. Yes, Katie would go back with her, and this man here, this good man, because Doug Scott was a good man, would likely be the last chance she'd have of marrying, for she was no beauty was Katie and she was past the age when she could pick and choose, if ever she had been that age.

As if she conjured Katie up by her thoughts there was a movement in the doorway behind Doug, and Katie entered the room. She looked first from one to the other, then gave her attention to Doug Scott, and her voice was abrupt as she said, 'Now I told you. I told you.'

'I know what you told me, Katie, but I've got the last word in this.'

Katie now looked fully at Tilly and Tilly at her, and Tilly's voice was low as she asked the question: 'If it wasn't for me would you stay with Doug?'

'Oh' – Katie tossed her head from side to side – 'you might as well say to me if it wasn't for the moon there wouldn't be any tides, it's a daft question.'

'Don't talk silly, Katie, answer me.' Tilly's voice was harsh now. 'Tell me, yes or no.'

Katie now became still. Her head turned and she looked at Doug, the tall, knotty-muscled, good-looking man, a man she had dreamed about all her life, yet knowing that dreams never came true, not for people like her, plain-faced, dumpy women whose tongues were the only things about them. And this wasn't always an asset, far from it. But this man wanted her, he had told her that he loved her; he had held her tightly in his arms and kissed her and laughed as he did so for he had to stand her on a block. Never again in her life would she get such a chance of having a man like him; never again in her life would she get the chance of having any man. What was there for her back at the Manor in the way of men? A butler? a footman? They wouldn't look the side she was on. No, at best it would be some oldish man who had lost his wife and had a houseful of bairns. But here was this good-looking, gay, vibrant man wanting her; and what was more, Miss Luisa was going to give them this house. Imagine her ever having a house of her own, and such a one. But against all this there was the severing of the bond, the strong bond that tied her to Tilly, Tilly Trotter that was, Tilly Sopwith as she was now . . . and who'd be the sole lady of the manor back home. But that wouldn't do her much good. The only solace in going home would be she'd be rid of her fear of Indians.

The very thought of an Indian chilled her blood; but again, with Doug to protect her, well, she imagined he'd see to it that no Indian would get near her all the while she was alive.

'Answer me, Katie.'

'All right, I'll answer you. Yes, if I wasn't concerned about you an' the bairns I'd stay along of Doug.'

'That's settled then.' The reply came quick. Tilly was looking at Doug now as she said, 'There's no need to talk about it any more, Doug, she stays.'

'Aw, ma'am!' His hand came out to hers and after a moment she took it; then they both turned and looked at Katie. She was standing with her head bowed on her chest, the tears were running down her face, and it was Tilly who sounded like the old Tilly, saying now, 'Stop your bubbling, there's nothing to cry about. And if I can cross the ocean on my own with two children, then I'll take word to your mother that you and' – she nodded towards Doug – 'and Doug will come over next year or the year after to see her.'

'Oh.' Katie threw herself against Tilly now, and they clung together for a moment. Then Tilly pushed her away towards Doug, saying now, 'Take her outside, she'll wake the children.'

She stood for a moment and watched the tall spare man with his arm about Katie's shoulders leading her down the steps; then she closed the door and leant against it and put her hand over her mouth. What would she do without Katie? Apart from the actual help with the children Katie was the only one she could really talk to, the only one who knew all about her and about everything that had happened to her. Oh Katie! Katie! Why had you to go and do this to me? I've had enough; I can't stand much more.

She pulled herself abruptly from the door, asking now as she generally did in self-criticism: Why had she to become Mark's mistress? Why had she to marry his son? Why? Why? Why?

She could give herself no answer except to acknowledge that Katie had to have the chance of loving too. . . .

Four days later at nine o'clock in the morning, she was standing on the deck of the ship. Willy was at one side of her, Josefina at the other. The deck was a-bustle with people, but it was as if she were entirely alone.

Through her misted gaze she could just make out the line of them on the dock: Luisa standing next to Mack; Doug Scott, his hand laid firmly on Katie's shoulder; they were all waving. Even Three, the proud obstinate Three was waving. She kept her gaze on Katie. The children were shouting, 'Bye-bye! Bye-bye! Aunty Luisa. Bye-bye, Mr McNeill. Bye-bye, Mr Scott. Bye-bye, Three. Bye-bye, Katie.' The last they shouted a number of times, 'Bye-bye, Katie. Bye-bye, Katie.'

Tilly did not call out, she had no voice. Anyway, whoever she called to, no one would hear; she was alone as she had never been alone in her life before. She had known loneliness at all levels, but in this moment the loneliness had turned to isolation. Why was it everyone she loved left her? Her granda, her granny, the parson's wife, Mark, Matthew. Oh Matthew! Matthew! Matthew. . . . And now Katie.

She forgot for the moment she was going back to John and Anna, two people who did sincerely love her. She could only think of the villagers and those ladies of the county who had scorned her when she was Tilly Trotter, spinster. Yet she had never thought of herself as a spinster until the check weighman had written it down on that application paper the first day she went down the mine. Tilly Trotter, spinster. Then she had become Tilly Trotter, mistress, mistress of a man; following which she had become Mrs Tilly Sopwith, wife. Now she was Mrs Tilly Sopwith, widow, and was likely to remain so for the rest of her days, that is if she were to carry out Matthew's last request of her. And of course, she would carry it out. It would be easy to do so for she couldn't see herself ever having any desire to marry again. Oh no! never.

The figures on the quayside were merely dots now. The children had stopped waving, they were tugging at her hands. She looked down from one to the other; then turning them about, she led them towards their cabin. There she sat on the side of the bunk and as she prepared to take off the children's outdoor clothes they almost simultaneously climbed up one on each side of her and they put their arms about her neck and Willy said, 'Oh! Mama! Mama!' Whilst Josefina resorted to the gesture which she used when she wanted Tilly's full attention, she put her fingers on her jawbone and turned her face fully towards her; and now her round bright Indian eyes were looking into Tilly's and what she said was, 'I love you, Mama.'

Tilly stared back at the child and for the first time she actually remembered Matthew's words, 'Go straight back home, and take Willy, but not Josefina.' And now she asked herself how she was going to explain this small fragile piece of foreign humanity to those back home. Josefina had said, 'I love you, Mama.' The child would call her Mama, and what proof could she give that she wasn't the child's mama; Josefina was a year older than Willy but not half his size. There was no birth certificate, nothing in writing to say who she was. Could she yell back at the tongues that would surely wag, 'She is my husband's bastard'?

'Mama.' The fingers were moving on the jawbone again.

'Yes, my dear?'

'I love you, Mama.'

'I know you do, dear; and I love you too. Yes, I love you, too.' And at this she pressed her son and her husband's daughter to her and, looking over their heads, her gaze went across the ocean and to that stretch of land between Shields and Newcastle and she muttered aloud with all the fervour of a deep heartfelt prayer, 'God help me . . . and her.'

TILLY TROTTER
WIDOWED

PART ONE

❧ The Veneer ❧

Mrs Matilda Sopwith stood against the ship's rail and watched the waters darken as the sun slipped behind the rim of the horizon. It had been an unusually calm day, in fact the weather had been clement for most of the journey, so different from that time almost three years ago when she had left Liverpool for America in this very same ship. Then, she and her small child and her friend, Katie Drew, had been tossed and tumbled about and made so sick that they had wished to die, and her small son had almost achieved this; yet the stormy sea and the plunging, rearing ship had not in any way affected her husband; he had seemed to revel in it, buoyed up by the fact that he was going back to the land he loved, the land, he had once said, in which he wished to die. And his wish had been granted him, but much, much sooner than he could have expected.

She swung her mind away from her husband and sent it spinning fast into the future that would begin on the morrow when the boat docked. She'd be met by her brother-in-law, John Sopwith, and his wife, Anna, both young, little more than boy and girl, at least to her mind; and there was no doubt that they would shower her with affection because she knew they were truly fond of her, for hadn't she been the means of bringing them together; two people who felt themselves scarred with defects over which they had no control, for what control had a young girl over hideous birthmarks? Perhaps in the man's case there was some measure for control for his cross was merely a bad stammer.

She could see them all taking the long journey back in the train; she could see the carriage meeting the train; she could see it bowling through the iron gates and up the drive to the manor house that lay on the far outskirts of South Shields; and she could already feel the welcome of Katie's mother, Biddy, and also witness the keen disappointment on her face when she realised that her daughter had not returned from America. But above all the pictures in her mind there stood out in sharp relief the faces of the whole Drew family and of the other servants when she entered the house accompanied not only by her small son Willy but also by a smaller child whose features claimed the ancestry of a Mexican Indian.

'This is my adopted daughter,' she would say to them. But why, their amazed gaze would ask, had she to adopt one such as she, for everyone knew creatures like her weren't really human beings, not like English human beings, and were merely born to be slaves.

Could she then say to them . . . could she even ever say to Biddy Drew, Biddy who, like her daughter Katie, knew all about her and had been her friend and confidante for years, could she say to her, 'I did not adopt her, Biddy, she is my husband's bastard'? No, no; she could never put a slur on Matthew's name, although in the ordinary sense a bastard was no slur on the man, simply on the woman who bore her, that is if the child was white; but to be dark-skinned with strange unblinking eyes, a skin that seemed to flow over the bone skeleton beneath it, a mouth whose lips lay with gentle firmness one on the other seeming to forbid the tongue to speak, and then the hair, black, straight, its sheen making it shine like a military boot, and all encased in a tiny body. There could be no acceptance whatever for such.

Yet she wasn't worried so much about Josefina's acceptance into the house as she was worried about her effect on the villagers. It was unfortunate that the child, who was as far as she knew about four and a half years old, should have the stature of one hardly three, unfortunate because she knew what would be the outcome of the villagers' diagnosis once they looked on the strange piece of humanity: Tilly Trotter had been up to her tricks again. She could even hear their concerted voices: 'My God! To think of it, having the effrontery to bring back another of her bastards. Wasn't it enough she had been the cause of the death of two men before disgracing herself by becoming the mistress of a man old enough to be her father? Then, when he was hardly cold in his grave, what did she do? She married his son and goes off to the Americas; and here she is come back as brazen as brass and showing off her latest effort.'

As if she could hear the voices and see the faces, she turned sharply round from the ship's rail and leant against it for a moment before walking quickly away up the deck. As she made to go down the companion-way the captain stood aside at the bottom of the steps and waited for her, and bowing his head slightly towards her, he said, 'Only another few hours, ma'am. You'll be glad when the journey is over.'

'Yes, I shall, captain; but I would like to thank you now, in case I don't see you later, for the effort you have made to make us comfortable during the journey.'

'No effort at all, ma'am, it was a pleasure. And yet I wish I hadn't had the pleasure, that circumstances had turned out differently for you, for you've been so tried in your short time away from the old country. I remember your husband well. Pardon me for speaking of him, ma'am, I don't want to arouse any memories, but I'd just like to say we, my officers and the crew, thought he was a very fine gentleman.'

'Thank you.'

'Will I see you at dinner tonight?'

'Would you excuse me, captain? I don't like to leave the children for too long.'

'I understand. Yes, yes, I understand; and I'll have something substantial sent to your cabin.'

'It is very kind of you and I thank you.' She inclined her head towards him, and he, in return, bowed his, and she went down the steps, along the corridor and into her cabin.

The cabin was the largest on the ship and one which the captain had allotted to her use much to the chagrin, she had discovered, of a Mr and Mrs Sillitt, a couple who were used apparently to making sea voyages and who had travelled on this particular ship a number of times.

It was as much to avoid Mrs Sillitt as her need to be with the children that had caused her to refuse to join the captain in the last meal on board. Mrs Sillitt was partly of French extraction and, therefore, her loyalties were divided. Scarcely a meal had passed during the voyage without she touched on the subject of the recent Crimean war, at times delving into it as if she had actually witnessed the battles of Alma, Balaclava and Inkerman. The lady hated the Russians with a fierce hatred, and some of her hatred seemed to have rubbed off on to the English for which her husband bore the brunt. It appeared at times as if she was accusing the poor man of having ordered the weather to freeze the soldiery to death, for everything that had gone wrong was attributed to the British, and was not her husband English, in fact Dorset English; and being apparently ineffectual inasmuch as he suffered in silence, he represented for her the inefficient British Command. The captain had at an early stage given up the fruitless argument, but not so the first officer who was a Scot. This man had confided in Tilly privately that he had little time for the English as a whole but God knew he had less time for the Frenchies whose main occupation seemed to be causing revolutions and making Napoleons. The latest one, who called himself Napoleon the Third, strutted around like a little bantam cock on a midden. No, the English, be what they may, were preferable to the Frenchies. And what's more, he could name a dozen women from the Liverpool dock front whom he'd be pleased to eat with in preference to sitting down opposite to Mrs Sillitt.

Mrs Sillitt's chatter had in a way floated over Tilly's head, that was until three evenings ago when she brought up the subject of 'the blacks'. She had brought Tilly sharply out of her reserve by saying in her naturally loud overbearing voice, 'Do you think it's wise, Mrs Sopwith, to take a black child into the country? Although slavery has been abolished in England since the beginning of the century, there's still a suspicion in some quarters that black children are being used in the old way.'

Her remark had stilled the conversation at the table and also caught the attention of the diners at the other six tables in the room.

Tilly had stared hard at the woman, then said stiffly, 'I am returning home with my adopted daughter, madam,' but before she could continue Mrs Sillitt, smiling tightly, said, 'Yes, yes, I know, my dear, we know of your situation, but I'm only offering the suggestion that it may not be wise seeing that she will be brought up in close proximity to your son. Black and white don't go together. Never will. I merely put it as a suggestion.'

'Then I would rather that you kept your suggestions to yourself.'

This rebuff did not penetrate the hide of Mrs Sillitt, and she was about to make another retort when her husband, seeming to drag himself out of obscurity and making his entry as explosive as a gunshot, glared at his wife as he hissed, 'Mind your own business, woman! Just for once, mind your own business and get on with your meal.'

As the first officer said later, if everybody had burst into cheering he wouldn't have been at all surprised, but oh, he wished he could have put his ear to the keyhole when the couple were alone in their cabin. Yet, he pointed out to Tilly, did she notice that the bold lady actually did as her husband bid her, although, mind you, she had looked as if she was going to burst asunder at any moment.

Since that meal a few nights ago the problem of Josefina had taken on a more definite shape in her mind, and the shape encompassed the years ahead and what might come out of the close proximity between the children. Mrs Sillitt had opened up another avenue of concern.

Yet as she sat on the side of the bunk and looked down on the sleeping face of Josefina she asked herself what else she could have done, and the answer came, she could have done what Matthew told her she must do, return home alone with Willy and leave his flyblow behind.

And it was strange to think now that that penultimate request of his had been unthinkable, whereas his dying request, the request that had made her swear that she would never marry again, had been easy to comply with.

She put her hand out and stroked the black shining plait lying over the small shoulder; then she rose to her feet and looked into the other bunk that was now on eye level with her. Her son was sleeping soundly, one fist doubled up under his chin. He was beautiful to look upon, so beautiful that the sight of him always brought an ache to her heart. Although when he was born he'd resembled his father there was now no trace of that resemblance in his features. He had her eyes. Oh, his eyes. The ache turned into a sharp stab that seemed to pierce her ribs. Perhaps in a very short while he'd be unable to see what she looked like; one eye was already sightless, the other gave him but dim vision, and yet no one looking into them would guess that they were not capable of normal sight. For a moment the incident that had injured his eyes rose before her. She saw herself in the market place, the child in her arms, and there was Mrs McGrath drunk and brawling, and when the sodden woman wielded the stick at her, she had ducked her head to avoid it, only for her son to take the blow. A baby of but six months he had been then.

Oh, those McGraths. They had been the curse of her life. All except Steve, the youngest of them and now the under-manager of the Sopwith mine. He had been her friend from childhood days. He had suffered for her, as his crooked arm proved, he had suffered for her because he loved her. Yes. Yes, Steve McGrath had loved her. And three years ago she had almost taken advantage of that love and offered to marry him to escape the passion of Matthew, because even in her own eyes it seemed a sin to be marrying the son of the man to whom she had acted as mistress for so long and whose child she had only recently borne.

Would she be pleased to see Steve? She got no answer to this question, except to give herself another question: Would she be pleased to see anyone?

Although she had recovered from the breakdown that followed on Matthew's death, there was a great void in her which she felt would remain with her always for she could never see anyone filling it, except her son.

She now touched Willy's hair; it was getting fairer every day. She lingered a moment longer gazing at him, then she turned from the bunk and attended to the packing.

A few hours now and she'd be in England, home, home which meant Highfield Manor, the place where she had gone as nursemaid all those years ago, the place from which she had been twice turned out, the place to which she was now returning, not as mistress of Mr Mark Sopwith, or as wife of Mr Matthew Sopwith, but as a widow and owner of the house and estate and the mine besides. She was financially a very rich woman . . . rich in everything that didn't matter.

<h1 style="text-align:center">⋘ 2 ⋙</h1>

'S . . . s . . . soon be there, Tilly. S . . . s . . . soon be there . . . s . . . soon be home.'

John Sopwith turned from the window of the swaying coach and looked across at Tilly and his wife sitting hand in hand then with his arms out he encircled the two children kneeling up on the seat beside him, and when Willy, bobbing up and down, shouted excitedly, 'Horses, Mama. Look, horses, galloping horses!' John said, 'Yes, horses, my boy. Why are you so . . . so surprised? America is not the only pl . . . place that has horses.'

'We had lots of horses, sir.' Willy had turned and was looking up into John's face, and he, bending towards the child, said, 'I am Uncle Jo . . . John. Say Uncle John.' And the boy glanced at his mother, and when she gave a little smile and a small movement of her head he looked back at John and repeated, 'Uncle John.'

Josefina had now turned from the window and was looking at John, and she too repeated, 'Uncle John.'

Her words were clearly defined. She was speaking English yet the inflection of her voice stamped her as foreign as much as did her dark solemn appearance.

When she put up her hand and tapped John gently on the nose he burst out laughing. Then looking across at Tilly he said softly, 'She's an unusual ch . . . child. I can understand why you wanted to . . . br . . . br . . . bring her . . . back with you.'

Yet even as he spoke he knew he was merely being polite because for the life of him he couldn't think what had possessed Tilly to bring this coloured child, this strange-looking coloured child, back home. This child did not look like any coloured person he had seen before. But he had seen pictures and drawings of American Indians, and there was something of the Indian in the hair and eyes. Yet she did not appear altogether Indian.

He now lay back against the quilted leather of the seat and with only half his mind he listened to his wife explaining the changes she had made in the house and stating that she hoped they would meet with Tilly's approval. For the rest, a strange thought had entered his head and he was chiding himself for it, albeit at the same time expanding it. Four years old, Tilly said the child was, yet she had the stature of a child not yet two. To his mind she was too tiny to be four years of age, she was more like an infant. Tilly had left this country almost three years ago. . . . No, no! He now thrust the thought from him. There was the child's voice; she certainly spoke as a child of four might.

He centred his gaze on his wife now. She was so pleased to have Tilly back. There was little female company of her own age or station near the Manor. There were neighbours, yes, but Anna didn't make friends easily; she was still very conscious of her affliction, especially so with anyone outside the household. Yet looking at her now from his position there was just the merest sign of the purple stain rising above the lace collar of her blouse. It was only when she was undressed that the frightful birthmark covering one entire shoulder and part of her breast gave evidence of the burden she had carried since she was a child. Yet he loved every inch of her skin with a passion that seemed to grow in him daily. He had known when he married her that he loved Anna, but he had never imagined himself capable of the feelings that possessed him now. In a way he felt his feelings for his wife almost matched his dead brother's mania for Tilly. Why had Matthew to die? And how had he died? He was longing to talk to Tilly about his brother, to know every detail. All she had told them so far was that he had been wounded in an Indian raid and had died of his wounds.

'I never thought to see these gates again.'

The carriage had turned into the drive and Tilly was now bending forward looking at the line of rowans, their greenery about to burst fresh and bright. Spring wasn't far off. For a moment she felt a stirring within her as if the coming season itself had touched her. Then it was gone, replaced now by a quivering anxiety, for in a few minutes she'd be meeting Biddy and, however pleased Biddy would be to see her, she wouldn't be able to understand that she'd come back without her daughter, for of all her children, Tilly knew, as strongly as she would deny it, Biddy had favoured the one she had chastised most. She had boxed Katie's ears as a child, shouted her down because of her chattering, ordered her about as if she were still a child when she was a full-grown woman, and had done all this to hide the fact from the rest of her family that she favoured this particular plain, podgy-looking daughter.

The carriage came to a stop at the foot of the steps and there they all were, all the members of the household, most of whom she recognised: all the Drews, Biddy looking the same as when she had left her, her work-worn back still straight, her big lined face, usually unsmiling but now with a look of bright expectancy on it that caused Tilly to gulp in her throat against the disappointment she was about to bring to her. There was Peg, the eldest of the girls – she must be near to forty and she was the best-looking of the bunch. She had been married and widowed. And there was Fanny, the youngest. What was she, twenty-five? And Arthur, a sturdy man in his thirties; and he was the youngest but two of the seven Drew men. And that was Jimmy, who must be about twenty-eight now. Bill, she understood from one of Anna's letters, had left and had gone to sea. That had been a surprise. She had thought he might have joined his three older brothers in the Durham mines. Betty Leyburn was still here, and Lizzie Gamble. She had been engaged as under-housemaid just before they went to America. And there were two strange men. The younger of the two, a man of about forty, was now opening the door. He was the new footman then. And the portly man with the grey hair at the top of the steps must be the butler. At one time she would have smiled to herself at the evident way he was showing to all those present that he knew his place in the servants' hierarchy.

The children had scrambled to the open door of the coach and she watched the footman extend his arms and lift Willy down to the drive. She also noticed that he hesitated for more than a moment at the sight of the dark child, and that when he did place her beside Willy his eyes remained on her before he swung about and extended his hand to help her down from the coach.

Almost immediately now she was engulfed by the whole Drew family. This was not a meeting between mistress and staff, this was a meeting of friends. But as quickly as it had begun so it ended. With one arm around Tilly's shoulders, Biddy Drew looked towards the carriage and to where stood the young master and mistress she had served during Tilly's absence; and then she was looking at Tilly again and her voice was a whisper as she said, 'Katie?'

'It's all right. It's all right, Biddy.' Tilly was quick to assure her. 'She's well and happy, very happy. I've got a lot to tell you. . . .'

'*She hasn't come back with you?*'

'No. No, but she'll be coming later on. She's married. Let us go in.'

The Drew family gazed at one another, their eyes saying, Our Katie's married? Then at the children, particularly at the dark child, before they all followed Tilly and John and Anna up the steps.

At the front door Tilly was greeted by the butler. His manner as correct as one would wish, he bowed towards her, saying, 'I am Francis Peabody, ma'am.'

Again Tilly wished she could smile. How was she to address Francis Peabody? Call him mister or Francis, or merely Peabody? And this she did, but gently, saying, 'Thank you, Peabody.'

Then they were in the hall, and she stood for a moment looking around it. It was a beautiful sight, so beautiful. She hadn't realised before how beautiful this house was. Even in America when she had longed to return here she hadn't visualised it as she was now seeing it. Nothing had changed; Anna hadn't altered anything, not even to move one piece of furniture. She turned towards Anna and found her hand extended, and she gripped it, and she knew in this moment that here she could have a friend, a confidante; and yet she also knew that she could never talk to her as she had done to Katie, or as she would do to Biddy. She was the lady of the manor but beneath the veneer and the education that Mr Burgess, the one-time tutor of her husband and his brothers and sister, had imposed on her was the child, the young girl, the granddaughter of William and Annie Trotter, two very ordinary people who had brought her up.

She looked down for a moment on the children. They were standing side by side gazing upwards to where the stairs led into the gallery. Their mouths were slightly agape, their eyes wide. The house was as new and surprising to Willy as it was to Josefina, for he could have no memory of it. And when he turned and, looking up at Tilly, said, 'It is a big house, Mama,' she said, 'Yes, dear; it's a big house.'

'Shall I take him . . . them upstairs, Tilly . . . ma'am? The nursery is ready.'

She turned and smiled at Fanny Drew, who was as perplexed as the rest of the household by the small dark addition to it, and in this moment too, so excited that she had forgotten that the old family friend, Tilly Trotter, was now their mistress. Of course, she had been their mistress for years before, but on a somewhat different footing.

'Yes, Fanny, take them up. Thank you. Their day things are in the small trunk, the other luggage will be following.'

Fanny nodded and smiled and held out her hands to the two children; but her right hand being on Willy's left side he did not see it and she had to lift it up, and as the child was drawn forward he turned and looked towards Tilly, saying questioningly, 'Mama?' and she, nodding towards him, said, 'It's all right. Fanny will take care of you; I'll be up in a moment.'

Following this, the servants, taking their lead from Biddy who had uttered no word since coming into the house, dispersed.

It was in the drawing-room when Anna was helping her off with her hat and coat that Tilly felt suddenly weak. Her legs gave way, her mind became a void, and the next thing she knew she was sitting on the couch with John and Anna bending over her, their faces showing their anxiety . . . Wh . . . what is it, Tilly? D . . . d . . . do you f . . . f . . . feel ill?'

She shook her head. 'No, no. Please don't worry; I'm not ill, it's . . . it's just reaction, relief I think that the journey is over.'

'You almost fell, dear, and you've lost all your colour.'

She caught hold of Anna's hand and pressed it gently.

'It's nothing. I . . . I was rather ill after Matthew died. My legs go weak now and again, I think I'll go and have a wash. And then I must talk to Biddy; I could see she was in a state. But' – she smiled weakly now – 'before I do anything at all, do you think I could have a cup of tea?'

''Of course. Of course. Of course. What am I thinking about?' Anna rushed to the bell-pull near the fireplace and tugged at it; and presently, when the door opened and Mr Francis Peabody sailed into the room, she said, 'Bring a tray of tea immediately, Peabody.' The butler inclined his head and, gravely turning about, went from the room, and Tilly closed her eyes and it came to her that life could hold other problems besides those stemming from the big issues, such as the one of having two mistresses in the house. And then there was Mr Peabody. No, not Mr Peabody, merely Peabody. How would he react to her sitting at the kitchen table chatting to the cook, laughing with Peg and Fanny. But then, after all, the latter needn't trouble her for she didn't think she'd ever laugh again. . . .

After drinking a cup of tea she did not go upstairs immediately; instead she went into the kitchen where it looked as if Biddy was awaiting her entry, for she was standing to the side of the table looking down the long room towards the green-baized door. Her hands, joined at her waist, were gripped so tightly that the knuckles showed white. Peg and Fanny Drew were also in the kitchen and they too stood waiting for Tilly to approach.

Going immediately to Biddy, Tilly pressed her hands apart and gently pulled them from her waist and, holding them tightly, she said, 'It's all right. It's all right, Biddy, Katie's all right, I've a lot to tell you. But first' – she now glanced at the girls – 'I want to say how glad I am to see you all again. I . . . I never thought I would. . . . Sit down.' She drew Biddy to the settle, and when they were seated both Peg and Fanny came and stood in front of them, and Fanny in her soft voice said, 'You weren't just sayin' she was married, were you, Tilly? She's not dead, is she?'

'Dead! Don't be silly, Fanny. Of course not! She's married.' Tilly now turned and looked at Biddy and she shook her old friend's hands up and down as she said, 'She's married, Biddy. It . . . it all happened at the last minute. She wasn't going to stay. You see. . . . Oh it's a long story. After Matthew died I had a kind of relapse and I wasn't aware of very much for months, and then when I got on my feet my one thought was to come home, and the very day before we left – Katie was all packed, not a word about staying – Doug came to me, Doug Scott. He's a cowboy. Not like an English farm boy, oh no. Anyway, he told me that he loved Katie and Katie loved him, but that she wouldn't stay because she felt her duty was to come home with me. Well now, Biddy' – Tilly dropped her head slightly to the side – 'what could I do? Could I have said yes, she must come home, when I knew where her heart lay? And what's more, Biddy, she'd never get a chance again like Doug.' She turned and smiled at the girls now, saying, 'He's a handsome fellow and seems twice her size . . . well, I tell you, he's six foot three. And Luisa, she's Mr Portes's daughter who now owns the ranch, is promoting him and giving him the house that we lived in. We had it specially built for ourselves. She's very fortunate, Biddy. But the main thing is she's happy, and she says they'll come home next year, or perhaps the following one, because Doug's not short of money.'

Biddy sighed now, then said, 'I was looking forward to seeing her, Tilly.'

'I know you were, Biddy, but she would never have got such a chance here.'

'Nobody'd get such a chance as that here.' Peg's head was bobbing as she spoke. 'I wish you had taken me with you, Tilly.'

'Be quiet you!' Biddy, sounding her own self, now turned on her daughter, saying, 'And not so much of the Tilly, I told you all yesterda'. You'll forget yourselves one of these days, and in front of company.'

'Oh.' Tilly now flapped her hand towards Biddy, saying, 'It's lovely to hear my name again.'

'People should know their place; they've been told often enough.' Biddy now rose abruptly from the settle and went towards the open fire, and Tilly pulled a small face towards the girls and they both grinned at her.

It was as Biddy bent and lifted the teapot from the brass kettlestand that she said, 'I was sorry to hear of your loss, lass,' and her daughters nodded their heads confirming the statement. When their mother passed them and added as she placed the teapot on the table, 'You seem fated, lass, for sorrow,' the pain that seemed to lie just beneath Tilly's ribs stabbed through and she lowered her head and bit on her lip, and when Peg's hand came on her shoulder it took an effort to stem the tears gushing up from the back of her throat and into her eyes, and she said thickly, 'I'll go and have a wash. I'll be down again later.'

'Aye. Aye.' Biddy had not turned towards her, and the girls stood silently by as she walked between them, her head still bent, and went up the kitchen, through the long passage and into the hall.

Seeing the hall empty, she stood for a moment, her hand about her throat, trying to compose herself.

'You're fated, lass, for sorrow.' It would seem that Biddy was right; in fact she had merely voiced the thought that had been in her own mind since Matthew died. Oh, Matthew! Matthew! Would the longing for him never leave her? . . . And yet it was little more than four years ago that she had stood in this very hall and said, 'Oh, Mark! Mark!' after Matthew's father had been carried out.

And then there was that day in the far past when she had run to Simon Bentwood, the farmer, after hearing that his wife had died, feeling that his arms would be widespread to greet her. And what had greeted her? The sight of him naked in the barn consorting with a woman far above his station, and her as bare as on the day she was born. That first love had died as cleanly as if it had been cut off with a knife. Yet it had been love, a love that she had fostered from when she was a child.

There had followed the twelve years with Mark as his mistress and mistress of this house. And she had loved him too. Oh yes, she had loved him too. But was that love anything compared with what she gave to his son? There was no way to measure love against love. When it was present and filled the time, it was all. But how many times could one love? She didn't know. What she did know was, she had loved for the last time.

✑ 3 ✑

The days that followed were, in a way, tranquil. She fell into a routine. Three weeks had passed and she had never been outside the gates; nor had the children, but they were content, in fact in their element. The garden had become a world to them. They were spoilt by Arthur and Jimmy Drew and also by the new coachman, Peter Myers. He had taken the place of Fred Leyburn who, with his wife Phyllis and brood of children, had moved to Durham where a windfall of a cottage had been left to Phyllis by an aunt.

Then there was the stable-boy, Ned Spoke. Peter Myers had already threatened him with a beating for running with the bairns and acting the goat as if he were a bairn himself instead of a thirteen-year-old lad.

It was at this time that Tilly, fearing that the children were beginning to run wild, spoke to Anna about the matter of their education. This she had decided to take upon herself, as there seemed nothing for her to do, for as much as Anna made an effort to let go the reins of the household, the habit of the last few years was strong and when the young matron found herself giving the orders she nearly always ended with, 'Oh, Tilly, I'm sorry, I'm sorry,' until the apologies had become rather embarrassing, making Tilly feel inclined to take the easy way out and say, 'You carry on as always.' But then, where would she be? What would her position become in this household? She owned the house, she owned the estate, she owned the mine.... That was another thing, the mine. She had only a few days ago expressed the wish to go to the mine and this had seemed to shock both John and Anna. The mine was no place for her now, not in her position. In any case, it was being run very efficiently by the manager and his under-manager.

They seemed to forget, that is if they ever remembered, that she had once worked in the mine.

And about the under-manager. She thought that in some way Steve might have made a point of coming to the house to welcome her back. Was he not a tenant in her cottage? Yet why should he wish to bring her back into his life? From the beginning she had played havoc with his feelings, not intentionally, oh no, never, for she had made it plain to him that she would never feel for him other than as a friend. And who knew now but that he was married or at least might have someone in his eye.

She was feeling very unsettled in herself; as Biddy would have exclaimed if she had confessed her feelings to her: 'You don't know which end of you's up, lass.' And there was Biddy herself. She was the same yet not the same. She still did not seem to have got over the disappointment of Katie not returning, although she'd had a letter from her and one enclosed from Doug. Her only comment on this had been, 'He seems a decent enough fellow.' Then she had added in her caustic manner, 'But I can't see our Katie on a horse, she'd look like a pea on a drum.'

But now she was talking to Anna about the children. 'I'm going to engage a nursemaid,' she said; 'someone sensible, young enough to play with them but old enough to keep them in their place when needed. In the mornings I'll take them for lessons, Willy already knows his ABC, but Josefina doesn't take too kindly to learning I'm afraid.'

'They're so very young yet, Tilly, and they're enjoying the garden and playing. Must you start them on lessons?'

'I don't think you can start them too soon, Anna. You know, when I first came here John was four years old and Mr Burgess had him reading nursery rhymes. The first one I heard John read was "The Little Jumping Joan":

> Here I am, little jumping Joan,
> When nobody's with me I'm always alone.

And when he finished it he always put his head back and laughed.'

'Did he stammer then?' Anna's voice asked the question quietly, and Tilly lied boldly, saying, 'Yes, much more than he does now. Oh' – she shook her head – 'much more because now he can reel off sentences without a hitch, and that's all your doing.' She inclined her head towards Anna, and Anna replied simply, 'I hope so because I love him, I love him dearly, and I never forget that I have you to thank for him, Tilly.'

'Nonsense! Nonsense! You would have met up without me.'

'No, we shouldn't and you know it. When you asked me to come back that day I had intruded on you, hoping like some simpleton that you could give me a cure for my birthmark, I know now your mind formed a plan of bringing us together. John needed someone and I needed someone.' She leant over and gripped Tilly's hand. Then after a moment she said, 'There's only one thing bothering me, I . . . I show no signs of having a child.'

'Oh, there's plenty of time, that will come. Remember I was with John's father for twelve years, well . . . eleven years before it happened to me, so don't worry your head, just go on being happy.'

'Oh, I am happy, Tilly. I never imagined there could be such happiness in life. I....'

They both turned as a knock came on the door and it opened, and Peabody was standing there.

'A messenger on horseback has brought this letter for you, madam. He says it's urgent,' he said, holding the letter out as he walked slowly towards Anna.

Getting up, she took it from him and opened it. She read a few lines; then her face showing her concern, she looked at Tilly, saying, 'It's from Aunt Susan. It's Grandma. She has taken a bad turn; I must go at once.'

'Of course. Of course.' Tilly now looking at the butler said, 'Tell the messenger to return and say Mrs Sopwith will be there as soon as the carriage can take her.'

'Yes, madam.' Peabody inclined his head towards Tilly. Then as he went to turn away she stayed him, saying, 'Order the coach to be got ready immediately, and then send word to the mine and ask Master John to return home as soon as possible.'

She noted herself that she did not say 'The master' because there could be no master of the Manor until Willy took his place, and that would be years ahead. . . .

In the confusion of the next few hours Tilly seemed to step back over the years. It seemed as if she had never been away from the house. The reins were in her hands once more and from the moment she saw Anna and John into the carriage she knew with that strange knowledge that could be termed intuition, or foresight, or even witchery, that they had gone to stay, and that for the first time she could now act as mistress, legal mistress of the house.

⤺ 4 ⤻

A fortnight later Anna's and John's belongings were taken to their now permanent residence in Felton Hall, beyond Fellburn. The old lady had had a stroke and Anna felt that she should be near her. Tilly was under the impression that John wasn't too happy at leaving the Manor; but wherever Anna was there he wanted to be, and as he said to Tilly, what made her happy satisfied him. John seemed to have matured greatly since he married.

The day following their final departure, Tilly interviewed a girl from the village. Her name was Connie Bradshaw. She was the daughter of the innkeeper who, so she informed Tilly without much regret in her voice, had died last year, and her mother was no longer at the inn but living in a cottage on the outskirts of the village. She was a sprightly girl, free spoken, as Tilly found out when she questioned her.

'How did you know that I was enquiring for a nursemaid?'

'"Twas round the village, ma'am.'

It was odd, Tilly thought, how a whisper in the house could travel to the village, and that over two miles away and none of the staff seeming to visit it.

'Have you just left a position?' she asked the girl.

'Well, not rightly a position, ma'am. I was workin' in the bar for me mam after me da died, but she gave me no pay an' then she got slung out.'

'Slung out? . . . Why?'

'Drinking more than she sold, ma'am.'

'Oh!' The candidness of the girl caused Tilly's eyelids to blink and she looked to the side for a moment. She only faintly remembered Mrs Bradshaw and had a picture of a blowsy woman, loud-voiced and running to fat, and so she could understand this girl wanting to get away from her parent and to better herself.

'Your name is Connie?'

'Aye, ma'am.'

'Well, Connie, I shall take you on trial for a month. Your temporary wage will be two shillings a week. Should you suit at the end of that time then your wages would be ten pounds a year, together with uniform and your choice of tea or beer as refreshment. You will have leave to go to church on a Sunday if you wish, and one half day holiday a fortnight and one whole day a month.'

The girl's face was bright as she replied, 'Eeh! that sounds good to me, ma'am. I hope I'll suit. I'll try anyroad.'

'I'm sure you will. Good-day, Connie.'

'Good-day, ma'am.'

She had interviewed the girl in the morning-room and after allowing enough time, as she thought, for her to get along the passage and to leave by the kitchen, which way she had entered, she herself left the room and made for the kitchen, meaning to give Biddy the orders for the day's meals, but she stopped just before she opened the kitchen door to hear the girl exclaim loudly, 'I've got it! On trial for a month I am. Ain't there no housekeeper here? She asked all the questions hersel'. Well, I suppose she knew all the answers seein' as she was in my place once.'

'Get yourself along, miss, and it'll surprise me if you reign a month.'

That was Biddy's voice, and Tilly remained for a while standing where she was before turning about and going back into the morning-room.

She had made a mistake in engaging that girl, yet she had felt sorry for her having to work in a bar for nothing, and then putting up with a drunken mother. But she was from the village, and she should know by now that no villager wished her well, except perhaps Mr Pearson. Yet what had his son done? Appeared out of the blue in the wilds of Texas and exposed her past to all who would listen. But she couldn't blame Mr Pearson for that; you should never blame the parents for what their offspring did. Look at Mark's daughter, Jessie Ann. She had been the sweetest child but she had turned out a little Tartar of a woman. What would be her thoughts now, she wondered, knowing that her father's mistress, whom almost literally she had thrown out of this house, was back in it as its rightful mistress this time. It must be gall to her.

About that girl. Well, she had only taken her on for a month; she would wait and see. But now she must arrange her days, at least her mornings, in the schoolroom and the first thing she must do was to get suitable books. There wasn't a book in the library that she could use to instruct Willy and Josefina. At one time there had been dozens in the nursery, but when the second Mrs Mark Sopwith decided to leave her husband and take the children with her they had taken their books along with them.

But she knew where she could lay her hands on books of instruction for the young, in the attic at the cottage. After Mr Burgess died she had spent days clearing the rooms downstairs and packing the books under the roof; all she had to do was to go along there and select what she needed. . . . And risk running into Steve? Well, she'd have to meet him sometime. And why need she be afraid of meeting him? No need whatever.

She would go along one afternoon between one and three because if he was on the back shift he would likely still be down below, and if he was on the fore shift he would most likely be on his way there. Still, why try to evade a meeting, they were bound to come across each other some time; so the sooner the better and get it over with.

She left the room and went to the kitchen and the first words Biddy said were, 'I think you've taken on something there, lass.'

'I've told her it is only temporary, for a month.'

'That's just as well. Doubt if you'll put up with her for a week, she's all tongue. And you know who she is?'

'Yes, she's Bradshaws' daughter from the inn.'

'A pair if there ever was one. He died of drink an' she's goin' the same way.'

'So I understand, but the girl didn't seem to want to follow in her mother's footsteps.'

'She's got her mother's tongue. . . . Anyway, it's your business but I'm tellin' you this, lass, if she starts any of her antrimartins back in the hall' – she inclined her head towards the wall and the servants' hall next door – 'I'll slap her down quicker than you can spit.'

Tilly smiled as she said, 'You do that, Biddy, it'll save me a job.' It was odd, she thought, yet comforting how she dropped into the old colloquial way of speaking when talking to Biddy. 'Now about me dinner, I don't feel very hungry today so. . . .'

'If you ask me, you never feel very hungry. Now look' – Biddy pointed – 'there's a lemon sole that'll melt in your mouth. There's some veal cutlets an' all. Now I'm gona do those for you and you're gona eat them. Do you hear me?'

'I hear you.'

'Here.' Biddy jerked her head, a sign for Tilly to go and stand close to her, and now Biddy's voice was a mere whisper as she said, 'Has his nibs been at you?'

'Peabody?'

'Aye. Who else?'

'No. Why should he be at me?'

'To get his daughter in here as nursemaid. The footman, Biddle, let on about it.'

'He has a daughter . . . Peabody?'

'Four.'

'No!'

'Aye. And you know what he was aiming to do just afore you came home?'
'No.'
'Get the lot of them here. His eldest one's tickin' forty and she's a housekeeper in Newcastle somewhere. He'd been on to Master John about a housekeeper sayin' that it wasn't right for an establishment like this to be run by a cook.' She now thrust her her thumb into her chest. 'Then his second eldest daughter is a widow with one bairn, and the other two are in service. The youngest, just on seventeen, would, he imagined, be just right for the nursery. Oh, when he knows about our Miss Connie Bradshaw the poker'll drop down his spine and right out of his backside, and he'll crumple up 'cos, let's face it, that lass's as common as clarts. He thinks my brood's bad enough. Oh aye, he does.' Biddy nodded vigorously at Tilly who now bit on her lip and lowered her head; for the first time in many, many months she had the desire to laugh.

Oh, it was good to be home, good to be with Biddy, good to be with real people. Not that John and Anna weren't real. Not that Matthew and Mark hadn't been real. But there was something about Biddy and her brood that presented life without veneer. There was no pretence. You hadn't to act in her presence, you just were. But she knew that if she were acting correctly as the mistress of this house she should not be standing hobnobbing with her cook; nor should she have the desire at this moment to fall against her and put her arms around her and say, 'Oh, Biddy! Biddy! hold me close, comfort me.' In fact she shouldn't be in the kitchen at all, she should, as that girl had said and as Peabody expected, have a housekeeper and leave the ordering to her, for was she not Mrs Matthew Sopwith.

No, no; she wasn't, not really, not underneath. Under the façade she knew who she was, and always would remain so, she was simply Tilly Trotter.

The sun was shining when, a week later, she rode out of the courtyard, and not side-saddle but astride the horse. It was the first time she had been on a mount since she had returned, and she was aware that the men were watching her covertly from the stables, as was Biddy and most of the staff from the kitchen windows.

She sat relaxed, as Mack McNeill and Matthew had taught her. The stirrups were long, her legs almost straight. Her riding breeches were grey, her high boots and coat brown; except for the bun of white hair showing behind her soft felt hat, the one that she had worn when riding out from the ranch, she could have been taken for a young man, a slim, straight young man.

As Biddy, her face close to the window, muttered to her daughters: 'In the name of God did you ever see anything like it, the change a pair of trousers can make in a woman! And it'll do her no good at all to be seen ridin' like that, astride a beast for all the world like any man.'

It was Jimmy Drew who opened the gates for her. He had been working at the end of the drive trimming the hedges, and, what was unusual, he never spoke as he watched her ride through, although she said, 'Thanks, Jimmy. Thanks.... Lovely day, isn't it?'

She wasn't unaware of the stir she had made in riding out in such a fashion, and she knew her slouched hat, which was at variance with the smartness of her coat and breeches, would itself cause comment should she meet any rider. But what matter, she was used to comment. And this is how she had been taught to ride; and this is what she had worn when riding side by side with Matthew.

Oh Matthew! Matthew! If only he were here. Last night she had dreamed and the dream had been so real that she had turned in the bed and snuggled into him and just as always happened when she had turned to him he had loved her, and she had woken rested and put her hand out to feel him, and when realisation hit her she had pressed her face into the pillow and sobbed.

But crying was for the night; you faced the day calmly. You had two children to educate and a house to run . . . a difficult house to run, a house that was staffed partly by her friends and partly by professional servants. It hadn't been difficult for Anna and John to keep the harmony between the two factions but it was going to be so for her, for she knew she wouldn't be able to favour her friends without annoying her professional staff, few as they were.

She put her horse into a canter and rode so until she came to the lane leading from the main coach road. Here she quickly drew the animal to a walk as she saw in the distance a woman and three children scrambling up the bank. They had been gathering wood, which was made evident as they pulled the bundles into the narrow ditch at the side of the road, and when she came abreast of them they stared up at her as one, their eyes unblinking.

'Good-afternoon.' She smiled at them, and it was after a moment that the woman replied, 'Afternoon, ma'am,' at the same time bobbing her knee.

As she rode on there came over her a strong feeling of nostalgia for the days when she herself had gathered wood, not only gathered it but limbed it from the trees and sawed the branches up before dragging them home, and then had the satisfaction of seeing a roaring blaze at night as she sat before the fire between her granda and grandma. But that was another life, another world.

When she eventually turned a bend in the narrow lane and came within sight of the cottage it was to see a horse tied to the gatepost, and her acquired knowledge of horseflesh told her it was a good animal and beautifully saddled. She also noticed that the hedge bordering the side of the cottage had been allowed to grow to almost twice the height she remembered it, although the top had been kept trimmed, but as she turned from the lane and rode up by the side of it she could just see over it and towards the front door of the cottage.

She was pondering in her mind whether to ride on and return later when the door of the cottage opened almost abruptly and a woman stepped on to the pathway, and following her came Steve. She did not immediately recognise the woman but she recognised Steve, although his head looked to be bandaged and his face was smeared with coal dust. The woman had turned and was looking up at him where he was now standing on the step above her, and it was with a start of amazement, not untouched with horror, that Tilly now recognised her.

It must be all of seventeen years since she had last set eyes on this woman, and then she had been lying naked in the barn with Simon Bentwood. Strangely, it was this woman who had decided the course of her own life; in a way, it was her she had to thank for the position that she now held as mistress of the Manor, for if on that day she hadn't seen her lying with Simon Bentwood, he and she herself would have come together and she would have been a farmer's wife and happy to be so.... Life was strange, terrifyingly strange. But what was that woman doing here? Indeed, what else but trailing a man! She was noted for it. She remembered her nickname, Loose Lady Aggie.

Tilly slid from the horse and took its head to keep it quiet. She did not want to be found here by either of them and it was no use riding on because the path which simply circled the garden would eventually bring her back into the lane and in full sight of them.

She listened as Lady Myton spoke. Her voice was as she remembered it, high, haughty, the words clipped. 'You're foolish, you know that,' she said.

'I don't see it that way, m'lady.' Steve's voice sounded cool.

'It's a good position, you'd be in charge of the stables. There are nine hunters in there altogether.'

'As I understand it you have very good stockmen already.'

'Yes, I had, but Preston has left and his place is open.'

'Then why not move the next man up?'

'He's not capable enough.'

'Well, I can assure you, m'lady, he'd be much more capable looking after hunters than I would. My knowledge of horses is practically nil.'

'I saw you riding the other day, you handled the animal well.' 'Oh, him!' There was a slight note of laughter in Steve's voice now. 'Only because his back's as broad as a fireplace settle, and he's too old even to trot. His days were over in the pit and he was on his way to the slaughterhouse; I felt he would save my legs the three-mile walk twice a day, so I took him on.'

'You're making light of your achievements.'

'Not a bit of it, m'lady.'

There followed a pause now and Tilly heard their footsteps going down towards the gate; then Lady Myton's voice again: 'You are turning down a great opportunity. Do you know that? And anyway I understand you were thinking of leaving the mine?'

'I think you've been misinformed, m'lady.'

There was another pause before her voice came again, saying, 'It's a tinpot mine, doesn't even pay its way.'

'Again I think you've been misinformed. It's doing very nicely for all concerned.'

'Until it's flooded again. And look at your head. I understand there was a fall this morning?'

'Just a slight one. These things happen every day in mines.'

'And two men taken to hospital?'

'Just broken bones, nothing to worry about really.'

Again there was a pause, and when the woman spoke Tilly could only just make out her words. 'When we last met I indicated that I could be of great help to you; and you know, you are the kind of person that could be of great help to me. It would be a reciprocal situation.'

There was a longer pause before Steve's voice came to Tilly, saying, 'On that occasion, m'lady, I'm sorry to remind you, I pointed out that you had picked on the wrong man.'

There was now the grating of the horse's hooves on the rough road and the sound brought a feeling of panic to Tilly. If the visitor rode back in the direction of the mine all well and good, but if she decided to take the coach road then she would pass by the path and almost assuredly she would glimpse her.

As there came to her the words 'You're a fool, Mr McGrath. Do you know that?' followed by Steve's answer, 'Yes. I'm well aware of that. Have been for years,' she pulled the horse forward and was making quickly up by the side of the hedge when she heard a loud, 'Well! Well!' and, looking over her shoulder, she saw Lady Myton sitting on her horse staring towards her. As they looked at each other over the distance Tilly realised that the woman had recognised her, and this was made evident when her ladyship's voice rang out, saying, 'Mrs Sopwith, about to enter by the back door. If I remember rightly you have a habit of turning up at inopportune moments. The way is clear now.' She thrust out one arm in a dramatic gesture. 'He's yours, for the time being at any rate. I've always balked you, haven't I? Ha! Ha!'

As Lady Myton spurred her horse up the path, Tilly was aware that Steve had parted the top of the hedge a little way back and was peering at her in amazement; then almost instantly he seemed to be by her side.

'Oh, I'm sorry, Tilly, I never expected you. I mean . . . well' – he hunched his shoulders and spread out his hands – 'what can I say? Here; let me turn him about.'

He turned the animal about and into the lane and tied it to the gatepost where Lady Myton's mount had been fastened a moment ago.

Now they were walking up the path to the cottage and she hadn't as yet spoken.

'Here, sit down.' He pulled a chair from underneath the table, and she sat down thankfully and looked at him as he bent slightly above her. He was smiling, his eyes shining, his black hair above the bandage was ruffled, his shoulder muscles were pressing against his shirt; the belt that supported his trousers didn't cover a stomach bulge; he was a very presentable man and she could understand how he attracted Lady Myton.

As if he had picked up her thoughts he put his hand to his head where the bandage was stained as he said, 'That woman! She's a menace, and she's as brazen as a town whore. I'm sorry.' He flapped his hand now. 'But I'm so surprised to see you. Of course I knew you were back and we'd come across each other sometime, but to be on the doorstep so to speak.'

'And at the wrong moment.' It was the first time she had opened her lips and she smiled at him and he smiled back at her as he said quietly now, 'Aw, Tilly, it's good to see you and to hear your voice. How are you?'

'Oh, getting along, adjusting.'

'I hear you had a rough time of it out there.' His eyes rested on her hair where it showed under the turned-back brim of the hat, but he made no remark on it.

'Yes, you could say that, Steve.'

'I was very sorry to hear about Mr Matthew, very sorry indeed. You can believe that, Tilly, I was.'

'Thank you, Steve.' She looked to the side for a moment; then her glance went round the room and she said, 'You haven't altered anything.'

'No; why should I, it was just right to begin with'

'You still like living here?'

'Nowhere better. In one way I've never been so contented in me life. Look, I'll just have a sluice and then I'll make you a cup of tea. The fire's bright.' He thumbed towards it, and impulsively, she said, 'You go and have a sluice and I'll make the cup of tea.'

'You will? Aw, Tilly!' He jerked his head at her. 'It's as if the years have dropped away. I'll do that. Do you remember the day the bucket fell down the well?'

'Yes, yes.' She laughed at him as he went down the room and out of the bottom door. She didn't, however, go immediately to the fireplace but stood looking around her, and for a moment again nostalgia hit her and she had a longing to be back in this cottage with Mr Burgess sitting on the couch there nodding over his books, and Willy lying in the wash-basket by the side of the fireplace. She hadn't realised how peaceful she had felt during that interlude between Mark and Matthew.

Automatically her hand went to the mantelpiece for the tea caddy; and yes, when she opened it there it was half full of tea. As he said, he hadn't altered a thing. Dear Steve. But she must be careful, very careful, she must raise no hopes in that quarter again.

A few minutes later when he came into the room his face was clean and shining; his hair was combed back and the bandage was off his head showing a two-inch cut across his brow sealed now with dried blood, which caused her to exclaim, 'Was the fall bad?' Then turning her head to the side, she muttered, 'I couldn't help overhearing some of your conversation.'

'I'm glad you did, Tilly, else you might have thought otherwise . . . got the wrong idea like. . . . But about the fall. No, it was nothing. Two fellows were trapped, one got his shoulder put out, the other . . . well, I think his leg's broken but it'll mend; we got them out quickly.'

'Is the mine paying?'

'Aye, yes. Oh yes, especially this last year. Master John has done a good job. He belies his looks that young fellow if I may say so, and the men think highly of him. There's hardly a day goes by but he shows his face, and that's something in a mine owner. Well, what I mean is' – he gave a quick jerk of his head – 'I know he's actin' for you, but the men look upon him as the boss and although he's got a longer trek now comin' from his wife's place he still turns up.'

'I'm glad the men have taken to him. He's a good young man in all ways, but I'm sure things couldn't have worked out so well without the help of you and Mr Meadows. By the way, were you thinking of leaving?'

'Er . . . well no. No, no, not at all . . . and leave this cottage and everything? I'd be daft now, wouldn't I?'

She stared at him, this Steve McGrath whom she had known from a boy who had pestered her with his attention until she had shocked him off by becoming the mistress of Mark Sopwith. That Steve had been a kindly nondescript character, persistent in his attentions, but nondescript; but this Steve, well, he could be a man of the world. Put him in different clothes and she could see him talking with the best of them. He sounded confident, knowledgeable, which thought brought her to the reason for her errand here. And so as he turned from her, saying, 'You've mashed the tea then. I'll pour out. And you still take milk?' she said, 'Yes. Yes, please. And . . . and I must tell you the reason why I came today. You see I'm in need of books, school books; I'm going to start teaching the children.'

'Well, you've come to the right place, Tilly; they're all just as you left them. Well, that isn't quite true.' He now paused with the big brown teapot in his hand. 'You see I've been going through them, at least some of them. I'd have to live a couple of lifetimes afore I'd manage to read that lot up there' – he lifted his head towards the ceiling – 'but the more I've read lately the more I've realised what a learned man Mr Burgess must have been, because most of the pages have pencil marks or queries on them. He must have read most all the light hours of his life.'

'Yes, I think he did, Steve. As for me, I've always felt indebted to him and that indebtedness increases with the years because besides teaching me so many things, he taught me what to read. You can waste so much of your time reading stupid matter.'

'You're right there; but I don't think he possessed a book that you could put the name stupid to. You know, I think he would have made a good member of parliament, and on the side of the working man too. Did you ever read the notes that he made on Malthus? By! some of them were scathing, especially those touching on what Malthus said about catastrophes, wars and famines and such being the natural means of preventing overall starvation. . . . My! if he'd had his way there wouldn't have been any bairns born because every bairn meant another mouth to feed. He was a stirrer was that Malthus. I used to sit here at nights' – he pointed to the rocking chair now – 'and get all worked up about him, real hot an' bothered.' As he put his head back and laughed Tilly gazed at him, her face straight. She hadn't read anything about Malthus but she remembered the name now and hearing Mr Burgess explaining to Mark the Malthus theory, his idea being to bring about an ideal life for the few.

'Is your tea all right?'

'It's lovely, thanks. Have you read any of Shakespeare?'

'Oh aye. Oh yes. By! there was a writer, wasn't he?' He now sat down at the opposite side of the table to her and, folding his arms on it, he leaned towards her, saying, 'I can put this to you, Tilly. You see I can't talk to anybody else about it because I'm like a being set atween the devil and the deep sea. The lads back there' – he jerked his head – 'wouldn't understand what I was getting at; even those who are now learning their letters on the quiet, and if I was daring to open my mouth to me betters' – he made a face here – 'you can imagine their reaction, can't you?' He now straightened his back and took up the pose of a man sitting at a table with an enlarged stomach and his voice matched his stance as he said, 'What the devil is the fella on about? Give them an inch and they take a mile. Only way to manage 'em is keep 'em down. Keep 'em down.'

Tilly put her hand over her mouth and laughed quietly and as she did so she felt the tense muscles in her body relaxing. Oh, it was nice to talk to one of your own sort, an intelligent one. And now he was speaking again.

His arms once more folded, he said quietly, 'As I was about to put to you, did it ever occur to you when you were reading a lot, Tilly, of just how ignorant you were of all the things that went on in the world afore your time, and just how ignorant everyone else around you was? Did it? Did it?'

'Oh yes, Steve, yes.' She shook her head slowly from side to side. 'I know I'm still ignorant. I think you only start to learn when you realise you're ignorant, it's your ignorance that drives you on.'

'Yes. Aye, yes' – he nodded at her – 'that could be true. Yet I was thinkin' the other day when I was listening to the lads down below, if they all had the chance to read and write would it get home to them that they were ignorant? Would they take advantage of it? Do you know I doubt it, I doubt it, Tilly. I think some men are made in such a way that they cling to their ignorance. "I know nowt but I'm as good as thee, lad". You know, that sort of thing, sort of "I'm not gona learn, on principle." Mind your eye, I don't think women would take that attitude; I think if women got the chance they would learn.'

'Oh, I don't know if I agree with you there, Steve. All a woman really wants, in the first place that is, is a husband and a home and bairns. All the ordinary woman wants is warmth and enough to eat for herself and her family. A woman will work all her life to get security, as it were, for those belonging to her.'

He sat back in his chair now and his lips went into a twisted smile as he said quietly, 'What about the Lady Mytons?'

'Oh, they're a type on their own, bred of their own class.'

'Well now, it's me that doesn't agree with you there, Tilly, for I don't think they're a type on their own. Her type is found in every class of society from the gutter upwards.'

'Well, you certainly sound as if you know.' She was smiling at him but when she saw the colour rise to his brow she actually laughed aloud, and he self-consciously with her, and he said, 'Well now, Tilly, don't get me wrong; I didn't mean I'd had experience with people like her in every class. But I do keep me eyes and ears open, and all I can say is she's not alone. And when you do get somebody like her she's worse than any man. . . . Eeh!' He rose to his feet now, saying apologetically, 'I shouldn't be talkin' to you like this.'

'Why not?' She looked up at him. 'We're old friends, Steve, we've known each other for a long, long time, and we're not children any more.'

'Yes, you're right there, Tilly.' He stood gazing down on her. 'And eeh! by! it's lovely to see you again an' to talk to you. And it goes without saying you'll be very welcome in your own house' – he spread his arms wide – 'any time you've a mind to come, because I'll not be able to take the road the other way unless I come as a messenger, will I?'

She wanted to say again, 'Why not? You may call any time you like,' but what had she warned herself of just a short while ago? They were old friends but the friendship must remain old and not be renewed in any way. She rose to her feet now, saying, 'May I go up and sort out the books?'

'It's your house, Tilly.' His voice was level and slightly flat now. He pointed to the ladder, then added, 'When you've got what you want give me a shout and I'll bring them down for you.'

'Thanks, Steve.'

She had her foot on the first step of the ladder when he said quietly, 'That outfit suits you. You don't see the like of it round here.'

'No, I suppose it is surprising, but it's common in America and it's a very comfortable way to ride.'

He nodded at her and she went up the ladder and into the attic where his bed was. It had been roughly made and there were no clothes lying around. He was naturally tidy, like a sailor might be, one who was used to a small space. Well, thinking back to his early days he had been used to a small space, a cubby-hole in the roof, if all tales were true. Yet that being so it was a wonder he hadn't gone the other way and strewn his things far and wide. He was a surprise was Steve in all ways; there was not the slightest connection between the man and the boy.

She went to the far corner of the attic and she could see at once that the books had been sorted over but she quickly found what she wanted. A moment later she knelt down on the floor and called, 'Steve! Would you take these please?'

Having reached up and taken the books from her, he placed them on the floor, then, his arms extended, he steadied her as she came down the ladder.

It was the first time in years that she had felt his touch, in fact she couldn't remember him ever putting his hand on her; she could only visualise him standing suppliant and pleading for her love. Now, surprisingly, he must be so self-sufficient he didn't need love of any kind or else he would surely have been married before now.

'How you going to carry these, you can't tuck them under your arm? Look, I'll make two slings and they'll hang at either side of the saddle.'

'Yes, yes, that's a good idea. Thanks, Steve. And I'll have to be getting back.' She took a fob watch from the pocket of her short riding jacket. 'Twenty to three. Dear, dear, how the time flies. The children will be racing round looking for me.'

'How is the boy?'

'Oh, Willy? He's fine.'

'Are his eyes improving?' He asked the question quietly and she looked into his face which was straight now and then her head drooped as she said, 'The sight has completely gone in one eye and the other is somewhat affected, but I'm afraid time isn't on his side with regards to his sight going completely.'

'I'm sorry. Oh I am, Tilly. I'm sorry to the heart. And I can tell you that feeling isn't unmixed with guilt when I think me mother is responsible. By! the things our family have to answer for. I want to stop believing in a hereafter except for the fact that if there's no justice beyond they'll get off scot-free. I used to think our George was decent, or would have been if he'd got the chance, but his youngster, Billy, is another Hal by the things I hear he gets up to.' He looked down towards the floor now as he said, 'Me mother turned up at the door here one day. I didn't ask her in, and I said things to her that day that she would have brained me for a few years earlier. You know' – he smiled wanly now – 'when I was a lad I used to imagine she had stolen me as a bairn because somehow I didn't seem to link up with any of them in that house. And when our Hal gave me this' – he now lifted his left arm which he was unable to straighten from the elbow, he added with bitterness, 'I swore that one day I'd get me own back on him, and I did, didn't I?'

'Oh, Steve!' She swallowed deeply in her throat. 'I was to blame for that.'

'No! No!' The words were emphatic. 'I would have done it some time or other;

I meant to kill him and I haven't the slightest regret. Perhaps I'll have to pay for that too if there's a beyond, but I'll willingly do it. He would have died in any case that night left out alone as he was on the fells, with his back broken, but I saw to it that I despatched him afore the weather got him. Now don't worry, Tilly' – he put out his hand towards her but didn't touch her – 'I've never lost a moment's sleep over it. I became a man that night, and it's odd but I seem to have grown from then on both upwards and outwards. I feel free of the lot of them now.'

As she stared at him she wondered if he really had forgotten what he had said when he came to propose to her. 'I killed our Hal for you, Tilly,' he had said. 'What I did to him I did for you.' Had the years blotted out that memory? She imagined it must be so, and it was just as well. Oh yes, it was just as well.

During the time it took him to rope up the books neither of them spoke, and it wasn't until they were going down the path that she said, 'I'm so glad that you're settled in the cottage, Steve. I would have had to sell it, or let it to someone who wouldn't have looked after it as you have.'

He half paused as he turned to her, saying, 'You'd sell it?'

'I don't know. I don't think. . . .'

'Well, we can talk about it later, can't we?'

'Yes, yes.'

'Talking of buying cottages or houses, I had a stroke of luck a few years ago.'

'Yes, what was that?'

They were standing by the side of the horse now. 'Well, you know the people I lodged with when I worked in Durham, a Mr and Mrs Ransome? Well, the old lady died, and he was lost without her, and one Bank Holiday he took me with him to a cottage right out in the wilds of Northumberland, nothing but hills around it, and on the hills nothing but sheep. He had been brought up there. It wasn't much more than a little but and ben, nothing like this one' – he jerked his head backwards – 'two small rooms, a loft and a couple of shippams and most of the place dropping to bits. Well, from that day we got into the habit of going up whenever we could and doing a bit of repairing. I could have got a job as a stone-mason by the time I'd finished; and oh, it was and still is lovely up there, in the good weather that is. By heck! come the winter it would freeze the nose off a brass monkey. Anyway, to cut my long story short, when Mr Ransome died what did I learn but he'd left it to me, the cottage and ten acres. Sounds marvellous doesn't it, but you've got to see the land. It's all stone and you can't do anything with it except run sheep on it, and then only a few. But there you are, Tilly, I'm a land-owner. Doesn't that surprise you?'

'It does, it does indeed, Steve; and I'm very happy for you.'

'Funny thing life, isn't it? Neither of us had a brass farthing or as much as a penny to start with, and now we're both well set, you most of all. And there's nobody more pleased for you than I am, Tilly.'

'Thank you, Steve. Thank you.'

They stared at each other for a moment, both smiling. Then without further ado he bent down, took the sole of her high boot in the palm of his broad hand and the next moment she was astride the horse, and he was looking up at her, saying, 'You make a fine pair. I'll swap him any day for the old dodger back in the field.'

She laughed, saying as she did so, 'Bye-bye, Steve,' and he answered, 'Bye-bye, Tilly.'

The horse had taken but a few steps when she turned and looked at him. He was no longer smiling and for a moment she seemed to recognise the expression that was usually on the face of the boy he had once been, and it disturbed her. But only for a short while, until she reached the Manor.

She had handed the horse over to Peter Myers and when Biddle met her at the top of the steps she had allowed him to relieve her of the books, but she had no sooner entered the hall when Josefina, jumping down from the second stair and evading Connie Bradshaw's hand, rushed towards her, crying, 'Mama! Mama! she slapp-ed Willy. Mama, she slapp-ed Willy.'

Taking hold of the child's hand, she said, 'Quiet! Quiet! Josefina.' Then looking towards where Connie Bradshaw was holding Willy by the hand she asked quietly, 'What is this about slapping?'

'I just tapped his hand, ma'am.'

She stared at the girl for a moment; then reaching out, she took her son's hand and drew him to her side, saying to him now, 'Have you been slapped, Willy?'

The boy hesitated a moment as he peered up at her, his lids blinking over his brown eyes, and he replied, 'I was naughty, Mama.'

She had noticed this about her son that he never answered a question by yes or no but generally gave a reason. It was a queer trait in a child and it nearly always pointed to his attempting to avoid trouble both for himself and others.

'Why were you naughty? What did you do?'

'I pulled at nurse's chain...'

'He touch it, Mama, she nasty, grab it and slapp-ed him. She slapp-ed him hard, Mama.'

'I didn't, I didn't. I tapped his hand, that's all.'

Tilly looked at the girl. She wasn't wearing a chain of any kind. Naturally she wouldn't while on duty. She didn't, however, go into the question of what kind of a chain Willy had been pulling, but instead said, 'Please don't raise your hand to the children again. If they're naughty come to me immediately and I shall deal with them. You understand?'

'Yes, ma'am.'

'Well now, take them up to the nursery. I'll be there shortly.'

'She naughty, Mama. She naughty.'

'Quiet! Josefina. No more. Now be a good girl, go along with Willy.'

Both the children went dutifully away with their new nurse, but not silently, for Josefina's mutterings could be heard even when she reached the gallery.

Tilly turned now to where Biddle was still standing holding the books and she said to him, 'Take them to the nursery, please.'

'Very good, madam.'

As she watched the footman ascending the stairs she wished Anna hadn't gone to the expense of rigging out both him and Peabody in such flamboyant uniforms. Breeches and gaiters didn't somehow go with the atmosphere of this house.

She sighed and pondered for a moment whether to go into the kitchen as she was or go upstairs and change. Having decided on the latter, she slowly mounted the stairs and as she made her way across the balcony and along the broad corridor, Josefina's high piping voice came to her, and she smiled to herself ruefully. Things didn't change all that much; it seemed no time since Matthew and his two brothers and his sister had run wild up on that floor and chased each other screaming down the stairs and along this very corridor.

Again she thought, Oh, Matthew! Matthew! for Matthew had loved her from the first moment he had seen her; he had been ten and she sixteen, and later he had died loving her; but he had laid the rest of her life heavily on her.

Immediately on entering the room she stopped and looked towards the bed on which she had lain with his father, but never with him, and she asked herself why she should have thought that, Matthew had laid the rest of her life so heavily on her, for hadn't she made up her mind she could never love again and so the promise she had made to the dying held no burden for her. . . . Or did it?

She had got out of her riding clothes and put on a dressing-gown, and, sitting before the mirror, she pondered the fact that she was only thirty-five but her hair was as white as driven snow. It was the hair of an old woman, yet she hadn't a line on her face. As she rose from the stool, pulling tight the cord of the dressing-gown around her thin body, an impatient voice within her muttered, What did it matter what she looked like? One needed to have pride in one's looks only for a husband or a lover, and she'd had both and now she had neither. So be it.

⚫ **5** ⚫

'Look, Ma, I saw her shaking little Willy as if he were a rat. If the other one had been there there would have been hell to pay, but Miss Josefina had run down to the lake. I saw it all out of the gallery window.'

'Well, if she had really hurt him he would likely have yelled out.'

'He doesn't, Ma. I've noticed that about him, he doesn't. Miss Josefina makes up for it, I'll give you that, but he holds his tongue about things. He's funny that way, an' it's sort of old for a bairn of his age.'

'Well – ' Biddy went on straining the stock through a sieve as she said, 'Give her enough rope and she'll hang herself; you can't do anythin' without proof and don't you go carryin' tales, our Peg.'

'I don't go carryin' tales, but I hate to see little Willy. . . .'

'Master Willy.'

'All right, Ma, Master Willy. And anyway, I don't forget meself beyond the kitchen door, and I'm not talkin' to anybody but you. Now.'

'An' mind who you are talkin' to.' Biddy stopped her straining for a moment. 'Don't use that tone to me.'

'Oh, our Ma, you never change.'

'No; that's one thing about me; as I was yesterda' I'll be the morrow. An' when I'm on, what were you and Myers gassing about in the yard a minute ago when you should have been about your work?'

'Oh, he was tellin' me that he had met up with the Mytons' coachman when he stopped for a pint in the Black Horse t'other night. And what do you think of the latest, Ma?'

'Well, I won't know till you tell me, will I, lass?'

'You know who her ladyship is after now? You'd never guess.'

'No, I'm no use at guessin', so spit it out.'

'Steve McGrath.'

Biddy let the strainer drop into the clear liquid, then jerked it out, saying, 'Never!'

''Tis true. She does, she is. She waylays him on his road back from the pit.'

'She's a maniac, that woman . . . Steve McGrath. Eeh! who in the name of God will she have next? She had the master at one time, then she had Farmer Bentwood; and now Steve McGrath of all people. . . .'

'Oh, them's not all. Their coachman told Myers that one of the stable lads . . . well, he wasn't all that young, he was nineteen, but he did a bunk one night 'cos she kept coming up in the loft after him, supposedly wanting to have her horse saddled, sometimes around two o'clock in the morning.' Peg started to giggle and Biddy said, 'God above! She should be locked up.'

'An' speaking of bein' locked up.' Peg now nodded at her mother. 'That's what she's tried to do to his lordship. The coachman said she'd had a doctor there to have him put away, in fact two of them, but the old boy talked so sensible like an' acted the same way that the doctors were flummoxed an' said they could do nothing until he became dangerous, an' dangerous he's become if the rumour is right.'

'What rumour?'

'Well, the coachman said the old fellow's taken to ordering the coach practically every day and he takes his shotgun with him. He's known all along about her carry-on, but till now it's just seemed to slide off him. But since the doctors came he's changed. The coachman said it was funny 'cos although he seemed to talk more sensible like he acted more mad, if you know what I mean.'

'No, I don't.' Biddy now took the strainer and threw it over into the sink as she called into the scullery, 'You, Betty! These dishes will be walking out to meet you if you don't clear the sink . . . and now!'

As the voice from the scullery shouted, 'Comin' Mrs Drew, comin',' Biddy walked to the far end of the kitchen towards a round baking oven set in an alcove, and opening the door gently she peered in before closing it as gently again. Then turning to find Peg at her elbow and sensing that she was intent on imparting something of a private nature, she asked under her breath, 'What is it?'

Peg now glanced down the long kitchen towards Betty and she waited until the girl had scooped up an armful of dirty dishes and disappeared into the scullery again before she said, 'I hear they're startin' on about Tilly again . . . in the village.'

'Startin' on about Tilly! What now?'

'About the little one.'

'Well, what about the little one?'

'Aw, Ma!' Peg's voice was a mere whisper now and she shook her head from side to side before she added, 'Well, you know Tilly says she's well on past four, but I ask you, does she look it? She's so tiny and she hardly looks on three. Of course, she talks older but that's with being a foreigner and learnin' her English from Tilly.'

'What you gettin' at?'

'Well, Ma. Aw, don't you see what they're sayin'? They're sayin' it's hers.'

Biddy drew her head back away from her daughter's and into her shoulders and said, still in a whisper, 'Don't be so bloody soft.'

'I'm not, Ma, I'm not soft. And don't put on so much surprise either, 'cos hasn't it occurred to you it's funny that she should bring such a bairn back with her? Even our Authur said the other night, white people don't do that kind of thing, pick up Indian bairns, I mean adopt them when they've got one of their own, and he says by what he hears from fellows who've been over there that the Indians are looked on worse than the niggers.'

'But the bairn's not Indian, just Spanish or Mexican or some such.'

'Aye, you've said it, Ma, some such. Mind, not that I'm blamin' Tilly. She could have been raped. Aye she could by all I hear, 'cos, as our Arthur said, women are classed no better than cattle over there. And he's worried about our Katie.'

'He's not the only one.' Biddy turned and went back down the kitchen with Peg close on her heels. But at the table she stopped and, her face grim, she looked at her eldest daughter as she said, 'This business about the little dark 'un being Tilly's, well, I'd stake me life on it there's not a happorth of truth in it. Why, seein' how Master Matthew doted on her he would have murdered anybody who touched her.'

'Perhaps he did, Ma. How are we to know anything? She doesn't talk about what happened out there. The only thing we can gather is it must have been pretty awful to turn her hair white. Anyway, it doesn't matter what we think, it's them villagers, you know what they're like, nothin' seems to change them, father to son, mother to daughter. The witch business still clings to her.'

'What's that?' Biddy cocked her ear to the side and Peg said, 'It's the little 'un screaming; you can hear her a mile off.'

'Well, I've never heard her from down here afore. Look, get yourself upstairs and see what's afoot.'

As Peg hurried out of the kitchen and into the hall Tilly came out of the library and they looked across at each other before both running to the stairs and up them. As they reached the gallery the screams came louder, mingled now with Willy's childish crying and the voice of Connie Bradshaw.

Tilly was first up the nursery stairs and as she rushed through the open door into the day-room she stopped for just a second to take in the scene before her. Willy was lying on the floor nursing his hand and crying loudly, but in the far corner of the room Connie Bradshaw was shaking Josefina in the same way a terrier would shake a rat, and the child was screaming and kicking out with her feet.

'Put her down this minute!' Tilly's voice thundered through the room, and Connie Bradshaw actually dropped the child to the floor, and Tilly, rushing forward, picked her up and cradled her in her arms while she glared at the nursemaid, crying, 'How dare you! How dare you!'

'She tore at me, she tore at me face. Look!'

Tilly looked at the girl's face. There was a long scratch down one cheek, and it was actually bleeding.

'You must have done something very bad to her that she should react in that way,' Tilly said emphatically.

'Ma-ma. Ma-ma.' Josefina had her hand on Tilly's jawbone stroking it rapidly – it was a gesture she always used when she wanted her whole attention and now through her crying she spluttered, 'Beat Willy. Beat Willy, Mama.'

'I didn't, I didn't, you little liar you!'

'Be quiet! And don't you come out with such terms here.'

'Mama! Mama!'

Peg had picked Willy up from the floor, but pressing himself away from her hands, he groped towards Tilly, crying, 'Your box. Your box, I was looking at your box.'

'What box, dear?' Tilly now put Josefina down and picked up her son and again said, 'What box, dear?'

'From the toilet, on the table, Mama, the pretty box.'

'In her pocket, Mama, box in her pocket!' Josefina was screaming the words now as she pointed at the nursemaid, and Tilly, looking at the girl, demanded, 'Show me what you've got in your pocket.'

The white starched apron that reached from the girl's waist to her ankles and which had a bib with the straps crossing over her back and buttoning on top of her hips, had two large pockets. Connie Bradshaw now stuck her hands into them, saying as she did so, 'I've got nothin' in me pockets but what's me own.'

'Then you needn't be afraid of letting me see what belongs to you.'

The girl's jaw tightened and she thrust out her chin as she said, 'I've got a right to what's mine. Me ma says everybody's got a right to what's theirs. I know me rights, you can't search me, I've got nothin' belongin' to you. You'll get wrong if you accuse me I have.'

Tilly now looked towards Peg and said, 'Ring the bell for both Peabody and Biddle, please.'

Peg now went to the corner near the fireplace and pulled the rope twice before pausing and pulling it again three times.

It was Biddle who entered the room first and he stopped within the door and stared at his mistress, then at the scene before him; but he said nothing, and neither did Tilly. Presently, the butler arrived puffing slighty, and he, too, stood without speaking for a moment. When he did speak, all he said was, 'Madam ... you rang?'

'Yes, Peabody. I want you to witness Peg searching this girl.'

As Peg moved towards the nursemaid, Connie Bradshaw backed from her, saying, 'You lay a hand on me and I'll scratch your eyes out.'

'We'll see about that.' As she spoke Peg's hand came out and caught the girl a ringing slap around the ear, and before she could retaliate Peg had her up against the wall and was thrusting her hand into one of the pockets. Then she pulled out a small enamel trinket box. It wasn't more than an inch across and about the same in depth, and as she handed it on her open palm to Tilly she said, ''Tis off your table, ma'am.'

Taking the box, Tilly stared at it; then shaking her head, she said, 'No, this one is from the china cabinet surely in the drawing-room?' Turning now, she said, 'Biddle, will you please go across to this girl's room, take Peg here with you, and search her belongings.'

'I'll have the polis on you, yes, I will. I didn't take that box, I didn't. It was that little black sod picked it up from off the table, and I took it from her and was gona take it back, I was.'

'Do as I ask.' Tilly nodded from Peg to Biddle, and they left the room.

She herself remained standing awaiting their return, the children pressed tightly against her skirts, and Peabody, standing apart, kept his gaze on the still-defiant girl as if he were viewing something that smelt.

The five minutes seemed endless before Peg and Biddle returned, when the footman, holding out his hands to Tilly, said, 'She had made a hole in the underside of the mattress, ma'am. These were in it.'

Slowly Tilly picked up from his palm the locket and chain that Mark had given her years ago, it was one of the few pieces that his wife hadn't managed to take with her. The locket was silver with a gold filigree surround, the chain supporting the locket was of fine gold. She hadn't missed it because it was kept in a box among other trinkets in the bottom drawer of her dressing-table. From his other palm she took up, first a miniature portrait of a baby. It showed Mark's father at the age of one year. It had lain from the time it was painted until now in one of the cabinets downstairs. Next and lastly, she took from his hand two gold rings and a brooch. The rings had been presents from Matthew. They, too, had lain in a box, or rather in a velvet case, at the back of the top drawer of the dressing-table.

She turned slowly and looked at the girl. She must be stupid. How did she expect to get away with this? But then of course, anyone with access to the bedroom could have been blamed, Peg or Fanny, Lizzie Gamble or Betty. On Sunday, which was her half-day, she would have taken the things home and her mother would have disposed of them, and she would have returned as brazen as brass. No, she wasn't stupid, she was cunning.

'Do you wish to call in the law, madam?' Peabody did not say 'the police' or even 'the polis', but 'the law', and she looked at him for a moment before saying, 'No, Peabody; we won't call in the law but I would ask you and Biddle to go into her room again to make sure there is nothing more there.'

'Very good, madam.'

Both men inclined their heads towards her and left the room; and now Tilly, looking at Peg, said, 'You will stay with her, Peg, until she is outside these gates.'

'I want me money afore I go; I've been here over three weeks.'

'You have forfeited any right to your probationary wages; you are lucky you won't find yourself in the house of correction this night.'

'Aw! you. I'll have me ma on you for me six shillings, she'll sort you out. Anyway, I wouldn't have stuck it here. Me ma always says you shouldn't work for them worse than yersel.'

The girl moved from where she had been standing against the wall down towards the nursery table and as she went to pass Tilly she glared at her as she said, 'It's right what they say in the village about you; not satisfied with havin' a blind bastard you had to go whorin' with a bloody nigger.'

For a moment Tilly seemed to stop breathing. Then there rushed through her body a torrent of anger. It was like fire in her veins. She was facing Alvero Portes again, diving at him, tearing at his face; she was firing point blank at the Indians. The girl before her seemed to sprout buffalo horns, her face was painted, and she sprang at her, delivering a blow first to one side of her face, then the other. What she would have done next she didn't know had not Peg torn her back from the girl and thrust her down into a chair before almost flying to where Connie Bradshaw was leaning against the wall holding both sides of her head with her hands and with tears now raining from her eyes, and she shouted at the girl, 'Out! Out!' and swinging her round, she pushed her out of the door and on to the landing; and there, meeting the butler and the footman, she cried at them, 'She went for the bairns!' and then added, 'and . . . and the mistress.'

'She did?' Peabody drew himself up to his full height and, looking down on the spluttering girl, he said one word, 'Scum!'

The word seemed to return the girl to her defiant self and she yelled at him, 'I never did! I never did! She hit me. Like a mad 'un, she was, crazy. But I'll have her. Me ma'll have her for it, you'll see. . . . Aye. Aye, just you wait 'n see.' Her voice trailed away as Peg pushed her down the stairs.

Peabody and Biddle entered the nursery, and the sight of his mistress sitting at the table, her head held in her hands while the children, crying loudly, clung to her waist, caused the butler to become ordinary and human and to say softly, 'Come, madam, come. Don't distress yourself, You, Biddle' – he turned to the footman – 'take the children downstairs; Mrs Drew will see to them. Put them in the servants' hall.' Then turning to Tilly again, he said, 'Take my arm, madam. This has been a most unfortunate occurrence.'

'I'm all right, thank you. I can manage.' Tilly rose from the chair and stood supporting herself against the table for a moment; then she looked at the elderly man and said, 'Thank you. Thank you, Peabody. I . . . I think I will go to my room. And yes, if you would see me there I should be grateful. And then would you ask Mrs Drew to come up to me, please?'

'Certainly, madam. Certainly.'

As she walked, with the aid of Peabody's arm, she felt that her legs were about to give way beneath her. Those waves of rage always had a weakening effect on her. Dear God! what she might have done to that girl if it hadn't been for Peg. But the knowledge that the village had started on her again had made her lose control. Would anybody believe her now if she were to say that the child was Matthew's, his flyblow? No. The only one who could speak the truth was Katie; and it wasn't likely that she would ever come back to this country again. Although she had promised Biddy that Katie would come on a holiday some time, she knew in her heart there was little chance of it. Katie could not endure the sea and Doug Scott could not endure to be away from the life to which he had been bred.

Scandal had touched her once again and this time it would be worse than before. To brave the scandal of a white bastard had been bad enough, but to have a dark foreign one added to her score was something she didn't know how she was going to contend with. Matthew had been right. Oh Matthew! Matthew!

ᥱᥬ 6 ᥬᥱ

'Bloody trollop! Put the devil on horseback an' he'll ride to hell. Never was a truer word spoken. Bash me daughter, would you, you dirty trollop! Come out o' there an' I'll sort you out!'

Peabody was at the hall window looking over the terrace down on to the drive where stood the drunken woman, and as Biddle came hurrying up to him, he turned his head towards him and said, 'It's that girl's mother and she's as drunk as a noodle. What do we do with her?'

'Get her away before the mistress hears her, I hope.'

Biddle made towards the front door. Biddy came hurrying out of the kitchen and across the hall, saying, 'Hold your hand a minute. Leave her to me; I can deal with the likes of her. You go out there an' she'll have your fancy toggery off your back quicker than it took you to put it on, I can tell you that.'

'But she sounds a vicious woman, Mrs Drew.'

'Well, what am I just telling you, Mr Peabody? But if she starts any of her games with me my two lads will be behind me, and they'll give her the Highland fling down the drive and out of the gates, I can assure you of that. But I'll be obliged, Mr Peabody, if you'd see that the mistress stays up in the nursery until the coast's clear.'

'As you say, Mrs Drew. As you say.'

There was no doubt who was in charge of this situation and when Biddy pointed towards the door, Biddle almost jumped to open it. And then she was standing on the terrace looking down on the bloated face of the prancing, shouting and gesticulating woman.

'Aw! she sent ya out, has she? Frightened to face me, is she? The dirty, whorin' upstart!'

'I'll give you two minutes to turn an' get yersel' down that drive and out through them gates, Bessie Bradshaw. And if you don't make a move I'll have you carried out.'

'My God! look who's talkin'.' The woman put her head back and laughed loudly. 'Daft old runt! You know what they say in the village about you? You close your eyes to the goin's on to keep your family set-in. But I'll not close me eyes, no, I'm goin' to the polis. She battered my lass. You should see her face.' She slapped at her own cheek now as she ended, 'Out here.'

'Your girl attacked her.'

'Bloody liar!'

'There are witnesses. And let me tell you something, Bessie Bradshaw, if it wasn't for the mistress your lass would be in the house of correction this minute for the stuff she stole.'

'*What!*' The woman now stood swaying, her head poked forward. 'What you say? My lass stole? You're a damned liar!'

'I'm no liar. Two of the staff and they weren't my lot either – searched her room and found a number of valuables stuffed in the mattress.'

'My lass stole?'

It was evident to Biddy that this news had come in the form of a shock to Bessie Bradshaw, for the woman screwed up her face as if in protest, then said, 'You tellin' the truth, Biddy Drew?'

'Aye, I'm tellin' the truth. And there's those inside there' – she jerked her head back towards the house – 'who would go to court an' swear to it an' all. And it would be nothing less than three years she'd get, and lucky at that.'

The woman now half turned away and looked about her. She saw the two men standing at the entrance to the stable yard, she saw the faces at the hall windows; then, her eyes lifting slowly upwards she saw the lone figure outlined against one of the narrow windows that bordered the top of the house and, recognising it, her anger returned and she rounded on Biddy again, crying now, 'Aye, well, about this 'ere last business, I'll deal with Connie. But there's one thing she hasn't done yet, she hasn't stood without her shift on cryin', Come on, Tom, Dick or Harry,' this way, this way. Tis a whorehouse she should be in, your missis. Worn hersel' down to skin an' bone with it, she has. All in together, girls, never mind the weather, girls. Shameless bitch, bringin' her black bastard here.'

Biddy was down the steps facing her now and crying, 'Shut your mouth and take your trip!' the while pointing down the drive. 'Now get goin' or I'll do what I promised first off.'

'Aw, to hell with you! An' the lot of you. You'll sizzle in hell's flames. Drink's one thing, but loose livin's another. I'm no loose liver, never have been. Nor me lass. Stealin'! Don't believe a bloody word of it.' She shook her head before she turned about and shambled away, her voice receding with her steps.

Biddy waited until the woman was lost to her sight round the bend in the drive; then, beckoning her sons to her with a jerk of her head, she said, 'Take a dander down there and see she gets out. And I'll have a word to say with you, our Jimmy, as to how she got in. Those gates should be locked.'

'They are locked, Ma. She must have got over the wall down by the wood; it's no more than four foot there.'

Biddy shook her head. 'Well, go on after her,' she said; 'and see she goes out the same way she came in.'

Her sons hurried away to do her bidding, but she did not return to the house by the way she had come out; instead, she walked slowly through the courtyard and so into the kitchen, and there, looking at her daughter, Fanny, she said, 'I wonder what next. At her very door! Aye, I've said it afore and I'll say it again, that lass draws trouble towards her as a flower draws the bee. She never goes out to meet it, it just comes to her. Like the season that brings God's little apples it comes to her.'

'You're right there, Ma. You're right there.' Fanny nodded. 'I'll make a fresh pot of tea, and I've set her tray. Will I take it up?'

'No; I will.'

'Well, I'll carry the tray up the stairs for you.'

'Aye, you can do that, for of a sudden I feel tired, sapped.'

Fanny picked up the tray and preceded her mother out of the kitchen, along the passage, across the hall and up the main staircase, but when they reached the gallery, Fanny turned and whispered, 'Will I put it in her bedroom or take it straight up to the nursery?'

Biddy thumbed upwards, and by the time she reached the nursery floor she was panting and so she stood and inhaled a number of deep breaths before following Fanny into the day-room.

Tilly was alone, the children were having their afternoon rest, and when Fanny put the tray on the table and went to pour the tea out, Biddy shooed her away with a wave of her hand.

Neither of them spoke until Biddy, taking the cup of tea to Tilly, where she was still standing in front of the window, said, 'Here, lass, drink this.'

But Tilly did not turn to her and take the cup from her, she raised her arm and, leaning it against the edge of the deep frame of the window, dropped her head on to it and began to sob.

Quickly putting the cup down on the ledge, Biddy turned her about and, holding her tightly in her arms, murmured, 'There, lass. There, lass. Take no notice, she's scum. They're all scum in that village, every blasted one of them. The devil's run riot through their beds for years, for every one – man, woman and child – in that damn place has got him in them. Come on, lass, come on. There, dry your eyes. Look.' She pressed Tilly away from her and with her bare fingers rubbed the tears from her cheeks, saying loudly now, 'You're the lady of the manor, lass, you're above the lot of them. You can buy and sell them; with the money you've got you could buy the whole damn village and turn them out on their backsides. Just think of that now. Here, come on, sit down and drink this tea.'

Tilly sat down and she drank the tea, and after a moment or so she looked at Biddy and said 'How am I going to live down this latest, Biddy?'

'Be yourself, lass. Go out and hold your head high. Take them both with you wherever you go. If you've got nowt to be ashamed of, it won't show in your face.'

Tilly became still as she looked straight into Biddy's eyes and said slowly, 'Josefina isn't mine, Biddy; she is the offspring of a Mexican Indian girl, a very young girl, and a white man.'

'A white man?'

'Yes, I said a white man.'

'Somebody you knew?'

Tilly's gaze did not flicker, she made no movement for almost thirty seconds, and then she said, 'Yes, someone I knew, Biddy.'

Slowly Biddy's gaze fell away from hers and, picking up the silver teapot, she poured out another cup of tea, and when she handed it to Tilly she said, 'You've got nothing to be ashamed of, lass. If you ask me, much to be proud of. You'll win through. You'll win through.'

ఎం 7 ౷

On the following morning Tilly had another visitor and his presence caused a greater stir than had that of Bessie Bradshaw.

She'd had a disturbed night and had slept late – on Biddy's orders no one had attempted to waken her – and it was almost ten o'clock when she came down to breakfast, but not before she had visited the children in the nursery.

The morning was soft. She looked towards the long window at the end of the breakfast-room. It gave on to the side terrace and the sloping lawn that led down to the lake. She could just glimpse the sheen of the water and she thought how peaceful it all looked, but empty, solitary; yet she realised that this was but a reflection of her inner feelings.

Last night she had lain for hours pondering on her life, a life that could be said to be uneventful looked at from the outside, but which underneath the surface had been filled with tragedy since she was a child: her father dying in strange circumstances; her mother fading away afterwards; then herself being brought up by her grandparents on stolen money that had lain hidden for years; her persecution by the villagers, through which, inadvertently, she had been the cause of the death of two men; her succumbing to the love of the owner of this manor, and her constant attendance on him for twelve years until the day he died; then her bearing him a child, and finally marrying his son.

She had fallen asleep before her thoughts had begun to revive memories of this last episode in her life; and for this she would have been thankful, for what she tried not to think about at night were those short years spent in America because then, just as her husband had had nightmares about frogs,. so she would have nightmares about Indians and mutilated dead people and a child's brains splattered about a post.

There was a tap on the door and Biddle came into the room, almost scurrying towards the table in his haste, and in a voice little above a whisper he said, 'Madam, there . . . there is a visitor.'

'A visitor? Who, Biddle?' Her voice was flat.

Biddle swallowed. 'It is Lord Myton, ma'am,' he said.

She rose to her feet, repeating, 'Lord Myton!'

'Yes, ma'am, and . . . and I think you should be prepared for the fact that, that he is . . . he is not quite himself, ma'am.'

She was moving towards the door as she said, 'How did he arrive?'

'By coach, ma'am.' Biddle seemed to spring forward now and open the door for her. And then she was in the hall looking at what she termed an apparition, for there stood an old man dressed in a heavy riding coat which covered a long blue nightshirt. On his feet were bedroom slippers and on his head a high riding hat. His face was unshaven and his wrinkled chin and cheeks showed a stubbly bristle of some days' growth. His eyes set in deep dark hollows appeared bright but their light was lost as he screwed them up when inclining his head towards her and doffing his hat, which showed his pate to be quite bald. But what caught Tilly's attention more than his appearance was the gun he carried under his left arm.

'Ma'am . . . sorry . . . to trouble you . . . ma'am.' His words were spaced. 'My card.' He fumbled in the breast pocket of his coat; then looking to the side, he said, 'Howard. My card for for . . . the lady.'

Stepping forward and playing up to the situation as if he had practised it daily, Peabody said, 'Madam has your card, my lord. She would like you to come this way.' He looked at Tilly, his eyes wide, and she, making a small motion of her head towards him, said, 'Yes, of course.' And now holding out her hand to Lord Myton, she directed his shuffling walk into the drawing-room.

'Kind of you, kind of you.'

'Not at all. Do please be seated.' Tilly indicated an armchair, then watched the old man slowly lower himself down into it. He still held his hat in one hand and the gun under his other arm, and when Tilly said, 'May I take your hat, sir?' he handed it to her, muttering, 'Yes, yes.' But when, without speaking further, her hand reached out to the gun he pressed it tightly to him, saying now in a high squeaky voice, 'Oh no! Oh no! Not that. Not that. Sit down. Sit down.'

She sat down opposite to him, and she remained quite still as he peered at her. Then seeming to have come to a decision in his mind, he said, 'You're all right; don't look like a whore. She's one. Oh aye, all her life. . . . Is she here?'

'I don't know to whom you are referring?' Tilly lied now.

'Her, of course, me wife, the bitch. Always a bitch, but gone too far this time. My God! Aye. Aye.' He now leant towards her and, his voice dropping to a hissing whisper, he said, 'Trying to put me away. D'you know? Trying to put me away, insane.' He bobbed his head once more, then repeated, 'Insane. And you know' – again he bobbed his head – 'I must have been all these years – insane. But I laughed. Didn't matter, didn't matter . . . long as she was at t'other end of table, amusing, made me laugh. Oh yes – ' He drooped his head, and it was some seconds before he repeated, 'Made me laugh.' Raising his head again, he grinned at Tilly now as he added, 'A sense of humour. Bawdy, aye, like a man, bawdy. That's why I took her, good company, bawdy.' Again his head fell forward and now he muttered, 'I was no use to her. Didn't matter, didn't matter . . . No. No; but not with a pit fella. Aw now, not with a pit fella!'

The last words had ended on a shout and he repeated, 'Pit fella, lowest form of life. Sunk to that, pit fella. . . . Kept tag of her amours. Aye, yes. An earl'n a guardsman in town. Gentlemen. Gentlemen. Always gentlemen in town. But here. God Almighty! Like a stag in the rut. Sopwith first one. . . . Your man, wasn't he, your man? Mistress to him. Kitchen slut they said you were . . . come up. Don't look it. Don't look it. He did a damn good job on you if you ask me. Then the farmer. Oh aye, the farmer. Then Turner and Drayton and on and on.' He turned his head to the side and looked around the room and, his mind diverted for a moment, he said, 'Nice . . . nice. Taste here. Good taste.' Then bringing his watery gaze on to her he said abruptly, 'You do this?'

It was some seconds before she could answer. 'Just the upholstery and drapes.'

Again he was looking around him. 'Very nice. Very nice. But her. Yes, her, aye.' He nodded at himself as if recollecting his thoughts; then pointing his finger at her, he said, 'John Tolman. Yes, John Tolman. His wife, you know . . . you know Joan?'

Tilly shook her head.

'She nearly tore her hair out . . . Agnes's. Scrapped like fishwives. Yes, aye, they did.' He began to chuckle now. 'Then Cragg, Albert Cragg, you know. You know what?' His body began to shake with his chuckling and he bent almost double but still keeping his eyes on her as he said, 'She must never have looked at faces. God! no, 'cos you know Cragg?'

Did she know Cragg? And did she know Tolman? Yes, she knew them, but more of their wives, the women who had looked upon her as if she was mire beneath their feet.

'Three good stable lads. Aye, three good stable lads I lost. But what matter? Menials are there to be used. What's good for the goose is good for the gander.' His body was again shaking. 'Should be what's good for the gander 'tis good for the goose, eh? . . . Eh?'

Suddenly becoming still and his voice issuing in a growl from his throat, he said, 'Where is she? She's here!'

'No, I'm afraid she's not, milord. Your wife is not here.'

'Don't lie to me. She knew I was after her 'cos she had sent for those damned fellows again to have me barred up. Burton said she had ridden off to the pit fella's cottage, but when I got there they were gone. Lad said he had seen them riding towards here. Now, don't you hide 'em. It's the finish, I've stood enough. Disgrace, a pit fella!' He drew saliva into his mouth and looked for somewhere to spit, but after a moment he fumbled in his pocket and drew out a green silk handkerchief. Having spat into it, he made an attempt to pull himself to his feet. But Tilly was already standing in front of him and, her voice soothing, she said, 'Lord Myton, please listen to me. I can assure you on my word of honour your wife is not here, and I can assure you too that you are mistaken about . . . about her association with the . . . the pitman.'

'No? No?' His lower lip curled so far over that she could see the stumps of his diseased teeth in the side of his gums.

'I swear to you, Lord Myton.'

He looked up at her now for some seconds before asking in a childlike voice, 'Well, where can she be?'

'I have no idea.'

'I'm dry.'

'Oh, I'm sorry, I should have offered you some refreshment. What would you like?'

'Brandy.'

'Brandy it shall be.' She hurried to the fireplace and pulled at the bell rope, and as if Peabody had been standing outside the door it opened and she said to him in a voice that appeared calm, 'Would you please bring the decanter of brandy?'

'Yes, madam.'

It all sounded so normal, and the normality was continued when a few minutes later the butler placed a tray by the side of his lordship and poured out a good measure of brandy which he handed to the old man. Lord Myton gulped at the brandy, and after he had emptied the glass he shivered, smiled a weak smile and said, 'My drink, brandy.' He handed the glass back to Peabody who looked at Tilly, and she made a small motion with her head towards the decanter and he again poured out a good measure, but this time he left the glass oh the tray. Looking at it, the old man did not pick it up immediately but he said, 'Good. Good.'

The butler was turning away when he hesitated as there came the sound of voices from the hall. They had caught Tilly's attention too and she, looking hard at Peabody, said, 'Will you please stay and attend to his lordship for a moment?'

'Yes, ma'am.'

'Excuse me.' She bowed towards the old man, and he, picking up the glass of brandy, said, 'Yes, yes.' At the moment he seemed oblivious of where he was except that perhaps he thought he was at home for, looking at Peabody, he muttered, 'Should be a fire in the grate.'

'It's warm outside, milord.'

'It ain't warm inside, not inside me t'ain't.'

By the time Tilly had closed the drawing-room door behind her he had already thrown off the rest of the brandy.

In the hall stood Biddle, Peg, and the visitor, who should be none other than Steve.

Walking towards her and, straight to the point, Steve said, 'Is the old man here?'

'Yes.' And she added in a whisper, 'And where is she?'

'When I last saw her she was haring back home to Dean House where she expected to find the doctors. Apparently she sent for them first thing this mornin'. The old fellow had been on the rampage all night looking for her. He had a gun.'

'He still has and he's in a very odd state. Come in here a moment.' She turned abruptly and led the way into the dining-room, and when she had closed the door on him she said immediately without any lead up, 'He suspects you and her.'

'Me!' He screwed up his face at her.

'Apparently you are her latest choice, and she has made it pretty evident, hasn't she?'

'Now look here, Tilly; you believe me, there's nothing. . . .'

'You needn't protest, Steve; I believe you, but the old man'll take some convincing. Have you met him?'

'Never. Never set eyes on him.'

'Well, that's one good thing because . . . well, I really think he means business if somebody doesn't get that gun away from him.'

'What brought him here anyway?'

'From what I could gather he understood that she and you were making for here.'

'What!'

'That's what he said. One of his men told him that she had gone to your place. He must have got it out of the man at gunpoint I should imagine. Anyway, when he didn't find you or her he questioned a boy on the road, who said he had seen you both riding towards here.'

'I rode with her as far as the coach road and I told her plainly I wasn't accompanying her any further but I'd have a look round for the old fellow on my own. The last time I saw her, as I said, she was haring back towards Dean House, and it was as I was making me way roundabout like to the mine, 'cos I'm on turn in an hour, that I met Richard McGee and I asked him if he'd seen anything of the Myton coach. He said he had passed it not fifteen minutes gone heading for here; at least it was on this road and so I put two and two together. . . . Look, Tilly, as he doesn't know me, do you think I can persuade him back into the coach because I can't see you handling this on your own?'

She paused a moment, staring at him, then said, 'Yes, perhaps you could help. If once you could get the gun away from him he'd be easy to handle, but whatever you do don't let on that you work at the pit. Miners in his estimation are the lowest form of life and it's because he thinks his wife has' – she lowered her chin whilst keeping her eyes on him – 'an association with one such that has created the last straw.'

'Oh!' He raised his eyebrows while making a small nodding motion with his head as he said in mock politeness, 'Thank you very much for telling me, Tilly.'

She smiled wryly at him now. 'He's just finished his second large brandy and he's in the state that he might have thrown it over me had he been told that I, too, once worked with the lowest form of animal life.'

'Yes. Aye' – Steve's face became serious – 'that takes some remembering. I can't imagine you ever being down below, Tilly.'

'Oh I can. I can remember every moment of it vividly still. But come on –' again she smiled at him and made her first attempt at a joke for many a long day as she said, 'I do hope he hasn't shot Peabody, we were just beginning to understand each other.'

'Aw, Tilly.' He pushed her lightly on the shoulder and they stopped for a moment and, looking at each other, laughed quietly; then, her voice serious now, she said, 'I don't see how I can find any amusement in this situation.'

'It'll be a bad day when we don't see the funny side of things, Tilly.'

She nodded now and led the way out of the dining-room, across the hall and into the drawing-room, and it was immediately apparent that Lord Myton was giving Peabody a lesson on his long sporting gun. It was evident too that their presence was very welcome to Peabody for, moving quickly out of range of the pointing gun, he glanced from one to the other as he almost stammered, 'W . . . will I serve some re . . . refreshment for the gentleman, madam?'

'No, thank you, Peabody; I'll call you if I need you.'

Bowing slightly, the butler made his escape, and both Tilly and Steve looked towards Lord Myton who was sitting leaning forward, his left hand cupping the long barrel of the gun, while the forefinger of his right hand stroked the trigger. He was looking towards the fireplace as if aiming at the banked flowers stacked there.

'Would you care for another drink, milord?'

'Oh. Oh' – he looked at her – 'it's you. No, no; I don't think so. No – ' he smiled a toothless smile now as he added in a normal tone, 'if I start on it too early I don't enjoy me dinner and I do like me dinner. Never lost me appetite. Strange that, isn't it?'

'No, not at all; I'm very glad to know you still have a good appetite. Would you care to stay and have a bite with us?'

He seemed to consider for a moment, then said, 'Well, yes, ma'am, yes, and thank you kindly. What are you having today?'

What were they having?

Oh yes, yes; she recalled quickly, then said, 'It's rather a plain meal but very appetising; there is spring soup, saddle of mutton, asparagus and the usual vegetables' – she nodded at him – 'and we'll finish with baked gooseberry pudding and cheeses.'

'Sounds nice, very nice, not wind-making.'

Tilly swallowed and glanced at Steve before she said, 'I don't think it'll be wind-making.'

'Strong digestion. Always have. . . . Who's this?' The question was addressed pointedly at Steve, but before he could answer Tilly said, 'He's a friend of mine, milord, a . . . a lifelong friend.'

'Workman?' He turned his eyes on her. 'Lifelong friend?'

'Yes, milord, a lifelong friend. I was once a working woman, you remember?'

'Oh aye, yes,' he chuckled; 'from the kitchen, from the kitchen. Yes, yes. Don't sound it though.' Of a sudden his joviality vanished and he demanded, 'Where the hell is she? She's not going to make a fool of me this time. Where's she, eh? Her fancies have caused her to stoop low in the past but not as low as this, no, no.'

As his left hand jerked the barrel upwards Tilly said softly, 'Would you like to rest, milord, before you eat? There's a comfortable couch in the little sitting-room off the. . . .'

'All right here. You want me out of the way?' His white brows were beetling.

'No, no, no, of course not, milord.'

'Pleasant woman.' He turned now and addressed Steve. 'Pleasant woman. I like pleasant company; but one can't always be laughing. What do you say?'

'You're right, milord; one can't always be laughing.'

'You sound like a workman.'

'I am a workman, milord.'

'What are you?'

'I am an engineer.'

'Oh. Oh, engineer?' The old man's eyes widened, the wrinkled skin stretched as his head bobbed. 'Engineer. Bridges?'

'Er . . . yes, milord, bridges.'

'Oh indeed! Bridges. Railroads; they need bridges over and under. Oh yes, yes.'

'Could I help you into the next room, milord.'

'Help me? Why do you want to help me, you're not of my household, are you?' He now narrowed his eyes at Steve, then shook his head, saying, 'No, can't recollect seeing you before. No, of course not, you're the workman, engineer, building bridges, yes. Aye.' He now swung the gun round and laid it across his knees, where his great coat had fallen open exposing more of his nightshirt. Then raising his head, he looked at Tilly and in the politest of tones he now said, 'Would you please leave the room, madam, I wish to go to the closet?'

Tilly showed no surprise, she neither blushed nor swooned, the reactions one would have expected from a lady of the manor, but what she said was, 'The closet is at the end of the corridor, milord. If you would allow my friend to assist you, I will show you the way.'

The old man stared at her again, then made a chuckling sound in his throat before saying, 'Ain't no lady, that's evident; no lady'd show me to the closet! Funny, but that whore of mine could sport naked, oh aye, aye' – his head was wagging now from side to side as if throwing off denial – 'I say, an' I know, sport naked she could, but throw up her hands in disgust if she opened the door and saw me on the closet. But you wouldn't, would you, ma'am?'

'No, milord.'

'No, she wouldn't.' He now nodded to Steve, but just as Steve was about to make some remark his attention and that of Tilly's also was brought to the door from beyond which there came the sound of an altercation. But it didn't penetrate to the old man until the door was thrust open and there, seeming to fill the whole frame, stood his wife. She was arrayed in a plum-coloured riding habit, a high velour hat perched on the top of her dyed hair. Her face looked suffused with anger. Behind her were standing two men, their heads and shoulders alone visible to those in the room until she moved forward; and then their sober dress proclaimed them to Tilly immediately as doctors.

The old man did not move from his seat except to turn his head in his wife's direction; that was until she marched forward crying, 'Stop this capering and come on home this very minute!' and then he spoke, his voice sounding so ordinary and sane that Tilly's eyes were drawn from his wife and on to him as he said, 'Stay where you are, Agnes! Stay where you are!' and as he spoke he slowly moved the gun into a position in which it was pointing straight at her.

When the two gentlemen accompanying her now made a move towards him, he said sharply, 'You, too!' and he shifted the barrel of the gun just slightly but enough to encompass the three of them. Then he spoke to the nearer one, saying, 'Brought the papers with you, all signed and sealed, eh, to put me in the madhouse? Is that it?'

'Now, sir.' The voice sounded oily. 'We just want to see you well settled in your bed, nothing more.'

'You're bloody liars, sir. And don't move! I'm warnin' you. You see, what you've all forgotten is that I've nothing to lose, I'm near me end and I know it. But I thought to go out of life as I've lived it, laughing at it on the side. And I would have done, but she went too far. Pit fella she took a pit fella. Me grooms I'd tolerate, but a dirty pit fella! And you threw him in me face, didn't you? Bragged you could get 'em from the top to the bottom.'

As the old man's lip curled, Steve drew in a long breath and cast his glance down towards the floor; but his head jerked upwards almost immediately as Agnes Myton's voice, screaming now, cried, 'You're mad! You don't know what you're saying. Doctor – ' she turned to the man at her right hand, crying, 'This is what I've told you about, delusions, delusions, accusations, all lies, lies. He's got to be restrained; I can't stand any more of it.'

'Did you hear what she said?' The old man now turned his head slightly towards Tilly, while keeping his eyes on the three in front of him. 'She said she can't stand any more. Ain't that funny? By the way, I wanted to go to the closet, didn't I?' He paused, then gave a sound that was like a high laugh before he added, 'Doesn't matter, not now, doesn't matter. Wind'n water, that's all we are, wind'n water.'

'Give me that gun.' His wife was stepping slowly towards him now and he said, 'Yes, I'll give you the gun, Agnes. Aye, yes, I'll give you the gun 'cos I'd hate to enter hell alone.'

Tilly heard herself scream out as she saw the quivering finger pressing the trigger, then at the moment the explosion rocked the room she watched Agnes Myton clutch with both hands at the bosom of her habit. She watched her mouth open wide as if in amazement. She watched the woman's head move from one side to the other as if to look at the doctors as they held her, then slowly slump in their embrace. But they had hardly laid her on the floor before there came another report, and as Tilly looked towards the old man she again screamed for she was back in the Indian raid. In a way she was seeing what she had imagined Alvero Portes to look like after the Indians had finished with him, for Lord Myton had placed the gun under his wrinkled chin before firing the second barrel.

❧ 8 ❧

Well, it was to be expected, wasn't it? Wherever she is somebody dies. Two of them this time. A lord and lady, a murder and a suicide. Well, as they all said in the village, it proved it didn't it? There was something odd about her. It went right back on her great-granny's side; they'd all been touched with witchery.

They counted up the deaths and tragedies that lay at her door, they recalled her immoral doings, they reminded each other that she had ruined Farmer Bentwood's first marriage, then when his wife died and he didn't ask her to marry him she had put a curse on him that turned him to drink and whoring. Now he was married again with a little daughter of his own and had gone steady these past three years. Well, he had done right up to the time Tilly Trotter, or Sopwith as she was now named, returned from the Americas. And what had happened? He had gone on the spree again. Oh yes, there was something about her, something bad, and folks were wise to give her a wide berth.

And those sentiments were also expressed by old Joe Rawlings's daughter to the second Mrs Bentwood herself. Peggy Rawlings had called at the farm for some milk and in a roundabout way had brought up the tale of the coroner's inquest last week on the two dead gentry. 'Miscarriage of justice, that's what me dad says, Mrs Bentwood. He said they should have brought that madam up for indirect murder like she should have been brought up years gone by, for people die like flies when they're near her. It's witchery me dad says.'

The second Mrs Bentwood had surprised Peggy Rawlings by saying, 'I don't believe in witchery, witchery is just ignorance.'

As Peggy said to her dad later on, 'She was a bit snotty, so I got a bit snotty with her and I said to her, Farmer Bentwood believes in witchery, her witchery. He suffered from it, and you watch out you don't an' all.' Then she had added, 'She looks the quiet sort, his second wife, but I think she's deep under it. Well, I've warned her, so it's up to her. . . .'

Later that night Lucy Bentwood, looking at her husband across the supper table, said, 'What happened at the inquest last week?'

'What happened? How should I know?'

'You went; I know you went.'

'All right, if I did, what about it?'

'Nothing, nothing.' She smiled at him. 'I just want to know what happened.'

'What always happens at inquests, they prove the people dead.'

His wife continued to stare at him for a moment before resuming her eating and she wasn't surprised when he pushed his plate away from him before he had finished his meal and without an excuse got up and left the table. She watched him through the open door making for his office at the other side of the small hall, and she herself stopped eating and sat with her hands folded on her lap.

She loved this man and she had imagined that he loved her, not that she thought for a moment that she was the be all and end all in his life. She knew that he'd had other loves, many of them, if all the hinting tales were true, but this Mrs Sopwith, Tilly Trotter as she once was, seemed to have been the first love in his life and she'd always had a strange influence on him, being responsible, so she understood, for turning him from a kindly generous-hearted man into a drunken, roistering boor. Yet since they had met on that momentous night outside the theatre in Newcastle when she had slipped on the icy pavement and he had caught her and held her he had become for her the man he once was, kindly, thoughtful and loving. He was ten years her senior and she had known that she was past the acceptable marriageable age; but he had treated her like a young girl, and she had felt like a young girl and given him a daughter. And this had seemed to bring an added joy into his life, that was until two months or so ago when Mrs Sopwith returned to the manor, a widow now.

Three times in the last month he had got drunk. Could there be any truth in the tales of her power? Had she put a curse on him?

She almost overbalanced her chair as she sprang up from the table. She was no ignorant villager, she was well read, thanks to her parents' care; also she was sufficiently cultured to pass herself quite well on the piano and at the embroidery frame. She wasn't going to let such stupid thoughts get a hold in her mind. If Simon was returning to drink, then there was a reason for it, and it would have nothing to do with witchery.

Simon, sitting in the office and drawing hard on his pipe, might not have agreed with his wife at this stage in his life. Years ago as a young man he had defended Tilly Trotter against the accusation, but having experienced the effect she had on men, particularly himself, he was beginning to think along the lines of the villagers. There was some strange quality in her that upset a man's life. All those years she had been Mark Sopwith's mistress he himself had gone through the tortures of the damned; and when Sopwith died and she was turned out of the Manor, her belly still full of him, he had offered to father her bastard. And what thanks had he got in return? Scorn. Yet at one time she had loved him; oh yes, he was sure of that, she had loved him. When he looked back he realised that she had loved him even before he had come to the knowledge of his love of her. He had imagined that his feelings were merely those of a big brother protecting the young sister, but on the very night of his first marriage, to Mary, his eyes had been opened, and he hadn't been able to close them since.

He had just about managed to face up to that situation when she was shameless enough to marry the son of her late keeper, and her six years or more older than him! By! that had shaken him to his very core. What he would have done if she hadn't gone off to America right away he dare not think. Gone and set the whole bloody manor on fire likely because he had seemed to go mad at the time. Then he met Lucy and he had to admit that Lucy had resurrected some remnants of decent manhood in him. Under her love he saw reflected the man he had once been, the young, outspoken, upright farmer who would do a good turn for anybody; and then when she had given him a daughter life had taken on a new pattern, a new meaning. He had sworn on the day his child was born that he would cut out drinking altogether, and he meant it. But what happened? Tilly had to come back, a widow now, and free to marry again; that was if anybody would take her with a second bastard at her skirts. The tale that the black piece was older than her son wouldn't carry water. It was rumoured that young Sopwith had died through the wounds he got in an Indian raid. That, too, was just hearsay; likely he died fighting over her as other men had.

God in heaven! He rose from the chair and began to pace the small room. Why couldn't she have stayed where she was over there. What was it in her that got into a man, turned his brain?

When he had heard the rumour that her hair was white, as white as the driven snow, he had thought with some comfort, Well, she'll look like an old woman now, but last week, standing at the back of the crowd as he had done many years ago when she had appeared in another court when the judge had asked if she was a witch, he had seen her come out on the arm of the young Sopwith, and her hair was indeed white, but she was no old woman. If anything the whiteness had added to her fascination. He had never thought her really beautiful, she was too tall to be beautiful, taller than most men, yet there was something in that face that outstripped beauty; there was a magnetism about her eyes that looked at you yet didn't seem to see you for they were looking through you, into you, and beyond. And who should be walking behind her but young McGrath. He still thought of him as young McGrath, yet he was a man, taller and broader than himself now, except round the middle. He had always been her shadow, had Steve McGrath, since he was a youngster spewing his calf-love all over her. Was he in the running now? No; Master John Sopwith wouldn't, surely, tolerate that association. And yet what, after all could Sopwith do, she was mistress of the whole place, and she must have come into quite a packet too from her husband. It was incredible that she, Tilly Trotter, whom as a child and young lass he had at one time kept from starving, should now be in this position. It maddened him, really maddened him.

He stopped now in his pacing and stood near the corner of his small desk with his finger nails digging in the underside of the wood. He knew he had come to a turning point in his life, that either he could revert to his drinking bouts which would likely cause her nose to curl, or he could go on upwards, which would mean that he could do what he had wanted to do all those years ago and buy the farm. With what Lucy had brought with her he now had more than enough, and for extra land at that. But buying the farm would mean getting in touch with her. Aye, well, that's what he would like to do, come face to face with her and show her that whatever power she had wasn't strong enough to ruin him.

The decision made, he sat down again and, placing his elbows on the desk, he dropped his face on to his hands, and his teeth ground against each other and his lips pressed tight to stop her name escaping, but his mind groaned at him, Tilly Trotter! Tilly Trotter! God blast you!

෬ **9** ෭

Tilly made the acquaintance of Lucy Bentwood one day towards the end of June. They came upon each other in the middle of Northumberland Street, Newcastle, and, strangely, they took to each other, although they exchanged only a polite greeting.

Tilly had been persuaded to leave the house to accompany John and Anna to the city. Anna was to see her lawyer with regard to her grandmother's estate. Her grandmother had died a month ago, and from that day her daughter, Anna's Aunt Susan, who was in her late forties, had taken to her couch and decided she was in decline, and so it was left to Anna and John to settle all the legal affairs.

Tilly had left them at the solicitor's office in Pilgrim Street, the arrangement being that they would meet in an hour's time and have lunch together. In the meantime, she herself was bent on doing some shopping for the children.

She had not wanted to leave the house at all for since the day of the inquest she seemed now to have dropped back into the lethargy of the time following Matthew's death. She was aware that if it wasn't for the children she, like Anna's Aunt Susan, would have needed little persuasion to take to her couch for then she would less likely become involved in another's life.

Over the past few weeks she had almost come to believe that there must be something in what the villagers said about her, inasmuch as she seemed to attract death. She had heard Biddy going for Peg who had been repeating some gossip from the stables that it was odd how Lord Myton had chosen her drawing-room in which to commit murder and suicide; why hadn't he done it in his own house? And what was Steve McGrath doing there? Hadn't she been poison to the McGraths all her life?

It was as she turned from looking at the display behind the great new plate-glass window of a shop that she came face to face with Simon Bentwood and his wife.

At first she did not look at the young woman but at the man who had been her first love. He was now in his middle forties but he looked fifty or more; his face was florid, his girth on a level with his chest. His clothes were good – he had always dressed well – but there was no semblance of the young man who had touched her heart all those years ago. As she glanced at the woman at his side, who looked young enough to be his daughter, she hesitated, not knowing whether to go on or to stop. The decision was taken from her when Simon said, 'Hello, Tilly.'

She swallowed before she could answer, and then, her voice low, she said, 'Hello, Simon.'

'This is me wife.' He put his hand to the side and Lucy Bentwood, staring at her, inclined her head, then gave the slightest bob of her knee. This gesture seemed to incense Simon, for having first spoken in an ordinary tone, he now almost growled at his wife, 'No need for knee-bobbing here, woman. Tilly and me know each other too well for that. Isn't that so?' His face had taken on a deeper hue, and because she felt sorry for the woman she answered him in a quiet level tone, saying, 'Yes, we were well acquainted when I was quite young.'

'Acquainted!' He laughed now, his head jerking up and down. 'Funny word to use that, acquainted.'

When into his laughter his wife's quiet tone came, saying, 'I am pleased to meet you, Mrs Sopwith,' Tilly looked at her and, seeming to ignore Simon completely, answered, 'And I you, Mrs Bentwood.'

Lucy Bentwood smiled now at the tall lady, because that's how Tilly appeared to her, a lady, and aiming to make amends for her husband's manner she proffered: 'We're up for the day. I'm going to shop for some material to make dresses for my little girl.'

'That is a coincidence.' Tilly smiled towards her. 'I, too, am shopping for my children. How old is your daughter?'

She did not include Simon in the question and his wife answered, 'Just on two, ma'am.'

Again Tilly was aware of Simon's displeasure at this latest address, but this time when he broke in on their conversation his tone was less aggressive: 'I've had it in mind to come and see you these weeks past, Tilly,' he said.

'Yes?' She turned an enquiring glance on him.

'It's about business.'

'Oh!'

'"Tis about the farm.'

'You want repairs done?'

'No; more than that. I'm thinkin' of buying it if that meets with you.'

'Oh!' She raised her eyebrows, at the same time turning her gaze for a moment on his wife; then she said, 'Well, it's something that needs to be looked into, but if you would just let me know when you are coming we could discuss the matter.'

'Fair enough.'

Tilly now stepped to the side and, looking at Lucy Bentwood, she said, 'Good-bye, Mrs Bentwood.'

'Good-bye, ma'am.'

Tilly made no formal farewell to Simon, nor he to her, she merely inclined her head, then walked on, but she was hardly out of earshot before Simon Bentwood said to his wife, 'You drop the ma'am when speaking to her, she's no better than she should be.'

'I don't think I could.'

'Why?' He paused again and stared at her; and she, with the strength of character which he had already come to suspect lay under her quiet, even serene demeanour, said, 'Because no matter what is said about her, she appears a lady. Before opening her mouth she appears a lady, more so afterwards.'

'My God!' He looked as if he were aiming to toss his head off his shoulders; then leaning towards her, he said, 'You know what they say about her, don't you?'

'Aye, yes, I've heard it all, but as I see it, so to speak, Simon, it's nothing but second sight. My grandmother had second sight: she saw my grandfather dead six hours before they brought her the news, and he had died not half an hour's run from her door. The horse shied, the carriage wheels went back on him and that was the end, and she had seen it and told me mother, as I said six hours afore.'

'Oh, be quiet!'

'Just as you say, Simon. Just as you say.'

'And don't use that laughing tone at me.'

'Did you think I was laughing, Simon? Well, I can tell you I wasn't. I'm only trying to keep a calm head in a very odd situation because that lady just gone back there caught more than your imagination years gone, not only from what I heard and the little you told me yourself, but from the look on your face whenever her name's been mentioned and in your eyes as you looked at her not a minute gone. No, Simon, I'm not laughing. And what I'll say here and now should be, I think, kept for a private place, not in the middle of Newcastle, but it's in me mind and here at least you can't bawl your denials, so I'll say it, and once it's said I'll mention it no more. 'Tis this. The part of you she once had I fear she's still got, but she had it afore I met you, and I've given you a child. And again I say this, 'tis no place to tell you in the middle of a street but I'm bearing you another.'

She was pulled to a stop and he stared down at her, into her kindly eyes, and he knew shame as he had never known it before; and he cursed Tilly Trotter and her returning into his life, for here before him was his wife, a young woman whom he had been lucky to wed, and she was wise and good. Yes, very wise and very good, for at this moment he recalled how Mary, his first wife, had taken his affection for Tilly Trotter: it had poured vitriol into her veins and made her mad at times with jealousy.

He did not say, 'I'm sorry, Lucy,' what he did do was to take her hand and draw it through his arm as he muttered, 'Let's go home; we can shop another day.'

Meeting Simon had in a way been equally disturbing for Tilly. She no longer found that the sight of him disgusted her; she had looked into his face without seeing the picture that had been in her mind for years, that of his nakedness sporting with the plump white body of Lady Myton. She must already have accepted that his conduct had been no worse than that of her going to Mark, or, what must have appeared worse still, of her marrying Mark's son. And was he any worse than Matthew lying with that small enigmatic-looking Mexican girl, whose child she had taken on to herself, the child who had already brought her trouble by the fact that she herself was being named as its mother?

No, what was past, was past with Simon; he was a man as other men. That he had grown coarser was a pity, but now that he had taken to himself a wife, and such a one, augured good for his later years. . . . And he wanted to buy his farm.

She remembered vaguely her granny saying that it was the desire of Simon's life to own his own place. Well, if he came in a proper way and offered a reasonable sum, and she would not quibble over the amount, he would own his own farm. But in granting his desire she knew she would be doing it not so much for him but for his wife, that young woman with the pleasing manner, the open honest face, the young woman who had addressed her as ma'am. She liked her; under other circumstances she would have wished for a closer acquaintance. But that was impossible.

She did her shopping; met Anna and John, and after a substantial lunch, which she didn't enjoy, she expressed the desire to return home. In a way she knew she was disappointing Anna for the arrangement had been that they should visit the galleries; but all she wanted was to get away from this city that reminded her only of police courts, and men who looked at her from top to toe the while their eyes seemed to strip her of her clothing.

It was a fortnight later when Peabody announced, 'Mr Simon Bentwood, ma'am.'

Tilly rose from the seat in the drawing-room. She did not say, 'Hello, Simon,' for he would surely have replied, 'Hello, Tilly,' she just inclined her head towards Peabody, which motion told him his presence was no longer needed.

When the door had closed on him, Tilly, looking towards Simon who was standing just within the room, said, 'Please take a seat, Simon. I've had the fire put on' – she motioned her hand towards the fireplace – 'this last week of rain has called for fires.'

'Yes, yes, indeed.' His tone was polite, even deferential, and if he had owned to the truth he was at this moment feeling a little awed; it was the first time he had been inside the manor house. His yearly rent had always been collected by one servant or another; not since his father's time, when the manor boasted a steward, had anyone from the farm gone to the house to pay its dues.

The carpets and furnishings were making an impression upon him, and at the back of his mind he was telling himself that these had been her surroundings for years, and in a way she had taken on the patina of the furniture about her, a veneer that had caused Lucy to call her ma'am. Yes, yes, he could understand that one would become different living in these surroundings.

When he was seated he looked to where she was standing to the side of the hearth with one arm outstretched, her hand resting on the marble mantelshelf, and standing like this she looked at him and said, 'What can I offer you to drink? Would you like something hot or a whisky, or rum perhaps?'

She watched the muscles of his cheeks working as his tongue pressed his saliva into his throat. 'A cup of tea would be welcome, thank you.'

She half turned and, lifting her hand from the mantelshelf, she extended it backwards and pulled on the piece of broad thick tasselled red velvet that hung down by the side of the wall.

A moment later the door opened and she looked towards Peabody and said, 'A tray of tea, Peabody, please.'

'Yes, ma'am.'

She does this every day, Simon thought. It comes natural to her. It was unbelievable when he looked back to the lass she had been, sawing, humping branches twice as big as herself, digging that plot of land. How would she have turned out if he'd had her? Not like this for sure, she'd have been a woman, a mother of a family, respected, whereas now, for all this grandeur, her name was like clarts, and she was feared and hated, aye, you could smell the hate of her in the village, when her name was mentioned. If she had known what was to become of her, would she have picked him or this?

Peabody brought the tea in, she poured it and handed him a cup and he drank it, and then another, and still he hadn't brought up the reason for his visit. It was she who had to say, 'You have come about the farm, Simon?'

'Aye, that's it, I've come about the farm.'

'Well, I've been thinking it over and I've talked it over with John because he helps me run the estate' – she smiled deprecatingly now – 'and I have decided that you may have the buildings together with fifty acres.'

'Fifty acres!' His shoulders went back. 'But there's all of seventy-five acres to it.'

'Yes, I know, and the rest can still remain for your use but as rented land. You see in this way it will in fact square the land off as the farm and those fields jut out on the east side of the estate.'

'I'd rather take the lot.'

'Yes, I suppose you would, Simon, but that's all I have to offer. It's up to you to decide if you want it or not.'

'Oh yes, I want it, that's why I'm here. If you think back to the early days, Tilly, you'll realise I've always wanted it.'

She made no reference to the early days but said, 'With regard to the price, of course the stock's your own but the outbuildings are in good repair and Mr Sopwith . . . Senior' – she swallowed here – 'had, I remember, two new byres put up for you, and also a small barn.'

She immediately wiped from her mind the picture that the mention of a barn conjured up, and went on, 'Then there's the house. John tells me that it was repointed for you some two years ago. A new well, too, was dug. And so his suggestion of four hundred pounds would not be exorbitant.'

John had suggested seven, it was she who had brought it down to four, and Simon before he had left the farm this morning had said to Lucy, 'They'll want eight for it, if a penny.' But then, of course, he had expected the whole amount of land.

Tilly watched him rubbing his chin with the side of his hand as if considering her offer. It was a man's way. He must know that the terms were favourable, but this she supposed was business, and no one ever thanked you for giving them a bargain.

'Well, aye, yes, I suppose I'd be willing to settle for that.'

'I'm pleased. It's good to feel you own your own home.'

'Aye, it is. Well, you should know, Tilly.'

He slowly turned his head and looked about the room, and she said stiffly, 'In a way this is only entailed to me, it will be passed to my son when he's twenty-one.'

As he stared at her she felt the colour rising to her face. She knew what he was thinking: her son had no claim to a stick here, he was an illegitimate child. Her voice sounded cool and her words clipped as, looking back at him, she said, 'It has been arranged in law, he will inherit.'

'Oh. Oh, well, that's good enough.' He now rose slowly to his feet and, again looking round the room, said, "Tis a splendid room. The ceiling in itself is something to look at.' He was staring upwards at the medallions linked with garlands within ornate squares when there came the sound of high delighted screeches, seemingly from above his head, followed by the soft thumping of steps running down the stairs.

Looking at him with a slight smile now, Tilly said, 'The children, they're on the rampage. This is what happens if I leave them for too long.'

'Do you look after them yourself now?' The 'now' indicated that he knew all about Connie Bradshaw and she answered, 'Yes, in the meantime, but I have a new nursemaid coming next week.'

He looked towards the door when the squeals came from the hall and he said, 'They seem to he enjoying themselves.'

He'd hardly finished speaking when the door burst open and Willy ran into the room, one arm extended, his head to the side, an action he used nearly always when he was running. 'Mama!' he cried. 'Mama! Josefina is going to whip me.' He was laughing as he flung himself against Tilly's legs; he then ran behind her as Josefina came racing up the room like a small dark sprite, and for a moment there was a game of tig about Tilly's skirts, until she cried, 'Enough! Enough, children! Do you hear me? We have a visitor. Willy, stop it!' She slapped at her son's hand and he became still; then she caught hold of Josefina's arm and, shaking her gently, said, 'Enough! Enough! Now, no more!'

Their laughing and giggling died away and they stood now, one on each side of her, looking at the guest.

'Say how-do-you-do to Mr Bentwood, Willy.'

The boy paused a moment, put his head back on his shoulder and to the side, screwed up his one good eye; then, his hand outstretched, he said politely and slowly, 'How-do-you-do, sir?'

There was just a second's pause before Simon reached out and took the boy's hand and, his voice sounding gruff, replied, 'I do very well, youngster.'

'Are you a rela . . . relation?'

'No.'

'Are you from the mine?'

As Simon was about to reply again, Tilly, reaching out, drew Willy back to her side, saying, 'Don't be inquisitive, Willy.'

'I was only asking, Mama.'

'I know you were, but it isn't polite.' She now half smiled at Simon; then looking down at Josefina, she said, 'This is my adopted daughter. Say how-do-you-do? Josefina.'

It was Josefina who stepped forward now and, as politely as Willy had done, she too said, 'How-do-you-do, sir?'

Simon made no reply, he just stared down at the tiny elfin figure below him, searching the brown face, the black eyes, the straight hair for some resemblance that would connect her with Tilly. And he imagined he saw it in that indefinable something that Tilly possessed; added to which the child looked much younger than her son and was hardly half his size. The fact that she spoke clearly mattered nothing: children often spoke well at two years old, and the strong foreign burr gave the impression that she was older. But she wasn't older than the boy. Anyone with half an eye could see that.

He almost started as the child said, 'Don't you want to take my hand, sir?'

He looked at Tilly. She was looking at him, her face stiff and just as he was on the point of putting out his hand the child suddenly and impetuously threw herself against him and, gripping his leg below the thigh, looked up at him as she cried, 'You are very big man and you smell like Poncho. . . .'

The next second the child would have landed on her back on the floor had not Tilly sprung forward and caught her. In one motion she swung the slight form up into her arms, and glaring at Simon, she said bitterly, 'You should not have done that!'

'Why not? I could understand that one' – he nodded towards Willy who was now squinting up at him, the lid of his good eye working rapidly – 'but I think you went too far with this one. I've heard it said that the Indians rape women; well, if they did you, then you should have come into the open and people would have understood. You must think folks are simple, or as ignorant as pigs, but the dimmest knows that no white adopts a black bairn. Buy 'em for slaves, aye . . . or houseboys as they are called, but adopt, no! And for you to look down your nose on me for my one mistake. My God! you've got a nerve. I'll say you have that . . .'

'Get out!'

'Aye, I'm going. I knew this would happen.'

Tilly again reached out towards the bell rope, and as she did so he turned towards her, his lip curled in disdain. 'You needn't ring for your lackeys, I can walk out without them aiding me. An' let me tell you one thing afore I go. I'm sorry I ever put the word love to you. Beddin' with your own kind I could understand, or being taken down by a wild man I could understand that an' all, but not to try to pass it off as you're doing. Do you know something, Tilly?' Glaring at her, he thumbed towards Josefina. 'That makes me want to spit.'

He had pulled the drawing-room door open, but he did not close it behind him, and she watched him marching past both Peabody and Biddle. She watched him turn his head and bark some words at Peabody, then he was gone.

She didn't move until Peabody entered the room and, closing the door behind him, said softly, 'Are you all right, madam?'

Slowly she lowered Josefina to the floor, saying, 'Yes, thank you, Peabody.'

He came and stood quite close to her. 'Are you sure, madam? Look. Sit down, madam, and I'll pour you a cup of tea' – he put his fingers on the silver teapot – 'it's still hot.'

She sat down and when he handed her the cup he said, 'Do not trouble your mind about such a man, he's no gentleman. It is the first time in my career that I have been referred to as a lackey.'

'I'm sorry, Peabody.'

'It's not your fault, madam, that some men cannot help but behave as louts. I will take the children now, madam, and see that Biddle takes them walking in the garden. The rain has stopped. We'll wrap them up warmly.'

'Thank you, Peabody. Go along, children.' She made a small movement with her hand and they both quietly did her bidding.

Alone she sat with her eyes closed. She saw herself sitting in the wagon supporting Matthew's blood-stained body, and she could hear his words, 'Go home. Take Willy, and leave her behind.' Matthew had known what he was talking about. Yes, yes, indeed, he had known what he was talking about.

➷ 10 ➹

Christine Peabody turned out to be a very good nursemaid and a girl with a pleasant personality, so much so that she overcame Biddy's initial dislike of her; she happened to be the butler's youngest daughter and Biddy had prophesied she was the thin end of the wedge for his other three daughters, but that remained to be seen. The girl was very good with children. She could be playful, but she could also be firm. She was so good with them that Tilly had a great deal more free time on her hands, and this enabled her to read more and . . . ride more. She was finding an increasing enjoyment from her association with horses. Accompanied by Peter Myers and Arthur Drew, she even went to a horse sale. Myers, having dealt with horses all his life, had a knowledge of horseflesh and on that occasion helped her to choose a three-year old mare well broken to the saddle. The mare was lively and needed exercise, which necessitated her taking it out daily.

On a number of occasions during the months that followed she met other riders. The first time it was a group of six gentlemen, all well mounted but both horses and riders bespattered, indicating they were returning from the hunt. They all moved to the side of the road to allow her to pass and each one of them doffed his hat to her while keeping his eyes riveted on her face, albeit vitally aware that she was wearing breeches and sitting astride a horse like any man.

The occasion she met up with a party of four, two ladies and two gentlemen, the gentlemen again moved to the side, but the ladies had kept to the middle of the narrow bridle path, and in order to pass them she had to take her horse into the ditch; true, it was a shallow ditch, but the fact that they would not make way for her told her more plainly than any words how she was considered by the gentry of the neighbourhood.

There was a joy in riding: the feel of the horse's muscles beneath her legs, the power of its stride, the idea that it was soaring her heavenwards when it jumped a hedge and the exhilaration it created in her as it galloped over a free field, the wind whistling past her ears, down her throat and up her nostrils seeming to have a cleansing effect on her. However, after a time her rides became merely physical exercises, so leaving her mind free to grope; and she knew she wanted a companion.

Anna preferred to ride behind the horse in the comfort of a carriage; when she sat on the back of one it was merely to trot. But John sometimes accompanied Tilly; and these occasions she found most pleasurable, the end of the rides finding them panting and laughing, very rarely talking.

There was, she knew, another companion she could have had on her rides.

Sometimes, when returning from a ride she had come across Steve, and he had accompanied her back to the coach road, but no further, for almost always he would be black.

The last time they had met in this way he had said laughingly, 'I'm getting a feeling for horseflesh; I think I'll go to the market one of these days and get me one with four legs, not that I'll do away with old Barney here because we've come to an understanding. We have long conversations, you know, old Barney and me.'

It was strange about Steve, he could make her laugh. This mature Steve could make her laugh whereas the young Steve had mostly irritated her; but this she knew had been because of his pesterings of love.

Of late, she'd had to curb a desire to take a ride or even a walk to the cottage and just to sit quietly there. She knew where he put the key. It was the same place where she herself used to leave it, a good hidey-hole. There were no doubts in her mind why she wanted to go to the cottage and to talk to Steve; it was simply for the company, someone of her own ken as she put it, someone who understood her language, the language she used when she hadn't to stop and think. But that was as far as it went, and this being so she knew it was unfair to put herself into his presence unless there was a good excuse for doing so, for after all, at bottom, he was still Steve and underneath the man was the lad who had loved her. And he might still be there; it wasn't fair to bring him to the surface.

*

Biddy said, 'Why don't you have a party at Christmas, lass, and come out of yourself? Look; you've been in black long enough. As long as you still wear black you're still in the grave with him. Let the dead bury the dead, as the saying goes. Get Master John over and Miss Anna. And don't tell me she can't leave her aunt, her with two nurses to see to her. They could, you know, wrap her up and bring her over. The bairns would soon bring her out of herself and get her off her couch if I know anything. How old is she anyway?'

'Oh, late forties.'

'God Almighty! and puttin' herself on a couch. But then it always happens. I've seen it again and again: women who've never had a man, they've got to have attention from somebody, so they take on a sickness, and other people, mostly their relations, have got to run their legs off up to their knees an' are often in their own boxes afore their charges. Oh aye, I've seen it happen, in mud huts and in mansions.'

'Oh, Biddy!' Tilly looked across the settle where she was sitting in the kitchen to where the big-boned elderly woman was rocking herself briskly backwards and forwards in the rocking chair. This was the time of day she looked forward to: the children were in the nursery asleep, the rest of the staff had gone to their rooms, except perhaps Peabody or Biddle or whoever's turn it was to lock up, and at this time of the evening she would sit opposite Biddy and they would talk; or rather she would listen, for Biddy seemed to store up all the odds and ends of the day and pour them out on her and, as was her wont, she would jump from one subject to the other. But no word she said was idle chatter; there was always the wisdom of common sense in most of what she said or, as now, a subtle hint, a subtle plea for one of her daughters.

'It never did anybody any good to live unto themselves. Gives them too much time to think about what's not happenin' or what's going to happen. There's only one thing sure in this life and that's death, but most people meet it halfway, even get ready for it in their middle life by making a nightgown for their laying-out or a shirt for their man. Then they sit and think about it comin'. Half the trouble in the world comes through people who have time to think. As me mother used to say, our mind's like a hen's nest, every egg you put into it is hatched. If the egg's been tread properly then the chick will be all right, but if it's not, sitting on it, brooding on it, what do you get? Just a big stink. What I'm sayin' is that it's not right to live alone, nor live in the past.... Now there's Steve over there in that cottage living by himself. 'Tisn't right. If our Peg had her way he wouldn't be long alone.' She nodded at Tilly, saying, 'Aye, that's how it is with her. And she been married and widowed. But the want is strong in a widow. And it's funny, isn't it, it was the same with our Katie. Our Katie would have walked on hot cinders for Steve but he never looked the side she was on. Of course, there was you in those days, Tilly.' Again she nodded. 'But now things are different, positions are different. Our Peg would make him a good wife if he had the sense to see it. I think he only wants a nudge, somebody to tip him the wink. Aye well' – she looked at the clock on the high mantelshelf – 'it's about time I was making for me bed. Aye.' She pulled herself upwards and ran her finger round the shining globe of a copper pan, one of a set of eight all in a row on the mantelpiece, and she nodded her head at it, saying, 'I'll get that Betty working on those pans the morrow. Look at that dust on them!' She held out her finger towards Tilly, but Tilly could see no difference between the colour of the gnarled finger and any dust. Rising to her feet she said, 'You're too finicky, Biddy.'

'Aye, well, you'd have something to say, ma'am, if you found a dirty kitchen.' Biddy had said the ma'am with a grin and Tilly flapped her hand at her, replying in kind, 'All right, my woman, see that they're clean tomorrow.'

They smiled broadly at each other before Tilly, turning away, said, 'Good-night, Biddy.'

'Good-night, Tilly lass. By the way. . . .'

Tilly paused and Biddy, loosening the strings of her white apron, said, 'Don't you think it's about time I had a letter from our Katie?'

'Oh, I shouldn't worry; you'll be gettin' plenty of mail for Christmas and more than mail I suspect.'

'What do you mean by that, more than mail?'

'Never you mind. Wait and see.'

'She's not comin', is she?'

'No, no; not that, Biddy. I told you perhaps next year.'

'Aye. Aye. Good-night, lass.' She turned away on a sigh, and again Tilly said, 'Good-night, Biddy.'

In her room, Tilly sat before the dressing-table taking down her hair, and she paused with a hairpin in her hand and stared into the mirror. What was she to do, give Steve a hint that Peg was there for the asking? Perhaps he was aware of it already. Anyway, from what she knew of the man Steve, he wouldn't appreciate any hints like that; if he wanted something he would go after it. If he had wanted Peg he would have had her before now.

Yet it was right what Biddy said, nobody should live alone. But she'd have to live alone. Yes, for the rest of her life she'd have to live alone. But then not quite, she had the children, she had her son, her own son, and she had in a way a daughter, a little dark much-loved and loving daughter. Yes, and one who would one day grow into a dark young woman, with all the needs of a young woman, perhaps intensified by the nature of that very colour.

The eyes looking back at her through the mirror became large and as if they had spoken she said to them, 'Sufficient unto the day is the evil thereof.'

⌘ 11 ⌘

November was mild. It was all agreed they were having better weather these past two weeks than they'd had at times in the middle of the summer. On two consecutive Sundays the sun had shone and she had ridden through the park with the children as far as the spot where the cottage had once stood.

She had already told the children that she had once lived at this spot, and each time they came to it they forced her to stop and plied her with questions about it; as today, when Willy, sitting straight on his pony, his head to the side, looked to where the old outhouses still stood almost obliterated now by the undergrowth and asked, 'Would my grandmama and grandpapa have loved me?'

Tilly, surprised at such a question, looked at her small son and said, 'Yes, yes, of course; they would have loved you dearly, Willy.'

'Would they have made a fool of me?'

'A fool of you?' She narrowed her eyes at him. 'What do you mean, make a fool of you?'

'Well, I heard Jimmy say that grandparents always made a fool of grand-children.'

'Oh. Oh' – she smiled broadly at him now – 'what Jimmy was meaning to say was that all grandparents spoil their grandchildren.'

'Oh.'

'Mama.'

'Yes?' She turned to Josefina.

'Would they have loved me, Willy's grandpapa and grandmama?'

'Oh, yes.' Tilly, her voice very gentle now and her head nodding, gazed at the diminutive figure on the small pony and said, 'Very much. Oh yes, they would have loved you very much.'

'Even because my face is different from Willy's?' The child took her hands from the reins now and tapped her cheek.

The smile slid from Tilly's face as she said, 'They would have loved you for yourself.'

'Not because you are my mama?'

It was a strange question, and Tilly paused a moment before answering this wise and perceptive piece of humanity. 'No, not simply because I am your mama but because you are yourself.'

The child now turned her gaze away from Tilly who was peering at her and, looking straight ahead, she repeated, ''Cos I am myself.' Then looking back at Tilly, she asked, 'Do people always throw stones at people who are not the same colour?'

'No, no, of course not. But who has been throwing stones?' She looked now at Willy, but he remained silent; then again she was looking at Josefina and repeating, 'Who has been throwing stones?'

'Christine said not to trouble you, she said they were silly boys.'

'When did they throw the stones?'

Josefina pursed her lips and shrugged her small shoulders but remained silent, and Tilly turned to her son and, her voice stern, demanded, 'Willy, tell me, who has been throwing stones.'

'Some children, Mama, from beyond the gate.'

'When?'

He considered for a moment, then said, 'Sunday.'

'Last Sunday?'

'Yes, Mama.'

'And before that?'

'Yes, Mama.'

'Can you remember when?'

'On . . . on fair day, when they were on holiday, they had on their Sunday suits.' He nodded at her.

She now reached out and moved aside the hair covering an inch long scar on his brow, just above the jagged line left by the rough stitching of the wound that had caused his near blindness, and she recalled a day some weeks ago when she had come into the hall and found Christine Peabody talking rapidly to her father. The children were standing between them and when she enquired if there was anything wrong it was Peabody who had answered, saying, 'Master Willy ran into a branch, madam, when he was playing. He has cut his brow a little.'

'Did a stone do this, Willy?'

The boy's eyelids were blinking as he muttered, 'Yes, Mama. But it wasn't Christine's fault, she ran out of the gates and chased the boys.'

Tilly felt her body slumping down into the saddle for a moment, but only for a moment; then she was sitting bolt upright. All her life she had suffered from the village and the villagers and because of Josefina they had another flail with which to beat her back. But Josefina was one thing, and her son another. The village, in the form of Mrs McGrath, had blinded her boy in one eye, and that stone could have taken the little sight that remained in the other, for the cut in his brow had gone deep and it was just above his right temple. Another half an inch or so and it could have been the eye itself.

As she felt the old surge of temper rising in her she swung the horse around, saying to the children, 'Come! we're going for a ride.'

Obediently they turned their ponies and trotted by her side, and when they cut on to the main drive and went towards the main gates neither of them cried as they might have done excitedly on another occasion, 'Are we going to ride far, Mama?' They remained silent.

At the lodge she drew rein and called, 'Jimmy! Jimmy!'

She knew it was Jimmy's day off, and when he appeared at the door dressed only in his trousers and shirt he quickly buttoned up the neck of his shirt as he came down the path, saying, 'Yes, Ti . . . ma'am?'

'Would you mind going back to the stables and telling Arthur or Myers, whoever is available, to saddle a horse and follow me as quickly as he can.'

'Yes. Yes, ma'am, yes, of course. Which way will I tell them to go?'

'I'm making for the village.'

The young man's eyebrows shot up as he said, 'The village!' and he repeated in amazement, 'The village!'

'Yes, Jimmy, the village. Tell him I'll wait at the turnpike. Go at once will you as I'm in rather a hurry.' As she spoke she took out her watch and looked at it, and after gaping at her for a moment, Jimmy turned and, just as he was, he rushed up the drive.

Her watch said half past eleven. Most of the villagers would be at the service, and all the children too, and if Parson Portman was anything like the usual preachers it would be three quarters of an hour before the church emptied.

Jimmy, in obeying her orders so promptly, had forgotten to open the gates, and she had to dismount and open them herself. It did not matter for, not wearing a habit, her remounting proved no obstacle.

Out on the road, she walked her horse, and the children's ponies followed suit. They had gone some distance when Willy asked tentatively, 'Are you vexed with me, Mama?'

She turned her face towards him and swallowed the lump in her throat before answering softly, 'No, my son, I'm not vexed with you.'

'Who are you vex-ed with then?' This question came from Josefina, and Tilly, now looking at her, said, 'Not you, my dear, either.'

'Are you vex-ed with the village?'

'Yes. Yes, I suppose you could say I am vexed with the village.'

'Are you going to chas ... chas ... ?'

'Yes, I suppose in a way you could say I am going to chastise them, dear.' And she added bitterly to herself as she looked ahead, 'And not before time. For once I'm going to live up to my name. God forgive me!'

They hadn't been waiting long at the turnpike when Tilly heard the sound of galloping hooves behind them and Arthur Drew came riding up to them.

Drawing his horse to a halt, Arthur breathed deeply for a moment before he asked, 'You all right, Tilly?'

'Yes, yes, I'm all right, Arthur.'

'There's something you want me to do?'

'Yes, Arthur.' She paused. 'I want you to ride say two or three lengths behind us as I go into the village, and when we stop you stop. I simply want you as a show of strength, if you get my meaning, sort of prestige, the lady of the manor taking her children for a ride accompanied by the groom. Do you follow me, Arthur?'

He didn't quite, but he knew she was up to something. The Tilly he knew never put on airs, but she was playing the lady now all right, and he'd support her with everything in every way he knew how.

'I should have got rigged up in me best,' he said.

'You're all right as you are.' She looked at his breeches tucked in his top boots. The boots could have had a better polish on them, but what matter, he was the servant following his mistress. That's how it should be today.

'Have you got a large white handkerchief on you?' she asked.

'Aw' – he made an apologetic movement with his head – 'I've got a hanky on me but I'm afraid it isn't very white.'

'Oh, it doesn't matter, Arthur; I have the very thing.' She unloosened the top button of her riding jacket. It was without revers and was made very much in the style of a Texas Ranger's coat, buttoning right up to the neck. Pulling a narrow cream silk scarf from around her neck and leaning towards Willy, she said, 'Take off your cap, dear.'

She now proceeded to wind the scarf twice around his head, slanting it downwards to cover the cut at his temple, and when he protested, saying, 'But, Mama, it isn't bleeding,' she said 'I know that, Willy, but I want you to keep this on. Here, give me your cap.' She now placed his cap to the back of his head leaving the scarf much in evidence.

Again she looked at her watch, saying now, 'There's plenty of time, we'll take it slowly.' She glanced back at Arthur explaining, 'I want to be in the middle of the village when the church comes out.'

Arthur made a slight motion with his head. His mouth opened and closed, and then he said, 'Why? Why, Tilly?'

For answer she said, 'How long will it take us to get there, fifteen minutes?'

'Aye, that should do it.'

'Very well, off we go. And children' – she looked from one to the other – 'don't ask any questions until we are back home. You understand?'

Willy was the first to say, 'Yes, Mama.'

But Josefina said, 'No questions, Mama?'

'No questions, Josefina, not until we reach home.'

'Yes, Mama.'

'Well now, come on.'

Her head up, her back as straight as a ramrod, she now urged her horse forward. It could have been that she was leading an army into battle, and in a way she was. She knew that when she faced her enemies what she would put into them would not be the fear of God, but that of the devil. It was the only weapon she had, and she meant to use it for the sake of her children.

The village street was curved. Some of the houses were very old, their foundation stones having been laid over two hundred years past. The houses at the end spread out to form a square in the middle of which was a large round of rough grass where at one time had stood the market stone, but all that remained of it now was a flat slab, itself almost obliterated by the grass. At one side of the square were small cottages fronted by gardens, the opposite side was taken up by a number of shops, in the middle of which stood the inn.

Not all the villagers attended church, some went to chapel. The church and cemetery lay back from the road at the east end of the village; the chapel, a new erection, was, as it were, cut off from the village by being situated down a side lane; but whether by accident or design both services began at the same time on a Sunday and also ended approximately at the same time. It was laughingly said that the minister of the chapel had a runner waiting outside the church to inform him when the parson was drawing the service to a close. However that may be, both sets of worshippers, at least those on foot, generally managed to straggle into the village square at the same time as they made their way home.

So, as usual today, in twos and threes they emerged in their dark Sunday best either from the side lane or through the lychgate, but all of them stopped in their tracks, only to be nudged forward by those behind them, for there in the middle of the green was a woman sitting on a horse; she was flanked on each side by a child on a pony, and behind her at a respectable distance sat a man in the clothes of a groom.

It took but a few minutes for the older inhabitants among the thickening throng to recognise the rider. The younger ones had to grope in their minds, but even they soon realised this was the woman that all the stir was about.

After their first pausing some of the villagers began to move towards their respective houses, defiance in their step which was lacking in their faces, and it was as the first couple entered their gate that Tilly, in a voice that was not loud, but each word clear and distinct and which carried to everyone present, turned to her son and, pointing across the square, said, 'That is the inn, Willy, where Mrs Bradshaw used to serve. You know, her daughter came to look after you and struck you and stole my jewellery, so I had to dismiss her. And next to it is the baker's shop. The Mitchams lived there.'

She was aware that her son was straining to stare at her, his mouth slightly open, his face red. She was also aware that most of the people had stopped and that they, too, were staring at her, and most of them too had their mouths agape, and their eyes stretched wide. But as if she were unaware of them and now moving her arm to the side, she said, 'Willy, where you see the board swinging that is the wheelwright's shop. The wheelwright's name was Mr Burk Laudimer. His son has now taken his place.' She could have added at this stage that these people blamed her for killing his father, but she went on, her finger now pointing here and there, 'That is the carpenter's shop. Mr Fairweather owns that and he lives in a cottage' – she turned her head and her body moved slightly in the saddle as she pointed behind her, adding, 'over there.' In her turning she saw Arthur Drew's face. His eyes, too, were wide, almost popping out of his head.

She was again pointing in front of her, but now leaning towards Josefina as she did so and saying, 'You see that cottage there, Josefina? There lives the gravedigger. You know what a gravedigger is? He is a man who buries the dead.'

She could see that Josefina was on the point of asking a question, and so she turned from her and went on naming names, pointing out houses; and lastly she pointed along the street to where at the end of the row of shops was the blacksmith's, and it did not escape her that outside the door stood George McGrath and his son, taller now but whom she recognised as the boy who had broken the cottage window and accused her of killing his Uncle Hal and calling her witch.

She had lost count of the people she had named, she only knew they were all standing transfixed gazing at her, as they might have done at something at a fair, but without the enjoyment that sight would have elicited. And it was at the precise moment when she was about to give them an ultimatum that there pushed through the crowd, his black robes flapping, Parson Portman.

She had, of course, heard of Parson Portman but she had never met him; apparently the Manor was out of bounds to him, but now there he was standing not three yards from her looking up at her and she down at him.

When she spoke to him her voice was polite and had the inflexion of the gentry, which surprised him. He had heard so many tales of this woman and none good, yet she had the face of a . . . he dare not say angel, so substituted in his own mind, a beautiful creature with the strangest eyes he had ever seen in a woman.

Parson Portman was an educated man. He was a bachelor from choice, for he had seen too many of his kind struggling to support a wife and yearly increasing family. He loved the creature comforts which included good food, wine and a large fire, and a man in his position didn't usually come by these things unless he had been able to buy himself into the church. Being one of eight brothers, his people had educated him but that was all they had been able to do for him. And so, knowing on which side his bread was buttered, he aimed to keep in favour with his more wealthy parishioners and no one of these but had held the Manor and its occupants in disdain for years.

He had been assigned to this parish following his predecessor's departure in disgrace through his wife's escapades, joint escapades, so he understood, with this very woman here. She had corrupted the parson's wife, so the tale went, but now working it out for himself, this woman in front of him could have been little more than a child or a very young girl when the incident happened. Yet from the look of her he could imagine that she could have a strange power over both men and women: possessed of the devil they said she was, and that death attended her wherever she went.

What was he to do? How was he to deal with the situation? Why was she here, attended by her children and her groom? What did his parishioners expect him to do, put a curse on her?

What she had said to him was, 'Good-morning, sir.' And now some moments later in answer to her greeting, he replied, 'Good-morning, madam. Can I be of any assistance to you?'

She seemed to consider for a moment, then said in no small voice now, 'Yes, oh yes, Parson, you could be of great assistance. You will I am sure have heard of me, and, of course, you will know that I am a witch and have been persecuted because of my particular talent.' She now looked over his head and around the gaping faces; then looking down on him again, she went on, 'Not only have I been persecuted, but my sort also. Perhaps you are aware that my son' – she put out her hand now towards Willy – 'is almost blind. This was done by one of your parishioners. He has just a little sight left in one eye. Well, not satisfied with this, the children of the village have been sent . . . directed apparently to finish what their parents started.' Now she swiftly put out her hand and whipped off Willy's cap showing his bandaged head and, her voice rising, and again looking at the scattered crowd, she cried in a voice that the young Tilly might have used 'A well aimed stone tried to finish the job. Well now, sir,' – once more she lowered her head and looked at the parson – 'I have come to the village to give them an ultimatum: the persecution stops or else I shall use the powers that they ascribe to me, and the first one in future who lifts his hand against us, or even his tone, I shall deal with in my own way.'

The whole square was silent; the fact that a mongrel dog stood immovable on the edge of the green staring up towards her only added to the eeriness.

When she turned her fierce gaze down on to the parson's face it looked blanched. She saw him wet his lips, move his head in bewilderment, then put his hands out as if he were about to appeal to her; she did not allow him time for she dug her heels into the flanks of her horse and the beast turned obediently and moved off the green on to the roadway. The children following suit came slightly behind her. Lastly, after he had stared, in his turn, in amazement at the fear-filled faces of those nearest to him Arthur Drew followed his mistress out of the village.

Tilly, as after any emotional experience, expected to feel slightly sick. She expected her body to tremble, her legs to be so weak that they would not support her, and in this particular case that they would have possessed no strength with which to guide the horse. But she felt none of these things, what she did feel was a great sense of elation which lasted all the way back to the Manor. And when as soon as they were inside the house the children wanted to clamber about her and ask questions, she quietly passed them over to Christine and, saying to Peabody, 'Have a glass of wine and some biscuits sent up to my room, please,' she walked steadily across the hall and up the stairs.

But Arthur Drew in the kitchen sat at the table and wiped the sweat from his brow and looked at the faces of his mother and his sisters as he said, 'Ma, it was the weirdest thing I've ever experienced. I tell you, she sat there on that horse and the things she did! She named everybody in that village, at least all of them that had had a go at her. And then it was like the heavens had opened and there was the parson, and she talked to him, called it an ultimatum. But I tell you, every soul in that village knew she was offering them a curse. Eeh! Ma.'

'Here, drink that.' Biddy pushed a mug of ale towards him, and she watched him drain the mug dry before she sat down and said, 'I can't take it in, the very fact of her going into the village. What brought it on do you think?'

'I don't know, Ma. The only thing is, as I said, she bandaged young Willy's head up just as if it had happened this mornin'. But 'twas the way she spoke. I tell you, Ma, I wasn't on the wrong side of her but she still put the fear of God into me. You know, I can't help but say it, there's somethin' in her . . . Tilly.'

'Don't be so bloody soft, our Arthur!'

'I'm not being bloody soft, Ma.' He had risen to his feet. 'You weren't there.'

'Well, she's no witch. God! you've known her long enough.'

'Aye, I have, an' there's nobody I like better, but I tell you, Ma, she's got somethin' that the ordinary woman hasn't. And I can't put me finger on it no more than anyone else can, but it's there.'

'Aye, it's there, and it's nowt but attraction as they call it. Some women have it and some haven't; she's got a bit more than her share, that's all.'

'Well, have it your way, Ma; the only thing I can say again is you weren't there. But I'd like to bet me bottom dollar that there won't be any more trouble for some time in the village.'

'Well, that's something to thank God for this Sunday anyway. By! I'll say it is 'cos she's had more than her share.' It was Fanny nodding at him now. 'From as far back as I can remember people have been at her. I only wish I'd been there.'

'I only wish you had, our Fanny, instead of me. Yes. Yes' – he nodded slowly at her – 'I only wish you had. But I'll tell you this, I wouldn't want to sit through that again.'

'What did the parson say to her?'

Arthur had made for the door and he turned. 'Nowt. Nowt. He just looked as if he had been struck dumb or put under a spell or somethin'. Aye, that's it. Like the rest of 'em, put under a spell.'

'Good for Tilly, 'cos he's never crossed the door. It would queer his pitch with the pious nobs he toadies to. Good for her.'

'Ma, I'll say again, you weren't there, and to my mind it wasn't good for anybody.'

᥆᥍ 12 ᥆᥍

There was a change in Tilly. The Drews had remarked on it, Peabody had remarked on it, and Tilly herself remarked on it. Since the Sunday she rode into the village square and prophesied doom and tribulation for anyone who would dare to persecute her or hers in the future, she had, as it were, brought to the surface her fear of the villagers, and with such a melodramatic effort too, for she was fully aware that she had played on the melodramatic and used it to aid the effect of her warning. Yet as she had ridden out of the village there hadn't been a vestige of the old fear left in her; in fact, she had the idea that she had distributed it among all those present that morning.

The change in her was made evident when she no longer bypassed the village on the way to Shields but ordered Ned Spoke or Peter Myers, whoever was driving the coach, to go directly through the village. Also, at times she rode horseback through it, but never alone, always she would be accompanied by one of the men acting as groom. But quite frequently she rode alone to visit Anna and John.

It was Anna who said to her a few days after the eventful Sunday, 'Is it true what I'm hearing, Tilly, that you went to the village on Sunday and waited for the church coming out and addressed them?'

Tilly could not help but laugh at the term used for her haranguing Parson Portman's and Mr Wycomb's congregations and she answered, 'Yes, quite true, Anna. But I wouldn't say I addressed them, rather put the fear of God in them . . . or the devil. Yes, the latter is more like it, the devil. They've associated me with him for so many years that I felt it was about time I gave them proof of his power.'

'But why? Why?' Anna had questioned, her head shaking from side to side. 'There has been no trouble lately.'

'No? Willy was struck in the head with a stone; in fact it was almost on his eye, his good eye. I was unaware that the stone throwing had been going on for some time; it was kept from me so I wouldn't worry. Well, that's how these things start. The next move could be setting fire to the barns . . . or even the house. Oh, don't shake your head like that. Remember . . . or perhaps you don't but I've already been burned out once. They have persecuted me for years and if I intend to go on living at the Manor, and I do Anna, I'm not going to have the children brought up in fear. If anyone's going to hand out fear in the future it'll be me.'

Anna's eyes had widened, her face had stretched as she said, 'It sounds so unlike you, Tilly. You've always seemed to crave peace and you've never been the one to retaliate.'

'That was because I was so fearful of them, petrified of them and what they might do. Yet on looking back, I remember after they burned the cottage down and my granny had died because of it, I lay on the straw in the woodshed and I can recall vividly imagining myself standing in the middle of the village screaming at each one in turn, denouncing them and instilling fear into them. It has taken a good many years for that desire to bear fruit. You know, they say if you wish and think on a thing hard enough you'll get it in the end, but that saying doesn't take account of the work, and in my case the anxiety and fear in between.'

John, too, was a little shocked at the stance Tilly had taken. His concern, however, was mainly with regard to her safety. 'They c . . . could have set about you, Ti . . . Tilly. There're still some w . . . wild ones in that village,' to which, touching his shoulder, she had answered with tenderness, 'John, you know that some brave men are afraid to walk though a graveyard at night. Well, I've turned into the graveyard for that entire village,' and to this all John could say was, 'Oh, Tilly! what a simile, you . . . you a graveyard. Oh Tilly! . . .'

However, one person, but only one, saw the funny side of the incident, and that was Steve.

During the past month Tilly had made two visits to the mine, once accompanied by John, and once on her own. John, in a tentative way, had suggested that she did not visit the mine unaccompanied. 'It wasn't seemly,' he had said.

To anyone else she would have answered, 'Why not? I'm the owner, it belongs to me, why shouldn't I visit it and speak to the men who work there?' But she merely smiled at him and said, laughingly, 'Remember, John, I'm no lady.' And to this, he had screwed up his eyes, tossed his head to the side and, his stammer more evident again, he had spluttered, 'D . . . don't say su . . . such things. Tilly, you are as g . . . g . . . good a lady as ever I've . . . I've met. It m . . . maddens me when you dep . . . dep . . . deprecate yourself. I am con . . . concerned for you simply, be . . . be . . . because you are a l . . . lady.'

Dear John. Dear John. Sometimes she thought, of all the Sopwiths he was the best and the kindest. Perhaps, she told herself, she thought that way because he was uncomplicated, he had inherited none of the passions of his father or his brother. In a way he and Luke were alike in temperament, as Matthew and Jessie Ann had been.

They would see Luke soon. He had written to say he was coming, that he was getting leave from his regiment at Christmas and would spend a few days with them. He had never seen Willy since she had returned home and, of course, he hadn't set eyes on Josefina, and she naturally wondered not a little just what his reaction to the child would be. Yet it didn't trouble her.

On this particular visit to the mine, she had talked with the present manager, Mr Meadows, and she sensed that he, like John, didn't welcome her presence. On this occasion the men were coming out after doing a shift and a half, and she had wanted to know why they had been called upon to do the extra work. There was a little water coming in on the B level, Mr Meadows had said. And she had surprised him by answering, 'There was always a little water coming in on the B level. In my opinion it's time that area was closed off.'

The sharp retort the man was about to make was checked by his remembering that this woman had once worked down this very mine and had for days lain with the owner behind a fall, the same fall that caused the man to lose both feet. And so he said, 'There's been a lot of work, repair work, done on B section, madam.'

'Then why are you still having trouble?'

God! he thought, the questions women asked. 'Because, madam,' he said slowly, 'this whole mine runs by the side of and in some parts under the river.'

'I'm aware of that, Mr Meadows,' she had answered; 'and that's why, I repeat, that section should be shut off.'

'Then you'd better talk the matter over with Mr John, madam.'

She looked at the men who were passing her. They were not only black from head to foot but they were also wet, the wet coal dust was covering them like a black glaze.

She stopped two men. 'What's your name?' she asked, looking at first one then the other.

'Me name's Bladwish, ma'am, Bladwish.'

'Bill Thircall, ma'am,' said the other one.

She smiled at them now before saying, 'How bad is it down there?'

'Oh, not all that bad, ma'am. Bit of water. We've got it in time; it'll take somethin' to get through that now. The river'd have to burst its banks first.' He laughed.

She looked from one to the other. They must have been down there sixteen to eighteen hours; they looked worn out yet they could still smile, still have a cheery word. And what were they going home to? A two-roomed cottage, a hovel really, like the Drews used to live in, which at one time she had gladly shared with them. Well, that's something she could do, and would do: she'd build a new row, two rooms up and two rooms down, and a dry closet in the yard. Yes, that's what she'd do.

As the two men touched their foreheads and moved away she turned and was about to speak to the manager, whose expression was anything but pleasant, when she saw Steve coming up the drift towards her. He was accompanied by three workmen. They were talking and nodding at each other, but when Steve glimpsed her he seemed to pause for a moment before leaving the men. Coming towards her, he touched his cap and said, 'Good-afternoon, Mrs Sopwith.'

It was the first time he had addressed her formally, and she answered in the same vein, 'Good-afternoon, Mr McGrath. I hear you're having some trouble.'

'Oh, nothing to worry about.' He glanced towards his superior, then said, 'There's one thing sure, wherever it comes in it won't be in that spot again.'

'Don't you think that section should be closed?' she now asked.

'No, no.' He shook his head in a wide movement; then looking at Mr Meadows, he said, 'You don't think so, do you, sir?'

'I've already had my say to madam.' The manager now turned to Tilly, adding, 'If you'll excuse me, madam, I must be about my business;' then glancing at Steve again, he said, 'I want you in for the fore shift.'

It was a moment before Steve answered, 'Right;' then looking at Tilly, he said, 'Can I give you a step up on your mount, Mrs Sopwith?' and she answered, 'If you please, Mr McGrath.'

When she mounted she looked down at him and said, 'Thank you' before turning the horse around and taking it up the muddy bank past the stables, the lamp house, and the office.

She had noted Steve's hesitation when Mr Meadows had told him he expected him to be at work for the fore shift. Like the men, he had likely been below sixteen or eighteen hours. It was now late in the afternoon, in fact it was dusk, and the fore shift went in, she knew only too well, at two o'clock in the morning. From where he lived it would mean getting up at one if he intended to make a meal before going out; and what he would have to do, the men would have to do. Nothing seemed to improve in mines, time, pay or conditions. She had heard of men in other pits striking and she could understand why. Oh yes, only too well she could understand why.

In a thoughtful mood she walked her horse, thinking, I've enough money to raise their wages, I could cut down their hours. Yet she knew, as kindly as John was, he'd be very much against this, for any alteration in pay or lessening the men's time would bring other coal owners, such as Rosier, about their ears. Bonded men were little better than slaves; in fact, looking back, she considered the four male slaves on the ranch in Texas had in many ways lived better than some of her own miners.

But she could alter things, give them decent places to live in, and rent free, she must talk to John about it or perhaps Steve.

As if her thinking had conjured him up, she heard the clip-clopping of the hooves of the old horse on the road behind her and, turning, she drew her horse to a standstill to allow him to come abreast. He was riding the animal bareback and as he jogged to a halt, he said, 'That's the first time he's ever trotted. Do you know, I tHtink he could gallop if he was put to it. There's life in the old boy yet.'

She smiled at him, then said, 'You must be very tired.'

'Oh, not too bad; not too tired to brew a cup of tea if you'll come in?'

'No, thank you, Steve. It's getting dusk, and if I'm not back before dark they'll have the bellmen out for me.'

They rode on in silence for a few minutes, and then he said, 'Nice to see you taking an interest in the mine, Tilly.'

'Yes.' She half turned her head towards him. 'It's one thing taking an interest but another thing entirely, I imagine, to get anything done, I mean make changes.'

'Oh' – his chin jerked up – 'you mean Mr Meadows. He's a stickler for the rules. I suppose I shouldn't say it but he's frightened of the death he'll never die. To my mind he shouldn't be in this business at all; either you're made for it or you're not. Not unlike being in the army, where you've got a better chance of surviving if you come up from the ranks, so to speak. It's all right being conversant with the technical stuff but if you don't get the feel of a seam before you touch it, then there's something missin'. Still, the way things are suits me: I see to below and he sees to up top, most of the time anyway. You're sure you won't come in for a cup of tea? It won't take a couple of minutes.'

They were nearing the cottage gate now and she shook her head, saying, 'Another time I'd be very pleased to. In fact I must come again and gather up a few more books, if that's all right with you?'

'Oh' – he jerked his head – 'now don't be silly, Tilly . . . if it's all right with me, it's your cottage. By the way' – he put his head slightly to the side – 'you're looking better, brighter. Your riding likely does you a lot of good. And as I haven't seen you for some time, I must congratulate you on one ride you took.'

As she returned his gaze she pretended she didn't know to what he was alluding and her voice had a query in it as she said, 'Yes, and what ride was that?'

'The day you put the fear of God into them in the village.'

'Oh that! Do you think that's the right term?'

His laugh now rung out as he answered, 'No, somehow I don't. An' there's one thing I can tell you, you acted like a dose of senna on half the churchgoers that morning. And through the bits of tittle-tattle I've heard here and there I don't imagine you'll have much trouble from that quarter in the future. Your fame's spread even as far as Pelaw. On the way back from Newcastle last week I dropped in at The Stag to have a drink. I've never been in that pub afore, so they didn't know me, and talked freely among themselves. And I can tell you this, Tilly, they were mostly for the stand you made, for you know, like the way Shields feels about Newcastle, Pelaw and up the line feel about Shields, and the villages.'

'Well, that's good to hear anyway, it means I won't have a hunting party coming from Pelaw.'

'No; nor nowhere else, if you ask me. As one of the fellows said, he had seen you once and he wouldn't mind having a witch like you sitting at the other end of the table any day. Aw! Tilly' – his voice suddenly full of concern, he put in quickly, 'I just said that to reassure you. I mean. . . .'

'I know what you meant, Steve. And don't worry, the name doesn't trouble me any more, in fact I think I'll cultivate it. Yes' – she nodded her head – 'that's what I'll do. Anyway they've dubbed me a witch for so long I feel there must be something in it.'

'Never! You've got as much of the witch in you, Tilly, as I have blue blood.'

'You think so?'

'Sure of it.'

'Then tell me, Steve' – her voice was serious now – 'why has the name stuck to me, why have I been persecuted because of it?'

'Oh' – he leant forward and stroked the horse's grizzled mane, then moved his lips one over the other before slanting his eyes towards her and saying, 'It's because you've got something, a sort of an appeal. No, no' – he now shook his head – 'that's not the word. Attractiveness, I suppose, would be better. Better still' – his voice sank on to a low note as he ended – 'fascination. Aye' – he nodded his head – 'I think that's the word that fits you, fascination. You've always had it. Don't ask me what it consists of, I don't know, it's just you.'

Her voice as quiet as his, she said, 'It's an attribute I could have well done without, Steve.'

'Aye, from your point of view you would say that, but not from others, Tilly. No, not from others.'

She lowered her head and remained silent, which prompted him almost to shout, 'Look! we're out here nattering when we could have been indoors in the warmth, you're sure. . . .?'

She was sitting bolt upright, the reins tight now in her hands as she said, 'Bye-bye, Steve. I'll pop along one day for the books.'

He didn't speak until the horse had taken a few steps, and then he answered 'Do that, Tilly. Do that.' His voice was so low that his words came only faintly to her.

She put the animal into a trot and then into a gallop, and all the while her mind kept pounding with the rhythm of its hooves: fascination, fascination; and she knew that the fascination for her still held with him, and she told herself once more that she must keep clear of him for his own sake, and that if she visited the cottage it would have to be when he was out. But, on the thought, the feeling of loneliness welled in her; of all those about her, with the exception of Biddy, with whom she would like to be on friendly terms it was him; because whatever the tie was, it was there and had been since they were children.

∝ 13 ∝

Christmas was a gay affair, made so not only by the children but by their new Uncle Luke. This tall man who crept on all fours and chased them and elicited from the children screams of delight as he pretended to be a monkey and sprang on to couches and over chairs. Not only did the children enjoy him, but so did John and Anna and Tilly, and indeed the whole of the staff were for him: was he not a soldier who had fought the Russians, those strange and terrible people who lived on another planet? Besides that he was a gentleman, a gentleman who had a civil word for them.

As they said in the kitchen, they doubted if this house had ever heard such laughter and known such gaiety. And they themselves added to it. From Betty up to Biddle and Peabody they each in his own way contributed towards the happiness that prevailed in the house during the holiday.

It was only at night when lying alone in her bed and the echoes of the laughter had died away that Tilly would whisper, 'Oh, Matthew! Matthew! If only you were here.' Yet at the back of her mind she knew that if Matthew had been present, the atmosphere might not have been so gay, so free. Matthew had to dominate the scene, he would have had to set the pace, play the practical jokes, as he had done from a boy; yet like most practical jokers he was unable to accept being made a fool of, of being laughed at in return.

John, for instance, had always been laughed at because of his stammer. He was used to it. And Luke, she had found during the last four days, possessed qualities that had hitherto lain hidden. His way with children was delightful. He let them rumple him, climb all over him. This was new to them, for the man that Willy faintly remembered as his papa had never played with him, and the man that Josefina remembered as her papa had hardly ever looked at her. This uncle was certainly a revelation to them and, like all children, they took advantage of it, so much so that on Boxing Day there were tears when Christine was ordered to take them to the nursery and prepare them for bed.

For the first time that Tilly could remember Willy had disobeyed her, saying openly, 'I don't want to go to bed, Mama, I want to play with Uncle,' whereupon Luke put in, 'If you don't do what your mama tells you then I'm going to pack my bags and call for the carriage and ride away, right to the sea, and there I'll board a boat and you'll never see me again.'

The response had been quite unexpected for both Willy and Josefina had thrown themselves upon him, the tears flowing freely and crying, 'No! Uncle Luke. No! Uncle Luke.'

When peace was restored and the four adults were left in the drawing-room, John, nodding at his brother who was now lying flat out on the chaise, said, 'I think it's just as w ... well you've only g ... g ... got another f ... few days, otherwise Tilly would have to give ... give you notice and.... Just l ... l ... look at you! For a sol ... sol ... soldier of the Queen, you are a mess ... mess.'

'Oh.' Luke stretched out his legs and put his hands behind his head as he said, 'It's wonderful to be a mess, this kind of a mess;' and rolling his eyes backwards, he looked up at John who was standing at the head of the chaise and, his voice quiet, even serious now, he said, 'Don't put a damper on me, little brother; you have no idea what this spell has meant for me.' He brought his head down now and looked towards where Tilly and Anna were sitting on the couch that ran at right angles to the fireplace, the open hearth showing a great bank of blazing logs, and he asked, 'You don't mind, Tilly, do you?'

'No, Luke, I don't mind. Of course I don't mind.'

'I suppose I have gone a bit far ... daft.'

It was Anna who spoke now, saying, 'I wish more people could show their daftness in a similar way.'

Luke rose on his elbow now and grinned towards her as he said, 'Thank you, sister-in-law. And if you'd care to engage me when your family comes along I should be delighted to offer my services free.'

When Anna hung her head slightly, John's eyelids blinked rapidly and, his stammer evident now, he said, 'You're a f ... f ... fool, Lu ... Luke. Always were and ... and ... and always will be. Come on, Anna, let's go and s ... see the children to bed, then g ... get on our way.'

He held out his hand to his wife, turning his head and glaring at his brother as he did so.

As soon as the door closed on them, Luke swung his legs from the chaise, pressed his shirt into shape under the lapels of his coat, ran both hands over his skin-fitting trousers, then smoothed his hair back before saying, 'Did I say something wrong?'

'No, not really.' Tilly gave a slight shrug of her shoulders. 'Anna is just a little conscious of the fact that there is no sign of a family yet. But as I've told her' – her smile widened now – 'it took me almost twelve years.'

'Yes, yes, it did.' He nodded at her, and their laughter joined.

It was strange but she found she could talk very easily to Luke. Of the three brothers she would have said she liked him the least. He had always appeared a very self-contained person; he knew what he wanted to do and he did it with the minimum of fuss.

She watched him now rise and come towards her, and when he sat down in the corner of the settee he looked at her for a few moments before he said, 'This is the first time we've been alone together since I came home. Funny that.' He raised his eyebrows. 'I said home. Although I spent all those years away in Scarborough, then in the army, I still look upon this house as home.'

'I am glad of that.'

'Tilly.'

'Yes, Luke?'

'I've never mentioned Matthew, being half afraid it might be too painful a subject to bring up. . . . Is it still?'

'No, Luke, no. Talk about him if you want.'

'John tells me he had a terrible time. What I mean is you both had, I think you most of all.'

When she remained quiet he wetted his lips before lowering his head and muttering, 'You're more beautiful with your white hair.'

And again she made no answer.

He raised his eyes to her as he said, 'You'll marry again of course?'

'No, Luke, never.'

'Oh.' He jerked his chin to the side. 'That's nonsense. Anyway, I can't see you being allowed to remain single.'

'Nevertheless, I shall.'

'Why?'

'I can't tell you why, only that I shan't, I won't . . . I . . . .'

'Don't be silly, Tilly.' He leant forward, one hand pressing deep into the pile of the cushions as he brought his face almost within an inch of hers. 'Love doesn't last a lifetime. It can't, not unless there's someone on the other end to keep the fire stoked. You loved Matthew, all right, I admit that, and he loved you. No . . . no' – he now made a single swift movement with his head that spoke of denial – 'he didn't love you, his feelings for you could only come under the term of mania. He was so eaten up by you, even as a boy, it wasn't normal.'

'Don't say that, Luke.'

'I must say it because it's true, and you know it's true. He would have put you in a cage if he could just to keep you to himself. And in a way, yes' – he nodded at her – 'in a way, I can understand his feelings. But it wasn't ordinary love, and you shouldn't let the memory of it rule your life. Tilly' – he caught at her hand and she let him hold it – 'I'm going to ask you something, a question, but I think I already know the answer. . . . It's simply this, why did you adopt Josefina?'

All the muscles in her face seemed to be twitching at once, she couldn't take her eyes from his. Her mouth was dry and she ran her tongue round her lips before saying, 'Because her mother didn't want her and . . . and she was such a tiny thing so, so in need of care.'

'No other reason?'

Again she moved her tongue around her lips before saying, 'No.'

'You're lying, because I know that nobody in their right senses adopts a dark child, not one such as her, except a missionary might. She's not an African, she's not Chinese, she's not Spanish, nor is she pure Indian or Mexican. There'd have to be some very grave reason for you to take such a child into your life.' He released her hand now and, turning from her, he lay back against the couch and spread one arm along the head of it as he said, 'When Matthew came back from America we met only once. We had a long day together and as usual when two men meet the conversation reverts to the pleasures they have had or missed. I asked him what the American women were like. I remember his answer wasn't very flattering. One of the ranchers had three hefty daughters and, excuse the coarseness, but I remember he referred to them as three mares waiting to be sired, but not without the ring. He said the only beautiful women were half-castes. I asked him if he had known any of them, and by using the term "known" I was indicating something deeper, and I remember he made a face before using a certain expression which told me that he had been in contact with at least one of these women. Then the fact that he refused to enlarge upon her, and that his manner became abrupt, seemed to suggest his association with one person had had consequences that he wished to forget. Well now, Tilly,' – he turned and looked at her – 'I must admit when I first set eyes on Josefina she gave me a bit of a shock and I asked myself the question that everyone must ask when they see you and her together, why did this woman adopt such a child, a child that looks like a little foreign elf, a beautiful elf, but a strange creature? Why? And after thinking back I knew I had the answer. She's Matthew's, isn't she, Tilly?'

Her eyes were wide and unblinking and when her lips trembled he caught at her hand again, saying, 'Poor Tilly. Dear Tilly, to shoulder his flyblow. . . .'

'She's not a flyblow!' The sharpness of her reply almost startled him, and he said rapidly, 'I'm sorry. I'm sorry. Believe me, Tilly, I'm sorry.'

'If she's a flyblow so is Willy.'

'Tilly! Tilly!' He had pulled himself towards her and was gripping both her hands now. 'Tilly, you are the most wonderful woman on earth. Do you know that? And I'm going to say this to you. I won't ask you to forget about Matthew because you never can, but don't hang on to the past. Marry again. Promise me' – He shook her hands up and down now as he repeated, 'Promise me you'll marry again for I can't bear the thought of you being wasted.'

She slumped back against the couch now and her voice was weary as she said, 'I can't. I can't, Luke.'

'Tell me why. Is there a reason, not just your feeling for Matthew?'

It was on a long-drawn-out breath that she said, 'Yes, there's a reason.'

'Can you tell me it?'

She turned her head and looked at him. If she didn't give him a reason he would probe.

He broke into her thoughts, saying urgently now, 'It isn't that you're ill in any way?'

'Oh no, no.' Again she let out a long breath, and now she said, 'I promised Matthew on his deathbed that I would never marry again.'

He drew his chin tight into his neck and screwed up his eyes as if getting her into focus before he exclaimed, 'You what!'

'I don't need to repeat it, Luke, you heard what I said.'

'I hope I didn't. You said that you promised Matthew on his deathbed not to marry again? Don't tell me he asked you to give that promise.'

Her lids were lowered, her chin was on her chest when he said, 'Good God Almighty! But yes, yes – ' He let go her hands now and sprang up from the couch and paced the length of the long rug that lay before the open hearth as he cried, 'I can hear him doing it. Yes, I can hear him doing it. Promise me no other man will ever touch you, Tilly. Let me take my mania to the grave with me.'

'Luke! Please, Luke.'

He was standing now, his legs apart, his arms spread wide, silent, just standing gazing at her; then his arms flapping to his sides and his heels almost clicking together, he said, 'Damn him! He was my brother and I say to you, Tilly, damn him wherever he is for the selfish, self-centred maniac he was. As for you to give him that promise, what were you thinking of?'

'I was thinking of him dying. And under the same circumstances I would do the same again.' Her voice was quiet.

He bent towards her as he said, 'You've got a long life before you, Tilly. You are lonely; one can see it in your eyes. You laugh with everything but your eyes. And think of the years ahead. Knowing this, can you say you would give the same promise again? By God! if I wasn't your brother-in-law, Tilly, I would see that you broke that promise. Do you hear me? A man can't marry his brother's wife, and even if he could you might think that to run the whole gamut of our family was a bit too much, but if it was within the law, Tilly, I tell you that I'd wear you down, because I, too, have loved you, not like Matthew, that maniac, or like my father in need of solace, but as an ordinary man loves a woman. . . . Oh, don't press yourself away from me like that. Nothing can happen between us, I'm well aware of that. And I haven't lived a saint's life because I couldn't have you. Oh no; I've enjoyed a number of women; and it's because I've done this I know what you're missing. And let me tell you' – he poked his face towards her – 'that's what you need at this very moment. And because I'm sure of this I beg of you, forget your deathbed promise and take yourself a husband, a man who'll be a father to those children because that's what they want. Their need in a way is as great as yours.'

When he straightened his back the sweat was running down from the rim of his hair over his temples and, his voice quiet now, he said, 'This is the moment I should apologise I suppose and say I'm sorry, but I'm not a bit sorry, Tilly.' He took a step back from her and they surveyed each other in silence until he said, 'I'll leave you to think over what I've said. Tell yourself, Tilly, that the dead are dead, and there's nothing as dead as a dead man. I am haunted at night by the dead I have seen and by the fact that there can be nowhere for them to go: the heavens couldn't hold all the dead that have died in battle and by plague and massacre. There's no place for the dead in which to survive even in spirit, Tilly, so they have no power over you. Matthew is dead. He will never know whether you have kept the promise he extracted from you or not. Your struggle to keep faith with him is as senseless as if I were to say to you now, I am going to shoot myself because I remember that my friends dropped dead around me.'

Her head was bent again and she felt rather than saw him walk up to the head of the couch, and when she heard the drawing-room door close she opened her mouth wide as if she were about to scream; then she pressed her hand tightly over it, but she did not now say, 'Oh, Matthew! Matthew!' rather, her mind cried, 'Oh dear God! help me. Help me.'

◦ **14** ◦

The children cried when Luke departed. Dressed in his uniform once more he did not look the same man who had clambered over the furniture like a monkey, chased them up and down the stairs, rode the rocking horse in the nursery, and generally enchanted them; yet the uniform did nothing to hide the man from them, the father figure, and they clung to his legs until they were forcibly removed by both Tilly and Christine.

When the nursery door closed behind them, Tilly led the way down the stairs, saying, 'You have spoilt them,' and he answered, 'If playing the father to them has spoilt them, then I am found guilty.'

She did not answer this, but hurried on across the gallery and down into the hall. It was the first time he had made reference to the conversation they had held in the drawing-room four days previously, four days which she had found to be very uncomfortable. She had no doubt within herself that if it hadn't been for the law Luke would have pressed his suit, and then what would she have done? Father and two sons. No! No! It wasn't to be thought of. Anyway, she had no feeling for Luke other than as the brother of her husband and the elder brother of John. She had more, much more tender feeling for John than for Luke. She was glad he was going, but he stirred her mind in the most uncomfortable way, and not only with regard to the children. But it was right what he said, they missed the presence of a man, a father; but as she would never be able to supply that, she must in some way endeavour to bring into their lives the male element.

The thought of Steve was rejected at once, yet it was the first name that came into her mind, for she imagined Steve would be good with children. No, she knew what she was going to do once she was rid of Luke. And now here they were standing face to face at the front door. The carriage was waiting on the drive. Myers had lowered the steps, Biddle was standing on the terrace; Peabody flicked a speck from the back of Luke's collar, then moved back and stood at a respectful distance. Luke took her hand and, his voice soft, he said, 'Good-bye, Tilly. This has been a most memorable visit for me.' And out of politeness, she said, 'You must repeat it as soon as possible.'

He made no answer, but leaning forward, he put his lips to her cheek, and as he did so a shudder passed through her body because for a moment she imagined him to be Matthew: he had the same body smell, his mouth was the same shape.

Her fingers felt crushed within his grasp. She could have winced with the pain but she made no sign, and then he was gone, running down the steps. He did not turn and look at her again, but she saw him looking up at the nursery floor; then the carriage was bowling down the drive.

Biddle came hurrying up the steps and into the hall and, closing the door quickly after him to shut out the bitter wind, he was about to chafe his hands when he noticed his mistress standing in the middle of the hall. He stopped and looked at her enquiringly; then he could not keep his eyebrows from rising slightly as she said, 'I would like to speak with Ned Spoke. Bring him to the morning-room, please.'

. . . . 'Yes, ma'am.'

As Tilly made her way across the hall to the corridor leading to the morning-room she was well aware that Biddle and Peabody were exchanging glances and wondering why she wanted to see the stable boy.

She had already given everybody their Christmas boxes, generous with them, too, she had been. What was she wanting with Spoke?

Young Ned Spoke, too, wondered this as he was thrust into the changing room by Biddle, told to take off his boots and to choose a pair of slippers that were likely to fit him from a row set against the wall, then ordered to lick down his hair, straighten his jerkin, and to mind his manners when speaking to the mistress.

Ned Spoke had not answered Mr Biddle. Mr Biddle was a footman and you didn't backchat footmen, but he followed him obediently through the kitchen, past Mrs Drew who wanted to know what was up but got no reply from Biddle, and into the corridor, then into the hall, across it and there he was standing in what he termed a grandly room, the carpet so thick he felt that the large slippers on his feet were lost in it.

'Thank you, Biddle.'

Biddle went out and closed the door and Ned Spoke stood looking at the mistress.

'Sit down, Ned.'

'What! I mean, should I, ma'am?'

'I've told you to.'

Ned slowly lowered himself down on to the very edge of a chair and stared wide-eyed at his mistress, and he would have said that his eyes couldn't stretch any further but they did as he listened to her talking.

'You used to like playing with the children, didn't you, Ned?'

'Aye, ma'am.'

'Why didn't you continue to play with them?'

'Mr Myers stopped me: I was wasting time, ma'am.'

'Well now, in future, Ned, I want you to play with Master William every morning for at least an hour. If it's bad weather you can go into the big barn, but if the weather is at all mild I prefer you to play outside.'

'Play, ma'am?'

'Yes, play, Ned, wrestle and. . . .'

'Wrestle!' The end of the word seemed to jerk the boy's head up and he gulped, then gulped again before he whispered now, 'Wrestle, ma'am?'

'Yes, that's what I said, wrestle.'

'But I can't wrestle properly, ma'am. Well, what I mean is, not like me Uncle Phil. He's got prizes for it.'

'Your Uncle Phil has prizes for wrestling?'

'Aye, ma'am; he's a champion.'

'Indeed! And where does he live?'

'Hebburn, ma'am.'

'Hebburn, so near?'

'Aye, ma'am.'

'When is your next leave, Ned?'

'I had it last week, ma'am.'

'Well now' – she smiled at the boy – 'you may take another leave tomorrow morning and I want you to go and ask your uncle to come and see me with the idea of giving you real lessons in wrestling so that when you wrestle with Master William you won't hurt him in any way, but he'll learn from you. Will you do that?'

The boy's mouth was agape, his eyebrows, which were inclined to points, seemed to be straining to disappear into his hairline, and again he gulped before he said, 'He works in Palmers, ma'am; he ... he could only come on a Sunday 'cept in the summer when the nights are lighter.'

'Well, tell him he can pick his own time. And when we meet we can arrange his fee.'

'Wh ... what, ma'am?'

'I mean we can discuss what he will charge for his lessons. Tell him that.'

'Aye, ma'am.'

'And another thing: while you are playing with Master Willy, Miss Josefina will be skipping and playing hop-scotch.'

When the boy's face took on a look of utter perplexity, Tilly said on a gentle laugh, 'I won't expect you to play hop-scotch or skip with Miss Josefina, Christine will be there to see to that; but I'd like you to be altogether when you are ... well, having a game.'

'Yes, ma'am.' His next words, however, seemed to come out of the mouth of a very small boy, not of this gangling thirteen-year-old youth, when he said tentatively, 'But Mr Myers, ma'am?'

'I shall see to Myers, Ned. Don't worry about that. I shall also tell him that I want you to learn to ride so that you can accompany Master William when, later, he is able to ride out on his own.'

When Tilly got to her feet, the boy came up from the chair as if he had been stung, and he walked two steps backwards before bowing his head to her and saying, 'Thank you, ma'am,' and, his face breaking into a broad beam, 'Thank you, ma'am.'

She knew she was being thanked not for the wrestling part of his order but for the fact that he was going to be given the chance to ride a horse, and for a moment she recalled the negro slave, Number Three, whose life was saved because he had sneaked out at night just to touch a horse, for if he had been in his hut he would have been massacred with the rest in the Indian raid.

Ned Spoke almost ran across the hall, the passage, then the kitchen, oblivious of the staff waiting to know what the mistress had had to say to him, for he was telling himself that only last week he had been about to give in his notice because his father had said he could make more in the pit. He hadn't wanted to go down the pit, but there was little excitement in his present job, and Mr Myers was always at him, but now, by golly! every day to play with the young master and then to learn to ride. Eeh! he couldn't believe it. . . .

Nor could the rest of the staff when they heard. Even Biddy was strong in her protest to Tilly, saying, 'Is it true what I hear, you're goin' to get the bairn learn to wrestle?'

'Yes, it's true, Biddy.'

'But he's little more than a baby yet?'

Tilly stared at Biddy for a moment before she said quietly, 'In a few years more, Biddy, and under other circumstances he'd have been able to go down the pit.'

'Oh' – Biddy had swung herself round – 'those days are past now. And anyway, seeing who he is he should be brought up like a gentleman. That's my opinion, if you want it.'

'I'd rather see him brought up like a man, Biddy. He's already handicapped but he's going to grow big and strong. Well, I want him to be able to use that strength should the occasion arise. And what is more – ' She had turned away and looked out of the window on to the stable yard as she ended, 'I have learned over the holidays that he needs more than a nursemaid and a tutor, he needs a man's company, a boy's company.'

'Well' – Biddy now flounced back again – 'a lad like Ned Spoke isn't to my mind edifying company for the likes of him.'

'For what I need Willy to learn Ned and his uncle are the right people to teach him.'

'And the little youngster is going to skip and play hop-scotch an'll?' There was a sneer in Biddy's voice. 'Might as well have her brought up in a back lane; or perhaps you could find some flags and chalk up a hop-scotch on them for her.'

'Yes, perhaps I could, Biddy' – Tilly was smiling tolerantly at the old woman now – 'but I'm afraid I'd have a job. Still, the next best thing is the stone flags in the corner of the barn. I'll have them cleared and they can play on them there.'

'My God! I've heard it all. It would never have happened if Master Matthew had come back with. . . .'

'No, it wouldn't, Biddy.' Tilly had turned on her now, her voice conveying deep hurt and anger. 'Everything would have been different if Matthew had come back as you say; but he didn't come back, I'm on my own, I have the lives of two children in my care and I'm doing what I think best for them. I said Willy was handicapped, but not half as much as is Josefina. For the first time in our acquaintance, Biddy, you're not being very much help.'

As Tilly stormed her way up the kitchen, Biddy leant over the table, her head bowed deep on her chest, and although she said aloud, 'I'm sorry, lass,' it didn't carry. The flouncing figure went out of the far door and now Biddy groaned

aloud as she muttered, 'You've gone too far this time. You should practice what
you preach, woman. You're always on to the others about knowin' their place.'
Putting out her hand, she now groped towards a chair and, flopping down on
it, she muttered, 'I'm tired. Oh God! but I'm tired.'

It was the first time in her life that she had ever expressed those words aloud.

The following morning, like any housekeeper or ordinary servant, Biddy knocked
on the morning-room door, and when she was bidden to enter she went in
slowly and, standing some distance from Tilly, who although she had finished
her breakfast was still seated at the table, she stared at her for a moment before
swallowing deeply and saying, 'I've come to apologise – ' she was on the point
of adding 'lass' but substituted 'ma'am', and on this Tilly closed her eyes tightly,
gave such a hard jerk to her head that a bone cracked audibly in her neck, before
getting to her feet and, taking Biddy by the shoulders, she actually shook her,
saying, 'Don't! For goodness sake, woman, don't! Never, never do that Biddy.
Never apologise to me, not you! There'll never be any need for that between us.
Oh! you old fool.' Now she pulled the older woman into her arms, and Biddy
returning the embrace, they held tightly for a moment; then almost embarrassed,
they pushed away from each other, Tilly, her voice almost rough now, saying,
'Sit yourself down.'

'No, lass; I've got a lot to do, I'm up to me eyes in the. . . .'

'Sit down. That's an order.'

When Biddy was seated Tilly took a chair opposite her; then leaning forward,
she gripped Biddy's hands as she said, without any lead-up, 'It was Luke. You
see, when he was here he had such an effect on the pair of them' – she jerked
her chin upwards indicating the nursery – 'and we had . . . well we almost had
words about them. He – ' She looked away now as she went on, 'He said that
they both, not only Willy but Josefina too, needed the presence of a man in the
house, they were surrounded by women, they were being brought up by women.
Anyway, he set me thinking, and the best I could think of was that Willy should
have a playmate who could also instruct him in games. You see, Biddy, I'll never
be able to send him away to school. As things are, all I'll be able to teach him
in the physical line will be how to sit a horse, and he can do that already, so
I want him to be able to box, run, wrestle with the best of them. Do you
understand?'

'Aye, lass, aye; yes, I understand now.'

'And it won't hurt Josefina to be able to stand physically on her two legs
either.'

It was Biddy who smiled now and said, 'Well, I doubt she'll ever be more
than a bantam-weight, Tilly.' When they laughed together, Tilly said, 'No, perhaps
not; but she's wiry and she's smart up here.' She tapped her forehead. 'She's
miles ahead of Willy in that way.'

'Huh!' Biddy was on the defensive. 'You're not sayin' Willy's dim?'

'No, no; far from it, but she's got a brightness of mind that is . . . well, the only
way I can explain it is by saying it's very un-English, she's as knowledgeable
and keen witted as a child twice her age and she has a sort of sensitivity, a kind
of knowing that is very unchildlike. Anyway' – she squeezed Biddy's hand – 'I

have no intention of sending them both to the fair or the hoppings.'

'Well, that's something to be thankful for.' Biddy now rose to her feet and, changing the subject completely, she said, 'About New Year, is Master John and Miss Anna coming?'

'Not to stay, Biddy. They wanted me to go across there, but I couldn't really think about leaving the children for a couple of days, so they are popping over on New Year's Day for dinner, that is, weather permitting. There is a smell of snow in the air. Don't you think so?'

'Yes, I do. I was just saying the very same thing to meself this morning when me bones began to rattle when I got out of bed.'

'Well, that's your own fault.' Tilly now pushed her towards the door. 'There's no need for you to rise before eight in the morning, Peg can take over nicely.'

'It's a habit, lass.'

'Well, it's a habit you'll soon have to break.'

'When that time comes order me a wheel-chair, will you?'

'Go on with you!' Tilly pressed her out through the door and into the hall and as she watched her walking away it dawned on her that Biddy was an old woman. She must be seventy if a day, but she wouldn't admit to any age. The saddening thought came to her that if Biddy retired or died there would be a gap in her life that no one else could fill, because, whether she had realised it or not, from the first time she had met her she had looked upon this woman in the light of a mother, and as they had been drawn more and more together Biddy had taken the place of a mother, the only real mother she had ever known.

As she made her way up to the nursery she told herself she would get Peg and Fanny to one side and tell them that they must lighten their mother's load in the kitchen and see that she kept off her legs more.

Her granny used to say work never killed anybody, not perhaps outright but it led them by both hands to the edge of the grave.

ෙ 15 ෙ

They were preparing for a New Year's party in the servants' hall. Lizzie Gamble and Betty Leyburn had been infected with the giggles from early morning and by afternoon had passed them on to Peg and Fanny; even Christine Peabody, when out of her father's sight and hearing, hugged herself at the thought of the fun they were going to have at the party.

Peter Myers's brother who played the fiddle had been invited and he was bringing along his friend who played the concertina, and both these males were unmarried; also Biddy's eldest son, Henry, and his wife and their two children were coming, and Alec and his wife, and Sam and his wife.

So it must have appeared to Mr Peabody that the Drews were having the monopoly in the coming entertainment, for he had approached the mistress to ask if it would be possible to invite his brother and his wife, who lived in a village outside of Hexham in Northumberland, to be his special guests. But having come so far would it be in order that they could be accommodated for the night? And to this the mistress had replied, most certainly. Some of the Drew family too would be staying overnight and so he could give orders that rooms were to be aired and beds warmed in the west wing.

This left only Biddle; and he surprised everyone by asking if he could bring his mother and father. As Fanny laughingly said, fancy Biddle having a mother and father. Well, she supposed he had been born at one time. She had then gone on, still giggling, to relate to her mother that Biddle had said he would like to invite his parents because he had no female appendage. She had made great play on the word and mimicked him. Then her laughter becoming filled with a self-conscious embarrassment, she had added, 'He asked me if I would dance with him, an' all.'

Biddy had looked at her daughter for a long moment before she said, 'Well, he's a man underneath his uniform and I suppose you could do worse,' which had elicited a great, 'Oh, our ma! Me and Biddle?' And Biddy had repeated, 'You and Biddle. Beggars can't be choosers, not when they're gettin' on a bit, they can't.' And again Fanny had said, 'Oh, our ma!' then stormed out of the kitchen, the skirt of her stiff print dress bobbing with each movement. But in the passage she had paused for a moment and looked towards the stillroom where Mr Peabody and Mr Biddle usually had their morning tea. Then she looked back towards the kitchen door as if viewing her mother through it; after which she wagged her head and hurried along the corridor, a tight smile on her comely face. It could be a leg up, he could become butler if old Peabody snuffed it. It was worth considering. She gave a little hitch to her step, pulled the waist of her apron straight, patted the back of her starched cap, then went into the servants' hall where two long tables were covered by starched white cloths, and on them Betty and Lizzie were laying out the extra crockery, cutlery and glasses, all loaned from the dining-room. . . .

Tilly, of course, had promised to attend the party and to see the New Year in with them, but not wishing her presence to put any restraint on them, she told herself that after drinking in the New Year she would take leave, for once she was gone then, she knew, the fun would start.

While Mark was alive, she had often listened to the laughter and song seeping up through the thick walls into their bedroom. A servants' party was allowable on New Year's Eve, and if it continued on into the early morning of New Year's Day it would have been a very mean master who would have checked it.

Mark had been no mean master but she knew that he had been irritated by the sound of gaiety and the distant thump, thump as they danced their way through the night. Of course, she had understood that the prancing about must have been a special kind of agony to a man who had been deprived of his feet, and never once during the eleven New Years that she lay by his side did she by word or sign show how she longed to be down in that hall among the Drews dancing in the New Year.

It was strange, she told herself, that she had never been to a New Year's party, not where there was meat and drink and dancing. She had seen the New Year in standing between her granda and her grandma; she had seen it in from the window of this very bedroom year after year. Then she had seen it in in America; but never, like other folk, had she known any jollity, and so in a way she was looking forward to tonight and the party. She would, under the circumstances as mistress of the house, not be able to let herself go as she once would have done, but nevertheless she told herself she would enjoy the happiness of those around her, especially the Drews, for besides being her friends, they were, she considered, her family.

She was coming down the lower part of the main staircase when she saw the dining-room door open and Fanny start to run across the hall, only to pull up at the foot of the stairs and, with head slightly bent, say, 'I'm sorry Til . . . ma'am.'

Tilly looked down on her for a moment; then, her head shaking as her lips compressed, she walked to the foot of the stairs before she said, 'And so you should be. Thank your lucky stars I'm not Peabody.'

The words were uttered in an undertone and issued with mock censure which caused Fanny's head to lower still further and her teeth to clamp down hard on her lower lip before, sedately now, she continued walking across the hall towards the kitchen.

Tilly was smiling to herself as she went towards the drawing-room, then her head turning to the side, she glimpsed between the heavy tapestry curtains draping one of the long windows, a rider dismounting on the gravel below the terrace. Going sharply to the window now, she recognised John and was also aware at this moment that Peabody had appeared as if from nowhere and was making his way towards the front door. It was as if he had smelt a visitor, or perhaps his hearing was so acute it was attuned to any unusual noise outside.

He had the door open as John came hurrying up the steps, and as Peabody reached out for his hat and cloak John thrust him aside with a wave of his hand, while addressing Tilly, saying, in a more than usual flustered fashion, 'Glad I f . . . f . . . found you in. Thought you might have g . . . g . . . gone to New . . . Newcastle.'

'What is it, John?'

She looked at his bespattered clothes, even his face showed streaks of dirt. He was leading the way now towards the morning-room – he seemed to have forgotten for the moment that he was no longer playing master – and Tilly, after a quick glance at Peabody, followed him, and not until they were both in the room and the door closed did he turn to her and say, 'It's the mine. I . . . I thought you should know. There's b . . . b . . . been an . . . an accident.'

'Oh no!' She put her hand across her mouth, then asked, 'Is it bad?'

'B . . . b . . . bad enough. One man dead, three . . . b . . . badly injured. B . . . B . . . But there are still f . . . f . . . four others down below.'

'When did it happen?'

'This . . . this morning. L . . . L . . . Last shift. They ge . . . ge . . . get careless at holiday times. It's always the way. He stumped round from her and walked to the end of the room, his hand now gripping his brow; then coming back to her again, he stood before her and his body seemed to sag as he said, 'I d . . . . . .

d . . . didn't want to trouble you but off . . . officially you are the owner, Tilly, so you had to know.'

'Of course. Of course. Where . . . where has it happened, which road?'

'Number four.'

'Number four?' she repeated. 'That's right opposite to where it happened to . . . to. . . .'

He nodded now at her, saying, 'Yes, Tilly. It's a f . . . f . . . faulty seam. And McGrath w . . . w . . . warned us. Well, at least he told Meadows. I c . . . c . . . came upon them discussing it, but Meadows w . . . w . . . wouldn't have there was anything wrong. I've never had m . . . m . . . much faith in Meadows; he never w . . . w . . . went down enough, left it all to Mc . . . McGrath. McGrath is a good enough fellow but he hasn't the responsibility and n . . . now they're b . . . b . . . both down there. . . .'

'What do you mean, both down there?'

He swallowed deeply, then swallowed again, before he said, 'They've been cau . . . caught, and two other m . . . m . . . miners, they were fur . . . further along the road."

One hand cupping her cheek now as she stared at John, but without seeing him for she was in the dark again holding Mark's twisted body, groping for stones in the blackness to support his back, tapping endlessly on the wall of rock, dropping off to sleep only to be woken by Mark's groans and at times his screams; and now Steve was down there hemmed in. Was he, too, trapped by the arms and legs . . . or his complete body?

'I'll have . . . have to get back, Tilly, but I thought. . . .'

She gave a jerk with her head as if coming out of sleep; then putting her hand on his shoulder, she said, 'Sit down a moment; you must have a drink. And . . . and listen, I'm coming back with you.'

'No! No!'

'Yes.' The word was definite. 'I'm the owner, and being so I should be there. But look' – she turned her head now towards the door – 'I've got to give them all' – she now waved her hand backwards – 'some other excuse for leaving because they're having a party tonight and they are all excited and if they knew about the fall it would spoil everything because the men would go immediately along there. As you know, they were all miners once. But they can't do anything, can they?'

'N . . . no, no. All that c . . . c . . . can be done is being done.'

'Well now, listen.' She wagged her finger at him. 'I'm going to ring for Peabody. He will get you a drink. In the meantime, I'll tell Biddy and the rest that . . . that Anna is not well and she wants to see me, eh?'

'Yes, yes, you c . . . c . . . could do that. B . . . B . . . But they'll find out t . . . tomorrow, if not before.'

'Yes, I know they will, but let them have a bit of jollification tonight. You see they've invited families and friends and they've talked of nothing else for days. I . . . we mustn't spoil it now.'

She reached out and pulled on the bell, and almost immediately there came a tap on the door and Peabody stepped into the room. But he didn't speak, he just looked at Tilly and waited, and she began, 'It is most unfortunate, Peabody, but

Mrs Sopwith isn't well and she would like to see me. I'm sorry that I'll miss the party but I'll leave it all in your hands. You must see that everybody enjoys themselves.'

'Yes, madam. Of course, madam.' His eyes flicked from her to John, taking.in his bespattered apparel, and she knew by the look on his face that he had not entirely believed what she had told him and so, on an impulse, she put in quickly, 'We must take you into our confidence, Peabody. What I have said is merely an excuse, there has been an accident at the mine. But if I let this be known to the staff, you understand that they will feel it their duty to postpone the party.'

Peabody stared at her for a moment, then said, 'I understand, madam, and I shall do as you wish. May I say that I hope the accident isn't serious.'

'I am afraid it is, Peabody.'

'I'm deeply sorry, madam. And may I add that I think it is very commendable of you to consider your staff in this way and that your gesture will be appreciated.'

She nodded at him as she said hastily now, 'Please get Master John a glass of brandy, and on your way give orders for my horse to be saddled. I shall step into the kitchen and tell them before I go to change.'

'Very good, madam.'

A few minutes later Peabody returned to the morning-room with a tray and a decanter of brandy and, after pouring out a good measure, handed it to John, saying, 'May I ask, sir, if there are any casualties?'

'One d . . . d . . . dead and three injured so f . . . far.'

'Dear, dear! And on New Year's Eve too. Strange, strange – ' He shook his head before adding, 'You would have thought that death would have left madam alone on this particular night of the year at any rate. Now wouldn't you, sir?'

'What? Oh yes, yes.'

John sipped at the brandy, then watched Peabody walk slowly from the room. Odd fellow, but then any man must be odd to want to become a butler. What had he said? You would have thought that death would have left Tilly alone on this particular night of the year. What a strange thing to say.

✌ 16 ✆

The light had already faded when they reached the mine, a slight drizzle was falling and it lent a lustre to the numerous lamps swinging backwards and forwards among the men milling around at the entrance to the drift.

After dismounting, Tilly and John pressed through the crowd of women forming a rough half-circle between the stable block to one side of the drift entrance and the offices and storerooms at the other. The half-circle was broken by the rolley way that led down into the drift from the level land above, and John had to make way for Tilly as she walked it until the way was blocked by wagons and the women crowded to the side of them. There must have been thirty or more women and children on one side of the wagons alone, yet there was no sound coming from them. Not even the children were crying or whingeing, and Tilly recognised the anxiety that creates silence, and she didn't break it as faces turned towards her but looked back into the wide staring eyes with understanding.

Then they were at the mouth of the drift and John was asking, 'Anything fur ... further?'

One of the men said, 'We're making progress, sir. We've just come out for a breather, the other lads have taken over. Can't work more than four abreast down there and ... and the air's heavy.'

When Tilly, without speaking, moved past them to make her way into the drift, one of the men put his hand on her arm and said, 'Oh no, ma'am, no, 'taint safe in there yet. They're propping up as they go but it ain't safe.'

'How many men are there down there, I mean in the rescue team?'

'Oh' – he turned and looked at his mates – 'about twelve of ours and half a dozen Hebburn men.'

'Hebburn men?' she repeated. 'No one from Mr Rosier's mine?'

'No, ma'am. An' there would be more from Hebburn I think but they're scattered like. You see it's a night for jollification an' there's only the safety men left, and ten to one they'll be bottled. But Rosier's fellows would have come if they'd known, no matter what he says, but as I said, ma'am, they go visitin' the night and nobody'll likely go back till middle shift the morrow.'

She now looked past the man and up the slope to where the band of women were divided by the wagons and, nodding towards them, she said, 'What about the women?'

'What do you mean, ma'am?' It was another man speaking now.

'Couldn't they take a turn going in and helping?'

'Huh! you've never been in there, ma'am; you're up to your waist in water in parts an' your sweat's helpin' to raise the level. You've never seen owt like it, ma'am.'

'Yes, I have seen something like it, and so have those women standing there.' She turned abruptly from them and, looking at John now, she said, 'Come along.'

It was he who had hold of her arm now, saying sternly, 'Oh no! Til ... Tilly. No!'

'Yes, John, yes.' Her voice was as loud and as stiff as his and, wrenching her arm from his, she surprised one of the bystanders by grabbing his lamp from him and hurrying into the darkness.

John was stumbling by her side now protesting all the way, and she stopped abruptly and, her voice quiet, she said to him, 'I know more about this mine than you do for the simple reason that I've worked in it. I've walked along this very road, day in day out for months. And I've experienced a fall. You seem to forget that. Now let us go and see what the trouble is.'

Fifteen minutes later she saw what the trouble was. At first the men took her for another man, seeing that she was in riding breeches, but when she spoke they gaped at her open-mouthed and one of them, straightening his back after lifting an enormous piece of rock and handing it to his mate behind him, said simply, 'Ma'am.'

'How's it going?'

'Slow, ma'am.'

Her voice had caused a pause in the rhythmic passing of the stones, and in the light of the lamps she looked at the wall of rock some yards ahead, then asked, 'Have you heard anything?'

'Oh aye, ma'am, aye.' Several of them nodded. 'They're there all right, but it's far back. There's a lot down, it'll take some time yet.'

She looked down at her feet, she was standing calf-deep in water but, unlike the rest of those present, she didn't feel it for the soft leather of her riding boots came up to just below her knees. But the men around her hadn't only wet feet, they were wringing to the skin right up to their waists, and their upper bodies were naked. She turned to John who was speaking to one of the men. He was saying, 'How long do you think . . . think it will be before you g . . . g . . . get through?' and the man answered, 'Couldn't tell sir, not at the rate we're goin'. The road's narrow and the stones have got to be moved well back, else as you see they would soon block this way.'

While John and the man went on talking she stared at the wall of rock before her and beyond which were Steve and the manager and two other men, and it wasn't likely with a fall such as this that they would have been able to save a light. And then there was the lack of air. Half an hour could make all the difference; five minutes could make all the difference between life and death when you were short of air. If anything should happen to Steve she would have lost her only lifelong friend. The thought came to her like a revelation. There was no one alive now that she had known as long as Steve, there was no one in her life had been so faithful to her as Steve, there was no one she could talk to now as she did to Steve. If anything should happen to him a new aloneness would enter into her being; only Biddy and Steve were her kind of people and Biddy was old and could die tomorrow. But Steve was young . . . well, in his full manhood, and he could die tonight.

When she turned about and ran stumbling back through the water of the drift John, coming behind her, cried, 'Ti . . . Tilly! Ti . . . Tilly! wait. What is it?'

So swift was she running that he still hadn't overtaken her before she came out of the drift and into the open air. Straightaway, pushing her way through the men, she made for the women and, lifting her lamp high, she yelled into their amazed faces, 'How many of you have worked down below?'

To her surprise no one answered her for the moment; but then a hand went up here and there and a voice said, 'Me, ma'am. Me, missis.' Of the crowd on this side of the wagons not more than eight responded; and when, having squeezed herself between two bogies, she put the same question to the women on the other side, she wasn't aware that she was speaking in a voice no longer representing Mrs Sopwith but that of Tilly Trotter, the girl before she had come under the guidance of Mr Burgess, the tutor, and what she cried was, 'Will you come below an hour at a time an' help move the stones back?'

'Aye, aye. Oh aye, ma'am. Anything's better than standin' here waitin'.'

But when the women moved up abreast of the men near the mouth of the drift they were halted with gruff cries of, 'No bloody fear! you're not goin' in there,' and 'Those days are gone.' And 'It's men's work. Now get back, the lot of you!'

'If I can go in there they can.' Tilly was facing them. 'For the first turn I'll take eight women with me. We'll do an hour at a time.'

Of a sudden silence fell on them again, at least on the men. They stood stiffly staring at this woman who had made a name for herself, and a queer one at that, but she owned the mine and was willing to go in and hump with the rest, which was something when all was said and done, and her living soft for years.

When the women pushed their way through the menfolk there were no more protests and Tilly said quietly now, 'Just eight of you.' And on this she went ahead, John again by her side and muttering now, 'My G ... G ... God! Tilly. If anything should hap ... happen to you.' And now looking at him tenderly and because of the concern on his face, she whispered under her breath, 'Nothing can happen to a witch, John, that she doesn't want to happen.'

And as he said, 'Oh, Tilly, things li ... li ... like that c ... c ... can court dis ... disaster,' she thought painfully, Yes, maybe you're right. All her life she had courted disaster and this might be just one more time, and a voice cried from deep within her and from out of the pit blackness she remembered so well, 'Hang on, Steve. Hang on.' And it sounded as if she were talking to Mark, encouraging him to live, to keep breathing.

The first shift of women worked like Trojans. They passed the stones back right to the junction of the roads where they were piled up against the walls.

Against John's protest, she also accompanied the second batch of women in; but within a short time she had to come out and rest. It wasn't because her arms or her back were aching, it was the constriction in her chest. Her lungs had been free of dust for years and she was taking badly to it now. She sat in the office quite alone for a time to recover herself. John had gone in again with another shift of men and what was most gratifying was that pitmen from other mines were making their appearance in ones and twos having heard in a roundabout way of the disaster. There were men from as far away as Felling who had walked the six miles in the rain to help.

When she looked at the round-faced clock on the office wall she thought there must be some mistake for it couldn't be twenty minutes to eight. Surely she hadn't been here all of four and a half hours.

The thought brought her to her feet and she picked up the lamp and went out into the night again. The rain was coming down steadily now but she found it cooling on her face. As she neared the entrance to the drift she felt the excitement: there was no silence now but a combined chatter.

'Ma'am! Ma'am! I think they're nearly through. They can hear the knockin' clearer.'

She said nothing, but hurried through them and, almost running down the rolley way, she came to the junction where the women turned to her with their sweat-smeared faces eager with the news. 'They can hear 'em plain, ma'am. Heard a voice they did.'

She passed through them and into the water which now flooded into the top of her boots, but which did not make her shiver for it felt warm, and she looked to where a man was shouting into the stone: 'That you, sir? You all right, sir?'

She did not hear the mumbled reply and she only just stopped herself from shouting, 'Ask if Mr McGrath is all right.'

A man turned to her now and said, 'Another hour, ma'am, at the outside should see us through.'

'Good. Good.' She nodded at him and smiled, and he jerked his head at her and with renewed energy began to lift the great blocks of stone as if they were house bricks.

It took more than the hour to get through to the trapped men. It was quarter to eleven when they pulled the first man through. He was unconscious but still alive. The second man had a smashed arm and a broken ankle. The manager was in a very bad way, having been pinned down by a beam. The only one who had apparently escaped injury was Steve, but after he had helped to ease the manager through the hole and had himself crawled through he swayed as the men helped him to his feet. But saying, 'Thanks, lads, thanks. I'm all right, I'm all right,' he stumbled unaided towards the junction. And it was there that Tilly saw him, and he saw her. He might have passed her but for the fact that, hatless, her white hair, now looking a dirty grey, caught his eye. He paused before walking towards her and saying casually, 'What do you think you're up to?'

And she, swallowing deeply and blinking at him, said just as casually, 'I'm after a job.' The men and women around laughed, but their laughter was high, and had an unnatural sound.

When John, addressing Steve, said, 'Are you . . . are you all right, Mr McGrath?' there seemed to be a pause before Steve answered, 'Yes, yes, I'm all right, sir.'

Tilly's eyes now travelled over Steve. There was no sign of injury on his arms or face but she could see that he must have been up to his neck in water for a time for he was still wearing his shirt and there was a deep rim of black scum around the collar, and she knew enough about the pit to remember where the water last touched it always left its mark. As she stood there the years fell away from her and she was back in this junction watching tiny children crawling out of the side roads, some of the roads no higher than three feet, which didn't allow for a child to stand up, not if he or she was over six years old. She saw them dragging the iron harness from between their legs or pulling the leather band that was attached to the skip from their foreheads and then dropping where they stood, some of their faces wet with sweat, others with tears, and surprisingly one or two here and there had laughter on their lips.

The law had been passed in 1842 prohibiting children from working in the mines but little or no notice was taken of it in many quarters, for who was to know what went on down below, and inspections, like miracles, happened rarely. Often, too, the men of the family were with the masters in this, for how, they reasoned, could a man be expected to bring up a large family on a pitman's wage. No; a shilling a week was a shilling a week, however it was earned.

When she herself had come to work down here late in 1838 the sights, the stench, the weariness, the labour, the long hours in dimness, the vileness of the language, the exposure of the human body in all its undignified postures, and the almost animal viciousness of some of the workers, coupled at the same time with a comradeship which would herd them together in times of stress, brought into her awakening knowledge a side of humanity dragged out of human beings by the environment they were forced to live in. Only in after years, when looking back, had she realised the lessons she had learned in those long months below ground.

'C ... C ... Come, you're all in.'

She blinked and turned to John who had taken her by the arm, and when he said, 'I'll ge ... get you home and then. ...' she cut him short, saying, 'No, no; there's no need. I'm all right; Anna will be waiting for you and worrying. I'll ... I'll ride back part of the way with Steve.'

She turned her head to where Steve was walking a little behind her and she asked, 'Will you be fit to ride?'

'Aye.' His answer was brief.

And now John turned to him and said, 'W ... W ... Would you be able to see Mrs Sop ... Sopwith home, McGrath?'

Again Steve paused before answering, when he merely said, 'Aye,' not even adding 'sir' now.

Tilly cast her glance back at him and because of the dirt covering his face she could not see the expression on it nor that in his eyes for his head was bent slightly forward and his gaze directed towards the rough track as if, she thought, he was making sure of where he planted his feet. Once more she wanted to ask, 'Are you all right?' but John was speaking again: 'I really think I sh ... sh ... should go b ...... back with you at this time of night; McGrath w ... w ... will want to get cleaned up and rested. It must have been a pretty stiff time in there.' He turned and glanced at Steve, but Steve was still looking towards his feet.

'John, please' – she tugged at his arm 'I'll be perfectly all right. It's you who needs to get home and rested. Now say no more, Steve will see me to the gate and with a bit of luck I may be able to join the New Year party after all.'

'The staff p ... p ... party? Yes' – John nodded at her – 'and we have guests c ... c ... coming too as you know. But this has certainly put the damper on it for me. If only that one hadn't died, and Mr Meadow in s ... s ... such a bad way.' He hung his head. 'The others, well, they can be p ... p ... patched up, but I hate to lose a man in the m ... mine.'

She nodded at him in silence now; she had forgotten about the first man they had brought out. What was his name? Fox. Andrew Fox. Well, she would see to his widow and children. She could do that, and she could erase the fear of the family being turned out on the road. She would give the wife a pension.

As she walked up the rise into the open air where the sky was high with stars now for the rain had stopped, she looked upwards for a moment as she thought. It's as if I had just come back.

'Now you're sh ... sh ... sure, Tilly?'

'Oh, John' – she shook her head impatiently at him – 'get on your horse and get home. Tell Anna a happy New Year from me. I'll pop over as soon as possible.

Come along, let us get the horses.' She made to move away, but then stopped and waited. The women and men who had followed them out of the drift, seeing her standing there, stopped one after the other; and when the last one had put in an appearance she spoke to them, saying simply, 'Thank you very much. Thank you all very much. And I'm sure you men will realise what a great help your women have been to you tonight. And those you have rescued will I am sure want to thank you, too, when the time comes. Please tell Mrs Fox not to worry, she and her family will be seen to. What is more I can tell you now, I intend to build two new rows of cottages in order to house you in better conditions.'

No one spoke until she said, 'Good-night to you all,' when, as she turned away there was a chorus of, 'Good-night. Goodnight, ma'am. Happy New Year ma'am. Thank you, ma'am.'

When they reached the office, John, as if just remembering something, turned to Steve and said, 'What about the p . . . p . . . pumps? that water is deep down there.'

'I'll see to that afore I leave, sir. Sanderson, Briggs, and Morley will deputise for the night; they'll see to things and I'll be back first thing in the morning.'

'Oh, well. Thank you, McGrath. Thank you. You've had a l . . . l . . . long ordeal and must be very tired.'

'Not when you reckon some of the falls, sir. This one was just a matter of a few hours. I'm sorry about Fox though; he was a good man, in many ways.'

'Yes, yes he was. And you yourself were lucky to c . . . c. come out unscathed.'

Steve did not reply for John had turned to Tilly asking, 'Now are are you sure . . . ?' only to be cut off by her voice, weary-sounding now, saying, 'Yes, yes, John, I am sure. Now please get yourself home.'

'W . . . W . . . Well, if you insist. Good . . . Good-night, my dear.'

'Good-night, John.' She put her hand on his arm and guided him to the door where he turned and called, 'Good-night, McGrath.'

'Good-night, sir.'

Alone with Tilly now, Steve, pointing to a chair, said, 'Sit yourself down, Tilly; you look just how I feel. Would you mind waiting another ten minutes or so?'

'Not at all. Go and do what you have to do.'

Without further words he left the room. With his going her body seemed to slump, and she bent forward and looked at her hands. Like her clothes, they, too, were black with coal dust. When she touched her face she could feel the grit on it and she guessed that her hair would no longer be looking white. Of a sudden she felt weak, almost faint. Twisting her body round, she put her forearm on the rough wooden desk that fronted the window, the window at which she had stood and given in her name before making her first trip into the mine. 'Tilly Trotter . . . spinster,' the keeker had said. That memory seemed to belong to another life. But tonight's memory was fresh in her mind and it was with a deep sorrow that she thought: Why do people have to work and slave like that, to run the risk of being trapped or of dying in the dark? And the answer that came to her was simply, money. Yes, that was it, money. Wasn't she herself making money out of the labour of these people? Yet were she to close the mine tomorrow, would it help them? No, their condition would be worse than that which they suffered when working down below, for if they were allowed to spend their days above ground the majority of them would starve for there wasn't enough work to be had for them.

Sighing now, she leant her forearm on the desk and laid her head upon it. . . .

It was some twenty minutes later when she was startled by a touch on her shoulder and Steve's voice saying, 'You all right, Tilly?'

'Oh yes, yes. I . . . I must have dropped off.'

'And no wonder. Well, the horses are ready. Come on.' He took her elbow and raised her up; then lifting the lantern from the table, he led the way out.

The horses were standing in the yard and after fastening the lantern to the side of his saddle, he came round to where Tilly had one foot in the stirrup and, putting his hand under her other heel, he helped her to mount.

When they reached the cottage she drew her horse to a halt, saying, 'Come no further, Steve, you're worn out. Just give me the lantern and I can make my way.'

When he didn't answer her, she peered at him, saying, 'What is it, Steve?' and when her hand went out and touched his shoulder and he visibly winced and drew his head down, she said again, 'What is it?'

'Nothing, nothing. Come on.' He went to urge the horse forward, but she swiftly leaned across and pulled on the reins, saying, 'You're hurt. Your shoulder? Get down. Get down.' Without further ado she dismounted and went to his side and, tugged at the bottom of his coat, saying, 'Come on, get down.'

Silently now he obeyed her; then leading his horse, he took it through the gate and up the path, and she followed.

When the animals were housed in the rude stable and he muttered, 'They've got to be seen to,' she said, 'Go on in, I'll see to them.' Again she was surprised when he obeyed her. Quickly she brought water and hay for the beasts, then hurried into the house. Steve was sitting in the old rocking chair to the side of the banked fire. He was leaning forward, his elbows on his knees, his hands slack and joined between them. Without any preamble she stood in front of him and said, 'Where are you hurt?'

Simply he answered, 'My back.'

'Here, let me get your coat off.'

When he pulled himself to his feet she eased off his coat. His striped blue shirt was black, and she noticed right away that the front of it hung loose but the back seemed stuck to his skin, and when she touched it she saw his teeth clench and his face muscles knot.

'Why didn't you say?' she said harshly. 'You should have gone to hospital with the rest and seen the doctor. Was it the stone?'

He moved his head once, then said abruptly, 'Aye, it pinned me for a time.'

Swiftly she went to the fire, took the bellows and blew into the bottom bars. Then she lifted the lid of the big black kettle that was standing on the hob, dipped her finger into it and, finding it hot, took it up and, hurrying into the scullery, she groped in the dark for the tin dish that in her day she had kept under the sink – as Steve had once told her he had never altered anything – and so she found it immediately.

A few minutes later she set the dish of warm water on the mat before the hearth, then said to him, 'Get on your knees.'

Slowly he obeyed her.

Again and again she wrung out the towel and placed it across the torn shirt on his back, taking off the coal dust while at the same time soaking the garment loose from his skin.

When at last she was able to pull the shirt over his head, her own features screwed up at the sight of his shoulders. There were three deep cuts on them and, added to this, the skin had been sheared off for some six or eight inches across the shoulder blades.

'Oh, you are a fool you know, Steve. What do you think you're up to? Playing the brave man with a back like this! It looks flayed.'

He gave no answer but made to rise from his knees, only to be checked by her, saying, 'Look, stay where you are; these cuts have got to be cleaned or else you're in for trouble. I must get some fresh water.'

When she returned from the scullery, he was no longer on his knees but sitting on a low cracket in front of the now bright fire, and when she began to bathe the raw coal-dust-infested flesh he made no movement whatever. She had been about to say, 'Am I hurting you?' but she knew that to be a silly question. He must be going through agony for she was having to rub at the raw flesh to get the dust free. What he needed was to lie in water. Now if it had been summer he could have gone into the river. But it wasn't summer, it was New Year's Eve. Strange, but she had forgotten it was New Year's Eve.

After she had cleaned the wounds as best she could, she said, 'What I need is fat. Have you got anything at all like that?'

'There's a jar of goose dripping in the cupboard.' He jerked his head, and to this she said, 'Oh, good; good. There's nothing better.'

Gently now, she pressed the goose fat into the raw patches of flesh; and then she asked, 'Where do you keep your clean shirts?'

When he pointed to the bedroom and said, 'In the chest,' she looked towards the far door, saying, 'I'll have to take the lantern for a minute.'

She was surprised when she lifted the lid of the chest to see what she imagined to be about a dozen shirts lying in a neat pile. He looked after himself, did Steve. And that was good. She liked that.

In the room once more, she went to put the shirt over his head but he took it firmly from her hands and, getting to his feet, he put it on. Then for the first time he spoke lightly, saying, 'I'm not going to tuck it into these,' pointing to his dirty trousers, and he walked from her towards the bedroom. But there, in the doorway, he turned, saying, 'You could do with having your own face washed, Tilly.'

'Yes, yes.' She smiled wearily at him. 'I think I'll do just that. And then a cup of tea wouldn't come in wrong, would it?'

'No, you're right there, it wouldn't. Take the lantern into the scullery with you, the fire is enough light for me.'

'Yes, yes, I will, Steve. . . .'

It was about fifteen minutes later when they sat, one each side of the hearth, sipping gratefully at mugs of steaming tea that had been laced with whisky, and after Steve had drained his mug he leant forward and, looking towards the fire, said, 'I've known some New Year's Eves but this is the strangest.'

'I think I could say the same, Steve. What time is it?'

They both lifted their gaze to the high mantelpiece and almost simultaneously they said, 'Ten to twelve.'

'We should be hearing the hooters soon.'

She nodded at him, 'Yes, yes. I've forgotten the sound of the ship's hooters. . . . How you feeling now?'

'Much better; a lot of fuss about nothing.'

'Nothing!' She turned her head to the side. 'Good job you can't see your back. And you won't be fit to go in in the morning.'

'Oh, don't you worry. Never fear, I'll be there in the morning.'

'I think you should see a doctor.'

'After you've been at me?' He smiled at her. 'I don't need any doctor now. Anyway, I've got good healing flesh, it'll be as right as rain in a few days.'

'That's as may be.' She reached out now and put her mug on the wooden table, then said, 'There's one thing I do know, you're not moving out of this house tonight again. I'll make my own way home.'

As she rose to her feet he too rose, saying quietly, 'And there's one thing I know an' all, and that is you're not making your own way home. What will happen if you meet up with some of the lads out on the spree bringing in the New Year from here to Gateshead?'

'I can be home within half an hour, and I don't suppose they'll start their rounds much before one.'

She had been smiling gently but now the smile slid from her face as she saw the expression on his, and when he said quietly, 'Stay and see the New Year in with me, Tilly,' something in his voice caused her to lower her gaze. Stay and see the New Year in with me. It sounded an ordinary request; but what happened when the church bells rang and the ships' hooters blared, when the factory buzzers shrilled into the night? You shook hands, you looked into faces as you said a happy New Year, a happy New Year, and those you loved you kissed. Yet she couldn't be so churlish as to refuse his request. And anyway, they would see the New Year in together were she to allow him to accompany her home. Yet she knew in her heart it would be a different thing to stand in a room, the door closed, waiting for the first sound to herald in the New Year, the year that was to bring happiness, work and money galore, the seeming fervent desire of every ordinary Northerner, for hope sprang eternal in their breasts.

Her decision was, however, taken from her when from a distance, like that of a hunting horn, came the sound of a ship's siren, and Steve, turning and looking at the clock, said, 'It must be slow. Come. Come on Tilly,' and took her hand and drew her to the door and there, pulling it open, they stood looking out into the starlit night, with the sounds of sirens, hooters and bells filling the air.

Her hand still in his, they had stood for some seconds silent when, turning to her, he looked into her face and, his voice soft, he said, 'A happy New Year, Tilly.'

'And the same to you. A happy New Year, Steve.'

He had caught her other hand and was holding them tightly against his breast now and when he murmured, 'Oh, Tilly, Tilly!' she went to withdraw from his hold, but he gripped her hands still more firmly, and with the sound of a break in his voice he muttered, 'Every New Year that I can remember, Tilly, I've wished only for one thing, and you know what that is. No, no; let me speak, just this once.'

Still retaining his hold on her, he drew her back into the room, pushing the door closed with his foot as he did so, and now to her bent head he said, 'Part of me, the sensible part of me keeps ramming it home that the situation for me is hopeless, worse than ever it was, you the lady of the manor, me little more than a hewer down the pit... well, only a couple of steps up and likely to remain there. Forget her, I've said. Marry, I've said. And I've tried; God knows I've tried. Twice I've been on the verge of it, only to withdraw because it wasn't in me to make another woman's life a hell. One can put up with one's own hell but inflicting it on somebody else, that's another thing. But now for the other side of me, the side that lives in a dream. This side sees a man who doesn't work down the pit, who speaks well, dresses well, can carry himself in any company. This man can go to the lady of the manor and say, "I love you, Tilly. I've always loved you. Marry me." But this fellow only comes alive at night, and he's never there in the morning. But it's night now, Tilly.... No! No! Keep still; just let me hold your hands, just this once, please!' His voice had risen from a murmur and the last word was not asked in the form of a plea but more of a demand, it was as if he were saying, 'You owe me something for my constancy over the years,' and it brought her head up and her eyes, misty now, looking into his. And as she stared at this man whose love had been an irritation to her in her youth, there came over her the most strange feeling, and somewhere in the far recesses of her mind a voice was repeating: How many times can we love? It was a question she had asked herself on the very day Matthew expressed his passion for her, and she knew that she loved him although she had loved his father, and once long, long ago she had loved Simon Bentwood too. And now this feeling was rising in her again, this warmth, this desire to enfold, to be enfolded, this longing to be at one and the same time a wife, a mother, mistress, and friend.... But she knew that all she could ever be to this man, to this man whom she was seeing with new clear eyes, all she could ever be was a friend.

Yet more than friendship must have seeped upwards into her eyes for the next moment she found herself for the very first time crushed within the circle of his arms. The thumping of his heart reached through her clothes and penetrated her skin, and when his lips fell on hers and covered her mouth she neither succumbed nor resisted. She was only aware that at one point she had the desire to put her arms about him but told herself that his back was sore – she hadn't said to herself, 'You mustn't do this.'

After he released her lips he still held her tightly, his breath seeming to come from deep within his lungs, and it was some time before he said, 'I'm... I'm not going to apologise, Tilly, I've done it. It'll likely be all I'll ever have of you, but it's something to remember.'

When his arms finally released her, she staggered and he had to clutch at her again. Then he was sitting her in the chair near the fire once more. He did not sit opposite her but remained standing, looking down at her; and now he said, 'Say something, Tilly.'

When she didn't speak he said, 'I'm going to tell you something. Deny it if you like, but I know it's true. You in your own way are as lonely as I am. And another thing I'll tell you. You've changed your opinion of me of late. Once you saw me as a sop of a lad, at least soppy over you. I pestered you. If I'd had more sense I might have made better weather of it. And yet, no; you have to work out your own destiny. But now you're back, not where you started, true, yet on the same ground. But at the top of it. Master John, though, and all his kin, no matter how good they are, they're not your type, Tilly, not your people. You look like a lady now, you talk like a lady, you act like one, but underneath I still see you as Tilly, Tilly Trotter. Will you tell me something truthfully? Look at me, Tilly.'

Slowly she raised her head to him, to this Steve McGrath who looked every inch a virile man, and the beat of her heart quickened, and what he was saying now was, 'Imagine you had come back, but not in a high position, and I was as I am today and you were seeing me differently, would there have been a chance for me?'

She closed her eyes tightly now and her head was bowed again as she said, 'Oh Steve! Steve! don't ask me such a question, because I cannot answer it. I . . . I can only tell you I'd be happy to have you as a friend.'

'Aye well' – he gave a short laugh and sighed deeply – 'that's something. But that'll only be until you marry again.'

Her head jerked up quickly now and, her face straight, her voice sharp, she said, 'I'll never marry again, Steve.'

'Don't be silly.'

It was odd but that is what Luke had said, don't be silly; and now Steve went on almost to repeat Luke's statement: 'You won't be able to help yourself. Anyway, men won't let you,' he too said, adding, 'I'd like to take a bet on it that within two years' time there'll be a man in the Manor sitting at the head of your table.'

'You'd lose your bet, Steve, definitely you'd lose your bet.'

He bowed his head towards her and his eyes narrowed now as he said, 'You seem very sure of that, Tilly.'

'I am, Steve.'

'Why? There must be a reason.'

'There is.'

'Can you tell me?'

Could she tell him? Twice in a week could she divulge the promise she had made to Matthew? Yes, she could. She would have to, if only to stop him hoping. Looking up at him, she said, 'I promised Matthew on his deathbed that I'd never marry again.'

'You what!'

It was odd, men's reactions seemed to be alike. Even his features had taken on the expression which had been on Luke's face.

'You mean to say your husband asked you not to marry again?'

'Yes.'

'Well' – he shook his head slowly from side to side – 'all that I can say now is that you must be slightly crazy if you stick to it.'

'A promise to the dying is a promise, Steve.'

'Aw, to hell with that!' He swung round from her, then back again, pointing at her now and saying, 'Look, Tilly. It nearly broke me up when you married him. I hated his guts then; that was nothing though to what I feel about him at this minute. But I'm going to say this, rather than live your life alone I would come to your wedding the morrow. What kind of a man was he anyway to make you promise such a thing? A selfish bugger at best. That's swearing to it, but that doesn't describe his mentality. To my mind it's just as well he died because he would have had you caged.'

It was really uncanny how alike his reactions were to Luke's. She rose to her feet now, saying wearily, 'I'm tired, Steve, very tired,' and the sound of her voice and the look on her face made him immediately contrite and he said, 'I'm sorry, too, Tilly. I've forgotten what you've been through an' all the night. You're the one who should have been taken home and washed and seen to. I'm sorry, I really am.'

'Don't be, Steve. I'm glad it's in the open, and you're right when you say I'm lonely. I'd be happy and proud to have you as a friend, Steve, always, but at the same time I don't want you to waste any more years on me. There are so many women who would jump at the chance of you.'

'Aye well, you'd better get them lined up and I'll sort them over.' He smiled a twisted smile; then holding out his hand, he said, 'I say again, Tilly, a happy New Year.'

As she put hers into it she replied, 'And to you, Steve, and to you, and many of them.'

PART TWO

 cons80 Below the Skin cons80

৩ 1 ৫৯

Lucy Bentwood straightened up and looked down at the broad expanse of her husband's naked back and she said, 'For goodness sake, Simon, stop whingeing like a bairn without a bottle!'

'Don't you dare use that tone to me – !' The next word, 'woman!', was stifled by a sharp cry as he tried to turn from his face to confront his wife. Resting on his elbow, his body now half turned towards her, he gasped, 'You think you've got me where you want me, don't you, half paralysed? You wouldn't have taken that tone a few. . . .'

The flat of her hand on his shoulders thrust him downwards, and with laughter in her voice now, she said, 'I've always taken that tone with you, and you know it. If I hadn't, I wouldn't have been able to suffer you.'

When he made no comment on this statement, the smile slid from her face and, reaching out for a bottle of liniment, she poured some on to the palm of her hand, then applied it to his spine, and as she rubbed her hand rhythmically up and down his back she thought with a sadness that she never showed to him of how true her words had been, for if she hadn't laughed at him she would, many a time, have cried because her patient and happy nature had been sorely tried by him in so many ways; not alone by the scrapings of his love that he gave her but which she felt was compensated for by the son and daughter she had reared, but with the knowledge that his mind was filled with the want of the woman who had beguiled him from her very childhood and whose memory until a few years ago had driven him again and again to bouts of drinking.

The night he fell off his horse in a drunken stupor and lay in the cold ditch for hours she took to be a blessing, for from that time his back had been affected, so much so that he was in constant pain, there were times when he couldn't move for days on end. Even when he was mobile he found it agony to walk the farm. No longer could he ride a horse, and the jolting of the pony trap was agony to him, so his visits to the village and the inn were few and far between. But what she was more thankful for was that he could not now keep an eye on his daughter.

He had always been possessive of Noreen, but from the day her young brother inadvertently told his father that they had met up and talked with Mrs Sopwith's pair, life had hardly been worth living. Noreen was only fourteen at the time and her brother not yet twelve, they were mere children, but his reaction was such that, had he heard they had been behaving indecently with the young couple from the Manor, his wrath couldn't have been worse. What her daughter's life would have been like if her father hadn't happened the accident, Lucy didn't dare to think because Noreen had inherited some of his own independent spirit and from the beginning had baulked at the bit he had put in her mouth.

But now she was riding free – Lucy turned her head and looked towards the bedroom window as her thoughts followed her daughter – she hoped not too free. She knew where she was at this minute and she dreaded with a great dread that the knowledge of what her daughter was about would ever reach the ears of her father. Yet if she knew Noreen, the time would come when she and her father would stand face to face and the truth would be out. And then God help them all.

Noreen Bentwood was of medium height; her hair was a deep rich brown and thick with a natural wave to it; her eyes were hazel and set in sloping sockets in her oval-shaped face; her skin did not look delicate but slightly weathered; her cheeks were red, as was her large well-shaped mouth. She carried herself straight and placed her feet firmly, her walk always suggesting she was off to some place. And on this particular Sunday afternoon she was certainly off to some place for she was going to the burn, to what she termed the little island. It should happen that the little island was the same spot hidden by the half-circle of scrub where Steve McGrath had fished as a boy, and where one day he had sat watching a salmon, protecting it as it were.

Every Sunday for the last two years, except when the snow lay so thick that it was impossible to get to the bank, she had made this journey, and on each occasion she had met and talked with Willy Sopwith, sometimes for minutes only, other times as long as an hour.

Nearly always, on her journey, she would recall the first time she had come upon him. She was then almost fourteen, and it was on a Sunday too. She and Eddie had been walking by the river bank. They had rounded the curve by the bushes and there saw this young man sitting fishing. She remembered how he lifted his head upwards at their approach; then rising from the bank, he had stood peering at them with his head to one side. And she knew this was the son of their landlady, the woman who had made a name for herself, the woman whom her father hated because he had once loved her and she had turned him down. This information she had managed to get out of her mother only recently, when she asked the question, 'Why does Dad hate Mrs Sopwith?' and her mother, who was always honest with her, told her why. The information lowered her opinion of her father yet another peg because she considered her mother to be a wonderful woman and her father a fool for still entertaining thoughts of a notorious lady while possessing a wife such as he had.

Noreen had always felt that she was older than her years and when on that Sunday the tall fair-haired young man said, 'Hello, little girl,' she forgot, or chose to ignore, the attitude a tenant-farmer's daughter should pay to the gentry who owned their land and answered, 'Little girl yourself! I'm coming fourteen, and there's nothing I can't do on the farm, and I intend to learn blacksmithing.'

She had expected him to laugh at her but what he said was, 'I'm sorry. I didn't realise you were such an age, or so talented, but I wouldn't go in for blacksmithing if I were you . . . well, not if I had your voice.'

At this she had ignored her brother's tugging at her arm and replied, 'What's wrong with my voice?'

'Nothing, nothing at all; it sounds a lovely voice, I'm sure you must be able to sing.'

She had paused while staring at him, then had said in a modified tone, 'Well, yes, yes I can sing. I sing in the choir and I've sung solos.'

'I wasn't wrong then?'

She had found nothing to say to this and she had been about to walk towards him to see what he had caught when around from the far end of the bushed river bank there came 'the other one from the house'. She had seen her before from a distance, in fact she had seen them both from a distance but never close enough, as now, to speak to. She transferred her stare to the slight figure approaching them, and noted with amazement that the girl, who was about her own size, which was then five feet, appeared much smaller because she was so thin. Everything about her was thin, her body, her face, her hands, her feet, she looked like a large chocolate-coloured doll, a beautiful chocolate-coloured doll. When she spoke it was not to her but to her adopted brother, so called, her father said, and her words, clear and high sounding, were, 'What have we here? Did you catch them, Willy?' Then she laughed, and her laughter, like her voice, was something that Noreen had never heard before, they were both strange, musical, she couldn't put an exact name to the sounds except that they recalled some of the notes Mr Byers struck on his harp. But what she did know instinctively was that she didn't like the dark individual. She guessed she'd be snooty, high-handed, and this urged her to shout, 'No, he didn't fish us up, miss, but he could have you, by the looks of you.' And on this, she grabbed her brother's hand and, turning about, walked quickly back round the bend and along the bank, her step causing Eddie to run and to protest, 'Aw, give over, our Norah, you're pullin' me arm out.'

It was this incident that Eddie had related innocently in his father's hearing which evoked such wrath as they hadn't before witnessed in him. . . .

It was a full year later when Noreen next met Willy Sopwith. She was with the dogs at the far end of the land. A sheep had become caught up in the wire fencing and she was trying to extricate him. The wild barking of the dogs had drawn the attention of a rider on the top road. Glancing up, she saw him and she knew by the way he turned his head that it was young Sopwith.

He dismounted and came down the bank towards her, but she went on with what she was doing, and Willy said, 'Can I give you a hand?' and to this she answered briefly, 'You'll have to get over the fence and push him from yon side.'

And this he did; and after the sheep was free and racing down the field bleating with relief, they stood looking at each other. She had grown considerably during the past year and he remarked on this, smiling as he said, 'I had better not make the same mistake I did at our last meeting,' and she, finding herself smiling back at him, said, 'No, you'd better not.' Then peering towards the wire, he said, 'Couldn't one of your men have come and done this?'

'They're at the market, and Father has hurt his back.'

'Oh, I'm sorry.'

It was on the point of her tongue to say, 'I'm not,' and she knew she would have been speaking the truth because over the past year her father had hardly let her out of his sight. He had always wanted her alongside him, much more so than he ever wanted Eddie, which seemed strange to her. But of late she hadn't even been allowed to go to church on her own. Although he himself never entered the place he took her there and waited for her coming out again. As she had remarked to her mother, he had become like a jailer. But this last week she had known freedom and had revelled in it, as she was doing at this moment.

Looking up into Willy Sopwith's face she saw that he was beautiful and a great pity arose in her for his condition. She knew the cause of it had been them McGraths from the village, yet some of the older folk said it would never have happened if his mother hadn't been a witch. She had seen his mother out riding but to her the odd things about her were her hair which was very white and that she sat a horse like a man and wore breeches. Otherwise, like her son, she had a beautiful face.

He had asked, 'What is your name?' and she had answered, 'Noreen. But I don't care much for it, I prefer Norah.'

When he said, 'I'm Willy Sopwith,' she answered, 'Yes, I know.' And then he had laughed. He had put his head back and laughed, and while one part of her felt annoyed, another was amazed that with his handicap he could be so cheerful. He seemed a happy individual. She didn't know many men who were happy, in fact she didn't know any men who were happy.

When she had demanded 'What's funny?' he had stopped, then after a moment said, 'You know, really I couldn't say, it was just . . . well, how you took the wind out of my polite introduction.'

There had followed a pause, and then he had said, 'Do you go to the games?'

'Yes, sometimes.'

'I might see you there then?'

'Are you showing something?' she had asked.

'No, no.' He shook his head; then added, 'I like to watch the wrestling.'

'Wrestling?' A memory was stirring in her. She had heard that the almost blind fellow from the house boxed, or fought, or did something like that with one of the hands.

'You sound surprised.'

'Yes, well, I am a bit. I . . . I thought it was only the rough 'uns who went to see wrestling and things like that.'

'Well, perhaps I'm a rough 'un.'

'You don't look it, you don't look . . . well.'

'Well what?'

'Well, the type that would be interested in wrestling.'

'Oh! Now let me tell you, miss' – he had assumed a pompous air – 'it is said that I am quite good at the game, myself, depending upon my sparring partner.'

'Indeed! Indeed!' She, too, had now assumed an attitude and when she added, 'My! My! the things you hear when your ears are clear,' he laughed again and she with him.

And that's how it began.

During the following year they might not meet up for weeks, and then it would be only in passing, but she learned a lot about him during that time. She learned, to her further amazement, that he did a stint at the mine, some three days a week, and that he also went into Newcastle to study engineering. But how he managed this with his one good eye, which didn't seem to be all that good the way he had to peer through it, amazed her. But what surprised her most was his cheerfulness. With a handicap such as his she wouldn't have been surprised if he had been morose and had shunned people; but he seemed to like company, and he was never at a loss for an answer, or to ask a question.

Then came her sixteenth birthday. Her mother had bought her a new coat and bonnet. The coat was grey cord with blue facings and a cape to the shoulders, and the bonnet was blue velvet trimmed with grey. She had never had anything so smart in her life and she felt that all eyes were on her when she stood up in church to sing on the Sunday morning. When the service was over she had hurried away because there was no father waiting to escort her home; not even Eddie was there to accompany her, for he was in bed with a cold. So she was alone when she met up with Willy.

He wasn't astride a horse today, nor was he sitting on the bank fishing, he was walking slowly along the road accompanied by a dog; and it wasn't a presentable animal, not like their own sheepdogs. He was the first to speak, saying, 'Why, hello. It's you, isn't it?'

'Yes, it is me,' she had answered pertly. 'Who else?'

'Well, you must excuse me if I didn't recognise you at first, you look dressed for town and very pretty.'

'Which means I suppose that when I'm not dressed for town I don't look pretty?' She was smiling as she spoke and she expected him to laugh, but on this occasion he didn't. With his face to the side he stared at her before saying, 'I meant no such thing. I've always considered you pretty, more so, rather beautiful at times.'

She could give no answer to this; no one had ever told her she was bonny, let alone beautiful. The little mirror in her bedroom had assured her that she was . . . all right, perhaps not as pretty as Maggie Thompson from the village, but much better looking than the Rainton twins.

Into her silence he now asked quietly, 'Will you be out walking this afternoon?'

'I may be,' she said; 'I cannot promise. My mother will be making me a tea, it's my birthday.'

'Oh, may you have many, many more. How old are you? Seventeen?'

There was a moment before she said with apparent reluctance, 'No, sixteen.'

'Yes, of course.' It was as if he were recalling the day she had stated emphatically that she was nearly fourteen.

The dog surprised her now by coming up and sniffing at her and when he licked her gloved hand she patted his head, saying, 'He's a friendly fellow. What breed is he?'

'An Irish hound.'

'What's his name?'

'Pat. You couldn't call an Irish hound anything else, could you?'

'No.' She laughed gently, then said, 'I must be on my way. Good-bye.'

'Good-bye.'

She knew that he hadn't walked on but was standing still and this caused her step to go slightly awry and she had to check the desire to run. But she told herself, she was sixteen and her running days were over, she was a young woman and from now on must act the part, no matter how she might feel inside. . . .

She didn't manage to see Willy that afternoon. Her father was out of bed and he never let her out of his sight, not on that day or for some weeks that followed. But when at last they did meet again by the burn it was as if only hours had passed since they had spoken for, standing close to her, he held out his hand and she placed hers in it; then they sat side by side on the bank and talked.

And so it would happen whenever they could meet he would take her hand, that is if the dark one wasn't with him. But as time went on she seemed to be there more often than not and when this happened Noreen would merely pass the time of day with them, then walk on. Strangely the dark girl now never spoke in her presence, even though she stared at her all the while.

This form of occasional Sunday courtship continued. She would be eighteen on Tuesday and today she was going to the river and she prayed that she would find him alone, for the time had come, she knew, for something to be said openly between them. Of late she had felt that if he didn't speak and so enable her to declare her love for him her body would burst asunder. She knew that he liked her, more than liked her. She could feel it in the touch of his hand, she knew it by the way his narrowed gaze lingered on her, yet he had never spoken one word of love, not even of tenderness. Perhaps, like her, he was afraid of the consequences of a declaration. She knew that her father's wrath, should he ever hear of her association with this particular Sopwith, would be something that her imagination could not even visualise. And on Willy's side there was his mother.

His mother she knew wasn't a good woman, well not morally good, everyone said so. For years she had been carrying on with the manager of the mine and, as people pointed out, she could build all the cottages she liked and give her pit folk pensions and their bairns boots and baskets of food at Christmas, but that wouldn't wipe out her sin in the eyes of God. Apparently she had always been a bad woman. Hadn't Willy himself been born out of wedlock after she had been mistress to his father for years. And when he died she went and married his son. And when the son died she returned home with a brown baby that she said she had adopted. Taking all that into account, she was really an awful woman, and yet she must admit that the glimpses she had had of her seemed to belie all these facts. She wished she could meet her and form her own opinion of this woman. She wasn't afraid of meeting her, not like some of the villagers who'd walk a mile rather than run into her.

Well, if Willy spoke she'd have to meet her, wouldn't she? And oh, she hoped it would be soon because every time she was near him the feeling in her was like that of a smouldering fire, which only needed the touch of his lips to burst into a flame. But when that happened the flame, she knew, would engulf not only her but a number of others; and there would be screams of anguish from all sides, particularly from her father. But she felt strong enough to face the consequences, any consequences, if only Willy would speak.

⤶ 2 ⤷

It was on this same Sunday morning that the matter of Willy's association with Noreen Bentwood was being brought into the open at the Manor, and not by Willy or Tilly, although she wasn't entirely unaware of what was going on, but by Josefina who, in an unusual burst of rage, had screamed her denunciation.

It should happen that Josefina had made arrangements to go and visit John and Anna who were entertaining for the week-end Paul and Alice Barton, a brother and sister whose home was in Durham. The Bartons were what was known as a county family and whereas the county didn't visit Mrs Tilly Sopwith, there was no such barrier at the home of Mr John and Anna Sopwith.

Josefina found Paul Barton good company; he was a foil for her wit. Besides playing a good game of whist and croquet, he was good to watch at cricket.

Of late there had been a great restlessness in Josefina. She couldn't herself put a name to it, she only knew that she was tired of the Manor and the way of life in it. No one with the exception of John and Anna ever visited. If she or Willy wanted to meet people they had to go out, not that that really worried her because she didn't care much for people. With the exception of Willy and her mama there was no one she really cared about. And then the feelings that she had for these two people appeared, as it were, to be set on different platforms in her mind.

For her mama she had an affection, but the feeling she had for Willy she knew to be that which a woman has for a man. She also knew that Willy did not view her in this light but looked upon her more as a sister. And this, coupled with her knowledge that her mama was not really her mama, had caused to grow in her the feeling that she did not belong to anyone in this country. And so there had formulated in her mind a decision concerning her future. Her life presented her with two roads: if she could not walk the one she desired, then she would take the other stoically, and in doing so she might in the end be compensated and the strange void in her be filled.

But in her cool reasoning she had forgotten to take into consideration that in her small exquisite body were traits of mixed heritage, whose reactions civilisation had merely dampened down.

The arrangement of the house had been altered over the years. Tilly continued to use the bedroom which had always been hers, and the dressing-room adjoining and the closet. She'd also had a guest room turned into a private sitting-room and it was here she spent most of her time, here she kept the books that concerned the running of the household and also those concerning the business of the mine.

Gradually she had taken on the management of the mine, though not the practical side. This she still left to John and Steve and his under-manager, Alec Manning; but over the years she had come to know more about the business side of it than any of them, and this knowledge she had gradually imparted to her son. She had also encouraged him to take an active part in the running of the mine, for from a boy he had shown interest in it, and knowing that a choice of careers for him would be limited she saw his interest as a godsend to them both, imagining that whatever happened she would always have him by her side. Even if he married he would want her to remain on here. Well, where else could she go? or would she go, even though there were times when she wished she were miles away.

All her life she seemed to have been alone; yet not quite alone, for it was true what Steve said, all her life he had been there, and was still there. And for many, many years, too, there had been Biddy.

Biddy had been dead these last ten years, but as good as Fanny and Peg were, they could not make up for their mother. They had not the wisdom or the warmth. Loyalty, yes. Oh, she couldn't ask for more loyalty than she still got from the Drew family; and since Fanny had married Biddle, he, too, had joined the clan, as it were, and defended her name against slander.

It was odd that her name had still to be defended. And yet what had she done over the past sixteen years that would call for defence of her except that she had made an open friend of Steve.

When in the quiet of the night her body ached for the closeness of another human being and she imagined a face looking at her from the pillow, she told herself she was a fool, all kinds of a fool, and cruel into the bargain, for what had she given this man in return for a lifetime's devotion? Nothing but her hand, and at rare odd times her tight lips.

Yet she knew that if she were to stand up before the altar and swear unto God that nothing else had transpired between them, God would not believe her. And after all, who would blame Him?

She wondered at times how Steve managed to continue in this situation. She wondered if he had a woman on the side, someone whom he took up to that cottage in the hills. Twice he had taken her there but on each occasion the tenants had been present. They were a Mr and Mrs Gray. Peter Gray had been a lead miner who had had to leave the mine when the lead began to poison his system, but he was a man who was very handy and he had extended the cottage on both sides and made a fine job of it. Over the eleven years he had lived there the cottage had grown to twice its size with the addition of a wash-house, a cow byre and a stable, and all built lovingly with the stones he and his wife had gathered from the hillside. But two years ago Peter had died, and Nan, his wife, now an old woman, had gone down into the valley to live with her son. And not once since the cottage had become empty had Steve suggested that he take her up there. Yet she knew that every other week he took leave from the late shift on the Friday night until the Monday morning. She also knew that he paid not infrequent visits to an inn on the Gateshead road, and the reputation of this particular place was anything but savoury.

And what did all this amount to? That he had a woman. And who could blame him? Not her; although the thought of it stabbed at her and created a pain of jealousy which she would have attributed to a young girl and not to a woman of fifty. But she didn't look fifty, she didn't look anything like her age. Nor did Steve. Steve was a year younger than herself but he could pass for a man in his late thirties. There was not a grey hair in his head and his body was straight, which was unusual in a man who had spent so many years going down the drift. But he looked after himself did Steve. As he had once said laughingly to her when she had seen him running across the hills, 'I've got to keep up with you.'

He often ran with Willy. Willy had to have a guide when he was out running, for the sight of his good eye was slowly deteriorating, and it gave her a keen pleasure to see them both together. Willy liked Steve. But then Willy liked most people. His nature was so kind and embracing that she feared for him at times. Only the good die young, it was said, and she was afraid that the gods might claim their own.

And then there was Josefina. Josefina liked Willy, and Tilly sensed at times that she might even more than like. Yet you never really knew what Josefina was thinking. As a child she had been open in her love, demanding affection, but as she grew to girlhood and then touched on womanhood a strange reserve seemed to have settled on her. She looked a lot but said little. She had formed disconcerting habits: one such was sitting perfectly immobile for an hour or more at a time. It was as if the real being in her had gone away and left the outer casing without life. On one such occasion she had touched her shoulder, and Josefina turned and looked at her and said enigmatically, 'Why did you do that, Mama?'

'Do what?' she had asked her.

'Bring me back.'

'Bring you back?' Tilly had repeated. 'From where?'

'I don't know.' Josefina got up and walked away leaving Tilly very troubled. Yet within a short while she had returned to her sharp-tongued witty self. And the incident was forgotten, until it happened again. . . .

Of late there seemed to have been a barrier growing up between them. She was worried about Josefina. And now on this particular Sunday the years were rolled away by a succession of shouts that were touching on screams, and they were coming down from the nursery floor. Tilly's head jerked backwards. It was as if there were two children up there again and Josefina was having a tantrum because Willy was laughing at her. But there were no children up there now. The whole nursery floor had been given over to Willy. The old school and playroom was now a music room because he loved playing the pianoforte. Also he was quite proficient on the violin. His bedroom was next door.

The room across the landing, where Tilly herself had once slept, he had turned into a small museum in which every article was made of brass, from coal scuttles down through candlesticks and horse-brasses to miniatures of all kinds of animals. Everything was brass. It was a strange hobby, one which was started by Ned Spoke's uncle, the man who had taught him to wrestle. On Willy's fourteenth birthday, Ned brought him a brass horseshoe for luck; and with that the collection had begun.

When something heavy hit the floor above and Josefina's voice rose to a shrill scream, Tilly ran from the room, along the corridor, and up the stairs to the nursery floor, and for a moment she put her hands over her ears as the voices of both Josefina and Willy came at her. Then she was in the music room and amazed at the sight before her, for there was Josefina flinging music books and sheets here and there, tearing some in the process.

'Stop this! Stop it this instant!' Tilly was herself yelling now. 'Josefina, do you hear me! I say stop it!' At this the girl paused for a moment; then suddenly lifting up the violin that was lying on the top of the piano, she swung it in an arc and sent if flying against the oak cupboard that stood against the far wall.

'Oh no! No! You're mad. You're a bitch. Do you hear? You're a bitch.'

Tilly became still as she stared at her son now who was on his knees on the floor, his hands searching for the pieces of the broken violin that John had bought him on his sixteenth birthday and which was an excellent instrument and had cost a great deal of money. But it wasn't that that was freezing her emotions, it was that this gentle son of hers should be so aroused that he would call the girl he thought of as his dear sister, a bitch. She had never heard him use a swear-word or an uncouth sentence in his life.

Her head swung towards Josefina, who had rushed across the room and was standing over him. She had taken no notice of Tilly's presence, it was as if she considered they were still both alone, for now she shouted, 'I'm a bitch, am I, not to be classed with your pig and cow girl? All right, I'm a bitch, but you, Willy Sopwith, are a bastard, a stupid one-eyed bastard.'

There were times in Tilly's life when she knew that she herself had been so consumed with rage that she became unaccountable for her actions, like the day she sprang on Alvero Portes and tore at his face. And now she had sprung again and had gripped Josefina by the shoulders and actually swung her from her feet into the middle of the room, and was shaking her as if she were a rat as she cried at her, 'Don't you dare! Don't you dare use those words to my son! Do you hear me?'

Josefina's head became still for a moment. Fury still spitting from her eyes and her lips, she yelled, 'Well, he is, he is a bastard. Besides his sight you have kept him in the dark . . . about that, and other things an' all.'

Tilly gaped open-mouthed at the slight, dark bundle of rage wriggling in her grasp; then she thrust her away with such force that the girl almost overbalanced, only saving herself by gripping the edge of the piano, at the other side of which Willy was now standing, the broken violin in his hands but not looking at it, for his face was turned to the side, his head moving slightly as he took in the two misted figures before him.

The sudden and unusual burst of temper was ebbing from him and flowing into him now was a deep sickness lined with sorrow, not so much for himself and what he was hearing, but for the two people that he loved and who were stabbing each other with words, for now his mother was crying at Josefina, 'He's no bastard, but you are. Do you hear, girl? You are! You are my late husband's bastard. Why did I adopt you? Not because your mother didn't want you, for she knew she would be able to make use of you. No; I took you because I thought it was my duty. But I'm going to tell you something now, girl, and you've brought it on yourself: I don't think my husband fathered you. He swore he didn't but your mother and her father and brother wanted money, so they named him. And your mother was a loose woman. Now think on that, who's the bastard?'

My God! My God! Tilly put her hand to her head and, turning about, staggered to the wall and leant her face against it. What had she said? What had happened? In a few minutes of anger she had destroyed the girl's life. Their association had been wonderful until this very day.... No, it hadn't. A denial came at her. For some time now Josefina had been changing and the girl's attitude towards her had at times been marked.

Slowly, she turned about and now leant against the wall again and looked from one to the other. Their faces were no longer convulsed with anger. Both seemed to be holding the same expression as they stared at her, and the only word she could put to it was, amazement.

Piteously now, she said, 'I'm sorry. I'm sorry,' then letting her gaze rest on Josefina, she said softly, 'Forgive me. Please forgive me.'

Josefina blinked her eyes, then turned and glanced at Willy before looking at Tilly again, and when she spoke it was as if she hadn't been screaming her head off minutes before for her voice sounded cool and calm and what she said appeared as if she had given the matter great thought, not that it had been thrust upon her only minutes before. 'There is nothing to forgive. I, too, should say I'm sorry. And what you have told me is not such a surprise as you may imagine, only I wish I had acted as I felt inclined to some time ago and brought the matter into the open. The only difference your revelation has made is for me to reappraise how I feel inside, and how I appear outside, for I have realised that I am not wholly Indian or Mexican or even Spanish, but I have never imagined there was English blood in me. I'm inclined to believe what you said that your husband did not father me. If he did it would make our relationship' – she now glanced at Willy – 'rather complicated, and I don't know how you would term it. Seeing that Willy was born of one man and I of his son, we cannot therefore be half-brother and sister. I don't know what we can be' – she shrugged her shoulders – 'that is if I was born of your husband, which, if I am to go by my inner feelings, I would repudiate.'

Tilly stared into the small, exquisite face. The way she spoke, the words she used, were alien to how she looked, but if ever she'd had doubts before she doubted it now that Matthew had ever sired this girl. And so what was their relationship? If there was nothing of Matthew in her then she would be free to have Willy . . . to marry Willy. There, it was out, the secret fear that she had kept hidden for years, because she had known that Josefina loved Willy. This had been demonstrated since he had met up with Simon's daughter, not only met up with, but become very interested in. This, too, had been a source of worry, even more so than Josefina's affection for Willy, for she could imagine how the bitter, frustrated Simon Bentwood would look upon his daughter favouring her son, and he with his handicap.

She wondered if ever life would run smoothly for her, that she'd ever have a day to call her own, go where she liked, act how she liked. Yes, act how she liked. And if she could only act how she liked at this moment she would take up her skirts and flee from this house to the cottage and throw herself into the arms of Steve. Yes, yes, throw herself into his arms, into his bed. Strange how years could alter one's feelings. Of all the loves in her life there had never been one like the present, one that exchanged so little yet was so fiercely strong on both sides, like a subterranean torrent ever flowing in search of an outlet.

'May I speak to you alone . . . Mama?' The last word came hesitant from Josefina. This didn't go unnoticed by Tilly, and she stared at this girl who had in a way ceased to be her daughter even by adoption and, looking towards Willy, she said, 'Would you excuse us, Willy?'

Willy scrutinised them both for a moment through the narrowed lid of his eye, then turned abruptly and left the room. And now Tilly and Josefina were alone, and almost immediately the girl began to speak. 'Don't look so worried, Mama,' she said; 'it all had to come into the open sooner or later. It's really later because I've been thinking a lot about my beginnings for a long time now and waiting for the opportunity to talk to you about the matter. But I'd rather it hadn't been in this way.'

'Well,' Tilly sighed, 'why did you bring it about then? Why were you screaming at Willy?'

'Oh that!' Josefina now turned her back completely on Tilly and, walking to the window, she stood looking out for a moment before she said, 'I wanted him to ride over to Uncle John's with me. The Bartons are going to be there, Paul and Alice.' She turned her head slightly now in Tilly's direction. 'You know Paul is the only man who has shown any real interest in me; not that I imagine he could ever bring himself to ask me to marry him, but his manner is natural when talking to me. He does not. treat me like a black servant when I don't speak, or show embarrassed surprise at my intelligence and choice of subjects when I do. If you remember, Mama, for a time a few years ago the county doors were opened slightly for us to squeeze through, but apparently their curiosity being satisfied, they were closed again, that is with the exception of the Bartons. But it really didn't matter because – ' She turned her head to the window again and paused before continuing, 'I was quite happy to be at home here as long as I was with Willy. He was all the company that I wanted. But I suppose you know, Mama, I love Willy and if, as you say – ' Again her head moved so that she could see Tilly, and then she ended, 'If, as you say, you don't think your husband was my father, then I am no relation to Willy and there would be nothing to stop us marrying, except one thing: he has always seen me as a sister and he has been led to think of me that way. But – ' She now walked towards where Tilly was standing and her body seemed to become even smaller with the admission that she dragged from her lips as, with bowed head, she said, 'There's another thing, he loves that Bentwood girl.'

If in an unemotional moment Tilly had been asked which girl she would choose for her son she would, if she were to answer truthfully, have said, 'Neither.' But at this moment, if forced to make a choice, she would have plumped for this dark exquisite creature before her, who was now wringing her heart with the unusual expression of sadness on her face, for with this girl Willy's choice would bring no repercussions, except perhaps raised eyebrows from the county folk and expressions of 'Well! what do you expect of that set-up?' from the villagers. But for the Bentwood girl, she guessed that Simon Bentwood would rather see his daughter dead than married to her son. The jungle telegraph worked both ways and over the years she herself had inadvertently, and sometimes deliberately, listened in as the messages dropped into the kitchen quarters. Simon's tirades against his daughter in his drunken bouts was general knowledge, but it never ceased to amaze her that such love as he professed for herself could turn into a red raw, deep uncontrollable hate. That his wife held no such feelings she had personal evidence of, for on the four occasions they had met during the last fifteen years they had stopped and spoken amicably, both enquiring after the other's children and both knowing that under different circumstances they could have been friends.

Of the daughter in question Tilly knew nothing, except that she was a bonny girl with an open countenance. She had passed her when out riding but they had never exchanged a word. She wondered now how she would react to this girl if she ever became her daughter-in-law and, presumably, mistress of this house.

Her whole body jerked, whether at the thought that had come like a violent stab into her mind or at the shock of Josefina's words, for she had just said, 'If I can't have Willy, I am going back to America to find my people.'

Tilly's mouth opened and shut twice before she brought out, 'You . . . you won't find them in America. Well . . . I mean not the America from where I brought you.'

'Why not?'

'Because they are . . . they are mostly white people there now.'

'And I wouldn't be accepted, is that what you're saying?'

'Yes, that's what I'm saying, you'd never be accepted, not as an equal.'

'Well, I could find my own people and be accepted there I suppose.'

'You . . . you could not endure the life of your own people.'

'What about the Spanish? I can remember speaking Spanish fluently when I was little.'

'That . . . that was the language a lot of Mexicans adopted because they were integrated.'

'So, no one would have me, is that what you're saying?'

'I'm being truthful, Josefina, for your own good. You are here, you belong here. You. . . .'

'No, I don't! That I do know.' The anger was back in her tone. 'I have known for a long, long time that I've no place here, and that only Willy could have made my life tolerable. Well, say what you like, I mean to go back and find out for myself how I'll be received. I won't have to ask you for any money, you have been more than generous to me with my allowance over the years, and I have spent very little of it, seemingly because, well, I suppose that some day I knew the time would come when I would leave. And the time has come.'

'Josefina!' Tilly held out both her hands towards the small figure, saying pleadingly now, 'Wait! Wait! If you must go back then you must, but . . . but let me make arrangements. I've kept in touch with Luisa McNeill over the years. And there is also Katie. She will welcome you and help you.'

Josefina remained silent. Her dark eyes looked bright but not with the moisture of tears. Tilly had never seen her cry; not even after tumbles as a child she had never cried; yelled and fought, yes, but never given way to tears. But now she saw her throat swelling and she watched her gulp before she spoke. 'Will you write to them straightaway?' she asked quietly.

'Yes, this very night.'

'Thank you.'

As Josefina turned away, Tilly had the desire to pull her back and into her arms as she had done when she was a child. As a child she had demanded to be held, to be petted, to be loved; but there was nothing of the child in Josefina now, only a cool aloofness that held one at bay and which was the result of deep conflicts of colour and race, a race that had its beginning in the past so far back that all that surged to the surface now was a strange uneasiness.

After the door closed on Josefina Tilly sat down on the music stool in front of the piano. About her feet were slithers of broken wood, some a polished brown, some showing a plain surface. As she stared down on them, the thought came to her that they represented her life, for every now and again back down the years something had broken her happiness, dashing it to smithereens. Superstition, jealousy, death had all played their part, and now love, young love had suddenly flared into passion with the result that not only was she going to lose her adopted daughter but there was every possibility that she would soon lose her son. And he was the only human being she loved in life. . . . Except, of course, Steve. The 'of course' passed through her mind as if her feelings for him were an established and open fact instead of a secret pain known only to herself.

When she heard the handle of the door turn, she looked over her shoulder and watched Willy enter the room. He did it slowly, turning and closing the door and seeming to pause a minute before making his way towards her. Then one hand resting on the side of the piano, he stood peering down at her. She did not return his gaze but kept her eyes lowered towards the floor once more; nor did she raise her head when he said, 'Is it true that I was born out of wedlock, Mama?'

The question sounded so precise, as if a character in a book had suddenly become alive and was speaking his lines. She almost gave voice to a shaky laugh. 'Is it true that I was born out of wedlock, Mama?' Not as one of her own people would have said, 'What's this I'm hearing! Look! I want the truth, am I a bastard or am I not?' but, 'Is it true that I was born out of wedlock, Mama?'

In an ordinary way she should have been amazed at this moment that her son was still in ignorance of the true nature of his birth. He was nearly twenty years old, he was a man, a big, handsome-looking man; not even near-blindness nor the scar across his brow left by the blow that had inflicted him with the blindness detracted from his good looks, and all his life, at least since she had put him in the care of Ned Spoke, he had shown a desire to mix with people, and mix he had. He had attended the fairs and the hill races and the markets. This being so, you would have thought that somebody would, perhaps when in drink, have referred to him as a bastard; but apparently no one had. Perhaps the condition of his eyes had evoked pity; added to which the very fact that he went down the mine and showed that he wasn't afraid to use pick or shovel when learning the ins and outs of the business had caught the admiration of other men.

Yet it wasn't only with the common man he had mixed, he had, through John and Anna, met members of the county and these, as she knew only too well from personal experience, could convey an insult while smiling into your face, or the inflexion they laid on a few simple words could set a mind wondering. Yet he had escaped all this and here he was asking a question, the answer to which, had she been wise, she would have given him years ago.

She raised her head and, looking up into his deep brown eyes over which the lids were blinking rapidly now, she said tensely, 'Yes, it's true. I lived with your father for twelve years and I nursed him every day of that time. He had, as you already know, been in an accident at the pit which deprived him of his feet. His wife would not divorce him. When she died he wanted to marry me but I said no. I was of a different class. I felt unfit to take on the position of his wife . . . that is legally. You were conceived very late in our association. I would have married him then to give you a legal name but he died.'

'And then you married his son?'

These words were ordinary sounding now, but with a note of condemnation in them, and she replied more stiffly still, 'Yes, I married his son. I married him because I loved him and he was a young man. I had never known the love of a young man.' At this moment she did not think of Steve, but apparently her son did for his next question brought her up from the seat so swiftly that she almost overbalanced and her voice was loud as she cried at him, 'No! I am not having that kind of association with Steve.'

'You're not?'

'No, I'm not!'

'Well, I'm surprised that you aren't because he cares for you.'

She was silent for a moment before she said, 'And what gives you that idea?'

'Well – ' He sighed and turned from the piano now and walked away from her towards the table as he said, 'I may be almost blind but I can still see a little; and then again I don't discount my hearing. He talks of you. I have learned more about you from him than from anyone else. At one time I imagined he was my father.'

'Willy!'

'Oh' – he swung round now – 'don't say it like that, Mother, as if you were shocked. I've always imagined that nothing could shock you; you know so much of the world, and have gone through so much. It would have been the most natural thing that you two should come together now and again. I understand it must have been difficult for you both, you in your position, he in his, but I thought . . . well' – he shrugged his shoulders and stretched out his arms while she stared at him.

The young man confronting her now seemed a different being from the one who had entered the room a few minutes ago and said, 'Is it true that I was born out of wedlock, Mama?' And now she watched him sigh deeply as he went on, 'What does it matter how we were born, where we were born, and even who begot us, it's how we act that matters. You, I think, have acted for other people's good all your life and without much thanks. Most people seemed to have wrought havoc on you, and I'm, apparently, going to be no exception when I tell you that I'm in love with Noreen Bentwood and mean to marry her, that is if she'll have me.'

He took a step nearer to her, his face to the side now, with one eye peering at her, his voice soft as he said, 'I'm sorry if I'm hurting you. I never want to hurt you. I know how you view Bentwood and I've never got to the bottom of why he hates you so much except that you turned him down more than once, but I suppose that would be enough to make any man hate. She's . . . she's a nice girl, Mama, a lovely girl . . . say something please.'

She had to force herself to bring out the words, 'If . . . if she makes you happy that's everything. Have you spoken to her?'

'No. Oh no.'

'No?'

'No, not a word. And . . . and I don't think I've given her a sign because . . . well' – he gave a short laugh – 'I'm not exactly the catch of the season.'

'She'd be the luckiest girl alive to get you, and I would think she knows it.'

'I wish I could think like that. She's been kind to me and – ' He turned away now and walked towards the window saying, 'There's no one I've known that I've felt more at ease with.' He did not add, 'except yourself' and she closed her eyes tightly and bit on her lip. 'We've sat on the river bank and I've held her hand, just held her hand, and it's filled me with a feeling of. . . . Well, I can't explain it. I suppose one could say peace, and yet no, not peace because there's a turmoil inside me when she's near. And what's more, she takes away that awful feeling of being disabled. I feel whole when I'm near her.'

He stopped speaking and she saw his face tilted back as if he were looking towards the sky. He seemed gone from her entirely, and the pain in her chest was as if a mill was grinding against her ribs. She had never imagined he felt himself handicapped, he had always been so cheerful, so outgoing as if he took his lack of sight as a natural thing. Her pain increased as realisation seeped into her that her son had not gone from her this day but rather some long time ago; perhaps the very first time he had met up with Noreen Bentwood.

'Say something.'

She had not realised that he had turned from the window but she could not do as he asked, and now taking her hands, he pleaded, 'Please, don't be upset, nothing has changed between us. What has happened today doesn't matter. I'm only sorry it has had to happen this way. If Josefina wasn't such a spitfire none of this would have come about. I'm sorry I called her a bitch but I was so mad at her when she broke my violin, and all because I wouldn't go to Uncle John's with her.'

Tilly bowed her head. It was strange how some men could be so inwardly blind. He had no idea of Josefina's true feelings for him; and it was better that he should remain in ignorance.

When he put his arms about her and kissed her she held him tightly for a moment before saying, 'Go and make your peace with her, she's very unhappy.' She did not add, 'She won't be here much longer;' enough was enough.

When the door had closed on him she stood perfectly still in the middle of the room, then lifting her hand, she pressed it tightly over her mouth as if to prevent the words escaping from her lips, for her mind was crying, Oh Steve! Steve! He was the only rock in her life, the only being who had never changed. She wanted to fly to him, fling herself into his arms and cry, 'I'll marry you,

Steve. I'll marry you.' At this moment the promise she had made to a dying man appeared foolish and futile, and her reason for not having broken it earlier was, she knew, because she'd had two children to bring up, then two young people to see to and guide; but now both of them were gone from her life, cut off as surely as if they had packed their bags and taken separate coaches to separate railways, they had gone.

She must see Steve, she must. Perhaps he hadn't gone to his cottage. Well, if he had she would stay and wait for him. Oh yes, she would wait. Whatever time he came back tonight she would be there waiting. Had he not waited for her for years?

From the top of the stairs she called down to Biddle and gave him orders to have her horse saddled. Then going to her room, she swiftly changed her clothes. Fifteen minutes later she was galloping down the drive, through the main gates and on to the coach road. But she did not continue along it to the turnpike as she had done at odd times before, she jumped her horse over a ditch, then over a low field gate, rode him around the border by a dry stone wall until they came to a part where the wall had broken down. Taking him gently over this, she set him into a gallop down a shallow valley and up the bordering hill. On the top she drew him to a stop for a moment, not only to give him a breather but to view the surrounding land. Away in the far, far distance to the right of her she could see a narrow silver streak, that was the River Tyne. Away to the front was soft undulating farmland. Then her eye was drawn slightly to the left and below her where the land dropped again, and her gaze became rivetted on two riders. One was unmistakable, as was his mount. Steve's horse was a fourteen-year old mare which ten years ago she had helped to choose. She was broad in the back and made for weight, but the horse walking alongside her was a sleek animal, evidently a hunter, and its rider was sleek too. But she wasn't a young girl. She had her face turned towards Steve and she was laughing, they were both laughing, he into her face and she into his. The sound of it came to her as if carried on a patch of wind, and now the mill grinding against her ribs worked faster as she saw Steve lean from his saddle, his hand outstretched. She could not see what he did with it, but its direction left little to the imagination – he was placing it on that of his companion.

Oh God! God! She turned her horse slowly about and the seemingly unaffected part of her mind said, 'Why do you always say, Oh God! God! when you're upset? You never pray, so why do you appeal to Him now?' But appeal to Him she did and, looking upwards, she asked, 'What have I done this time?' and the answer seemed to come to her from every corner of the wide expanse of sky, saying, 'You left it too late. You left it too late.'

⤜ **3** ⤛

Noreen was sitting by the burn gazing into the water. She had been sitting like this for almost an hour now and she told herself she would wait another five minutes and then she would go.

She waited ten, fifteen, and she had risen to her feet when she heard the rustle of footsteps in the dry grass, and the snuffling of the dog, and quickly she put her hands to her bonnet, straightened it and dusted the grass from her coat, and then he came round the corner and towards her.

'Hello.'

'Hello.'

'I'm . . . I'm late.'

'Yes, you are.'

He laughed gently now. Any of the other young misses he had met he was sure would never have given such a forthright reply. They would have said, 'Oh, are you? Well, I've just come,' or some such nonsense. He held out his hand to her and he knew it was trembling, and when her fingers lay within his palm he knew that she was trembling too. His head to the side, he bent down towards her and as he did so it seemed for a second someone had lit a lamp in front of her face.

'You've got a new bonnet on,' he said.

'You can make that out?'

'Yes, yes. I see it plainly in my mind. And you too. You're . . . you're very beautiful.'

'No.' Her voice sounded flat now. 'I'm pretty but not beautiful.'

'I think you're beautiful.'

'Well, I'll not argue with you.'

'No, you'd better not.'

They both laughed; then he said, 'Am I allowed to say that blue suits you? It is a new coat and bonnet, isn't it?'

'Yes, my mother bought them for my birthday . . . it's my birthday on Tuesday, but it being Sunday she gave them to me today to wear.'

'Yes, I know when your birthday is.'

'I never mentioned it to you so how do you . . . ?'

'You told me the day you were sixteen, and you had a new bonnet and coat on then.'

'Did I?'

'You did and you know you did. You pronounced it as if you had gained a century.' Again they were laughing; and now he drew her cautiously towards the river bank and, as they had done so often before, they sat down side by side on it.

She reached out now and drew a paper-covered parcel towards her, saying as she did so, 'I've brought your books back. I like the Dickens stories, but they're sad, aren't they?'

'Yes, they are; but they're true to life.'

'How do you know because you've hardly been away from the big house?'

'I've been to London.'

'You have!' There was awe in her tone now.

'I have.' His tone was deliberately pompous. 'And what's more, I have heard Mr Charles Dickens reading his own stories from the stage.'

'You haven't really.'

'Yes, I have. My Uncle John and Aunt Anna, Mother, and Josefina, we all went to the St James's Hall one night and listened to the great man. It was most enthralling. I felt so sorry when he died; 'twas as if I had known him personally.'

'He is dead then?'

'Yes, he died about three years ago.'

'Aw, I'm sorry too. I hate to hear of people dying. I never want to die, I want to go on living and loving. . . .' She stopped suddenly and her fingers jerked away from his.

After a moment he leaned towards her and said softly, 'You love someone, Noreen?'

Her head was bent, her hands tightly clasped.

'Yes.' Her head was nodding now.

'Do I know him?'

There was a pause before her answer came. 'Yes.'

'What's his name?'

When she didn't answer, he asked gently, 'Can't you tell me his name?'

'No' – she was shaking her head now – 'he's got to speak first.'

'Perhaps he's afraid to, this person you love. You see I know all about being afraid to speak my mind because I, too, love someone very, very dearly. But I'm . . . I'm handicapped. I couldn't imagine her ever really loving me, being sorry for me yes, being a companion to me, a friend, but I couldn't ask her anything more until . . . well, I wouldn't want to frighten her and lose her friendship.'

'Willy.' She was kneeling by his side now gazing at him, and he swung himself round so that he, too, was kneeling, and as he whispered her name she said again, 'Willy. Aw Willy.' And then their arms were about each other and his lips were on hers, hard, tight, and she was clinging to him as if she would never let him go.

It was minutes later when, still clinging together, they sat once more on the edge of the bank; and Willy now brought from his pocket a small box and, handing it to her, he said, 'A happy birthday, my dear, dearest Noreen.'

Slowly she pressed the spring and when the lid opened there lay a brooch in the shape of a half-moon and lying in the crescent was a star. The moon was set with small diamonds, the star too, but at its central point there lay a ruby.

'Oh . . . Oh!' . . . Oh! Willy. I've never seen anything so beautiful. Oh! thank you. Thank you.' Her arms were about him again. Once more their lips held; and then he said in a tone full of emotion, 'You'll marry me, Noreen?'

'Oh aye, yes, Willy.' Each word seemed to be balanced on wonder, and again she said, 'Oh yes, yes.'

'When?'

Slowly now she sank away from him while still retaining hold of his hand, and she looked across the water as she said one word 'Father.'.

From the thicket behind them a prone figure slowly edged itself backwards and if the couple on the bank heard the rustle of the grass they put it down to a rabbit, but the dog heard it and when he made towards it, Willy commanded him to stay.

Randy Simmons was more of the weasel type than a rabbit, and he grinned and nodded his old head as he muttered to himself, 'Aye, aye, *Father*.' News of this would mend his back for him. Aye, by heck, it would. He could see his master skiting up to that Manor and tearing it apart. Just let her say it to him once again, 'You're as lazy as you're long, Randy Simmons,' and he'd put the shackles on her all right. He'd split on her, her father'd hear about it in any case, sooner or later.

Father. She had a good right to say it like that, the little trollop. By! it'd make a story in the pub, the witch's blind bastard and Bentwood's lass. 'Twas about time there was a bit of excitement round here, things had been too quiet of late. Aye, much too quiet.

'Girl! look at your coat. It's all grass stains, you'd think you had been kneeling in it.'

'Mam! Mam!' Noreen pushed her mother's hands away. 'Stop fussing and listen, I've got something to tell you ... listen ... listen ... Willy has asked me to marry him.'

'Willy?' Lucy screwed up her eyes as if she had never heard the name Willy before, and one thing was sure, she had never heard it from her daughter's lips.

'Willy Sopwith.'

'Willy Sopwith?'

'Mam, don't act on as if you didn't know.'

'Well, I didn't know it had gone this far.' Lucy's voice was now a harsh whisper and she glanced about her as if afraid of being overheard. Then grabbing her daughter by the shoulder just in case this fear should be realised, she thrust her forward, saying, 'Get upstairs.'

When they were standing in the back bedroom Lucy peered at her daughter as if she were finding difficulty in seeing her. The light in the room was dim, it being the original upstairs room of the once two-roomed cottage that had first stood on this site, and on the brightest day the light merely filtered into the room through the two narrow windows that were set like armoury slits in a castle wall; and the walls, all of two foot thick, did resemble those built as a fortification. Noreen could have had any of the other three vacant bedrooms in the house but she preferred to stay in the one which had acted as her nursery when a child.

'You're mad, girl. You know that, you're mad.'

'All right, I'm mad, but we're going to be married.'

'When, in the name of God?'

'I . . . I don't know exactly, but we are. He . . . he wanted to take me to see his mother today, and when I wouldn't go he wanted to come here. . . .'

'Come here! Oh!' Lucy held her head between her two hands and she rocked herself from side to side as she said, 'He'd go for him. You know that, he'd go for him.'

'Well, he might find his match if he did, Willy's no weakling.'

'He's almost blind, girl, at least from what I hear . . . Is he?'

'Yes.' The answer had come firm and clear, and as Lucy looked at her daughter she recognised that she wasn't arguing with or trying to persuade a young girl, because Noreen neither looked nor sounded a young girl, she was a woman. She had always been older than her years and much wiser than one would expect from someone of her age, but the revelation did not deter her in her pleading, in fact it seemed to make it imperative that her daughter should see sense before it was too late. 'Look,' she said now; 'give yourself time. Tell him you must think it over, have time. . . .'

'I have thought it over, and for a long time now, and I've given him my word. Anyway, I want to marry him. If I don't. . . .'

'*Oh no! No! Oh girl, no*! Lucy had put her hand up as if to ward off something fearful, and now she cried almost in anguish, 'Not that, girl. Don't tell me that you *must* marry him. How could you!'

'Mama!' The word was almost a bellow. 'You're barking up the wrong tree.'

Lucy closed her eyes and her body seemed to slump; then looking at her daughter again, she said, 'I'm sorry, lass, I'm sorry, but I could stand anything except that. The disgrace of that, at least for you. Aw no! No! Aye – ' she managed to smile now as if in relief – 'things will work out, at least I hope to God they will. But do this for me, lass, don't mention anything yet. And don't go running off because that might be all right for you and him but your dad will go up to that house and there would be murder done. I tell you you don't know how he feels about . . . about that woman.' Her head was down now and her lips were trembling and it was Noreen's turn to feel concern. Putting her arm around her mother's shoulder, she said, 'I . . . I do know and . . . and I think he's mad, mad in so many ways, mainly for not appreciating what he's got in you, for what I've seen of her . . . she's got no figure, nothing, she's as flat as Willy himself.'

They stood in silence for a moment, Lucy her head still bent, Noreen looking towards her bed. When she spoke she asked a question: 'Do you think, Mam', she said, 'that Dad's not right in the head, because nobody sane could act like he does about something that happened years and years ago, and be normal?'

Lucy now moved from her daughter's hold and towards the door and she had the knob in her hand as she said, 'He's sane enough in one way but mad in another, because some women have the power to turn men's brains.'

'I don't like her.'

'Looking sadly at her daughter, Lucy said, 'Well, if you're hoping for her to be your mother-in-law it's a sad look out for the future, because there's an old adage that says, a wife is but the second woman in a man's life.' And on this she went out.

⤜⧽ 4 ⧼⤛

For the past two months Tilly had avoided meeting Steve except when she visited the mine, and even there she managed to arrange for a third party to be present.

She knew she was afraid to be alone with him, in case she might upbraid him for enjoying another woman's company and in doing so reveal her own feelings towards him. And this she knew would be most unfair for the situation between them was of her own making. She could have married him any time within the last sixteen years but now it was too late.

A meeting had just taken place in the office with regard to the building of new repair sheds, also the renovation of the stables. There had been present John, the under-manager Alec Manning, Steve and herself. Some of the under-manager's remarks had been disturbing. He was a modern young man, not afraid to open his mouth, and he said openly that it was very little use spending money on new buildings when the roads inside were almost worked out. Better, he thought, to open new seams.

She had been surprised that Steve had not downed him. His silence on the point seemed to suggest he was of a similar way of thinking. Then why, she thought, hadn't he spoken up. Her own thoughts became agitated as she realised that his mind was not wholly on the business in hand.

John had been emphatic against spending more money on exploring new drifts until he was absolutely sure there was nothing more to be had out of the present ones.

The meeting had ended with nothing settled because no two of them seemed to be in agreement on any point.

She came out of the office and stood talking to John, aware at the same time that Steve and his under-man had gone into the lamp house. Steve hadn't spoken to her privately except to wish her a good morning.

John brought her attention to him swiftly by saying, 'Mc . . . McGrath is not . . . not himself these days. I fear there m . . . m . . . might be some . . . something in the rumour after all.'

'What rumour?' Her voice was sharp.

'Oh, just that I heard he was th . . . thinking of leaving the pit and taking up f . . . f . . . farming. I understand he's got some kind of a f . . . f . . . farm.'

'It's merely a cottage.'

'Oh yes, yes' – he looked closely at her – 'I f . . . f . . . forgot you've b . . . been there. And it isn't a f . . . farm of any k . . . k . . . kind?'

'No. The land's useless for farming. A few sheep perhaps but that's all. When did you hear this?'

'Oh, s . . . s . . . some time ago, in fact I c . . . c . . . can't remember wh . . . wh . . . where it was or who m . . . mentioned it. But there, I think he w . . . w . . . would have told you about it, w . . . w . . . wouldn't he, Tilly, if there w . . . w . . . were any t . . . t . . . truth in it?'

There was an underlying meaning to his words which she wasn't slow to recognise, but she ignored it, saying, 'Well, I happen to be his employer, but then it is often the employer who is the last one to be brought into the picture. . . . How is Anna?'

'Oh, as usual.' He looked to the side before returning his gaze back to her and saying, 'I've s . . . s . . . suggested to her that we adopt a b . . . b . . . baby.'

'How did she take it?' Her voice was soft now, sympathetic.

'N . . . N . . . Not at all well, T . . . T . . . Tilly. In fact, it brought on one of her ner . . . ner . . . nervous bouts again.'

'I'm sorry. But you know, John, children besides bringing blessings also bring pain.'

She watched him shake his head sadly now as he said, 'She, and I too, would gladly su . . . su . . . suffer the pains.'

'Has she talked the matter over with her doctor?'

'N . . . N . . . No, Tilly, and I w . . . wouldn't suggest it to her, n . . . n . . . not again. I d . . . d . . . did once allude to it but it's such a de . . . delicate matter. You understand?'

'Yes, yes, John, I understand. Well, give her my love. And I'll expect to see you both on Friday. Insist that she comes, won't you, John, because it will be the last time she will see Josefina.'

'Th . . . Th . . . That girl, she must be m . . . m . . . mad and ungr . . . gr . . . grateful in . . . into the bargain.'

'No, no, John. It's natural I suppose, she wants to see her people and the country from where she sprang. It's a natural desire. And she can always come back. I've told her this is her home, she can always come back . . . Well, there's Robbie with your horse.' She pointed, 'Good-bye, John.'

'Good-bye, Ti . . . Ti . . . Tilly. See you Fr . . . Fr . . . Friday.'

They parted: he mounted his horse and rode away; she now went to the stables.

As she approached the wide double doors she was met by Steve leading both her own and his mount out. Without a word he assisted her up into the saddle and the next minute he was riding by her side, and not until they were clear of the pit head and on the road did she speak, and then she said, 'You've changed the shift?'

'Yes, some days ago.'

Again there was silence. At one point the road narrowed until their mounts had to walk close together, and when his knee touched hers, he said, but without looking at her, 'Why have you been avoiding me, Tilly?'

'Avoiding you?' She had turned her head towards him, and so she was aware of the angry hue that had come over his face before he exclaimed, albeit in a lowered tone, 'Oh, for God's sake, Tilly, don't put on your drawing-room manner and your polite asides. I say you've been avoiding me, you know you've been avoiding me, and I want to know the reason.'

So he wanted to know the reason. Being Steve, he wouldn't settle for anything else. Well, what would she say to him? Tell him the truth: I've been avoiding you because I'm jealous, because I can't bear the thought of you being nice to another woman? And what would his answer to that be? 'You're too late, Tilly, you should have thought about this years ago, even a few months would have made all the difference. I'm a man, I need someone.' And she had no doubt that he slaked a particular need during his not infrequent visits to his cottage on his long weekends and to the inn on the high road. And she couldn't blame him for that, oh no.

'Come in a minute.'

She turned to him in surprise. She hadn't realised they had ridden so far in silence. She allowed him to help her down, watched him as he tied her horse to the gatepost, and then she preceded him up the path and stood aside while he placed the key in the lock, turned it and opened the door.

When she entered the room the proceedings went as usual. He put the bellows to the fire, he took up the black kettle from the hob, went into the scullery, and in a short while returned with it and pushed it into the heart of the coals, then went again into the scullery, and she sat listening to him getting the thick of the coal-dust from his hands and face. But today his ablutions seemed to take longer and when he came into the room she saw that he had also washed his hair; it was lying flat and gleaming on his head.

He came and stood in front of her, but he did not speak for some seconds; and then his words were directly to the point. 'Out with it, Tilly,' he said; 'you owe me this at least.'

Well, here was something she could make use of without giving herself away, so she repeated his last words, 'I owe you that at least, you say. Well, perhaps you owe me something too, Steve. If you are thinking about changing your job, shouldn't I have been the first to know?'

'Changing my job? Where did you hear this?'

'Does it matter? . . . Is it true?'

'It is and it isn't, so to speak. It could be true but on the other hand it could be just a rumour.'

'As is the fact that you may be thinking of getting married?' There, she had jumped in with both feet but without giving herself away. He was looking down at her, straight into her face; but his expression told her nothing. His next words did however: 'Yes' – he inclined his head towards her – "I've been thinking about it for some time now, some long time in fact.'

'You could have told me.'

'Yes, I suppose I could, but what would you have said?'

'I – ' She kept her eyes fixed on him as she took her spittle over the lump in her throat, then continued, 'I could have wished you happiness, you deserve happiness.'

'We very rarely get what we deserve, Tilly.'

'May I know her name?'

'Oh' – he pursed his lips – "her name doesn't matter very much.' He was turning away as she said, 'Well, I've seen her face so I would like to put a name to it.'

He stopped in the act of making a step; then his right foot seemed to descend slowly to the floor and he remained immovable for a moment not speaking. When he turned, it wasn't towards her but towards the fireplace where the kettle was spluttering its boiling water on to the now glowing coals, and he lifted it up and placed it on the hob, then straightened his back and reached for the tea-caddy from the mantelpiece before he asked, 'When did you see her?'

'Oh, you were out riding together some time ago.'

The tea-caddy in one hand now, he stretched out the other hand for the brown teapot which was standing on a corner of the delf rack to the side of the fireplace, and he said slowly, 'Ah yes, yes; that would be one Sunday about seven weeks ago. It was the first time we had ridden together.'

He turned his head now and looked at her over his shoulder and his face was bright. He was smiling, the lines at the corners of his eyes were deep, his mouth was wide and the expression on his face pained her to such an extent that she wanted to cry out against it. She couldn't remember ever seeing such a look on his face, not even on that night long ago when they watched the New Year coming in together, and he had taken her in his arms and kissed her.

'Well now, where's that milk? As if I didn't know.' He went to the cupboard beneath the delf rack and took out a can. Lifting the lid, he sniffed at the contents and said, 'It should be all right, I only got it last night, 'tisn't turned yet.'

She watched him pour the milk into the cups, then take up the brown teapot and pour out the tea. After handing her a cup, he picked up his own and, taking it from the saucer, he raised it as one would a glass of wine in a toast, and he waited as if he expected her to do the same. After a moment she did so and forced herself to say, 'I wish you every happiness, Steve. You know that.'

'Not more than I wish myself, Tilly. Not more than I wish myself.' The smile slid from his face and he was placing the cup on the table when the sound of a galloping horse drew his eyes towards the window, and, bending his length downwards, he said, 'It . . . it looks like one of your lads. It is, it is. It's Ned Spoke. What now?'

She had risen swiftly to her feet and they were both at the door when Ned came running up the path. He stood gasping for a moment before he could say, ''Tis trouble, madam. I . . . I was on my way to the mine, then I saw Bluebell.' He thumbed back towards the horse.

'What is it?' She had gone down the step and had hold of his arm now, and again he gasped before he said, 'Mr Bentwood, he . . . he came crashing in. Mad he was, clean mad like a raving bull. He knocked Mr Peabody over, clean over. Then Biddle tried to tackle him. 'Twas then that Master Willy came on the scene. He . . . he, Mr Bentwood, sprang on him and got hold of him by the throat, so Peg said, but Master Willy, being good at throwing people off, got free. But he didn't raise his hand to him. He tried to speak, Peg said, to calm him down. But then Mr Bentwood came at him again and knocked him flying.'

Tilly now ran down the path calling as she did so, 'Is . . . is he hurt?' and Ned, coming after her, cried, 'His face is busted a bit and he hit the bottom of the stairs and went out like a light, but he came round again.'

'Wait! Wait! Tilly; I'll be with you.' Steve was now running to the stable, buttoning his shirt neck as he went, and he mounted his horse almost at the same time as Tilly did hers, and within seconds was galloping after them. . . .

The house seemed in chaos, it was as if the whole staff had gathered in the hall. It was Biddle who came forward now to her, saying, 'He's all right, madam. Don't worry, he's all right. He's recovered. We put him in your room.'

She did not stop to ask questions but flew upstairs and into the bedroom to see Josefina holding a cold compress to Willy's face. He was sitting on the edge of the bed and since the compress was covering his good eye he turned in the direction of the opening door and, sensing her before she spoke, he said, 'Don't worry, don't worry, it's all right.'

'Oh my God!' Tilly had lifted the compress away and looked at the darkening surface of the skin from the top of the eyelid to well below his cheekbones, taking in the split at the corner of his upper lip which was still bleeding. 'We must get the doctor.'

'I've already sent for him.'

She turned and looked at Josefina who added harshly, 'But who you should send for is the police. That man should be locked up, he's mad.'

'We want no police . . . or a doctor.' They both looked at Willy as he finished, 'Just leave me alone and I'll be all right.'

'You can't be left alone.' Tilly's voice was almost a bark. 'Have you any idea what has been done to your face?'

'Well, whatever it is it can't be worse than what has already been done to it, can it?'

They were the first real words of bitterness she had heard from his lips. Before, whenever he had referred to his blindness it was with acceptance. His nature was innately placid or had been; but over the last weeks she had noticed a change in him, a hardening. It seemed to date from the day of the upset with Josefina.

There was silence in the room for a moment, the only sound being that of water dripping into the dish as Josefina wrung out another compress. When she placed it against his cheek, she said, 'Well, this should bring home to you the fact that if you want to survive you'd better give up whatever thoughts you're harbouring concerning that gentleman's daughter.'

The reaction of his hand coming up and tearing the compress from his face was so rough that he almost caused Josefina to overbalance, and his voice now matching his action, he cried, 'He, or no one else, is going to stop me seeing Noreen and – ' he paused and his eye searched for his mother and held her gaze as he finished, 'marrying her.'

Again there was a short silence, ended by Josefina turning hastily away, saying with bitterness equal to his own, 'I hope you live long enough to accomplish it, that's all.'

As the door banged Tilly wrung out another compress and when she placed it on his face and he said, 'What's wrong with her these days?' she could have answered, 'If you don't know you are indeed blind. Can't you understand that the girl you have treated as a sister all these years is in love with you, deeply in love with you?' She could not have made a comparison, saying, 'And to a greater extent than Simon Bentwood's daughter,' because as yet she had no way of gauging the feelings of the girl, she only knew that she had so ensnared her son it could in the end be the death of him; and her mind gave her no other word but ensnared.

When a tap came to the door she turned her head, saying, 'Come in,' and when it opened Biddle stood aside to allow Steve to enter, and what struck her immediately was the incongruity of the two men, Steve in his coal-dust-stained shirt, a leather belt holding up his trousers, and Biddle in his grey and blue well-fitting gaitered uniform.

'How are you?' Steve was standing at the other side of Willy, and he, lifting his head, said, 'What does it look like, Steve?'

'Pretty rough to me.'

'Well, that's how it feels.'

'Something's got to be done about that man.' Steve was looking across at Tilly now, and Tilly asked simply, 'What?'

'I'm not having the police brought into this, Steve.' Willy made to rise from the bed while Steve, staying him with a hand on his shoulder, said, 'No; well, there's no need for that, not as yet. But if he thinks he can put the fear of God into you and everybody else he'll go on doing it. You've got friends haven't you? Phil Spoke, and Ned an' all, are not to be sneezed at when it comes to a knockabout.'

'I don't want that.'

'No? Well, you just might have to agree with it in the end. What I can't understand is how he got at you; using one of your holds you could have had him on his back because he's gone to wind. He's big but he's soft bodywise; you could have tossed him.'

'I didn't want to toss him.'

Steve let out a long breath and as it ended he said, 'I can understand that. But now, I think, looking at your face a steak wouldn't come in wrong until the doctor gets here.'

'A steak! I never thought of that, I'll get one immediately.' Tilly almost ran from the room; and with her going Steve lowered himself down on to the edge of the bed to the side of Willy and, his voice changing, he said, 'You'll have to be careful, lad; he'll not let you have his girl, not as long as he's alive.'

'Why? Why, Steve? All because of some silly thing that happened years ago.'

'Silly? Well, I wouldn't call it silly. What would you say if I came along now and took your lass away from you, from under your nose, and you had to watch her being happy with somebody else?'

'But it was so long ago; and he was so much older than Mama. I can't understand it.'

Steve gave a short laugh, then he said, 'You can't understand it ?Knowing your mother, being with her all these years, and you can't understand what it is about her that gets hold of a man?'

Willy bowed his head now; then his voice a mere murmur, he said, 'I can't bear the thought of her having had so many men.'

'Oh, you mustn't look at it that way, lad. Fact is, it isn't her who's had the men, t'other way round, they've had her, pursued her, persecuted her. One or two courted her, but they were few compared to the ones who would have liked to. Your mother is a unique woman, Willy, haven't you realised that? What do you think's kept me running after her, at her beck and call so to speak, since I was a lad?'

Willy slowly turned his disfigured face towards Steve and he peered at him for a moment before saying, 'You're a good man, Steve. She's lucky to have you . . . for a friend. I've . . . I've often wondered why you haven't married her. I've thought perhaps it might be . . . well, the difference in position, but knowing that much about her I know she doesn't lay much stock on position . . . You've never married, Steve?'

'No, never.'

'It's a pity, I think you should be.'

'Yes, you're right, I should be, and intend to be.'

'Married?' There was a quick and interested movement of his face which caused Willy to wince and put his hand up to his cheek and, as the door opened, Steve was saying, 'Yes, I hope to be married and not in the very far future. There's only one hindrance but I hope to overcome that.'

The room was quiet again and Tilly placed the steak over the whole surface of Willy's right cheek, and it seemed a long time before anyone spoke, and then Willy, his tone quiet, said, 'Steve has just been telling me he intends to be married.'

'Yes, I know.'

'You didn't say.'

'Oh, it wasn't all that important.'

The reply could have been taken as a slight insult or as merely an expression of ingratitude for a life of devotion, but to both the younger and the older man they conveyed neither of these things. Strangely, the same thought entered both their minds.

℺ 5 ℾ

The instigator of Simon Bentwood's memorable visit to the Manor was Randy Simmons. He had for some long time been looking for an opening through which to inform his master of what was going on between his daughter and 'that one up there's son' without exposing himself as a peeping Tom, or of bringing himself further into the black books of his mistress, for Mrs Bentwood had made it plain right from the beginning that she didn't savour him or his ways. However, because he had been so long employed at the farm he knew he stood well with his master.

So when it should happen that a letter was placed in his hands he, later when explaining it to the mistress, put it in his own words that inadvertently the master had twigged it.

As Tilly's grandmother had often said to her, no big event ever came about of its own accord, it had to grow, and such events matured from little acts or coincidences or, as in this case, just the changing of a sailing time of a boat going to America

Josefina was due to leave Liverpool on Thursday, the nineteenth of June, but because of boiler repairs not being completed on the particular ship the passengers had been transferred to a sister ship sailing on the high tide last thing on Sunday night, June the fifteenth.

Willy, who, of course, would be accompanying Tilly to Liverpool to see Josefina off, felt he must get word about the changed arrangements to Noreen. But how? He put it to Ned Spoke who had over the years become his friend and confidant, and it was Ned who said, 'Well, Master Willy, there's nothing like a letter for explaining things. I'll get one there for you without the old boy seeing it. I mightn't do it first go off but I'm bound to get the attention of one or other of the ladies sooner or later.'

But when Ned scouted the farm on his first visit he saw no one at all. Later the same day the only person he saw and the last one he wanted to encounter was Simon Bentwood himself. He was hobbling across the yard with the aid of a stick

The following morning he rode past the gate and there met Randy Simmons. To him Randy was an old man, a good farm worker. He had heard nothing against him except that he chatted a lot in the village inn. But then all the old codgers chatted a lot when they had a pint of ale in them. In an off-hand manner he enquired of his master and mistress, and to this Randy replied, 'Oh, all be gone into Shields. Me here, I'm king of the castle with only young Larry Fenwick to do me biddin', and he's as thick in the top thatch as a crumpled cow's horn.'

'Would you do something for me?' Ned asked.

'Aye, aye, lad,' Randy replied, 'if it doesn't cost money.'

'Would you give a letter to the young lass? It's private like, very private, you understand?'

Randy gazed up at the young fellow before grinning at him and saying, 'Oh aye, I understand, I understand a lot I do; nothing much escapes me. One eye over the fence and one ear under it, you learn a lot that way.' He jerked his head towards Ned, who replied with the same gesture that they understood each other; at least that's what he thought when he handed the letter over.

Two hours later Randy Simmons, on entering the kitchen, happened to drop the letter from his apparently flustered hand as he encountered his master.

'What's that?' Simon demanded and Randy Simmons grabbed the letter up from the stone flags, muttering as he did so. 'Nowt, master, just a letter.'

'Well, if it's a letter, let me have it.'

Randy placed the letter behind his back, saying, ''Tain't for you, master.'

''Tain't for me!' Simon repeated Randy's words, then held out his hands, adding, 'What letters come into this house are for me. Let me have it!' With the appearance of genuine reluctance Simmons handed the letter over, and then the world had seemed to explode in that farmhouse kitchen.

Reading part of the letter aloud to his amazed and now really frightened wife, Simon Bentwood ground out, 'My dear of dears, Ned will get this to you to tell you that, unfortunately, Josefina has to sail earlier than expected, so I shall be leaving on Saturday morning for Liverpool. But I shall be back on Tuesday.'

He held the single sheet of paper in both hands and, in his rage, shook it as he glared at his wife. Then with heightening passion he ended, 'My dearest dear, nothing or no one can separate us. Just cling on to that. You are mine and I am yours for as long as we may live, and after. I shall be there on Tuesday night as usual. Until then, my love, your own Willy.'

At this he crushed the letter in his hand as he screamed, 'As long as you may live. And begod! Your time is short, Master William Sopwith. If I have anything to do with it your time is short,' then he had made to rush out of the kitchen, but the cramp in his back caught him and he leant face forward against the wall and beat on it with his bare fists.

After some minutes during which he had continued to gasp with pain, he turned and, looking at Lucy, cried, 'Where is she? Get her!'

It said a lot for Lucy's courage when, standing stiffly, she said, 'Not until you calm down.'

'You! You! woman.' He brought himself with a great effort from the wall; then stumbling his way towards the dairy where Randy Simmons had already warned Noreen of impending disaster, having explained that it wasn't his fault, that he had been looking for her when he had come up with her father and became flustered.

Simmons had got no further with his mumbling apologies before the door burst open and without uttering a word Simon Bentwood grabbed his daughter by the collar of her dress and dragged her struggling and crying out into the yard and back into the kitchen; and there, throwing her into the old rocking chair with such force that but for Lucy's hand it would have tipped over backwards, he bent above her bawling now into her face, 'You dirty little strumpet you! To think I'm seeing you day in and day out and never guessed. I'm a bloody fool. Blind, like him. Well, listen to me, miss.' He had grabbed the front of her dress and brought her upwards to him. 'And listen hard. I'll see you dead first afore he comes within miles of you again, let alone touch you. Do you hear me? I'll kill him. Do you hear me? And happily swing for it afore I see you mixed up with that lot.'

'Then ... then you will ... you will swing, because he's for me, and me for him, no matter what you say.'

The blow from the flat of his hand knocked her backwards. And now Lucy was clawing at him, crying, 'Leave her alone or I'll take the poker to you!'

'Out of me way, woman!' With one backward thrust of his arm he knocked his wife flying and almost overbalanced himself; then hauling Noreen bodily out of the chair, he dragged her through the kitchen, across the hall and up the stairs. When she clung on to the bannisters he brought his free hand with such force across her wrist that she cried out. Kicking open the door of her room, he flung her inside and, looking at her where she fell, he cried at her, 'And here you stay until I have your word, whether it be days, weeks or months. I'll feed and water you like an animal but you won't move from this room until you come to your senses.'

On this he had gone out and turned the key in the lock. It was the first time in his memory that key had been turned and he had to use all his strength to wrench it around. And when it was done, he thrust it into his pocket and went outside, where he ordered Randy Simmons to saddle up the trap again. Then he made his way to the Manor.

ఆ 6 ౼

Willy, after all, did not accompany Josefina to Liverpool. The doctor having diagnosed slight concussion ordered him to rest for some days, and it was when the doctor was examining him that Willy asked him a question. 'Could a blow on my head improve my sight, I mean in the right eye?'

'Improve your sight?' The doctor pursed his lips, then said, 'I doubt it.'

'The last time you came about three weeks ago, I think it was when Lizzie Gamble broke her ankle, you were wearing this same suit were you not, doctor?'

The doctor looked down at his attire. 'Yes. Yes, I suppose so,' he said.

'I thought I detected a stripe in the material then. Rather unusual material, I thought, not . . . well, not a sober cloth, as it were.'

'No, you could say that, not a sober cloth.' The doctor smiled broadly.

'Well – ' Willy put out his hand and drew a finger nail down one of the narrow stripes of the doctor's coat, saying, 'At that time I couldn't really distinguish the colour of the stripe, but now I can see it's blue on a grey background. Am I right?'

'Yes, you're right.'

'Then that gives me the answer to the question I asked you. Could a blow on the head restore one's sight?'

'Ah! yes, yes. . . . But it may be only a temporary thing. As Doctor Blackman has already told you, in your right eye it's the nerves that are affected and bodily and mental strain can act on these. Then again, with the blow the retina could have been dislodged. And now moved again. I don't know.'

'But I have received a bodily strain, so to speak, and either the eye nerves have been affected, in reverse to what he suggested, or the retina has moved again.'

'Ah; yes, yes, could be perhaps.' Again the doctor was nodding his head. 'But I wouldn't rely too much upon the change.'

'If it's only the nerves that are affected, couldn't I have an operation?'

'On the nerves at the back of the eye? Huh!' The doctor laughed now. 'I doubt it. Nerves are funny things to play about with in any part of the body, but the eye is the most delicate. Still, let's see how long the improvement lasts, eh? and we might try spectacles again, although I know they were of little benefit to you before.'

'Just as you say, doctor. By the way, shall I be able to travel, I mean will this dizziness go within the next day or so?'

'Oh no, no, there must be no talk of you travelling for at least a fortnight. What you must do now is rest.'

So Willy said his good-byes to Josefina from his bedroom in the old nursery quarters where they had grown up together, and he was saddened to a depth that he hadn't imagined by the coming loss of her. The eruption on that particular Sunday some weeks ago was forgotten, at least by him, and he held her hands tightly as he looked at her, and with his improved vision he saw that she was very beautiful, exquisitely so. His throat was full as he said, and with a truth he was facing for the first time, 'I'm going to miss you, Josefina, so, so very much.'

She stared at him in silence. Her dark eyes were bright, seeming to give off a deep purple light. Her small mouth was pressed tight. But she didn't speak, and so he went on, 'Why must you go? We have been so close all these years. If we had been brother and sister the tie between us couldn't have been stronger.'

Now she opened her lips and her voice did not match her small, delicate frame but sounded deep and full of meaning as she said, 'But we are not brother and sister. Mama, as she said, has had her doubts all these years, in fact she is convinced that her husband had nothing to do with the makings of me. But this I think has only come to her of late, whereas for me I have known since I passed out of childhood that I in no way belong to this race . . . your race.'

'Oh, Josefina, don't say that. You'll always belong to us. You . . . you have a special place in my heart.'

'Have I?'

'Yes, yes.' He drew her hands towards his chest and pressed them there until she said with slow separated words, 'But not special enough.'

Both his eyes widened and the light that was without a hazy rim in his right eye saw the look in hers and slowly his hands released their hold on her and his head dropped forward while his mind cried, 'No, no!' and his senses cried back at it, 'Yes. Oh yes!' Josefina thinking of him in that way, and for how long? This was why she couldn't stand the thought of Noreen. Oh God! the complications and the hurts and the weight of guilt, for he knew now that he was responsible for her going.

She had risen from the side of the bed and helplessly he looked up at her and his next words sounded inane to his own ears as he said, 'It . . . it needn't be good-bye, you could come back for a holiday or we –' His voice trailed off for he could not add, 'Noreen and I could visit America.'

She stood looking down at him for a moment, her expression holding a look of slight scorn mingled with sadness. 'If I were contemplating coming back for a holiday,' she said, 'I wouldn't then be leaving now. As to you coming across there, that would be a waste of time, that's if you wanted to see me, for I don't intend to stay long on the ranch, I mean to find my own people. I won't be happy until I do, be they what they may. . . . Good-bye, Willy.' She leaned forward and as he reached up to kiss her cheek she placed her lips fully on his. It was the first time it had happened and their touch was like a spark from a fire alighting on his mouth, and instinctively his arms went up and held her tightly, and she to him; then, her hands on his chest, she thrust him back on to the pillow and, head bent, she ran from the room.

Slowly he lay back and stared before him. Josefina feeling like that.... And how did he feel? He moved his head slowly. He couldn't explain how he felt. He only knew that he was sorry to the heart of him that she was going and that he would never see her again.

When his gaze moved round the room, the images were dimmed again with the moisture in his eyes. 'I love Noreen,' he said to himself. 'Oh yes, I love Noreen.' And there was no doubt in his mind but that he did love Noreen. Yet why was he feeling like this about Josefina for his instinct was urging him to get up and to dash down the stairs and beg of her, 'Don't go. Don't go, Josefina.'

You couldn't love two people, not really, not at the same time, and in the same way. It was impossible.

He could not take into consideration that he was his mother's son and had inherited her problem.

⁊ 7 ⁘

'Mam. Mam. Do something, will you?'

'I will, lass, as soon as I can.'

They were each kneeling on the floor speaking through the keyhole.

'I'll go mad if I have to stay here much longer.'

'If you give him your word he'd let you out.'

'I can't do that.'

'Don't be ridiculous, girl; pretend, say you will, swear you will, and then once outside I'll get you away. I've got it all ready, I mean some things packed, and money for you.'

'Oh, Mam!' There was silence for a moment. Then Noreen's voice came tear-laden and trembling through the keyhole of the stout oak door, saying, 'Go to the police, Mam; they could make him let me out.'

'No, lass, no! I've gone into that. It's a private matter. A father is allowed to chastise his daughter, that's what the constable said.'

'Mam, I'm smelling, I haven't had a decent wash. It's ... it's thirteen days since I've been in here and my slop bucket's full again.'

Lucy turned her eyes towards the stairs and put her head to one side as if she were listening; but it was not for her husband coming home because he had just gone off to the market after having opened this door and thrust a meal inside.

This morning he had not brought any washing water because he was in a hurry. Whenever he did bring her a ewer he would shout through the door for Noreen to stand back, and do the same whenever he brought her an empty pail and took the full one out.

It was the full bucket of slops that Lucy was seeing in her mind's eye as she looked towards the staircase. Turning her head sharply back to the keyhole, she said, 'Listen, Noreen, listen. Now pay attention. He'll have had a drink when he comes in but he won't be full; he's wise enough not to overdo it because then I might get the chance to search him for the key. He's slept in the other back room since he put you in there. Now pay attention. I'll tell him you must have your slop bucket emptied. Now have it in your hand when he opens the door and make to put it on the floor within reaching distance of him, then swing it up and let him have it over him . . . Do you hear?'

'The slops?'

'Yes, yes.'

'Right, Mam. Right.'

'Then make for the door. I'll do my best to keep it wide. When you get downstairs go through the front room, I'll leave the right-hand window open, make for the cow field and the bottom gate. . . . You listening?'

'Yes, yes, Mam. Go on, go on.'

'Well, go to the old barn at the bottom, I'll leave the bass hamper of your clothes there and enough money to keep you going for some weeks. Make for the Jarrow turnpike. It's not far from there to the terminus where you'll get the horse bus. Do you follow me?'

'Yes, Mam, yes.'

'He'll never think about you going that way, he'll think you'll go straight to the Manor. But for God's sake, girl, if you value that young lad's life, don't go near that place. Do you hear me?'

There was a pause before Noreen's voice came to her, saying, flatly, 'I hear you, Mam.'

'And you promise you won't go there?'

'I can promise you that, Mam.'

'Because you know he'll kill him this time, don't you?'

Again there was a pause before her daughter said, 'Yes, I know that. But I'll tell you something, Mam. If I had a knife in here the night instead of a bucket of slops I'd drive it into him. I would, I would.'

'Oh, Noreen, Noreen, don't say that. He's acting like this because of his feelings for you.'

'Huh! feelings. It's not feelings for me, Mam, that's caused him to be mad, and you know it. He must have had some outsize opinion of himself when young and couldn't imagine anyone passing him over. He still can't . . . You know what's the trouble with him?'

'Enough. Enough. Listen. Listen.'

'I'm listenin', Mam.'

'When you get to Newcastle take a cab to Garden Crescent. Have you got that?'

'Yes, Mam.'

'There's a boarding house. It's respectable, it's run by a Mrs Snaith. Remember that, the name's Snaith. 2 Garden Crescent. Oh, if only I could get something under this door.' Lucy now actually clawed at the carpet that was tight against the bottom of the door. Although worn with constant rubbing it was still impossible to slip a piece of paper over it and beneath the door.

'It's all right, Mam. Mrs Snaith, 2 Garden Crescent, Newcastle. I'll remember.'

'And don't write me, lass, not here. Write to him and tell him he must never try to see you 'cos you're going to start a new life. . . . And you'll have to. You understand that?'

Lucy waited for confirmation of this, and when none came she said, 'Noreen! Noreen! you've got to forget him. If you want him to remain alive you've got to forget him. Get it into your head, lass.'

'If I ask him to come away with me he would, Mam.'

'Oh, come down from your cloud, lass, how would he earn a living away from the Manor?'

'He wouldn't need to, he'll have money of his own.'

'Not until he comes of age, lass. And then all these things are complicated. I think it's the mother who holds the purse strings there, and she's sheltered him all his life.'

'He's no weakling, Mam. You don't know him.'

'All right, he's no weakling, but he's an almost blind man, and how long do you think romance will last living a hole and corner life? You're sensible, you've always been sensible. He's been brought up as a gentleman; you yourself could rough it and your feelings remain the same, but it's different for a man, I'm telling you, I know. They are full of self-importance, from the smallest to the biggest. Aw lass' – she finished in a tearful voice – 'put him out of your mind. There are others in the world who will jump at you. You're young, this will pass.'

When no answering voice came through the keyhole, Lucy got to her feet and stood leaning against the support of the door for a moment, her eyes closed, her head bowed. Then bending again, she put her mouth to the keyhole and said, 'Put on as much clean underwear as you can,' after which she turned and opened the door of the wardrobe on the landing where most of Noreen's clothes were kept because the bedroom with its sloping roof would not allow of such a large piece of furniture, and taking from it a coat and a working cloak, she went downstairs and began to prepare for her daughter's escape.

On his return, Simon Bentwood was slow in getting down from the trap. Lucy watched him from the kitchen window and noted with relief that he was impeded as much by his back as by the drink he had taken.

With regard to the latter she was informed of the amount almost immediately for Eddie, scurrying into the kitchen, whispered, 'He hasn't had a lot, Mam, three pints and two whiskys. I was watching from the window. It's his back; he could hardly get up into the trap.'

Lucy made no answer but stood waiting for her husband's entry. The moment he entered the door she could see that he was suffering great pain for he had difficulty in lifting one foot over the step into the kitchen. Without comment, she watched him take off his hat and outer coat; then he sat down at the table, and cast his eyes over the bare boards before raising them to Lucy and saying, 'What's this?'

She answered straightaway, 'I'm not making any more meals in this house until that girl is cleaned up and is properly fed. She hasn't had a bite since breakfast, and worse, the room's stinking, her bucket is overflowing. If you don't come to your senses soon she'll die of a fever.'

He stared at her. Then, his tone without anger, even moderate sounding and slightly weary, he said, 'She could be out of there within minutes if she gave me her word, but until she does there she stays and nobody can do anything about it. Do you hear that, Lucy? Nobody can do anything about it. I'm her father and it's within my power to keep her under control as long as I like.'

She bowed her head and remained silent for a moment, and then said, 'Will you give her a clean bucket?'

When he made no reply she looked at him and with raised voice cried, 'Well, if you can't make the stairs let me take one to her.'

The very suggestion seemed to lift him from the chair, and when he was standing straight he said, 'Bring it to me!'

Immediately she went into the scullery and brought an empty pail, but as she handed it to him he said, 'Give it to the boy.'

This was a contingency for which she wasn't prepared; nevertheless she handed the bucket to Eddie and when his father pointed towards the door the boy went before him into the hall and up the stairs. It was a good minute later when Simon joined his son for he'd had to place two feet on every stair before being able to make the next one.

Now he was standing outside the door. Slowly he put his hand into his back pocket and, taking out a key, placed it in the lock. He paused a moment, then turning the key he pushed open the door, stood for a second before reaching out towards Eddie and grabbing the empty pail from his hand, then taking three steps into the room he faced his daughter. Her face was deathly pale, almost haggard looking, her eyes wide, staring, and her lips quivering.

Simon swallowed deeply, cleared his throat noisily, then said, 'Well, are you going to see sense, girl?'

When she didn't answer, only stared defiantly back at him, he thrust his hand behind him and said, 'Come and take the pail, boy.'

Now Noreen's gaze flashed to her mother standing on the landing, then bending swiftly she picked up the pail and as Eddie approached her she screamed at him, 'Out of the way!' and at the same time she heaved it upwards and threw the contents at the man before her.

Simon, aware of her intention just a second too late, had thrust out his arm towards her but when the avalanche of filth spewed over him he let out a most inhuman cry, staggered backwards, slipped, and with arms flailing in an effort to catch hold of something to break his fall he fell flat on his back and with an agonising groan lay there.

Noreen did not even see him fall for she was out of the door, past her mother and down the stairs; nor did Lucy go to the aid of her husband but, running after her daughter, she hissed, 'Don't forget the address. And pick up your cloak.' Noreen did not wait to give an answer to her mother. Like an escaping prisoner, as she certainly was, she flew through the sitting-room and out of the window, and as swift as any hare she made her way to the old barn where would lie her passport to freedom, freedom her mother would never have provided her with if she had known what she was carrying inside her.

8

'Mama. . . . Mama! please, please, be quiet. It's no use talking any more. I mean to go over there and find out what's happening to her. I went along with you last week when you asked me to wait, I've gone along with you this week when you've begged me to wait, but I can wait no longer. Unless she was tied up she would have got word to me in some way, I know she would. She's strong-willed, determined if you like.'

Tilly sank down slowly on to the couch and, taking a handkerchief from the pocket of her dress, she wiped the beads of sweat from her brow.

It had been hot all day, in fact June had been behaving as one expected it to do for the past two weeks; there had been no rain, the sun had shone all day long and the nights seemed to be almost as hot as the days.

All the windows on the ground floor of the Manor were open, yet no breeze stirred through the house.

She brought the handkerchief round her lips and, reaching out, picked up a glass of sherbet from the table and sipped at it. After replacing the glass on the table again she moved her lips slowly one over the other before she said, 'What you don't seem to understand, Willy, is that Simon Bentwood is capable of killing, and rather than have you have his daughter I'm sure he will attempt it, even knowing the consequences of such an act.'

'Mama' – he was bending down towards her now – "why did you have me trained in wrestling?'

When she looked up at him and made no reply he demanded, his voice almost on a shout now, 'Go on, tell me, tell me why you had me trained to defend myself.'

'Don't shout at me, Willy!' Even as she said the words she was surprised that she had to speak in such a way to this son who up to a few short weeks ago she had deemed to be the most even-tempered creature in the world, and when he slowly straightened his back and stood rigid before her she looked up at him and said patiently, 'Willy, you are dealing with a madman. How can I get that home to you? Simon Bentwood has become unbalanced.' She now put her hand out towards him and, gripping his wrist, she said, 'Do one more thing for me: wait until you hear from Steve. You said yesterday he was going to make enquiries.'

'I'm sorry, Mama, I can't. I can't stand another day without knowing what's happened to her. Do you know that I haven't slept for nights?'

No, she hadn't known that, but she used his words now, saying, 'Well, if that is the case, you're in no fit condition to meet up with that raving lunatic of a man.' Her voice had risen now, and she pulled herself to her feet and as she did so there was a tap on the drawing-room door. It opened, and Biddle stood there and announced solemnly, 'Mr McGrath to see you, ma'am.'

Tilly did not move towards Steve as he entered the room but Willy did. His hand guiding him along the back of the couch, his face slightly to the side, he hurried towards the mist-shrouded figure and as Tilly watched his hand go out to Steve, and Steve take it firmly within his and turn him about, then guide him back towards her, she experienced the grinding rib cage pain again which had nothing to do with her son's unhappiness but which recalled the words he had said to her some time ago: 'At one time, I thought he was my father.'

It was the first time she had seen Steve to speak to privately since their interrupted conversation. She had seen him twice since, both times he was on horseback and in the company of . . . the woman. And on the second occasion she knew that he had deliberately turned off the main coach road to avoid meeting her.

Acting the hostess, she said, 'Can I get you something to drink, Steve?'

To her surprise he accepted the invitation, saying, 'That would be welcome at the moment, Tilly. A beer, if that is possible.'

Yes, a beer would be possible, and from the cellar too, but it wasn't usually drunk in the drawing-room. However, marriage into the Drew family had so much altered Biddle's attitude that the request he should serve the guest with beer in this room would register no effect on his expression.

As she rang the bell Willy was saying to Steve, 'Have you heard anything?' and before the door opened Steve had answered, 'Yes. Yes, I have.' But once Biddle had entered the room he did not speak again; not until Tilly had said to Biddle, 'Will you please draw a fresh flagon of ale from the cellar and bring a platter of bread and cheese at the same time?' and only when the door had closed on the butler did he look from one to the other and say, 'I must warn you that it isn't pleasant news.'

Willy made no comment, and Steve went on, 'If one is to believe Randy Simmons's chat he's, I mean Bentwood's, got her locked up in her bedroom and she's been there for the past fortnight.'

'No! No!' Willy turned about hastily and made to walk towards the open window, and when he stumbled against the chair and it toppled over, Steve, rising hastily, made to go to his aid, but Tilly's hand on his sleeve stayed him, and when he looked at her she shook her head.

Now they both watched Willy swing around as he cried, 'Well, this is it! I'm going over there. Will . . . will you come with me, Steve?'

When there was no direct reply Willy shouted, 'All right! All right! I'll go on my own, but go I will.'

'Hold your hand a minute, wait! Wait. Come and sit down.' And saying so, Steve went towards him and drew him back to the middle of the room and pressed him down into a chair. He himself sat on the edge of the couch and, leaning forward, he gripped Willy's knee as he said, 'You've got to go careful in this business, Willy. If you barge into his house, even into his farmyard, and he does you a mischief you won't get much sympathy or even justice, you'll be at fault.'

'I don't want sympathy, and if there's any justice the police should go to the house and lock him up.'

'Now! now! wait. Put your studying cap on and think it out. It's a private matter; she's his daughter. What does she want to do? Well, she wants to run off with a young man. Now he doesn't see eye to eye with her about this, so what does he do? He locks her in her room. The same thing's been done countless times before, Willy, in an effort to make young lasses come to their senses.'

'She's ... she's not just a young lass, she's a very sensible person, clear headed ... she thinks. ...'

'Well, if that's the case she'll likely think of a way out of this situation. Look; will you leave the matter in my hands for another day or two? I'll take a walk round there and when he's in the fields, Bentwood I mean, I'll try to have a word with her mother.' His voice now went into a gritty growl as he added, 'And at the same time I'll collar Mr Randy Simmons and threaten to choke the life out of him if he carries any more tales. He's an old rat that fellow. He was a mischief-maker when I was a lad and the years haven't improved him. Well now, what do you say?'

'What's that? Aw no!' Tilly looked towards the door. They all looked towards the door from where beyond in the hall there came a sound as if Biddle had dropped the tray and the glass had splintered. But when there followed a commotion of scuffling and muddled voices, Tilly glanced quickly at Steve and he at her. Then they both ran towards the drawing-room door. But before they reached it, it was opened, not thrust open, but kicked open, and there, like an infuriated bull, stood the man who was in all of their minds.

'Where is she? Come on! Where is she?'

'Now, look here, Mr Bentwood.' Steve had taken a step forward, only to be checked by Simon Bentwood's voice bawling, 'You keep out of this, McGrath, this has nothing to do with you. Or then perhaps it has, you being her fancy man.'

The echo of his last word had scarcely died away before Steve had sprung over the distance between them. But all Bentwood's faculties were alert, the drink had worn off, his back for the moment had eased as it was apt to do at times, helped he had imagined by the cold sluice he had given himself under the pump to rid his body of the stink and filth of the slop bucket; so he met Steve's attack not with his fists but with his boot. Bringing it sharply forward he caught him in the groin and sent him reeling to the side in agony. Then he was in the drawing-room and advancing to where Willy was waiting for him, his body stiff, his arms slightly bent, his head turned well to the side.

The pose checked Simon Bentwood's onslaught and within an arm's length he stopped and again he bawled, 'Where is she?'

Before Willy could answer, Tilly's voice broke in, crying, 'She's not here. Your daughter's not here.'

Simon Bentwood did not take his eyes from the young man before him and again he demanded, 'Where is she? You dare to stand there and tell me she's not here, go on!'

'She's ... not ... here.' The words were spaced and firm; then Willy added more to them: 'But if she were here, I can assure you I wouldn't let you near her.'

'You! you blind son of a bitch of hell.' Now it was he who sprang, his right hand extended in the act of delivering a blow. But surprisingly it didn't reach its target and there was no one more amazed than Bentwood when he found himself spun round, his arms wrenched behind him and into a grip like that of a vice while a knee found the sorest spot on his spine, and, his body bent over, he was forced to groan aloud.

In the seconds it had taken this to happen, Tilly had raced from the room past Biddle and Peabody, who were attending to Steve, and it was only seconds again before she returned and, looking to where her son was still holding Simon Bentwood, she shouted, 'Let him go. Let him go, Willy.'

Willy could only dimly see the outline of his mother standing in the middle of the room. For the moment his vision seemed to have worsened and he imagined she was standing holding a gun to her shoulder. Her voice confirmed his dimmed image, for she now cried again, 'Let him go, and if he dares to raise a finger to you I'll shoot him.'

Slowly Willy relinquished his hold on the big, flabby figure and he could see enough to know the man stumbled some steps forward and groped for the support of the back of a high chair. He saw him straighten his back, then look slowly around the room.

Perhaps it was not only the sight of Tilly standing levelling a gun at him that raised the fury in Bentwood but the fact that she seemed surrounded by all her lackeys, for besides the two flunkeys three outside men were standing by her now. Two of them he recognised as the Drew fellows. And then there were the women crowding round the door, a host of them, all ready to defend her and her blind brat.

He fixed his gaze on Tilly now, then on a bitter laugh he cried, 'You would shoot me, would you? If I remember rightly you used to be against guns at one time, wouldn't hear of a rabbit being potted. But that was afore you crossed the seas and became a squaw. Did you shoot Sopwith afore he shot you for mixing it with the blackies? . . .'

The report of the gun startled him and lifted him from the ground for the bullet had passed through the pad of his coat taking the skin off his shoulder with it and had lodged itself in the panelling near the window behind him.

In the stillness that pervaded the room he put his fingers inside his jacket, and when he pulled them out they were wet. He stared at them for a moment, then looked towards her. She had the gun cocked again. She had shot him, Tilly Trotter had shot him. She could have killed him. Perhaps she meant to kill him. He wanted to say something but he was too shaken and he stood with his hand extended in front of him listening to her saying, 'I aimed for your shoulder. Now I'll give you exactly five minutes to clear my grounds, and should you ever enter them again, Simon Bentwood, I won't aim for your shoulder next time. One more thing, from this moment I give you twelve months' notice to quit your farm. . . . Arthur. Jimmy.' She did not look towards the men as she spoke but went on, 'See that this man leaves my property.'

When Jimmy and Arthur Drew approached him, Simon Bentwood, as if coming out of a dream, growled at them, 'Keep your place, you two. She hasn't finished me off yet; I'm still capable of dealing with lackeys.'

'Arthur.'

The command checked Arthur Drew from taking the battle further.

Simon Bentwood now moved from behind the chair and in passing down the middle of the room he had to come within two yards of Tilly and he paused for a moment as he glared at her and he said, 'I'll make a case of this, shooting's an offence. There'll be no one to meet you coming out of court this time. There's still justice here, and I'll see you along the line yet.'

Although she knew that his threat was empty because he was trespassing and had forced an entry into her house, she shivered as she recalled her ordeal the first time she had been in a court; and it was true, he had met her, he had been there to comfort her. He had been the only one to comfort her. But she couldn't imagine that the bulky form walking slowly through the door was one and the same man as the kindly thoughtful young Simon Bentwood. It was terrible to acknowledge the fact that love could have such power as to change a man into what Simon had become.

The room began to buzz: the girls were around her, Peg, Fanny, Lizzy, Betty, and Christine Peabody. 'Are you all right, ma'am? Are you all right; ma'am?'

'Yes, yes, I'm all right. Bring in some tea and . . . whisky,' she said to Peg, and to the others she said, 'Yes, yes, I'm all right. Just leave us.'

She placed the gun on the table and as her hands left hold of it she clasped them together in an effort to stop them trembling, before walking down the room to where Willy was standing beside Steve. Peabody and Biddle were still present and it was Peabody who said, 'I . . . I think, madam, that Mr McGrath should have attention.'

She had to lean right down in order to see Steve's face for he was bent over, one arm still hugging his waist.

'Is it bad?'

He made no answer, not even to move his head, and so she turned to Biddle and Peabody and said quietly, 'Can you assist him upstairs to the grey suite?'

'Yes, yes, ma'am.'

One on each side of him, they went to help him up, but he shrugged them off; and Willy, moving to the front of him, said quietly, 'Once you get straight you'll be able to walk, Steve. Look, lift your arms.'

Steve slowly raised his head and looked up at Willy and did what he was bid; and Willy, linking his forearms under Steve's oxters, gently brought him upwards, then placing one hand firmly on the bottom of his spine he pressed it, saying, 'That better?'

Steve gave him a sickly smile now as he said, 'Yes. Strangely it is.'

'Phil Spoke knew a trick or two.'

'He must have,' Steve nodded at him; then looking at Tilly he asked, 'You all right?'

'Yes.' There was a slight quiver to her voice but she repeated, 'Yes, I'm all right. Can you manage the stairs?'

'Thanks all the same, but if you don't mind I'd rather make for home.'

'But I think you should be attended to.'

'It'll . . . it'll just be a bruise. Winded me for a time.' He nodded at her.

She stared at him, then said, 'Very well, but you won't be able to ride.' She turned to Biddle now. 'Tell Myers to bring the coach round as soon as possible;' then turning again towards Steve, she took his arm, saying, 'Come and sit down.'

Slowly and stiffly Steve walked up the room, but when Tilly indicated the sofa he shook his head, saying, 'I think I'll be better standing, if you don't mind.'

She looked at him now in deep concern. 'I wish you'd stay and let me see to you.'

'Don't worry about me, I'm used to managing. It's yourself you've got to think about.' With this, he turned to where Willy was standing near him and, moving his head slowly he said, 'Now have you changed your mind about letting your friends deal with that maniac?'

Willy did not answer but facing his mother and Steve, he said slowly, 'She must have got away. Why didn't she come here to me?'

'Well, I should have thought that was obvious, lad, she knew she would endanger you.'

'Where could she have gone?' He turned his dim gaze from one to the other, and when neither of them spoke he said, 'I'll find her. She can't have gone all that far, she wouldn't know how, for she's never been further than Newcastle in her life.'

As Tilly looked at her son she hoped from the depths of her heart that his search would be in vain because instinctively she knew that if he were to find her he wouldn't enjoy her for long. One way or another, Simon would see to that, for she wouldn't always be there with a gun.

കൈ 9 ഇൻ

The village was agog. My God! she had started again, that one up there. She had shot the farmer now, and him just going asking if she had seen his daughter. And her fancy man going for him! Well, Farmer Bentwood had seen to him, laid him on his back for close on a week he had, almost put an end to his whoring too, so it was said. But to think she would actually take a gun up and shoot the farmer, him that had been so kind to her in her young days. Why, she had been the cause of his first wedding going wrong; hadn't she made a scene on his very wedding night, when he'd gone running to her aid and left his bride soured.

Old Mrs McGrath, now a toothless hag, retold the tale for the hundredth time to her grandson, even going as far as to brag it was her hand that had taken the light from the witch's bastard's eyes. But her own son had warned her an equal number of times to stop her chattering, and he warned her now to keep the door closed and her voice down when she spoke of that 'un up there, because, say what you like, she had power. It had already been proved in both ways in their very own family; hadn't she killed one of them off and raised another to a position he would never have reached on his own, for what had that young snipe learned in a pit that he himself and his brothers hadn't. Looking back, he reminded his mother that her youngest son hadn't had a word to say for himself when a lad, timid he had been, skinny, undersized, and look at him now, six foot if an inch and broad with it, and learned they said, book read, and spoke no more like the rest of them. Now who but one with a strange power could have brought that about? he asked his mother yet again, so it behoved her to speak in whispers when she was alluding to that 'un.

The day following the events at the Manor Randy Simmons brought the news to his master that his daughter had been seen tearing towards the turnpike road the night before, and the same pair of eyes had watched her wave down the horse bus before it reached the turnpike; and she had been alone except for a bass hamper that she carried.

After hearing this news, Simon Bentwood looked for his wife and found her in the dairy, her arms turning the wheel of the churn. She didn't stop her work when he came and stood close beside her. Putting out his left hand, for his right one was hanging stiffly by his side, he gripped her free arm and said, 'You manoeuvred it, eh?'

Lucy stopped wielding the churn handle and, taking up a large wooden spoon from the bench to the side of her, she brought it down sharply across the knuckles that were gripping her flesh.

At this, he almost screamed at her, 'Go on! woman, put my other one out of action. Is that what you're aiming at?'

She walked away from him, placing the churn between them, and then she said, 'Yes, if you handle me in such a fashion again, yes. And aye, I did manoeuvre it. I wasn't going to see you drive my daughter mad up in that slit of a room, so I told her what to do. Throw filth over him, I said, because what was in her bucket would match your mind.'

'Be careful, woman! careful. I warn you.'

'You can warn me of nothing, Simon Bentwood, no more, no more. I've put up with you for years because I loved you. I've lived with the fact that your mind was on that woman every minute of your waking hours and I tolerated it because, as I said, I loved you. But no more, after the way you've treated your daughter and aimed to break her spirit into submission because you couldn't bear to think that she would find happiness with the son of the woman that spurned you. I could see you dead tomorrow and not mourn.' She paused now and stared into his face. His brows were beetling, yet the expression on his face seemed to express more pain than rage, and when she ended, 'I never in my life imagined I would say those words to you, but they're true. And I will add to them this: from now on I'm no longer your wife. I'll cook and clean and work, but I'll no longer share your bed, not ever again. You'll have to find solace elsewhere, Simon, to ease the hunger in your heart, but it'll never again come from me.'

She ran her hands down each side of her white apron before ending, 'Now if you'll leave me I'll finish the butter, but if you don't then you can get your henchmen to come and do it for you.' She watched his lips part slowly, his mouth open wide as if gasping at the air. She waited for him to speak but no words came. His lips closed, he made an attempt to straighten his back; then winced inwardly at the pain before turning away and walking slowly out.

She did not turn to watch his going but, gripping the handle of the churn again, she swung it down and up; and now her own mouth was open wide and the salt tears were raining from her eyes down into it.

Tilly visited Steve on each of the first three days after the incident at the house. She had wanted to attend him but he had pushed her off as if she were a young girl who had never witnessed bare flesh, so she arranged for Peter Myers to see to him. But it was from the doctor she derived the extent of the injury Steve had received. The impact had split open his groin almost two inches and it had to be stitched; moreover, his whole hip was bruised.

Tilly had arranged for Fanny to ride over in the trap, taking a hot meal to him and, whilst there, to tidy the cottage. She would like to have carried out the latter duties herself, and doubtless would have done if Willy hadn't been claiming most of her time.

Willy had become a problem. Never had she imagined this quiet son of hers could become so intense and show such determination. In a strange way she could see Matthew in him, for Matthew's one aim in life had been to conquer herself; it seemed now that this trait had also developed fast in Willy. He was more like Matthew's son than Mark's but, of course, she should not be surprised at any traits that made their appearance in her son that resembled those in Matthew, for were they not half-brothers?

Willy was determined to find Noreen, and his main idea was that the best place to look for her would be in Newcastle. But he couldn't search alone, and so without even asking his mother's leave he had ordered Ned Spoke to take him in, not on just one or two occasions but every day. He had not even enquired if she would need the coach. This annoyed her, and so she brought it into the open on the evening of the fifth day.

It was almost dark when he returned. She had gone to the drawing-room door to watch him entering the hall and she saw by the way he walked and the groping movement of his hands held out before him, that his sight at this stage must be very dim, and so she directed him towards her, saying, 'Have you had anything to eat?'

He lifted his head and, walking more steadily now, he crossed to her, saying, 'Yes, we had a bite around teatime.'

She looked from his pale, dust-covered face to his equally dust-covered suit, which spoke of the miles he must have tramped round the city, and certainly not in the main thoroughfare, and she had the desire to put her arms about him and comfort him, while at the same time she knew, should she do so, she would be seeing the boy he once was and not the man he had become.

She walked just ahead of him, her voice leading him into the middle of the room and to the couch, and there she said, 'What will you have? Some soup and cold meats?'

'No, no, I want nothing to eat, but . . . but I'd like a drink, a whisky.'

The surprise she felt she didn't show in her voice as she repeated, 'A whisky?' He hadn't been a spirit drinker, not even a wine drinker, if he drank anything it was the usual ale.

She had rung the bell and Biddle had brought in the tray and decanter. She sat down on the couch and, following a moment's silence, she said, 'This can't go on, Willy.'

'Why not?'

'For so many reasons.' She turned her body towards him and her voice was sharp now: 'You'll wear yourself out. Moreover, Ned is wanted here, as is the coach. You did not even ask if I might need it.'

There was silence again for a time before he answered, 'No, I didn't because I thought you would understand. Anyway, I would think I was past the stage where I've got to ask permission to use the coach. As for Ned, I was under the impression that you gave him me as a guide years ago. He is my man.'

If in the future were she to try to pin-point the time when her boy finally went from her, she knew it was now on this beautiful June evening, two days after his twentieth birthday with the scent floating in from the garden, with the air still and the house quiet and seemingly at peace. The love that was tearing at her son had thrust itself between them, severing the bond that had linked them from his birth, and with this knowledge the pall of aloneness settled on her once more. Had there still been Steve in the background waiting, his patience of years proving his stability, the pain would not have been so acute.

Josefina gone, Steve gone, and now Willy. What was it about her that time and again thrust her out into the wilderness? What had begun it all, this thing that caused her to be misjudged, ostracised, that caused men to love her and hate her and often brought death in its wake? Money . . . yes, money. She felt herself nodding at this realisation. It was as if for the first time her eyes had been opened and she saw from where stemmed her fate, the stolen money, stolen by the McGraths, and discovered by her grandfather and taken from its hiding place by him and Simon Bentwood's father and hidden in the well of the farm. And it was she herself who, as a child, innocently revealed to old woman McGrath, Steve's mother, that she possessed a sovereign, a sovereign to go shopping with when it was known that her grandfather had never worked for years, and they were supposed to live from hand to mouth. From that day the McGraths had planned to recover what they thought was theirs, and when all else failed Hal McGrath had determined to get his hands on the money by marrying her. That had been the beginning. And yet not quite: There had been her desire too to read and write. This had brought her within the vision of the parson's wife, and the parson's wife, who was young at heart, had besides teaching her her letters, taught her how to dance, and with dancing the image of the witch had been born. And it was strange when she came to think of it, she had never danced since. She was now fifty years old and she had never danced. She had faintly hoped to do so on that New Year's Eve years ago, but that was the night the mine had been flooded, and that was the night Steve first kissed her as they stood together watching the New Year come in.

'Will you want the carriage tomorrow?'

'What?'

'I said will you want the carriage tomorrow?'

'No, no.'

'I can go in the trap, it makes no difference.'

'No; take whichever you want.'

'I'm sorry.'

'It's all right . . . Go to bed. I'm going up too.'

Willy pulled himself to his feet and when he was facing her he said slowly, 'I can't help myself, Mama, I wish I could, but she's . . . she's all I want from life. It's odd, the feeling she creates in me when I'm with her, it's . . . it's as if I'd come home. I can't explain it. I . . . I understand how Josefina wanted to return to Texas.'

He stopped speaking and turned his head to the side now as if Josefina had suddenly appeared, and he recalled a dream that had been vivid in the night, but had escaped him on awakening leaving only a vague, confused feeling, But now he was remembering it, because in his dream he had been searching in an unknown place and it wasn't for Noreen but for Josefina. He put his hand to his head. Sometimes over the last few days he had thought he wasn't only going stone blind but stone mad.

When he felt the touch on his arm he allowed himself to be led from the room and up the stairs. All his life he had been led here and guided there, and he now felt a fierce urge to throw off the arm that he had leaned on for years and scream to the gods to give him light, at least light enough that he would never need hers or anyone's guiding hand again.

↶ 10 ↷

During the weeks that followed and slipped into months there grew in Tilly a feeling of helpless despair as she watched her son get into the coach that was to take him to Newcastle or Gateshead or Sunderland or Durham. His search had taken the form of a mania; he had become the object of gossip to the extent that bets were laid on his finding young Noreen Bentwood before her father did, because it was well known that Simon too was searching, not so frequently perhaps but with more advantage.

During the last two weeks however, there had been days when the carriage had not gone out and Willy had stayed at home and spent the time in his rooms or walking in the gardens. He could do this alone because he knew every path and turn up to where the land drifted away into fields.

These days had brought relief, she knew, to Ned Spoke, for she guessed he had become weary tramping the streets, his eyes continually searching. But when she had questioned him about the procedure he had made no word of complaint for she knew he was devoted to Willy. This the young man had demonstrated when once she said to him, 'See that he gets a good meal when he's out, Ned,' to which he had replied, 'He won't go into an hotel, ma'am, because you see I can't sit with him, my being dressed as I am. And then I'd be like a fish out of water eating in them places, so it's usually rough grub, pies and peas, or pork dips an' such, but it's fillin' an' wholesome and he eats.' And he added, 'Well, he knows he's got to, ma'am, if he wants to go on.'

Occasionally Steve would relieve Ned. At least on half a dozen Sundays he had acted as Willy's guide. The last time was the Sunday just gone. It had been a very wet day. September was nearing October, the trees had turned, the grass was yellowing and the land was getting ready for the winter, and on their return Steve had remarked on this, saying to her, 'Something'll have to happen to put a stop to this afore the winter sets in or you're going to have a sick man on your hands, Tilly.'

When she had said, 'But what can I do?' his answer had been, 'I don't know, I don't know. What has to be done he'll do himself I suppose.' And then he added, 'The pity of it is he thinks if he doesn't have her he'll never have anyone. He can't imagine anyone else wanting him, not in his condition. This is what makes the whole thing so very difficult. I've told him, or words to the effect, that there's more fish in the sea than have ever been caught, but that slid off him.'

More fish in the sea than have ever been caught. He must have come to the same conclusion with regard to his own affairs. He himself had picked on another fish, hadn't he?

Since this business of Willy's daily treks had come about, Steve had made no further reference either to the woman or to marriage, but she knew it must be very much on his mind because she had seen the woman at the cottage twice during the week he had been ill. Her horse standing at the gate had been the cause of her turning her own animal about and riding back home. On another occasion Fanny had told her, 'I didn't stay to do anything, ma'am, because the lady was there again.'

Fanny hadn't said the woman, but the lady, and Fanny knew a lady when she saw one.

Tilly knew it in herself that she dreaded meeting Steve's 'lady', and because of this she generally took a different route when going to the mine. Here, she saw him at least once a week when on a Friday he, his under-man, John, and herself held their meeting in the new office buildings she'd had erected. Previously Willy had made the fifth member at the meeting, but no longer, and his absence would be commented upon by John as if it were the first time he had not put in an appearance.

John, as dear as he was, could be very irritating at times, Tilly found, especially when he voiced openly what he thought of Willy's behaviour. Inconsiderate to say the least. And the whole thing lacked dignity. Chasing a farm girl! Well, that's what it amounted to, didn't it? She didn't come back at him and say that if Anna had been a farmer's daughter and had showed an interest in him at the time when he imagined that no one would ever want him or love him because of his stammer he, too, would have done the same as Willy was doing now, for she knew from experience that the years dimmed memories of failings and one's reactions to them. That was why the old could never understand the young.

Then came the day when Tilly met Steve's lady. It was at the beginning of

November. She herself was feeling at a very low ebb for she had nursed Willy through a severe cold that had bordered on pneumonia. One good thing had come out of this, for now he seemed to realise how fruitless his search was. He was physically weak and mentally dispirited and on this particular morning when the post arrived she was glad to see two of the letters were from abroad. One was in Katie's handwriting, the other Josefina's.

Over the last few weeks she had dealt with her mail at a small desk she'd had placed in Willy's bedroom, and now entering the room, she said cheerfully as she held up the mail, 'Two letters from Texas.'

'Oh?' His interest sounded as weak as he looked. She did not immediately open the letters but went to the fire and, taking up the tongs, placed more coal on it. Then pulling her chair towards the brass fender, she placed her feet on the rim, reached out to the desk to the side of her and picked up the first letter. It was Katie's, and it began simply:

'Dear Tilly, I take pleasure in answering your letter. I am pleased to say I am very well at present and so is Doug. Miss Luisa, too, is well, although she misses Mr Mack very much. We all miss him very much, Doug most of all I think, but as my ma would have said, Tilly, one's sorrow can be another's joy. Which isn't a very nice thing to say at this time, but you see it's like this, Miss Luisa has taken Doug into partnership, and that is a big thing, isn't it, Tilly? Just fancy, Doug in partnership on this ranch. But, of course, he's taken it as another excuse for not coming to England because since fencing off the land there's thousands of heads of cattle to be seen to. Eeh! it's a sight, Tilly . . . the drives. And to think there wasn't a single head of anything left after the war. I said to Doug the other day, you would enjoy it, the riding; as for meself, you know me, Tilly, I'm not built for a horse.

'Now about Miss Josefina. Well, like I told you in my last letter, she only stayed here a few weeks and spent most of the time asking our Mexicans where she could find her mother. Then, off she went and I really thought, Tilly, I would never see her again for it was plain to see that she had her back up against white people. Well, I suppose that was only to be understood for, going by the looks of her, she is a half-breed and you know what things are like out here. Well, three weeks ago there she is come back getting off a scrub cart, dusty and tired and looking smaller than ever, and she looked different, so sad. Well, it was like this, Tilly. She finds her mother and was horrified, that's her own word. I hope I've spelt it right. Well, she said she was horrified at the conditions under which her mother lived and she wasn't pleased to see her, I mean her mother wasn't pleased to see Josefina. All she wanted was money. And she told her that she wasn't born of Mr Matthew but the man who fathered her was called Abelorda Orozco. He had once been a short-timé hand on the ranch. He was living with her there in the house and whatever he was like must have come as a shock to Josefina for she found it difficult to speak about him, Tilly. And you know what, Tilly, she started to cry. Even as a child, although it's years ago, I never knew Josefina to cry, and I couldn't imagine she'd ever be given to crying.'

Tilly stopped reading the letter and looked over the top of it towards Willy. Indeed, Josefina must have received a shock and be in great distress, for she herself, too, had never seen her cry, not even on that day of the great outburst, nor when she had finally said good-bye to her on the boat, and they had held each other tightly for a moment and looked into each other's eyes. There had been a mistiness there, but no tears.

She returned her attention to the letter:

'Miss Luisa will be pleased to have her stay for she is lonely. She spends a lot of her time up here ... Miss Luisa. The latest is she is talking to Josefina about starting a school of sorts. There are now about ten Mexican children in the huts and quite a number scattered further afield, and you remember Number Three? well, he married a half-breed Mexican about ten years ago. But I think I told you that. And he has five children but they don't look half-breeds for they're all pure black and lovely bairns. At times with one and another the place seems swarming with bairns, it's like being back home and, oh Tilly, how I long to come back, just for a little while, not for good 'cos I've got to like it out here. Well, I had to, hadn't I? Well, Tilly, no more news now 'cos the men are riding in and that bloke of mine will go and eat one of his own horses if the meal isn't on the table. Give my love to all of 'em ... I'd better tell you afore I finish, Tilly, that I've written to Peg and told her I'd love to have her out here. I hope you won't mind, Tilly, but I long to see someone of me own. You know what I mean. Love again, from Katie.'

As she placed the letter on the table, Willy turned his head slightly towards her from the bed and said, 'Well?' And she answered, 'I haven't opened Josefina's letter yet. That was from Katie.'

'What has she to say?'

'After I've read Josefina's letter I'll read it to you.'

Josefina's letter began:

'My dear Mama, Strange but I still think of you as my mama, yet I have just recently returned from seeing my real mother and my mind is still saying, she was right, she was right, meaning you, for I haven't yet got over the shock.

'I imagined when we met she would take me to her heart. I was prepared for her and her family being poor, but not the kind of poor I was presented with, dirt, laziness, squalor, and a way of life that I am ashamed to put into words, yet I shouldn't be because I know I was born to it.

'I am ashamed to admit now that I left the ranch with hardly the courtesy of a thank you to either Katie or Luisa and they both had been very kind to me, but when I returned humbled in spirit I was brought low by their reception of me which was so warm and welcoming.

'Luisa had ideas with regard to me putting my education to use. She talks of starting a school here for the children of mixed races. I should be enthusiastic at the prospect but I am only half-hearted with regard to it. I feel I must still be in a state of shock.

'With regard to what you tell me about Miss Bentwood, I cannot believe that she will be gone for good. If she loves Willy then she will return. Or if he loves her ... as I know he does, he will make the means to find her.

'I miss you, my dear Mama, more than I can tell you, and over these past tempestuous days I have made comparison and thought how lucky are the people who work under your care.

'My love to you and Willy, Josefina.'

The movement she now made brought Willy's attention to her again. 'It was a long letter,' he said.

'Not as long as Katie's ... which do you want to hear first?'

'It doesn't matter ... Well, let's hear what Josefina has to say.'

So Tilly began to read Josefina's letter, but she noted before she was half-way through it that Willy had turned on his side, his face towards her, and that the look of despondency had for a moment left him. She omitted to read out the part concerning himself and Noreen, and as she ended he said immediately, 'She should come home.' Then after a moment's silence he added, 'Does she know about Noreen?'

To this she answered briefly, 'Yes, I wrote her.'

'And she hasn't referred to it?'

There was a long pause before she said, 'No.'

She watched him lie back on his pillows, she watched his hand move across his usually clean-shaven chin that had a deep shadow of stubble on it for as yet today he hadn't shaved and he would allow no one to do it for him.

His voice was low as he said, 'She sounds different, broken somehow, her spirit gone.' He turned his head slowly towards her again. 'She was always high-spirited, wasn't she?'

'Yes, yes, she was.'

'You know, we lived together all those years and appeared so close but I've thought of late that I never really understood her, or her need ... her many needs.'

'That wasn't entirely your fault, she had a secret self. I was excluded from it, too. I've wondered lately if it's a good thing to take people from the environment into which they are born. Heredity is in the blood and it will out in the end, yet, if I hadn't taken her, imagine the life she'd be leading now. One does what one thinks is best. But then, what is best? I know one thing, unless you are born into the class no amount of self-education is going to prepare you for acceptance into it.'

'You could grace any class.'

He had held out his hand towards her as he spoke, and she rose from the chair and took it; and she stood in silence for a moment looking down at him before she said, 'There's never been more than half a dozen people in my life who have believed that, but thank you, dear.' She bent down and kissed his cheek, then said on a sigh, 'Well, it's Friday again, I must get to the mine. I'll send Ned up to you. The papers have come from Newcastle. He can read you the headlines. And I won't be long, a couple of hours at the most.'

She was going towards the door when he said quietly, 'I miss you.'

She paused and turned her head over her shoulders and answered as quietly, 'I'm glad to know that.' But even while saying it she knew in her heart that she was now but a poor substitute, for what he needed.

The meeting was over. It had been much the same as usual, even briefer because John was not there to ask questions and raise irrelevant points which he felt he must do to prove his interest.

After the meeting she had gone some way into the mine accompanied by both

Steve and Alec Manning. She had talked to the men and here and there enquired after a family, congratulating a Mr Morgan who told her that his son had got a book prize for reading at the village school and his daughter a certificate for her regular attendance at Sunday School.

This over, they walked up out of the drift, there to see on the road beyond the huddle of stables and outhouses the woman. She was seated on her horse and she and the animal appeared as a beautiful picture in a grubby frame.

As she walked slowly to the top of the drift, Tilly kept her eyes fixed on the woman. She knew that Steve had glanced quickly in her direction, but she did not look at him. Her whole attention was on the creature before her, and she saw her as creature, a beautiful creature. She was attired in a dull brown corduroy velvet riding habit. Moreover, she was riding as a lady should, side-saddle. The whole made her own attire with top boots and breeches mannish and gauche in comparison.

'Why! Phillipa; I didn't expect you.' Steve had gone on slightly ahead of her and was now holding the woman's hand, and she, looking down at him laughing, said, 'We just returned last night. I came by the cottage, but you weren't there. And your fire's nearly out. Do you know that?'

'Huh!' He was laughing as he looked up into her face. Then seeming to remember Tilly, he turned and said, 'My dear, this is Tilly . . . Mrs Sopwith. I've mentioned her to you.'

'Yes, yes.'

The woman was nodding down towards Tilly now, but Tilly stood looking up at her making no movement until a hand stretched out; and then she had to force herself to lift her own, and as this was being shaken the woman said, 'I am very pleased to meet you, Mrs . . . Sopwith. And pardon me for saying it but I must do so right away, I admire your attire. It's so sensible.' Then releasing Tilly's hand, she looked at Steve as she ended, 'I'm going to have an outfit made like that.'

'It won't suit you.'

'No? . . . Why not?'

'Because . . . Well – ' He turned and grinned at Tilly now. Then looking back at the seated figure, he laughed out loud as he said, 'You're bursting out all over, you've got to be slim, flat, before you can wear breeches like Tilly here.' He jerked his head towards her while still looking up at the woman.

Flat, which really meant unwomanly. That's how he saw her. Oh, let her get away out of this.

'I must get my horse. It . . . it has been nice meeting you. Good-bye.'

'Oh . . . oh no, you don't.' Steve had his hand on her arm. 'We'll both get our horses and we'll all return to the cottage. I want you two to get to know each other. It's about time.' On this he looked up at the woman, saying, almost with a command, 'You stay put, we'll be back in a minute.' Then taking Tilly's arm, he hurried her across to the stables. But once inside, she released herself and, facing him, she said, 'What if I have no wish to become further acquainted with your lady friend?'

'Well, Mrs Matilda Sopwith' – he was poking his head towards her – 'for once I'm disregarding your wishes. Yes, for once in my life I'm disregarding your wishes. Now get that into your head. The time has come for plain speaking and I can't do it here, so if you'll allow me.' He bent down and she put her boot on to his hand, and the next minute she was in the saddle and riding out of the stable.

The journey to the cottage was lively, but she herself took no part in the banter. The grinding pain was in her chest again. Men were cruel. All men were cruel, but at this moment she thought Steve was the cruellest one she had met as yet, for he was getting his own back for the years of dalliance, for that's how he must have looked at the time he had spent at her beck and call. And now he was paying her back, proving that a man past his prime but who could still be taken for forty was able to capture the affection of this young woman. She might be touching thirty or thereabouts, but she was still young . . . and beautiful, with a figure that could not carry breeches and a riding jacket, and was much more alluring to a man because of it. . . .

They were in the kitchen. The kettle had boiled; she, the woman Phillipa, had made the tea. She seemed to know where everything was kept in the cottage, and when the three cups of tea were poured out it was she who handed one to Tilly, then one to Steve. And as she picked her own up from the table, Steve went to her side and, putting his free arm around her waist, pulled her tightly towards him. And like this they confronted Tilly as she sat barely able to hold the cup and saucer steady in her hand. And then his next words almost sent them flying, for what he said was, 'Tilly, meet my daughter, Mrs Phillipa Ryde-Smithson.'

Tilly gulped, such a deep gulp that it brought her chin moving towards her shoulder and her right hand jerking to steady the saucer that her left hand had almost let drop. She looked up at them. They were both grinning at her, for all the world like two children who had sprung a surprise on an elder.

When she found her voice all she could manage to say was, 'Your daughter?'

'Yes, Tilly, my daughter.' The grin had gone from his face. He looked at her steadily before adding, 'It's a long story. I'll get down to it shortly, but in the meantime I'd like you two to get to know each other, and so if you'll excuse me I'll take my cup of tea into the back and have a wash.'

It would be difficult to say if there was ever a time when Tilly had felt more embarrassed than at this moment. She could find no words with which to express her feelings. Nor apparently could Mrs Phillipa Ryde-Smithson. But it was she who spoke first. Drawing a chair up to the table, she sat down and she tapped the saucer with her spoon and kept her gaze fixed on it as she said, 'As Steve said, it's a long story.'

Tilly noted that she had called him Steve, not Father. 'And he'll tell you the tale much better than I can as he knows more about it, but all I can say is that I am very proud that he is my real father although Daddy, as I call him, is a wonderful man and I love him dearly. But they also know that I have a special affection for Steve, and strangely they have too.' Now she lifted her gaze to Tilly and her large grey eyes twinkled as she said, 'It was very naughty of him to keep you in the dark. You thought I was his woman, didn't you?'

Tilly felt the colour flooding over her face and she said on a slightly defensive tone, 'Well, not exactly his . . . his woman, I thought you were to be married. He gave me that impression.'

'Naughty of him! Very naughty of him! He's a tease, you know.'

No, Tilly didn't know that Steve was a tease, but what she was gathering, and quickly, was that this woman, this daughter of his, had undoubtedly been brought up among the class. Her manner, her way of speaking all portrayed this: the words naughty, very naughty, the way she said them, he's a tease, all held an indefinable something that spoke of a different world, a world in which she herself lived but was not of it because she hadn't been born to it. This woman was Steve's daughter and Steve had been a working boy and was still a working man, yet this girl had evidently been brought up in an environment which had soaked into her until now she appeared . . . of the blood, so to speak, which belied the conversation with regard to heredity that she'd had with Willy just that very morning.

'Your son is not well at present?'

'No; he, I am afraid, has just escaped pneumonia but he is recovering.'

'I should like to meet him some time if I may.'

'You will be very welcome.'

There was a silence between them now, until Steve's daughter broke it by putting her head back and calling,' Have you dropped down the well?'

'No, m'lass, I haven't dropped down the well.' Steve came out of the scullery rubbing his hair with a towel, and Phillipa, getting to her feet now, said, 'I must be off. Lance is meeting me with the coach in Harton at three o'clock. He's attending a meeting on the Lawe with sea captains and such about some cargoes.'

'How long are you here for?'

'Oh, a week at the most.'

'What about your horse, if Lance is meeting you?'

'Oh, we'll stable it and one of them will pick him up tomorrow. By the way, Lance would like you to come over on Sunday if you've nothing better to do.'

'I have nothing better to do.' He smiled at her.

'Well, good-bye' – she had turned to Tilly – 'I was going to say Mrs Sopwith, but may I call you Tilly? I've always heard of you by that name.'

'I'd be pleased if you would. . . . Good-bye.'

'Good-bye.'

Tilly watched Steve throw aside the towel, rub his fingers through his hair, then escort his daughter to the door and down the path. She saw him put his hands under her oxters and heave her upwards, and although the rampant jealousy of this young woman had gone, the sight of the tenderness with which he treated her and the friendliness that existed between them, which was almost like a comradeship, touched some sore point in her heart and she turned from the window and went and stood before the fire, looking down at it, waiting his return.

His face was straight when he entered the room. And it remained so while he poured himself out another cup of tea and sat down on the settle; then in a sober manner he said, 'Sit yourself down; you're in for a long session.'

Seated before him, she kept her eyes intently on his face. When he was young his affection had created in her an irritation mingled with pity because of the love she could never give him, and as a man his concern for her had created in her nothing but a deep thankfulness, until it had grown into something much stronger, but never had she felt resentment against him. Yet at this moment when she knew that she must still be in his thoughts as dearly as ever and that her rival, so to speak, was no rival at all, she felt an irritation rising in her that bordered on aggressiveness, and just as it happened at other times in her life when she'd had the urge to strike out, so now she wanted to bring her hand across his face, which, had she done so, would no doubt have revealed to him her true feelings more than any words might have done.... All these months he had been laughing at her; the secret that she thought she held was no secret at least from him; he had made her suffer in imagining that he was tired of being the friend, the sustainer in time of trouble, and was putting a definite end to it.

As he put the empty cup back on the table he broke in on her thoughts, saying, 'I don't suppose you remember the day I came to the house and stood round near the wall and I told you I loved you and even tried to blackmail you into returning some affection by reminding you I'd killed our Hal for you ... eh?' He brought his eyes to hers but she made no answer, and he went on, 'No, it's likely too far back to remember. And it's of no consequence. Anyway, from then I still kept on hoping, that was until I heard you'd taken up with your master. It was then I left home and travelled about a bit. I was in lodgings when I met Phillipa's mother. She was the same age as me, just on nineteen, and it was strange but I'd never had a woman in my life afore because, you see, I only wanted you.'

She didn't lower her eyes and cast her glance down on this, but she looked straight at him and listened to him now as he continued, 'I was scared to death when I knew Betty was going to have a baby, and her brother and father were for hammering me and dragging me to the church. But I couldn't face it. I did a bunk. And so did Betty. She went to Hartlepool to an aunt of hers who wasn't very fond of her parents. It was in a roundabout way that I heard the child had been born and that it was a girl and that it was to be put out for adoption. Funny, but that did something to me. I sought Betty out and told her I was making decent money and would support the bairn. She agreed. She was working in a mill at the time. Then within a couple of months she wrote me and told me that she had met a lad who was willing to marry her but that he wouldn't take the bairn on and so she was again going to put it out for adoption. Now it's strange how things come about, but the owner of the mill had a daughter who had been married eight years and without the sight of a child in view and, as things get about, she had heard of the obstacle to Betty's marriage while she was visiting her father. She and her husband lived on the island of Jersey. So Betty was approached with regard to the adoption. But at the time she didn't know who it was who wanted the child, she only knew it was going to a very good home. So she told me that she was going to let her go. Well, what could I do? I remember going to see her, and there was the child in the cradle. And I knew then that I didn't want to let her be adopted but that there was no other course open. By the way, the name on her birth certificate was Mary not Phillipa, but it should happen that her adoptive grandmother had been named Phillipa and her new mother decided to call her that.'

'Well – ' He now rose to his feet and went to the mantelpiece and took a pipe from the rack and from a tin a long plug of tobacco; then sitting down again, he proceeded to shave the end of the plug into his pipe as he went on, 'Time passes. It has a habit of doing that, but every now and again I would think of the child: she would be three; she would be four; she would be ten; what was she like? During all this time I'd had a longing for bairns, for a family of me own, and twice I'd been right on the rim of getting married. Oh yes' – he nodded at her as her eyes widened – 'within a fortnight at one time. And I had to run again.' He smiled wryly now. 'She was going to have me up for breach of promise, that one. I settled with her for nearly all me savings. The other one was sensible, she knew I wouldn't make a good husband.

'When Phillipa was eleven her adoptive mother died, but before she did she told her who her real parents were. Well, the news was a shock, as could have been expected, to this young girl. But she was filled with curiosity, and so she makes a trip from Newcastle to Hartlepool on her own and there she found that her own mother had died the previous year and her husband years earlier, but that she had a father, a real father, who was alive. The old aunt gave her this information. Her father's name she learnt was Steve McGrath and the last that had been heard of him was that he was working in a pit further north.

'Anyway, two years later when she's on holiday from her private school, and was supposed to be visiting a school friend she finds me, so it was about seventeen years ago when a young and beautiful girl knocks on the door. I can see her now' – he turned his head to the side – 'standing very upright, straight faced, just about there' – he pointed to the table – 'and saying, "I'm Phillipa Coleman. My real mother, I understand, was named Betty Fuller, and you, I understand, Mr McGrath, are my father."

'You know, Tilly' – he leant towards her now, the look in his eyes was soft and tender like they must have been on that day – 'if God had opened the clouds and dropped an angel at my feet I couldn't have been more surprised, or pleased. But pleased isn't the word to describe my feelings on that day. This girl, this lady, because she looked every inch a young lady, was my daughter, and, you know, it was strange but from the word go we clicked, just like that.' He snapped his fingers. 'And that's how it's been ever since. Well, the next visitor I had was her adoptive father, Jim Coleman, a man who loved her as if she were his own. Well, we talked, and the outcome was I was invited to his home, his mainland home. He had two, one in Newcastle, strangely enough, and the one in Jersey; and stranger still, we became friends. Then there came on the scene Mr Lancelot Ryde-Smithson. That's a mouthful for you if you like. He was the man who wanted to marry her. She was sixteen and he was seventeen years her senior, but she loved him and he doted on her. He was French on his mother's side and a charming man, and very wealthy into the bargain. Well the Ryde-Smithsons are, aren't they? You know' – he nodded at her 'the steel-works and such.'

Ryde-Smithsons, the steel-works and such. Yes, indeed.

'Anyway, Mr Ryde-Smithson and I talked. We were men of different worlds, but almost the same age and we understood each other. And that's how it's been up till now. I was at their wedding, a big affair, just before you arrived home from America. It was held at her father's place in Jersey. And you know, Tilly, it was a wonderful feeling to be accepted by everybody, but ... but mostly by her and Lance. He was a great man, he still is. They live in France most of the time. I've been there to their home and played with me grandchildren. Aye, grandchildren, I'm a grandfather. Two lovely children, Gerald is twelve now, and Richard ten. And you know something more, Tilly? If I had any sense I'd have been away from your mine and this place years ago because I've had offers that would make a man dizzy, and from Mr Coleman, an' all. And why haven't I accepted any of their offers? Well, Tilly, some people would say it is because I am a bloody fool. And sometimes I thought they were right. Oh yes, yes.' He shook his head and, his face unsmiling, he repeated, 'Yes, yes; many a time I thought they were right. And not more so than early on when you went off abroad with Mr Matthew. That nearly finished me. Well, it did finish me, and I've asked myself time and time again why I stayed on in this place in that bloody little mine because, Tilly, it is a bloody little mine; bloody in more ways than one. There's hardly a day goes by but I fear to see water rushing towards me. Oh yes, I know everything's been done that can be done, but nevertheless it is a bad-tempered bloody little mine. And this cottage' – he waved his hand round – 'very nice, very nice, but I exaggerated its charm when I first came into it. And you know why, I've got no need to tell you, it was just so that I'd be near you. Anyway, your presence was full about me here, you'd lived in it. Then off you go to the Americas, so why did I stay? There was Phillipa and Lance and Jim Coleman, all of them wondering what on earth was the matter with me, turning down a nice house in Jersey or a fine house in Jesmond as Jim Coleman once offered me. But not for nothing of course, he was a business-man. As he said, he wanted someone who could handle men, and apparently, Tilly, I have that talent. And there I was letting it go rotten here, so to speak.' He sighed now and, looking into her face, he said, 'I'm laying it on thick, I know, but I've waited a long time, Tilly. And over these last years acting as your sort of henchman, friend of the family, yet not accepted at the Manor because of what one might hear from the village, that damned narrow-minded sanctimonious little cesspool. I sometimes think of this place, you know, Tilly, when I'm sitting in Jim Coleman's dining-room at a table that's laden with silver, some pieces so heavy the weight would fill a skip, and accepted there, an' all. But here I'm Stevey McGrath, son of that old hag in the village, with a brother that's got a reputation that stinks and a nephew that's been along the line twice. Anyway, Tilly, there it is I've had me say. It's been grinding in me for years. And I've got to say this, I don't think . . . well in fact, I know I couldn't have stood the situation as it's been between you and me if I hadn't had Phillipa as an outlet, so to speak, for the strain's been hellish at times. So there it is Tilly.' He looked at her softly for a moment without speaking, and at this point she could have dropped into his arms, but he began again, and what he said now brought her slumped body straight and tightened the muscles in her face. 'And now, lass,' he said, 'I'm going to give you the ultimatum I should have given you years ago. You marry me or I take the belated offers and move. I'll give you a little more time to think it over because there's the responsibility of Willy and next year he'll be coming into his own I suppose, and if he were to marry, well, that would be one of your problems solved. Yet if Noreen doesn't turn up I doubt if there's much hope of marriage coming his way, and so you might feel obliged to stay with him. But whether you'd see me as dowager master of the hall' – he pulled a face here – 'dowager isn't the right word but you know what I mean. Anyway, it's up to you. I might as well tell you while I'm on, Tilly, that I've had a very good offer and it's open until February next. That leaves you three or four months to sort things out finally, although I'd be happier if I could know by ... well say December.'

Tilly stared at this man, this person standing before her whom she had grown to love as she imagined she had never loved Mark or Matthew, and he was talking about his love for her in a fashion that one might use in a matter of business, small business, for his statements had been cool, concise. He had made no attempt to take her in his arms and kiss her, no attempt to speak of his need of her or give her the opportunity to speak of her own need of him. She couldn't sort out her feelings at the moment, she only knew she felt utterly deflated while at the same time hurt, and angry.

For a moment he appeared like the old Steve when he put his hand out and gripped hers, saying, 'Don't look like that, Tilly. All this I know has come as a bit of a surprise to you, but life's like that. You should know better than anyone that life is full of surprises, especially where feelings are concerned. Anyway, my dear, it's up to you.'

Yes, it was up to her.

Slowly she pushed his hand away from hers and, rising to her feet, she looked into his face and she repeated her thoughts and his words, 'Yes, it's up to me, Steve. Thank you.' She inclined her head towards him and she took no notice of the pained and troubled look that came into his eyes but, turning from him, she went towards the door, opened it and walked slowly down the path. She knew he was close behind her but she didn't look at him, not even when he helped her up on to her horse, not until he said, 'Tilly' and the name was filled with a deep plea did she turn her gaze to him and say quietly, 'I'll be seeing you, Steve.' And with that she rode off.

ເອ 11 ອຸ

He was gone from her, as surely as if he had married that woman who had turned out to be his daughter. The Steve who had coolly given her an ultimatum was in no way related to any of his other selves which he had presented to her over the years. All these had held that quality of kindness and devotion that she had come to expect. Never, never could she have imagined that Steve would change, not towards her, for hadn't he been obsessed with her, and that was the word, obsessed with her from when he was a boy, in a way as much as Matthew had been.

But Steve *had* changed, and not a little of the hurt inside her was due to the fact that she didn't know anything about this other Steve. The man who had presented the ultimatum was a man of parts, a man who mixed with the gentry, while she herself who had lived with them, been mistress to one and married another, was still on the outside of the charmed circle wherein moved the class. But he was mixing with them, thick with them so to speak, for the Ryde-Smithsons were class, and the Colemans, oh yes.

For years now she had longed to be one with this man and she knew that she had deluded herself into thinking that marriage to him was impossible because of the vow she had given to Matthew never to marry again, for inside herself she recognised the truth, and the truth was that the shadow of that vow had grown dim, very dim a long time ago, and that one of the real reasons that had kept her from marrying Steve was merely the fact that she couldn't see him acting as master in this, a manor house. Yet she knew now that he had in a way as much experience of such houses as she had, more in fact, for he had been accepted by their occupants: as he had so graphically stated, he had sat at their table where one piece of silver was so heavy it would weigh a skipful of coal.

The Steve who had dedicated his life to her was no more and she could blame no one but herself for the loss, but the hurt this knowledge brought to her was intensified by the fact that during his periods of frequent absences at week-ends he had not been relieving his needs up in the cottage in the hills with some woman, or indulging in the inn on the high road, but was being entertained by his daughter and her people. She would have rather, much rather, known that he was assuaging his natural appetite than playing the father and being accepted by a class of people with whom she had imagined he could never mix, the class which, incidentally, ignored her.

He had given her until December to decide. Well, she had decided already.

In the weeks that followed this revealing day Tilly's spirit had risen up in her, especially so at night when, her pale reflection staring back at her from the mirror, she had cried at it: Who does he think he is anyway? Steve McGrath who has hounded me with his love all my life now to give me an ultimatum? And to say he couldn't have borne the situation between them if he hadn't had the consolation of his daughter. It was galling to think now that she herself hadn't really held him all these years.

On one occasion she had paced the floor for hours and the soft padding of her steps had penetrated upwards, and Willy, sleep eluding him too and with ears highly attuned to every sound in the house, had made his way downstairs and, knocking on her door, he had called, 'What is it? What's the matter?' and she had answered, 'Nothing. Nothing.' Then after a moment he had asked, 'May I come in? I can't sleep either.'

She had stirred up the fire and they had sat side by side before it in silence for a time, until he said, 'It's Steve, isn't it?'

She was sharp to answer, 'What makes you think that?'

'Because I suppose my ears have taken over from my eyes and I read a lot from inflexions, and yours has very little warmth in it now when you talk to him.'

She hadn't answered him for a time, then said, 'We had a difference,' and to this he replied, 'Well, I hope for both your sakes it doesn't last. He's a good man, Steve, you know, Mama. There's not a better. He's honest, true, and he's been a good friend to you . . . and to me.'

Honest? she had thought. Devious would be a better word to apply to him.

Changing the subject, he had said suddenly, 'I have a feeling, Mama, that Noreen is dead. I dozed off while I was reading and I saw her. She looked changed, really grotesque, but I put my hands out to her and she slapped them away. Then I opened my eyes and the feeling became stronger. It was as if she were in the room with me. But there's a certainty in me now that we'll never come together.'

'Don't say that, dear, just keep hoping. We could hear any day from the agent we engaged; he has already traced her to two places since she left the lodgings.'

Willy had said nothing to this but had risen from the chair and made his way towards the door. There he had said, 'Goodnight, Mama,' and she had answered simply, 'Good-night, Willy.'

And then he had added, 'Think about Steve.'

Think about Steve? If she could only stop thinking about Steve. . . .

And now it was December. The snow had come early this year. Twice there had been heavy falls. They'd had no post for three days, but on midday on this Wednesday Jimmy got through to the village and met the carrier and returned with a sheaf of letters, one of which was addressed to Mrs P. Crosby.

After giving Biddle the letter to take to Peg, Tilly went up into her room and the first one she opened was from Josefina. It was short and very surprising and right to the point. It began simply:

'Mama, I am coming home. I have booked my passage and sail early in January. I cannot wait to leave this land and be once again with you, and with Willy, even with his wife, if Miss Bentwood has returned. I imagined that a rejected love was the most cruel thing anyone could suffer, but I have discovered that there are feelings that can be injured more deeply. Rejection of one's colour can carry sufficient hurt but when you carry the imprint of two on your countenance then the hurt reaches depths which you didn't imagine lay within you.

'I realise now that you protected me, even cosseted me, and I long to return to that protection. Your loving Josefina.'

Tilly sat back in the chair and covered her eyes with her hands for a moment while her teeth pressed into her lower lip. It was as if a daughter of her own flesh was expressing a longing to be with her again. After what had happened of late with Willy and Steve, especially with Steve, Josefina's return would be all the more welcome, and she experienced a feeling almost akin to joy as she thought of them both being in the house again with her, Willy perhaps seeing Josefina in a different light, that is if Noreen didn't appear on his horizon again. And as day had followed day she had become more assured that this latter would not happen.

She had just opened the letter from Katie, which confirmed what Josefina had written, when there came a tap on the door and when she said, 'Come in!' Peg entered.

Immediately Tilly sensed her confusion, and she guessed before Peg spoke what was causing it.

'Can I have a word with you . . . ma'am?' There was always a hesitancy with all of the Drews between her title of ma'am and her name, even after all these years.

'Of course, Peg. Sit down.'

Peg sat on the edge of the small padded couch that stood crossways in the middle of the room, and she drooped her head and unclasped her hands before, suddenly groping in her pocket, she drew out a letter, saying, 'I've had word from our Katie.'

'Yes, I thought it would be from her.' Tilly nodded, then slapped at the letter in her own hand. 'I've had one too.'

'You haven't read it then?'

'No, not all yet.'

Again Peg looked down. Then her voice a mere mutter, she said, 'She's sent me the money for me passage, she wants me to go out. What am I to do?' She raised her eyes now and looked straight at Tilly.

'What do you want to do, Peg?'

Peg glanced to the side; then lifting her hand, she straightened her cap, pushing at the starched frill that covered her ears before saying, 'I'm not ungrateful. Believe me I'm not ungrateful. You've done so much for all of us, but I'm gettin' on, Tilly, and somehow I'd like to end me days with our Katie. I'm sorry.' Peg's head dropped lower until Tilly said softly, 'Peg, look at me.' And when Peg had lifted her head she went on, 'I'm not going to say I won't miss you, I shall, there'll only be Fanny left, but you've got to live your own life. And there could be a lot of it left to you yet, for you're so sprightly and don't look half your age. And so you write straight back and I'll do the same; and I'll also make arrangements for your passage on the next boat out.'

'You won't want me to serve me notice?'

'Don't be silly.' Tilly now got to her feet, Peg also rose, and they stood confronting each other as Tilly said, 'There's no need to talk of notice between you and me or any of your family, my family, because that's how I consider you all, as my family, the only real one I ever knew after I lost the old people. And what's more you'll not go out empty-handed, you'll go out as a well-dressed, well-endowed woman. And if the men are after you for nothing else they'll be after you for your money.' She now punched Peg playfully in the shoulder. But Peg, bowing her head again, began to giggle like any young girl until her laughter suddenly sprang into tears. And then they were holding each other, Tilly, too, crying now as she said, 'There, there. It'll be a wonderful life for you. You'll enjoy it. Just think what it's done for Katie.'

After a moment they separated and both stood wiping their eyes, smiling now, and Peg said, 'What about them Indians?'

'Oh, well, I should think by now they're all dead and buried. Katie's man has likely polished them off. Oh' – her voice became serious now – 'don't worry about the Indians. As Luisa said, the Civil War was worse to put up with than the Indians. There's great things going on out there. I often think how different my life would have been if Matthew had survived. We would have had our own big ranch and thousands of head of cattle and horses, and' – she nodded towards Peg now – 'that's what you could have one day, you'll see. There's lots of lonely men out there.'

'Oh, Tilly. Oh no, not me. Never again; not at my age.'

'Don't tell them your age, well, knock ten years off. Anyway, Doug's a big man now being partner with Luisa, a lot of marvellous things can happen and will happen to you. Well now, go on downstairs and tell the others. I doubt if the lads will be pleased. Yet on the other hand – ' she pulled a long face and nodded towards Peg as she ended, 'they might take a leaf out of your book and the rest of them follow you. And then where will I be?'

'Oh, there's no fear of that, Tilly; the lads know where they're well off. Aye, as our Sam often says, it was a lucky day for the Drews when they *drew* up alongside of you that special Sunday.'

'And a very lucky day for me, too, Peg, oh yes. But go on now.'

'Thanks, Tilly. I'll never forget you. None of us ever will.'

The room to herself again, Tilly stood looking towards the door. Peg had said she would never forget her. That was very magnanimous of her because at times if she hadn't hated her she must have disliked her when she saw her as the stumbling block between Steve and herself, for Biddy had made no secret of the fact that in her opinion Steve would have taken up with Peg had Tilly been out of the way. But Tilly had known this would never come about because Steve would never have stayed in this quarter of the country if it hadn't been for her, even before he discovered his daughter. . . . *Oh, his daughter.* She turned away with an impatient twist of her body and went to the desk and finished Katie's letter, which told her exactly what Peg had just said.

The remainder of her mail was dealing with business. After she had gone through all the letters and filed them for answering she rose and went to the window. It had started to snow heavily again, big white flakes, falling slowly and so thickly that she couldn't see down into the garden. She sighed deeply. At this rate the road could be blocked again and they could be hemmed in for days, even weeks. There seemed nothing to look forward to, until she reminded herself of Josefina's coming. And on this she gathered up two letters from the desk and went out of the room towards the attic floor and the studio where she could hear Willy playing the piano. He spent most of his time now playing the piano or the violin. He seemed to find comfort in the pieces that he chose, all slow movements. That was how he must be feeling about life, slow, tedious. And for her, too; oh yes, yes, for her too it was slow, and tedious.

୶ 12 ୭

There was a fug of warmth in the room which contrasted with the bitter snow-driven wind outside.

It was just on one o'clock. The street grating, under which and supported by two planks of wood was a piece of plate glass, at no time allowed very much light into the basement room, but today it could have been a brick wall so thick was it covered with the black slush from the treading feet.

The lamps fixed to the walls on each side of the table were so placed that they illuminated only the table itself and the double oven fireplace exactly four feet from the end of it. Perhaps this was as well for they shut out from Noreen Bentwood's gaze a regiment of cockroaches and fearless rats that infested the margin of the basement. So dim were the outskirts of the room that to the vermin it must have been constant night, and the cockroaches, if not the rats, seemed to take this for granted. The two cats that should have been parading the premises were so satiated with food that they slept most of their time, except at night when they escaped to pursue their instincts.

Proggle's Pie Shop was situated in an alley off the waterfront. It was open from six o'clock in the morning until twelve at night and was never known to be empty. It was also known that Proggle never kept his cooks longer than two to three weeks at the most. This latest one though had stuck it for seven weeks, but of course that was because her belly was full and she was for the House. But like many before her, she'd leave that visit until the last second if she was wise.

It was also said that the pastry which had lately come out from Proggle's kitchen was the best the customers had ever tasted.

It was this fact and this fact alone that had caused Proggle to keep the lass on so long and to grant her concessions, such as letting her start at eight in the morning and finish at eight at night. At three halfpence an hour and her food, he considered he was paying her well. And so good a hand was she at pastry-making he had offered to take her back when her confinement was over, that's if she could get someone to take the bairn for adoption. He had talked the matter over with her, saying, 'What you mustn't do, lass, is put it out to farm, 'cos if it hasn't got rickets when it goes in, it'll have 'em sure as God made little apples when it comes out, for no matter what you pay those bitches they feed the bairns nothing but pap, mouldy bread and whey, sucking at pap bags all day long tied in their boxes. Rabbits in backyards have more scope than those bairns. I've seen 'em; so don't have it put out, lass, have it adopted, or send it back to your people, 'cos whoever they are they brought you up right. I can see that in many ways.'

He was kindly, was Joseph Proggle, when kindness would benefit him in the long run, but he was right about the baby farmers. Noreen had seen this for herself. There was one place two doors down from where she lodged where the children didn't cry out aloud, they merely whined in chorus and continuously.

Noreen lifted up the heavy sneck of the oven door and drew out the iron shelf on which were two dozen round pie tins, the pie crusts raised with a shiny crown from the colouring of burnt sugar with which they had been brushed.

When she reached the table she did not slide the shelf on to the edge of it, as she usually did, but dropped it with a light thud; then one hand on the corner of the table, the other hugging her waist, she bent over for a moment while drawing in deep breaths of the stifling air.

It was some seconds later before she straightened herself and, taking up another iron sheet filled with pie tins, she placed these in the oven. Following this, she took a ladle and went to the fire again and there stirred a thick mass of peas simmering in a huge black iron kale-pot, before returning to the table once more, tipping out the pies on to a wooden tray which she then carried to the end of the room where, inset in the wall, was a lift. Placing the tray in this, she knocked twice on the wooden side, and a minute later when she saw the shelf move upwards she turned away and, going to the table again, took from a brown bowl a great slab of pastry, threw it on to the floured table and began to roll it out.

She was only half-way through this process when again she stopped and once more one hand was gripping the edge of the table and the other hugging her waist. It couldn't be, not yet, if her timing was right. And oh yes, she knew that was right. There were another three weeks to go. So what was this strange pain that was gripping her now?

Pulling a box towards her, she sat down on it and clasped her hands on the table top and, looking to where a narrow black mass was moving backwards and forwards against the far wall, she whispered, 'Oh God! don't let it happen so soon. Oh God! God!' As she moved her head the tears sprang into her eyes and rolled down her cheeks; and now, her chin drooping towards her chest, she whispered, 'Oh, Mam. Mam! Oh, Mam. Mam!'

She did not think of Willy. Strangely, she rarely thought of Willy these days. At first the temptation to write to him had been so great that she had actually stamped a number of letters and got as far as the post office with them. But there she remembered her father, and she knew that if Willy were to take her back to the Manor – for where else could he take her – he would not live long, as her mother had suggested, to enjoy his triumph.

For some time now she hadn't cared whether she lived or died; in fact, there were nights in that dreadful little room she had rented with the sound of all human activities penetrating her ears far into the night, she had prayed that she wouldn't see the morning.

Of late there had come over her an apathy. The only person she wanted to see was her mother, but at the same time she knew that her own condition would horrify her, at least at first.

'Now, now! what's up with you, lass?' Joseph Proggle had come down the steps in his slippered feet, and his approach startled her. Jumping up from the box, she muttered, 'I . . . I was only resting, Mr Proggle, just for a minute.'

He peered at her in the dimness, saying, 'You're not comin' on, are you?'

'No, oh no' – she shook her head emphatically – 'I was just a bit tired.'

'It's early in the day, lass, to be tired, not yet on one, an' the shop packed to suffocation. They're pushing them down scalding, they are. Those peas ready?'

'Yes, Mr Proggle.'

'Well, dish 'em up an' get another lot on 'cos the way the weather's shapin' it's gona be a full house. And I've got an order for six dozen pies for the night, sailors havin' a beano along at the Blue Sail.'

He peered at her as she stood rolling out the pastry; then he said, 'I'll get Jenny Blackett to come in and give you a hand round teatime. How's that?'

'Thank you, Mr Proggle. It'll be a help.'

'She can clean up if nothin' else. . . . My God! look at that cheeky bugger.' He took an empty pie tin from the table and heaved it at a rat that was making for the middle of the room. 'What's those bloody cats up to?' He now took his foot and kicked at the larger of the two cats curled up to the side of the oven and when it awoke with a squeal he cursed it further, crying, 'You'll end up as pie meat, me lad, if you don't do your job. You don't feed 'em, do you?' He had turned to Noreen now, and she shook her head, saying, 'No, no.'

'No; that's right, don't give 'em a scrap, let 'em work for their livin' else we'll have that bloody inspector here again. . . . Inspector!' He spat on the floor, then said, 'Well, hurry up, lass. When is the next lot due?'

Noreen turned and nodded towards the other oven and paused before she said, 'About five minutes, Mr Proggle.'

'Good, good. Send them up straightaway.'

She nodded again, then went on with her rolling.

It was around about this time in the day that Simon Bentwood left his horse and trap at the farrier's with instructions to the man not to unharness the animal as he would be no more than half an hour before he was back, because with the change in the weather he'd have to take the road home as soon as possible.

But the conditions in Newcastle were nowhere near as bad as they had been when he left the farm. Although it was snowing here there were no drifts, the streets and roads were just black slush. He made his way down to Market Street past the new Law Courts and into Pilgrim Street where he stopped before a doorway on which was a curved brass plate indicating a number of offices therein. On the third floor of the building he knocked on an opaque glass door, then went in.

A clerk was sitting behind a small desk. He did not look up immediately, he was writing in a ledger, his hand moving slowly, and his paper cuffs hanging almost two inches below the frayed sleeve of his jacket made a small grating sound not audible until Simon stood looking down on the bent head in silence as the man continued to write.

'You deaf?'

The hand moved over two or three further words before the head lifted, when the elderly clerk, looking over the top of his glasses, said, 'Not that I'm aware of, sir.'

The tone immediately aroused the aggressiveness in Simon. 'None of your bright lip, mister,' he said. 'You tell your boss I'm here.'

He watched the man rise slowly from the chair, go towards another glass door, knock on it, then enter the room.

It was almost three minutes later when he returned. Stepping aside he left the door wide, saying, 'Mr Robinson is free now to see you . . . sir.'

Simon gave him a scathing glance as he passed into the small office where the agent was sitting behind a long substantial-looking desk and on an equally substantial-looking leather chair, and he greeted Simon affably, saying, 'Ah! Mr Bentwood. Good-day to you. It is strange that you should come at this time.'

'Why? You have news?' Simon sat down opposite the desk, and the agent, nodding his head briskly, said, 'Indeed! Indeed! And I would have had it out to you but for the weather.' He did not add his thoughts: 'and to Mr William Sopwith at the same time.' Hansom his clerk and he had a small wager on who would reach Proggle's pie shop first. Mr Sopwith had the advantage of a carriage but this man sitting here had the fury of a father to give wings to his feet.

'Well, get on with it, what do you know? Have you found her?'

'Well, yes and no. . . .'

'Yes and no? What answer is that to give! You have or you haven't?'

Mr Robinson sat back in his chair and tapped his fingertips gently together as he said, 'It all depends on a name, a change of name. We have found three young women who apparently don't want to be found. One goes under the name of Hannah Circle, which is not her name at all; likewise Mary Nugent; and the third one is a Miss Lucy Cuthbertson. Each of these young women has a reason for not wishing to be found. . . .'

'*What did you say?* Lucy Cuthbertson?'

'Yes, Lucy Cuthbertson.'

Simon was now leaning forward in his chair. 'What's she like? How old?'

'Well, it's very hard to gauge a young person's age when they are with child, as are these three young women, but Miss Cuthbertson. . . .'

'What did you say?'

'I said Miss Cuthbertson. . . .'

'Afore that. With child you said?'

'Yes, that's what I said, Mr Bentwood. Now as regards this young lady, she could be eighteen, twenty, twenty-two, what can one say, because the position she holds at present is, I should imagine, very taxing. I have only seen her twice, and then in a dim light when I presented myself as a vermin inspector in her kitchen.'

'You what!' Simon's eyes were screwed up.

'A vermin inspector. One has to take on different guises in this business. I had heard there was a young woman working for a certain pie maker near the waterfront and that she was near the time of delivery, so last week I presented myself, as I said, as a vermin inspector. Does the name Lucy Cuthbertson ring a bell for you, sir?'

Simon was staring down towards the floor through narrowed lids. She was going to have a child. His Noreen was going to have a child. And who could be the father but that blind bastard. He would kill him. Sure as he was sitting here he would kill him. But to get to her first, to get her home. Oh yes, to get her home. He blinked and said, 'It was her mother's maiden name.'

'Oh.' Mr Robinson's eyes widened. 'I think we are on the right track then, sir. Anyway, I would suggest that you go to the shop and ask to see her. Do you know where Proggle's Pie Shop is, sir, on the water . . . ?'

'Yes, yes.' Simon had risen to his feet. 'Who doesn't know Proggle's Pie Shop?'

As Simon now made hastily towards the door, Mr Robinson rose to his feet, saying, 'I trust if the young woman is whom you hope her to be, you will call and settle your account . . . or should I send the bill on to you?'

Simon paused for a moment, turned his head and said, 'Don't worry; either way you'll be paid.'

'Of course, sir. Of course.'

In the street now, his walk almost a run, he dodged in and out of people on the crowded thoroughfare and slithered as he crossed the road between the packed vehicles; then his breath coming short and sending out waves of mist to mingle with the thickening snowflakes, he came to a stop outside the pie shop and stood for a moment, his eyes closed, while the appetising smell of the pies filled his lungs as he drew in a deep breath before pushing his way into the crowded shop.

It was some minutes before he could get to the counter. At one end of it a young boy was scooping ladlesful of mashed peas into bowls while at the other end a small sharp-faced, greasy-haired man was swiftly bundling pies into sheets of newspaper seemingly with one hand, while with the other placing numbers on tin plates that were being held out to him by the customers, and, like a magician with a third invisible hand, he was taking money and returning change.

When Simon managed to push his way along the counter and to stand before him, the man glanced at him for a moment, saying, 'Plate or paper?'

'Neither. I want to see Lucy Cuthbertson.'

As if some unseen clockwork had stopped the movements of his hands, Mr Proggle looked at the well-dressed man before him, who by his voice was not a gentleman, but by the cut of his clothes was certainly someone of quality. Swiftly resuming his serving, pushing the paper-wrapped pies or the plates this way and that, he asked, 'Why do you want to see her?'

'I'm her father.'

Again the hands came to a temporary halt and the man, now jerking his chin upwards, said, 'Oh aye. Well, you'll have to prove that.'

'I'll prove it, where is she?'

'You'll have to wait, I've got me hands full.'

Simon now looked over the heads of the crowd of men, women and children and his eyes came to rest on a dark hole that led into the shop, and so, pushing his way through the throng, he paused at the top of the stairs and glanced back at Mr Proggle, who was staring towards him; then he descended into the cellar kitchen. . . .

The first glimpse he had of his daughter, his beloved Noreen, pierced him as would a knife driven into him by a friend. His lass who had been brought up as good as any lady working in this filthy hole. She had her back to him but there was no need to wonder if he was on the right track.

When Noreen turned from the oven, the big iron shelf in her hand, and saw him standing in the dimness at the foot of the stairs she had to take two running steps in order to avoid dropping the shelf and its contents on to the floor. Then she stood leaning against the corner of the table staring at him, some instinct born of the tie of blood urging her to fly to him and throw her arms around him and feel the protection of his strength, while the knowledge of his temper and the possessiveness of his love brought her back straight and her face stiff as she watched him approach slowly into the radius of the lamps.

When he didn't stop at the end of the table but kept coming on she backed from him towards the ovens, saying as she did so, 'You lay a hand on me and I'll scream and I'll have that shopful down on you.'

'Aw, lass! lass!' The tone of his voice, the sorrow in it, the compassion in his look, took the stiffness out of her entire body, and when he stopped within an arm's length of her she saw that his whole face was quivering.

His voice low now, even pleading, he said, 'I'm not going to lay a hand on you, all I want is for you to come home.'

Again there was the urge to throw herself at him, but the realisation of why she was here in this filthy verminous, stinking place came to the foremost of her mind, and she cried at him, 'And be made to toe the line again, locked up? Or perhaps you haven't noticed' – she now slapped her stomach hard – 'I'm not alone any more, I'm carrying Willy's bairn. And what'll you do if I go back? Kill him, as you promised? or will you send for him and say marry my daughter and make an honest woman of her? But before you contemplate doing either let me tell you that it was me who did the wooing. Oh yes, you can droop your head, I wanted him, I wanted his child. I thought in my ignorance that if you knew I was bearing you'd see things differently. But you went mad before you even knew we had come together. And now you say come back?'

Simon still kept his head bent. He knew he wasn't dealing with a girl any longer but that here was a woman who would go her own way no matter what he did or said. But all he wanted at this moment was to get her back into the shelter of his home because unless he succeeded in doing that he would have lost for good, not only her but Lucy also; and of late it had come to him that strangely he needed Lucy, for lying alone at nights he had realised that what he had thought of as her complacency, good-humoured complacency, had been a form of strength, deep strength. And she had shown him to what depths that strength could carry her these past months, for as sure as he would have killed Willy Sopwith had they met up, she would have done likewise to him if he had laid a hand on her. And he knew now that he needed her, he needed her as much as he needed Noreen, more in fact, because Noreen would, he hated to admit, have inevitably gone from him one day to another man. But Lucy would always have been there. She was there now, and yet she wasn't there, but once she had her daughter back and knowing he was the means of bringing her back quietly, peaceably, accepting the condition she was in, she would return to the once pliant wife he had come to rely on while not realising it.

He said quietly, 'Your mother misses you. She's not herself any more, she wants you back. And there'll be no trouble. I promise you. I give you my word on it, there'll be no trouble.' He did not add, 'As long as Sopwith keeps out of the way,' for he knew he wouldn't be accountable for his actions if he were to come face to face with the fellow, for the desire to pay off the score between Tilly and himself was still burning in him and could only be achieved through her son.

'Do you mean that?' Noreen's throat was swelling, and he answered, 'I do.' But when she said, 'And you won't tie me down in any way?' there was a slight pause before he repeated her words, 'I won't tie you down in any way.'

She now dusted her hands one against the other, then looked from side to side, saying, 'I'll . . . I'll be leaving him in the lurch, he's. . . . ' She got no further; evidently in pain she pushed past him and gripped the edge of the table and again her hand went round her waist.

Now Simon was holding her, saying, 'What is it?'

She shook her head, unable to speak for the moment; when she did she answered simply, "Tisn't due for three weeks.'

'But the pain, how long have you had it?'

'A couple of days.'

'Come; get your cloak.'

As Simon spoke Mr Proggle entered the kitchen, saying, 'What's this? What's this? Now look, where you off to?' He put his hand out towards Noreen, but it was Simon who answered, saying, 'She's off home where she should have been all the time.'

'She . . . she can't go like this, she's by the week. She's leavin' me in a pickle and I won't pay her, not me. I can claim for the four days; by the week she is.'

'What does she earn a day?'

Mr Proggle seemed surprised by the question and the fact that the man was putting his hand into his pocket, and he muttered 'Penny ha'penny an hour. Good wage at that; six shillings that is.'

Slowly Simon counted the six shillings on to the table; then staring at the man, he said, 'You should be prosecuted for keeping anyone working in this hell hole.' He pointed now to a cat chewing at the carcass of a rat and to the beetles scurrying around the skirting board, and his lip curled away from his teeth as he said, 'Slaves have better quarters.'

'A man has to earn a livin'.'

'You mean, has to make a fortune. And that's what you're coining up there' – he jerked his head – 'and out of the unfortunates. Out of me way!' He threw his arm wide and nearly knocked the man on to his back; then with his other hand around Noreen's shoulders he pressed her forward and up the stairs. And now guiding her through the shop amid the curious glances of the customers, they made for the street. There she stopped and, turning her face upwards, she let the snowflakes fall on it for a moment before gazing down the narrow cobbled road towards the waterfront and the dim shapes of the masts of the boats lying along the quay.

'I've got the trap at Fuller's, do you think you can walk that far?' She nodded but made no reply; nor did she resist when he put his arm around her shoulders and helped her up the slippery bank towards the main thoroughfare.

It was when they entered the farrier's and she saw Lady, her head tossing with impatience at being still harnessed to the trap, that she almost broke down and wept. Going to the horse who seemed to recognise her almost instantly, she laid her face for a moment against her cheek. Then moving towards the step of the trap, she was about to lift her foot on to it when again the pain seized her, worse this time, bringing her almost bent double, and Simon, holding her tightly, said anxiously, 'Shall I take you to a doctor?'

'No . . . no.' She straightened up. 'Just get me home.'

Home. It had a wonderful sound as she uttered it, and it sounded wonderful too to his ears.

Lifting her bodily now, he placed her in the trap, pulled the canvas hood – an invention of his own, he had made to keep out the winds – firmly into place; then having settled his account, he took his seat beside her and they moved out and began the journey home. . . .

When they crossed the bridge and left Newcastle it was as if they had entered another world, a white snow-bound world. Whereas the streets behind them had been lined with slush, the roads before them were bordered in deep white drifts, and the further they went towards Jarrow the deeper became the drifts and the harder the going. At times Simon had to dismount and kick the light snow away to allow the horse passage.

He had lit the lamps shortly after they passed through Gateshead and now at four o'clock in the afternoon the night had come upon them and it was impossible to see beyond the radius of light given off by the dim lamps.

Time and again he tucked the rug around Noreen and asked the same question, 'Are you all right?'

Sometimes she answered 'Yes', and sometimes she merely nodded. These were the times when the pains were gripping her. And she knew now, without having previous experience, that the child within her was trying to kick its way into life....

It was almost an hour and a half later when they reached the turnpike. At this rate another half-hour and they'd be home, but the road that lay straight ahead to the farm was now almost impassable with drifts three feet and more high. There was nothing for it but to take the side road. This would lead through the wood for at least half the remaining journey but there the trees would have taken a great deal of the snow and stopped the drifting.

He got down from the trap yet once again and turned the horse to the right and up the somewhat sheltered side road that led into the wood, the far edge of which actually bordered his own land or the land that he had thought of as his own and which he had been given notice to leave. But this thought did not enter his mind, all he wanted was to get his lass home and not least to witness Lucy's joy at the reunion.

He had been re-seated in the cart for less than a minute when from out of a snow-covered ditch to the right of them there sprang a young doe. How it had strayed down this far would never be known because the nearest herd was in Blandon Park, and that was all of eight miles away. When the horse reared, then tried to go into a gallop, Simon pulled on the reins and yelled, 'Whoa there! Steady! Steady girl, steady!'

But the animal was tired and frightened and it continued to try to go into a gallop; and for a number of yards it succeeded in an ungainly fashion, but then of a sudden it seemed to leap into the air before disappearing into the ground. As it let out an unearthly neigh both Simon and Noreen joined their voices to it as the trap, capsizing, rolled right over pinning them both beneath it....

They were all very still until the horse kicked out with its back leg, and as the hoof struck Simon in the middle of his back he made no sound for he was already unconscious.

There was silence again for quite some time; then Noreen, her voice like a faint whisper, said, 'Dad! Dad!' then louder now, 'Dad! Dad!' She tried to move and found her arms free but the seat of the trap was pinning her legs below the knees, and as she muttered, 'Oh God! Oh God!' her upper body relaxed and she lay back in the cushion of the snow, and her last conscious thought was, 'Well, I'm glad we made it up.'

❧ 13 ❧

When Steve came up out of the drift entrance he paused for a minute, saying to one of the men beside him, 'Good God, look at that! That's a contrast if you like. If you want to get in the morrow I can see you having to get your shovels out early on.'

The man nodded, saying, 'Aye, aye. The women kept it clear yesterday, but it was nowt like this. Aye, you're right, it'll be shovelling white instead of black.' He gave a throaty chuckle, then went on his way, saying, 'Night, boss,' and Steve answered, 'Night, Dick.'

In the office, Alec Manning was at the desk writing in the ledger, and Steve hanging his lamp on the wall said, 'It's been coming down thick and heavy, eh?'

'Yes; it started again about two hours ago.'

'Well, that was just about the time I went in. And by the way, they've got about another thirty skips extra out of that seam the day; must have been glad of the warmth.'

'Yes, I suppose so. And speaking of warmth, some of the fellows were at me about the free boots for the bairns come Christmas, and wondered if they couldn't have the money instead.'

Steve turned sharply towards him, 'Why is that?'

'Oh, they said the money could be spent on coats and such like and they can cobble the boots up.'

'Cobble the boots up?' Steve nodded his head. 'Or get a skinful with the money? I doubt if she'll agree to that.'

'I didn't think she would, but anyway they asked me to tap you so you could tap her.'

'Well, I think I can tell you what her answer will be afore there's any tapping done. The more you give some folks the more they want; they get an extra dollar at Christmas. Who else gives them that? You ask them that and tell them if they don't take the boots for the bairns they won't get the dollar. That'll make them think differently. Are they all in on this?'

'No, I don't think so; just Conroy, Wilson and McAvoy.'

'Oh, McAvoy. He'd see his bairns and his wife going naked, that one, as long as he could get his slush. He's the one who wouldn't send his lad to school, you remember? Anyway, I'm not bothering about them now, I'm ready for me bed. That's if I can get there. By the way, if I'm not in in the morning you'll know what's holding me up.'

'Don't worry, I'll be on hand. Rosie grumbles at times about the house being so near the pit, but this is one of the times I'm thankful it is. And so is she. And that's another thing, you know, you needn't make the journey home, there's always a bed there.'

'Thanks all the same, Alec, but there're two rabbits in the yard that need feeding, and three pigeons, not forgetting the cat. Of course the cat could have the pigeons, then finish up on the rabbits if the worst comes to the worst!'

They both laughed, then nodded at each other, saying, 'Well, good-night.'

In the stable, he lit a lantern, attached it to the side of the saddle, patted the animal while he laughingly half sang a verse from Cowper's hymn:

'God moves in a mysterious way
His wonders to perform;
He plants His footsteps in the sea,
And rides upon the storm.'

He was feeling happy tonight, yet on the face of it he had no reason to be. Tilly's attitude told him plainly what her answer was going to be. His plain speaking had made her mad, which, in a way, was a good thing, it all depended how you looked at it. He was spending Christmas with Phillipa and Lance and the children. He supposed it was this prospect that was affording him this feeling, yet all the time his mind, when not taken up with work, dwelt on Tilly.

When a voice came out of the darkness, saying, 'You're going to have a job further along, Mr McGrath,' he looked down into the two faces peering up through the falling snow at him, and he said, 'Well, you've managed it.'

'Just about, but it's worse further on. Doubt if the lads will get in from beyond the turnpike the night.'

The other man laughed now as he said, 'Never thought I'd say I'd be glad to get down below, but this is one time I will.'

'Good-night, Mr McGrath.'

'Good-night, Higgins. Good-night, Smith.'

He hadn't gone more than half a mile further on when he realised what the men meant for the horse was now up to its knees in snow in the middle of the road, and it wasn't drifting here. Some way before he reached the cottage he dismounted and ploughed forward on foot, leading the horse now, and it was just as he came in sight of the gate that another dark figure stumbled into view gasping, 'Is that you, Mr McGrath?'

'Yes, it is. Who's that?'

'Scorer, sir. Billy Scorer.'

'Hello, Scorer. Been finding the going hard?'

'Aye, I have, sir. And there's trouble back there, dreadful trouble. You're the first one I've met. There'll have to be help got. It's a horse'n trap tumbled into a ditch or a small gulley, and there's a woman and man pinned 'neath it. It was the horse that drew me attention, neighin' it was, cryin'.'

'Whereabouts was this?'

'Just off the turnpike, a couple of dozen yards just afore you get to the wood.'

Steve looked about him in bewilderment for a moment; then said, 'Well, I'll have to stable the animal, he couldn't get through in this. Hang on a minute, I'll come with you.'

'I think it'll take more than two of us. I tried to pull the woman clear but she seemed out for the count, didn't help herself. From what I could see with me light she didn't look hurt. I mean there was no blood or anything, but she's pinned somewhat.'

'I'll be with you.' Steve was shouting back now as he led the animal up the path and into the stable. There, pulling the saddle off him, he pushed him into his stall, placed an armful of hay and a bucket of water within his reach, then picked up the lantern and hurried out to join the man. . . .

It was a good half-hour later when they reached the side road. They hadn't met a living soul on the turnpike. There was a deep silence all around them and Billy Scorer remarked under his breath, 'Can't hear the horse now, but it's along this way; unless they've been found already.'

'I shouldn't think so by the look of the road.' Steve swung the light of his lantern over the smooth white surface ahead of them and added, 'Likely they'll all be covered by now.'

'No, listen; that's the horse again.'

They both made an effort to hurry now, lifting their feet high above the snow. Then the light of their lanterns showed up the tangled mass of horse, trap and two twisted figures.

'Dear God! what a mess.' Steve shook his head, then said quickly, 'Look; I think the first thing we've got to do is to get the horse out of the traces and then we can lift the trap, but we can't budge it as it is now. But wait, hold your hand a minute. Here.' Steve held his lantern out to Billy. 'Keep it high and I'll see what shape they're in.'

Slithering into the deep soft mass of snow, he let himself down to the bottom of the gulley; then shouting, 'Move it to the right. . . the light,' he saw dimly the face that looked as white as the snow in which it was pillowed but half-covered by the side of the trap, and now he whispered, 'Good God!'

Hanging on for support to one wheel of the vehicle, he swept the snow from around Noreen's face and shoulders. Then his hand going inside her cloak felt for the beat of her heart. He waited a moment, then let out a long breath before easing himself around her to the other figure. And here he expected to be confronted by Willy, but the man lying on his side, his head hatless, his face almost buried in the snow, showed him immediately who he was, and again he whispered, 'Good God! Simon Bentwood bringing his lass home and to end like this.'

He now pushed his way through the drift to where the horse lay, and as he did so he shouted up to Billy, 'Further along this way. Keep the light up.'

The horse was still, its eyes wide open, the look in them almost of human appeal. He patted its head, saying gently now, 'All right, all right, old fellow. We'll soon have you loose.'

Making his way round its head, he clawed himself up the incline which was less steep here, and now hastily said, 'Stick the lantern in the snow and help me get him loose. But look out for his legs; if he can rise at all he'll lash out.'

Once they had pushed the snow away from around the horse, the unloosening of the traces was a comparatively simple matter, but when the animal was freed it didn't kick and struggle to be up and away, and Steve had to prod the poor beast, saying, 'Come on, come on, on your feet. On your feet.'

It was some minutes later when he looked up at Billy and said, 'I think the poor fellow's had it.' But the animal, perhaps realising for the first time that it was free, gave a mighty snort and a heave and pulled itself to its feet to stand there quivering. In doing so, it moved the shafts of the trap and Steve, reaching quickly forward, grabbed at the iron frame that had supported the hood and, hanging on to it yelled, 'Pull back! Pull back!'

Seconds later they were both grappling with the frame and Steve was yelling again, 'Pull back towards you. This way to the left.' Then his voice again on a yell, he cried, 'Do you think you could hold it?'

'Aye, aye.'

At this he scrambled round to the back of the trap and there, bending low down, he thrust his hands into the snow and under Noreen's shoulders and gently eased her towards him.

Pulling her well clear, he laid her down, and then made his way to Simon. And to his surprise he saw that Simon was free. The half-buried cart wheel had missed him by inches. But it took him all his time to pull the unconscious form through the few feet to where Noreen lay. Once he had done so, he called to Billy, 'You can let go now.'

When the trap had sunk once more into the snow, Billy came round the end of it and, holding the two lanterns aloft, he asked quietly, 'They alive?'

'Yes; but they won't be much longer if they've got to lie out here. We've got to get help.' He gazed down for a moment on Noreen where, through her open cloak her stomach rose, and he added in his own mind, 'And quick!'

'But where from? Where's the nearest, would you say?'

'The Manor.'

'Aye, the Manor. But it'll take another half-hour to get there in this. By the way, the beast's got up the bank. Perhaps you could ride it.'

'No; it could never make it. I'll be quicker on foot . . . Will you stay with them?'

'Aye. Aye, of course. What else?'

'I'll be as quick as I can, Billy. But here.' He pulled off his thick overcoat, saying, 'Put that round her.'

'You'll freeze, man, in this.'

'Not if I keep running I won't. And look there.' He swung the lantern backward and forward. 'That looks like a shawl of some kind. Drag it out and cover them. But see to her. I'm away.'

Without any further words he scrambled up the bank, and when he came to the horse, standing mutely now, he slapped it on the flanks, saying, 'You'll be all right, boy, you'll be all right.' Then to his surprise the animal began to trudge after him. . . .

He was gasping for breath when he came to the gates. Finding them locked, he rattled the bars, then pulled violently at the iron bell-pull. But no one came out of the lodge, so he kept clanging the bell, and he was wondering if he should make his way along the boundary and climb the wall when he saw the glimmer of a light from a lantern in the distance.

Ned Spoke peered at him through the bars in surprise, then at the horse standing there before saying, 'Mr McGrath?'

'Open up, Ned quick; there's been an accident along the road. I want help.'

Within minutes they were hurrying up the comparatively clear drive and to the house, and at any other time Steve might have been brought to a halt by the fairy-tale scene of the lighted windows set amidst the white world.

He was kicking the snow from his boots and leggings when the door opened and Biddle, like Ned, exclaimed in surprise, 'Mr McGrath!'

Steve did not mince words but said briefly, 'Your mistress. Get her quickly.'

'Yes, yes, sir, Mr McGrath.' And turning to Christine Peabody, who was passing through the hall, he said, 'Tell the mistress Mr McGrath's here. 'Tis important. Quick now!'

Steve was still standing in the hall when Tilly came running down the stairs. She stopped at the foot and stared at him. The fact that he was wearing only his working jacket, breeches and leggings, and that there was snow still clinging to him, brought her hurrying forward now saying, 'What is it?'

'There's . . . there's been an accident. Can I have a word with you? We'll need men and . . . and a couple of stretchers.' He moved now almost ahead of her towards the breakfast-room, and when they were inside he turned to her, saying, 'It's Bentwood and the lass. He must have been bringing her home. The trap went into a small gulley. We've released them but they're both unconscious.'

When she put her hand to her mouth he said, 'There's something more I think you should know, the lass is full with a bairn and by the size of her almost on her time, I would say.'

The whispered 'No!' reached him and he explained softly, 'Now you can understand Willy's concern. Anyway, we've got to get them out of that as soon as possible. I don't know to what extent either of them is injured but they were both unconscious when I left them.'

'You, you want them brought here?' It was a question rather than a statement and tinged with disbelief and he said, 'Where else? The only other place is the Rosier pit cottages and you wouldn't have them go there, would you?'

'No, no.' Her voice was a mere whisper. She closed her eyes and shook her head. Then going swiftly to the door, she muttered, 'I'll get my things.'

'There's no need for you to come.'

'I'm coming nevertheless. If the girl's in the condition you say, well' – she turned her head and looked at him for a moment – 'the responsibility lies here as you've already indicated.'

'Willy. Will you tell him?'

'Not until we get back. He's up in his own room, he needn't know. Will you go to the stables and round up the men?'

'Well yes; but there's only four out there, isn't there? So you'd better tell Biddle to come along an' all, we'll need four for each stretcher. I've left Billy Scorer along with them. That only makes seven.'

'I can be the eighth.'

'Don't be silly.' He had turned on her, speaking as a man might to his wife, and she as sharply replied, 'I am not an old lady yet.'

'Aw, you know what I meant, Tilly. But there's no time for arguing, if you want them alive we'd better look slippy.'

If we want them alive! As she flew up the stairs and got into her riding habit and donned a thick coat and fur hat she endeavoured to press away the thoughts:

Did she want them alive, either Simon Bentwood or his daughter, the girl who was now carrying her son's child, her grandchild? And the honest answer she could give to this was, for Willy's sake she wished the girl to be still alive but not her father, for if he lived she knew that sooner or later she would lose her son.

It was almost two hours later when the men, stiff and frozen-looking themselves, carried the prostrate forms upstairs and into the rooms that had been prepared for them. While Biddle and Steve saw to Simon Bentwood, Peg and Fanny Drew undressed Noreen, and Lizzie Gamble, Peggy Stoddard, Nancy Garrett and Christine Peabody dashed up and down the stairs carrying water bottles and oven shelves wrapped in blankets, and during all this time Peabody stood in the kitchen dispensing hot toddy to the men; and Tilly faced her son in her bedroom and listened in silence as he stormed at her for having kept the knowledge of the accident from him.

Tilly was weary, she felt frozen to the bone. She had drunk a large glass of raw whisky, yet it seemed to have scorched only her throat.

'What would the men think?' he asked her now, and for the first time she answered him, saying, 'That you were better kept out of the way, you'd have only been a hindrance.'

'My God! the things you say to me!'

'Huh!' It was a weary sound. 'The things I say to you, Willy? Have you ever considered the things you have said to me lately? Ever since this girl came into your life you have hardly spoken to me but there has been a streak of recrimination in your words. Well now, what I'm going to say to you now holds no recrimination. Noreen has come back into your life, but she's not alone, she is full with your child, at least I would hope it's yours.'

He did not exclaim, 'What!' he did not immediately storm out of the room and grope his way to find her; he made no movement whatever; even the muscles in his cheekbones remained still; it was as if for the moment he had been deprived of life while being told he was the creator of it.

She rose from the chair and put her hand on his arm, saying, 'You didn't know?'

He drew in a long, slow breath, then made a small movement with his head; then said slowly, 'Where is she?'

'In the Blue Room. She . . . she has regained consciousness. She came to before they lifted her out of the ditch, but she's very weak and . . . and –' she pulled him to a standstill as he went to move away, then finished softly, 'the child is about to be born.'

'Aw no!'

'Yes.'

'The doctor?'

'We'll have to manage without one.'

She took his arm now and led him out into the corridor, down the gallery and into the west wing. This part of the house was rarely used but, as in the past, three or four bedrooms were always kept ready in case of visitors. Tilly had continued the practice although they hadn't been used for years. Now in two adjoining rooms the fires were blazing; Simon Bentwood lay in what was known as the Yellow Room and Noreen in the Blue Room.

When the door was opened in the Blue Room Tilly beckoned Peg out and Willy went slowly forward to where he could see the outline of the bed; then he was moving up by the side of it and now he was peering down into the white face and the eyes that were staring up at him.

'Oh, Noreen!' As he breathed her name he felt his mother pushing a chair for him and he sat down; and then his hands went out and cupped the face turned towards him, and again he whispered, 'Oh, Noreen!'

When she didn't speak or make any movement, he muttered, 'I didn't know. Why didn't you get in touch? This is terrible, terrible. Oh my dear, my dear.'

He was aware that the door had closed and that they were alone, and now he bent his head forward and placed his lips on hers, and when there was no response he asked softly, 'Are you in pain?'

'Yes.'

It was so like her not to waste words, his sensible, level-headed Noreen.

'Oh, I've missed you, Noreen. I've searched and searched day after day. Where were you?'

'Newcastle.'

'Newcastle?' He lifted up her hand now and brought it to the top of his chest and, pressing it there, he said, 'I went through every street in that city, every alleyway, every court. Ned got tired of looking – and you were there all the time. Oh my dear. My dear.' . . .

'Please, please don't cry.' It was the first animated sign she had shown, and she put her fingers up and touched his cheek. 'Don't worry. Whatever happens, don't worry.'

As he went to speak she placed her fingers on his lips, saying slowly and hesitantly now, 'Listen to me, Willy. Don't upbraid yourself ever, do you hear me? What happened was because I wanted it to happen, 'twasn't your fault, so you have nothing to reproach yourself with. Remember that.'

As he held her hand tightly between his own, his vision seemed to clear for a moment and he saw her face so different, so much older than the memory of it he had kept in his mind during these past months. Her cheeks were hollow, her skin looked grey. Then of a sudden he watched her features go into a grimace. He saw her teeth clamp down on her lip, and in this instant he recognised the face of the woman he had seen in his dream. When she brought up her knees and groaned aloud, he said, 'What is it? What is it, Noreen? I'll . . . I'll get Mama.'

She gasped and held on to his hand for a moment. Then her legs slowly straightening again, she said, 'Can . . . can you send for my mother?'

'Yes, yes, of course. 'He jerked himself up from the seat, almost gabbling now, 'We'll . . . we'll get her here.' He turned from the bed and groped his way hastily towards the door, for now his vision seemed so blurred he could not even see the outline of the room. Before he opened the door he was calling, 'Mama! Mama!' and a second later Tilly who had been waiting outside, said, 'Yes, what is it?'

He caught at her extended hand. 'Noreen . . . she's in pain, and . . . she wants to see her mother. Do . . . do you think we can get her through. . . .?'

Tilly did not answer immediately, and then she said softly, 'We'll do our best. You come away. Peg!' she called, and Peg came forward and Tilly said, 'Stay with her until I get back.'

In the hall she hesitated for a moment before saying to Peabody, 'Tell Arthur and Jimmy I'd like to see them.'

She knew that both men, like the rest, would be very tired for it had been no easy task, she knew personally, to carry those two stretchers all the way back here, but she also knew that if she were to ask the Drew men to walk into hell for her they would do it.

A few minutes later she was facing them saying, 'I know this is a bit thick and I hate to ask it of you, but she's in a bad way and she's asking for her mother. Do . . . do you think you could get her?'

Without hesitation it was Jimmy who answered, 'If it is possible we'll get her here, Tilly. There's one thing, it's stopped snowing.'

It was Arthur who now put in, 'And when we're that far, we'll call in in the village and pick up the midwife. If we can get Mrs Bentwood here, we'll get her here an' all.'

She nodded at Arthur now, saying, 'That would be a good thing if you could persuade her.'

'We'll persuade her all right.' Arthur nodded at her.

'Thanks.' She looked from one to the other and made a gesture towards them with her hand, then said, 'Wrap up extra well and take a flask with you.'

'Aw, we'll see to ourselves, don't worry.'

As they turned to leave, Steve appeared at the foot of the stairs. He did not speak but he beckoned to her with a lift of his chin, and as she approached him he said softly, 'He's conscious. I told him the lass was all right but he's asked for his wife.'

'I . . . I have just sent for her.'

He stared at her for a moment before saying, 'Well, I doubt she'll have to hurry, I think he's on his last legs.' Her eyes widened slightly as he added, 'I think his back's broken, and there's something gone inside, he's bleeding.'

She lowered her head now, and then she asked, 'Does he know where he is?'

'Oh yes, yes, he knows where he is. When he first opened his eyes and looked around he . . . he spoke your name, your old name.'

She did not ask how he had said her name for she knew it would have been laden with recrimination; yet Steve's next words belied her thoughts. 'He didn't speak it in bitterness,' he said; 'I think he knows his time is short and if it's in your heart to forgive I think you should look in on him, for no man should die in aggravation such as he's held for so long inside of him.'

She turned her head to the side and she kept it like that for some time, so long in fact that she became aware of feet and legs scurrying backward and forward across the hall; then lifting her head she looked at him and without a word passed him and walked slowly up the stairs. He followed.

When she opened the bedroom door she paused, and Steve had to press her forward in order to close the door. Then she was walking slowly to the foot of the bed. There were lamps burning on a table at each side of it and the lights seemed focused on his face like two beams. His eyes were open, the skin gathered in deep furrows at the corners as if screwed up against pain. His lips were apart and his tongue kept flicking over the lower one as if he were thirsty. This caused her to drag her eyes from him and say below her breath, 'Does . . . does he want a drink?'

But before Steve could answer the voice came from the bed, low and thick. 'No, I want no drink, I want nothing from you.' There was a long pause while their gaze linked; then his voice came again, 'You've . . . you've done enough for me, Tilly, haven't you? You've come in because you know I'm done for but you know in your heart you did for me years gone by. You ruined my life you did. And you know something?' His hand now came up and gripped his throat, and when he swallowed deeply Steve went to him and, bending over him, said, 'Don't talk.'

Simon swallowed again, then looking at Steve, he said, 'I'll talk all I want.' Now he turned his eyes again on Tilly and, his words coming slower, he went on, 'What I was gona say was, you were never worth it. You know that? You were never worth it. Lucy was worth t . . . ten of you . . . ten of you. Do . . . do you hear? Lucy was. . . .'

Again his hand went up to his throat; and now Steve, putting his hand under Simon's head, raised it slightly, then twisting to the side he took a glass from the bed table and held it to his lips. For a moment Simon gulped at it before pushing it aside, and when Steve laid his head back on the pillow he looked up at him and, after a great intake of breath, he muttered, 'She's done for you, too, hasn't she? Henchman, lap-dog, that's what she's . . . made of you.'

'Yes, very likely.'

The quiet retort seemed to silence Simon for a time. Then he said, 'My girl?'

'She's all right.'

Simon turned his gaze on to Tilly again who was now standing gripping the brass rail at the foot of the bed, and his voice a croak, he said, 'She's carrying a bastard born of a bastard. Well, you might get the bairn but . . . but you won't get her; I'm . . . I'm takin' her along of me.' His voice trailed away as a stream of blood ran slowly down the side of his chin, and as Steve bent over him, Tilly turned from the bed and stumbled out of the room and into the corridor. And there she made for one of the deep stone window-sills and dropped on to it and, her hand gripping her brow, she bowed her head.

Love and hate she knew were divided by a mere gossamer thread, but death was supposed to soften the emotions. That man in there had once loved her, and she him. Oh yes, she him. And it was she who should have hated him for being the instrument of shattering her girlish dreams. But she had never hated him, her feelings had not gone beyond dislike and revulsion. But her later rejection of him and the knowledge that she had become mistress to a gentleman had seemed to turn his brain.

'Come away from that cold seat.' She lifted her head sharply. For a moment she had thought it was Biddy speaking to her – Fanny was very like her mother –'and she allowed the younger woman to raise her up. But when she would have led her across the gallery and down the stairs, she stopped her and said, 'No, no, Fanny; I'll go to my room. Is . . . is Willy still . . . ?' She turned her head in the direction of the bedroom where Noreen lay, and Fanny said, 'Yes. Yes, he's with her. Don't worry about her, we'll see to her.'

'Is she in labour?'

'Well now, she's in pain and has spasms, but it's nothing like the labour I've had with either of mine. Look, you go and lie down or put your feet up anyhow on the couch. If anything goes wrong I'll call you. You've had about enough.'

As if their positions were reversed, Tilly walked obediently away from Fanny. Once in her room, however, she didn't put her feet up but kept them tramping the carpet. The only outward sound in the room was this padding sound, but inside her mind there was a great commotion. Voices were yelling at her, all her own but from different ages: as a child who had asked herself quietly why she hadn't anyone to play with, it wasn't only that the village was a way off; then the young girl screaming underneath the weight of Hal McGrath's body, yelling, 'No! Oh no!'. the nightmare of the stocks; the even greater nightmare of the courthouse and the question, 'Are you a witch?'; the voice that yelled in deep bitterness against those who had burned down the cottage; the loneliness that had cried out against the feeling that was engendered against her by the one-time staff of this very house. She had not cried out when twice she had been turned out of this place, that treatment had only filled her with sadness, but she had cried out greatly in bitterness when her son was blinded. Her cries had turned to screams when the Indians had massacred all but her and Matthew; but in the end they had got Matthew. All through her life she seemed to have been crying out, mostly against injustices. The loves she had experienced had always caused her in the end to cry out.

When the noises in her head became so loud, she gripped it with both hands and became still, saying to herself, 'Stop it! Stop it!'

This was not the first time she had experienced this cacophony of her own voices yelling against her destiny, but tonight there was a difference because all the voices, although yelling loudly, sounded weary. And she was weary, so very weary. Going to the bed, she lowered herself slowly on top of it and, turning her face into the pillow, she wept.

∽ 14 ∾

It was four o'clock in the morning but it could have been four o'clock on a busy afternoon for the house was abuzz with activity. The men had returned with Lucy Bentwood and the midwife around midnight. They were all exhausted, but Lucy would not rest until she had seen her daughter. The fact that Noreen was pregnant had come as an added shock to her; she had imagined the midwife had been called for one of the maids, neither of the Drew men had enlightened her otherwise. But as she had looked down on this almost unrecognisable girl pity and compassion had fought and conquered the feeling of dismay and shame.

When they were enfolded in each other's arms and Noreen was crying, 'Oh, Mam! Mam!' Lucy had been too overcome to utter any words, but her soothing hands had spoken for her.

Later, when she had stood by her husband's side and he had held out his hand towards her the very act had been one of supplication and it had surprised her. And when she placed her hand in his he whispered, 'Lucy, I . . . I found her,' she nodded; then said, 'Yes, yes, Simon, you found her,' and he must have recognised the note of forgiveness in her voice, for swallowing deeply again, he said, 'The child; take . . . take it home. Don't . . . don't leave it here.'

She could not say to him, 'It must be with its mother, wherever she stays.'

Again he had to gulp before speaking and, his voice a mere whisper now, he said, 'I'm . . . I'm sorry, Lucy. You . . . you were a good wife. You . . . you didn't deserve my . . . my treatment. And for what, I ask you? For what?'

'Don't talk; lie still.'

'I'm . . . I'm going to lie still for a long time, Lucy; will you say you forgive me?'

She could not see his face and her voice was breaking as she said, 'There's nothing to forgive. It's life and we've lived it as God ordained. Good comes out of bad.'

'You were too good for me. I . . . I should have had her, and she would have brought me more torment than . . . than I've gone through already . . . Wish there was time to show you I . . . I could be different. Hold my hand tight, Lucy.'

She held his hand tight and he closed his eyes and seemed to sleep. . . .

At one o'clock Noreen's labour pains had started in earnest. With Lucy on one side and the midwife on the other they urged her to press downwards, making encouraging noises, wiping the sweat from her brow, suffering the pain of her clinging nails. Then as the time wore on and the pains became more frequent her strength seemed to become less.

It was during one such period that Tilly opened the door and, beckoning Lucy towards her, said softly, 'Steve thinks you should go in,' at the same time motioning her head back towards the corridor. 'I'll stay here.'

Lucy paused for a moment, looked back towards the bed and the straining girl, then without a word she passed Tilly and made for the room along the corridor.

Tilly took her place at the other side of the bed from the midwife whose face was running with sweat, and the woman shook her head and muttered, 'Summit'll have to be done, she's about pulled out.'

Tilly did not ask, 'What?' but she bent over Noreen and said softly, 'Put your hands behind you, dear, and grip the bed rails.'

Almost immediately the midwife's voice came at her harshly, saying, 'She's tried that! I tell you she's got no pull left in her.'

Tilly looked at the woman. From the moment of her entering the house she had seemed to bring the atmosphere of the village with her. She must have come under protest or perhaps out of curiosity, but now she was looking almost as weary and tired as Noreen.

When Tilly spoke to her now it was as the mistress of the house. She said, 'You look very tired; go down to the kitchen and send one of the girls up.'

'And what could they do, ma'am, at a time like this?'

'As much as you're able to do at the moment.'

'Are you tellin' me I don't know me job, ma'am?'

'I am simply telling you that I think you need a rest.'

The woman straightened her back, then almost glared across at Tilly, saying, 'Well, don't blame me, ma'am, for whatever happens when I'm out of the room.'

Before she finished speaking there was a tap on the door and Peg entered carrying a tray holding bowls of broth, and Tilly, turning to her immediately, said, 'Take it across the corridor into the little library, Peg, please, Mrs Grant is going to take a short rest, then come straight back here.'

Although there was protest in the midwife's pose as she went out of the door, Tilly also gauged there was a certain amount of relief, for the woman had been on her feet for almost four hours.

When Noreen began to moan, Tilly caught her hands, saying 'There, dear, press down. Try. Come on, try.'

The girl made an effort to obey but there was little pressure in her straining and when she relaxed again, Tilly looked down on her in not a little alarm: if something wasn't done, she, too, would die. The thought brought her glance towards the far door and the dressing-room in which she knew Willy was pacing. It had taken Steve to get him out of the room and she herself had turned the key on this side of the door, but now instinctively she ran to it and unlocked it, saying as she did so, 'Come in. Come in.'

When he was abreast of her she whispered at him, 'She's ill, very ill, and weak. Take her hand; talk to her.'

She led him quickly to the side of the bed and when he placed his hand on Noreen's she saw that it was received with no answering grip, but Noreen turned her eyes towards him and said softly, 'Willy?'

'Oh my dear, my dearest, are . . . are you all right?' It was a stupid question to ask but it was a man's question, and her answer startled him.

'If . . . if the baby . . . is all right, let . . . let Mother have it, will you?'

When he made no answer she said again, 'Will you, Willy?'

'But . . . but you're going to get well; you're going to be all right. Won't she?' He turned his head towards the hazy figure of his mother standing at the other side of the bed, and when she didn't speak he gathered up Noreen's hand to his chest and pressed it tight against him as he muttered, 'Noreen! Noreen! you must get well. I . . . I need you. I love you.'

The only answer he received was a groan as another spasm of pain hit Noreen; at the same moment the door opened and Peg came scurrying into the room muttering by way of apology for not returning immediately something about the midwife knocking over the broth.

Beyond the open door Tilly saw Steve standing beckoning to her. Going quickly to him she pulled the door behind her and looked at him as he said softly, 'He's gone.'

She had been expecting this news yet it brought a strange reaction: she wanted to cry again and a voice from the far past came rising up from the depths of her, saying, 'Oh, Simon! Simon!' And the picture that now floated before her mind's eye was that of the kindly, considerate young farmer who had literally kept them from the borders of starvation for years; and following on this there came an accusing voice that had attacked her again and again, saying, 'What is it about me that changes people so?'

''Tis better this way; but it's odd that he should have to die in your house ... Aw Tilly!' Even the way he sighed on her name she took to be a condemnation of that which was in her and which could not be named.

Her back stiffened slightly and her voice conveyed the stiffness as she said, 'Would ... would you tell her ... her mother' – she inclined her head towards the bedroom door – 'she's needed?'

If he noticed her change of manner he ignored it and asked, 'How is the lass?' 'In a bad state, I should say.'

A sharp cry came from behind the closed door and he turned abruptly and hurried away leaving Tilly standing where she was voicelessly praying now: Don't let it happen to the girl. She wasn't thinking at this moment of the effect on Lucy Bentwood should she lose both her husband and her daughter, but of her own son and the burden he would have to bear if Noreen's death came about through the carrying of his child and the hardship she must have endured during these past months.

As Lucy passed her they exchanged a glance but did not speak, and when Steve, reaching out, opened the door for them the scream from the bed hit them and caused all their faces to move in protest. ...

As the late dawn broke the child was born. It was a girl and barely alive, but as it gave its first weak cry Noreen Bentwood joined her father.

৵ 15 ৶

The village was again agog. Nothing seemed to bring it alive as much as the happenings in the Manor surrounding ... *that one*. There had been shipwrecks in Shields when people standing helpless on the shore had watched men drown; there had been cases of cholera, enough to cause widespread apprehension of coming epidemics; there had been pit strikes; there had been strikes in the shipyards when the Jarrow men became a ferocious fighting horde, their anger ignited by injustice. Then there had been the local scandals. The daughter of a prominent business-man living not far from the village had run off with a stable hand, and she just fresh out from a convent education, and he not able to read or write, so it was said. And yet all these things great and small seemed to fade into insignificance whenever something occurred ... up there, through ... *that one*. And now God above! would you believe it, Farmer Bentwood searching for his daughter finds her working in the kitchen of a brothel, so it was said, and although her belly's full with the blind one's bastard he brings her home, at least makes the effort to. And she must have been willing enough to come with him. But then what happenes, some evil spirit guides him on the wrong road and there *that one's* fancy man finds them. And the result; aye dear God! – everyone in the village shook their head when they whispered the result – both to die in her house. But for the farmer to die there ... well, it was weird for she had plagued that man all his life. Hadn't she ruined his first marriage? And hadn't she tried to shoot him once? And now finally he dies in her house, and his beloved daughter with him. Was it not weird to say the least? they asked of each other. And had anybody reckoned up the people who had died after coming into contact with her?

They had waited to see her attend the funeral – it would have been just the brazen thing she would do – but she hadn't been there. Her son had though. Yes, and walking unashamedly alongside the poor widow, overshadowing her own son Eddie.

The villagers didn't go on to say that afterwards Lucy Bentwood had returned not to the farm but to the Manor; but they were up in arms at the fact that young Eddie had gone back and sacked Randy Simmons. Now what did you think of that, and him being on that farm since he was a lad? He had been given notice to quit his cottage an' all, no pension. Of course, everyone knew that Randy wouldn't starve, he had feathered his nest in one way or the other over the years, but that wasn't saying he should be put out of his cottage and no compensation. They were surprised at young Eddie though. But likely he had only been carrying out his mother's orders, for it was well known she never had much use for Randy.

But when it was all boiled down, it was still all connected with *that one* up there.

They sat one at each side of the fireplace in the drawing-room, each with a cup of tea in her hand, and when Lucy sipped at hers Tilly followed suit.

There were words to be said, matters to be arranged, but she couldn't find an opening. Yesterday this woman had buried her husband and her daughter, and the fault lay here in this house, for if her son had not given this woman's daughter a child then likely she would not have run away, and so there would have been no need for Simon to go in search of her. The snow would not then have got them, and they would have been alive now.

Only an hour ago when Willy had said for the countless time that he didn't want to give up the child, she had been forced to make him share the burden of the coffins he had followed yesterday. Unlike herself promising Matthew that she wouldn't marry again, Willy had said that he had given Noreen no answer to her request that he'd let her mother have the child because at the time he was stunned by the thought that she knew she wouldn't survive the birth.

Tilly was startled out of her thinking when Lucy said quietly, 'Don't carry the burden for what has happened on your shoulders, nor let your son carry it, it was inevitable. I don't know what Simon had promised her in order to get her to return home but I feel she would have demanded that in no way would he do any harm to your son. And knowing him, he would have promised her this whilst at the same time being determined to wreak vengeance for what had happened to his daughter. Although he had not known it, he had been in love with her. Oh yes, yes' – she nodded towards Tilly's widening eyes – 'he had in a way put her in your place.'

'Oh no, no! You're wrong there. He ceased to care for me many, many years ago.'

'He had never ceased to care for you.'

They stared at each other in silence.

'He was besotted with you. It was a bitter knowledge I had to accept, and it would have been easier to bear if he had acted normally and not tried to erase his feelings through hate, false hate.'

Remembering the last time she had looked down on Simon Bentwood's face and his words to her, Tilly was forced to say, 'I . . . I think you're mistaken. His hate was real, not simulated.'

'Then why did he die calling for you?'

Tilly made a movement to rise to her feet, then resumed her seat and, her head moving slowly from side to side, she said, 'It must have been in delirium because at our last meeting he told me exactly what I was worth to him, and his meaning was plain: he had wasted his life following the dross while ignoring the gold that was you.'

'He said that?'

'Yes.'

'And he meant it, and had he been spared to live you would certainly have come into your own.' Tilly looked down now on Lucy's bent head whose muttered words were scarcely audible: 'I stopped loving him a long time ago but I still cared for him and his needs. And then I stopped caring. That was the worst part, I stopped caring. I . . . I loved my daughter, yet in a way I was jealous of her, for I knew if he had had to make the choice who would have the last crust in a famine, he would have given it to her. Strange' – she raised her head now – 'he never cared anything for his son. Most men long for a son. And the boy was aware of his neglect from when he was a child. And I know now, and it is strange that I should say this, but my son is glad that his father's gone because his fear has been buried with him. He was afraid of him, you know.'

Lucy now took another sip from the almost cold tea; then putting the cup and saucer down on the table that stood between them, she said, 'At times I've pitied myself because I was being forced to live a life without love, and I envied you; but now I know that my life has been like a calm sea compared with yours and the injustices you have been made to suffer. Beautiful women like you have to pay the price for their beauty. In your case I think it's been too much, so what I say to you now, I said before, throw off any burden you might feel concerning my loss, because I shan't be unhappy: I have my son who I know loves me dearly, and because of your son's consideration I have a granddaughter to bring up. At the same time though, I shall remember that she has another grandmother here and also a father. And now I must be getting back.'

Tilly watched Lucy take the napkin from her knee and fold it up before laying it gently on the corner of the table. She watched her dust her fingers against each other, adjust the bodice of her black taffeta blouse, smooth down the sides of her thick black cord skirt; then as she slowly rose to her feet, Tilly rose also and impulsively now she held her hands out towards this woman who had suffered through her for years. And when she felt them taken and gripped the tears sprang to her eyes. They stared at each other for a moment in silence, until Lucy said thickly, 'I'll away and get her then.' And to this Tilly, being unable to speak, merely nodded.

Left alone, Tilly turned and stood gazing down into the fire. She knew that she should go in search of Willy for it was no easy thing she had persuaded him to do, and she knew, if she faced the truth, that persuading him to relinquish his claim on the infant was at bottom her own desire to be rid of the child, for at this stage of her life she didn't want to take on any more responsibility and certainly not that of an infant, for it would be herself who would have to bear the responsibility of its upbringing. Its presence, too, in the house would have been an obstacle to the plan that was forming in her mind, if it was not already formed, but which she would not at the moment bring to the fore. Even so, knowing all this, she still asked herself if she was really wise in letting the child go, for its presence might fill the gaping years ahead. Anyway it would always be near for what she meant to do was to give the freehold of the farm to Lucy and her son. This would achieve two things. It would ensure that her grandchild would always be near at hand, but more so it would go a long way to easing her conscience.

It was almost the New Year again and Steve had not asked for an answer to his ultimatum. Of course, he wouldn't, not under the circumstances.

He had been very good during this whole unfortunate business; in fact, for one period he seemed to be running the house, quite unintentionally she realised, for he was not trying to show her that he was capable of acting as her regent. Anyway, when he came for his answer it would be the same that she could have given him months ago in the cottage.

Of all the things that had happened to her emotionally in her life she knew Steve's defection was the most painful thing she'd had to endure. It was as if they had been married for years and that he had suddenly told her he had another woman . . . and had had her for some long time.

She closed her eyes tightly on the thought of how deep had become her jealousy of his daughter.

 **16**

She said to Willy, 'I don't think I can make the journey to Liverpool to meet Josefina; you'll have to go with Ned.'

'But she'll think it odd.'

'No, she won't. Tell her I'm not feeling very well, she'll understand.'

'It's a long way to come just to be greeted by me.'

Willy was sitting aimlessly in the big chair, one arm hanging over the side, his fingers moving slowly in the long hair of the dog at his feet, and Tilly wondered how long it would be before he would realise how much Josefina loved him. Sometimes she wondered if he already realised it. Last week he had suddenly said, 'Only five more days and she should be here – that's if the boat docks as expected. It'll be like old times.' Then he added, 'Can one really relive old times?'

'You can but try,' she had answered.

'She must have been very unhappy over there to want to come back because when she left she was so adamant that she would never return. . . . I missed her, you know.'

'Yes, I'm sure you did. And I did too.'

'I think I'll start at the mine again once she's settled in. I can't just sit here idling my days away. By the way, Steve hasn't been this week, has he?'

'No.'

'Was he at the meeting on Friday?'

'No; he has gone off for a long week-end with some friends.'

'Have you two really quarrelled?'

'No; why should we?'

'Oh, Mama, don't treat me like a fool. I've loved too, remember, I know what it's like, and Steve's love for you must be a very unusual love to have served you all these years.'

'Well, he's not going to serve me much longer.'

There, it was out.

'What!' The slackness left his body, he was sitting straight up in the chair. 'What do you mean?'

'He's got the offer of a new post, with Coleman's firm.'

'Coleman's the engineers?'

'Yes.'

'And he's going?'

'Yes; as far as I know he's going.'

'When did all this come about?'

'Oh, some time ago.'

'I can't believe it. Did he actually tell you this?'

'Yes, Willy, he actually told me this. And what you don't know, Willy, is that my dear friend has for some years been moving in high places. He has a daughter. . . .'

'What! Steve has a daughter?'

'Yes; she's a full-grown woman, over thirty, and she was brought up by the Colemans, and from there married into the Ryde-Smithsons. You don't get much higher than the Ryde-Smithsons.'

'*Steve! Our Steve?*'

'Yes, Steve. Our Steve.'

'Have you met his daughter?'

'Yes.' Tilly watched him sink back into the chair and nod his head slowly as he said, 'So that's what it's all about. Well! Well! Talk of surprises, I wouldn't have believed it. No wonder you have been feeling down. I'm sorry.' He pulled himself to his feet and made his way towards her, and when his arms came about her she lay against him for a moment, saying with a break in her voice, 'Such is life, Willy; it's . . . it's full of surprises.'

'And you've had more than your share. Well, I never thought he'd desert you, no matter how big the carrot was. I'm amazed, really I am. . . .'

There was a tap on the door and Biddle entered, saying, 'Mr McGrath has called, ma'am.'

'Speak of the devil.' The words were muttered before she nodded towards Biddle, saying, 'Show him in, please.' Then quickly she turned to Willy, saying, 'Where are you going?'

'Into the library. I don't want to be in on this, I might forget how good he's been to me and say things I'd be sorry for later.' He now turned from her and groped his way steadily down the long drawing-room to the door at the end, and as he went out of it Steve entered the room from the other end.

He gave no immediate greeting until he was standing in front of her, and then some seconds passed before he said, 'Nice to see the sun out, isn't it, even though it's struggling?'

'Yes' she turned her head towards the long window – 'we could do with some sunshine.'

'How are you?'

'Oh, I'm all right . . . Sit down.' She pointed to the chair opposite, and when he had sat down she resumed her own seat.

He was looking very spruce, very smart. He was wearing a new suit, she noticed, pepper-and-salt colour and of a good tweed. He had short gaiters over the tight trouser bottoms; his boots were brown and highly polished. At his neck he was sporting a gold tie pin in the shape of a riding crop. His hair was well brushed, still brown on top but greying at the temples. His face was lined but more with character than with age. Yes, he would cut a good figure in the society in which he was about to move; his daughter would have no need to apologise for him, oh no.

That he was returning her appraisal was given with his next words, 'You look peaky,' he said.

Her back stiffened still further. 'Well, if you remember I've been, in fact we've all been, through rather a trying period.'

'Yes, yes.' He nodded pleasantly at her. 'I could say we have. Yes, I endorse that.'

I endorse that. He was using words that would fit into his new way of life. The bitterness gathered in her, forming a knot in her chest, not a little with the knowledge that there were worlds dividing the once adoring lad and this sophisticated man.

'Are you up to talking business?'

'Yes, I'm up to talking business.'

'Good.' He was smiling at her again. His whole attitude seemed to point to his being well satisfied with himself and when he said, 'I'd better get on my feet, it's usual isn't it when one comes a-courting?' Her mouth fell into a slight gape. He was making fun of her, and to say the least it was in very bad taste. She listened to him in amazement as he now said, 'About me ultimatum.'

Perhaps it was her irritation and feeling of annoyance that made her remark, even bitterly, to herself that in spite of his polish he still reverted to the idiom 'me'.

'What's it to be?'

She stared at him for almost a full minute before rising slowly from the chair and facing him and, as slowly, saying, 'I think you're already aware of the answer.'

'Aye.' He looked to the side and raised his eyebrows. 'Yes, I felt that's what you would say after the way I put it to you. I'm not surprised. Well now, that's out of the way.' He opened the last button of his jacket, pulled the points of his waistcoat down, then said, 'Me other business. It's about the cottage, I want to buy it.'

Rage was rising in her. He had dismissed her refusal as the merest trifle, not worth a second's consideration. She had never thought there would come a time when she would hate Steve McGrath almost as much as she hated his brother, but it was almost upon her. And he wanted to buy the cottage! She repeated now in cutting tones, 'You want to buy my cottage? You're sure you don't want to buy my mine too?'

'Well, not at the present, Tilly; funds wouldn't run to that.' His smile broadened. 'But I can manage the cottage and the alterations I have in mind.'

'Oh –' her lips pouted, her head wagged and she repeated, 'alterations you have in mind.'

'Yes. It is poky, you must admit, so I thought of sticking on a parlour. Not a drawing-room' – he looked around the room, his head making a waving motion the while – 'just a nice comfortable parlour. The present room I'll turn into a kitchen, for that alone, and I'd like a little dining-room and a couple of bedrooms up above. I would arrange all the windows to be mostly at the back, because it's a very nice view from there, isn't it, being on that bit of a rise? I've also seen Mr Pringle who owns the fields at the bottom. He's quite willing to sell a few acres because they run soggy in the dip and the cattle get bogged down there sometimes in the winter. When I've been thinking about it, I've had to laugh to meself because that's how manors and big houses started, didn't they, mostly anyway, from a little cottage and a bit added on here and there? This very house' – he waved his hand about – 'I learned recently had only eight rooms when it was first built, and now how many has it got? I bet they can't count them. Of course, I won't be able to achieve it at one go but that's the kind of pattern I've worked out. So what about it, eh?'

She just couldn't believe her ears. There was something wrong here. What did he want the cottage for and all the extensions if he was going away? She tried to speak but her words were choking her and she had to swallow deeply twice before she could bring out, 'Why do you want to buy the cottage if you are taking on a new position?'

'I never said I was taking on a new position.'

Again she swallowed. 'You indicated in your ultimatum that if my answer didn't suit you, you would then take up Mr Coleman's offer. Such a lucrative one you gave me to understand.'

'Oh that! And aye, it was very lucrative, as you say.' He jerked his chin upwards. 'But I told him straightaway no. I never had any intention of taking it on.'

'But you said. . . .'

'Aye, I know what I said.' His voice had lost its bantering tone. His face was straight now and the muscles began to jerk in his cheekbones, and then he muttered thickly, 'I had to do something to bring you to your senses and to stop you actin' like a young lass who didn't know her own mind while all the time you did. I was sick of being played about with, being used, I wanted to know where I stood for once. And now I do.'

As she watched the stiffness leave his face and a twisted smile draw up the corner of his mouth, the anger in her swelled. To think he had put her through all this for months, and on top of all the other trouble. He had been laughing up his sleeve at her while knowing what she must be suffering.

She could have been yelling at the sightseers who were looking at the burning cottage, or staring at Alvero Portes before she sprang at him, or standing in the square confronting the villagers, her anger was as deep as any she had felt before, and she reacted to it.

When her hand came slap across his face he staggered back for a moment, then covered his burning cheek with his palm. Slowly now his mouth opened as he stared at her; then a most unusual thing happened. It took the fire out of her anger and she slumped like a pricked balloon when, his head going back, he let out a great roar of laughter. It rose and rose and the tears gushed from his eyes as it became louder.

Willy heard it in the library. It brought him up from his chair but he didn't move towards the drawing-room; but it caused him to smile, the first time his features had moved in this direction for weeks.

The laughter was heard as far away as the kitchen and caused Fanny to exclaim, 'Oh, isn't that good to hear somebody's laughing?'

It caused Peabody in the hall to unbend so much that he forgot himself and addressed Biddle as Clem, saying, 'Well! well! Clem. What do you make of that?' And what any of them would have made of the scene in the drawing-room would be hard to say, for now Steve was holding Tilly tightly in his arms. His face was wet, his mouth wide and his eyes looking straight into hers, he was saying, 'You don't hit a man unless you either hate him or love him, and there's one thing I'm sure of, you never hated me. Aw Tilly! Tilly!' Again the laughter slid from his face and, his voice thick and coming from deep in his throat now, he said, 'I haven't any need to tell you how I feel, you've known it since I was a lad, but I must put it into words. I love you, Tilly, with no ordinary love because I've lived you and breathed you since I can first remember. You've never been ordinary, not even as a lass, and when you became a woman . . . well, you had something, and all the men who met you knew it. It is a strange quality you have about you, Tilly. But I'll say this for you, you've never played on it because I'm sure you don't realise you've got it. It's a kind of power you have, either to make or to break a man. And you know, that's been proved. But I didn't want it to happen to me, the breaking I mean. Although taking the crumbs you've dropped over the years has been hard, I've put a face on it just to remain near you. Discovering Phillipa as I've said afore, helped, but nothing or no one could fill your place. I was rough on you a few months ago but I could see it as the only way to end this impasse because what I don't want, Tilly, is you as a mistress. Many a man would say I've been a damn fool because with a bit of manoeuvring that could have come about some years ago.... Don't move.' He shook his head at her. 'You're not going to get away. And deny it as much as you like I know I'm right, and you do an' all. I want you as a wife, Tilly. I've always wanted you as a wife, and that's what you're going to be to me at last, isn't it? Willy will eventually marry Josefina, it's a foregone conclusion. You know that as well as me, and you'll have to be prepared for more tongue-wagging ... Oh aye. And those two as much as they love you they won't want you here. You'll have to face up to that too. That's why we're going to live in the cottage.'

She was limp within his arms. She wanted to say something, upbraid him for the way he had gone about this business, but all her mind was saying was, 'Oh, Steve! Steve! Oh, my dearest Steve!' She wanted to say the word 'dear' or 'dearest' aloud, words that he had never heard her apply to him, but she was unable to speak, so she let her lips speak for her. When she placed them on his there was a space filled with stillness before his grip became like a vice and her whole body seemed to merge into his for a moment, two moments, three, a passage of time going right back to their childhood.

They were both different beings when still holding her he pressed her gently from him and, drawing a deep breath, said, 'Tilly. Tilly. Mine at last. I ... I can't take it in yet, but I will.... Oh Tilly!' There was a break in his voice. Then as if in an effort to cover his emotion he reverted to a jocular tone as he said, 'I've got a name for the house when it's finished: Trotter Towers. What about that?'

'Trotter Towers.' She bit on her lip and said again, 'Trotter Towers.' Her mouth went into a wide gape. '*Trotter Towers.*' When a great gurgle of laughter rose from where it had lain dormant for so long and they fell against each other once more, their mirth mingled and the house became alive with it.

'Oh Steve! Steve! *Trotter Towers. Trotter Towers. Trotter Towers.* You and me in *Trotter Towers.*'

The fears of the years seemed to slide from her as, as if in one of the Brothers Grimm's fairy tales, she saw the tower rising from the stones of the cottage and, standing guard, was Steve, and as long as he was there she knew she would be safe against attacks. She was wise enough to know she'd still be attacked, for even when she changed her name from Sopwith to the once hated name of McGrath, she'd still be known as Tilly Trotter. But what matter; she was loving again and being loved. Oh yes, she was being loved, by this man who had never stopped loving her.

Her body was lost in his again, she had no breath, no desire to think except that she was loving for the last time, and it felt as if she'd never loved before.